INVITATIONS
FROM
AFAR
A NEED TO KNOW

a novel by

LINDA A.W. KING

authorHOUSE®

AuthorHouse™
1663 Liberty Drive
Bloomington, IN 47403
www.authorhouse.com
Phone: 1-800-839-8640

Published by AuthorHouse   05/31/2012

ISBN: 978-1-4772-0388-0 (sc)
ISBN: 978-1-4772-0387-3 (hc)
ISBN: 978-1-4772-0386-6 (e)

Library of Congress Control Number: 2012908462

To my family
Dave, Rose, Doug
who always believed in me

Acknowledgments

My husband R. David King visualized many chapters that I read aloud to him on road trips. His editorial help was invaluable, and his overall encouragement was constant.

My daughter Rose Davis offered me concrete suggestions and helped in many practical ways.

My son Doug King gave me upbeat and insightful perspectives on writers' work styles.

Dave Chapman was more than generous with his time and talent in providing empathy, suggestions, proofreading, and editing.

Nolie Mayo, Ph.D., read and discussed the manuscript with me. She said it was ready to go.

My granddaughters Ava and Grace Davis kept my creative juices primed by requesting that I tell them more stories.

Barbara Bailey helped me with an East Tennessee dialect.

John Gorman, Ph.D., and Sally Jordan encouraged me with my earlier material.

Solarship *Copernicus*
Friday, 2:45 p.m. CDT

"There's something you need to know." From Houston, Max Marsh called the *Copernicus* for the second time in one flight day, an unusual deviation from routine.

Commander Jackson Medwin replied, "We are so ready for home. Tell me our mission's been declassified, and everyone knows what we've found."

Jack and his three crewmembers certainly were capable of maintaining silence regarding every aspect of their mission, if necessary, for the rest of their lives, even Jana Novacek, the youngest, the one he felt the most responsibility to protect. Jack did not consider the secrecy necessary or desirable. Yet, declassification was not his call.

As the video transmission sharpened, Jack experienced a heightened alertness when noting Max's strangely somber expression. Although Max in his faded plaid shirt looked like he had just stepped out of the old West, he enjoyed a sterling reputation at Johnson Space Center. Jack felt thankful that his friend, a brilliant perfectionist, was the computer systems specialist for this mission.

Yet, why was Max calling now? By procedure, he called only once during each wake cycle, the term for a flight day that often varied in length on a long space mission. Mission Control, referred to simply as Houston, continuously received all of the solarship's readings on many separate channels, and if anything was troublesome, then CAPCOM, the capsule communicator, not Max, should have called.

•

1

The time delay was lasting longer than the transmission turnaround. Jack realized that Max was deciding whether or not to divulge something. Finally, Jack said, "Whatever it is, just tell me."

Max replied, "Follow procedure XY12A. That's X-ray, Yankee, One Two Alpha."

"Wilco," Jack said. That meant, "I have received your message; I understand it and will comply." At that moment Jack realized something was seriously wrong. The video screen blurred before the transmission abruptly ended.

XY12A was Max's signal for Jack to open the private, secure channel that bypassed Mission Control. No record would be left of any communication on that channel. Max never before had asked Jack to initiate a secret conversation. Yet, after the security leak a month ago, Jack taped the code on the main console so he would have quick access if the need arose. Now, he spoke. "Y E L I A B N A L A * * * *"

The response came back. "Not a valid address." He tried again, enunciating each letter carefully, and for each asterisk saying, "star."

As he waited, he did not speculate on what Max might tell him. Instead, he allowed himself to think about his family. In five days, the *Copernicus* would dock at the spaceport that orbited synchronously with the International Space Station. After nearly a seven-month mission, he and his crew soon would be home.

It was many seconds before Jack got a response. "Hello, this is Max. The video is not clear."

"What's up?" Jack asked.

Again the delay was lasting too long. Max still was deciding. Finally, he quietly announced, "There may be an explosive device—a bomb—heading toward you."

"What? Who would consider such an act? We're talking big bucks. At the very least, sabotage like that requires lift-off and guidance capabilities. It also requires knowledge of our trajectory." His mind flew, trying to make sense out of what Max told him. Finally, he said, "Should I presume that Houston is working the problem? Does

CAPCOM not want to worry us?" Jack tried to joke. "And you, on the other hand, are worrying us."

"It's not like that," Max replied. "Today, someone totally outside JSC brought me the coordinates where you'll be tomorrow afternoon at 1600 hours. That's when the bomb supposedly impacts the *Copernicus* in a little more than 24 hours."

"What's Director Clayton doing about this situation?" Jack asked.

Silence on Max's end stretched longer than the normal transmission delay. Finally, he answered, "I'm checking out some things on my own before going to him."

Jack rapidly evaluated this startling information. Later, he would evaluate more slowly and carefully. Until this moment, he had trusted Max's judgment completely, but now his friend of all people had chosen not to tell the JSC director. It made no sense.

As far back as the initial planning stages, Max had been included in the small circle of people who knew not only about the secret mission but also about its main goal. A thought too horrible to consider came to Jack, but for now he pushed it away and proceeded in another direction. "Who told you this? How credible is the person?"

"Highly credible. This is a secure transmission, I hope, but, still, I'll not mention the name. I'll tell you this much, and then you'll figure it out right away. Last fall, shortly before you went into isolation for this mission, someone wanted to meet you. The three of us went to lunch."

"Yes, I remember," Jack replied, noting that Max's caution extended to not even mentioning the name of the restaurant.

"This morning, that person learned about a bomb plot and was concerned for your safety. He asked me if his information—a set of coordinates and the corresponding time of tomorrow afternoon at 1600 hours—meant anything. A bomb hurtling in space toward you, I thought, was impossible, but to reassure him, I checked out the numbers he brought me. Everything lined right up."

3

Jack seldom felt confused, and he did not like the feeling. Only a small but growing group within JSC and another small group high up in government knew about their secret mission. Fewer knew about the mission's main goal.

On the other hand, Jack thought, the *Copernicus*'s stealth shield and cloaking devices were not infallible. Neither were their other techniques to avoid detection. Their burns, the fuel expended for course corrections, were planned carefully with detection avoidance in mind. Yet, telescopes all over the world and more orbiting Earth were operated by astronomers and amateurs, always hoping to find something out of the ordinary. However, if some group were tracking them, the *Copernicus* would appear as an unidentified object in the heavens, not as an identifiable solarship. Jack asked, "How did . . . this person know about our mission."

"Easier than you think," Max replied. "This person thought there could be a mission. Remember the security leak last month?"

"Of course," Jack replied. "That would have been the perfect time for Director Clayton to get permission and announce our mission, even with the extraordinary ramifications."

"True," Max said, the corners of his mouth quivering. "Mission Control decided not to tell you that the rumors have intensified, even in the mainstream press."

"Then the secret's out, and the world knows about us," Jack said. "I'm glad."

"Not this way, Jack. Top management has verified nothing. The secret's distorted."

"Describe."

"Not now, Jack. You have enough on your plate."

"If our 'secret' mission is common knowledge, then the whole bomb thing could be nothing but another rumor by someone who gained access to our trajectory. What are the worst rumors?"

"One deals with contamination," Max replied. "Some scandal sheets are running with the idea that your crew is contaminated."

"Director Clayton himself needs to make a public announcement immediately and put frantic minds at ease."

"If only he could," Max replied. "I've recently heard that his request to declassify your mission has been denied."

"That's bad. That's very bad."

"Another rumor deals with Jana. Several papers and TV commentators continue saying the most vicious things about her. They have focused all their hatred on her. They say she has taken over control of the *Copernicus*."

It angered Jack that she was the target of wild speculation. Yet, Jana was such an easy target. She had no advanced degrees like the other astronauts, not even an undergraduate degree, just two years of college. Jana was the first person from the new, abbreviated training program, and by far the youngest person to fly in space. To know why she had been selected rather than any of the hundreds of far more trained and experienced astronauts, one would need to understand the entire purpose of the mission and Jana's unique qualification, not something easy to explain. For this specific mission, her presence had been crucial. If one did not understand, it would be so easy to make up bizarre reasons for her being on the mission.

Jack put his concerns about Jana aside and focused on the bomb situation. He said, "If people believe a contaminated crew is returning to Earth, there must be extreme fear. Yet, fear is far removed from having the resources to launch a bomb."

"My contact knows of significant financial resources, but I dare not say more about money sources even over this channel. Where is everybody?" Max asked.

For a second, Jack caught sight of the confident, reassuring Max who could solve most any problem and put anyone at ease. "Fawzshen is here in the cabin. I'll get him involved immediately. Lauren and Jana are in the garden module in the cargo bay. Stay on this channel."

"I have been talking with Max," Jack said in a loud voice as he glanced toward Co-commander Fawzshen who was braced against a window, taking pictures.

The Asian man waved Jack closer. "Come here, my friend. This view is most incredible. Earth is a perfect jewel, blue and round, and the moon hangs so close."

Jack glanced in the direction where Fawz pointed. The earth and moon were breathtaking to behold against the blackness of space. Jack realized Fawz had not heard any of the transmission. In the noisy solarship with low air pressure, sound did not travel well. Jack said, "Max asked me to follow procedure XY12A. He's on that channel, now"

"To secretly contact Max!" Fawz raised his brambly brows. "This is most troubling." Fawz's dark eyes grew wide as he abandoned the window, secured his camera, and quickly moved toward Jack and the main console. "That channel bypasses Mission Control."

"Yes, and you need to know what Max has just told me."

Once Fawz was in front of the monitor, he greeted Max and listened carefully as their computer systems specialist concisely explained the situation.

Jack turned toward Fawz and asked, "Any ideas?"

He replied, "If a bomb is out there, our two meteoroid detection programs would alert us. The main program finds every meteoroid within approximately a 20 to 24-hour range. If an explosive were on a rendezvous trajectory with our ship, we still would have about a 10 to 12-hour warning, assuming standard velocities. That should give Houston time to save our ship. JSC has access to thousands of experts who would help us." As an afterthought, he added, "And a few days ago, Houston even sent us an updated meteoroid program."

Max yelled, "I decided not to send that update to you. Your existing program was more than adequate and well tested. You know we don't frivolously send updates in the middle of a mission."

"I'll look at it," Jack said. He turned toward the keyboard of the master computer and typed in a few commands. Since the two meteoroid programs always ran in the background, he checked the tag title of the main one. "Here it is, 'Advanced Meteoroid Detection, Version 6.1.0A Update, programmer: Denise Morneau,' and, listen to this, 'approved: Filbert Grystal.'"

"Fil doesn't have that authority. I'll check into this right away," Max said, his voice metallic and shaking with concern. "Give me an hour, and then call me back. Use the same passcode." Max terminated the transmission.

Jack felt an energy growing within him. It was not unpleasant, more hormones from the adrenal glands kicking in, he figured. "Damn," he thought. "Our lives are in danger, and I like the feeling." That, however, was the extent of Jack thrashing himself. To Fawz, he said, "I assume you saved the prior version."

"Correct!"

"Run an analysis of the differences between the two."

"I'll take care of it," Fawz replied.

Jack could count on Fawz no matter how challenging this situation became. His friend for over twenty years was as reliable, steady, and brilliant as anyone he knew.

The two had met as graduate students at the prestigious Houston Aerospace University. Fawz, the crown prince of a small mountainous kingdom named Rhatania, returned to his own country after graduation. In the intervening years, he visited the US several times, and on one occasion stayed for a year and trained before flying on an international mission.

Even though a prince, Ph.D., and highly experienced pilot, Fawz's title of co-commander was largely ceremonial. He easily deferred to Jack's decisions. In fact he deferred more easily than several other astronauts that Jack had commanded. This man accustomed to such power and privilege simply worked hard and did his job, completing his tasks with flair and ingenuity. Jack thought Fawz's attitude toward work had much to do with his concept of protocol.

"Jana and Lauren should be back by now," Jack said.

Fawz did not reply because he was deeply involved in his work.

Jack checked the video monitors of the modules lined up in the cargo bay, each connected to the next one. He changed views until he located Mission Specialists Jana Novacek and Lauren Adams inspecting the lettuce garden.

Jana and Lauren both were rookies, as if one could be considered a rookie after a seven-month mission. Jack rarely thought of them that way. Now, he wondered if either of them could handle whatever the next 24 hours might bring. He would need to count on them. Under the worst conditions, the four astronauts would be alone, trying to save themselves with no help from Mission Control. Jana and Lauren would do fine. He could not imagine either one of them falling apart.

Jana was strong without the appearance of muscles. Her hazel eyes, at times green and other times gray, were enhanced by the bluish cast of the whites. Her distinctive eyes danced and missed nothing. She was always observing, always thinking, yet still enthusiastic.

It was fun having such a bubbly young person around, and Jack sometimes envied her emotional peaks, which in no way interfered with getting her work done. He had seen her become as analytical and tough as the most seasoned astronauts.

Jana sometimes stayed up into her sleep cycle writing on a small notebook computer. He wondered if she perceived the trip in the same manner he did. Every now and then, he had an urge to read her private journal. What would a young woman, a 20-year-old rookie without a traditional background, write about? She showed her journal to no one.

Lauren also wrote on her own time, but these addendums to her required JSC reports she gave to Jack and the other crewmembers for comments. Lauren at 29, although several years older than Jana, still was young to be selected for such a plum assignment. Lauren, no-nonsense, efficient, yet pleasant, was picked for this major mission over far more experienced candidates specifically because of her social sciences background. She also had the traditional background—pilot's license, advanced technical degrees—but her degrees in both sociology and linguistics plus her extensive field experience in anthropology were what made her stand out among the astronauts. She was selected solely because her skills would come in handy if the crew fulfilled the mission's primary goal—to find intelligent life. That primary goal was the major reason as far as Jack knew for the mission's secrecy.

Had the mission been publicized, Lauren would have been good for public relations, adding definite glamour to the program. Her appearance was striking, statuesque, and elegant with well-toned muscles and a flawless dark complexion, but she was not the kind of woman that a man would dare compliment regarding her looks. Before the mission, a fellow astronaut in Houston had been hopelessly smitten by Lauren, but as far as she was concerned for the wrong reasons, her looks and her status. That astronaut, Filbert Grystal, had not easily accepted her rejection of him. She had wanted more in a relationship.

Then, Jack remembered something significant. The astronaut in Houston smitten by Lauren, Filbert Grystal, was the same person who had sent the *Copernicus* the updated meteoroid program without Max's approval. He also had been involved in the security breach a month ago but had been quickly exonerated in that snafu. Jack considered Filbert a self-absorbed, egotistical jerk, who was so different from the positive stereotype most people held of astronauts.

Jack breathed deeply. He could not allow himself the luxury of wildly speculating and constructing a conspiracy theory. There was another side to Filbert. He seemed truly dedicated to the Space Program, and, furthermore, the support staff liked him. Filbert had gone to bat more than once for programmers whom he considered underpaid. Jack suspected Filbert had a tender spot somewhere in his arrogant heart.

Why were Jana and Lauren taking so long? Jack zoomed for a close-up and noticed they were talking and treating what they thought was their last task of the wake cycle like a leisurely stroll, except they could not exactly walk. Jana propelled herself along with the handholds while Lauren pushed off against the decking. They stopped and inspected some field greens to make sure that their precious plants were happy. Then, they dawdled and talked some more. They had just finished working twelve hours, and now they thought it was time to recreate.

Jack decided against using the microphone in the garden module. His words bouncing against the metal walls would sound like the voice of God. Instead, he talked into Jana's wrist communicator. "Finish the inspection quickly," he said. "We have a new assignment."

He would have to tell them. He did not want to. He wanted his astronauts to have a memorable mission they would savor all their lives. All their lives, he thought! How long?

Unexpectedly, his entire life tumbled before him. He recalled a pleasant childhood, filled with hiking, camping, and white water canoeing adventures. When he was a young teenager, the life of the International Space Station was indefinitely extended. Within not so many years, five space stations orbited the earth, one a factory where spaceships, minishuttles, and larger solarships were assembled, and another, the spaceport where the ships were docked. The biggest ships such as the *Copernicus* never got any closer to Earth than the spaceport because they were not built to withstand liftoff from Earth. There also were three moon bases, two fully functional and one being constructed. It went from the minimum to abundance in space.

Jack knew he had been the luckiest person in the world at the best time in history when he was chosen to command the Mars I mission, two ships with seven crewmembers each. Director Clayton, then new at his post, let it slip that Jack had been selected as commander partially because he was photogenic, had a good smile and cobalt blue eyes, projected an image of sincerity, and probably could be groomed to become a national hero. This information briefly disturbed him and became a minor secret in his life. He told his wife, Shirl, about it but no one else.

Since the Mars I mission had been televised, his family as well as the whole world could watch his crew demonstrate everyday life on a solarship. Through private, secure phone connections, he enjoyed special moments with Shirl and his three young children practically whenever he wished. Finally, that crew shared the glorious moment with everyone on Earth of stepping on the surface of Mars and exploring the planet.

After that mission, he planned to stay on Earth and watch his children grow up. He became a spokesperson for NASA, the National Aeronautics and Space Administration. It was an easy time to encourage support for the Space Program, and, consequently, space exploration was well funded.

Good funding continued throughout the Mars II mission. As a public relations thing, Jack occasionally worked Mission Control and received great coverage for NASA on TV and the supernet. That job increased his longing for another major mission.

Despite the success of Mars II and despite all of NASA's other successes, within one year, funds dried up and times changed quickly. Different politicians in Washington! It disappointed Jack the way few things completely disappointed him. Soon, there were so few opportunities and so many astronauts.

Quite unexpectedly, the Ganymede mission opened up. The Rhatanian government footed a large part of the bill. The leadership requested Jack, partially because he was considered the premier astronaut and partially because Fawz and Jack had been good friends at the Houston Aerospace Academy and had stayed in touch throughout the twenty intervening years.

Unknown to NASA, the main reason the Rhatanians wanted Jack was because of their concept of fate. A few years back, Jack had displayed a Rhatanian museum catalogue on an end table in his living room, triggering a chain of events that culminated in this mission. That catalog was partially the reason Jana was on the mission, too.

This mission was so different from Mars I. He quickly realized how precious video communications with his family had been. Now, he so missed Shirl. Not telling her what the crew had found, possibly not ever telling her, would become a widening wedge between them. To his three children, he was an absentee father. Better than a non-existent one vaporized in a space explosion.

"I have compared the two versions," Fawz stated.

Jack did not reply. He needed a positive image, a vision to carry him through. Today, Friday, was rendezvous with the spaceport minus five days, tomorrow, Saturday, rendezvous minus four days. If they survived Saturday and avoided an unwanted rendezvous with a bomb, on Wednesday they would dock with the spaceport.

Jack found his vision. He closed his eyes and recalled the jolt of a solarship docking with the spaceport. It was not home but only 200 miles from Earth, close enough to behold the continents and blue waters.

Jack patted Fawz on the shoulder and said, "We'll do fine." He asked, "The new meteoroid detection update. Many differences with the old version?"

Fawz replied, "Most differences are minor. However, one significant thing—a time-dated subroutine that influences the main sequence—is written in a peculiar code. The tools I am using cannot fully analyze it. It seems to be a self-diagnostic check, but a diagnostic takes only a few minutes. This subroutine controls the main program for twelve hours tomorrow, the twelve hours exactly prior to the . . . the bomb's impact."

"Sounds ominous," Jack said.

"Indeed!" Fawz replied. "How do you wish to proceed? We could uninstall this new version and reinstall the old one."

"We'll talk to Max first," Jack said. "We have a completely different meteoroid program as our back-up. That gives us two ways to detect a bomb: The old version that we can reinstall and the back-up program. Go ahead and verify that it's functional."

"I have done that already," Fawz replied. "That back-up program works perfectly, but it is not sufficient. It searches for meteoroids within an approximate two-hour range, even less time for high velocity ones. If something were heading directly toward rendezvous with us, the range for detection would be cut to an hour or less."

Jack nodded in agreement.

Fawz explained, "In our potential situation, an hour is not enough time to make adequate plans. Imagine changing course to avoid a meteoroid only to discover that it's a bomb with guidance control that locks in on the *Copernicus* as the target."

"Good thing Max alerted us," Jack said, feeling more and more energized, the way a challenge affected him.

Fawz asked, "Who told Max about the bomb?"

"The Kazimier," Jack answered.

"The renowned religious leader!"

"Max and the Kazimier are close friends. They grew up in the same neighborhood. Before this mission, the three of us had lunch together."

"I remember you mentioned meeting him. What kind of man is he?" Fawz asked.

"Sincere, honest, I believe, also practical, intelligent, charismatic. And what a voice. That voice could move a mountain."

"He doesn't sound like a person who would kill," Fawz said.

"No, not at all. Definitely a man of peace."

"I am slightly familiar with the Kazimier's religion. A member of his flock could have confessed involvement in the impending sabotage."

"It's possible. A religious leader, the Kazimier, would try to prevent the crime," Jack said in a thoughtful voice. "He'd do whatever was necessary, but he didn't know if a mission existed or whether the scandal sheets had run amuck, so he went to Max."

Fawz added, "Then, Max pieced things together, his knowledge of our trajectory and the Kazimier's knowledge of a bomb threat and our coordinates tomorrow at 1600 hours."

"It could have happened that way," Jack said, "but we have no proof. We also don't know why Max didn't report this to Director Clayton. We won't do anything unless our meteoroid detection program or a properly working one finds something on a rendezvous trajectory with us. Meanwhile, we'll develop our contingency plans." As a dark thought pushed itself to Jack's consciousness, he added, "I just hope we'll have the support of Mission Control. I hope somebody there is not involved in sabotage."

They heard the distinctive sound of the safety door that separated the cabin from the pressurized modules in the cargo bay. Jana and Lauren bounced into the cabin. "What's going on," Jana asked, her voice filled with pleasant anticipation.

Jack took a deep breath. "If we weren't in this weightless environment, I'd ask you to sit down and announce that I've got something to tell you."

Momentarily, they all stared at each other.

Lauren asked, "Do I presume we have a problem? Or as you would say, Jack, an opportunity?"

Jack explained the situation and then said, "We have a major opportunity."

Jana shivered. "I'd call this a major problem."

Solarship *Copernicus*

3:57 p.m. CDT

Max warmly acknowledged Jack, Fawz, Lauren, and Jana before he said, "I've carefully checked the program Filbert sent you. It contains no viruses. It won't interfere with the functioning of your ship. That's the splendid good news."

"Fawz has been checking, too," Jack said, "and he found a strange subroutine that's time-dated for tomorrow. Is that the bad news, Max?"

"Yes, that's it! The subroutine in Filbert's copy is not in my official, signed-off master. Now, get this, that rogue subroutine deactivates the entire meteoroid detection program tomorrow for 12 hours. When you'll most need meteoroid—or bomb—tracking!"

"Damn!" Jack exclaimed. He rubbed his forehead. "I presume we should uninstall this update and reinstall the old version?"

"Yes, do it."

"I'll reinstall it right now," Fawz said as he swiftly moved away from the main console to a nearby computer.

"What's Filbert say for himself?" Jack asked.

"I talked to him before I knew his copy was tampered with. He told me that Denise Morneau, the programmer, gave it to him with the approval form signed by me. Indeed, I signed off on the program as being finished. However, if I had wanted it on this mission, I'd have delivered it myself to Mission Control with the required paper work. Filbert knows the procedure. He also knows we don't send you program updates frivolously in the middle of a mission without a good reason. When I insisted, he coughed up his copy, and after I got back to my lab, I compared his copy to my master. That's when I discovered they're different."

What does Denise Morneau say about all of this?" Jack asked.

"I can't find her. A co-worker thought she was on vacation, and another one said she's gone hiking in Tennessee. Her immediate supervisor's not in. Not unusual since this is Friday afternoon. I've left a message at his home, and I left another message for Denise, too, in case she's still in town. You know how things are around here on Friday afternoons. It's more than half deserted already."

"Could Filbert have added that subroutine himself?"

"That's possible, but I don't think so," Max replied. "He doesn't know much about programming, and the subroutine's pretty slick. After 1600 tomorrow, it erases itself out of the program without a trace. Totally no evidence! Unless one runs a compare program first with my unaltered master."

"Could someone else have added that subroutine?"

"Yes! Filbert could have given the program to anybody. It's hard to think of him as a saboteur. Yet, I have more difficulty thinking of Denise as a terrorist. She seems normal, smart, a little quiet, and a bit of a loner."

"Run a security profile on her."

"Sure, Jack, just a minute. This new security software is great. Here's her file. Everything looks normal. She's single. Likes to go hiking alone. That's a bit odd. Background check on her was done about a year ago. Subscribes to *PC World* and *Hiking Times*. Been to Mexico three times, Canada, twice. Oh, listen to this! She helps support several family members, a widowed mother, a younger brother, two sisters, and a sickly aunt. I don't have access to her salary, but judging by her GS level, she doesn't earn much."

"Because she's short on money doesn't mean she's involved," Jack said. "It could be her supervisor."

Max replied, "It could be a lot of people. Considering what's going on here, don't tell me about the plans you're making. Knowing you, they'll be extensive. I'll second guess you from here and help every way I can. Don't contact me anymore unless you feel that it's absolutely necessary. In the meantime, be careful whom you trust. That's my biggest advice to you."

As before, the transmission abruptly ended.

"Somebody inside JSC is trying to kill us," Lauren quietly stated.

"Not necessarily," Jack quickly said. "Someone on the outside still could have done this. If Denise Morneau sent Filbert the meteoroid program electronically, a hacker outside of JSC could have broken into the system and changed the program."

"On the other hand," Lauren persisted, "Director Clayton himself could be trying to dispose of us. A major mission's never been a secret before, and what we've learned may be too important to ever announce to the public. Even though we all know how to keep secrets, trusting us may be too big a gamble."

Jack thought that the director had more subtle means of disposing of them than a bomb. Furthermore, Director Clayton was not high up enough in the chain of command to order such a thing. He simply was the director of JSC in Houston. Still, the crew could not risk asking Mission Control for help. Before, if anything went wrong, they had ready access not only to the entire National Aeronautics and Space Administration but also to the contractors who worked for NASA. For now, however, the four of them were on their own, and they would need to operate even more as a team than they had done before.

Fawz rejoined the crew and said, "I have reinstalled the old version." Then he thought a moment and said, "I wonder how the *Copernicus* can outmaneuver a bomb. I need to think. This indeed is a challenging problem. Our ship is going extremely fast even though we are decelerating. A rendezvous is a tricky thing even under optimal conditions. It would be nice if the solution were as easy as changing our trajectory or our rate of deceleration."

"Fawz, you're a true aeronautics nut. We may be killed, and you're looking at it as an interesting aerospace problem to solve," Lauren said, but her voice was not harsh. It had gentleness to it. She added, "This might be the time for you to think about our destiny."

"It was our destiny to fulfill the purpose of the mission," Fawz replied. He half closed his eyes. "And that we have accomplished. Unfortunately, I did not see beyond that goal."

Lauren said, "I wish I believed in destiny right now and believed that it was our destiny to live."

Jana had been quietly listening. Now, she piped up. "We could send a message to Earth saying, 'If you're the one sending the bomb to us, please destroy it immediately. If you have any information regarding the bomb, please help us.'"

What a naive idea, Jack thought. He noticed that Fawz looked away, Lauren checked her nails, and that Jana's hazel eyes darted, taking in how they ignored her comment.

Jack knew at this moment they were not a team. Each crewmember was alone, with separate thoughts, each exploring a different avenue toward salvation, separate tangents, each important, even Jana's, any one the key, or more likely a combination of all their ideas, the right combination, and the timing of when to do what.

After all they had been through together, Jack felt he could read each of their minds: Fawz figuring out how the *Copernicus* could outmaneuver a bomb, Lauren wondering who had sent the bomb, and Jana hoping to send a message to Earth asking for help. They would get nowhere discussing everything at once, only bogged down. For now, they each needed to stay in their own worlds.

Jack said, "I have an assignment for each of you, and then we'll get back together in about a half an hour. Fawz, begin a high level plan for evading the bomb if we determine there is one." To Lauren, he said, "Develop a list of potential saboteurs."

Then, Jack looked at Jana. Her calling for help no longer seemed foolish or impossible. Yes, she came up with good ideas that seemed off the wall at first and sometimes so utterly simple. "Jana, if we decide to send a message to Earth asking for help, how would we go about doing it? What other communication access is available to us?"

Jana stared at the main computer monitor and tried to think like Max, but the idea would not leave her mind that she was not one of them. She did not belong on this mission. Jack, Lauren, and Fawz were her friends. They each thought well of her, she knew, but still, she was not really an astronaut. She had the title and pay of a mission specialist, but that was all. She had been incredibly lucky—in the right place at the right time and definitely with the right connections. The others were true astronauts. Jack had commanded the Mars I mission, Fawz had gone into space before and would someday—if they survived—lead an entire country (he would do a good job at it, too), and Lauren, who had more degrees than one could list, was so competent. Jana was proud to call each of them her friend, but now, facing imminent danger, they would need a real astronaut, not one who got her job because of much luck and a bit of guile.

She shook her head from side to side. Now was not the time for self-doubt. Jack gave her an assignment well within her ability. She recalled the classes she had taken from Max and hoped that she had absorbed some of his computer savvy. He had been an extraordinary teacher and among other things had taught her fearlessness regarding the onboard computers. She needed to recall something relevant that he had told her, but it hung at the edge of her memory like a name or word one could not quite remember.

Jana began working at a backup computer at the front of the ship. The only communication capabilities on the ship that she knew of might not be sufficient. The four astronauts communicated with Mission Control, officially with Max, and informally (probably outside of all regulations) with Max through his "unlisted channel." Now, Max felt it was too dangerous to continue using that channel. To talk with Mission Control, they touched the microphone or put on the headset, but the ability to effortlessly do these tasks was coded somewhere in the computer. Jana would find where.

She scrolled through a list of programs until she found a communications directory. Three subdirectories were listed as Houston, Personal, and Educational. The last two listings surprised Jana and gave her hope that Mission Control could be bypassed. Happily staring at the three listings helped Jana remember the important thing Max had told her. All the solarships had basically the same standardized programming. Missions on other ships had not been secret. That meant that the *Copernicus* might have the same communications capabilities.

Jana methodically began checking. As she thought, the Houston subdirectory was the programming for their official connections to JSC in Houston: two to Mission Control and their official line directly to Max.

Under the category called Personal were five listings: each crewmember's name next to a code, and a fifth with a row of question marks instead of a name.

Jana pressed her name, and her home phone number in Houston appeared. Could she call home that easily? She shivered. Then a message said, "JSC authorization required to activate this number. Press 1 to request authorization or press Cancel." She clicked the cancel button on the screen. She certainly did not want Mission Control's attention right now. She tried the same thing for Jack, Fawz, and Lauren's names and got phone numbers and the same response. Access to their families was set up but not activated.

Then, she pressed the question mark listing, and the computer message read, "Please print authorization code." If she knew the code, could she make a call? She wondered. Was this Max's private channel? She typed in the code Max had given her: Y E L I A B N A L A * * * *

The message appeared, "Press 'Proceed' to continue or 'Cancel.'" She pressed "Cancel." That was how Max had set up his private phone number. He had simply programmed in his secret channel along with the list of their home phone numbers.

20

Jana vividly recalled the day Max had given her the code. He had said, "What's something you will always remember, a name, perhaps, but not anyone in your family?" The name of her good friend Alan Bailey popped into her mind. That was more than eight months ago. Last month, when the crew felt the need to clarify what was going on back on earth, she rather easily had recalled the code.

The final category in the communications directory was named "Educational." Under that heading Jana found two supernet addresses with the word "Inactive" listed by each address. Crewmembers on a secret mission would not make educational broadcasts. Yet, the communications programming apparently was standard just like on other solarships. The supernet certainly would be the way to go. Jana wondered how one would activate inactive addresses. Would Houston need to do it?

She clicked on one of the addresses, and a message flashed on the computer screen. "Address active. Type of message desired: print only, audio and print, photographic quality, streaming video, motion picture quality." She stared back at the screen with unbelieving eyes and pressed "Cancel." The address reverted to the inactive status. Jana was ecstatic. They could activate the supernet at will. They could ask for help just like she wanted to. They could send a message to the whole world.

Seconds later, she realized they were days outside the range to access the net. By the time they were close enough, it would be too late. Yet, other solarships had broadcast from far away. The Mars crews frequently had broadcast over the net.

What had Max taught her? There was always more than one way to do something with computers. She recalled the day Max had shown her 15 ways to do the same thing. At the time, she had thought he was overdoing the lesson to make a point, but not now.

She did not need to be limited to computers. What other communications equipment did they have? The *Copernicus* was equipped with a videophone, surely an inactive one. She wondered if it could be activated as easily as the net was activated.

Jana glanced around the cabin at the rest of her crew. Lauren nibbled on a freeze dried Neapolitan ice cream sandwich, occasionally allowing a piece of food to drift away from her and then nabbing it back. Clearly, Lauren had completed her task. Fawz stared out the window, and Jack slowly somersaulted in space while studying a computer printout. From several feet away, it looked like a timeline.

When the crew met back together, Jack decided to save Fawz's analysis for last. His ideas for evasive action for their ship surely would be detailed and brilliant, but even Fawz could not possibly think of every contingency. Lauren's report by its own nature would be hypothetical. Jana's report would be concrete if she found anything. The idea to broadcast to earth was beginning to sound appealing.

He glanced in her direction. Jana was bouncing around doing foot flexes against the wall, lightly pushing herself away, then grabbing a chair by the main controls and pushing herself back, waving the videophone in her hand, and acting as if she could hardly contain herself. Jack nodded for her to speak.

Jana said, "Luckily, our computers are programmed with two educational supernet addresses. We don't need JSC's authorization to activate them. One address is set up to broadcast over the net, and the other address is set up to receive messages from the net. However, we're too far from Earth to directly broadcast over the net.

"Now, listen to this. Here, we have our ship's videophone. It needs a code to activate it. I tried thinking up different codes and finally discovered that I can activate it with my personal credit card number.

"I thought we could use the phone to directly call those who can help us, but that function is blocked. Happily, the function to call the net and connect with a web address for broadcast only is not blocked.

"Our phone calls a communications satellite, and the satellite connects us with the net. We then can do a video broadcast over a web site to everybody in the world. There's a timing issue with the phone because our distance from Earth is constantly changing, but our computer can deal with that."

"How would our broadcast be found?" Jack asked.

"That's a difficult question. During your Mars I Mission, on the NASA bulletin board of web sites, a listing would read 'Mars Mission' whenever you made a broadcast."

Jack said, "I don't know how that worked. Houston took care of it. Our controllers took care of so much. Now, we could end up broadcasting without a net audience."

Jana added enthusiastically, "A listing might pop up on that bulletin board when we start broadcasting. It could be programmed to automatically do that. It might be listed 'Solarship *Copernicus*' or 'Ganymede Mission.'" Jana giggled. "How about 'Secret Mission Revealed?'"

Jana regained her composure. "I suspect our web site is listed as inactive on that bulletin board as there always were several inactive addresses. However, I found an option that will make the web address flash on and off. If the word inactive flashed on and off, even that would gain attention. Someone could be tempted to click on it."

Jana may have found a way. Jack felt as proud of her as if she were one of his own children. In fact, she most probably was his biological child. Jack seldom thought of her that way. He purposely categorized her as his friend and crewmember. Her parents were the people who nurtured her, those she called Mom and Dad.

Years ago, when he was starting his career, his best friends had asked him to be a sperm donor. Jack readily agreed. He had been flattered to be asked. They named her in his honor, Jack and Jana usually being a derivation of John.

Only five people knew, and Jana was not one of them. Now, it was far too late to tell her, and she must not ever know. With his friends' permission, he had told Shirl before his marriage, because withholding such a secret from his own wife would have been unfair.

23

Fortunately, Jana looked considerably like her mother. She even looked a little like her legal father, leaving open the possibility that he might be the biological father. The fertility specialist had assured the parents that their egg and sperm were not compatible and that Jana surely was the child of the sperm donor. They had decided against genetic testing. In this situation, ambiguity seemed like a good thing. However, sometimes Jack wished he knew with complete certainty that she was his own child because he wanted to be her father. This was one of those moments.

With great ease, he dismissed those familiar, but infrequent thoughts, turned his attention toward Lauren, and asked, "If a bomb exists, who is sending it to us?"

"You want a name?" Lauren lightly asked.

"A name would be good," Jack replied.

"A name might be easier than you think."

"Don't keep me waiting, then.

"I developed a list of potential saboteurs. I had eight categories. Any of them might have wanted to destroy our ship, but wanting to destroy us and having the ability to do it are two vastly different things. Who has the ability? More importantly, if a bomb is heading toward us, who is actually doing it? Then it occurred to me. The saboteur is only someone who launched a bomb during a certain timeframe: approximately three days ago. If only one thing were launched during that time, then, we've identified the saboteurs. We take appropriate action.

"The bomb probably would be disguised because most launches are not secret. It might resemble a probe or satellite of some sort. Probes often have explosives inside so that if they go off course, they can be destroyed before doing any damage.

"There are a limited number of launch sites in the entire world. We can ask Max to check what was launched about three days ago. If he finds nothing suspicious, then he checks satellites orbiting earth. Did one of them leave earth orbit and start traveling toward us? If he still doesn't find anything, then he checks what if anything was launched from any of the space stations.

"Now, here's a problem. Only a small number of people knew about our mission prior to the security breach last month. Of those, fewer knew about our trajectory, and no one knew that until about three weeks ago. Clearly, it takes longer than a month to manufacture a bomb disguised as something and reserve a launch date. These timing requirements point to an inside job, some group in the US or Rhatanian government."

Lauren frowned. "At present, I refuse to think that way. I searched for other possibilities. An off-the-shelf probe could be customized quickly, but to make arrangements with a launch company and to steal our trajectory takes time. If someone on the outside learned about us only a month ago, there hardly would be enough time to execute this treachery. Yet, it's possible.

"Then, I came up with a scenario. Suppose a probe built for a legitimate purpose was subverted to a new purpose, namely, to bomb the *Copernicus*. With that scenario, the saboteurs would have sufficient time. They would steal our trajectory data and reschedule their launch date so that the bomb could rendezvous with our ship. Maybe, I'm reaching, but I don't want our own people involved."

"Neither do I.," Jack said softly. "That's good work, Lauren." He was impressed that she had accomplished so much so quickly. She had far surpassed her assignment. He had not considered half of what now seemed so obvious.

He hoped that Max would think the problem through and conclude as Lauren had realized that only those involved with something launched about three days ago could be the traitors; then, Max would take whatever action was feasible. Yes, Max would figure that out. Jack would not risk calling him even on a secure line.

Lauren, Jana, and Jack turned their attention toward Fawz, whose overview was brilliant. Jack knew it would be. Yet, the details would need to be near perfect. When Fawz was finished, Jack removed a folded sheet of paper from his pocket. "I'll need input from each of you to complete this timeline."

"A real sheet of paper!" Jana playfully exclaimed. To keep waste to the minimum, the crew hardly ever printed anything but instead relied on their computer screens.

The four astronauts, enveloped inside the small world of their solarship, worked on their plans together. The bulk of their efforts would be focused on planning and executing their ship's evasive maneuvers. Three crewmembers would use the main computers for this work.

The fourth crewmember would need the videophone and an auxiliary computer to broadcast to anyone and everyone who found their web cast. Jack was beginning to doubt that the broadcast would work, but it was worth a try. He kept his doubts to himself.

Should we start broadcasting now?" Lauren asked.

"Not unless we find out something on a rendezvous trajectory with us. We need to be sure. We can reveal this mission to save our lives and our ship. We can do whatever is necessary to save ourselves, but Fawz and I can authorize emergency actions only if we're sure. That's procedure."

"The meteoroid detection program was deactivated. That seems like enough proof."

"Lauren, that's not nearly enough proof for what we're about to do."

"We're going to tell everything, aren't we? We're going to reveal secret classified information to everyone."

"That's the plan if we're all in agreement."

Fawz said, "Even if people learn of our existence, our message will not stop the bomb."

"It might," Jana whispered.

Lauren added, "Someone might have worked on a probe or a satellite who had no idea that its purpose was to destroy us. That person could step forward with valuable information to help us."

"Even if no one can help us," Fawz said, "we should proceed with the broadcast. People everywhere need to know about our discovery. Otherwise, if we perish, much of our knowledge could be lost. JSC has our reports, but they may never be declassified."

When should we start broadcasting?" Lauren asked.

Fawz said, "We know two variables. At 4:00 a.m. tomorrow morning Houston time, our meteoroid program begins tracking the bomb if it exists. At 4:00 p.m. tomorrow afternoon, unless we execute some fancy maneuvers, the bomb impacts the *Copernicus*."

"We'll broadcast the minute we know. If we find nothing, which is my fervent hope, then we'll keep looking. We won't let down our guard. Is there anything else?" Jack asked.

Lauren replied. "Tomorrow's Saturday. Lots of people surf their nets. We'll have a huge potential audience for our message. Yet, a powerful person or group simply could shut down our broadcast."

Jack thought for a moment. "Some laws governing the net pertain to freedom of speech. Anyone who terminates another person's ongoing message gets listed in a couple of official reports. It's like a spotlight shining on them. Not that those wanting to kill us care about the law, but they'd care plenty about being found out. People commit crimes in secrecy."

Jack again tried to shake from his mind that the broadcast would not reach an audience. Probably, when a scheduled web cast from space was in the offing, a web person at JSC took several preparatory steps at Houston's end. If the four astronauts were lucky, maybe an inactive address on a NASA bulletin board would blink. Could someone at a home computer then receive the web cast? Jack needed to proceed as if that could happen. His crew seemed so hopeful.

The four began working out the details for the broadcast. Once on the net, they would do two things: ask for help and tell about the whole mission from the very beginning. People needed to understand the impetus for the mission.

They would continue to broadcast until they were impacted by the bomb or until they avoided it. They would be on the net for many hours and could not talk extemporaneously that long. They needed to read something such as Lauren's official reports.

Jack studied Jana and exclaimed, "Your journal!"

She winced. "What about my personal, private journal?"

"Is it about the mission?" Jack asked.

"That's practically all it's about. I started keeping the journal the day you invited me to the party at your house."

"Is it accurate?"

"Oh, yes, it's very accurate. Jack, I know where this is leading, and it doesn't sound good. Lauren has perfectly wonderful reports she's prepared for JSC."

"Would you read your journal over the net if I asked you to?"

"Jack, you know I would. If that's my contribution to helping the mission, of course, I would do it." Jana concentrated on breathing slowly. She needed to tell him the truth. She would not whine. "I call it my journal, but it's not written like a journal. I took a couple of writing classes in college. It's written like a story."

"Better yet!"

Jana shook her head and said, "You're the commander."

"The press is saying terrible things about you. You could set the record straight."

"I told you I don't care what they think about me. They don't know me."

"But they soon will," Jack replied.

Solarship *Copernicus*

Saturday, 4:00 a.m. CDT

Jana suppressed a yawn as the four crewmembers watched the computer screen and waited. She had not once doubted Jack's abilities to protect his crew, and now she hated her negative thoughts regarding his leadership. Jack had insisted that they get some sleep. "You'll need your strength and full alertness tomorrow," he had said. And now, she had awakened tired, groggy, and aggrieved after fitful hours of sleep.

Almost out of a dream, she heard Fawz say, "We've taken this meteoroid program down to the most sensitive level, and nothing's there. Max's friend, the Kazimier, could be totally misinformed."

"The program may not be sensitive enough." It was Lauren's voice. "From this distance, the bomb is probably undetectable."

Jana half closed her eyes. She hardly could continue questioning Jack's order to read her personal journal over the net. She did not explain to him that she often wrote about her friend Alan, who was waiting for her back in Houston. Reading her journal to everyone would be difficult. Thoughts came to her in a half dream-like state. She saw Alan's face before her. He held out his hand, and their fingers almost touched, but then she blinked and became aware of the ship's cabin.

As Jana became more awake, she reevaluated her feelings and understood that Jack's order was a minor thing when compared to their present situation. Still, her negative feelings about him did not dissipate until the thought came to her that most of all Jack wanted to save the crew, but if they survived, he wanted to continue being an astronaut. She knew they all wanted that. He said that her journal could serve as a counterweight to all the rumors and provide political damage control. Jana had no idea what he was talking about. She would simply trust his judgment.

Lauren, Jack, and supposedly she herself scanned a computer monitor, looking for an object, a dot, the bomb. Fawz had moved in front of another computer screen. Jana focused her bleary eyes on Fawz's monitor. He was reading an on-line instruction manual.

Fawz said, "Override the multi-directional search and focus on small areas of the sky at a time. That should increase the program's sensitivity."

"Done," Lauren replied. "Still nothing. We don't know its velocity, or when or from where it was launched, just where it's supposed to be this afternoon. It's hard to select the areas to search. It might help if I select one launch site at a time and do a search. I'll try the launch sites in Florida, California, Russia, and Europe."

Jack said, "Try the Texas sites, too. Darwin Industries launches lots of private satellites and probes."

A half hour went by. Then, they heard it, a small warning tone, barely a beep. A message marched across the screen. "Meteoroid within 24-hour range of the *Copernicus*. Unable to determine size." Then another 15 minutes. "Object on possible rendezvous trajectory with *Copernicus*." Another 10 minutes. "Object on probable collision trajectory. Projected collision: 11.1 hours at 1600 hours today. Consider this a 'Watch' category. **Alert**: Mission Control not receiving this data. Contact Mission Control for possible trajectory modification. **Danger**: Meteoroid shields unable to withstand potential impact."

"Your proof, Commander." Fawz said.

"Yes," Jack replied. "Our proof! Now, we'll plan for the worst case scenario. We'll plan as if this thing is capable of rendezvousing with us and also capable of tracking us down when we modify our trajectory."

Jana became wide awake and scared, but amazingly refreshed when the computer spoke in a pleasant voice, "Object on collision course. Consider this a 'Warning' category. Notify Mission Control immediately."

Jack hit the Override key on the main computer. He would not notify Mission Control. Not yet!

Seattle, Washington

3:00 a.m. PDT

(5:00 a.m. CDT)

George MacInturff anticipated catching the fastest hydro-ferry to Vancouver Island this Saturday morning. He had promised his wife Marge, and she soon would awaken and get dressed for tea at the Empress Hotel in Victoria. Afterwards, they would stroll around the harbor.

While waiting for her, George surfed the net. Since he had purchased every optional supernet package and because of additional net access his job provided him, he could access practically everything. He checked the NASA bulletin board, looking for something interesting from a space station or moon base. Moon Base II had just completed a routine maintenance and provided a written report. If that were the best choice he could find, George would read the report, but he preferred gizmos, motion picture quality presentations with vibrant audio.

As George further scanned the NASA listings, an inactive address flickered just once. As an experienced surfer, that caught his attention. Sometimes a flicker indicated the start of an unscheduled broadcast, a surfer's delight. He typed the address on his keyboard and received the following spoken message:

"Access to solarship nets required. Key in access code."

"What a find!" George said aloud. "I hope I can get in." His company did some work for the government, but nothing in aerospace. Yet, he had an access code. It was worth a try. His voice quivered.

"I cannot understand the command," the computer responded.

George toggled off the microphone as he felt his throat tightening. His computer might not recognize his verbal commands. He manually typed in his access code and then instructed the computer to find automatically the path to the address given on the NASA bulletin board.

"Sorry, Auto Path not available," his computer replied.

George licked his lips. He was into the system. As the supernet security chief for a large Seattle firm, he liked a challenge. He began working.

Supernet Broadcast from Solarship *Copernicus*
5:02 a.m. CDT

"Hello, this is Commander Jack Medwin speaking to you from the Solarship *Copernicus*. We are four days from docking at the spaceport. We believe an explosive device is heading toward us—to impact our ship in eleven hours.

"We want to live, and you can help us survive. If you personally can stop this attack, we implore you to do so. In helping us, you may put yourself in danger, so please be careful.

"If you personally do not have information about this sabotage against us, then please tell everyone you know to watch our broadcast. Tell them to tell everybody they know. We need as much attention as possible for our message. Someone you tell may be in a position to help us.

"Whatever happens to us, we want you to know the truth. There has been misinformation in the media about us.

"Our ship is not contaminated, and we are not contaminated. This bizarre rumor circulating in the media is absolutely false. In fact, the opposite is true. We presently are free of most bacteria, virus, or fungus, and that condition is quite rare because small creatures find the human body an excellent habitat. Completely erase from your thoughts any fear of contamination: biological, chemical, or any other type from us or from our ship.

"Our new knowledge will not harm you in any way. There are people who fear what we have found, people who fear change. Change is not always for the better. While this new knowledge is of the deepest, most philosophical nature, in no way will it affect our day-to-day lives now or in the future unless we as a civilization choose to allow that. We implore you to rise up as civilized people worldwide and protect those who never meant us any harm and who may now or in the future need your protection.

"Perhaps, if the mission had not been secret in the first place, we wouldn't be in the danger that we now face. But there were reasons for secrecy, reasons you will learn soon enough.

"We may look slightly different to you, but I assure you we are the crew of the Solarship *Copernicus*. Space travel as most of you know causes physiological changes. You might expect our faces to become a little puffier and bloated looking without Earth's gravity working on us. But that's only at first on a much shorter mission. We've been on our mission for almost seven months now. We've each lost some weight and have become paler."

Jack instructed the camera to follow his eyes and slowly pan the cabin. As he briefly acknowledged each crewmember, the astronaut waved and said a few words.

When the camera again focused on Jack, he said, "Other rumors circulating in the media deals with our youngest astronaut Jana Novacek. These rumors question her very being. Exactly who is she? Why she was picked for the mission? I assure you she is a normal young person, more of a dreamer than some, but one who became a superb astronaut and met all the challenges put to her.

"Jana has kept a personal journal from the beginning of her training. After you hear her journal, I believe you will understand the truth about her and the truth about our mission."

Jana moved in front of the camera next to Jack. Before he floated outside the camera's range, he whispered to her, "Speak slowly, and look up frequently from your reading directly into the camera. Of course, you'll do fine."

She whispered, "Thanks!" to Jack and then turned and faced the camera directly. "My name is Jana Novacek. I have lived right across the street from NASA's Johnson Space Center all my life until going on this mission. I've always wanted to be an astronaut, but I kept this ambition to myself." Her voice sounded too high pitched and thin, but she pushed on, hoping she could relax her vocal chords. Jana looked down at her notebook computer. She needed to start reading and tell strangers about her life. Maybe, she could talk a little longer, talk the whole eleven hours, and not read her journal at all.

"Commander Jack Medwin, Co-commander Fawzshen, and Mission Specialist Lauren Adams have become family to me. They treat me like an equal. Because they trusted me and allowed me to go on this mission, all of my greatest wishes have come true.

"This mission is worth dying for, but I don't want to die. For myself, it is one thing, but now I have another wish, to protect those who mean us no harm."

Jana glanced toward Jack, and he was nodding at her, mouthing the words, "Go ahead, start reading."

"Since our mission had been secret, I thought I wouldn't be reading my journal to anyone except maybe in the future to my own children if I ever had any. Instead, I now share it with you."

"I started keeping my journal almost a year ago last June when I first suspected that something big and secret was going on at JSC. I've written my journal as a story rather than as a diary. I never thought that I'd be reading it over the net. Yet, every word is as true as I knew or felt at the time."

Jana shivered and began reading the first page of her journal.

Jana's Journal

A courier hand delivered the invitation to me at work in a curious silver blue envelope.

Commander and Mrs. Jackson Medwin

cordially request the presence of

Miss Jana Novacek and guest

at a reception honoring delegates from

The Arctic Federation

at 7 p.m. on Friday June the third

at our home on Point Lookout Drive

Nassau Bay, Texas

RSVP   black tie

I decided to invite my friend Alan Bailey. He worked as a co-op student at an experimental garden run by SpaceTech, and I darted over there at lunchtime to invite him in person.

In the jungly garden within a small clearing, he leapt high in the air, brought his knees to his chest, and folded himself into a compact ball as he somersaulted once, twice, and a third quicker time before landing smoothly on the taut trampoline. A shard of sun filtering through bamboo highlighted his sun-streaked hair. When he noticed me, he leapt higher, showing off and defying gravity. Turning in midair, he faced me before jumping off the trampoline onto the spongy moss ground covering.

"That's quite a job you have," I said. "Don't tell me, leaping on the trampoline causes air currents to help the plants grow better."

"That's a theory with possibilities," Alan replied.

"Your boss is over at the farm? And you're playing."

"He's in a greenhouse right over there. The hired hands are encouraged to exercise at lunchtime. We need to keep fit to climb the trees, you know, measure the biomass and count the insects."

I usually liked to talk to Alan about his ideas and theories for growing plants on the moon, but this day I had other things on my mind. I announced, "I've got some delectable news."

"The gazebo?" he asked, which was a special place to talk. "I'll get us some lunch first." I waited while Alan went into the main building and returned a moment later with two salads, the latest gifts from the garden. I had been to lunch here before, and the bounty from this garden was quite tasty, unusual but tasty.

We weaved our way through the jungly garden to the bougainvillea entwined gazebo and settled down on plump green cushions.

I took a bite out of the greens. "Delicious. And how many of these plants can grow on the moon?

"Maybe three. One for sure. It'll need some help, lots of help getting started in the lunar soil, and it'll grow inside an atmospheric dome, too."

If I asked, Alan would tell me the botanical name of every green in the salad and the temperature range in which it could survive. "The one that can survive on the moon is probably this blue lichen looking thing," I said, pointing to the least appetizing of the greens.

"Nope." He pulled a delicate leaf out of his salad and held it admiringly. "Believe it or not, it's this one." He then gazed expectantly into my eyes. "Okay, what's the *delectable* news?" he asked, barely mimicking my word.

"This Friday night, we're invited to a reception at Jack Medwin's house."

His eyebrows arched and his brown eyes grew darker. "Jackson Medwin, Commander of the First Manned Mars Landing?"

"That's Jack."

"You get a summer internship at JSC, and two weeks later you've wrangled a choice invitation like that?"

"I told you I was doing a good job," I replied teasingly.

"You told me that you finished your entire assignment for the summer in four days. Now, that impresses me."

"Don't be impressed. Now, I'll tell you the truth. Somebody grossly overestimated how long the job would take."

"I'd suggest keeping that little gem to yourself," Alan admonished.

"You're the only one I've told. Now, my supervisor doesn't know what to do with me. This past week, I've mostly run errands—been a gopher—go for this, go for that."

"Are you terribly bored?"

"I'm far too happy for boredom. The letter, the one I've been waiting for, came over the net this morning right before I left for work. What a morning! First the letter and then at work the invitation to Jack's party."

"The letter? Was it the one from Houston Aerospace Academy?"

"Yes, I'm accepted."

In one spontaneous motion, Alan moved our salads out of the way, stood up, lifted me up, took me in his arms, and hugged me. It was only a bear hug, but we both backed away, seemingly stunned. We were just friends, good friends. "Congratulations, Jana. That certainly puts you on the fast track, early admission to graduate school, and not just any grad school. Houston Aerospace Academy's very prestigious, where the best astronauts have gone, very expensive, too."

"Remind me to ask you to write my resume. You want the truth. I was the very last person to get accepted for this fall, and that's only because someone else decided not to attend. I know this because I called the school every day to check on my status. I can't imagine anyone declining such a school." I sat down and picked up my salad.

"What about a better offer?" Alan asked.

Our eyes met. The better offer could be sitting across from me, munching an exotic salad. I shook my head. I needed a clear focus on my future. Alan was so easy to talk to. I could tell him practically anything, but not how I sometimes felt about him. I needed my life uncomplicated, uninvolved, and clearly in focus, at least for now.

"What time is the party?"

"It's at 7:00. Now for more truth. My summer internship has nothing to do with why we're invited. The reason is a little more straightforward than that. Jack and Shirl Medwin are my parents' closest friends. For years I baby-sat their three kids."

"Your parents' closest friends? You seem to tell me everything, and still you have more surprises."

"I do tell you most everything." Reassuringly, I added, "It's just too much like bragging to throw his name around. I've done way more than my share of boasting for one day. Sorry."

"I don't mind if you boast. I'm glad you're happy. What kind of reception is it?"

"A formal shindig for foreign dignitaries."

"Dignitaries! From where?"

"That part is non-specific, a JSC method for keeping important visitors unpublicized and safe from harm. The invitation merely says the dignitaries belong to the Arctic Federation. They could be representatives of the Federation itself, but they also could be visitors from a specific country, even a head of state who happens to belong to the Federation."

"Sounds mysterious."

"Want to go?"

"Sure, why not?"

To be completely fair, I added, "The summer dance we've been talking about is on Friday night."

"I know," he said. "However, I think you'd rather go to the astronaut's thing. Wouldn't you?"

"Yes, I would."

The way he gazed at me, the hint of a smile breaking through, was a clue that he might have guessed my life's ambition, to go where Jack has gone and beyond, to the asteroids, to the moons of Jupiter, further to Titan, and onward to the edge of the solar system. This I kept locked in my heart, even from Alan. He knew, of course, that I wanted to work in the Space Program, but I had not told him my specific dream of being an astronaut for a major mission.

If I verbalized my dreams, would Alan laugh at me and remind me of the great numbers that had the same ambition? I hoped he would not laugh, but, still, I could not tell him, not yet.

Alan said, "A formal reception! That gives me an idea; there's something I'd like to show you." I unfolded myself from the gazebo seat and followed Alan past a reflection pool to a gnarled live oak tree. Delicate golden orchids grew profusely from a moss-lined limb.

Seattle, Washington
3:15 a.m. PDT

George MacInturff gloated over his luck and skill in accessing an unscheduled message from a solarship until he realized that the crew was issuing a plea for help, an SOS over the supernet. He wanted to help, but he knew nothing about recent launches. Furthermore, a space vehicle carrying a bomb toward a solarship would have been launched with the utmost secrecy.

It grieved him to think that Jana Novacek's life would end in less than eleven hours. So unjust! Jana was not at all like the tabloids described her but instead a young woman resisting her feelings and trying not to fall in love. His wife Marge often called him sentimental. She was right, but the compassion in his soul was because of her and because their love had worked out so well.

He turned the volume up. Jana had a nice voice, kind of young and bubbly, but he heard fear, too; sometimes, she lost her modulation and her pitch went up an octave.

How could he help? He could send e-mail messages, but to whom? Who could help her?

He had no intention of losing his connection with the *Copernicus*. Therefore, he would not try even one other task on this computer; co-processing opened up the remote possibility that the computer would crash.

He spun his chair until he faced his second best computer. A stack of messages awaited him, one with an urgent tag on it. He glanced at the urgent one. It was from his church headquartered in Houston.

To: All members
From: The Kazimier

Brandon Lane is no longer affiliated with us and is not authorized to collect funds on our behalf. The Kazimier will announce the name of a new Chief Financial Officer at a later date.

We are not now nor have ever been affiliated with the Flame Foundation. Furthermore, we express no opinion on the Flame Foundation.

For clarification, call the office during regular business hours or call 713-555-7356 day or night.

The e-mail from the Kazimier sounded like it had been drafted by an attorney, George thought. Probably an embezzlement, but he had never heard of the Flame Foundation. He could not deal with the rest of his e-mail messages now.

The crew of the *Copernicus* needed his help, but how could he proceed. With all his net savvy, all his access, and all the best computer equipment, still, he was at a loss. He spun his chair back around until he faced Jana. "I'll help you," he said to her image on the screen. "There must be a way."

Jana's Journal

Rare golden orchids were woven in my hair on Friday night when Jack Medwin ushered Alan and me into his dramatic living room. Jack radiated confidence and charm. Thin, yet muscular, with steady cobalt blue eyes, and an expression of sincerity, one would believe anything he said.

In a slightly elevated voice, Jack said, "I hear you're making quite a splash at JSC." He cleverly left out my status of "summer intern." A few heads turned toward me. That was Jack. In one sentence, he made me feel like I mattered and even that I belonged at this VIP reception.

Shaking Alan's hand, he said, "So, you're Jana's friend, Alan. I've heard fine things about you, son."

Jack's words startled me. How would he know about Alan? Maybe Dad had mentioned that I was bringing Alan.

Motioning his arm toward the far side of the room, Jack said, "The dance floor's over there, and the band starts in a few minutes. Food's scattered around." Then, Jack stepped forward to greet the next guests.

We entered the sprawling, domed living room and stood alone. Alan in a dinner jacket looked like he belonged. I hoped I, too, blended in. I wore Mom's new blue silk dress with subtle gold trim, a designer outfit she had not yet worn. Had she been home, she would not have loaned it to me.

I nudged Alan to look up. Shoulder to shoulder, we gazed through the immense glass dome that opened onto the early summer dusk.

I felt close to the heavens. For a brief moment, I could see myself working on an important project in the Space Program.

Below the dome, gigantic space photographs—some of Mars but also many computer enhancements of Jupiter and its moons—dominated the walls. I wondered what had happened to the subdued art collection that usually nestled between the pairs of tall French doors. Missing also were the other collections of rare old books and museum catalogues from around the world that usually adorned the end tables. I had so enjoyed browsing through those museum catalogs and even had managed to get Jack's kids interested in them, too.

Beyond the French doors, a brick loggia ran the length of the living room, and beyond the loggia, lights reflected off Clear Lake. A few people roamed outside into the muggy Texas dusk.

Inside, the crowd grew louder as people exchanged greetings. Many gestured toward the pictures and tilted their heads up to admire those higher on the walls.

"Do you know anybody?" Alan asked.

"Not really. I've seen some of these people before when I baby-sat Jack's kids during other parties." I pointed up to the balcony that flanked the high-domed living room. "From up there, the kids and I watched astronauts, mission controllers, trainers, and managers." I shivered. I was actually about to mingle with a room full of people who shared my interest in space exploration.

"Were Jack's other parties like this?" Alan asked, his eyes darting from one person to another.

"No, this one's more formal and bigger, too."

I did not see Dad anywhere. I spotted Jack's wife, Shirl, but she seemed busy introducing people to each other. I slowly scanned the living room for someone I might personally know. No luck. Then, I saw a face familiar only from newspaper articles. "Look, the one heading in our direction is Lauren Adams. I've read about her in the news. Of course, she's a pilot, but she's also studied sociology, anthropology, and linguistics. Strange background for an astronaut."

A rich, vibrant voice said, "You must be Jana Novacek. I'm Lauren Adams."

She knew my name. How curious! Choosing my sophisticated voice, I said, "I'm glad to meet you."

Alan lowered his voice to introduce himself. "I'm Alan Bailey."

Lauren projected no-nonsense attractiveness. Her smooth dark complexion glowed, but, yet, she seemed not to be wearing make-up. Abundant curly hair framed her face and dared not disobey her. She was slightly taller than I and somewhat heavier, not overweight, but she looked like she was exactly the weight she wanted to be.

I felt instant rapport with her. Our lives were worlds apart, separated by years, education, and training. Still, the feeling of rapport lingered.

Lauren gazed toward the wall to the right of Alan and me. "These photos turned out so well. I've seen only the 8 by 10's until now. Would you like to see my favorites?"

"You bet," Alan answered instantly.

She pointed toward a giant photo. "See Jack's footsteps on that red Martian soil. To me, this is second in a series, the first being the moon landing way back in 1969."

Lauren, Alan, and I moved to the next picture. Pointing to an area on a Martian plain, Lauren stated, "That's where they intend to erect the first Mars Base."

"And outside, a grain similar to wheat might grow right out in the open," Alan said. "Martian soil is loaded with nutrients. Some think the first crop will struggle to survive, but it could thrive. SpaceTech is experimenting with plants that endure minimal atmosphere, low sunlight, and the absence of a magnetic field. Even plants that take in nutrients from the Martian dust storms."

"Crops on Mars," Lauren said. "I like that." As we moved around the room, Lauren seemed aware of my mood, feeding it, commenting on the pictures, and weaving dreams.

"Isn't it about time for another major mission?" I blurted out, my voice sounding too bubbly and denting my shield of sophistication.

"That it is, that it is," Lauren said with enthusiasm. "The work we did building the space stations and moon bases was vitally important." She continued, "All the planning, all the effort, and all the hard work have increased our chances for success. Now, we're ready. The foundation is in place." As Lauren spoke, her voice softened, "I guess every astronaut yearns for a major mission. That's my goal, too."

From the glazed look on her face, I knew we shared common ground. Her chances of flying a major mission were a million times greater than mine, and yet the odds still were not in her favor. She would probably visit some of the space stations and might even get to a moon base once or twice during her career. Yet, she seemed so confident. Maybe, she knew something.

"If it's time for another major mission, what's the delay?" I asked.

"Money! Most everyone at NASA thought approval of the space appropriation supplement would be a routine matter." She paused. "Unfortunately, Senator Quagly has other ideas. He's fighting us with every fiber of his being." She and I exchanged glances. "So you're thinking, 'What's new about that?'"

"That's exactly what I was thinking," I replied. Senator Quagly fought NASA for every appropriation; that was how he got the nickname of Quack, Quack.

"The new twist is our new president. You could put her scientific knowledge on the head of a pin." Touching her thumb to her forefinger as if holding an imaginary pin, she explained, "Quagly sees his chance to cripple NASA, a chance he hasn't had in a decade." Optimistically, she added, "Of course, NASA is attempting to educate Madame President."

"I hope you succeed," Alan said.

"I certainly hope so, too. But never despair. There are other means of financing our work." Her eyes sparkled as if she knew some secret information. I had seen a similar look on Dad's face many times, but particularly before the Mars II Mission was announced. He often was required to conceal highly classified material from Mom and me.

Alan asked, "Other means of financing, like private investors or foreign governments doing a joint project with NASA?"

"There are ways," Lauren said almost too casually, like a flower closing its petals.

Although I had just met Lauren, I knew she would not reveal any more. Dad behaved in a similar manner when I became too inquisitive.

As Lauren, Alan, and I commented on the photograph of another Martian plain, the best looking astronaut I had ever seen breezed up to us. I recognized him only from press releases, photos showing him with Jack and the other premier astronauts. "Lauren, I've been looking for you," he said in a melodious voice.

"Hi, Filbert," Lauren replied nonchalantly.

"I stopped by to pick you up, but you had already left." Underneath his smooth, melodious voice, a slight whine filtered through.

She arched her left brow in response.

"I told you I was going to pick you up." His facial expression seemed a mixture of delight to see her and anger that she had not waited. He totally ignored Alan and me.

Lauren's vibrant voice dissipated into a flat monotone. "Filbert Grystal, I'd like you to meet Jana Novacek and Alan Bailey."

Filbert made an exaggerated turn toward us. We were a distraction he did not want. As much as it apparently pained him to acknowledge us, in his melodious voice he said, "Nice to meet you."

He turned back toward Lauren, but she was gone, having executed a magician's disappearance into the crowd. He craned his neck, bobbed his head in all directions, and then reluctantly turned back toward us, waiting for one of us to talk.

"Do you fly many space hopper missions?" I politely asked.

"They save the top astronauts for major missions," he arrogantly answered. "I'll probably go on the next one." He looked directly at me and waited expectantly.

It occurred to me that he wanted me to fawn over him and flatter him, but I had no intention of behaving like a simpering fool. "And when will the next major mission be?" I calmly asked.

He glared at me, all semblance of his syrupy charm gone. Then he turned to Alan. "You want to know, too?"

"Of course! I also want to know where you're going. To Mars? One of the asteroids?"

Baring his teeth, Filbert said, "Such information is classified. You children should know that." He lingered over the word "children," slowly hissing it out. He glared at both of us but to me said, "Are you the baby-sitter?"

Before I could answer, he turned quickly and wended his way into the crowd.

Filbert punctured the happy mood we had shared with Lauren. Alan and I easily were the youngest people at the party.

I wondered if Alan felt out of place. "We could leave," I suggested. "We can go somewhere else."

"Can you believe the nerve of that guy? Alan asked. "We were bystanders, witnesses, I guess, of his futile encounter with Lauren, and he took it out on us. Look, Filbert's across the room glaring at us."

"Where?"

"See, the 'Gristle' is leaning against the wall by the dance floor."

My eyes met Filbert's. "He certainly doesn't have the winsome personality one would expect of an astronaut." Alan and I both knew that in addition to their other duties astronauts were ambassadors for the Space Program. I added, "He wanted me to flatter him."

"I'm glad you didn't."

"He wouldn't have treated anybody who mattered that way."

"We matter." Alan took my hand. "Come on, Jana, cheer up. Want to dance?"

We sauntered across the room toward Filbert. His face seemed composed, but, as we got closer, a slight crimson spread from the hollows under his cheekbones. We neither paused nor acknowledged him.

Dancing with Alan, I soon forgot about Filbert and everything else but the beat and Alan's grace. How easy it was to follow him, even when he improvised every tenth step.

As we stepped off the dance floor, Dad greeted us. "I'm glad y'all are already making yourselves at home." Dad threw in a little Southern accent whenever he was ill at ease. "Sorry I'm late; it's been four and five meetings every day this week, constant interruptions, and only evenings left to get anything done. I guess the Rhatanians haven't arrived yet."

"Rhatanians?" I asked, recalling pictures I had seen of that mountain kingdom.

Dad said, "I just found out about the Rhatanian visitors this afternoon. There are three of them, the crown prince, the princess, and the chancellor."

Although Dad might not know all the details, he was at a high enough level that he knew days or weeks in advance about important foreigners who put JSC on their agenda. If Dad did not have a need to know, there must be something different about tonight's visitors.

"Mr. Novacek, why would Rhatania be in the Arctic Federation," Alan politely asked.

"I can't imagine why they joined, but I do know that they joined only recently."

Something intriguing and very specific about Rhatania hung at the edge of my memory, but it remained elusive. Instead, I recalled that countries touching the polar circle or having economic interests in the polar circle formed The Arctic Federation–the US, Canada, Greenland, Denmark (as protectorate of Iceland), Norway, Sweden, Russia and countries affiliated with Russia, and Rhatania. Rhatania did not touch the polar circle, and I could not imagine what its economic interest in the area could be. I knew that Rhatania was a rich, prosperous country that had a good reputation in the world community.

Dad nudged my shoulder and nodded in the direction of the foyer. He said, "The Secret Service has arrived."

About a dozen men and women in dark suits waited just inside the foyer. Apparently, upon signal, they gravitated to strategic points throughout the house, eyeing everyone. One stood behind Dad, Alan, and me.

Jack strode toward the band, took a microphone, and tapped it with his pen. "Attention!" People gradually stopped talking and drifted toward Jack. "As you well know, heads of state often include JSC on their official visits. Tonight, we are pleased to be hosting Prince Fawzshen, his wife Princess Regney, and Chancellor Li Shuwen of the Kingdom of Rhatania. They will be arriving momentarily. Some of you may already know Prince Fawzshen since he's flown on a NASA mission. In fact, he was educated in this country, and he and I were classmates and friends at the Houston Aerospace Academy.

"The Rhatanians will form a receiving line here on the dance floor. The band has been practicing the Rhatanian national anthem and plays quite a stirring rendition, I might add."

As the band filled the air with a stimulating and mysterious melody, the double front doors opened, and three rather simply dressed people advanced toward the dance floor and quickly formed a receiving line. An astronaut next to each royal personage introduced the honored guest.

Since the line of guests curved around the dance floor, I had a pretty good view of the royal party while Alan and I waited our turn in the receiving line. The royal couple and the chancellor were all attractive, dressed in subdued clothes, and perfectly groomed, except the prince had brambly eyebrows. All three of them looked definitely Asian and like pictures I had seen of people from northern China. An aura of power and dignity emanated from each of them. Still, the prince resembled a regular person wearing a very fine suit.

The prince was not a mere figurehead. Someday he would rule a small prosperous country. I could not imagine what it would take to successfully run a country: keep it functioning and safe from harm.

I was glad I had commandeered Mom's best dress and that Alan had given me rare golden orchids. This would be my only chance ever to meet royalty.

Finally, it was our turn. I hoped the prince would not ask what we children were doing here. An astronaut friend of Jack's introduced me to Prince Fawzshen, and the Prince said, "I have been wanting to meet you, Jana Novacek."

I was so taken back with his comment that I do not remember what I responded. I decided that must be his form of greeting to each person when he leaned past the astronaut between him and the princess, tugged at the princess's sleeve, said something almost inaudible to her, and nodded toward me.

Princess Regney said to me, "You are the one." I was not sure if that was what she really said. She said it so softly with a British accent like she was thinking out loud.

I almost replied that she must have me mixed up with someone else. Instead, I said, "I hope you'll enjoy your visit here."

She replied, "I now believe it will work according to our wishes."

I had no idea what she was talking about, but I simply nodded, as it was time to move on and meet the chancellor who also seemed extra friendly. I felt both exhilarated and bewildered.

Surely, I misinterpreted the royal comments, but the minute Alan and I moved away from the receiving line, he said, "The prince and princess were entranced by you."

"That was fun," I replied, downplaying whatever had just happened.

After the formalities, people surged forward and clustered around the royal party. The noise level intensified.

I yelled, "The other parties for important visitors were so different."

"Oh! How?" Alan asked.

"They were . . . friendly, but subdued." I pointed up to the balcony and reminded Alan that I had watched lots of them from up there.

"This isn't subdued," Alan said.

"I know. Tonight's different. It's also different from the lively parties that Jack and Shirl throw for the JSC crowd. Tonight, there's urgency in the air. Can you feel it?" I asked.

"Urgency?" Alan mocked, but then he added, "I feel it, too. These people seem frantic to impress the prince and princess. I wonder why."

"Oh, Alan, look!"

A man in a worn cowboy hat stood just inside the double doors. He wore old jeans and a faded plaid shirt, like he had just come off a trail ride. Maybe he was a bum crashing the party. Yet, he appeared totally at ease. He casually removed his hat.

Jack saw him and moved rapidly across the room to intercept. Would Jack smoothly lead the gate crasher to the door?

Jack and the cowboy shook hands. They talked as Jack led him across the room to the prince. Who would dare show up late for such special guests?

The cluster around the prince respectfully backed away as Jack presented the cowboy to the royal group. The prince and the cowboy exchanged greetings with a shake of the hand and a nod of the head. At closer range, I recognized the cowboy as being Max Marsh, a star JSC computer systems specialist.

Alan and I found a table laden with food. Alan dragged an artichoke leaf between his teeth, and I munched on a carrot stick. I noticed the Rhatanian chancellor trying on the cowboy's hat and realized the strange urgency in the room had dissipated. It was as if Max Marsh had a soothing, disarming effect on the other guests.

From out of nowhere Lauren appeared and said, "Do you mind if I borrow Alan for a minute? I want him to meet someone."

For a moment, I stood alone in the midst of voices. I saw Jack talking to Prince Fawzshen and Princess Regney. All three of them looked back at me. I walked over to the French doors and, seeing the canopy of stars, stepped outside.

The moon was almost full and pale orange, a wonderful color usually reserved for fall; yet, despite the brilliance, the stars shone through and reflected off Clear Lake. Tonight, the sky exuded a magical unreal quality as if Van Gogh had just intensified each heavenly body with a brilliant touch from his brush. I sat down on the porch swing in the shadows.

My thoughts were disrupted when Prince Fawzshen and Princess Regney strolled onto the porch, talking in a melodious language. They stood at the waist high brick rail. Prince Fawzshen mumbled strange words, gloating, a tone recognizable in any language. "Chri Anri. Chri Anri. Zum Du Der Leri."

He leaned over the porch rail and stared out over Clear Lake, seemingly talking to Princess Regney but also to himself or to the almost full moon and the stars. It was the brightest of nights, and I could see his profile clearly. His brambly eyebrows jutted forward, forming right angles with his forehead and casting shadows on curious dark eyes.

They knew I was out here because they had been looking in my direction when I stepped outside. Just to be sure, I stood up and gave the swing an extra push, making it squeak a little louder. I eased over beside them and said, "Sirius A and B are my favorite stars."

They turned around from the porch rail and seemed surprised by my comment. Was I being too forward? I was relieved when the Prince replied, "It will be long time before we get to stars; I prefer planets because they are accessible."

"Please join us, Jana," Princess Regney said. She knew my name! Jack must have reminded her before they came outside, but then I remembered her almost inaudible comment to me in the receiving line when she had said, "You are the one." She sat down on a porch glider and arranged her dress in one smooth gesture.

"I'd be delighted to join you," I said, surprised by my relaxed voice that rolled out. I sat down next to her, and Prince Fawzshen sat on the swing that faced the glider. I asked, "Are you enjoying your visit to the US?"

Princess Regney said, "We like your country very much. I would like to meet people and look, look, look at everything. However, I will have few days of intensive shopping. My relatives each asked me to purchase a memento of your fine country. To them and to me too, the United States is quite exotic. You perhaps could give me ideas where to shop."

"Oh yes, we have several shopping malls. Some of the older ones like Baybrook may interest you, or the Galleria on the other side of town. I'd be happy to take you there."

The prince and princess exchanged glances. I had overstepped my bounds. How could I have been so dumb? One must follow rules of protocol when interacting with royalty. I, however, had no idea what any of the rules were. Finally, Princess Regney said, "That is most thoughtful of you, but you will be busy next week."

She certainly was polite about declining. I had not meant to be pushy, merely helpful, and I felt they both understood. I did not feel embarrassed anymore, only relieved that I had not insulted them.

"Jack tells us you are doing well as a summer intern," Prince Fawzshen said.

"I was assigned a coding project," I simply said. I decided to take Alan's advice and keep quiet about someone's miscalculation in estimating how long the job would take.

Princess Regney said, "Jack also told us that you received a special honor."

"Special?"

"When you were in the high school."

It took me a minute to figure out that she was referring to a school requirement. NASA had given our school space on the hopper, and hardly anybody had entered in the area of crystallography. Then the local paper ran an article on the projects selected to go up in the hopper, and my picture had been in the paper. To explain that such an undeserved honor was merely a matter of luck seemed like a bad idea. I simply said, "It was a crystallography project."

Price Fawzshen leaned forward, "What are your career goals?"

The setting was perfect for the proclamation I was about to make. Something I had not even told Alan. A bright moon. A canopy of stars. A royal audience. The voice of determination and confidence blurted out. "I want to be an astronaut." If that was not enough, I added, "Major missions."

Princess Regney's joyful reaction surprised me. She clapped her hands lightly with excitement and laughed, almost with a sigh of relief, an airy tinkling laugh. "How simply perfect. You wish for a mission into space!"

She looked so pleased. She must have thought that just because I wished to become an astronaut that I would become one. Overnight! If she wished something, it could happen. For her wishes and reality marched side by side. But for me, becoming an astronaut meant successfully completing Houston Aerospace Academy followed by special training and finally much luck. She quietly inquired, "Will you miss your family when you go on a mission?"

"My mom is a jet pilot. She's gone for a week or more. Mostly to Edwards Air Force Base. When she returns, the time we spend together is so special. Guess you might say I'm accustomed to being away from family."

"And that young man you were with, your beau?"

What a deliciously old fashioned word. Alan? A beau? I had to be truthful. "He's a friend." As I said the word "friend," I knew he meant much more.

"There is vigorous training to become an astronaut." Prince Fawzshen said. "When the craft lifts off and Earth fights to claim you back, one must be in superb physical condition. Are you fit, Jana?" He sounded so serious.

"Do you exercise much? Aerobics?" Princess Regney asked.

"I exercise a lot, swim, jog, and do gymnastics on the trampoline."

They exchanged glances, the kind of exchange I had seen between Mom and Dad when sharing an unspoken thought. They talked with me quite a while and asked many questions about my family, college, my summer internship at JSC, and even my flying lessons.

All their questions seemed so strange and reminded me of an interview. I almost asked why they were so curious about my life, but then I thought of protocol rules unknown to me and the possibility of offending visitors with different customs. Instead, I changed the subject.

"What's your country like?" I asked.

"It is cold, austere, and marvelous." Prince Fawzshen spoke proudly.

Princess Regney said, "We have a summer home high in the mountains beside a lake. We swim and boat. Sometimes, we ride horses and hike through the forest. You must tell us when you can visit."

Was this an invitation from a Princess? One I had just met? I thought of Mom and of all her flying perks and how possible it would be to visit. I almost said, "We might just do that," but then caught myself just in time. Maybe that was their way of being polite. I simply replied, "Thank you for the invitation."

Princess Regney shifted her weight in the glider and turned her head so that she was looking straight at me. "Your eyes are like ours," she announced.

Both the prince and princess had dark brown eyes with thick, dark lashes while my eyes were hazel with rather pale lashes. "I don't understand," I said.

"Look in the mirror. Look very carefully. Then you will know," Princess Regney said and smiled.

Just then Jack strolled outside and joined us. "How's everything going?" he asked.

Prince Fawzshen answered, "Everything is A-Okay. A-Okay."

Later, Alan and I found each other by a dessert table. I asked him about Lauren's friend whom she wanted Alan to meet, and he said that the person didn't seem particularly interested in speaking with him. I told him about the prince and princess and that the princess had said that my eyes were like theirs. I did not mention a strange idea that had popped into my head: Lauren had found someone for Alan to talk to because the prince and princess wished to speak privately with me.

Such an idea bordered on delusions of grandeur. Yet, the prince and princess certainly had been inquisitive. To distract myself, I asked, "You want to meet Jack's kids? They're probably upstairs in the game room."

"Sure, why not?"

We found all three of them sprawled out on the floor, each holding an electronic hand of cards.

"This is Alan." I said. "And here we have Brad, Mark, and Stacy, my beach buddies."

Stacy carefully looked over Alan and then put her card screen face down in front of her. To me, she asked, "Is he your boyfriend?"

Alan and I glanced at each other, and I giggled. "He's my friend."

"Sure, that's what they all say," Stacy replied.

"Perceptive little person," Alan said. He sat down on the floor next to Stacy, and asked, "Who's your boyfriend?"

Stacy stared down at the floor and mumbled, "I don't know."

Brad and Mark carefully stashed their card screens in secure spots. Brad, the eldest, allowed Mark and Stacy to tease me for a while about Alan. Surprisingly, Alan did not mind. Finally, Brad said to me, "You look like a movie star." The two others laughed and giggled.

"Okay, guys, what's going on?"

Brad, between chuckles, tried to answer. "I went downstairs to forage for food. That conceited astronaut Filbert pointed to you and asked if you were the baby-sitter. Imagine us with a baby-sitter! But don't worry, Jana, I told Filbert you were one of the special guests."

"Special! In what way?" I asked, but Brad looked away, pretending not to hear me.

Stacy, the youngest one, said, "Dad doesn't like Filbert."

Brad declared, "Dad never said that." Brad's demeanor quickly changed from that of a carefree child to the senior officer in charge.

"But Brad," she implored. Then, quickly to me, she asked, "Did Uncle Fawz say anything about your eyes?"

Brad lightly elbowed her in the ribs. "Be quiet!"

I shivered. "What about my eyes, Stacy?" I could feel the little hairs on my arms standing up.

"Uncle Fawz asked questions about eyes. Eyes like yours." Stacy puffed up with pride. "I told him about your eyes. Uncle Fawz said everything would work out."

"What did he mean?" I asked.

"Hush, Stacy," Brad ordered, his voice sterner. To me, he said, "We don't know what he meant. Dad told us not to repeat anything that Uncle Fawz said at dinner that night."

"But Jana is like family. It's okay to . . . ." She broke off and looked guiltily at Brad.

Mark patted Stacy on the shoulder. "It's okay. You didn't tell anything important."

Brad authoritatively said. "Dad can't tell us anything really important. He trusted us with a little, and we let him down. We failed him. We failed Uncle Fawz, too."

"It sounds like you all know Prince Fawzshen pretty well," I said, half soothing the situation and half fishing for more information. When they exchanged nervous glances, I quickly said, "It's okay, never mind."

Brad, now that he had the other two firmly under his control, thought a moment before speaking. "It's okay if we call him Dr. Fawz. He says that's a title he earned, but he likes us to call him Uncle Fawz. When Princess Regney and Chancellor Li Shuwen go back to Rhatania, Uncle Fawz will stay on at the hotel. That's not a secret."

I resisted the temptation to prod further.

As soon as Alan and I were out of earshot of the three children, I whispered, "Something highly classified at JSC involves Prince Fawzshen."

"If so, why this big party?" Alan thoughtfully asked. "Wouldn't he rather keep a low profile?"

"I don't think so. It's almost a JSC tradition for foreign dignitaries to attend an event at Jack's house. If there were no party, people would say, 'Why are they keeping Prince Fawzshen tucked away?'"

"So, instead, Jack shows him off?" Alan asked, still not convinced.

"And another thing, Jack and Shirl have house guests almost nonstop. Most of their relatives have visited them, I guess, to be close to the first person whose footprints rest on the red Martian soil. If Prince Fawzshen, Jack's friend, were staying only a short time, wouldn't he, too, stay here in this house?"

Alan shrugged and said, "Maybe not." Then he brightened. "Your job at JSC! Because of your job, you might find out why Prince Fawzshen is here. What do the people at NASA call it when a task requires knowledge about classified information?"

"A need to know," I answered and shivered as more irrational thoughts came to me.

"Now, what's this about your eyes?" Alan stared into my eyes and thoughtfully said, "How fascinating your eyes are. They're usually hazel, but they're green tonight. Occasionally they're blue, and sometimes even gray. They're lovely magical eyes.

Solarship *Copernicus*

5:22 a.m. CDT

As Jana read her journal over the net, Jack, Lauren, and Fawz concentrated on their plan for evading the explosive. Then, a monitor beeped. Jack read the supernet message almost with disbelief. He was pleased. At least one person with enough computer savvy to send a reply to a solarship had picked up the broadcast. Lauren and Fawz floated toward the computer screen.

The reply simply read, "This is George MacInturff from Seattle, Washington. What can I do to help you?"

Jack marveled at the simple reply. Not only had George MacInturff received their message but also he had sent a reply to them over their second supernet address. This took knowing his way around the net. With so much security on the net, Jack had been concerned whether people would know how to wend their way through the net and not be intimidated by scary security messages. He also had wondered if those receiving the broadcast would need advanced interface options. He thought they probably would. Until that moment, Jack had doubts, which he had kept to himself, that anybody who could help them would receive their message. If their plight were not so deadly serious, Jack would have found it humorous how an individual, possibly on a home computer, could contact a multibillion-dollar spaceship.

Jack, Fawz, and Lauren quietly analyzed how to respond while Jana continued reading her journal.

"If we send a message directly to him, we could put his life in jeopardy," Lauren said.

"Also, our message to a specific supernet address would alert Mission Control if they don't already know." Jack hated to think that people he knew had issued orders to destroy the *Copernicus*. "What are we buying, anyway? Time to get worldwide attention! If people within NASA are involved, under worldwide scrutiny they most likely would abort their plans."

The crew had variations of the same conversation throughout the early hours of that wake cycle. They did not wish to publicly alienate JSC because NASA could be totally innocent of this whole mess. If so, the crewmembers wanted to continue being astronauts. Jack wondered if that any longer was possible now that the crew had gone public. After a quiet discussion, they decided how to respond.

Jack motioned Jana to find a stopping spot in her reading. Then he exchanged places with her in front of the camera.

"This is Commander Jack Medwin of the Solarship *Copernicus*. We have been broadcasting for a little while, and you on Earth who are watching this may want to know specifically how you can help us. Perhaps your name is George, and you live in the Pacific Northwest. What can you do? Call all your friends! Tell them to call all of their friends. The more people who watch this broadcast, the more likely we'll find someone who knows something. Someone with the power to stop this attack on us soon may be watching."

Seattle, Washington
3:32 a.m. PDT

George blinked. Commander Jack Medwin had gotten his message and was telling him what to do. He was filled with a noble feeling, but that quickly faded. Jack's message was basically the same as when George had first found the broadcast from the *Copernicus*. George did not consider himself dense, but he had been thinking about helping the astronauts directly rather than merely spreading the word.

He rubbed his chin. Why was NASA not broadcasting, too? Why had a NASA representative not come on the net? How incredibly peculiar that highly trained astronauts on a solarship needed his help.

He commanded his computer to search for possible coded messages. Nothing. He needed to contact people right away, but how could he do it efficiently?

Few of his friends had advanced interface options with their nets. Even if they did, fewer still would have the required government access. Was Commander Jack Medwin aware that only a small percentage of net users could access the broadcast? Maybe the Commander knew something he did not.

Was there another way? Logically, there should be. Government clearance should not be a necessity because the *Copernicus* was neither blocking access nor encrypting the broadcast.

George spun his chair around until he faced his second computer. Like a starburst, he had a brilliant idea and quickly tried it. No luck. He tried again. He knew many techniques. He plodded on. On his eighth try, he was in. In retrospect, the path seemed obvious to him. Now, people could access the net without advanced interface options and without government access.

He had lifted that major barrier for his friends—better yet, people, lots of people, aerospace people, people everywhere—to access the *Copernicus*, but he did not know how to proceed. He printed out Jack's message, and the words "watch" and "watching" jumped out at him.

Then as if out of a fog a thought came to him. What did lots of people watch? TV! He would call the TV stations. Would they pay attention to him? He would sound like a nut case if he told them that Commander Jack Medwin from the Solarship *Copernicus* had asked a George from the Pacific Northwest for help and that he was that George. Yet, TV definitely would be the way to go, and the most persuasive person he knew could call the TV stations for him.

"Marge," he yelled, "come here quickly."

Marge emerged from the bedroom calling out, "Yes, yes, I know we've got to catch the hydro-ferry. Tea at the Empress will be jolly fun. I'm ready to go."

Oh, no, George thought. He had forgotten all about their planned jaunt to Vancouver Island. He glanced toward her, and her appearance practically took his breath away. After all these years, she still was a beautiful woman. Someone else could save the astronauts. He was taking his wife to tea in Canada.

He stood up. How charming she looked, anticipating a trip to Victoria. He would be firm. "Call everybody you've ever known in the whole world," he ordered. "But call the TV stations first."

"What are you talking about? We'll miss the early morning ferry."

"There's something we've got to do first. Honest, I'll make it up to you. We'll go somewhere quite incredible, but not this morning."

"Where?" she asked, willing to bargain.

"I don't know. I can't think about it now." George hardly knew where to begin. Under the best of conditions, it was hard to say "no" to Marge. But now, she probably was one of the few people in Seattle who did not have even a passing knowledge regarding rumors of a contaminated solarship. Furthermore, she did not know that responsible newspapers now were saying that a secret mission indeed was in progress. George explained the situation as quickly and carefully as he could. When he decided that she understood, he coaxed, "Come here, Marge; look, it's that young astronaut, Jana what's her name."

"I'm not going to be co-dependent with your addiction to the net."

"You like the net, too."

"I can take it or leave it. I have a life outside that little box of transistors."

Transistors were twentieth century technology, but George did not have time to banter with her. He loved Marge, his colorblind artist, and now he needed her true talent, the ability to sell anything to anybody.

"Please, Marge, watch the monitor. That's Jana, the astronaut. See how she reads and how she looks straight at the camera every now and then. She's no actress." George thought it best not to mention that he sent a message to the solarship and that they had replied. "The crew is in dire danger, and they need our help, now."

"Yeah, yeah. Think of our phone bill! You could be watching all this on the space channel, for free, too."

"Maybe, turn it on, would you?"

Marge clicked the TV remote to Channel 51. There was a picture of a space taxi and explanations of the 6,000,000-mile maintenance check.

"Marge, this whole mission's been blacked out. This is their first transmission." George knew he was not getting through to her. Marge's life primarily was her art, some interaction with other artists, and her love for George. If she had wanted, she could have sold computers to people who had no written language and could barely count. Instead, she worked steadily as a red/green colorblind artist.

George tried tact. "If you make the phone calls for me, I'll mix paint for you for a month whenever you want, on demand, so to speak."

"This is important to you?"

"Oh, yes, and extremely urgent. Call the network TV channels, the cable news stations, and the other major channels, too. And foreign TV stations. Call them, too. Tell them this path and this address." George wrote it down and checked it carefully. "If their engineers don't know how to pull stuff from the net onto TV, have them call me. I've found a really slick procedure at the last net security conference."

"Where's the extraordinary place you're going to take me?" Marge asked.

"Someplace great," George replied offhandedly. "After you're finished with the TV stations, call all of your friends, but keep it short with each one. Call our friends in Houston first. Several private space exploration companies are down there. Do we know anybody near any other launch sites? Cape Kennedy? The launch sites in California? Foreign launch sites? Your friends will be grateful to you and indebted, too."

"Don't patronize me, George," she said as she headed toward another part of the house. "What about NASA? Do you want me to call them?"

George thought maybe a split second. "No, don't call them." He figured if they authorized it, they knew.

George was determined to do more while Marge called the TV stations. TV was the best way to go; yet, many people far preferred the net and rarely turned on TV. He must reach those people, too. The net security chiefs he had met at the recent conference probably would be an ideal group to contact, and he recalled that several of them worked for aerospace firms. George placed a storage device with all their names and e-mail addresses into his second computer. He sent them all an urgent e-mail and asked them to forward it to everyone in their companies.

He remembered the net security chief from Darwin Industries in Houston had been a particularly pleasant, yet highly conscientious young woman, and now he recollected that Darwin Industries launched private satellites. He quickly typed a personalized e-mail to her, but before he pushed the send button, he figured that she would want to check out the authenticity of the astronauts' message for herself. Since she would have advanced interface options and required governmental access, he included the documentation so that she could verify that the astronauts' message indeed was coming from a solarship.

He realized that some other net security chiefs might also wish to verify for themselves the message's authenticity, so he sent them all a second urgent e-mail with documentation included. His mind flew. He remembered the Kazimier's message about a probable embezzlement and thought about the church's mailing list, a cross section of people throughout the world, a significant percentage right in Houston, the city of private space exploration firms.

Whoever was at the church office on a Saturday morning might not take independent action. It was worth a try, however. He quickly composed an e-mail letter, listed all his supernet credentials, and verified that the broadcast from the Solarship *Copernicus* was authentic. He explained precisely how church members could access the broadcast, and he ended by imploring the Kazimier (or whoever at that moment was in charge at the church office) to immediately forward the message to every church member, emphasizing that time was everything. It was a far different letter than those he had dashed off to security chiefs with whom he already had established credibility.

He visualized a church secretary reading his e-mail, dismissing it as something from a crackpot, and hitting the delete key. As soon as Marge finished calling the TV stations, he would ask her to call the church.

What next, he thought? He could go into a chat room on the net and tell people about the broadcast, but would he reach large numbers of people at a time? What else? He needed several large e-mail lists, but had access to only one. He could send an e-mail message to everybody in his own company, but his company did not have any aerospace contracts. He could not think of anything better to do at the moment, so he pulled up his company mailing list, slightly modified what he had sent to the security chiefs, and pressed the SEND ALL button.

George then turned his attention back toward his best computer. He listened to Jana's voice as she read from the screen of a notebook computer. Her wild fluctuations in pitch were gone, an indication, he hoped, that her level of discomfort had decreased. He saw her not as she was portrayed in some papers but as a young woman who had known nothing about what she was getting herself into.

Jana's Journal

The morning sun scorched down on me like a steam machine. The temperature easily could reach a humid 100 degrees today. I was programming Dad's new lawn mower when Alan jogged toward me. "How about a swim later today?" he cheerfully called out. As he got closer, he said, "I've got some work at the SpaceTech garden today. Want to meet at the pool later this afternoon, say about four?"

"Sure, that sounds great." Under the morning glare, last night's party at Jack's house seemed gossamer and insubstantial. Had Alan said my hazel eyes were lovely? The way he gazed at me now, his eyes not as piercing, but less focused and accepting, he had said it. "I should have the house all spiffed up by four. Did I tell you that Mom's due home tonight?" I rolled my eyes, and both Alan and I laughed.

It was Dad's and my modus operandi, but Alan knew about it. When Mom went out to Edwards Air Force Base in California, Dad and I neglected the house. Then, just before she was due home, we would go on a whirlwind picking-up, cleaning-up, and yard-sprucing spree. Dad usually spruced the yard, trimmed shrubs, and applied Instabright while I tidied up inside the house. But today Dad was changing a program in his hydrocar, so I was not sure how much outside work would be left to me.

Alan bent down to the grass, picked a blade, and rubbed it between his thumb and forefinger. "Slowgrow 417." Green residue was on his fingers. "It's been fed large quantities of Instabright."

"That's probably true," I nonchalantly said. Dad was not much into plants and shrubs, but what we had was green, verdant green, brilliant green. Alan's SpaceTech garden was a work of love, while our yard was neat, well-trimmed, and bright, but uninspired, except for the lawn. Soon, the lawn would become its own work of art, a monochrome, three-dimensional picture—I had chosen a Mayan calendar—of various heights, thanks to Dad's new computerized lawn mower.

Alan said, "I'll help you cut the lawn. It'll be done in a nanosecond."

It would take more like an hour, and I would be drenched in sweat. It was thoughtful of Alan, but I did not want him to see me looking so unkempt. I shook my head. "Thanks, but I'll do this myself."

"I'll meet you at four, then." He turned away and jogged about fifteen feet before turning back. "I had a great time last night," he said.

"So did I," I replied.

Then he waved cheerfully, and I watched him move from sunlight into the sharp morning shadow of an oak tree, back into sunlight, the sun catching his hair, then into the smaller shadow of a skinny pine. I liked the way he moved with an agile quiet confidence past the neighboring homes, twice turning to look back at me. For a second, I longed to jog with him. I would cut the grass later; no, it would be far too hot then. A white hydrocar, barely a few inches off the ground, drifted lazily down the street past Alan.

I turned on the mower. The hum reminded me of last night's voices, individuals heard against the background of the lively crowd. I thought about Lauren and the photographs of Martian landscapes. I thought about Prince Fawzshen and Princess Regney, and I relived our conversation on Jack's porch under the stars.

Why had Jack Medwin, the most respected of all the astronauts, invited me, a summer intern, to a party of astronauts and JSC contractors in honor of the Rhatanians? Jack, his wife Shirl, and my parents were the best of friends, but still, it was not a family party. I knew the answer, but it was too strange to contemplate. He had wanted me to meet the prince and princess, but why?

Turning my attention toward the lawn, I pretended the mower was a power source pulling me along an alien meadow as I scanned for signs of intelligent life. Thoughtful beings should be here somewhere if they could tolerate such heat. I enjoyed turning a grueling task into a pleasant activity. It certainly was hot. My hair stuck to my face, and blades of grass flew onto my damp ankles. The grass smelled sweet and clean.

Barely above the mower's hum, I heard the distinctive hissing of a hydrocar settling down at the curb. As I turned around, the doors of a white hydrocar with a NASA emblem buzzed open; Jack and a slim Asian man agilely leapt out. I gasped in amazement at seeing the man; yet, I did not recognize him.

I shut off the mower, pushed strands of hair off my sweaty forehead, and walked toward them. I was trying to place the Asian man. Did he work Mission Control? Was he someone who worked with Dad? As I drew nearer, I recognized the dark eyes accentuated by brambly eyebrows; it was Prince Fawzshen, crown prince of his kingdom and the object of all last night's excitement. In a casual knit shirt and summer slacks, he looked slimmer, smaller, like a normal person, and not majestic at all. Yet, there still was a dignity about him and a bearing of someone accustomed to power.

"Dad should be back any minute," I said.

As I led them onto a brick walkway toward the front door, I remembered the house needed straightening. I told myself I would think of something. Prince Fawzshen probably had never seen a cluttered house. A castle I had visited near London flashed into my mind: gleaming marble floors, rosewood and needlepoint furniture, and every item in perfect order.

We were almost to the door before an idea came to me. The screen porch was straightened and reasonably attractive, filled with Dad's bright green Instabrighted plants. The plants were too green, looking like they might reach out and devour all in sight, but they would do.

I led them past the front door to the side of the house. As I ushered them onto the screen porch, I turned the controls for the overhead air jets to maximum speed. I turned on another control to cool the water that circulated through the white tubular furniture, comfortable, flexible, porch stuff that, when activated by body heat, molded itself somewhat to the occupant's shape. Dad was ever so fond of gadgetry.

I wished Dad were here. He would know what to do. How does one behave toward a prince? I had no idea, but last night seemed to go well enough. I would think of Prince Fawzshen merely as Jack's friend. Then I remembered that Jack's children told me he liked to be called Dr. Fawz because that was a title he had earned. I simply would think of him in that manner.

I waved my hand toward the white porch furniture. "Please, sit down. What would you like to drink? Would you like some lemonade whiz?" The voice that came from me sounded like someone else speaking.

"The lemonade whiz intrigues me. I will choose that."

"I'll take a lemonade whiz, too," Jack said.

As I dashed into the house, I left the kitchen door slightly ajar, allowing more cool air to flow onto the porch. I leaned over the kitchen sink and splashed cool water onto my face before filling two glasses with lemonade whiz.

Outside, I handed them each a glass and said, "That was a terrific party last night. I'll never forget it."

"Beginnings people rarely forget," Dr. Fawzshen said.

What a strange comment! Maybe it was his translation of a foreign idiom into English.

Jack frowned and moved his bottom lip up, half covering the top one. Rarely have I seen him any other way than perfectly at ease. Maybe it was the heat. Quickly, Jack reverted back to his delightful self and said, "The kids were pleased you stopped by and said 'hi.' They still talk about all the places you took them." That was the Jack who could make anyone feel important in a second.

"We had some great adventures together," I said, remembering the trips to Galveston on the monorail and the dangers we got into that Jack and my parents never discovered.

Neither one said anything. Obviously, they were looking for Dad. "Dad should be back in a few minutes. He's gone to the hydrocar supply store."

"His hydrocar's broken?" Jack asked. "I've never heard of one of those things breaking."

I replied, "You know Dad; he's trying a new program that'll make it run even more smoothly."

Jack grinned. "That's an engineer! Actually, we dropped by to see you." Then he asked, "how're you enjoying your summer job, Jana?"

"The programming assignment was fun, but now it's over."

"What are you doing now?" Jack asked.

"Mostly running errands for my supervisor."

"Far from enthusiastic you seem. Correct!" The way Dr. Fawzshen pronounced "correct" with a hard "K" sound was so charming that I suppressed a giggle. This was beginning to sound like an interview again.

I certainly was far from enthusiastic, but I could not explain to them or to me this yearning I was feeling for something more. I was quite lucky to be working at JSC, errand person notwithstanding. "My summer job will pay for some airplane rental. Mom's been giving me flying lessons."

The porch air jets were doing their job, the furniture was cooling, and the air from the house helped, but still it was a bit uncomfortable. I watched Jack gulp down his lemonade whiz. Dr. Fawzshen already had finished his. I wondered if I should invite them inside amid the clutter. "How about some more lemonade whiz?" I asked and dashed into the house with their glasses.

I poured lemonade whiz into their glasses as a disappointing thought struck me. Dr. Fawzshen was going to ask me to baby-sit his children. Their interview last night was about that. Maybe according to their custom, only a person with a certain kind of eyes, eyes like theirs, whatever that meant, could tend the royal children. I should have figured it out when that arrogant astronaut Filbert asked if I was the baby-sitter.

A few years back, how I had enjoyed baby-sitting Jack's children, and Jack had said I was the best sitter ever. Brad, Mark, and Stacy were the younger brothers and sister I never had. It had been fun, but now it was time to move on.

When I went back outside into the heat with the whiz, I asked, "Where is Princess Regney?"

"Reg shops for presents to take home to our relatives."

I had to know. "Are your children with her?"

Dr. Fawzshen chuckled. "Our children are babies. What precious babies they are." He grinned softly.

I persisted. "Is someone caring for them today?"

"Correct. They are home in Rhatania with the nanny," Dr. Fawzshen said. "Today, Reg will have a jolly busy time. United States is a most exotic country." He glanced over at Jack. "I talk much, and we have important business to tend."

Jack said to me, "We've known each other your entire life, and you've never told me your life's ambition."

"My life's ambition?" Dr. Fawzshen or Princess Regney must have told Jack about last night's conversation.

"That you want to be an astronaut."

"With all my heart!" I exclaimed but quickly softened my unrealistic enthusiasm with a more casual comment. "I went to space camp twice. It was great."

"I believe we can find you a different job at JSC," Jack said.

"What kind of job?"

They exchanged glances. "This, I consider the fast training program for astro . . . ." Dr. Fawzshen stopped abruptly.

I thought he was going to say that wonderful word "astronaut." I knew of no program for students or interns to train with astronauts. "How do I apply?"

"The first step is a preliminary physical by a JSC doctor." Jack spoke quickly as if he did not wish to think and risk changing his mind.

"When?" I asked.

"Tom Keenan is working today," Dr. Fawzshen said. He touched his eyelid and looked directly into my eyes. I shivered, but it was a shiver of joyful anticipation.

Dr. Tom Keenan was the personal physician to the astronauts, not all the astronauts but only those who were involved with current missions. Why would he give the physical for a student training program? I was mystified.

Jana's Journal

Palm trees swayed softly as late afternoon shadows danced across the neighborhood pool. A small thatched roof building, housing the dressing room and the speed delivery tube, created a big trapezoidal shadow. Near the shallow end of the pool, a mother and two little children gathered up towels, rafts, and pool toys, and slowly sauntered away. Not another person was in sight.

I so wished Alan had waited for me even though it was after five. I wanted to tell him about the incredible things that had happened today. I wanted to believe in something wondrous. But reality crept in. Most likely, Jack was helping Dr. Fawzshen locate a gopher: go for this; go for that; run the copy machine; run the library search terminal; get on the net, find a document.

Then as Alan stepped out of the trapezoidal shadow, the late afternoon brightness backlit him and framed his sun-streaked hair. He appeared like a magnificent angel gliding toward me and holding something in each hand. At that moment, Alan and I were the only people in the world. I felt warm and joyous all over.

"I'm glad you waited for me," I called out. "Sorry I'm so late. I did try to call you."

"You said you would be here." He shrugged, as if the hour delay had been nothing although I knew he was busy, working his co-op job at SpaceTech and taking two summer courses at the university. He handed me a "cool pac" carton from the speed delivery tube.

I quickly opened it. "Raspberry yogurt, my favorite. What perfect timing, too," I said. He must have spotted me from the top of the high dive.

We lounged on pool chairs and munched our icy yogurts. I wanted to tell him everything but hardly knew where to begin.

He took a few bites of yogurt and then said, "There's a neighborhood dance on Friday night, right here poolside. Would you like to go?" The assurance in his voice pleased me.

"Yes, most definitely," I said. My feelings toward him were embarrassing to admit to myself.

"We'll have a great time." He sat his yogurt down on a little table and leaned toward me, looking at me so lovingly. But then he said, "How did you get the pressure patch on your arm?"

"I had a physical at JSC this afternoon." I explained that Jack and Dr. Fawzshen's visit most likely meant a different summer job, probably helping Dr. Fawzshen.

"Why would you need a physical to help Dr. Fawzshen?"

"It was strange. At first Dr. Keenan—that's the JSC doctor—treated me like I was an inconvenience. He drew blood from my arm and put the sample in a little machine. Then he went into an office adjacent to the lab and made a phone call. He left the door open, but he faced the window with his back to me and practically whispered into the phone. The sound must have bounced off the window because I could hear every word he said. You know how sound sometimes travels in strange ways."

"You listened?"

"Of course. He told a woman to meet him at the marina in about a half an hour, that he had another damn blood specimen to analyze, this time a rush job he was handling himself. He doubted if Jack would find anyone with the blood component he was looking for."

I decided against telling Alan that Dr. Keenan referred to me as a frail young woman who could not pass the physical even if my blood contained the component.

"Then what?" Alan asked.

"After he finished the phone call, he came back into the lab and checked the machine. He coded something into the machine's computer, and it printed out results. He said something under his breath that sounded like, "Jack will be thrilled about this." To me, he said, 'I need to run this test again and verify the results.'"

His attitude toward me changed completely; he became friendly and said that I needed a stress test. It was thorough. I must have the most thoroughly checked out heart of anybody, including, I guess, professional athletes and astronauts. I walked fast on the treadmill, sped up, and then ran at various speeds, all the time wearing monitors. Even the air I exhaled was measured.

"Next, I took a physical dexterity text, standing on one foot and hopping in place, things like that, then a hearing test, really, really soft sounds. The hearing test reminded me of the woman waiting for Dr. Keenan at the marina. I couldn't exactly remind him to call her so instead I said that I needed to call someone to say I would be delayed. I tried to call you, but still that didn't jog his memory. Apparently, he had forgotten all about her.

"After that, he tested my eyes; it was more thorough than a visit to the eye doctor. Dr. Keenan did a lot of peripheral vision checking. Objects approached from the side, and I had to indicate as soon as I saw them."

"What kind of objects?"

I giggled. "Asteroids, rocks, spaceships. The graphics were pretty. There was a lot about color and shades, too. Is this color like that color? Then Dr. Keenan said something about blue sclera. He wasn't an ophthalmologist, but my blue sclera certainly was pronounced. I asked him what blue sclera was, and he said, 'The eye whites have a bluish cast.' I asked if Dr. Fawzshen had blue sclera, and he kind of stammered and said he didn't know."

"Your eye whites really are bluish," Alan said surprised. "Maybe, that's why your eyes are so . . . so lovely."

I liked it when Alan complimented me, but I simply said, "Do you remember if Dr. Fawzshen or Princess Regney has bluish eye whites?"

"That's not something I'd notice. Why does it matter?" he asked.

"I don't know. I think it does matter, and I think it matters a lot." I shook my head from side to side. "Then, Dr. Keenan said that security usually does fingerprinting, but since this was a rush job, he'd fingerprint me himself."

"That's bizarre!" Alan exclaimed.

"He pulled up a program on a computer and had me place each hand on the screen. I noticed him reading the instructions as if he hadn't taken fingerprints before. Then he told me to roll each finger from left to right inside squares drawn on the screen."

"A doctor doing fingerprinting? Jack's certainly in a hurry," Alan said, shaking his head.

"What conclusion does all of this lead you to, Alan?"

He was silent for a minute before he said, "That's a heck of a lot of testing for someone to search for data from the supernet," he said. "Why do you need to see so well? Have bluish eye whites? Have something magical in your blood. Hear so well? Have so much stamina? Have a security clearance? To make copies?"

"That's how I felt, that this was . . . was a . . . ."

Alan quickly sat up. He smirked. "Go ahead, Jana; say it."

"I felt this was a preliminary test for an . . . astronaut."

"That's what you really want, isn't it?" Alan asked.

Why not tell Alan? Dr. Fawzshen and Princess Regney already knew, and now so did Jack. I said, "Yes, yes! That's what I want."

He didn't laugh. In fact, his eyes sparkled, and he smiled slightly. As his smile quickly faded, he still seemed pleased but also sad and thoughtful, almost distressed as the corners of his mouth turned down, as if a shadow had fallen across his face. He gamely resurrected a smile, but not his confident smirky smile, and said, "You can do it."

Since Alan now seemed more distressed than pleased, I added, "I probably didn't pass the physical."

"As healthy as you are?"

"On the treadmill, Dr. Keenan asked me to run faster and faster. Finally, I couldn't run any faster. He turned off a hand held computer and seemed disappointed. I thought, 'So it ends here, and I don't know what I've lost.' Then I had an idea. I said that I might not run really fast but that I've got lots of endurance."

"Good fast thinking, Jana; did that help?"

"Yes, he flipped his computer back on and let me run on the treadmill about fifteen or twenty minutes, I guess, to see if I was telling the truth."

"What was his reaction then?"

"Dr. Keenan said I certainly had endurance. I had the strangest feeling that, if at all possible, he wanted me to pass the physical and was truly glad I had mentioned endurance."

"They want you!" Alan said cheerfully, having recovered from his distress regarding my career goal. "Now, what is NASA going to do with you? There's the SpaceTech project. You could be a test pilot for one of their minishuttles."

"Alan, senior astronauts will test them."

"But after that, civilians for 'the minishuttles that fly themselves.' Why not you?"

"The civilians will be highly experienced licensed pilots."

"If it's not the SpaceTech minishuttle, let's see, that leaves the best adventure of all."

"And what might that be?" I was intrigued.

"The best is the one with the Rhatanians." Alan leapt up. "They need you because 'you're the one.'"

"You overheard Princess Regney say that?"

Alan nodded.

I said, "You know that's not logical. Princess Regney could have been referring to anything." But my soul was soaring. It could be possible. For one moment I believed. I looked up at Alan, my friend, and felt thankful that he had woven a magical world for me. "Thanks, Alan," I said, "thanks for not laughing at me."

Solarship *Copernicus*

6:05 a.m. CDT

After a scheduled communication with Houston, Jack removed his headset and secured it on the console. He wondered why Houston still was unaware that he or Jana had been on the net continuously for the past hour. He also wondered what Max was doing on their behalf. Obviously, Max had not told anyone at JSC that there was a problem, or CAPCOM, the solarship communicator, would have asked Jack some pointed questions. Jack followed Max's lead and did not even allude to the supernet broadcast.

Jack would tell Houston during the next communication, but he preferred that CAPCOM ask him. How could Mission Control not know? Granted, under normal conditions, today was the last chance for the flight controllers to take a holiday. Tomorrow, if they survived today, the *Copernicus* would cross the moon orbit and then be so close to Earth that they all would be on alert for satellites and space garbage. The controllers would be working double shifts. Today, the team could be slim.

Jack could not afford the luxury of pondering any longer. He studied the timeline that he and his crew optimistically had worked out for their survival. Then, he folded the sheet of paper and put it in his pocket.

His next task was to decide whether Jana should proceed with her journal or whether she should read Lauren's notes or even the top secret NASA reports. That latter option would have even more repercussions for the crew. For the past hour as he tended to several tasks, the bits and pieces he heard of Jana's journal pleased him. Would

81

it counter and squash the tabloid speculations about her and about the mission?

Jack turned his undivided attention toward Jana and laughed aloud when she described her medical exam of nearly a year ago at JSC. He had forgotten that Jana had initiated additional treadmill tests by telling Doc Keenan about her endurance, thereby propelling forward the entire chain of events that led her to the *Copernicus*. Resourceful little soul! If she had been less resourceful, at this moment, she would not be in imminent danger. Jana might be attending a Saturday morning class at Houston Aerospace Academy while only dreaming of space flight.

Jack wanted the terrorists to see and hear the crew, specifically Jana, and to understand that not one of them posed a threat to the world. Neither did their discovery. Whether these facts mattered to the perpetrators was currently unknowable to Jack. Someday! He wanted to know if there were to be a "someday" for the four of them.

Jack breathed deeply as his spirits soared. Jana's journal would do just fine. Happy to be alive and embroiled in a life or death struggle, he became even more alert, feeling attuned to the souls of the three other crewmembers, as if these souls were melding into a greater spirit, rising above ego, above self, to work together as a flawless team. Such a thought he would not mention, but he knew they felt it, too.

His crew all believed in their own power over their lives and even power over this situation. Realistically, their only power, he thought, might be to alert people everywhere about the terrorism in progress against the *Copernicus* and this small crew of international astronauts on a peaceful, scientific mission.

It was almost time for Jana to play a video of Jack explaining their situation and pleading for help. Earlier in this wake cycle, Jack had prepared several announcements for Jana to intersperse with her reading. That way, he could keep on with his work. Now, however, Jack decided to make an outrageous comment. What blatantly wrong thing would get Mission Control to respond to their supernet broadcast?

He needed something the outside world would not recognize as outrageous, also something that would spook the terrorists, whoever they were, and throw them off stride.

Jack motioned to Jana to find a stopping place. She pointed to her computer screen and then held her thumb and fingers a few inches apart, indicating that she would stop soon.

As she read, Jana referred to herself as "the one." Jack wished she had not done that. He had wanted the supernet audience to see her as a regular astronaut, not as "the one," but in truth she was "the one." Yet, that reference did not mean what the tabloids made it out to mean. Jack briefly reconsidered his decision about her journal but then decided that he simply would trust her judgment. He needed to charge ahead with his tasks.

Jana finished reading and moved out of the camera's range. Jack propelled himself in front of the camera. He described the danger the crew was facing and asked people everywhere for their help. He explained that the explosive heading toward them could have been launched from Earth or Earth orbit about four days ago.

In a nonchalant tone, he said, "We soon will be in a tight orbit around the moon. From there, we'll transfer into our lander and descend to the landing pad at Moon Base II." He added a few more comments about how they would return to Earth from the moon.

Every word he said about the moon landing was completely false. In actuality, they now were in a decelerating fall toward the spaceport, the satellite orbiting merely 200 miles from Earth.

If his comments about the moon did not get Mission Control's attention, his next statement would rock them. "If you can help us or if you know anybody who can, please call Johnson Space Center in Houston, Texas." As an afterthought, he added, "In the United States . . . of America."

Jack drifted away from the screen but then quickly moved back. Calling JSC could be exceedingly dangerous for whomever tried to help them. He said, "Please help us all you can. At the same time, protect yourself from the terrorists."

Jack wished he knew more about the operations of the supernet. He wondered if Mission Control or a governmental power had quietly shut down their broadcast in such a secret way that there would be no record of their transmission.

Yet, at least one person knew, a George MacInturff from Seattle. He had even replied to their message. Jack wondered how much of each crewmember's future rested in MacInturff's ability to alert people who might help them survive this wake cycle.

Jack pulled the hard copy of his timeline back out of his pocket. In his computer, the timeline was quite detailed, but the hard copy version he had printed was top-level information, an overview, nice and clean, with a few major milestones. The timeline seemed to him like a talisman. On that sheet of paper, their salvation appeared routine. It was anything but routine.

Jack floated toward Fawz and Lauren who had been calculating several possible maneuvers the *Copernicus* could execute to evade the bomb. Lauren whispered that their work was ready for Jack's preliminary review.

For now, Jack simply would check their calculations and logic, but within the hour, he would choose one option so the crew could have time to work through the rough spots and give it a better chance for success. Yet, with this caliber of decision, selecting an option usually required input from a team of experts. He could overlook something critical and, yet, obvious to one of the crew. Surely, with their lives in the balance, the crewmembers would speak up. However, they generally deferred to him so easily, behavior he usually appreciated, but not now. To Lauren and Fawz, Jack simply said, "Name your best option for evading the bomb. Then, tell me about the other options."

Fawz liked Americans. Most he knew were so confident. Even the insecure ones accomplished the impossible.

He censored his urge to declare to Jack, "If changing the trajectory does not solve our problem, we have no way out of this situation." Instead he said, "Sacrifice the lander to protect our ship. If we carefully control the trajectory and velocity at launch and afterwards, the lander will continually shield the *Copernicus* from the bomb's line of sight. The bomb's telemetry will see only one object, the lander. The *Copernicus* will stay hidden far behind the lander. Then, the lander will take the bomb's direct hit, and we will be saved."

"And the ensuing debris cloud, how will we be protected from that?" Jack asked in an even voice that did not reveal his reaction.

Lauren said, "I've been working on that. Our lander's got a strong belly with a crumple zone for safety. We could cushion the belly more by programming the meteoroid shield in that area to vary its protection level, that is, set up a vibration at the exact moment of impact. This could confuse the bomb's explosive mechanism. With luck, the bomb might not explode at all. Then the problem would be far less complex, like a collision with a small satellite.

"On the reinforced top side of the lander, we would pre-program the meteoroid shield for maximum protection to keep the bomb or its particles from passing through. The smaller debris particles would deflect away from the *Copernicus*. If any of the larger debris particles passed through the meteoroid shield, their velocity would be reduced."

In a bland voice, Jack asked, "What are the potential problems?"

Fawz replied, "The view from Earth might pick up two distinct objects, and the bomb could have multiple warheads. No terrorists who know anything about the *Copernicus* would send only one warhead.

"Any more problems?" Jack asked.

"Since the lander has been beefed up, we do not know its exact mass." Fawz declared, "That is critically important! We could crawl into the lander and estimate a mass for each change."

Fawz read that wild, faraway look in Jack's eyes that meant, "It's a go." As Fawz explained their other options, he noted that Jack listened

85

carefully, trying to be logical and impartial. Jack would think everything through and ask more questions. In the final analysis, Fawz figured Jack would sacrifice the lander.

Glad to be with three Americans, Fawz rubbed his brambly eyebrows. This crew had no understanding, whatsoever, that the situation was impossible. They confidently charged ahead. Just for today, he would behave like an American. He chuckled.

Jana's Journal

It began as a pleasant "Mom is home" day. Outside on the screen porch, Dad, Mom, and I, always in a festive mood when Mom had just returned, were having brunch: waffles, strawberries, and sweet grapes Mom had brought from California. A slight southerly breeze off the Gulf enhanced the balmy, not yet hot morning air. The porch plants, a few potted trees and a hanging assortment of ivies, ferns, and succulents, rustled lightly and reflected our mood, seeming fuller, healthier, less omnivorous, and even greener than yesterday, thanks to the magic of Instabright in Dad's determined hands.

Beyond the porch, the precision manicured yard stood at attention, and, inside, the house sparkled. The whole place was orderly, cared for, and loved. I liked my environment better this way.

Patiently, I waited for Mom to talk about her assignment at Edwards Air Force Base. Finally, Mom matter-of-factly described her latest testing series. After a few, terse comments about her work, she switched to other topics, mutual friends she had seen and the California weather.

Something had happened! Otherwise, now she would tell us in detail everything that was not classified about her test flights. She knew how much her flying stories intrigued Dad and me. What had happened in California? A near brush with death? Glancing furtively at Dad, I noticed his forehead ridged slightly as his skin paled. Probably, he knew more than I about what had happened. He seemed scared, scared but proud of Mom. She truly was a terrific pilot, but, sometimes, I wished she had a safer job.

Mom heaped strawberries onto her waffle. She looked fragile, but her muscles were as strong as titanium and her nerves, an even tougher fiber. Even so, she could not talk about it, not yet. Her brain needed to digest, analyze, and compartmentalize THE DANGER so it would not interfere with future test flights. At least, that was how I figured it. At times like this, I did not ask questions.

In a week or so, she would talk. As I visualized a vibrating plane quivering over the Pacific, I could almost hear her words. "The jet seemed okay. I was putting it through maneuvers. I went into a tight turn, and the jet started vibrating. It was getting harder to handle. I eased the plane slowly out of the turn, it fighting me all the way, and then decided to take it back in. Getting back to base, my next turn was wide and so gradual. There still was a slight vibration, but it was under control, barely."

I was glad she was okay. I could wait to find out what really happened. I liked Mom's flying stories, usually savoring each word and trying to piece together gaps, classified things she could not reveal. I drifted into a daydream: in the cockpit next to Mom, I took over the controls, looking down through cirrus clouds at the fast moving Earth below, and then gazing up at the welcoming blue. I took the plane up higher and higher where it was not designed to go and at the correct angle flew it free from the atmospheric sea. Out the window the wing skins of tough titanium alloy glowed a soft pink.

I was jolted out of my reverie by a tapping on the screen door. There was Jack. Dad jumped up to let him in, and I darted into the house for another table setting. After some enthusiastic greetings, Jack sat down with us, between Dad and me and directly across from Mom. He declined the waffles but helped himself to a small bunch of the California grapes.

Between nibbles, he said, "The way you saved that plane, really something. A new chapter for the flight manuals."

"Thanks, Jack. The news, it seems, traveled faster than I did," Mom said lightly.

Neither spoke another word on the subject. I figured Jack knew she was not ready to talk about it, yet. Soon, they discussed people Mom had seen. Several of the pilots were thinking about switching over to another contractor who most likely would be awarded a bigger slice of the aerospace pie.

I was not particularly interested in all the details about contract negotiations. Instead, I wanted to leap into the conversation and ask Jack about my JSC job but decided to be patient and wait. I hoped I had run long enough and fast enough on the treadmill yesterday. I tried to give myself more patience by thinking this was the weekend, and probably Jack had not received the results, yet, from Dr. Keenan.

I swished the last morsel of waffle into maple syrup and then speared the last strawberry on my plate. I was ready to take a bite when Mom said, "Jana tells me you might have a different summer job for her at JSC."

I could not restrain myself any longer. I put down my food filled fork and blurted out, "Did Dr. Keenan give you his evaluation? Did I pass the physical?"

"Your speed on the treadmill was slower than standard," Jack replied.

"Oh," I said, feeling a strange sense of loss for an unknown job.

"Don't worry," Jack said. "Dr. Keenan fortunately decided to test your endurance, and that more than compensated. It certainly was a stroke of luck that he thought about endurance, or I wouldn't be here right now talking to you about a job. We've gotten a waiver on your running speed."

A waiver! What kind of job was this? "Then I've got the job?" I asked.

"Do you want it?"

"I don't know what it is," I replied. "If it's working with Dr. Fawzshen, it could be something special."

"More special than you know," Jack said.

I shivered with delight, thinking about all Alan and I had talked about yesterday at the pool.

"But we'd need your parent's permission."

"Jana's an adult," Mom quickly said. "She's almost 20 years old. She makes her own decisions."

"I know how old she is," Jack said, "but Jana is a student, living in your household, and being financially supported by you. And she is under 21!"

"Yes," Mom said.

"According to international laws governing space travel, we need both parents to sign a waiver, saying you won't sue NASA, the manufacturers of any of the hardware, or any foreign governments involved. It's the same kind of waiver we ask spouses of astronauts to sign."

Wow! I could barely believe what Jack was saying. When I heard the words "space travel" and "astronauts" echoing and reverberating in my head, my heart thumped so rapidly that I could hear it. How could such a thing be possible?

Mom leaned forward. "Tell us more."

Jack seemed at a loss. Even his posture seemed less than his usual military bearing. He seemed to occupy less physical space. I shivered again. Yesterday and today were the only times I had seen Jack exhibit anything other than total confidence. Finally, he said, "You heard we were awarded the SMT contract yesterday. Imagine, announcing a contract on Saturday."

Dad replied, "That SpaceTech group probably doesn't know what month it is, much less the day of the week. How many sunrises and sunsets a day do they see? Eight? Nine? From what I hear, they're determined to make the minishuttles successful."

Jack said, "They're proud of their product. That's for sure. Working with them could be difficult. Quite difficult. They believe their shuttles are extremely well designed. Extremely well built, too. They're pushing for minimal astronaut testing before the civilian training begins," Jack said.

I wondered if my job involved the minishuttles. I wanted them to quit rambling, but it seemed they purposely were delaying whatever Jack had to say about my job. I might have to guide them, but I needed to wait for my chance.

Mom said, "I can't help remembering a few years back, NASA gave out contracts and did not bid on commercial ventures to maintain financial strength."

"Times change," Jack said, his facial expression somber, the sparkle in his eyes missing. "Of course, we could do so much more for the future if we had adequate funding. So we'll work with others, commercial ventures, other countries."

Other countries! I thought about the enthusiasm toward Dr. Fawzshen at Jack's party.

During a lull in the conversation, I seized the opportunity. "Tell me about my job?"

Jack looked directly into my eyes. "Part of our contract with SpaceTech is to test their preliminary training manuals for the minishuttle pilots. We would like you to study the material. Also, we'll provide you with special tutors and supplementary material."

Would I pilot a minishuttle? Savoring such a thought, my heart soared. I dared not ask because I wanted to hold the thought tenderly as long as I could, but Mom quickly asked, "Would Jana pilot a minishuttle?"

"No," Jack said firmly. Mom sighed in relief as my hopes thudded to a crash landing.

Mom said, "So Jana studies the material and then takes some tests or maybe does a few drills on a simulator. That sounds safe enough. It should be an interesting summer for her."

Jack's frown was barely perceptible; this was not going as he wanted. "Myra, you're hardly a role model for a safe job," he said jokingly, but he was serious, and Mom picked up on it.

"What's going on, Jack?" Mom asked.

"Not something we would enter into lightly," he replied cryptically. "You both still have current top secret security clearances?"

My parents nodded that they did. My mom added, "Even Global Top Secret."

"I thought so. Now, Jana, I have a document for you to sign. Jack pulled the crisply folded sheet of paper out of his pocket and handed it to me. Under my authority and supervision, it gives you a temporary security clearance, a single project clearance, until NASA completes a formal security check on you and we get the paperwork processed."

With Jack's pen in my hand, I was ready to sign when I glanced up. Dad gave me his eagle eye, just like when I was a child, that certain look that meant to behave appropriately. But how? Of course, read the document carefully before I sign.

I read the Temporary Authorization for Top Secret Security Clearance. It was for one project and only one project: The US-Rhatanian Joint Mission. I would agree not to reveal the information to anyone unless the other person also had a Top Secret Security Clearance on this specific project as well as a need to know. I signed my name. My eyes met Dad's again; he nodded slightly in approval. I handed the signed form to Jack. My parents did not know what it said.

Jack's confidence returned when he asked my parents, "Have you heard any rumors about a secret mission?"

Dad said, "Not until your party on Friday night; then, I knew something was in the works. I'm usually briefed about upcoming missions, but not this one."

I tried to project calmness and self control. I dared not speculate. Maybe there was a simple explanation, but my thoughts again soared higher and higher.

Jack said, "The people involved with the project have been kept to the barest minimum." I wanted to blurt out what I knew but bit my lip to keep quiet as Jack announced, "It's a joint mission with the Rhatanians."

"Rhatanians!" Mom exclaimed incredulously. "I know that they're a rich little country, but what could they possibly have that we need?"

"Believe me, Myra, any other country with space capabilities gladly would have jumped at the opportunity the Rhatanians offered. Prince Fawzshen, my long-time friend, could have gone to the Europeans, the Russians, the Chinese, or the Japanese. With all the budget cuts going on here, we're lucky to have gotten the Rhatanians."

"What's their offer?" Dad asked.

"They have verifiable and astounding information."

"Is it a patent or a process? Some small countries have achieved such amazing technological feats."

"I can't say, at present," Jack answered.

I closed my eyes and thought of lifting off in a Space Taxi from Cape Kennedy. I quickly shook my head. I needed to stay alert and not drift off into dreams.

"How does Jana fit into this," Mom asked, her voice shaking.

Jack put his hands together, palm to palm. "We have been looking for a person over the last several weeks." Jack thought a minute. "A month ago, one of our four astronauts training for the mission developed asthma, an adult onset type. First, she developed an aspirin allergy after doing some testing on the centrifuge. Shortly thereafter, her allergies became generalized, and our physicians determined she should not be flying around in spacecraft. We think the centrifuge precipitated her problems.

He frowned. "We have the backup crew, but when the astronaut became ill, we decided to search for a person who more closely fit the newly-determined requirements of the mission.

"We checked our pool of astronauts for one who has a specific rare blood component. We found no match. The blood typing is not something we do routinely, but the newly isolated Blue Factor or BF is linked to an eye condition called blue sclera. We found no match until yesterday."

A shiver went up my spine, and my hands became clammy as I remembered what the doctor had said about my blood.

Jack continued. "Far more people have blue sclera than have the Blue Factor, but people who have the blood component probably also have blue sclera. We've gone to several local ophthalmologists and optometrist and asked them to contact patients with pronounced blue sclera. We've tested about forty people so far, and not one has had BF. The eye doctors thought they merely were helping JSC accumulate information."

Mom incredulously asked, "You would have taken any one of these forty people as an astronaut? You would have taken someone off the street!"

"No, that's merely the starting point."

"And Jana has the Blue Factor?" Mom asked softly.

"Yes," Jack said.

Mom just sat, drumming her fingers. "Will this factor make Jana a better . . . a better astronaut?" she asked.

"No, not at all. But in ways that I can't go into, it makes her uniquely qualified for this specific mission." Then, he looked directly into my eyes. "Of course, Jana, you understand this is a long shot. You're well aware that astronauts traditionally train for a year and bring strong backgrounds with them. You certainly won't need to know as much as a pilot. If you successfully complete all of your training, your category will be mission specialist."

A mission specialist! I was not a geologist, medical person, or US senator. For now, my best approach was to say as little as necessary and look intelligent.

"There's more," Jack said to me. "Because of the short time frame for training, approximately four months, you would live on site and have no contact with family or friends for about three months. This would help you and JSC to determine how well you handle separation."

Mom said, "Someone has thought about many variables. It sounds like you want this to work out."

"Oh, yes, most definitely," Jack replied.

"What's the destination of the joint US-Rhatanian mission?" Dad asked.

All eyes were on Jack when he announced, "The mission is to a moon of Jupiter. I can't divulge which moon."

Jupiter, my heart soared. I wanted to leap into the air. Humans to cross the asteroid belt, me, Jana, being one of those humans. I could have been acting crazy if Alan and I had not discussed such possibilities yesterday afternoon. "Be calm, be rational," I told myself. So I sat at the table, I am sure with a silly expression on my face, but I was not leaping around, and I was not saying ridiculous things.

Mom quickly said, "That sounds dangerous."

Dad jumped in and said, "Not one Space Program in the entire world has attempted anything like that. That's too huge a leap. After our manned Mars missions, there needs to be lots of intermediate steps before a manned Jupiter mission. There're many asteroids to explore first. Jupiter is incredibly far away, about 365 million miles. And how about the bow shock effect when entering Jupiter's magnetosphere? Equipment could malfunction."

Jack said, "Many people feel the same way you do. That's one reason for the mission's secrecy. As I said before, because of international laws governing space flight, we do need your permission."

I quickly glanced around the table. My parents were wonderful, but they also wanted me to stay alive. I had to be careful. I could influence them if I worked it just right.

Mom and Dad stared at each other almost as if in a state of shock. I noticed the soggy remains of waffles on their plates and on my plate. Finally Dad asked, "Jana, how do you feel about this?"

"I definitely want to do it," I said as firmly as I could. I would not whine. I would not beg. But somehow I would get them to say "yes." Right at that moment, I felt both my parents were perched practically on neutral, evaluating, Dad slightly toward "no," and Mom slightly toward "yes."

The rest of my life awaited their decision. This could be my only chance to become an astronaut. Years from now, assuming that I excelled at the Houston Aerospace Academy, assuming I got accepted into the Space Program, then assuming I got accepted to fly, assuming I got accepted into the major mission division, then maybe I would get the exact chance I had right now. The future was too many assumptions. It could be now or never. Mom and Dad had to realize what a rare opportunity this was.

"Who is the commander of the mission?" Mom asked, still in her evaluative role.

"I will be commander," Jack said.

Mom smiled slightly. I imagined a gauge in her head moving from "barely yes" more into the "yes" range. The Mars I Mission under Jack's commands had been book perfect. Later, the other astronauts on the mission had said that Jack fixed problems even before they or Mission Control knew any existed.

Mom still was on guard. "Picking somebody by blood component sounds so primitive, so archaic, not worthy of the twenty-first century. People should be judged by their skills. If a blood component is indicative of traits to make one a better astronaut, then that I could understand."

Jack said, "Myra, I generally agree with what you are saying. I can't go into the reasons in this particular case."

Mom asked, "Why didn't management go to the armed services. Surely of all the qualified pilots in the Air Force or Navy, there must be several who have the Blue Factor."

I silently thought, "Good heavens, Mom, whose side are you on?"

Jack said, "That was our first thought right after we screened our own pool of astronauts, but this is a secret mission. To do a massive testing, we would need justification. Many more people would know about our mission. Also, we talked to two of our attorneys, the only two who are fully apprised of the situation. They suggested getting the position filled as quickly and as quietly as possible."

I thought over and over, as if my thoughts could influence them. "Don't discuss it. Just say 'yes.'"

"If Jana succeeds with the training, would she become a member of the mission?" Dad asked.

"Probably yes. The Rhatanians definitely want Jana. NASA tentatively goes along with their wishes."

"You mean they want someone with the blood component?" Mom asked.

"No, they specifically want Jana. The Rhatanians are very bright, very logical, but they also believe in fate and destiny. They 'knew' she would be the one even before we tested her blood."

I recalled the moment in the receiving line when Princess Regney had softly said I was the one. Jack's comments left me with odd questions, but now was not the time. Mom and Dad did not put stock in things like fate and destiny.

"They knew?" Mom asked incredulously. "Now, that's weird!"

My eyes met Jack's. I slowly shook my head from left to right. Fortunately, Jack stayed quiet.

Finally, Dad said, "We'll need to think about it and talk it over with Jana."

"Of course," Jack said.

How could Mom and Dad leave this momentous and life changing thing hanging? I stated clearly and firmly, "I want to do this."

"I know you do," Mom said kindly. "We've got to look at all sides."

"Okay," I said. This was not the moment to push. If I pushed, it could be them against me. They must not feel coerced; I was not above coercing them, but it would not work. All I had to do for now was keep my mouth shut. I knew that, but still I blurted out, "I want more than your permission. I want your blessing." I covered my face with my hands and told myself to be quiet.

Jack left with the understanding that I would call the next morning. I went up to my room. I carefully closed the door and let out a soft yell they could not hear. Then I did two cartwheels, landing lightly so that no thud would be heard downstairs.

I could barely wait to call Alan, to see his face when I told him he was right, that indeed there was a joint US-Rhatanian mission. I ran a comb through my hair and touched the panel on my videophone. Then I realized that I could not tell Alan, my dearest friend, because I had signed a top-secret security agreement. Alan had neither a clearance nor a need to know anything about this mission. I quickly turned off my videophone.

I wondered what he was doing at this moment. He had probably gone to the SpaceTech garden to feed his plants ground up volcanic rock soaked in his newest concoction. Then I remembered. Alan had told me he was working a double shift today.

It was just as well. Would I ever be able to tell him? "It's true, Alan, it's true," I thought, as if my thinking would somehow let him know.

I was far from Alan but also far from space, my life hanging in the middle. I thought I was free to make my own decisions, but now the freedom was gone, back into my parents' hands, people who wanted to keep me alive.

An hour passed before I heard Dad's voice calling me. Had they made up their minds already? Such a quick decision boded poorly for me. I ran downstairs and then composed myself before entering the living room.

Mom sensed my anxiety and quickly said, "We are still discussing and we need more input from you."

Oh, no! I thought. They were getting into psychological stuff. Stay calm, I told myself. "I want to do this," I said slowly and clearly, carefully enunciating every word. "As you know, my plans are to become an astronaut. For whatever the reason, it's a break for me. It's my chance to leapfrog ahead, and I would like to take advantage of it."

"We know you do, Jana," Mom said gently.

"Hypothetically speaking, suppose you went through the training . . . . This is untested material," Dad said.

"Yes," I said. Don't waver, don't back down, I told myself. I knew where they were leading. Now was the time to impress them with my adult maturity. "Suppose I can't handle it? Is that what you were going to ask me?"

Dad seemed pleased that I had read his thoughts. "If that were the scenario, how would you feel?"

They would expect me to take a little time before answering, but I was not examining my soul for an answer. I was figuring out the answer they wanted. When they got into psychological stuff, which luckily was not often, I felt like an alien. It was time to answer. The truth would have to do.

"I would feel terrible. I would be truly disappointed, to be so close and not to make it." That was the truth, but maybe not the answer they wanted.

My parents exchanged knowing glances, but they hid their thoughts from me. They wore their masks, the bland expressions they assumed when they concealed things from me, the lips purposely held expressionless, the brows pulled back in the opposite of a frown, and the eyelids slightly more open than the relaxed state.

"The astronaut who had been in training and then got sick. How do you think that person felt?"

"Horrible," I said. "Still I would rather go through the training and risk terrific disappointment than not try at all." I flashed my most winsome smile at them and added, "This desire must be in my genes."

"Well, jury, what is it?" I thought. Their masks were slipping; they were pleased; the truth and the answer they wanted happily coincided.

Dad said, "Mom and I need to talk some more."

I went back to my room and began feeling hopeful, but, still, it would take time for them to work it through. I would go out and do something to distract myself. I would go windsurfing on Mud Lake.

I felt cheerful until I thought of something so devastating that they would never approve. Money! Taking the "long shot" chance for a goal

99

beyond my best dreams meant relinquishing my place at the Houston Aerospace Academy; yet, my entering the early admission program would save my family two years of tuition. If the Rhatanian thing did not work out for me, would Mom and Dad spring for two more years of college? Making such a request of them would be outrageous, but that was exactly what I was about to do. I reluctantly opened the door to my room.

Downstairs again, I quickly explained the financial implications. I do not remember exactly what I said. It all poured out, but I volunteered to work for as long as they wanted me to help with the tuition. I think I made more promises.

The next morning, my eyes unsealed as dawn filtered into my room. A short time later, numbness encased me as if I needed to steel myself and could not deal with emotions.

I put breakfast under the hydrator lamp and thought if they did not come downstairs soon, Dad would be late for work. I stepped out onto the porch to check the table setting. I had chosen a sky blue tablecloth (they could not help but notice the symbolism in that), dishes the color of a full moon, and an Indian vase filled with red roses and white periwinkle from the garden.

Through the glass porch door I saw Mom. She appeared dejected, older, like she bore a great burden. Enough numbness left me that I felt my stomach muscles tighten.

I said to myself, "I can be brave, I will be brave, I am brave. No whimpering, no begging, no sulking."

When she glanced through the glass door and saw me, she tried to brighten up and actually managed a half-smile. She opened the door and said in her friendly manner, "Breakfast looks yummy. Dad will be down in a minute."

The next thing I knew, Dad was downstairs. They were smiling at each other and at me. I instantly knew.

Dad said, "It's time for you to call Jack and tell him everything is A-Okay."

"For the training and for the mission," Mom added.

"I'll work so hard; you've made the right decision."

"I hope you'll feel that way a year from now," Mom said, her face looking shadowy. I dared not question her comment because I certainly did not want her to reconsider. Then as if sorry she cast a shadow on our joyous moment, forcing cheerfulness into her voice, she said, "We've shown you the world. Now you need more. What's left, we cannot do for you. We only wish you the best."

"Oh, thank you. I love you both. I'll succeed. You will be proud of me."

"We're already proud of you," Dad said. "Do this for Jana, the astronaut."

When I called Jack, he said, "You can't begin to understand how happy this makes me." Then, I realized that it went beyond blood, eyes, and the idea of Rhatanian fate. Jack, himself, also wanted me to be on the mission. I suspected that he had exerted his considerable influence on my behalf. I hoped that I would not disappoint him.

Later in the day, doubts crept into my every thought until I visualized myself inside a gleaming solarship and said aloud, "This is possible. It's all possible."

Webster, Texas (Near Johnson Space Center)
6:35 a.m. CDT

Jerome Westlake clicked on his TV to find a girl in an astronaut's blue daywear reading something. She looked somewhat familiar. He pressed his remote to another channel, and there was the same girl. He tried another channel, the girl again. He took a closer look; she resembled Jana Novacek, the girl in the tabloids, the girl he had seen in the JSC cafeteria, but this girl's face was thinner. Then a name flashed at the bottom of the screen, Jana Novacek, Astronaut on the Solarship *Copernicus*. What was she reading, some kind of story, and why?

Jerome was certain he had sat across from Jana Novacek in the JSC cafeteria on several occasions. He had even timed his lunch breaks in hopes of running into her. She was pretty in a quiet way, and he had tried to talk to her. He remembered she had been polite, but preoccupied, like someone who already had a boyfriend or who had something heavy on her mind.

He had been mildly interested in all the tabloid stuff about a secret mission. Indeed, three astronauts and Jana, a summer hire, had been unaccounted for, and Director Clayton refused to make a statement about whether or not a secret mission was in progress. Why had the director stonewalled it? Now, watching TV, he wondered what the astronauts had encountered that JSC tried to hush up. He had discounted the tabloid stuff about alien beings. Now he wondered. Some tabloids emphatically stated that Jana was a space alien. He absolutely knew that was not true.

Commander Jack Medwin came on the screen. Jerome recognized the Commander immediately, even with a thinner face. He had seen clips of Jack Medwin from space on other missions.

"We are one day out from Moon Base II, and we are in imminent danger. As I speak, an explosive device is heading toward our solarship with impact expected at 4 p.m. Houston time. We implore you, citizens of Earth, if there is anything you can do to stop this, if you can stop this yourself, then deactivate the explosive. If you have information that might help, then contact the Johnson Space Center or the CIA."

After the Commander's announcement, Jana Novacek described how her family gave her their blessing for the mission. Jerome could understand that. If his own family held control over something he wanted that desperately, they would help him, too. They would not stand in his way.

Jerome's head began to throb, and he became filled with an enormous sense of guilt and responsibility. All the disparate pieces of the past several weeks crashed together in his mind—stolen JSC flight data, the gray car, the man in electronics store, and now an explosive device heading toward the solarship and its passenger Jana Novacek, that frail girl in danger, reading, looking up, looking straight at him. The young man started hyperventilating. No, he did not have time for this; he had to think.

What possibly had led him to steal the data? At the time, it made sense to him. Fresh out of college, he had been promised that he could work with flight trajectories, but instead he was given the job of system administration. At work, one computer was different than the others he administered. It was a high security computer, and he did not have access to its data or its network. One day, he thought there had been a spyware intrusion into that computer. He immediately reported it to his supervisor, and quite a short time later a man named Max wearing a cowboy hat and plaid shirt came from another building to check on it.

Only later did he learn that Max was the top computer guy for missions. That fact piqued his curiosity. At first he resisted the urge, but he soon spent his spare time working with that computer until he broke into the system and accessed a goldmine of flight data information. That was exactly what he needed to test a trajectory program that he had written on his own time at home in hopes of impressing his boss.

One day he brought in a mass storage device from home and backed up all the trajectory data. After work, his hands were clammy on his steering wheel, and he felt that he might hyperventilate as he approached the guard gate. Cars were subject to random searches. If stolen data were found on him, he would be immediately fired and worse. Fortunately, the guard waved him right through. At home, he would declassify it himself by rotating all the coordinates ten degrees.

He knew all along he should not be stealing that JSC flight trajectory data, but soon he regularly backed it up and took it home. He drove right past the guard gate without a thought until he started noticing the same gray car behind him. Several times, he looked for the gray car in the parking lot at JSC but did not see it. One day driving home from work, he made a sudden and unexpected turn. The gray car did not follow him. After that, there was no gray car behind him. But sometimes he thought he saw it two or three cars behind him. Then he did not see it anymore, but that was after his apartment was burglarized.

He tried to remember the sequence of everything, maybe unrelated. First, there was the gray car, then the chance encounter in the electronics store, and then the burglary of his apartment.

The young man remembered clearly the only other customer in the electronics store, a man in green sweat pants. It had been a chance encounter. Or was it? He trembled. Yes, that was the day that he had made the sudden and unexpected turn. That gray car could have doubled back.

The man in green sweat pants had drawn him into a conversation, and Jerome told him that he worked with flight trajectories. As soon as the words were out, Jerome knew he had made a mistake. He had an uneasy feeling but then shrugged. After all, the man did not know him or where he worked; however, he decided he should be more discreet in the future.

A few days later his apartment was broken into and thoroughly ransacked. The only important things missing that he could tell were his mass storage devices. One even had been removed from his computer. He was way behind in rotating the flight data, thereby declassifying it, as he had promised himself he would do. Thus, some highly classified material had been stolen.

At the time Jerome had rationalized that whoever had stolen the storage devices from him would not know the significance of them. The thief merely would sell them or use them himself. Yet, the mass storage was not particularly expensive. Then, Jerome remembered something he did not want to remember. He had set the security alarm before leaving his apartment on the day of the burglary. At the time, he had convinced himself he had forgotten.

He should call JSC, but he would lose his job, worse, might be accused of a crime, yes, would be accused of a crime. Indeed, he had committed a crime.

The young man stared through the TV screen into Jana's eyes. Even in the astronaut's daywear, she looked fragile.

He should call his supervisor, he thought, but then he began hyperventilating again. He went into the kitchen and put his head in a paper bag. After his breathing normalized, he convinced himself that the incidents were all unrelated.

Jerome went back to the TV but as he watched Jana read, he decided to take action. He looked up the main JSC number and slowly dialed it. A recorded announcement said, "The JSC switchboard is closed until Monday morning. If you know your party's extension, please dial directly."

Maybe he would do nothing after all, but then he took his phone out of his pocket and looked up his supervisor's phone number.

Jana's Journal

Not long after Jack's party for Dr. Fawzshen, I had packed my clothes, a few designer outfits Mom had loaned to me, and my computer gear and had moved into a small but elegant apartment at JSC in quarters reserved for visiting scientists. Even though much astronaut training went on at Ellington Field, Jack and Dr. Fawzshen decided I would have a lower profile here at JSC. Besides, this apartment was available, and many of my classes would be right at the Space Center.

I paced around the study and bedroom past Polynesian furniture and wall murals of moonscapes into a most stunning bath. The tub with jet sprays and shower were surrounded by an indoor garden of palm trees and blooming orchids. The orchids reminded me of Alan's SpaceTech garden.

The government's appropriations ranged from extreme frugality to adequacy to some ostentation (only twice) right after the two Mars landings when NASA was held in such high esteem by the public. This complex must have been built during the ostentation building. I reminded myself to thank Jack and Dr. Fawzshen for such fine accommodations.

I continued pacing, thinking, and waiting: waiting until the time for my first class, orbital physics taught by "to be announced." Already Jack's party seemed long ago.

I roamed around the quarters remembering Jack's words. "It's a long shot." Clichés about my situation danced in my thoughts. I had gotten "my foot in the door" or specifically my body into JSC, and now, the rest was up to me. What a scary idea! I thought about the astronaut's corps: more than 400 brilliant, superbly trained men and women. I thought about the academies bursting with qualified candidates: the Houston Aerospace Academy would graduate almost 200 this week, people smarter, more mature, and better educated than I would be any time in the near future. Yet, I had a shot, and they did not.

All Dr. Fawzshen knew about me was that I wanted to become an astronaut. Jack knew more, but what was there to know? Jack had been my friend all my life. When his three kids decided they were too old for a sitter, I became their social director for a while. Life was much less complicated then. I thought up different places to take the kids, to putt-putt golf, into downtown Houston to the museums or the circus, and to Galveston for an afternoon at the beach. In those days, I had the monorail and hydro bus schedules practically memorized.

One of their favorites was Space Center Houston right next to JSC. They would find their dad's pictures and make enthusiastic comments while people gave them skeptical glances, and I acted nonchalant. Being a good sitter hardly qualified me to become an astronaut. Or did it? Jack and Shirl counted on me to keep their children safe and happy.

Yet, my good fortune tangentially had something to do with baby-sitting because Stacy had noticed my eyes and told her Dad. I was here at JSC because of my eyes and because my blood contained a specific, newly-discovered component, facts too odd and strange to attempt any type of analysis.

Unexpectedly, a wave of loneliness washed over me. I so wanted to call Alan, talk with him, see his face before me, his brown eyes, his smirky smile, his sun streaked hair. He would encourage me, tell me I could do it, and tell me it was possible. However, part of my training was handling separation. For at least three months, I could not see or talk to Alan, my parents, or anyone other than the people I would be working with or those whom I ran into at JSC. I would not leave the JSC grounds unless accompanied by someone who was training me. However, I could leave with prior approval from Jack or Dr. Fawzshen to go to a designated place.

I roamed around the study. In front of a pink Mars scene, free standing from the wall, a large workstation was fully equipped with a state-of-the-art computer, a printer, a fax hookup, probably supernet connections, a phone, and a document shredder. On the phone was stuck a note. "Remember, for authorized NASA use only." On the computer a similar note read, "The e-mail for authorized JSC use only."

I wondered if it was okay to use the fax. I sat down at the desk and flipped on the computer. I would fax a note to Alan.

Dear Alan,

Remember at the swimming pool when you filled my head with so many possibilities. Because of you, I didn't act like a fool when the opportunity beyond my best hopes simply was handed to me. I'm now at JSC. I actually have a chance. I wonder how much of a chance. I'm full of doubts. I need your reassurance.

I pressed the delete key and watched the words disappear. I could not tell Alan nearly that much. I tried another note.

Dear Alan,

What we talked about is true. I won't be able to see you for a while. Miss you already.

Jana

I selected a decorative border of rockets and stars, keyed in Alan's number, overrode the return address fax number, and selected "None

Given." When I was confident that Alan could not trace the fax back to this apartment at JSC, I pressed the Send button. In a few seconds if Alan were home, he would be reading the note.

Then, I sat down with my textbook, *Highlights of Orbital Physics: A Training Manual for SpaceTech Minishuttle Pilots.* In a couple of minutes, it would be time for my class.

As I crossed the JSC grounds, it reminded me of a college campus with lots of buildings surrounded by nicely landscaped grounds. The grass was almost as green as Dad's. In the distance, a tram full of tourists headed toward Mission Control.

My first class at JSC would be in one of the oldest buildings. I walked down the corridor of a musty smelling, disreputable building and entered a small dingy room. The classroom consisted of dim overhead lighting, a few metal tables, and a portable blackboard. I sat down at a scarred metal table and waited.

It was time for orbital physics to begin. I looked at my schedule and checked the room number again. I wondered what my instructor would be like. Would he or she be patient? Would I be able to understand?

The most handsome astronaut I had ever seen entered the room, and my brain said, "No, no, no." I felt nauseous. I thought of the words of Jack's kids, "That conceited astronaut Filbert." I tried to get a grip on myself.

"Janice, so nice to see you again. I met you on Friday night at Jack's party. My name is Filbert," he said in a melodious voice.

"I'm Jana, not Janice. Are you my instructor?" I asked, trying to sound pleasant.

"Yes, I am. Jack wants only the best for you," he said without the least hint of sarcasm. "He wants this to be a private one-on-one class. We'll be zipping right along. A regular class would be far too slow for your needs."

I needed a positive attitude and fast. I tried to give myself a quick brain washing by telling myself this: Filbert had been spurned in front of Alan and me at the party, so he took it out on us. He had nothing against me personally.

My brain did not believe what I was telling it. I settled on looking studious and alert.

Filbert immediately launched into a lecture without going into any of the normal, preliminary stuff such as class goals, his expectations, and my background, if any, for this course. His voice was pleasant and melodious. He drew pictures on the blackboard and talked and talked, but he might as well have been talking in Hindustani. I took notes but did not understand a thing. Had this not been my first class of my entire training, I might have spoken up and asked questions. I decided I could study the material in my apartment at night, reread the textbook, and figure it out.

Upon leaving, I noticed the classroom was located near a convenient side door to the building. When I opened the heavy door, it creaked and squeaked loudly. Then it clanked behind me upon being closed.

That night I struggled through the problems by following the sample problems and by combining the samples, but I lacked any level of understanding. The next day I was determined to ask questions and once started to say something but he motioned me not to interrupt. That evening, the problems took even more time because I totally lacked understanding about what I was doing. The same situation went on for a week. I thought of that building as a dungeon and the squeaking and clanking side door as the dungeon door.

At the same time, I was taking another class, physical conditioning, from the astronaut Lauren, the one who had spurned Filbert. Lauren and I worked on preliminary aerobic, agility, and coordination exercises together. That class was going well. Soon we would drive to Ellington Field where I would try the simulators. After that, it would be a ride on a very special plane, the KC-135X.

In a week or so, I would start computer classes with Max Marsh as soon as he had some other tasks under control. Max was the "best there is" according to Jack and Dr. Fawzshen and performed feats of magic with computer networks.

I did not want to be thrown out of the program because of Filbert and orbital physics. With proper training I knew I could master it. I would go to class early, wait for him, and then ask questions before he launched into yet another non-stop lecture. If he insisted on starting his lecture, I would point out that it was not time for class.

At the creaky outer door, I was pleased to see a maintenance man repairing it. He held open the door, and it did not make a sound. When I got near the open classroom door, I heard voices and decided not to barge in. I would wait in the hall. Then I heard my name. It was Filbert's voice.

"That little Jana is trying to hang in there. Oh, I've got to give her that; she certainly tries. I'm afraid today's material will snow her, really snow her. I'm planning to give her a test tomorrow, and by Friday it's possible she could be washed out of the program." Filbert snickered. "And then a real astronaut can go into that slot."

"Are you that astronaut, Fil?"

"There's the list. My name is next on the list."

"But you're not a member of the back-up crew."

"Neither was she," Filbert replied.

"Some say the list is a fiction, that it doesn't exist. Have you seen the list?" the friend asked.

"Not personally, but it exists."

"You get rid of Jana, and then you don't get it anyway. And they need her."

"Why would they possibly need her?"

"To see that the solarship's designed well enough that a mission specialist with minimal training could take over if necessary."

"She's probably not going to be that mission specialist," Filbert said.

"You're teaching her with just this book? SpaceTech has supplemental material for practically all their subjects. I've been reviewing some of it for my department. They've got all sorts of interactive material for orbital physics, really fun stuff. Give that young woman a chance."

"She's had a chance," Filbert stated.

My first impulse was to barge in and tell Filbert I had heard everything. I felt myself getting angry all over. I started shaking. I wanted to scream. My rational self told me to calm down and think.

Filbert's friend asked, "What do you have against her? A summer intern thrown into an experimental program—she's probably insecure enough as it is. I would be."

"Oh, it's not really Jana. It's the whole mission. Why is NASA kowtowing to that wild-eyed Prince Fawzshen? We're America, and Rhatania is an insignificant little country. It's one thing to take foreigners but to let them dictate policy . . . ."

"Come, come, Fil, you're exaggerating."

"Oh, am I? NASA has a cadre of over 400 well trained astronauts. So many haven't been in space."

"So that's what's bothering you. You're in the premier category of major missions and you haven't been in space. You're not a rookie yet."

"It's not that. They give me the worst assignments, baby-sitting Jana every day, a baby actually. And when I'm lucky enough to work Mission Control, it's the night shift while JSC selects this Fawzshen and a child."

"They have also selected Jack, veteran of how many missions? Five, I guess." The friend talked soothingly. "For that matter, Prince Fawzshen is a graduate of the Houston Aerospace Academy."

"Oh, so he is. He probably charmed his way right through that school with his foreign manners and fancy titles. And why all this secrecy?" Filbert's voice had a harsh edge, which I had not heard before.

His friend's voice was so soft I could hardly hear. "Rumor has it that Lauren's going on the mission, too."

"No, that can't possibly be true."

"You know she's training for a mission and won't say which one. She's very competent."

"She's been an astronaut for not even a year. And she's got some weird, fluffy background in sociology. No, she's not going." Filbert's voice sounded almost like he was whining.

His friend decided to try a new approach. "It's not that important a mission. It's not a major mission anyway. They'll probably take the new solarship, the *Copernicus*, from the space factory where it's been assembled, test it out by orbiting the Earth for several days, and then park it at the spaceport."

"There's more to it than that. Why did Jack give such a big reception for Fawzshen? Why did he invite the kid? They're up to something, and it's bigger than a couple of days of orbiting the Earth."

I turned around and went back down the hall. The maintenance man held the door open for me again and said, "Change your mind, Miss?"

"Briefly," I said. Once outside, I marched over to a wooden bench by the lake. Four black and white ducks waddled hopefully toward me. They honked loudly. "I guess you guys are looking for food." The largest, boldest duck walked right up to me and nudged me with his orange beak.

Instead of being angry, I became numb. I did not have time for anger. I needed to act in as rational a way as possible.

I had just gained some valuable information. First of all, the crew, my crew, was going to be Jack, Dr. Fawzshen (who once had flown on an international mission), maybe Lauren (who was in training for a mission), and maybe me. The idea of Dr. Fawzshen himself flying on the mission had eluded me. Why would a crown prince again put himself at such risk? Secondly, testing out the Solarship *Copernicus* and then docking it at the spaceport sounded like a clever cover description. Even true. That test would be comprehensive, indeed, all the way to Jupiter and then back to the spaceport. I so wanted to be selected for that mission.

113

I could deal with Filbert. But how? If I told Jack and Dr. Fawzshen about Filbert, would they believe me? What kind of evidence did I have? An overheard conversation? That he consistently called me "Janice" instead of "Jana"? That the classroom was dingy and ugly? (Had Filbert purposely picked the building and the room?) That he was trying to not teach me? Jack and Dr. Fawzshen merely would consider me a baby with not enough endurance for the training, let alone the mission. Jack would recognize he made a huge mistake, thinking he could turn a baby-sitter into an astronaut.

I could look at everything another way. Filbert deliberately was trying to sabotage a certain part of the mission by not teaching me well. A saboteur certainly needed to be turned in. Maybe, I could tell Lauren. Yet, a poor teacher hardly can be classified as a saboteur.

A part of me wanted to run away and not confront Filbert, but a bigger part of me wanted to stay and fight if only I knew how. The ducks gave up on me and waddled away.

I tried to think of previous experiences that would help me. There were none. I thought about a ground training class I had recently taken for prospective pilots. The instructor explained how to know the wind direction at a desolate airstrip. There was no control tower, not even an air sock to read wind direction. How can a pilot get the needed information? Look which way the grass or trees are blowing. Look which way the cattle are standing. They stand with their backs to the wind.

This time I was the student above an alien airstrip without any power. To make a safe landing, Filbert must behave like a good teacher. Could I figure which way the wind was blowing?

There was no emotion left in me, only logic. I felt strong medicine flowing evenly through my veins. I marched back toward the building. The maintenance man still fidgeted with the door.

"That seems like quite a troublesome door," I commented.

"Think these hinges will have to go, maybe the whole door. So you're back, again."

"Say, can that door still clang?"

"You mean like this?" he asked as the clamor echoed down the hall.

I held my ears and said, "Yes, just like that."

As I entered the dingy classroom, Filbert's friend was leaving. Filbert beamed his impeccable smile and said, "Oh, you're early. We'll start right in. We have a lot to cover today."

He sat at his metal table and motioned me to sit down. I remained standing, towering over him. "I got here ahead of time to ask you some questions about the previous chapter."

"Sit down, Janice. My lecture will answer the questions," he said and then began speaking non-stop.

I interrupted him. "Filbert, it would help me if you answered my questions before the lecture."

He glued on his glorious smile. "Oh, Janice, we're not in high school. This is the real world." His voice sounded so soothing and convincing. "You'll be taking a test tomorrow, and I must prepare you for it."

"Sometimes, I feel like you're trying to snow me," I said, extending the "o" in "snow."

"You poor kid. The pressure's getting to you, isn't it?"

"I really want to learn this. I'm not a . . . baby."

He was silent for a moment. His perfect smile changed not one iota but an artery on his neck throbbed violently for a second. I could guess his thoughts. Could I possibly have overheard? When he spoke, his voice lost none of its luster. "Since you're early, we have time for one well thought out question."

He answered the question quite well before flying into his lecture. Twice during that session, his eyes clouded and his artery throbbed. Each time he slowed down and explained a point lucidly before launching back into his lecture.

Afterwards, we walked out of the building together. He stopped and examined the outer door. "The maintenance man's fixed the door," I said brightly. "He's been working on it all afternoon."

I did not know if he made the connection on what I was implying. He merely smiled politely and said, "See you tomorrow, Janice."

I said, "By tonight, I should have all the interactive stuff that goes with this book. I'm going to call SpaceTech right away."

Then, I noticed his neck artery throb.

Transmission between Houston and Solarship *Copernicus*
7:00 a.m. CDT

Surely, by now Houston knew of the supernet broadcast. Jack would find out soon enough. It was time for their transmission. It would take all his human relation skills to get Mission Control on his side. What kind of approach would work? Legalistic? That it was within his right as commander under an emergency situation to go on the net and reveal the existence of a secret mission? Righteous indignation? A bit of humor?

What was he thinking about? These people were his friends, or they had been. If the *Copernicus* or the crew were to be destroyed, would a different Mission Control, one that did not know the crew, be called in?

"What's going on up there? Are you having any problems?" asked CAPCOM.

"Problems? Is something showing up on your monitors?" Jack asked, keeping his tone bland and free from any a hint of sarcasm.

"All of our readings are nominal," Willie said and waited. That meant that each reading was within an acceptable range.

So this was it, the call Jack was waiting for, in a way dreading, in another way, anticipating the challenge. Jack studied the face of CAPCOM, a JSC astronaut, a rookie, someone he knew, a young man named Willie, in awe of Jack and in awe of the whole program. Jack hoped Willie was the sign he wanted that the danger was not coming from JSC. Jack breathed deeply. In his heart, he knew now that his own people were not trying to kill him. He just did not know how far "his own people" extended. Merely Max and Willie, all of Mission Control, all of JSC, all of NASA, the entire US government? His logical mind warned him to carefully study Willie's behavior and refrain from hasty evaluations of Mission Control. Yet, if Willie knew nothing about Jack's conversation with Max, how strange it would seem to Willie and to all of JSC for the four astronauts to take independent action. Jack hoped he could make his crew's independent actions seem normal and even prudent.

Finally, Willie spoke. "We've been getting phone calls from all over the world. Are you broadcasting over the supernet?" he politely asked.

"Yes, because we've determined that something is heading toward rendezvous with our ship, expected impact at 1600 hours CDT," Jack said. "Therefore, we have instituted emergency procedures. As part of the emergency procedures, we are broadcasting over the net."

"Oh, my God, sir, the broadcast really is from you! But why didn't you contact us directly? The meteoroid or whatever it is probably won't come within a thousand miles of the *Copernicus*, but just in case, we won't take any chances."

"Its trajectory indicates that its origin is the Earth. This makes the probability extremely unlikely that it is a meteoroid. That is why I am doing the worst case scenario and treating the object as if it is a bomb. That is why we're doing the broadcast."

"Sir, you don't think we're trying to . . . uh, abort the mission, do you?" Willie's eyes opened wide in sheer horror. "You don't think a . . . a bomb is coming from us?"

"That's one possibility, but definitely not a probability," Jack tactfully said. He wanted to get back to Earth safely, but he also wanted to continue his work with the Space Program, even if it required weeding out saboteurs.

"So you took action on your own. But why would NASA want to . . . ?"

"Think about it, Willie. Look at what we found on our secret mission."

"What can I do for you," Willie asked, drawing himself up to attention and firmly setting his jaw, apparently remembering he was CAPCOM and in charge.

"We need you to find out what was launched on Tuesday or Wednesday and then disarm it. Get the CIA and the FBI involved, too."

"Yes, I'll take care of it right away. You are correct, sir, in treating the object like it is a bomb."

"Remember that we estimate impact at 1600 today," Jack said.

"I wish we had more time. Wait a minute. I'll get a few things started. Then I'll need more information from you."

Jack watched Willie fly into action. He overheard a few comments. He heard Willie say, "Get the director down here fast. Track him down . . . . No, I won't read that stupid message to Jack. We have important things to deal with here."

Then, Jack's audio went out. Willie must have switched it off. As Jack watched the video, he became impressed and pleased with the young astronaut's behavior. If a group within NASA were trying to destroy them, Willie was not involved.

"I'm back, sir. All the wheels are in motion. I've even called in a more experienced CAPCOM to get us through this, sir."

Willie was doing just fine, Jack thought. "What was the message you didn't want to read to me?"

"It's nothing important, sir."

"Under these unusual circumstances, I would feel better hearing it."

"Okay," Willie said. He swallowed hard and picked up a piece of paper. "It's from Filbert. It says, 'Jack, you listen to me. Why is Janice reading her little diary on worldwide TV? Every TV station has picked this up. It's a circus here. We've had hundreds of calls telling us she's on TV. You are, too, begging for the public's help! First, we thought it must be an elaborate hoax. Do you know what Janice just finished reading? I'm gonna sue NASA and you, too, your royal buddy Fawzshen, and that Janice, each personally. My attorney tells me I have a great case. Lauren's totally innocent of this shameful deed. I know that.' Do you want me to continue reading this message, Sir?"

"Jana is on the net and on TV, too?" Jack asked.

"Yes, sir," Willie replied, "Every channel. I believe her transmission is on TV all over the world."

Jack was speechless. He sighed. As if in a concert hall during the crescendo of a symphony—it sounded like Beethoven's Ninth—he suddenly felt uplifted and free. However, his mind still warned him to proceed carefully. There were many small steps and a few giant leaps toward their salvation. "Read what else Filbert has to say."

Willie said, "It gets worse. Here's the rest of it. 'Are you getting even with me over that little transmission problem on Ganymede? I can't believe you'd stoop to such a low level. You, Jack, of all people! No, it's not the Ganymede thing. Your paranoia's got something to do with what Max and I talked about yesterday afternoon, doesn't it? That program update I sent you, the one that Max approved and signed off. So, I inadvertently stepped on Max's turf, but for you to respond like this!'" Willie looked directly into the camera. "It's signed 'Filbert.' I'm sorry about this, sir."

Jack dismissed Filbert's tirade except for another valuable piece of information. Filbert had most publicly reconfirmed the connection between himself and the sabotaged meteoroid detection update. Since the crew now was tracking the bomb, Filbert would realize that the crew had replaced that sabotaged update with a properly working one. Unless Filbert had no knowledge that it had been sabotaged in the first place. Yet, Filbert could be pretending that he knew nothing about it. Such a ridiculous message was thoroughly unprofessional unless Filbert was using offense as his defense. A guilty party could do that.

Filbert's tirade also publicly connected Max to the update. Was Max now in danger from the terrorists? On the other hand, if JSC was not involved, it seemed that Max had not yet gone to the director.

Would Max lose his job for withholding information? Max loved his work. Jack decided that he must concentrate on the task at hand and simply trust Max to take care of himself.

Jack asked, "Have you had any helpful phone calls, yet?"

"Maybe. We've had many calls, but we have just received a good one from a highly placed source. Right now, we have a Mr. Sandstrom of Darwin Industries on the phone with us. That company's headquartered here in Houston."

"I know a bit about that company," Jack replied. Darwin Industries, the largest private lift-off firm in the world, enjoyed a sterling reputation for safety. Sandstrom, a conscientious fellow, was the second in charge right under Charlie Darwin.

Willie said, "This is what we know so far. A Darwin employee, Sandstrom's chief of net security, called him this morning and assured him that she personally had checked out your net message. She certified to Sandstrom that it was coming from a solarship. She had been alerted to your broadcast by a counterpart, a net security chief for a large Seattle company."

So, Jack thought, could George MacInturff be that net security chief? If so, no wonder he had figured out how to contact the *Copernicus.*

Willie turned his head and spoke to someone. Looking back at Jack, he said, "I've just been handed the phone message. On Tuesday, Darwin Industries launched a payload for a company called LandSkyTech, a subsidiary of SpaceTech. My flight controller noted that Sandstrom sounds very concerned."

Jack had not heard of a SpaceTech subsidiary called LandSkyTech. So many companies had "Sky" in their names. "What's the payload?" Jack asked.

"A Saturn probe," Willie replied. "Sounds innocuous except for Mr. Sandstrom's concern. We'll thoroughly check this out."

"I know you will," Jack said and waited while Willie talked to someone.

"This is peculiar. Sandstrom said that right before he got the call from his security chief, someone from right here at JSC had called him with questions about recent launches. I don't know who that could have been."

Jack thought about Max but said nothing.

"Sir," Willie said, "Now that we know your broadcast is authentic, we'll check on launches from launch sites all over the world. We'll check the capabilities of orbiting satellites, too."

"That's an excellent idea, Willie."

"Sir, my people tell me we can't locate any meteoroid or object heading toward rendezvous with you. At this time!"

"I'll send you the trajectory data right now," Jack said. He simply had been waiting for the request.

"We may need to make a course correction for the *Copernicus*. Sir, that's what we'll probably recommend."

"I understand," Jack replied. He glanced at his timeline. Right on schedule.

"Sir, if the object doesn't make a corresponding correction, then our problem simply vanishes and you're home free."

"That would be nice," Jack replied.

"We'll do everything for your safe return. You will return safely!" Willie firmly declared. Then, he read another note he had been handed. "Sir, I have a message from Moon Base II. The people up there are in an uproar. They're not prepared for a lander. They don't like the idea of the unmanned *Copernicus* orbiting the moon, presumably passing right above their base." Willie sat up very straight. "The crew at the spaceport is prepared for you to dock there. Please proceed with those plans. They're increasing security protection for you, too."

Jack felt himself sinking, sinking into a heap of passivity as if all adrenaline had drained from his system. He wished to turn the entire situation over to Mission Control. However, he would do no such thing.

Jana's Journal

I jogged across the JSC grounds to my first class with Max Marsh, the computer systems specialist. The temperature outside still was pleasant (would peak later in the day), and the air smelled of freshly cut grass. As I got closer to the building I stopped jogging and began ambling slower and slower. I hoped Max Marsh would not dislike me as much as Filbert did.

As for Filbert, I had thrown all my effort into his class. The interactive material from SpaceTech had arrived quickly. It was clearly and even entertainingly written with lots of cartoon visuals. Unfortunately, it was at a simpler level than what Filbert was teaching me, but it definitely helped me with the basics. I thought that I was doing a little better in his class but got no feedback from him of whether it was good enough.

The newly cut grass reminded me of home, and if I were there, this problem would have vanished into thin air. Any number of people could have helped me including either of my parents, or I simply could have hired a tutor to teach me exactly what I needed at exactly the speed I needed. But now, once Max's class started, there would be less time for physics, so I was glad to have had the two weeks to devote primarily to Filbert's class.

Then I got the cheerful thought that Max could be as considerate as Lauren. So far, my physical conditioning sessions were going well because Lauren was kind, fun, and so helpful. Her attitude allowed me to relax around her and concentrate on my tasks. Also, I was pretty agile. Physical conditioning became a catchall term, not a standard JSC category, for a wide variety of training with Lauren. We already had started work on the simulators, which constantly tested my ability to pay attention and stay alert even though I realized the simulator work was at a basic level. I asked Lauren if she minded working on basic stuff and she said, "Oh, no, that's always good review."

She did not know why I was here at JSC training with her, but she accepted me, her student, with good cheer. I volunteered no information, and she did not question me. If anyone asked me what I was working on, I had learned from her to confidently say, "Special project." It indeed was my most special project in this world or any other. I wondered if she and I were training for the same mission as Filbert thought. I hoped so.

Even though my ambling had turned into a shuffle, I eventually found myself outside of Max's lab hoping for the best. I took a deep breath and knocked on the door, which had a keypad as well as a slot for a card.

Max Marsh looked like he had stepped out of a time machine. His face was rugged: lightly pock marked and deeply suntanned, as if he had never heard about the dangers of sun exposure. He wore an old leather cowboy hat, indoors yet, scruffy jeans, a faded plain shirt, and around his neck a small cone shell hung from a leather string. His eyes sparkled, and his air of confidence seemed to say, "I'm the best there is. I can dress any way I want."

"Salle is a big, dumb machine," Max Marsh said as he shook a computer about the size of a standard home computer. "Yet, it's tough and it's durable. Now, your turn."

I shook Salle rather gingerly.

"Naw, really shake it," he said. "Learn to have a healthy disrespect for computers. This model is exactly like the one that goes up in the hopper. Think how many g's it tolerates on lift-off. Furthermore, Salle is exactly like the computers in most solarship because we strive for standardization."

So began my first lesson in advanced computers.

While he looked like he lived in another century, his computer room sparkled with central processing units, video terminals, keyboards, and an assortment of printers, scanners, and other hardware I did not recognize. Salle and peripheral equipment—a large central video terminal and a dozen medium screens surrounding it—occupied several feet along one wall. On the opposite wall another computer looked exactly like Salle, and several smaller computers were scattered around the room. I could have been intimidated by so much hardware had Max not been so casual and friendly.

"Now, Miss Jana Novacek, tell me what you know about computers."

"A little bit about programming but mostly how to run different programs—word processing, data bases, research programs." I thought it best not to mention that I had a large collection of computer games in which I exhibited considerable expertise.

"What about troubleshooting?"

"Not anything."

"Networking?"

"Just enough to use the supernet."

"Anything about operating systems or hardware?"

"Not too much," I said, wondering how much more difficult my training would be for both of us.

"But I heard you were a splendid summer intern. Your supervisor told me you completed your programming job in only four days?"

Max expected a wizard, and instead he got me. Either the cowboy outfit or the friendly manner disarmed me. Or total fear that I soon would be submerged in lessons completely over my head. I had to be honest. I said, "My task for the summer looked like it would be complicated, but once I got started, it was pretty straightforward. It was . . . actually easy."

"The estimate for completing a task sometimes can be way off. But you do have two years of college?" Max asked, as if he were thinking aloud.

"I do," I replied, "But I was in an accelerated program in conjunction with the Houston Aerospace Academy. I've had two years of liberal arts and then I applied to the Academy where I would have taken computer courses, lots of science, and aeronautics. I hoped he was not too disappointed. "It's an experimental program," I added, as if that would make everything okay.

"And now you're in yet another experiment."

"Like a guinea pig," I replied, but decided to curb any more flip comments.

He said, "No preconceived notions! That's splendid! I won't need to unteach you half-truths and untangle the truth from the garbage." He nodded his head. "Sit back, relax, and think about this computer in front of you. It's not intelligent. It doesn't dream. It will not take over the world, at least not in the immediate future."

Max jumped around in front of the computer, almost as if he were doing a rain dance to an electronic deity. "Now, what does it do? It does exactly what its engineers, its analysts, its programmers, and its end users tell it to do. For one thing, it does mathematical calculations extremely rapidly. Thus, Salle is excellent for guidance control of a solarship. I know you're aware of exotic research computers and self programmable models."

Max walked over to a rather drab computer. "This one is loaded with advanced neural network software and other highly unique programs. It can practically think. It rewires itself as the situation requires, and only specialized, highly trained developers and programmers work on it. Unless it is handled with the utmost care, it becomes temperamental and very user-unfriendly. Someday, lots of safeguards will be developed for it. Eventually, it will become an industry standard. We had affectionately named it Prima Donna; now, that has become the official name for this particular platform with a particular combination of custom software.

"This top-of-the-line model preprogrammed from Houston goes on every mission. The main computers on a solarship are linked to it, but most of the time it does nothing. An astronaut would seldom if ever touch it. If it kicks in during a mission, which would only happen under the most extreme emergencies, an astronaut's job is to show restraint, leave it alone, and let it do its job. You also will leave this computer alone. Do you understand?"

"Absolutely," I replied.

"Now, here is another kind of computer. This one doesn't go on any of the missions yet. Any usage JSC has is in the research stage."

"I won't touch that one either," I volunteered.

"Good. You will only be touching Salle. There are many safeguards so you can be fearless."

He scrawled a picture with a felt tipped pen on a big pad of paper. "What's this?" he demanded.

Max's style was such a joyful relief over Filbert's monologue. Max did not seem to dislike me, and he did not mind his task of teaching me. I concentrated on being respectful. "It's a bug, sir, an insect."

"But what kind of insect?" he demanded, adding a line curved downward to his drawing.

"A mosquito?"

"Yes, this ordinary mosquito had as much intelligence as the most sophisticated, expensive computer of 30 years ago." Max quickly drew again. It was a low-to-the—ground creature with rounded ears and a long, skinny tail. " Now, what is this?"

"A rat? Rats are pretty smart," I said.

"Are today's computers as smart as rats? That depends on whom you ask. Some would say our standard computers are smarter than rats, and others say nowhere near as smart."

"At that rate," I said, "Computers will be smarter than people. What will happen, then?"

"Someday soon, we'll need to deal with such a contingency. However, for now, in certain respects, Salle is not as advanced as the mosquito."

"That could be reassuring," I responded.

"For example, Salle cannot be programmed to differentiate between a constant bombardment of multiple, ever changing variables, including some that have never been anticipated. That's when Prima Donna takes over to handle a difficult situation, at least in theory and in controlled tests. We have not used it yet for a true emergency on a mission."

Max patted Salle gently and said, "Poor thing. Salle is not glamorous but so trustworthy and does the real work on a solarship." He pointed toward a red switch. "Now, turn it on, and let's see what happens."

I flipped the switch. Five of the thirteen screens lit up simultaneously, and a most pleasant voice said, "Your handprint, please!"

I looked toward Max, but he merely pointed toward the larger central screen. "Handprint, please!" The voice seemed more insistent, or was that my imagination? A pale outline of a hand grew brighter on the central screen as I pressed my hand against the outline. The voice again sounding pleasant said, "Hold still for the retinal scan." I did not move. "Greetings, Miss Jana Novacek! Do you have any questions before we proceed?" Salle asked.

I felt so relieved that Max was starting his class off in such a relaxed manner that I was unable to suppress a little silliness. "I have been told you are a big, dumb machine. How do you respond to that?"

"I am very hurt. Will you apologize?" Salle asked.

Smart as a mosquito, indeed! Salle's response went well beyond anything I programmed into my home computer. When I powered up my computer, it said: "Hi Jana, are you ready to conquer the world today?" Regardless of whatever I answered, my computer then would say, "I'm glad to hear that."

Salle again asked, "Will you apologize?"

I glanced toward Max for advice, but he simply shrugged his shoulders. "I will not apologize today," I said.

"Let us proceed." I thought I heard a disappointed tone, even a sigh as Salle said, "Type TUTOR and hit the ENTER key."

After a few preliminary steps, I was running a flight simulation program in which I was an astronaut on board a solarship who needed to make a course correction with the assistance of Mission Control. Max sat at my side emphasizing what I definitely should memorize and what I could disregard.

At the end of the lesson after Salle was safely powered down, I asked, "How can a big dumb machine carry on an intelligent conversation?"

Max grinned mischievously and said, "Let me know as soon as you figure it out."

The first lesson had been so leisurely, so casual, and so much fun that the next day I was rather surprised that we were whipping through new material at warp speed as Max taught me the SPACE operating system. Sometimes, Max totally lost me as I felt like I had hit a wind shear, but without my saying a word, he would stop, carefully remove me from the crash site, dust me off, explain a point, and move on. Once I realized that Max would rescue me from each wind shear, I relaxed and my mind became like a sponge. People might consider Max a computer guru, but that day I realized he was a teacher extraordinaire.

After the formal part of the class, Max told me to select a program, study the tutor that went with it, and present the results to him on Friday. He crossed the room, sat down, and began working on an identical computer, which he called Salle Too.

I looked over the program titles, mostly two, three, or four initials, each with a cute little icon, but none indicating subject. I randomly picked a program, but when I pressed the enter key, the screen went blank. I waited. Nothing happened. I thought I heard soft laughter coming from Salle. Was Salle not cooperating because of yesterday's insult? Ridiculous! Yet, I definitely heard laughter as I selected another program from the list. The program's name filled the main central screen but try as I would, I could not access the tutor instructions. I considered apologizing to Salle, but that was when I noticed a tempting list of computer games. I resisted for a few seconds before calling up a game similar to Tetris.

An image of my Dad flashed before me as I recalled a Dad-type lecture. He once told me that the way employees use discretionary time was how to separate the really good workers from the average ones. I quickly dismissed Dad's image and wondered if I would be carrying his little mini-lectures around in my head forever.

I set the game level to novice and deftly arranged the little shapes as they tumbled from the top of the screen. I got high scores right from the beginning when a stabbing pang of loneliness struck and quickly enveloped me as I remembered Alan and I once had played the very same game using small hand held computers at the SpaceTech gazebo. I quit the game immediately.

The loneliness still had not subsided when I whispered so that Max would not hear me, "Okay, Salle. I'm sorry I called you 'a big, dumb machine.' You seem smarter than a mosquito, smarter than a rat, and I think smarter than I am."

I called up another program with three initials, again not having any idea what it was. *Voice Simulation Tutor* filled the screen. I quickly turned the volume way down and looked around to see what Max was doing. He was hunched over Salle Too's keyboard, totally involved.

Had I really called up VST or had Salle just given it to me? I could not remember for sure what initials I had selected since none of them had any meaning to me.

The first section of the tutor was a general overview on how Voice Simulation (VS) worked. I certainly was motivated to figure out how Salle talked to me.

The next day after the formal lesson was completed, I waited for Max to cross the room and begin his own work on Salle Too. Then, keeping the volume so low that I barely could hear it, I quietly attempted to learn VS. It soon occurred to me that VS would not help me to become an astronaut and perhaps Max would be displeased that I had not chosen a more important program.

On Friday, Max was busy working on Salle Too when I got to class. I quickly logged-on, gave a few special commands, and then powered Salle down. "The computer's off," I said.

"Well, turn it on," Max replied. "Don't tell me your love affair with Salle is winding down to friendship, and so quickly, too."

I hung back and Max asked, "Is Salle broken? Have all programs been wiped out of memory?" He spoke calmly as if such occurrences would not be catastrophic at all. "Is the operating system gone?"

I did not answer him. Max glanced at me suspiciously, left Salle Too, crossed the room, and flipped the red switch. "Hello, Dr. Marsh," Salle's voice greeted him. "I don't need your hand print today. I recognize your breathing, your blood pressure, and, of course, I can see you."

"What's my blood pressure today, Salle?" Max asked.

"At this moment, it is one twenty over eighty, sir."

"And what might I be wearing, Salle?"

"You are wearing a leather hat, sir, blue jeans, a cowboy shirt."

Max nodded approvingly. "The color of my shirt?"

"Plaid multicolor, sir. And now it is time for Jana's lesson. Please type Tutor and strike the ENTER key." Then, Salle laughed and laughed.

I was happy that I had covered enough vocabulary possibilities, but I could not tell whether Max was pleased or not. Had Max considered my time spent in silliness? For someone who could be so effusive, he merely studied me but finally asked, "What's your reaction to learning this program?"

"Pleasure," I replied, "but there's another feeling. When you first turned me loose, I thought that it's only the engineers and the programmers who have fun, and it's more routine for the end user. This program isn't simply the point and click stuff I have at home. It's more for a computer person. You've got to get into the program to understand it. With VS, I had a goal to make the computer carry on a conversation with you. In the process, something surprising happened to me. I entered the brains of the VS programmers and experienced their joy in creating something that works. I'm pretty sure there were two separate programmers, and I learned something about how those people think. I'd say one was quite innovative and creative while the other went more by the book."

Max nodded at me but did not say anything. I was hoping for a compliment. Why I valued his opinion of me or why I sought his approval, I did not know. I was not a child. Was I assuming that just because he was a highly respected computer expert and also a marvelous teacher that he could also predict my ability to succeed? The two were not related. I only needed to do my work, be respectful, and shake off my need for praise.

I thought he smiled slightly, but I was not sure. He seemed pleased, and then he said, "Splendid, Jana. I enjoyed the demonstration. And your analysis, too."

Like a flame, my confidence flared. As his flicker of a smile faded, my confidence died out. I reminded myself that he indeed had been pleased. For one precious moment I knew that I belonged, and I could succeed.

I drummed up courage and asked Max if I could spend extra time with Salle. He told me that only a few people had access to his lab, but without hesitation he gave me a key card and granted me permission to work with Salle anytime, whether he was there or not.

After that I hardly wanted to leave the computer room. My goal was not to become a computer wizard, but I was having so much fun learning about Salle and the intricacies of the SPACE operating system that I gave scant attention to everything else. Since I had barely gotten a handle on orbital physics by studying the supplemental material, I desperately needed to spend much more time with that subject. I tried to hold my focus steady and keep my goal firmly ahead of me, but the lure of Salle seemed beyond my control. I thought about talking to one of the psychologists who worked at JSC but decided that could prove risky.

Then something happened. I was working on Salle when my rational self and my wrist watch told me now was the time to stop and go study orbital physics. I had brought my textbook with me, but the interactive material that helped considerably was back at my apartment. Salle had a magical hold on me. I could not pull myself away. As I was deciding to stay a few more minutes, I heard the door unlock and open. It was not Max.

The man had piercing dark eyes, and immediately I could tell he was affable. "Hi, I'm Venzi. Where's Max?"

I told him that I did not know and that I could leave if he needed the lab. I introduced myself, and maybe because he was staring at my textbook, I explained that I needed to go and study my orbital physics.

He said with a fondness in his voice, "Ah, yes, undergraduate physics," and volunteered to help me sometime.

I was not likely to pass up help on that subject. I asked, "How about now?"

Venzi was taken back, but he seemed pleased by my request. He said, "That will work."

We went through all the problems, and for every question I asked, he explained things so precisely that I could hardly believe only half an hour had passed. I thanked him profusely and told him how clear and concise he had been.

Venzi laughed in a hearty, cheerful way that brightened and filled an already pleasant computer room. "No one has accused me of being clear or concise before. We must be on the same wavelength. I mean that in the colloquial sense. Here, let me demonstrate the Prima Donna."

"Will Max mind?" I asked.

Venzi's eyes grew wide, and he looked absolutely amazed at such an idea. "No, of course not."

I almost said, "You're somebody important, and I haven't a clue."

He must have sensed my thoughts because he said, "I'll tell you, Jana. I lead a charmed life. I also mean that in the colloquial sense. The center where I do research and here at JSC, I research exactly what I want, all because I'm interested in an area of physics that may soon yield practical applications."

"What's that area?" I asked.

"Time discontinuities. If something such as an unmanned satellite or space probe is lost in another time frame, how do you retrieve it? If the satellite has a Prima Donna computer with correctly set programs, the satellite can communicate with Houston and we can communicate with it. Then, we can retrieve the satellite or leave it where it is and retrieve information."

"That sounds exciting, like a time machine. How does it work?"

He thought a minute and said, "An analogy is something like the time delay on a phone system. Suppose you want to communicate with someone, say a friend, who lives a minute in the future, how would you do it?"

With barely a moment of thought, I quickly said, "I would send the message at a faster rate of speed than the rate that the friend's time frame is traveling. For example, a friend is walking away from you and you are trying to catch up. You walk faster than the friend," I said, realizing I was comparing his sophisticated physics with basic algebra, but he did not seem to mind. I also realized I had not touched on a phone analogy. I would not have dared say such things to Filbert. He would have shot me down in a minute.

Venzi simply said, "Now, let's look at the problem from several other frames of reference and other ways of seeing matter." Everything he explained seemed totally clear. I asked him so many questions that he finally said, "You ask more questions than my post-doc students."

"I'm sorry," I said.

"No, I like it. You are fearless intellectually, and that is good."

"I only have a few more questions. Is this material classified?" I asked.

"Fortunately, not yet. I consult with other physicists from all over the world. If it were classified, I couldn't be telling you about it, or in your case I probably could."

I shivered at that comment but did not pursue it. He had met me less than an hour ago. Perhaps, it was his way of speaking.

"You say that this is all theoretical." I tried to disguise a question as a statement.

"It's theoretical for now. JSC is allowing me to install certain programs on their Prima Donna computers that go onboard practically everything: their space stations, solarships, hoppers, and space taxis. Sometimes even their satellites and probes."

I knew Max was very particular about software that went on missions. I did not want to insult Venzi so I picked my words carefully, "How do you get the authority to have theoretical software on mission computers?"

"It comes from the director, but I must tell you that Max heartily approves."

I had heard that the director was an enormously practical person, but I did not realize he was forward thinking, too. Yet, lots of research was going on at JSC in fields such as propulsion and the life sciences.

Almost as if anticipating my unasked question, Venzi said, "I help out Director Clayton, and he reciprocates. About two or three times a year, the director asks me to look into a disputed area and give him my feedback on the subject. Sometimes, it's not my areas of expertise, and I tell the director that, but by my being with the engineers and managers and asking questions, the researchers involved work out their differences because they think I know the best course of action. Sometimes, they realize I don't know and fear my advice will mess up their work completely. Therefore, those who have been polarized begin working together.

"The director finds me enormously useful and thinks I walk on air. As for my theoretical work, he trusts that also will be as useful as my other work for him. Therefore, he gives me enough staff and funds and mostly encourages me to pursue my own interests. On faith, he sees that my programs are included on the Prima Donna equipment on the launches."

I was not sure someone whom I had just met should be telling me the secret aspect of his job description. I had asked but did not expect such an unvarnished answer. "Why do you do this particular job for Director Clayton? Is it to get special considerations?" I could not believe I was being so blunt.

"Gosh, no. It could appear that way. It certainly works that way." Venzi thought a minute. "I guess as a social service type of thing. I can't think of physics every minute, and ideas come to me when they're ready. I could be listening to a song or having a conversation. I could be driving in my hydrocar, and, gosh, there's an idea. I pull into a parking lot or onto the side of the road and write down my thoughts. Don't get me wrong. There's a lot of grunt work, too, as I imagine in many other fields, but then there's the magical, joyful moments of pure inspiration.

"I look upon this job for Director Clayton as helping JSC run smoother by solving problems or giving the people the impetus to solve their own problems. The first time was somewhat accidental. The director wanted my thoughts on a situation. Two different departments that needed to work together were entrenched in their opposing views. I helped them work through it. I liked being a logical, rational peacemaker and told the director I'd be happy to help like that again if there were another such situation.

"I tell people right up front, or more or less up front, that I'm checking into a situation for the director and that I will be reporting my findings back to him. I must say it cuts way down on my circle of friends, but I find they tell me what I ask.

"Now, let's look at this Prima Donna computer. It doesn't have any of the user-friendly interfaces. We'll be bold because I basically know what I'm doing. And I assure you Max won't mind."

He spoke a couple of words, and the Prima Donna came to life. The screen was full of programming code. He spoke a few more words and then read the first orbital physics problem. As he finished the last word of the problem, the answer appeared on the screen. "See, it does the same job your garden variety computer does, but it does much more. It almost thinks. Tell your physics teacher that you checked your problems out on the Prima Donna. That will make him spin."

I visualized Filbert being caught in a whirlwind. I wanted to say something mean about him but resisted the urge.

As if understanding my thoughts, Venzi said, "I surmise that you're afraid of your physics teacher. Fear impedes learning, and that's a neurological fact. A few well-placed comments about the Prima Donna will put you on more equal footing with Filbert."

Our eyes met. First, Venzi was pretending that he did not know who my physics teacher was, and then he referred to Filbert by name. Furthermore, in no way had I implied that I was afraid of Filbert. Maybe I was. Yes, I probably was.

"You're not accidentally here, are you?" I asked, realizing why Venzi had told me that he resolved interpersonal situations for the director.

He maintained eye contact, "Jana, I am not accidentally speaking to you about physics."

The director had sent him to solve a problem, and I was the problem. "You didn't tell me up front."

"I thought I just had."

"That wasn't exactly up front."

"Would you have allowed me to help with your orbital physics? Would you have asked all of your questions?"

"No, of course not, none of the above."

"How would I have learned what I needed to know?" he asked in a friendly voice.

"I feel like I've been tricked," I said.

"I'm sorry you feel that way, Jana. I feel like I'm helping JSC reach their goals. The stakes in this situation are very high."

I did not say anything. I just looked at him. Finally, he said, "I had dropped by to see my friend Max. Regarding your situation with Filbert, I was planning to speak with him first, but today you were here with physics book in hand and more than willing for me to help you. In fact, you asked me to help you. An ideal situation presented itself. Do you want me to apologize?"

I shook my no and cracked a smile, recalling how initially I had refused to apologize to Salle. I needed to get my personal feeling of hurt out of this. "What do you recommend that I do?" I asked.

"You need to know the director thinks highly of Filbert. Not too many people know that because he has not yet intervened on Filbert's behalf, but Director Clayton could and I think if the situation is right, he will. I would not recommend complaining to anyone about Filbert."

"No, I haven't done that," I said, realizing just how close I had come to complaining about him to Venzi.

"Apparently, you confronted him on a few occasions."

"Barely. That got back to the director?" I asked incredulously. I must have shaken Filbert up more than I thought. "What would you do?"

"Confronting him is fine. Stop being afraid of him. I'm not above a little intellectual intimidation when the situation calls for it."

"Wouldn't he see through that pretty fast, particularly since I don't know very much?"

"You know more than you think," Venzi said. "I'll give you a list of 50 physics terms. Memorize them and what they mean. Use them when the situation calls for it, and drop my name whenever you like. Tell Filbert I'm your friend. You can count on me to back you up. Contact me whenever you need help. Here's my card. I'll write my private number on it. If I'm in the middle of wrapping up my latest theory of everything, give me a few hours to reach a stopping point."

I took the card and thanked him profusely. Then I boldly asked, "Is helping me part of the director's assignment to you?"

"Oh, no, not at all," Venzi replied. "Why am I helping you? Gosh, I don't know. Yes, I do know. You treat me like a regular person. I like that. I've had preferential treatment all my life. Do you know what that's like?"

"I'm beginning to understand," I replied, thinking that my confrontation with Filbert had reached all the way to the director himself who chose to send a star physicist to investigate rather than take the word of his friend Filbert.

Venzi began telling me about himself. Here at JSC where he had few friends, he was glad that he could talk to Max about practically everything. At the international physics center where he also worked, his friends and colleagues were numerous, and his graduate and post-doctoral students held him in awe.

He told me the history behind his name, Venzi Suzaky. His family name sounded similar to Suzuki. To honor both physicists of the Gabriel Veneziano-Mahiko Suzuki string theory, his parents, physicists themselves, named him Venzi. He described childhood dinners with family when conversations were flavored with elementary particles, Penrose networks, loop quantum gravity, and all varieties of current and historical physics theories.

"It was as normal as talking about...." Venzi stopped mid-sentence and took a small hand held computer out of his shirt pocket and began feverishly keying in things. His behavior seemed most peculiar. I neither said a word nor moved a muscle. He focused on another world, apparently a joyful but intense place. He typed for about five minutes before he said, "I've been working on a perplexing problem, and now I have . . . I may have a solution. Sorry, I must rush back to my lab. Nice meeting you, Jana."

I nodded and waved but spoke not a word because I dared not interrupt his chain of thought with chatter. His idea could be lost forever because of a distraction.

The next day the fifty physics terms and clear definitions arrived via e-mail along with a note. "I've stumbled onto a breakthrough, I think. We shall see. The impetus was within those fond recollections of long ago dinner conversations. Glad you were so interested. Particularly glad you asked so many questions about all those theories." It was signed Venzi S.

After that, my fear of Filbert did not lift completely, but I no longer had reason to fear him. The orbital physics course began going better because I knew I could call Venzi if I got stuck. Knowing that, I relaxed, and the material seemed much less difficult. At the same time, I developed the will power and even the desire to log-off Salle and tend to my physics studies.

I memorized the physics terms and meanings that Venzi sent me, and finally one day when I was feeling particularly brave, I tested out one of the words on Filbert. Of course, he immediately challenged me. I knew he would. I held my own with him and then threw out Venzi's name. Filbert tried to hide his surprise that I knew Venzi, a brilliant physicist and the director's friend. Filbert's attitude toward me changed that very moment. He did not stop disliking me, but he realized that he could not mistreat me at will. His lectures even became more understandable although I still relied heavily on the interactive basic material from SpaceTech.

Soon, I not only understood orbital physics but also enjoyed it. Filbert resigned himself to the fact that the subject had finally become comprehensible to me. I asked him how I was doing, and he said that I was improving. I pushed a little and asked if I was doing well enough. Then he admitted that he had signed a JSC form certifying that I had learned the required material and that if I continued at the same pace, he would sign the final form. What a huge relief! I must have let down my guard for a second and looked really happy because then he said, "I've been told to be sure that you learn this material."

He waited for me to follow up on his comment, but I declined because the conversation could do nothing but deteriorate into issues such as my getting preferential treatment over many highly qualified people. Still, I was surprised that he had revealed that morsel of information. I wondered if word had come all the way from the director. After that conversation, he allowed his class to resemble more closely the interactive tutoring that I was supposed to be getting.

Once, he actually forgot how much he disliked me, and then I realized how much he liked physics. We shared a few brief moments of rapport while discussing trajectories. At some level there was a degree of warmth to him. Predictably, the rapport did not last, and by the next day we returned to our polite, but guarded interaction with each other. However, we stopped meeting in the dingy classroom and moved the tutoring sessions to his office, a pleasant, though slightly cluttered place. I almost told him that I had trouble being neat, too, but thought better of it.

One day I got an e-mail from Venzi entitled *Abstract: Space-Time Discontinuities*. Although only one page long, it was amazing. I e-mailed back and asked if I could read the entire document. He sent it to me almost right away. Every page was marked "draft." I understood about 20 percent of the ideas and 10 percent of the math. It was fascinating stuff. I called and thanked him. I also admitted how little I understood.

Venzi invited me to his office for tea and explained his paper to me with the math hugely simplified. He also taught me something called timing progressions, a mathematical series that would be required to move something from one dimension to another or from one time to another. He emphasized that his work was highly theoretical. He promised to send me some background material so everything would be more comprehensible.

I thought he would ask me how I was doing in Filbert's class, but I simply volunteered and told him things were going better.

In comparison to Filbert's, the classes with Max were sheer joy. About a month into my training, Max and I bantered back and forth about the finer points of reestablishing communications between a solarship and Mission Control. Max explained several causes for communications disruption: the actual physical location of the solarship in relation to the Earth and to communications satellites, solar flares, and simply certain calendar dates, specifically the equinoxes. When the sun was lined up a certain way on the longest day, June 21, or shortest day, December 21, or right in between, March 21 and September 21, communications satellites sometimes experienced problems. Then Max reviewed the many ways to reestablish communication if it did not happen spontaneously.

Since so much freedom in a formal learning situation still was a novelty to me, I continuously exerted the effort to behave respectfully toward such a brilliant and generous man. However, during that particular class I was having too much fun. I disrespectfully said, "Max, you teach me fifteen ways to accomplish each objective. One way should be enough?"

He did not mind my impertinence at all. He jovially replied, "That's a good comment, Jana. Let's take a hypothetical situation. Say, you've lost communication with Mission Control and . . . ."

We were interrupted by the intercom requesting Max to pick up the phone. He said, "Yes, of course, I'm always available to take a call from Madame . . . . I'll take it in my office."

When Max returned from his phone conversation five minutes later, the gaiety in his voice was totally gone, replaced by sadness. He got right back to instructing me. It was still on communication but a totally different lesson.

After a few minutes he sternly said, "Just because you have the opportunity to do something doesn't mean you should do it."

I replied, "If I get this particular opportunity, I'm going for it. I'm not going to hesitate. I'm not going to think twice."

Our eyes met and it quickly occurred to me that he knew my true status and not the cover that I had overheard Filbert and his friend talking about.

Solarship *Copernicus*

7:33 a.m. CDT

As Jana read over the supernet, her computer screen blinked red, her reminder to herself that she had come to sensitive material that must be skipped. She wondered if anybody watching would notice. She silently read as she quickly scrolled her screen through the entry.

Jana's Journal

(Not read over the net)

The next day, Max seemed like his jovial self again until it was nearly time for the end of the lesson. Instead of turning me loose to pursue a new program on Salle, he said, "Be careful whom you trust. People have their own agendas."

I considered telling him about Filbert but remembered Venzi's advice and held back. I said, "You're trustworthy, and you've been successful around here."

He replied, "I'm going to tell you something else about a solarship communicating with Houston."

"We've already had that lesson; remember, you've taught me 15 different ways."

"This one you someday may have a need to know."

"A need to know! You mean classified information, like a secret?" My head was too full of secrets already. Ever since I entered this training, I have had to be so careful about my words because I did not know who knew what.

"More precisely, top secret," Max said. "You'll know when it's time to reveal it to anyone else."

I said, "Please tell me." There was a certain delicious aspect to secrets, too.

"If you ever need my help, you can bypass Mission Control and call me directly. You might say I have an unlisted channel."

I could not fathom why any astronaut needed to bypass Mission Control, but it seemed best to stay quiet and listen. The corners of his mouth quivered, and he appeared so serious.

"I'll need to key in a code," he said as if talking to himself. Then to me he asked, "Give me a name or date that you can always remember, even under times of stress, not your birth date and not the birth date of anybody in your family; that would be too easy for someone to figure out. The name of a friend perhaps.

"My good friend is Alan Bailey."

"Let's reverse the order, and then we'll reverse the letters in each word. Okay, that will be Y E L I A B N A L A. For the rest, we'll add four stars. "Then we'll have the code: Y E L I A B N A L A * * * *

"This is a pretty simple code, but don't worry. When I receive it, Salle Too will automatically finish out the rest of a more complex code. You won't need to remember any of that. Max said, forcing joviality into his voice, "You never know when those characters in Mission Control go out for a coffee break."

I could not imagine any situation in which Mission Control would be unmanned, but I did not say anything.

"Let me show you what ol' Salle Too will do."

He leapt across the room and motioned me to follow him. He sat down at the computer and keyed in the code we made up. Next, he keyed in several other things so fast that I could not follow what he was doing.

He got up and said to me, "Now, it's ready for you. Jana, sit down right by Salle Too's keyboard and type in the code. Or simply speak the code slowly and clearly. When you get to an asterisk, say 'star.' You'll be calling me on my unlisted channel."

I clearly spoke the code. Salle Too beeped once, and the 13 monitors along that wall came to life.

Salle Too beeped again and the entire room with the exception of Salle became awash with light from many more monitors which all showed different data, but in its totality the room resembled a small Mission Control. Max turned up the volume, and we eavesdropped on the flight commander's conversation with a space taxi.

145

Why would an astronaut possibly need to go through Max and not Mission Control? Possibilities for Max's revelation welled up inside me.

After class, I staggered out into the bright Houston sunlight. Humidity bore down upon me like a weight. Did Jack know about all of this? Max had warned me and given me a way to protect the whole crew, if necessary, from something. If so, that meant Max believed that I already had been selected as a crew member. With that cheery thought, my fears and concerns lifted and dissipated into the humidity.

That day, I joined the tourists and took a good look at the Saturn rocket displayed in its own building at JSC. I visualized it transformed into a solarship and glistening in the distance, docked at the space factory, surrounded by the blackness of space.

Jana's Journal

The sun cast morning shadows as Lauren and I boisterously sang old flying songs as we drove to Ellington Field for my first flight on the KC-135X. I was scared but the singing suppressed sheer terror. Riding in her little hydro sport car helped, too. The top was down, and the balmy breeze smelled like the salt spray from the Gulf. It was a lovely morning for the most dangerous day of my life.

I sang louder and louder to control my fears. Lauren glanced over at me and patted me on the shoulder. "It's okay to be scared. Every astronaut who's gone up in this bird has been scared."

"Thanks," I said. So much for trying to conceal my fear. She saw right through my facade.

I wanted to ask her about the jokes regarding the KC-135X. More than once since I had been living at JSC, I had heard astronauts talk about the ride and laugh uproariously. I did not want to appear ignorant and ask them what was so hilarious. So I still did not know.

The X was patterned after the old KC-135A that earlier astronauts trained on. All of the astronauts since have trained on the old version or the X. The plane would go almost straight up, make an arch, and then go almost straight down. For the 25 or 30 seconds at the top of the parabola, I would experience weightlessness. We were planning to do the arch many times.

Lauren began chatting away. Her voice was warm and soothing, and I felt myself relaxing. She was the most cheerful person I had ever met. She seemed genuinely happy most of the time. Little things pleased her so much like finding out I knew the old flying songs. When she was low or blue, she was cranked down to about a normal person's outlook.

I was surprised when she switched gears into more personal issues. She said she had everything she could possibly want, except three things, one to go on a major mission and the other—a remote possibility—to live in a space colony.

"What's the third thing?" I asked.

She looked a little surprised at my question. I almost said, "It's okay, Lauren. You don't need to tell me." Instead, I kept quiet. She was quiet, too, but then said someday she might like to get married if she ever met the right person, but she was terribly selective. Maybe, true love was not meant to be. The wistfulness in her voice was gone in a flash.

A sensitive friend might have let it drop, but I was too curious. I had seen how easily men were attracted to her. It seemed as if she had many choices from which to make a selection. I asked, "How would you know when you found him?"

"I'd know immediately. So would he."

Trying to keep my voice bland and non-judgmental, I asked, "You mean love at first sight?"

"Yeah, I guess so," Lauren whispered slowly.

For the first time in my friendship with Lauren, I felt like the older one, the one with a little sense. "But you wouldn't know anything about the person."

"At that moment in time, we'd instantly know everything, everything that really mattered, each other's heart and soul."

"And what are the qualities of heart and soul that you'd want?"

"Honesty, kind heartedness, courage. I think there would be an understanding beyond passion, beyond language, a spiritual melding."

Practical Lauren was a romantic at heart? I could hardly believe it. She had her eyes on the road and did not even glance toward me. I studied her face beside me and even leaned forward to get a better look. Her eyes had a dreamy, glazed look like right before shedding a tear.

I was not feeling superior anymore to Lauren. I was remembering a moment with Alan that had been like that, in his garden covered with ice, the first time he had invited me there. A moment I would always remember but sometimes tried to minimize its significance. It was not exactly love at first sight because I had noticed him before at school, but even from a distance, he intrigued me.

I did not say anything. Neither did she. Then she lightened up a little and said, "It would be somebody who is lots of fun, somebody really interesting, somebody who knows more than I do about different cultures."

"You mean a sociologist?"

Lauren replied quickly. " I'd prefer an astronaut if . . . if I could find the right one."

"What would happen after that?" I asked.

"It would depend upon the circumstances. Maybe nothing."

It seemed that practical Lauren controlled her heart. Maybe, I, practical Jana, controlled my heart, too.

I lightly said, "You live in the right place. You have the right job to find Mr. Honest Astronaut."

Then, I told her that I missed Alan much more than I imagined I could. I emphasized more than once that he was just a friend. I abruptly stopped talking about him because I was pretty certain she did not know my status here. I did not think she knew that I was not supposed to see Alan or my family or anybody else except the people I worked with.

She said, "My lady doth protest too much." Fortunately, she did not pursue the subject but instead told me the history of the Clear Lake area, which I already knew. She said there had been Indians all around here, and it was a good thing that Armand Bayou had been preserved in the middle of all this technology. I half listened, not responding even to direct questions until I heard her say, "Did you know I have an Indian ancestor?"

"Texas Indians, Karanquas?" I replied, forgetting momentarily that a KC-135X awaited me.

"No, Oglala Sioux."

"That's impressive," I said, trying to remember my Indian history and place where that tribe was located. I, too, was a sucker for learning about other cultures.

"That's the tribe of Chief Crazy Horse," she said.

She wove more tales about Indian lore and explained how Crazy Horse had ridden zigzag like lightning to dodge the white man's bullets.

My fear had pretty much dissipated until we pulled onto the NASA side of Ellington, and there sat the KC-135X glistening in the sun and casting a long morning shadow on the runway. A pilot standing alongside the plane waved at us.

Lauren and I went to suit up in the standard issue coveralls. That was when Lauren presented me with pilot's coveralls as a gift. There even was a patch with my own name on it.

"This is a great gift, Lauren. It makes me feel like I belong."

"You're here. Therefore, you belong," Lauren firmly replied. "Let's board. We'll get a good spot on the plane."

I would follow Lauren's lead, relax as much as possible, and let myself be swept along with the breeze.

The plane was shiny and new, but it also had quite a utilitarian appearance. Once inside, there were no seats for the passengers, only padding on all of the walls. Lauren told me that the seats sometimes bolted along tracks in the back part of the plane had been removed. This way was better, she explained; we would have more room. Double shoulder harnesses with soft buckles were attached at varying heights along the walls. Lauren told me we would not need them. Instead, we sat cross legged on the floor. She instructed me to sit with my back very straight and my head resting firmly on my spine. I noticed airsickness bags attached with Velcro straps to the padded walls and was glad that I had followed Lauren's advice and eaten only a tiny breakfast hours ago, including a gingersnap cookie, which could help prevent nausea.

Pretty soon, about twenty people piled in. A few I recognized as astronauts. Lauren told me some were JSC employees and others were NASA contractors. They either sat cross-legged or knelt down. We took off and flew around. At first, it was like a commercial flight.

Then, the plane started climbing. Lauren told me look straight ahead, hold my head still, and focus on a spot above the heads of the passengers across from us. The plane climbed and climbed, it seemed like straight up. The pressure of gravity along the back of my head and spine pushed down upon me like a vise tightening.

Lauren said, "It's going to happen very soon." Suddenly, the pressure was gone, and we were experiencing weightlessness. Lauren somersaulted, like a diver, in midair toward the center of the plane. I joined in. Other people tumbled. Not being encumbered, moving freely, not having any weight on me anywhere filled me with such joy. My body seemed made for this microgravity. I giggled. Other passengers laughed and squealed with delight. This dreamlike state of my flying through the air lasted for many minutes, or so I thought. Lauren told me it only had been about thirty seconds.

The plane descended almost straight down and barely leveled at the bottom of the parabola before we climbed again, up, up, up, and again reached the top of the arch. I wanted the new moment of euphoric weightlessness to last forever. We made three more arches, and three more precious moments of weightlessness.

As we descended, I realized I was in a cold sweat all over. Even the palms of my hands were clammy. I had a tremendous urge to throw up. I tried to fight it back. "I will not throw up," I said to myself. The plane barely leveled before ascending. My stomach still was churning, but I had controlled it. Now, up, up with my stomach still full of its small cargo, into the arch, and then we descended straight down. I reached for an airsickness bag, but it was too late. My stomach suddenly and forcefully refused to obey my conscious commands. Vomit was everywhere: dribbling down my chin, on my new pilot's uniform, on the padded floor in front of me. Stomach acid burned my throat.

All I could think of was the pictures I had seen of astronauts walking off KC-135X, probably walking from this very plane, beaming and smiling and waving. If only I had prepared in some other way. Maybe I should have questioned Lauren more about preparing for over the top. I wondered how I had gone wrong. I should have skipped breakfast altogether.

I scanned the other passengers, and there was no evidence at all that any of them had thrown up. Then, a horrible thought came to me. I was not physically capable of becoming an astronaut. The vomiting was an indicator that I could not handle space flights. The thought never had occurred to me before because I was so agile and quickly and easily had learned all the exercises Lauren taught me. Orbital physics and even computers had been my concerns, certainly not physical training.

I thought I might cry, losing my dream, but I did not. My emotions became too numbed for such a reaction. I became steely cold. Physically, I had stopped sweating and was feeling much better. My stomach felt queasy but controllable.

Lauren politely asked if I felt up to a few more over the tops. Whether I was well or not, I knew the plane would not turn back on my account. Why not, I thought, on my last day of training to become an astronaut, I might as well go out in a cloud of competence and master the roller coaster. We went up and then into that wonderful moment of weightlessness which was even better than before because now I knew exactly what to expect. Then we went straight down. We tried it several more times, and my stomach was doing fine; my ears were doing fine. My clammy palms had dried up. The sweat stayed away, and I enjoyed the whole roller coaster ride. I was doing it, and I wanted to yell that I was feeling fine. I tumbled again and again like Lauren, the other astronauts, and even some civilians. Soon, it was time to land. I found out we had been flying over the Gulf for two hours, and I had no idea how much time had passed.

After we landed, I had to find out if I was disqualified as an astronaut. However, I did not think Lauren understood my status, and I certainly did not want to reveal any classified information to her.

"How do the astronauts handle this roller coaster?" I asked, keeping my voice bland and making it sound like a casual remark.

"What do you mean?"

"Do you enjoy it?"

"Sure, it's a lark." She stared at me quizzically. "You did really well, Jana. You can be proud of yourself."

"Thanks," I said, figuring she thought I did well for a civilian but not for an astronaut. "I'd like to take this ride again. I'll do better the next time." I had talked my way into the program by telling Dr. Keenan how much endurance I had.

Lauren simply replied, "There's not one scheduled."

I wanted to confide in Lauren and to tell her about my status here because I knew she was someone I could trust. I wanted to plead with her to give me another chance and to explain how much I wanted to become an astronaut.

Yet, I had unclear ideas about who knew what. I suspected that Max knew everything. Filbert had his suspicions. It seemed to me that Lauren only knew it was her job to teach me. I thought about a world without secrets or with very few secrets. What would that be like? All this secrecy was wearing me down. Yet, I had signed an agreement in the presence of Jack and my parents. I would abide by that agreement.

Two days after the ride on the KC-135X, a new training session in weightlessness, the submersion tank, began. As we drove over to the building, I plied Lauren with lots of questions about the submersion tank so this time I would be prepared, but she said she did not want me loaded down with other people's emotional reactions. She reassured me that most people found it a very pleasant experience.

153

The schedule for this training had been moved up by two weeks. I did not attach too much importance to the date change until I noticed that Lauren considered it quite significant. She refused to say why although she usually was quite open or as open as someone can be under the restrictions of tight security.

I suited up in something similar to diving gear. My suit had lots of pockets with Velcro fasteners and as soon as I was in the water, two trainers put weights in the pockets until I had achieved neutral buoyancy. I was floating under the water weighted down enough so I would not float to the top but not weighted down so much that I would sink to the bottom. When I finally realized the trainers were watching me carefully, probably making sure my oxygen tanks were functioning, then I relaxed, and the experience became pleasant indeed, somewhat similar to floating on top of the water.

I barely had been out of the tank, feeling that I had done it successfully, when I got a message delivered by courier to meet with Jack and Dr. Fawzshen the next day at Fawzshen's home for lunch. The message further said that my classes were canceled. Lauren was talking to one of the instructors and did not see that I had gotten a message. I had a really sick feeling that it was all over and that I was out of the program. I got out of my gear, got dressed, and then went to Lauren's car to wait for her.

As Lauren drove me back to my apartment, she mentioned something about how quiet I was, but she did not push it. She mentioned that I must be reveling in the awesome pleasure of the submersion tank. I told her that it indeed had been awesome. When she dropped me off, she said, "I'll see you tomorrow. It should be fun."

I fought back tears and simply waved at her. I did not have the heart to tell her there would be no classes tomorrow or ever. She would be notified soon enough. I wondered what the fun lesson would have been.

I also wondered about the luncheon at Fawz's place tomorrow. I simply would not go. It would be as hard on Jack and Fawz as on me.

They both wanted me in the program, but I knew they had rules to follow.

I opened the door to my pleasant apartment and stepped inside. I thought that it had to be the KC-135X. If only I had not thrown up. I had been doing so well in the computer and orbital physics classes, too. I had studied and crammed so much for orbital physics.

I would pack up my gear and go home. I started to pack and looked around and realized that I had kept the apartment reasonably neat. That had been a training program I had given myself, learning neatness in preparation for living on a solarship with limited space.

At that point, I became tearful and then had a full-fledged cry. I had not cried in a long time. I felt no relief afterwards but merely had red eyes and a headache. I thought about my Dad's words asking me how the astronaut felt who had been bumped from the program for medical reasons. I had said that she would feel terrible, and that was exactly how I now felt, terrible. There was a huge emptiness inside me of a dream shattered.

I went back to my packing and soon was finished except for the designer clothes my Mom had loaned me. They were still hanging in the closet. I had not worn any of them. My, they were beautiful clothes. I tried on a particularly lovely yellow dress, a perfect outfit for a luncheon. I looked older and like someone in charge.

I could be in charge of myself. A feeling of energy grew inside me. I would go to the luncheon after all and would wheedle politely. If that failed, I would be gracious. After the luncheon, I would send e-mails to everyone who had helped me, thanking even Filbert. He had helped me in his own way.

I had already missed out on the deadline for starting Houston Aerospace Academy, and, besides, I had relinquished my space. I would see if Jack or Fawz could get me another job at JSC until the spring semester at school started. With new plans, I began feeling better. Then, I sat down and did all of my orbital physics homework. I could be disciplined. I could be an astronaut if only given another chance.

155

Jana's Journal

Dr. Fawz said he would send a car for me but I did not expect a white stretch limousine. "This certainly is impressive," I said to the driver who promptly explained that it had the energy efficiency of a hydrocar.

We drove parallel to a tram load of JSC tourists who tried to stare in the tinted windows at me. Getting that kind of attention as a mystery person was fun. We drove out the South Gate and across the street to an old hotel where the doorman leapt to the limo to let me out.

Once inside the lobby, I was surprised to see Lauren waiting for me. I was usually happy to see her, but I did not want her to witness my humiliation.

She said, "For someone who just took a ride in a stretch limo, you certainly look glum."

I fought back tears, and she asked, "What's bothering you, Jana?" She led me over to a sofa in the lobby. We sat down, and she said, "We have a little time before the luncheon yet.

I blurted out, "All my classes have been canceled."

She laughed aloud and said, "I've never met anyone that dedicated before. You surprise me, Jana. Two days off will be good for you. Relax and enjoy life."

I became alert. "I thought my classes were cancelled for good. I even packed up all my gear."

"Oh, my, you thought you were . . . fired. I've got your schedule right here. See, here's your class for the day after tomorrow." She pointed to her wrist organizer.

"Wow, I made a huge assumption." I was feeling so much better that it did not matter that I also was feeling incredibly foolish. Surely, astronauts could not make dumb assumptions, or they would die.

Lauren softly asked, "Are you having problems in any of your classes, Jana? If so, we can get help for you. This is supposed to be an ideal learning situation for you."

"I'm not having problems in my other classes. It's just your class. I guess astronauts don't throw up."

"So that's it," she said. "Sure, they throw up. That's one of the big jokes about the roller coaster. I thought you knew. It's common knowledge! That's why they call it the Vomit Comet."

"I hadn't heard that."

"Your Mom's a pilot. You know old flying songs."

"Yes," I said weakly. Whenever I started to develop any confidence, I realized just how limited and spotty my knowledge was. I persisted, "But their smiling faces on TV standing in front of the KC-135X."

"A national hero is not going to admit to the entire world that the breakfast she consumed two hours earlier is now decorating the walls and ceiling of the KC-135X."

"I didn't see anybody else vomit," I stated, "and I checked, too."

"Most everybody on that plane except us was probably on some type of inner ear medication. The Life Sciences Division is always testing out a new or modified anti-dizziness drug. That's how most people get to fly on the Vomit Comet; they agree to test new medications."

I exhaled audibly, and Lauren looked like she wanted to ask questions like what was my purpose at JSC and why was she, a major mission astronaut, training me. I knew she did not resent training me. She was merely curious.

She talked about human physiology and how everybody suffers from airsickness to various degrees, some below the conscious level of perception. People can teach themselves to control the airsickness just as I had begun to teach myself. She told me about the cerebellum in the ear which controlled balance and helped people know which way was up. I basically knew all about the inner ear, but I felt so good about probably still being in the program that I just relaxed and listened. Then she mentioned the fear of falling instinct and said that primitive people probably lived in trees before they moved onto the savannas. And I thought, wow, how terrific technology was!

My mind wandered as Lauren's voice soothed me, and I thought about my parents, missed them, and wondered if Mom had thrown up in the beginning of her flying career and if she ever did anymore. Somehow, I could not picture Mom throwing up in an airplane. She was too much the professional. The lazy Sundays with Mom and Dad seemed so far away.

Lauren brought me back from my reverie. She said, "It's almost time for lunch."

I asked her if it was okay if I went up to Dr. Fawzshen's quarters alone because I had carefully reread my invitation to this luncheon, and it clearly stated that my classes had been cancelled. Maybe, Lauren had not yet received word. She agreed to stay in the lobby for a little while and make some phone calls. She also told me not to worry so much. She might worry, too, if she stood to lose as much as I did.

Dr. Fawzshen lived on the top floor in a suite of rooms overlooking Clear Lake. When I tapped at the door, it opened wide but I saw no one. A gentle breeze billowed gauzy sheers at the open windows and rustled strange fresh flowers that seemed everywhere. Small oriental rugs were spread around, and next to a hotel sofa were large silk floor pillows.

A strange metal tube about a foot in height and two inches in diameter shimmered on the coffee table. The tube seemed silvery, but as I observed, it became iridescent—forest greens and ultramarine blues—but then it turned silver again and reflective, taking on the golds and reds of the bright floor pillows. The cylinder, prominently displayed as if in a place of honor, looked eerily familiar. On the far side of the room by French doors next to a balcony, a table was ornately set for four.

Dr. Fawzshen stepped inside from the balcony of this oriental Shangri-La. He wore colorful, flowing clothes, probably Rhatanian ceremonial garb. As he strolled toward me, he said. "Jana, welcome to my humble abode."

I started to ask about the tube when Jack ambled out from the kitchen munching on something that resembled a fried wanton. "This food is super. If your cook made up some for the mission, I wonder if Food Tech would irradiate it and . . . ." Jack stopped mid-sentence. "Jana, welcome!"

He seemed genuinely happy to see me and not at all concerned that I had overheard him mention the mission. If they were planning to drop me from the program, then I thought that Jack's demeanor toward me would be less cheerful and more businesslike.

I greeted both of them and then asked, "What's this metal thing?"

Dr. Fawzshen replied, "Let us wait until Lauren arrives, and then I will tell both of you."

Jack and Fawzshen nodded slightly at each other. "You and Lauren, do you get along well?" Jack asked.

"Lauren is my dear, dear friend," I said. I quickly glanced at each of them. "She's a good teacher, too," I added. Were they still trying to decide whether to keep me in the program? That was a good sign if their minds were not yet made up. Then, I still had a chance.

Months ago, I had overheard Filbert and his friend speculate on the crew for a solarship named *Copernicus* being composed of Jack, Fawzshen, probably Lauren, and maybe me if I completed my training. This get together could be for the three crewmembers and the one potential crewmember.

When Lauren arrived, she asked me how I was doing. I told her that everything was fine, and she understood that I was not the recipient of bad news, not yet, anyway. I decided to take her advice, enjoy my two-day holiday, and not worry.

After various greetings and comments regarding the latest intrigues at JSC, we all sat down on the big silk pillows by the coffee table. The cook, an Asian man, brought out a platter of hot hors d'oeuvres and sat it down on the coffee table a safe distance from the glimmering metal tube.

Dr. Fawzshen leaned forward, lifted the glimmering tube off the coffee table, and cradled it in his arms as if it were a precious little baby.

"This artifact is over five hundred years old." He neither passed it around nor offered to let anyone hold it.

"My countrymen pride themselves on being good hosts and making visitors feel welcome. Many centuries before highways, railroads, and airplanes, our cities were quite inaccessible. The rare visitors who crossed the harsh mountains were usually treated magnificently and entertained lavishly. From these visitors our people received the only news of our neighboring countries.

"Twelve visitors came in a time of great hardship. Our people were embarrassed that they did not have much to offer, but they shared what they had. The visitors were so touched that they helped our countrymen find new underground springs and taught them new irrigation methods. They brought seeds for strange, wondrous plants that thrived in our soil. The visitors also brought gifts of gold jewelry and warm cloth.

"When our people asked them for news about our neighboring countries, they had no information. The visitors announced that they were from the stars.

"At the appointed time for their departure, a young man, the son of a high ranking duke, walked away with the visitors amidst a departure celebration. He planned to walk with them for a few days as a gesture of friendship and a sign of good manners. He returned within less than a day and said the visitors had entered a flying machine that had lifted straight up into the sky. He had watched until it disappeared into the heavens.

"The king did not like the attention the duke's son was getting, so he attributed the entire story to boyish exuberance, wishful thinking, or sheer laziness that the young man did not walk further with the visitors. The king attempted to make the duke and his son look very bad in the eyes of their countrymen. The young man stated that the visitors said they would return.

"After the king's criticism, the duke's son journeyed daily to the spot where the spaceship had lifted off, primarily hoping for the visitors' return but also wishing to regain his lost reputation. Within a few weeks, the duke's son announced that the visitors had indeed returned and had presented him with a gift. However, the visitors needed to return to their star immediately and could not stay. The duke's son stated that the visitors someday in the future would need the help of our countrymen. He then offered the king the gift the visitors had left, a very unique musical instrument that emulated the sound of the human voice. The king disliked the attention heaped on the duke's son and locked him in prison, claiming the musical instrument was evil. Since the duke was very powerful, after a few days his son was released.

"This incident caused a deep rift in our otherwise harmonious kingdom. The king left no heirs, and eventually the duke's son became king. Since many of our kings have not been above changing our chronicles to embellish the glory of their realms, our historians of later centuries thought the star visitors were a fabrication."

"Did the duke's son become a good king?" Lauren asked.

"Yes, excellent," Dr. Fawzshen replied.

"I presume he had a name?" Lauren softly asked.

Fawzshen straightened the sleeves of his native garb and looked away from us. "Correct! He was called King Fawzshen the First.

Lauren softly said, "And someday, you'll be King Fawzshen the Second."

Fawzshen did not respond to Lauren's comment. Instead he said, "As a boy in our kingdom, I was fascinated with the chronicle of the star visitors. When I came to Houston to aerospace school, Jack and I were in the same year and quickly became great friends. Jack shared my keen interest in history. I related the chronicle to Jack, and we speculated if it were the truth or a fabrication. If true, were there any artifacts left to prove the star people's visit? Would we find the gold jewelry or the warm cloth? Would we be lucky enough to recover the musical instrument?

"During a break from the Aerospace Academy, I began searching the archives. Visualize, if you will, room after room in cramped old buildings filled with furniture, clothing, musical instruments, the treasures of almost forty dynasties. The search would be long and tedious, not anything I could handle myself or even supervise because I did not know what I was looking for.

"I had other priorities in my life and did not pursue the historical search for many years. Then, an idea came to me. I would obtain help in going through the archives. I proposed to my father hiring specialists, and he immediately agreed, not to prove or disprove the space visitors, but because our country soon will celebrate our three thousandth birthday.

"My father had been thinking about building a new history museum to open concurrently with the trimillenium celebrations. The choice items from throughout the ages would be magnificently displayed. Everything else would be neatly catalogued for future exhibits and for historians. My father further decided the artifacts would make valuable resource material for filling in gaps in our country's chronicles.

"Finally, I had the financial resources to learn about the star visitors or to try. When I returned to your fine country to fly on an international mission, I hired an archeologist and an historian who specialized in Asian studies. After the mission, they went back to Rhatania with me and spearheaded the project. Many of my countrymen volunteered to help. I had no idea that so many of them shared my interest in the star creatures. Although the star beings were the impetus, our people developed an overall interest in our country's history.

"Now, several of our writers are involved with the project. Inspired by this new enthusiasm, we will write an accurate and comprehensive trimillineum history of our country to be released on the same day that the museum opens. Already, we have published a catalog of over a thousand choice items that we plan to display during the museum's inaugural exhibition."

As Dr. Fawzshen spoke, he stroked the metal tube. It had to be of the utmost importance, but it looked nothing like a musical instrument. I knew he eventually would tell us what it was. Meanwhile, I enjoyed his melodious voice, his intonations, and his utter joy in speaking about his country.

Jack had lots of museum catalogs at his house, and I recalled seeing one from Rhatania. Jack and I had talked about some of the items. We even might have talked about the metal tube.

I wondered why Dr. Fawzshen was telling us his country's history, merely to entertain us, or was there another purpose? Then I realized. The mission on which I might be lucky enough to be a crewmember was to find life, but I was thinking of small things, bacteria or fungi. Had their research uncovered something about the star visitors of 500 years ago?

The cook noisily bustled around the luncheon table, probably a signal to Dr. Fawzshen that lunch was ready. He said a few words in Rhatanian to the cook who disappeared into the kitchen and a moment later brought back on a silver tray four crystal goblets filled with something that almost had the color of orange juice but with a more golden hue.

"This special beverage, chun, comes from a tree that bears only a few fruit every year. We drink chun to honor new beginnings, a wedding celebration, the birth of a child, the start of a new business venture, or the beginning of a very important journey."

I heard "new beginnings" and shivered. I dared not hope. I still had another month of training, but it seemed as if Fawzshen were ready to make an important announcement. Today, right this minute,

I could learn if I had been chosen for the mission. Yet, a certain part of me did not want to know. I wanted to go on hoping and dreaming an improbable dream. In truth, the announcement could be about something else. I quietly listened.

"I do ramble," Fawzshen said. "As Jack often mentions to me, 'get to the point,' but he says it more tactfully in a host of euphemisms he has devised to help me fit in to your fast paced country." He glanced at Jack. "You are the Commander. Do you wish to make the announcement?"

"No," Jack replied. "We're here today because of your research, your historical find, your perseverance, and your ability to fund this mission. You do the honors."

A tension was growing within me. Just what was the announcement?

Dr. Fawzshen handed each of us a glass and then elevated his goblet. "A toast to us, Lauren, Jana, Jack, and myself, the crew, the four astronauts of the Solarship *Copernicus*."

I was stunned. Even though I had hopes, I could hardly believe my ears. Less than an hour ago, I thought I had been dumped from the program, and now I was a member of the crew. Then I felt tears of happiness trying to break through. With ever fiber in my being, I fought back the tears. An astronaut would not cry.

We clanked glasses together as Jack, Fawzshen, and Lauren beamed. I probably had a bewildered look on my face. Fawz sipped the beverage, and the rest of us followed. After the toast, I had recovered enough from the initial shock that I felt like leaping around the room. What I wanted so much and what I dreamed about so intensely had happened at a most unexpected time.

Dr. Fawzshen looked toward me as if I was supposed to say something. I resisted the urge to blurt out, "But I haven't finished my training, yet." My next urge was to yell, "Thank you, thank you, thank you!" However, I quietly sat on the pillow until I felt composed enough to say, "I am so happy and so grateful to each of you. I won't let you down. I'll do my best, always."

Yesterday, I almost had packed up my gear and gone home. That would have been the end of my opportunity here at JSC. Jack and Fawzshen simply would have thought that I had decided the mission was not for me. They would have been disappointed, and I would have been devastated.

Fawzshen said, "Lauren and Jana, you must be wondering why this whole mission has been cloaked in such secrecy. After lunch, you shall find out. First, let me congratulate you both. You worked together and, yet, followed your contracts on the need to know. Jana did not know that you, Lauren, would be on the mission, and Lauren did not know why she was training you, Jana. Not until today have both of you learned that Jana is the fourth crewmember. I commend your ability to keep a secret. You have proven yourselves."

We moved over to the luncheon table by the balcony. Before I sat down, I looked past the balcony at Clear Lake down below and remembered Jack's party and my conversation with Dr. Fawzshen and Princess Regney outside on the loggia that also overlooked Clear Lake.

Seated at the table, we chatted affably. Although I joined in the conversation, I mostly was absorbed with my own thoughts. During these past three months, I had thought there would be the training, the hope, and then the disappointment. Only on a few glimmering occasions had I truly believed I would succeed. The reality of my wondrous good luck would take time to filter through.

The food, native dishes from Rhatania, was delectable. One was a rice mixture wrapped in tender leaves. Others were precut fowl and seafood molded into the shapes of little birds and sea animals. Dr. Fawzshen proudly and carefully pronounced the name of each dish.

The breeze felt balmy against my face, the Rhatanian delicacies tasted more heavenly with each bite, and the conversation sparkled with light, cheerful repartee. I was there, but I also was an observer, a strange feeling, being there, yet being removed from the scene.

By the time lunch was over, we moved back to the plump cushions by the metal tube, and I was myself again. Fawzshen stood in front of the coffee table.

"Lauren and Jana, you both shall now learn the truly big secret. Beside the four of us in this room, only twelve other people in the world know the main purpose for our mission: my father, your president, the head of NASA in Washington, Director Clayton here at JSC, the physicist Venzi Suzaky, two NASA attorneys, and a few others. One of the others may surprise you. Dr. Max Marsh knows simply because he has been working so closely with us in preparing for this mission. He will continue to interface with us throughout the mission."

Fawzshen glanced at Jack. "You are the Commander; perhaps it is more appropriate coming from you."

Jack nodded in agreement, noting Lauren's and my anxiety. Jack said, "The purpose of our mission is to make contact with intelligent life from another planet or to find artifacts to confirm that life once existed there."

My heart thumped wildly. The purpose of our mission—to make contact! And not with a mold spore or bacterium, but living, apparently good sized intelligent beings. This was beyond anything I ever knew to hope for.

"The star beings?" Lauren asked.

"Yes! That is our specific goal. We have good reason to believe that advanced, intelligent life exists or did exist on a moon of Jupiter," Jack said in an even, calm voice, almost as if he were stating the temperature of the moon.

"We're hoping they still may be there," Jack continued, his voice resonating. "We theorize that scientists or explorers from a nearby star system set up a base to explore our solar system. Yet, they could have finished exploring hundreds of years ago and gone somewhere else."

He glanced over at Fawzshen. "Thanks to you and your countrymen, we have the basic information to proceed."

Dr. Fawzshen picked up the tube and caressed it. He said, "We Rhatanians have undergone name changes and changes of power, but essentially we have been the same people for thousands of years because we are so geographically remote. Throughout our history, occasional strangers have wandered into our country, were welcomed, and integrated into our society, but their number has been few because of our geographic inaccessibility. We Rhatanians are all related to each other and have rather complex genealogy charts. If any two people in our country wanted to figure out how they are related, they could. My father wants every one of our citizens to joyfully celebrate our trimillineum, and we hope to present our people with a very special surprise if . . . on this mission we discover something about the star visitors."

Lauren asked, "What is the relationship between the star creatures and the cylinder?"

"The American archeologist and historian wasted no time in training our volunteers. Soon, the team systematically catalogued items room by room. Since each team member was well aware of my special interest in the star visitors, when a volunteer came across a trunk of threadbare gowns for a young lady, he decided the period might be the correct time frame. At first he thought the trunk contained nothing but fragile clothes that had deteriorated throughout the years, but down near the bottom and carefully wrapped in scarves, hidden actually, was this."

Fawzshen held the tube straight out in front of him and then he carefully handed it to Lauren. "I want each of you to hold this cylinder," he said.

When Lauren handed it to me, I somehow felt different, as if someone else were present, maybe the Duke's son who had handled it five hundred years ago. The cylinder was warm, I guess, the heat from Dr. Fawz's hands. With my fingertips, I felt very slight ridges, but I could not see them. Holding the cylinder up close, I noticed writing for the first time, letters from the English alphabet, but also diacritical marks and additional letters, similar to additional Russian letters. Holding the cylinder securely, I moved it slightly, and the letters themselves changed color. Then, a strange feeling enveloped me that once before I carefully had held a cylinder just like this one.

"Notice how small the letters are," Dr. Fawzshen said. "According to our linguists, this document was written by someone not fully familiar with the Rhatanian language. We surmise the star beings themselves wrote this chronicle. It describes how much they enjoyed their visit with us, and how they hope that someday our people will pay a return visit when . . . ." Fawzshen stopped mid-sentence and looked directly at me and then directly at Lauren. "When we have mastered the art of space travel."

Fawzshen let the impact of that weigh on us while we drank sparkling water from the mountain springs of his country. "The aliens told where they lived, a moon of Jupiter. This was more than a century before moons of Jupiter were discovered."

"Which moon?" I asked. For three months, I had wanted to know which moon.

Fawz and Jack made eye contact and Jack said, "We'll reveal that to you once we're on the mission. If it were up to Fawz or me, we'd tell you now. Your not knowing until you need to know is part of our extremely tight security."

After a moment or so of awkward silence, Fawzshen said, "The document on this cylinder suggests many preferable dates for us to begin the mission. Those recommended departure dates were all a few hundred years ago."

Because of Filbert's orbital physics course, I instantly knew what Dr. Fawzshen was talking about.

"We have checked out the astronomical and aeronautical information, and it is correct. Their spaceships traveled at a far better clip than ours. So here we are. Any questions? Fawzshen laughed, "I do not guarantee that we will have the authority to answer."

Lauren immediately said, "This cylinder. You've verified its age?"

"We quite carefully verified the age of the clothes that were wrapped around it. The tests we chose were non-intrusive to the cylinder's integrity."

I wondered what Fawzshen meant by its integrity, but Lauren was off on another track. She said, "Is it made of something that we on Earth have the capacity to manufacture?"

Fawzshen answered gently, "We do not know its precise composition, yet. Additional tests could more completely reveal the cylinder's composition, but the tests could damage it, too.

I thought Lauren should not be asking these questions. NASA would not invest in this mission without thoroughly checking out the cylinder, but Lauren was in her extreme no-nonsense mode. I put my hand on her shoulder and thought, "Just take all this as a gift, Lauren, and be quiet."

But she was not quiet. Instead, she said, "The way you've described everything, the star visitors could look like us. That's pretty unlikely that creatures from a different star system with a different evolutionary history would look like people."

Fawzshen replied, "Yes, we have considered that. First of all, understand my countrymen. Back 500 years ago, our thoughts and ideas were not limited to rational concepts. The star creatures might not have looked human. Yet, a nonhuman may have seemed to a Rhatanian merely as a foreigner. Our people were pretty isolated, then."

Lauren raised her left brow, "I don't know, Fawz. People are going to recognize nonhumans."

He replied, "The only account contemporaneous with the time of the Duke's son is on this cylinder. There's no mention at all of their appearance."

"You have your own historical accounts," Lauren stated.

"Any historian within the intervening 500 years could have changed the original chronicles. Suppose our historians originally described the visitors as very strange, perhaps with wings. Then, a future historian under the direction of a future king might have 'updated' our chronicles. Correct!"

Lauren replied, "We can't communicate with most creatures right here on Earth, and yet 500 years ago, star creatures had perfect rapport with your countrymen." Lauren shook her head, "Don't get me wrong, I'm thrilled and honored to be on this mission. I guess it's possible that we can relate to advanced creatures from another world, but I'm a sociologist and really can't stop thinking like one."

"Any more questions?" Jack asked.

I had about a million, so many questions but still I did not know why I was picked, and what it had to do with my eyes. "Everything you've told us amazes me, but I guess I still wonder, 'Why me?'" I asked. "I know it's my eyes and the Blue Factor in my blood."

Jack replied, "Information on the cylinder specifies the identity of two crewmembers when we pay a visit to the star creatures. They specified that at least one person be from Rhatania. That much was clear cut and unambiguous.

"The other person was to have bluish eye whites or blue sclera and to be from another place in the world. The cylinder writings suggest that person might be found in Europe but not necessarily. The rest of the description for this person was mathematical and scientific but also untranslatable. Therefore, management went with what we knew, and an astronaut with a slight blue sclera was selected for our mission. Shortly before she became ill and withdrew from the mission, we received an updated translation."

"Correct," he said, "only because of our dedicated and diligent linguists. The original two scientists selected to help the linguists said the passage was scientifically untranslatable. Our linguists refused to give up. They found a renowned mathematician who though that the passage, indeed, was translatable and that a biologist or a geneticist might have luck. The latter two decided they needed a hematologist, a doctor who specializes in blood. Fortunately, the doctor selected was a researcher familiar with all the current work in hematology. The doctor quickly found the mathematics on the cylinder matched right up with a newly isolated blood component, so far found only in my people—the Rhatanians. The doctor thought the cylinder described a variation of the blood component, theoretically possible, but not isolated in anyone's blood—until Doctor Keenan tested your blood."

Jack quickly said, "We're talking about the Rhatanian language of five hundred years ago, not today's language. Word meanings change over time. (Compare Shakespeare's English with today's English, and that's about 500 years.) Remember, these words probably were written by star visitors not fully familiar with the language. We're not certain we know what they said much less what they meant."

"Do you have any questions, Jana?" Dr. Fawzshen asked, touching his finger next to his eye. He did not say anything else. Maybe, it was his intense expression or the way he moved his finger to his eyelid, but it was if I heard him say to me, "You are the one."

I shivered. My first thought was that somehow I was distantly related to Dr. Fawzshen even though he was Asian. However, a new, sobering thought quickly occurred to me that I might be on this mission because of a mistake in the translation. Suppose the linguists continued working on the translation and arrived at a totally different meaning? Would I be pulled from the mission? I immediately pushed such thoughts from my mind. How could I concentrate on training with my crew while holding onto such an idea?

I simply replied, "This is a lot to think about." I wanted to say more like, "Thank you, thank you for picking me."

Fawzshen briefly left the room and returned with fortune cookies in a crystal bowl. He passed them around. I cracked mine open and pulled out the little strip of paper. It said, "You will go on a long voyage." We joked about the messages.

"Any more surprises," Lauren asked in a lighthearted tone.

"There is one more surprise," Jack replied. "As I mentioned, Madame President is very concerned about the security of the trip. The solarship is almost ready. There will only be about two weeks for all four of us to train together before we begin another two weeks of isolation."

I wanted to jump into the air and yell "zowie," but instead I sat still while my mind raced on to meet aliens. We even talked about other aspects of the mission that afternoon.

Lauren said, "I guess you never found the musical instrument that emulated the human voice."

Jack and Dr. Fawzshen exchanged glances. "Yes, we found it." Dr. Fawzshen left the room again and this time returned with a glistening rectangular tray that appeared to be the same metal as the cylinder. It was about a foot long and three inches wide. He placed the metal tray on the coffee table. Then he carefully lifted the cylinder and placed it inside the tray.

"Look at this," Fawzshen said. "The cylinder does not touch on any side. It remains levitated."

Then, he touched the ends of the tray. Within a few seconds, the cylinder began spinning, and I heard sounds of the human voice, the tenor voice of a man, Asian words, rich in cadence, almost singing, almost pleading, then the voice of a woman, confident, yet sad, then voices of other men and women. Finally, at the end, all the voices joined together, half singing, half talking.

Dr. Fawzshen softly translated, "They are saying in unison, 'Fare thee well, dear people, we will meet again in the heavens beyond the broken and jagged rocks torn asunder.'"

Jana's Journal

Lauren called me on the phone the next morning. "How're you doing?"

"I'm still reeling from the shock. What a pleasant shock! Right at this moment, I'm figuring out what personal things to take. I'm taking my notebook computer for sure; that's the main thing I really must have."

"That's a good idea. Think I'll take mine, too. Max will need to verify that our computers won't interfere with any of the onboard electronics, but that shouldn't be a problem.

"Don't worry about personal items. You'll be given a list. If you like, I'll e-mail you my list. I'll get you some specialty products to try out, too, that are designed for space missions," Lauren said.

"That would be great. I'm sure I'm overlooking something as major as my toothbrush."

"There's a reception for JSC employees at the Gilruth Recreation Center this afternoon. You're invited. Would you like to attend?"

"Guess so." I thought a moment and then said, "I should decline the reception and get my gear in order for the mission."

"Get real, Jana. It's at least two weeks yet before we go into isolation," she said. "A pretty good window's coming up two weeks after that, but I bet that date will slip, too."

I did not want Lauren to know how cluttered my apartment could become. Two days ago while in tears, I had hastily thrown my gear into suitcases, and then yesterday after Fawzshen's luncheon while in a joyful state I had just as hastily dumped out the contents of the suitcases into a wobbly heap and fished out only items for the mission.

Now, I had an urge to put the apartment in perfect order. "I'll take a rain check on this reception," I said.

"Today's probably our last chance for a holiday, and that's only because Jack's been called to Washington. Jack, Fawz, and I have been training together on the simulator ever since Fawz arrived in Houston, and tomorrow you'll add intensive training with us to your schedule."

"That sounds intimidating! Also, thrilling, yes, very thrilling!"

"If you don't think you should spend today in play, look at this reception as a lesson in social graces, sort of like a necessary class," she coaxed.

"Me, needing social graces?" I asked. If Lauren wanted me to go with her to this thing, she probably considered me her friend and not merely her student even though she referred to the reception as a class. I could get the apartment perfectly straightened in less than an hour this morning. Furthermore, I had almost declined yesterday's luncheon, which would have been a disastrous mistake for me. I would not decline this reception. "I'd be happy to go," I said.

"We'll stay for exactly 30 minutes, but promise me not to leave the room where the reception is held."

"You're acting strange, Lauren, really strange," I said lightly.

"Humor me, Jana, and you won't be sorry. I promise you that."

That afternoon, Lauren picked me up in her hydro sports car, and we drove over to Gilruth. As we entered the lobby, two women sat at a table handing out name badges and checking names off a handheld computer. Behind the table a banner read, "SpaceTech."

A shiver went up my spine. As part of my training, I had not contacted my family or friends for three months, and I now realized that today the three months were up. Alan could be here. He had worked for SpaceTech during the summer. No, summer was over, and so was his co-op job at the garden. He would be back in school now.

The minute Lauren and I entered the big main room, my eyes were drawn up. Suspended from the ceiling was a model moon, complete with a realistic albedo and all the terrain, mountains, volcanoes, and moon bases. Suspended considerably lower were the five space stations. At the same level as the five stations and interspersed between them, smaller objects glittered. I looked carefully and recognized them as the SpaceTech minishuttles. Then, higher than the bases and higher than the moon were small dots of light in the form of constellations. Other slightly brighter dots of light represented the planets. All of the dots of light, in addition to representing stars and planets, also were thin, intense beams, the thinnest of spotlights, which all were directed to a spot in the center of the room. There, slightly elevated from the floor, far removed from everything else, and displayed like a giant crown jewel, a scale sized minishuttle shimmered invitingly.

Around the well-lit perimeter, separate booths housed various displays. The spacious, empty area between the perimeter displays and the central minishuttle model was almost dark, like a darkened dance floor, barely enough light to keep from tripping.

The SpaceTech people, positioned two or three to each display, all wore badges with their names printed underneath the words, "Welcome to the SpaceTech Minishuttle Expo." Alan's Dad worked for SpaceTech, too, but I did not see him. He was an engineer, and I figured most of these people were in sales.

I turned around to comment to Lauren who had been right at my side, but she quietly had disappeared. I was drawn to the scale version of the minishuttle. I strolled to the center of the room to check it over.

A SpaceTech woman in a pale coral suit asked me, "Would you like to ride in one of these?"

"Sure." I moved closer to admire it. "A shuttle without heat shields. Neat."

"Heat shields are not needed for the moon or for the any of the space bases. Only to enter the Earth's gravity, and these are not made for that purpose," the woman said, as if her words were memorized.

"Someday, minishuttles will be very popular and you could be riding in one."

I so wanted to brag, to tell her that soon I would be riding in a space hopper, a full sized one, and then after that I would be riding in a very large solarship, going on a far journey where no one had ever been before. But she would not have believed me. I could not resist saying, "I may need one of these in a couple of weeks."

She politely said, "The first production ones will be ready sooner than you think." She quickly turned away and began talking to someone else.

A voice from behind me said, "May I interest you in a minishuttle? Pick your color, pink, aqua, or how about lime green? Would madam like it monogrammed with a JN on the hull?" I'd know that voice anywhere. It was Alan's voice.

I wheeled around. There he was. That smirky smile, those dark eyes, the sun streaked blond hair, better than the Alan of my memory. He said, "It's been a long time, far too long."

I was stunned. All I could say was, "I think about you every day."

Alan flashed his smirky smile and said, "I know."

"You know!" I said jokingly, "That sounds a little smug."

"Oh, Jana," he said, gazing into my eyes. His voice became very soft. "It's strange. I can almost tell when you are thinking about me. Then, there are other times when I think about you, and you're not there. You're far away."

The three months that we had been apart melted away. I gazed at him, speechless, one of the few times in my life I was without words.

"I'm so glad you're back from wherever you've been or whatever you've done."

"Uh, oh," I said, almost involuntarily.

"You haven't gone, yet?"

I shook my head and said, "No."

Alan looked really sad. "Dad thought he saw you on site one day. He was too far away to tell for sure. So they're still training you for something."

I wished I could just tell Alan. Secrets were a problem to deal with. "This is difficult. I want you to know what is going on, but I can't talk about it."

"I could just talk, and you could nod your head 'yes' or 'no.'"

I started giggling. Alan had such a way of instantly making me feel wonderful. "You know I can't play that game, Alan."

"What do you want, Jana?"

"I just want you not to forget me, to know that I'll be thinking of you, wherever I am."

"I'm not going to forget you, Jana. I'm not ever going to forget you."

More than not forgetting me, I wanted him to wait for me; I wanted him to be here when I got back. How could I ask him something like that? Just because I was going on a great adventure did not mean I should ask Alan to put his life on hold. Yet, that was what I wanted him to do. I could not even tell him that I was going to be gone for such a very long time, maybe as long as a year.

Alan and I moved away from the minishuttle model as it was getting quite crowded in that area. We still were out in the middle of the floor, but it was a large area, empty except for Alan and me. I wanted to block out the rest of the room.

"Remember when we became friends?" I asked. "You invited me to see your yard. A frost had been expected the night before, and you had watered down all of your plants that night with your special concoction to protect them. The next day, you had invited me over. Ice covered everything, and it was an enchanting winter garden in Houston with frost on the lawn and icicles hanging from your plants. It was like a magical place, a dream place, and neither of us has ever stopped dreaming since."

"You were the only one I wanted to see it. Suppose you thought I was weird for inviting you to see the garden. But then I thought, you're either going to like the garden or not. You're either going to like me or not. I would take the chance and find out."

177

"I'm glad you took the chance. Otherwise, you still might be jogging past my house, not knowing, never our long talks in the gazebo that only you or I understand."

"And I wouldn't feel so very sad this minute. Happy to see you and sad that you're going."

"How did you get invited to this expo, Alan? Was it through your Dad?"

"No, Jack Medwin called me yesterday and said that he thought I would enjoy attending. I accepted immediately, hoping for the impossible, hoping to see you."

"I wasn't that astute at all. Lauren invited me this morning, and I told her I had other things to do."

"Do you think there's some JSC psychologist sitting around somewhere saying, 'Let Jana and Alan get together, a farewell, a public place somewhere, like a restaurant, no, a reception, limit the time, say an hour.'"

"Try a half hour. Maybe, it's just Jack and Lauren, working all this out, remembering what it is like to be young." I was thinking "and in love" but I did not say it.

"So, Lauren had to talk you into attending."

"Barely, once I knew she really wanted me to be here, I agreed. But still I didn't suspect."

"What was it you were planning to do this afternoon?"

I giggled. "I'm the same old me, I guess. I've finished the task already, and it wasn't fun. I've straightened the place where I'm living. I guess I should learn to keep my quarters neat. Heaven knows, I'll need to be neat on the . . . ."

Alan smirked and said, "I'll not follow up on that intriguing, unfinished statement."

"Thanks, Alan." Quickly trying to back away from what I almost told him, I said, "You don't have any problem keeping things straightened. Maybe, I could learn neatness from you."

"Don't worry about it. I'm neat enough for both of us."

178

Did that mean what I thought it meant? Of course it did! Why did I possibly want to go toward unexplored worlds when Alan in the flesh and blood was right here, right now? Alan, my best friend, could have been more if I had shown him any encouragement at all, but I had wanted my life uncomplicated and clearly focused. For Alan and me, there had been all the time in the world, time to go slowly, time to be sure, and time to get everything just right. Abruptly and unexpectedly, for the two of us, time ceased. Now, the clock again was ticking, but for how long?

Finally, he said, "You're going away, and then you'll be back. And we'll take up again right where we left off."

"That's what I would like, Alan. To take up exactly where we left off."

"Then, it's settled," Alan said cheerfully as he drew me into his arms. I felt the warmth of his body and the beating of his heart. Then he kissed me very lightly on the lips, and I kissed him back, and then it was a kiss filled with passion and longing. And I knew Alan was the person for me, forever. I wanted this moment to last into eternity. We stood embracing in the middle of a private, darkened dance floor, but the only music was in our hearts.

Momentarily, I blocked out the fact that we were standing under an artificial moon at an Expo that was getting more crowded by the minute.

"Let's get out of here and go someplace, just you and I," Alan said.

"Good idea," I quickly replied.

Right as we were heading toward the door, Lauren, like a chaperone of old, showed up. She greeted Alan and then to me said, "We'll need to leave in about five minutes. I'm going to take another look at the minishuttle, and I'll be right back."

"She's giving us a chance to escape," Alan said cheerfully.

"When she invited me to this expo, she wanted me to promise her not to leave this room."

"Did you promise?"

"No! I thought she was joking. I made no promises."

Alan took my hand. "Then, let's leave quickly."

I hesitated, "It's difficult enough saying 'good-bye' to you as it is."

Alan studied me carefully as his dark eyes grew more intense. He held my hand firmly as he started toward the door. I willingly followed, but then he stopped and faced me. "When will I see you again?" he asked.

"I can't tell you how much time I'm talking about, but it's considerable."

"Will I be an old man?"

"No, not at all."

"Will I still be young?"

"Yes, of course."

"Will I be finished college?"

"No, not close."

"Will I . . . ?"

"I touched his lips with my hand. "Okay, Alan, no more questions."

I wanted to kiss Alan again, to kiss him good-bye, but Lauren already was standing right there, right next to us, and the expo had gotten pretty crowded. So we just said good-bye, but we touched hands, and there was a spark of electricity that passed between us, strong electricity, and then I had hope, almost more than hope, almost assurance that Alan would be there when I got back.

As Lauren and I left the expo, I glanced back, and Alan was under the SpaceTech moon, watching me. I turned around and waved. He blew me a kiss, and I blew one to him. An arc of joyful energy flew between us. I hoped it would encircle us both and keep us safe while we were millions of miles apart, one from the other.

Later, I profusely and repeatedly thanked Lauren for her help in arranging Alan's and my farewell meeting, but I was thanking her for something else, too. I truly wanted to go on the mission as much as I wanted to go with Alan. And I was glad Lauren, like a guardian of the heart, had made the choice for me.

Suppose Alan had said to choose him or the mission. What would I have done? I was thankful he did not ask me to make such a choice.

Solarship *Copernicus*

8:50 a.m. CDT

Jack had a well-disciplined mind, and his thoughts seldom strayed from the work at hand, but now he glanced over at Jana reading about the SpaceTech expo. She was a spunky person, he thought, tougher than she knew and tough enough that he had gone to bat for her at the highest level. A meeting in the oval office was not something Jack would soon forget. It was Madame President, the head of NASA, and Jack.

At that meeting, Jack's admiration for Madame President was obvious. He was one of the few people who knew the purpose of her twice-weekly evening meetings. She worked with high-powered trainers on the basics of science, her original impetus being the environment. She became intrigued with how well the space stations, adjustable winged planes, and hoppers monitored the Earth's health. Madame President proved to be an apt science student as she developed a fascination with the Space Program.

Yet, she was considering canceling their entire mission and asked the head of NASA as well as Jack for their input.

"Madame President, the United States is being given a gift on a gold platter from the People of Rhatania," the NASA administrator said. "As you know, they're financing in excess of 80 percent of the mission."

"But golden strings are attached," she replied. "For the King, secrecy is a condition for the mission. I also am in favor of secrecy. However, if there's a security glitch, the secrecy issue could prove a huge embarrassment to our administration. The King may want to

182

maintain secrecy long after it is time for us to release the information." She faced Jack directly and said, "If word gets out prematurely, I need to count on you, Jack, as commander of the mission for damage control."

She was an imposing presence, and although Jack admired her, he managed to not become intimidated. He replied, "My first concern must be the safety of my crew and then the safety of my ship. My next concern must be the safety of the alien beings if we find any. We are seeking them out for peaceful purposes and not for conquest or subjugation. After those concerns are met, count on me fully for any and all damage control."

The NASA administrator winced at Jack's words but Madame President simply said, "That's fair enough. I appreciate your honesty. You're a brave man. Some in Congress, if they knew, would perceive a direct search for specific aliens based on an old cylinder as a ridiculous waste of money and others, as a downright reckless and dangerous thing to pursue. If we go forward with this mission, once we know what is out there, then we'll decide how to control the information."

The NASA administrator said, "If you go forward with the mission, this administration will achieve an amazing goal. If we find not one alien or one artifact, our astronauts will have traveled further than any manned mission has gone before. No one need ever know that our primary goal was a search for aliens. You know that our secondary goal is sound science. We will install permanent monitoring equipment on Ganymede to study Jupiter. The United States will be ahead of the Europeans, Russians, and Chinese.

Madame President's smile was most charming when she said, "We must not forget our partners, the Rhatanians. I am convinced that this secondary goal could benefit nations everywhere."

Jack knew Madame President was not just saying nice things. She cared about the world community and believed that civilization could improve. Jack, however, was not sure that the monitoring equipment would be much better than the many probes that sporadically had visited Jupiter at much closer range. He did not say anything.

The NASA administrator longingly said, "Imagine fulfilling our primary goal of our people being the first to make contact."

Madame President replied, "Many of our constituents would think making contact is a bad idea. The ramifications are unknowable. If we assume the aliens mean us no harm, the possibility of their more advanced ways of doing things could have a devastating effect on our industries."

Then Madame President looked directly at Jack and said, "I have a second concern. I have heard that one of the astronauts is rather young and has a non-traditional background. Do you perceive any type of problems with her, security issues or otherwise?"

"I can totally vouch for her. She will do fine," Jack said.

"That's all I need to hear," Madame President said. "Thank you for your input. We'll get back with you shortly with our decision."

Jack discussed the meeting with Fawz, and they both agreed to protect Jana and Lauren by not announcing that the whole mission might be scrapped. The women were so happy training on the solarship simulators with Jack and Fawz that there did not seem to be the need to worry them. The simulator training helped Jack keep his mind off waiting for Madame President's call. He also came to realize just how very much he wanted this mission, too.

The call from Madame President did not come shortly but a grueling two weeks later, right before they were scheduled to go into isolation. Now, he briefly listened to Jana read as she described the simulator training with such unabashed delight. It would have been different for her had she known just how tenuous everything had been.

Now, all these months later, Jack thought perhaps he was doing his best after all for damage control. The rumors like an infection had been growing unabated, and he had lanced the wound and freed all the rumors to dry up and blow away as something much stronger took the place of the festering wound. The damage control was the truth in step-by-step doses through a young woman's journal. Madame President might not be in the position to release the truth if the King wanted to withhold it. Jana was doing it for her.

Jack hoped that Madame President saw it that way, too. If she did not, then Jack had said that his first job was to protect the crew, and that primarily was what he was doing right now. Jack was glad he had not been wimpy that day and that he only made a promise he could keep.

With everything Madame President had to deal with each day, did she even remember his promise to her? He wondered if he would find out.

Jana's Journal

None of us talked. We merely sat in a row, keeping a low profile, as Jack had instructed us, each in our own thoughts in the hopper waiting room in Florida. Besides the four of us, there were sixteen other people, fifteen civilian employees with SpaceTech and one reporter SpaceTech had invited. All twenty of us were suited up except for our helmets, which we carried. We were ready to go. "Please, let's go now before I think anymore," I said to myself.

In a few moments, we would board the bus for a short ride to the launch pad at Cape Kennedy. This was the real thing, not practice on a simulator. I had been scared waiting to fly the KC-135X but nothing like my fear now as I waited to board the space hopper. My heart jumped wildly. I reminded myself to breathe and paced my breathing so I would not hyperventilate. I inhaled slowly, counting one, two. Exhaled, counting three, four.

I concentrated on my immediate surroundings. Jack, Dr. Fawz, and Lauren seemed relatively calm. I did not dare reveal my feelings, even to Lauren. I was racing beyond fear into an unchartered realm of terror when I noticed Lauren suppressing a silly smile. That little smile pulled me back from an unknown precipice. I guessed her feelings. After all of our training, we had made it. We were here.

Our small waiting room was separated by heavy acrylic windows from a bigger room. That window had to be strong enough and installed well enough to withstand shock waves every time a hopper blasted off. To distract myself, I asked Jack about that bigger room.

In a soothing voice, Jack told me in the old days that room had been filled with the press and family members of those going on the hopper. Nowadays, SpaceTech discouraged family from last minute farewells.

Jack knew I was scared. I did not want him to know. I wanted to lie and tell him I was okay. Instead, I said that the SpaceTech people seemed scared. They paced around, talking and laughing too loudly, even through the muffling effect of their helmets which some of them already wore. They were so hyped up. It was okay for civilians to be scared. However, watching them, my fear intensified. "Inhale, one, two. Think about something else. Exhale, three, four." I wondered which person was the reporter.

The last thing Jack and Fawz needed was a reporter. We wanted to call absolutely no attention to ourselves. That was why we were leaving from this hopper port here at Cape Kennedy on an old style hopper to make the whole thing appear routine.

The new space taxis launched in California attracted lots of media attention. Astronauts going on missions left from that facility. Except for our mission, of course! Employees of aerospace firms who worked at the various space stations launched from Florida in the older hoppers.

NASA management found out only two days ago that SpaceTech was taking up a reporter. That reporter would have been amazed had he known about the whirlwind he created, the high level NASA meetings, the name calling regarding how approval for the reporter had been granted on such a sensitive flight, and the phone calls to Washington. Jack and Dr. Fawz as co-commanders attended the meetings by video conference since our crew had been in isolation here at Kennedy Space Center for the past two weeks.

The source of the problem was traced to a NASA form on which the reporter listed "writer" as his occupation. Whoever approved concluded that "writer" meant "technical writer" for the SpaceTech manuals. That was not as blatant an error as it seemed since the SpaceTech people usually spent their two weeks in isolation taking seminars and reviewing the technical manuals. SpaceTech put a great deal of effort on their manuals and asked employees from all types of educational background to review them. So an outside writer, someone hired as a "contract laborer," would not seem the least bit unusual. Later, when the passenger list was finalized, his occupation was correctly listed as reporter.

Dr. Clayton and the KSC director both decided that at this late date denying the reporter would greatly distress the SpaceTech managers because they had so carefully orchestrated their publicity schedule. Furthermore, they had meticulously followed NASA's standard security procedures including a thorough background check of the reporter.

NASA management briefly considered changing our flight plans but decided that would call more attention to us and create scheduling nightmares. Yesterday, our "hold" was lifted, and we got our go ahead.

Jack said how odd the meetings had been because information about our mission varied, depending upon an attendee's need to know. Some thought the concern was merely to keep the test flight of the *Copernicus* a secret. A few knew about the actual mission, but very few knew about the mission's purpose.

Up to two days ago, everything for the hopper flight had been all set including our going up to the space factory on one of the few choice wider bodied ones. Jack was to fly co-pilot. Fawzshen, Lauren, and I would take pictures.

The picture taking was a slight ruse. The SpaceTech people would have no idea that our mission was anything more than a standard working mission for all five astronauts aboard, not just Jack and the pilot. Because of the photos, Jack arranged a few perks for us. To get specific photos that NASA needed, the hopper flight would take longer, and we would get more good views of the Earth. Best of all, our photography jobs guaranteed us the choice seats right across the front with the pilot. Those seats sold at a premium to the public, and companies like SpaceTech reserved them when available for their executives, akin to riding first class on commercial airplanes.

After all those last-minute meetings, here we were as originally planned, waiting for the Freedom II. Of the older hoppers, this was one of the few wider bodied ones. That made it less safe and more tricky when flying free of the atmosphere.

A hopper lifted off in a manner similar to a predecessor, the space shuttle. However, the hopper itself was a much improved machine.

My fear flared up again. I reminded myself to inhale. "One, two. Exhale, three, four. Keep breathing. Heart, slow down! Beat at a nice steady rate." I broke out in a cold sweat. I could tell even though enveloped in my space suit. "Distract myself. Think about being there already."

I felt a little light-headed. Suppose I fainted. "No, no, I immediately zapped such a thought." I would disappoint myself and mess up the scheduling of the entire trip. They could not carry an unconscious person onto the hopper. They would send my replacement up on the next available hopper. "Inhale, one, two; exhale, three, four." I handled the KC-135X. I could handle this. "Think about something, anything. I tried to think about SpaceTech."

Many people at JSC thought the whole concept of a minishuttle was ridiculous. Before SpaceTech started their minishuttle project, they were a very highly respected aerospace firm, on the cutting edge of technology, people who knew about those kinds of things said. Now with the two-person shuttle, they were regarded as having made a series of extremely unwise management decisions. To me, a two-person shuttle was a neat idea, why not one or two people dashing between space stations or between the stations and the moon. The minishuttles were supposed to be sturdy enough to venture a million miles beyond the orbit of the moon and even beyond. One person going that far alone sounded real adventuresome and downright scary. If the person became ill, there was enough remote control to safely bring the person back to the spaceport or the space factory.

NASA leased space on the space factory to SpaceTech and both the government and SpaceTech shared the high security facilities. NASA

189

built the massive major mission ships while SpaceTech assembled the minishuttles.

Good-bye, Alan. "No, no, don't think about him," I told myself. It was enough of an emotional drain being scared without being concerned about missing Alan or worse yet, never seeing him again or seeing him again and it being different, his not caring about me anymore. Of course, the more I tried to stop thinking about him, the more I saw his face before me. I replayed in my mind over and over what he had said under the SpaceTech moon.

Jack nudged me and said, "I've spotted the reporter. If he weren't so frightened about riding on the hopper, he would be over here by now. If his curiosity gets the better of him, be calm."

"Don't worry, if he says anything to me, I'll be very boring," I replied.

"Do you know him?" Lauren asked Jack.

"Yes. He's that fellow with red hair. His name is Eggvar Mesathistle."

"Are we going to have a problem with him?" She inquired.

"I hope not. He has the curiosity and skills of a fine reporter, except he mostly does publicity pieces, which are excellent. However, he then passes them off as news. SpaceTech will pay him the big bucks, and then he'll make a bit from the magazines and newspapers that publish his articles about the minishuttles."

"I doubt if those articles will be very objective," Lauren stated.

Five minutes later, the reporter's natural curiosity overcame his fear, and he sauntered over, acting casual and nonchalant, but bursting with curiosity.

"Commander Medwin, how are you, and what are you doing, flying on this bucket?"

"Doing my job," Jack said, noncommittal like.

"I declare, I thought NASA's star astronaut would rate the taxi." He then turned to me. "I say, young lady, space travelers are getting younger by the day."

"Guess so," I mumbled softly, hoping he would decide I was older than I looked.

"I declare, I would take you for a high school student."

"My husband and child would be amused." The words popped out before I realized what I was saying.

My crew turned their heads toward me. Jack registered surprise, Lauren looked shocked, and Fawzshen seemed confused. The reporter observed their spontaneous reactions to what I had just said. That was not good.

"Your crew doesn't know anything about you. You certainly must have trained together. Are you from a back-up crew?"

"No," I replied. I needed to make amends. I said, "We're separated. I mean that my husband and I are separated." Then I stopped talking. That would have to do. If I talked anymore, it simply would make matters worse.

The reporter squinted his eyes and said, "Something very strange is going on with you."

Fortunately, just then, someone from the SpaceTech group called, "Eggvar, over here." The reporter excused himself and crossed the room to the loud talking SpaceTechies.

I turned toward Jack and said, "Sorry."

"Don't worry," Jack said. "Since SpaceTech's paying his way up to the space factory, they'll want every minute of his time and attention. He'll reciprocate and deliver excellent propaganda. He'll probably forget about us unless something happens to refresh his memory." Jack's words sounded encouraging enough but his expression spoke of concern as he moved his bottom lip to cover the top one.

"Oh, my!" Lauren exclaimed. "You lie like the best of them."

"It just came out," I said, but I was figuring out why those words had been so available to me. It was wishful thinking. I wanted a life with Alan as much as I wanted this mission, and now he and I were indeed separated.

Just then, the flight facilitator walked into the room and instructed us to put on our helmets. I lifted my helmet up and put it over my head, and my heart started going crazy again. "Breathe," I told myself, "slow and easy." "Inhale, exhale." She proceeded to each person, checking the helmet and assigning seats. The four of us would have the best seats, right across the front, flanking the pilot on either side. We would have the whole front panorama plus the only side windows. Windows were what every space traveler wanted. She called out names, those in the back first, lining us up so we would not be crawling over each other. She would not be going with us.

I glanced back for a final look at Mother Earth through the glass windows to the vacant press room. There was someone there at the far end, an observer. It looked like, no, it could not be Alan.

When he saw me turn toward the window, the man moved forward. He walked like Alan. I wanted to see Alan so much that I imagined him there. Then the figure waved. I lifted my space suited lower arm to shoulder height and flicked my wrist. It was a secret wave. I did not want my fellow astronauts to look back and think I had divulged top secret information. I did not want my crew thinking that I had told Alan.

Was it Alan? I wanted to run to the window and find out. I was not brave enough. Instead, I turned and moved toward the door.

Right before walking out the door, I looked back again. I could not see that clearly, but I thought the man blew me a kiss. Then I felt a jolt of electricity pass right through the window. I could have darted back for a few seconds. Instead, I cupped my gloved hand under my chin and blew the person a kiss. At that moment, Lauren said, "Are you ready, Jana." I quickly turned and walked out the door.

We boarded the bus for the drive to the space hopper. I saw it on the gantry ahead of us, perched on the side of a large rocket and flanked by two fuel tanks. It looked just like the photos and TV footage of it. It looked totally familiar, but yet so different, because it was not contained within a photograph or a TV screen. It was huge, framed against the Florida sky.

Once on the elevator up to the hopper entrance, there was no turning back. Inside, the hopper was just like a simulator Lauren and I had trained in. But I knew the difference. This hopper was attached to a giant rocket. "Breathe, one, two, three, four." Then, something strange and wondrous happened to me. I relaxed. I was not as relaxed as sitting around at home, but I was not as tense as taking an orbital physics test from Filbert either. I thought, "All this training. Now let's enjoy this trip."

Mission Control talked us through the final countdown. Big puffs of steam rushed by the side windows. Then, all I could see was steam. The roar of the engines increased, and we were moving. The weight of gravity crushed down upon me, and the entire hopper shook violently. I felt like I was being jostled inside a food processor. Yet, the blades were unable to reach me because my well-toned muscles held my guts in place.

I had been trained for that very second and understood what had happened. The great rocket with the hopper firmly attached to it had wiggled and in the process shook off tons of ice. After that momentary wiggle, we were rising straight up through a puffy white cloud.

Two minutes into the trip, the hopper began jumping around as the second stage rockets separated. I had a slight nauseous moment but I repeated to myself over and over that I handled the KC-135X. I could handle this.

I had been well prepared for the wiggle and the separations. I was not prepared for the view below. Already we were passing over Africa. I saw only the slightest cloud coverage. Beneath large areas of clear sky, delicate greens, pale yellows, and muted browns formed a soft, impressionistic landscape as the pale blue ocean grew darker as it fell away from the shore. From up here, it looked like nobody had any troubles in such a paradise.

I did not know when we left the atmosphere because I was too busy taking pictures. I knew the angle had to be just right. Too slight and we would be back in the Earth's gravity, and too much and we would be in the wrong orbit or worse, heading out into deep space. With Jack, we were in good hands. "Just because you've done something before, don't get careless about it. Concentrate your efforts." I had heard Jack say that more than once. He would be alert enough to know when to override the computer.

As we orbited, we flew into the night and then in an hour or so later back into the daylight. The Earth grew smaller.

What amazing good fortune to be here in this hopper with my friends observing this awesome scene. We had gained altitude. The Earth looked like a soft blue globe wrapped in a thin layer of white gossamer. Fortunately for all of us, this hopper flight was taking longer than normal because NASA needed some pictures to update maps. They tracked so much from the air: like changes in the world's forests and crop size and health. Fawz, Lauren, and I each operated a camera. It was fairly easy work and did not interfere at all with my sightseeing.

Amid all this beauty, I got a nagging pain. I had been too much of a coward to run back to the window and wave goodbye to Alan. He had traveled from Houston to Florida to say goodbye. How could Alan have known? Easy! He had worked for SpaceTech this past summer. He could have learned of an impending SpaceTech flight in which the choice seats were not available. He could have correctly connected the dots. My behavior toward him had been unforgivable.

I comforted myself in thinking that maybe it had not been Alan. By then, I had my helmet on. It could have been someone else.

Fawz said to me. "We'll be docking in a few minutes."

All I saw ahead of me was blackness. Of course, I knew from Filbert and orbital physics that the space factory and the hopper were on converging courses and at some point ahead we would meet.

Then out my window I saw the space factory shimmering like an exotic bird with great gossamer wings, the solar panels. Was that our silvery solarship attached to a docking compartment waiting for us? I felt a soft thud as we docked, and soon the engines shut down.

Jana's Journal

We were free to exit the hopper. I unbuckled my seatbelt and lifted my arms. They stayed in the lifted position without my muscles exerting any effort. Cautiously, I put my hands on the seat rest and pushed off from my seat. I found myself levitated and not touching any surface. This microgravity was incredibly pleasant. I looked at my crew and recognized they also were filled with such joy.

We propelled ourselves through the airlock that connected the hopper to the space factory and into a softly lit cylindrical corridor. When the corridor branched, the fifteen SpaceTech people and the reporter went in one direction. The pilot led our crew in the opposite direction toward our ship. We tumbled and laughed as we proceeded.

"This is great," Lauren commented.

The pilot, eyeing her with interest, said, "Wait til you see your solarship. We're almost there."

The airlock hatch connecting our ship with the corridor was open, and the pilot went inside with us. The *Copernicus* was magnificent. Although it looked like the mock-up and simulator we had trained on, the real thing felt completely different because we were weightless. Now, every surface was usable because there no longer was a differentiation between floor, walls, and ceiling. In a certain way, the cabin resembled a small apartment designed for a weightless environment, with a bathroom, kitchen facilities for heating our space food, hammocks for sleeping, and lots of storage compartments. In another way, it resembled an airplane or hopper because the most prominent things were all the flight and navigational controls and computers at the front windows of our ship, similar but more complicated than the controls of an airplane. Four seats with belts in front of these main controls welcomed us. Flanked near these controls along both sides were two separate computers stations that were not networked to the main controls.

On the wall opposite the controls, storage compartments held securely packed supplies as well as the video and camera equipment. I basically knew what was supposed to be in each compartment. Our crew peeled out of our space suits and stashed them in the compartments specifically designed to hold these large, awkward items of protective clothing. Underneath, we were wearing our comfortable NASA blues. The pilot removed his helmet and tucked it under his arm. He kept his space suit on.

Almost as if on cue, we all rushed to the windows for a view of Earth, a mere 200 miles away. A side window yielded the best view, and we took turns at that window. Most of us were pretty talkative in our praise of our home planet, but Fawz was rather quiet.

After admiring Earth, we moved from our cabin into the first pressurized module inside the cargo bay. That module was mostly a storage room with closed compartments packed with food and supplies to repair the ship. Many items out in the open, such as food, repair equipment, and air tanks, were either netted or secured in place with straps. There was even the duct tape and another type of tape used to repair miniscule holes in the ship. A small hole most likely would be fatal to all of us, but under certain conditions, repairs were possible.

Connected to the far end of the storage module was the garden module, where plants were under growth lights. I noticed they were all carefully labeled. Some plants looked like the variety that grew in Alan's SpaceTech garden. I knew Alan's plants were fed anti-stress food to prepare them for strange environments.

The last module contained the *Falcon*, our lander. Jack had his hand on the lander's door latch, but he decided not to open it. Instantly, I realized why. The hopper pilot would realize that it also was fully packed for a landing. I knew about every item that should be inside the

Falcon, but we only could see a little by peering in the windows. Still, it was enough to know that the lander was ready.

If we were very lucky, in five-and-a-half months, the *Falcon* would land on the surface of Ganymede. Then, we would assemble the rover and explore that giant moon. If we were extremely lucky, we might even find descendants of those beings who visited Fawz's ancestors five centuries ago.

Inside the *Falcon* were two powerful communicators, a built-in one and a portable one that we would take with us in the rover to contact Houston while we explored Ganymede. Special accessories for the communicators were hand held phone trackers for crewmembers to speak to each other on the planet's surface or to track someone down who had become lost. I figured if we made it that far, we would stay close together and not go roaming off on our own.

The *Falcon* also carried modules that we would assemble into a monitoring station on the side of Ganymede that faced Jupiter. In addition, equipment to broadcast a live TV program from the surface of Ganymede to Earth was packed. The most mysterious item of all was a sealed box of gifts in case we found the living beings.

I thought, "Everything is starting right now, but it won't be over like a vacation. It will last for a long time, almost a year."

The captain said, "That's strange. The lander's all packed for a landing. I also couldn't help but notice that your ship is overflowing with supplies for a major mission."

I tried not to show any reaction at all by assuming my blandest expression. If the secret got out, would my greatest hopes simply be cancelled? I felt nauseated. My stomach knotted up.

Jack matter-of-factly said, "I haven't heard any announcement about a major mission. Have you?"

The captain stared at each of us. Then, he turned and peered into the window of the lander for a long minute. From where I was floating nearby, I had a clear view of his face. Something inside the lander caught his attention. The pupils of his eyes contracted for a fraction of a second. It was very fast, so fast that I could have missed it.

He knew a major mission could be in the offing, but he simply said, "They're hungry for visitors up here. They'll invite you to so many things. If you accept everything, you won't stay on schedule. Some of my other passengers had that problem."

"Thanks. I'll keep that in mind," Jack replied.

"Your ship's phone has just been activated. I gave the people up here your number. It's just standard protocol, but now, seeing what I've seen, it's good that I did. Otherwise, they'd be in your ship snooping around, saying they need to do a final check on this or that. And you're all packed, ready to go somewhere. Maybe, everybody up here knows where you're going, but I don't."

Jack asked, "Do you think this baby will hang together all the way to Alpha Centauri? That'll be some test flight."

That hyperbole broke the tension.

The pilot said that he would have shown us around this space factory, but he had to fly to the spaceport, pick up some people, and return them to Earth. Before he left, he said to Lauren, "Maybe, we could get together when you return to Houston."

She simply smiled sweetly and said, "I'm committed."

"It figures," he said. "Well, it was worth a try." He wished us a good test flight and then asked Jack, "Who's picking you up from the spaceport to take you back home? I haven't seen your names on the schedule."

Jack said, "We're not sure how extensive the testing will be."

Although the captain knew we were involved with something extraordinary, his bigger interest seemed to be Lauren. He said, "Well, it's always fun to spend a few extra days at the spaceport. Of all things, they even have a gift shop there." He knew the supplies he had seen were for far more than a few extra days. He simply downplayed what he already knew. He added, "Your gear's probably unpacked by now. Someone will deliver it to you soon."

As soon as he left, I said the obvious. "He suspects something."

"I know," Jack replied, "but he's a professional. He fully understands about the need-to-know."

Lauren asked, "What about getting together with the people up here? That's going to be awkward, particularly with this ship all loaded and more particularly since some of them loaded it. They'll have rather interesting questions. How can we simply say no?"

Jack was quiet, mulling over this development, but Fawz said, "We will attend their events and behave like everything is normal. We are here to take this ship on a test run. That is all they need to know."

"Of course, you're right," Jack said.

"What if SpaceTech invites us to something?" Lauren asked.

Jack and Fawz exchanged glances. Jack announced, "We will go."

That decision had barely been made when Jack started getting phone calls with invitations. He accepted one for this wake cycle from NASA for a reception and a tour of the assembly plant and one for tomorrow from the SpaceTech people for a luncheon.

Finally, we buckled ourselves into our seats across the front of the *Copernicus*. Fawz and Jack took the middle two seats. I sat next to Fawz, and Lauren sat next to Jack. The Earth was way off to one side. I could barely see it.

We checked in with Houston although JSC knew the hopper already had successfully docked with the space factory. Before we started the two-day series of pre-flight checks, Jack recommended to CAPCOM that our hopper flight pilot be reminded not to mention that he took us to the space factory. As far as the pilot was concerned, our being his passengers was classified information for him not to discuss with anyone. CAPCOM told us the pilot would be reminded before he ever reached the spaceport.

I figured the pilot definitely would be looking for Lauren in hopes she was no longer "committed." To me, everything about maintaining secrecy already seemed messy. Jack gave no indication about being concerned, but he must have sensed my concern because he reminded me that the NASA people here on this station knew not to mention to anyone else in correspondences and phone calls that we were here. As for the Space Tech people, they had a reciprocal agreement with NASA not to reveal who was here or what happened here. It worked to the benefit of both sides. SpaceTech's purpose was vested interest for trade secrets.

The problem was the reporter, Eggvar Mesathistle. CAPCOM reassured us that Space Tech had forcefully reminded him that everything he wrote needed their approval and that he was to write nothing regarding any of NASA's activities or people. Jack seemed comfortable with this whole messy arrangement.

Things were even more complicated because a manifest of cargo on each hopper mission to and from Earth was kept. This manifest also included a passenger list. Thus, anyone could know that we had gone up on a hopper to the space factory. Yet, people went up here for various reasons and stayed for months and months. The manifest of hopper flights between space stations was not made public. Neither was the list of people at a specific space station at any given time.

I hoped our secret would hold together until we were safely on our way to Ganymede. If it broke open sooner, I would not think about the ramifications.

I pushed my concerns out of my mind and concentrated on my job. Jack mostly spoke with CAPCOM, a flight controller whom I had not previously met, but several times, Jack interacted with Max on specific computer checks. Houston was automatically getting readings on about a hundred channels. If there were a problem, Mission Control would let us know.

We had plenty of redundancy. If our computers went down, which would be terrible, we could use two other smaller separate systems. In addition, hooked to the main computer system was a Prima Donna computer, which we were told not to touch unless we were specifically instructed to do so. I figured that Venzi Suzaky, the esteemed physicist and my friend, had done lots of work on that computer. As an integral part of the main computer system, it theoretically could fix them if we encountered serious problems and were out of touch with Mission Control.

For additional protection, we could talk to Houston on the back-up computers, also. Since this was a secret mission, certain methods of communication probably were not operative, such as the educational channels.

Our gear arrived while we were busy working with Mission Control. Someone stuck his head inside our cabin and said our gear was in the corridor outside. We found it secured to the walls. We unpacked and strapped our stuff inside the storage compartments. Everything looked so neat.

Since all our readings so far were nominal, we did not need to communicate with Houston for several hours. In our absence, Mission Control would watch over our ship through automatic readings.

Before our tour of the NASA assembly plant, Lauren announced to me, "We're not going to make the mistake again of your looking too young." She removed a makeup kit from her gear. I did not know she wore makeup. It certainly must have been expertly applied. I held the kit in one hand as she selected items.

"Frown," she ordered.

I complied. I held a mirror in my other hand while she drew furrow lines on my forehead with eyeliner and then softened each line with her fingertip. As Lauren made me look older, I recalled a fragment from a recurring dream: an elderly woman took off her makeup and then appeared far younger. Afterwards, the woman did a handstand. Only occasionally could I retrieve even that fragment when awake. I wanted to remember, but in a wakeful state, the rest eluded me. I thought it best not to mention a strange dream. Particularly now, I needed to appear like the stable person that I was. I pushed the dream away and watched Lauren work on my face.

"Lauren, this is ridiculous, but you're really enjoying it," I said and started to laugh at her efforts.

"Good," she said. "Now I see where your laugh lines go. I'll put some crinkle lines around your eyes." She floated back to survey her work. "Not bad," she said.

She could be successful and happy in a variety of environments. If she had her choice of anything all through history, I wonder what she would have picked. Probably to be here right now at this exact moment.

The NASA people were so pleased to see us. I wished they could have known where we were taking their ship. The reception included a tour of their assembly plant. Already, they were assembling another large solarship. Because the ships were so very large, they assembled one solarship at a time. However, smaller components for several ships were done in an assembly line fashion. As we toured, they asked us questions about Earth, but not about the weather because they could see that for themselves. Pretty soon, the four of us were separated from each other.

An engineer said to me, "Your ship is loaded with food for about a year, and specialty foods, too, like fried won tons." He gazed over at Fawz.

This was not good, but I was prepared. I assumed my blandest expression and asked, "Why do you think they did that?"

He thought a minute and said, "I don't know. It could be an issue of weight. Or maybe it's a new way of doing things, getting the ship totally prepared for a mission before the test flight. "

I felt relieved by his answer but still tried to stay emotionless as I thought of something innocuous to say. "Will the food keep?" I asked.

"Not indefinitely, but it keeps a long time. They're certainly doing things differently with this ship, lots of meetings I wasn't privy to. We've checked it and rechecked it, more checks than I can remember from before. It seems like they're being darn sure that the *Copernicus* will require only one test flight."

I asked, "How many test flights does it usually take."

Without hesitation, he said, "We usually need only one." He frowned and stared at me strangely. I had asked a stupid question to which I already knew the answer. Any astronaut, particularly one involved in testing solarships, would know that one test flight was the norm.

Grasping for something, I said, "I needed a little reassurance, hearing you say that." The more I talked, the bigger mess I was making.

He replied, "Yeah, don't we all. We all need a little reassurance."

Had he bought my comment? Was I was out of the woods? Would a trained astronaut admit to needing reassurance?

I hated all this secrecy and hated having to guard my every word. It could have been so different, a joyful send-off for a major mission.

Fortunately, at that moment, Jack called me over to him, and I excused myself. I hoped that engineer had not jumped to any conclusion. Secret trips were not something that NASA had undertaken before, so it would be unlikely that he suspected anything.

Then a thought came to me that I had been trying to push out of my mind. I did not want that thought, but the more I tried to suppress it, the more it popped out. The thought was this: if word got out that we were going on a secret mission, would the whole thing be cancelled? Madame President and the King had their reasons for secrecy, and would they still allow the mission if the veil of secrecy were torn asunder? I did not mention it to my crew. I did not want to burden them. Furthermore, it seemed like a huge leap from a fully packed ship to a secret mission.

After the reception, we went back to the *Copernicus* and continued checking it out in preparation for undocking.

The next wake cycle, Lauren again made me look older as we prepared to attend the luncheon with SpaceTech. This time, she overdid the make-up, and in the mirror, I looked considerably older and my skin tone was a bit gray. "Gee, Lauren, I look rather ugly."

"Oh, sorry, you do." Lauren took the make-up kit out of my hands. "Here, I can fix it."

Jack said, "There's no time for that. The luncheon's starting. Jana, you look okay."

We immediately left our ship and went through connecting tunnels to SpaceTech's facility where we were greeted most warmly. Now, according to Jack, this get together was simply a small group of managers who welcomed seeing people other than their own employees. Unfortunately, Eggvar Mesathistle, the reporter, was there, too.

Instead of being belted into chairs and sitting at a table as I might have thought, we floated around in little clusters, reminiscent of a stand-up reception. To myself, I named this a floating reception. Everyone had two decorative mesh bags holding an assortment of space food. The food in one bag had been heated, and in the other bag, the food was room temperature. I picked one item at a time and temporarily secured everything else in two pockets. Lauren had given me a good hint about space food: enjoy the food instead of comparing it to what it was supposed to represent before dehydration and rehydration. I found their food was totally satisfying, even delicious. If the situation were different, I would have requested that Houston order some of SpaceTech's food for our mission.

Eggvar Mesathistle, the reporter, was floating quite a distance from me. I knew he was watching me, but I did not make eye contact. I did not want to speak with him.

Afterwards, we toured their minishuttle factory and show room. Our crew took turns sitting in a prototype minishuttle that looked just like the one Alan and I had admired at the Gilruth Center. Fond remembrances of my farewell with Alan flooded back to me. I was almost in a dream state, wanting to keep remembering those moments, but Eggvar was waiting for me when I climbed out.

"Very nice," I said as I quickly moved away from him.

He followed me. "I declare, you're acting like you don't want to chat with me."

"Goodness," I replied. Of course, I was trying to escape from him, but under the circumstances I said, "How do you like this weightlessness?"

"It's quite enlightening," he replied, emphasizing the syllable "light."

I politely laughed at his word play, and we chatted innocuously for a few minutes, but I was totally alert so as to not say anything spontaneous.

"You seem tense," he said. "I know what will make you more comfortable." He led me over to a window and said, "This is the best view yet."

I blurted out. "Looking at the Earth, that's my favorite thing to do up here. It's so magnificent." I quickly regained control. He was a reporter, and this was not an innocent conversation.

"Thank you for showing this view to me," I said as I started to float away.

He followed me. "I declare, you look different."

I said offhandedly, "You look different, too. When we're first in microgravity, our faces swell up and so forth. I'm sure you know about that."

He squinted at me. "Something's going on with you. You look much older. How is that possible?"

I stayed calm and composed. "What a thing to say to a woman, that she looks older," I commented in as light-hearted tone as I could muster. I almost added, "Where are your manners?"

"Something's going on with you," he repeated. "You now look older than that gorgeous babe, Lauren."

"She certainly is gorgeous, and she's not married or engaged or even going with anyone." I said, hoping to distract him because I did not want to say something stupid and jeopardize our mission's secrecy. Lauren would know how to deal with him. "Would you like to talk with her now?"

He ignored my question. He would not be distracted. His eyes narrowed into slits, and he said, "What does this mean? You're aging at a fast rate before my eyes. Surely, your crew must notice."

Suddenly, his mouth dropped open, and his eyes widened as he registered what appeared to be shock and fear. Why would he possibly be afraid of me? Quickly, he hid his visible signs of fear. Then, drawing himself up and becoming taller, his expression became a combination between boldness and haughtiness when he said, "I make no promises to you. You can't help what you are."

He made absolutely no sense. It was like he had discovered a strange secret about me.

I said, "It's a reception in our honor, Mr. Mesathistle. I'm wearing makeup." My comment was too late. He already had made a decision about me, and it was a negative one. At this moment, even the truth would have made no difference to him. In any case, I certainly would not tell him the truth.

What about me could possibly frighten him, maybe the gray skin tone Lauren had applied to my face? I was tempted to find out. However, I thought better of it, excused myself, and floated away to join my crew.

I was relieved that he did not have a clue, but if he checked into my credentials, he could make a mess of things. An unpleasant thought occurred to me. If I got any publicity at all, JSC could send me back. If Eggvar Mesathistle caused trouble for me, I would become a liability for the mission's secrecy. How happy my replacement would be. I hoped that replacement would not be Filbert, my orbital physics instructor.

After my encounter with Mesathistle, I floated close by Lauren's side for the duration of the event. It could have been such fun chatting with these SpaceTech people about their minishuttle if I had not feared inadvertently saying something stupid and their finding out about the extent of our mission. There was too much to lose. I sensed Lauren felt the same way, too, because her demeanor was one of reserve rather than her normal confidence.

Later, I considered expressing my concerns to Jack about the reporter, but decided he should not see me as a whiny worrywart. The crew would not want someone on the mission worrying all the way to Jupiter.

After the SpaceTech event, we happily prepared for the test flight. We practiced with Mission Control as we ran so many checks. On the next wake cycle, we had the A-Okay for the test run. The NASA people showed up to bid us farewell. Clearly, some of them came to bid farewell to their ship. All of them touched the inside of the ship to wish us a safe test run. I wanted them to know that their bon voyage was for a very long mission, further than any astronaut had gone before. I felt sad, cheating them out of knowing the real destination of the ship in which they had put their time and effort. I believed that some of them sensed that this was far more significant than an ordinary test run. They sang us a bon voyage song that one of them had written recently. When I heard the words, I tried my best not to seem shocked. The song spoke of Mars, the asteroid belt, and the gates of Jupiter.

We closed the hatch and undocked. Undocking was a slight jolt, but slowly drifting away was so much easier on the body than the hopper blastoff.

We maneuvered away from the space factory for our two-day test run. I stayed very busy, and the thought only plagued me at quiet moments that the whole mission could be cancelled. Madame President and the King could change their minds. Mesathistle could interfere in some harmful way and expose everything. If that happened, I always would savor these days, but so much more was within our grasp.

The months of training blurred in front of me like an out-of-control slide presentation on fast forward: Filbert, my orbital physics instructor, being mean, trying to cut me out of the program; Venzi Suzaky, the physicist, helping me; Lauren and Max, being totally supportive and helpful; my assuming I had been dropped from the program and packing to go home; and Director Clayton, holding ultimate power over my chances at being an astronaut and, even now, continuing to be on this mission. My mental slide show abruptly ended because I now was getting some data from Mission Control and needed to pay close attention.

After many orbits of the magnificent and ever-changing Earth, the systems all checked out, and we were given the go-ahead for our mission. After making precise maneuver's and corrective burns, we left the safety of Earth's orbit.

"We're on our way," Jack said. What a glorious understatement that was. We toasted with chun, the special beverage from Fawz's country, for a safe and illuminating trip.

I breathed deeply and sighed in relief. Director Clayton could not change his mind about me now. No, he could change his mind and might very well do so, but he could do nothing about it. Clayton could not send me back to Earth. I finally was out of his reach. A huge burden had been lifted from me. I gleefully laughed aloud.

Barely a moment later, I promised myself that I would do as good a job as I possibly could so that Clayton would not regret an inexperienced person like me being on this mission. I vowed I would be worthy of my good fortune and be the best astronaut I could possibly be. I would be brave in the face of any contingency.

El Lago, Texas (Near Johnson Space Center)

9:35 a.m. CDT

Sharleen Rothwell had made more money on this one contract than on any other job in her entire career by merely using JSC data provided through the Freedom of Information Act to enable her customer to track a particular solarship and to pick up the astronauts' communications on their return to the spaceport. Her customer, a small startup company called LandSkyTech, could even broadcast to the astronauts.

She had worked contract labor with various JSC contractors and with some of the newly formed private space consortiums. LandSkyTech was a new customer. She had asked who recommended her. The answer was a name she did not recognize. Since she belonged to all of the right professional organizations and made many contacts, she nodded appropriately when the reference was mentioned.

She had an urge to check it out with JSC first, but what Jim Landres, the company president, offered her was so much she would not have to work for two or three years. She could vacation in Tahiti, live like a rich person, provide her child Emily with superb schools, build a bigger house, and have the best of everything. It was like winning the lottery.

Still, she initially had hesitated. He had offered her far too much money for the task. She realized that he knew next to nothing about trajectories, something basic in the aerospace business. She wondered why someone with so little knowledge was the president and owner of a company.

She also hesitated for another reason. B.G. Landres definitely seemed attracted to her. Since her marriage had just ended, was she simply scared to get involved? No, it was much more than that. Although Mr. Landres exuded charm and charisma, she sensed a relationship with him could prove dangerous. He seemed manipulative and controlling, which was bad enough, but how he read her emotions was downright scary. He immediately recognized how much she valued money, and that fact did not bother him at all. To nip any possibility of a relationship before she considered accepting the contract, Sharleen simply told him that she was married.

She barely could read his reaction. He seemed momentarily disappointed but then quickly turned his focus toward the job. If she had been younger or less experienced, she easily could have allowed herself to become involved with him.

Despite her reservations, she accepted the job after he assured her that LandSkyTech was a subsidiary of SpaceTech, a highly respected company. She then was required to sign a confidentiality contract with him, someone who was flaunting the Freedom of Information Act. How ironic! If she ever revealed anything about her job, she would be required to return all the money and face prosecution. As she signed, old sayings flew through her mind. "When something sounds too good to be true, it probably is." Then she said to herself, "This doesn't 'smell' right."

The data on the storage devices proved to be a mess. The back-ups were random with absolutely no documentation. After she sequenced the order of the storage devices, she worked day and night plotting the trajectory and extrapolating the continued path of a solarship. The data itself was strange. Some was real time for a five-and-a-half-month mission to Ganymede, and some showed a projected return of several months. Some data points had been rotated ten degrees, but the newer data, which also included the older stuff, had not been rotated. The latest data indicated a projected return of slightly more than three weeks from Ganymede to Earth? How was that possible? How, also, could astronauts go on such a long journey? That seemed way more complicated than the two successful Mars missions. Why would the mission be a secret? Sharleen put those thoughts out of her mind and dutifully finished her work. She explained to Mr. Landres that he would need the most current data to continually update the trajectory. He gazed longingly at her but simply thanked her for doing such prompt work.

Even though she had completed her contract and collected her money, Sharleen still felt queasy about the whole job. She had been working long hours and had not followed the news or watched TV, but that evening waiting at the grocery store checkout, she read a tabloid article claiming that JSC astronauts had landed on Ganymede. The article described situations that astronauts would not allow themselves to get into. Yet, there could be a kernel of truth. After all, there was an ongoing mission. She had plotted the trajectory.

In a moment of inspiration, she decided that a rival publication was planning to set the record straight and that LandSkyTech had been hired to eavesdrop on the astronauts during their return mission. It would be a publicity stunt. She thought no one could be harmed by picking up broadcasts from within the solarship. If anything, the astronauts, especially that young woman, Jana, would be exonerated from the crazy tabloid journalism surrounding them. Sharleen usually was a rational person, but the idea that she had actually done some good so comforted her that she examined the situation no further.

Now, she had money and planned to spend it. Sharleen knelt on her chair surveying below her on the dining room table preliminary architectural drawings for her new home. She had just returned from a meeting with her architect and still was wearing her new pale peach suit and matching heels. The sound of Mozart surrounded her. Then, the phone rang.

"Are you watching TV?" her friend asked.

211

"No!"

"Well, turn it on right away."

"What channel?"

"It's on every channel, I think."

She clicked it on. She recognized the astronaut Jana Novacek from the newspapers.

"So, it's beginning already," she thought to herself. Somehow, she had thought that her tracking would enable LandSkyTech to pick up only the audio. But the video, too, and how did her customer get the astronauts to cooperate? She wondered what NASA thought of the whole thing, a private aerospace firm dealing directly with the astronauts. Printed words marched across the bottom of the TV screen.

THIS IS AN EMERGENCY BROADCAST FROM THE SOLARSHIP *COPERNICUS*. IF YOU HAVE ANY INFORMATION, PLEASE CALL JSC AT 713-555-0378 OR THE CIA AT 713-555-2468.

The screen split. Jana was on one half, and Commander Jack Medwin was on the other half. Jana's voice faded, and Jack issued an urgent plea for help.

Sharleen's heart began pounding, and she clutched the back of her chair. She grew dizzy. Stay calm, she told herself. Did her plotting the trajectory have any relationship to an explosive heading toward the solarship? Who indeed was her employer, B.G. Landres? She activated her cell phone, clearly said "LandSkyTech," and anxiously waited for a response.

"That number has been disconnected," said a computer-generated young operator dressed in the latest fad clothes. She tried a second time and got the same results.

Sharleen's head swirled. Did she indeed have anything to do with the impending disaster? She had given LandSkyTech the projected trajectory of the mission. Trajectories can change, but her employer could obtain new information from another source. She remembered how carefully she had explained to B.G. Landres how to use the costly new software to feed in new information.

Sharleen listened to Jack's urgent plea for help. She once had been Jack and Shirl Medwin's guest, celebrating the safe return of the Mars II astronauts. She had partaken of the Medwin's hospitality, eaten their food, admired their artifacts from around the world, and chatted with their other guests. That had been quite a party. When she first received the invitation, she decided she had finally become known in the aerospace community.

Sharleen watched Jana read and thought that somewhere Jana had a family who cherished her, just as she cherished Emily. She listened to the wide-eyed account of the mission. Such innocence, yes, once she was innocent, but not when she took the LandSkyTech job. She had known what she was doing, not fully, of course. In her heart of hearts, eventually she thought she was selling out for a publicity stunt. She had taken a great deal of money for a little bit of work. She could be in trouble.

Her ex-husband could raise Emily. He was not such a bad sort. Emily would be okay. Sharleen remembered his scathing words toward her. "You'd work for anybody." She had vehemently denied that accusation, but his next words to her had been, "Do you know what that makes you?"

She called the JSC number flashing on the TV. It was busy. She called the operator to interrupt. The operator read a prepared statement, "As we speak, JSC is setting up additional phone lines. Please call back in a few minutes."

Think, think clearly, she ordered herself. Yes, she would go directly to the top and call Director Clayton's office. She had a classified JSC phone book that had been given to her to help with her work on a previous contract. She looked up Director Clayton's number and got right through to his secretary.

"He's in meetings all day." The secretary's voice sounded tired.

"It's very important. I'll come right over." She still had a valid JSC decal on her car.

"It's really bedlam here. They're sealing all the entrances."

She was feeling dizzy again. Think clearly, she told herself. "I'll be coming through the South gate. Would you please call the gate and leave me a gate pass?"

"Who is this again?"

She gave her name and then added, "My husband and I are personal friends of the director, and I have very important information regarding the Ganymede mission."

She grabbed her car keys and started for the side door of her house that led to the garage. Somehow, her sixth sense urged her to look out the front window. Two men got out of a car parked down the street. As she watched, they walked rapidly toward her house. One looked familiar, like someone she had worked with at LandSkyTech. "This isn't good," she thought to herself. She could get to her car, but wait, they could be the ones JSC wanted. If they chased her, she could get killed. Still holding her car keys, she grabbed her phone and purse and ran out the back door until she reached a shrubby area. It was a little spot where Emily liked to hide.

From a keypad in her purse, she locked all the doors and windows in her house and activated the alarm system. Then she called the El Lago police department and quickly explained the situation. She also suggested a possible solution. She would drive out of her subdivision very rapidly, and the men would dash for their car to follow her. As they sped after her, the El Lago police would nab them as if for a routine traffic violation. She and the police would bring the men directly to the South Gate of JSC for interrogation.

"You're not stringing us along, little lady?" the dispatcher asked her.

"No, I swear, this is true. This is urgent."

"You say your name is Sharleen Rothwell. Our computer shows you have more speeding tickets than anyone in the subdivision. Always in a hurry."

"Yes, that's me."

"We'll send a car right over."

"No, wait, they might escape." She went over her plan again, fully realizing that the dispatcher did not want to be told how to do his job.

"We can't hold them for speeding unless they do something else."

"Like what, kill me?"

"Are you in a safe place?"

"Yes, I think so." Sharleen could not see Emily when she hid in this spot, but Emily was a lot smaller, and the shrubs, azaleas backed by bridal wreath, had been trimmed recently.

"If they break into your house, then we could hold them. Stay on the line with me, and we'll wait. Are you scared?"

"Of course," she replied. But she was getting a feeling other than fear. Suppose she was wrong, that the men had dropped by to find out if she had given the trajectory information to anyone else or if she had not protected the data. LandSkyTech might think that she—Sharleen—was involved in a terrorist plot.

Through the shrubs, she saw a man walking between her house and her neighbor's. Now, he was on her back patio, looking around. Could he her? She was tempted to walk forward and greet him. She would explain that she had protected the data and that she was a full professional. The only thing that held her back was that she would look ridiculous emerging from her hiding place in the shrubs.

"What's happening now, Sharleen?"

"I can't talk," she whispered for the man was walking toward her. Then he stood in the middle of the yard for what seemed like an excruciatingly long time. Had he heard anything? A squirrel scampered up a tree. The man abruptly turned and retraced his steps toward the front of the house. Sharleen realized she had been holding her breath.

She breathed deeply and smelled the bedding soil around the azaleas. This was a perfectly good house; why did she always want more? She would admit to the dispatcher that everything was okay. He would have a few laughs with the policemen at the station.

Then the alarm to the house went off. "They're in the house," she said.

"I hear the alarm," the dispatcher replied.

She darted as fast as she could toward her garage, pushing the auto keypad as she ran, which opened the garage door, unlocked the driver's side car door, and started the motor of her car.

As she backed down her driveway, she snapped the phone into its slot on the dash. She said to the dispatcher, "They've got the house alarm deactivated already. They know what they're doing." She turned her car too soon. It screeched backward onto her well-tended lawn and then lurched forward across the driveway and over the curb into the street. "Tell your patrolmen to protect themselves; I can't begin to imagine how high the stakes are. I just hope I can make it out of the subdivision"

"Don't look back, Sharleen. We'll take care of those guys. Just drive like you usually do."

Johnson Space Center, Houston, Texas

Saturday, 9:58 a.m. CDT

Two El Lago police cars drove west along the shoulder of NASA Road 1 with their sirens blaring. In the first car Sharleen Rothwell rode in the front seat with Officer Ontiveres. In the second car rode two patrolmen in the front and in the back their two prisoners, the men who had broken into Sharleen Rothwell's house only minutes earlier. The two police cars cut in front of a long line of waiting cars and TV station vans and pulled up to the South gate of JSC. Sharleen figured the gate pass would be waiting for her, but it would be easier to try to get in with her JSC badge, long expired. No one ever looked at them that closely. The police cars stopped at the guard gate, and Sharleen flashed her expired NASA badge at the guard.

"Sorry, lady, JSC is closed down. We're not letting anyone in, even employees, without a gate pass. We're on Code 1 Alert, and we're checking every vehicle."

Sharleen firmly said to the guard, "I have a gate pass from Director Clayton waiting for me."

The guard checked his hand held computer, glanced at the two police cars, was unfazed, and said, "Sorry, there is no gate pass for you."

Behaving in her most official manner, Sharleen said, "We have urgent mission-critical information. It could save the lives of the astronauts. Would you please call the director for me?"

"Normally, I could, but you see that long line of cars behind you. My instructions are to direct everybody needing a gate pass to Building 2."

Sharleen sighed a practiced and usually most effective sigh, and the guard apologetically said, "It's pretty crowded in there. Everybody's trying to get a pass, but that's all I can tell you to do."

The two police cars drove over to Building 2 and pulled into "no parking" zones in front of the building. The standard method of getting a gate pass was going into that building, waiting in line, requesting the clerk to call the JSC person that the visitor wanted to see, getting authorization, and then getting a gate pass.

Sharleen got out of the police car and dashed into the building. As she entered, a frustrated person said in a loud voice, "We put people on Mars; why this ancient method of getting a gate pass?"

Another one said, "Yeah, I've been waiting in here over an hour."

A clerk at the front counter politely announced, "The phone system is experiencing an overload. Phone verifications are waiting their turns in the system's queue."

Sharleen decided they did not have an hour. As she was figuring out how to wheedle to the front of the line, she got a better idea. She rushed back outside and told the policeman in the first car her idea. In a minute, the three policemen were gathered around Sharleen outside Building 2.

"You want us to do what?"

She calmly repeated her idea. "We would just drive over to Space Center Boulevard. There's a tear in the fence. I've noticed it before. It's big enough for a person to get through. I'm pretty sure they haven't fixed it yet. Then, we'd just walk through the grounds until we got to the Administration Building. The building isn't that far from the tear in the fence.

"You want us to trespass on Federal property? We can't do that, Sharleen."

"It might save the astronaut's lives," she said. "Suppose that was your child in that solarship, the *Copernicus?*"

"I'm going back to the station. We'll lock up those two guys," one of the policeman said.

Sharleen sighed, trying for her most effective sigh ever.

"I'll go with you, Sharleen. It's my duty as an officer and a citizen. But I'll need one of you fearless guys to help." The other two policemen looked at each other and shook their heads. "Okay, you two squashed armadillos, just tell the chief that I'm waiting with Mrs. Rothwell for permission to go onsite. With the prisoners! Help me put joint restraints on them. Then, I can handle them alone."

When the policeman opened the door of the second car, one of the prisoners started yelling, "Hey, you left us in this hot car. The air was turned off. That's cruel and unusual punishment." However, the prisoners did not resist when the three policemen put joint restraints on their elbows, wrists, knees, and ankles. After Officer Ontiveres joined the two prisoners together at the upper arm with a Siamese restraint, he instructed them to get into the first squad car.

With sirens blaring, Sharleen, Officer Ontiveres, and the two prisoners roared West on NASA Road 1, made a left turn onto Space Center Boulevard, and turned off the sirens.

Sharleen quickly found the tear in the fence. The officer explained to the prisoners that they could wait in the car with the windows rolled up or they could behave themselves and accompany the officer. Sharleen lead the parade, the two prisoners "Siamesed" together at the upper arms were next, and the officer followed.

With a minimum of bending and twisting, they easily maneuvered their way through the tear in the fence. As they trekked across the field, Sharleen became aware of what she was wearing. Her mind had been flying in too many directions before for her to even notice that she still was in high heels and nylons and wearing a suit meant for air conditioning, not for sun and heat. Fire ants crawled up her legs, biting her through the nylons. As she walked, she bent down and picked off the fire ants.

One of the two prisoners started complaining in a loud voice. "You've made a big mistake, arresting us. We were on official government business. We work for a CIA agent."

"Sure you do," the officer said. "Just remember that you have the right to remain silent."

"You're in big trouble. You're a cop, and you're breaking onto the Space Center grounds. Did the doll put you up to this?"

"Shut up!" the officer said.

Sharleen, who had been trying to keep quiet and concentrate her thoughts, suddenly got an especially nasty ant bite. She lost her patience and said, "I've seen both of you more than once in LandSkyTech's facilities. You had come to see the owner, B.G. Landres."

"You don't know anything. That's not even his name," the prisoner said.

The other prisoner sharply jerked his restrained biceps and said, "You nitwit. Be quiet."

Sharleen persevered, "If he's not B.G. Landres, who is he?"

"He's a CIA man. That's his cover."

"Owner of an aerospace firm, a cover? That sounds pretty ludicrous," she said.

As they trekked across the field, unknown to any of them, a news photographer with a telephoto lens took several pictures of Sharleen, her two prisoners, and Officer Ontiveres.

They had finally reached the wide area leading to the steps of the Administration Building. It was more impressive than most of the other buildings. Flags on tall flagpoles blew in the slight breeze.

Before entering the building, Sharleen took a compact out of her purse, powdered her face, combed her hair, removed each shoe, checked for fire ants, polished each shoe with a facial tissue, smoothed her suit, and marched into the building as if she herself were the director. She then remembered that the officer had two prisoners to struggle with, so she went back outside and held the door open while the officer escorted his two prisoners inside.

A guard, always on duty inside that building, swiftly made his way toward her group. She flashed her expired badge, clipped it onto her suit, and said, "These people are with me."

"But they need to be badged, too. You need to go back to Building 2 and get them badged."

"This is an extreme emergency, and the director is expecting us," Sharleen said and sighed sweetly.

"You need to go back to . . . ."

The officer said, "Aren't you Juan Rivera? We went to Creek together. Time is everything, Juan."

"Oh, yes, I remember you," the guard said. "Go ahead and go up. I'll call the director and tell him you're on your way."

Once, safely on the elevator, Sharleen said, "That was a lucky break, knowing the guard."

The officer loudly said, "Yes, wasn't it." To Sharleen, he whispered in her ear, "Never saw him before. Just read his badge. People all the time think they recognize me. Since two nearby high schools have Creek in the name, I tried my best guess."

The prisoner said, "Now you're going to make out with the doll in the elevator! What pinheads you people are."

As they walked into the director's reception room, the secretary looked up at the policeman, the two prisoners, and Sharleen. As she read the badge, she said, "Oh, I'm so sorry. I forgot to call the gate. It has been chaotic around here."

"No problem," Sharleen said brightly. "Here we are."

"The director has been going strong all morning. He's in his office now having a bite to eat."

"It's pretty urgent. Maybe, I could bring him up to speed while he's having lunch. My husband and I are good friends with him." That was a gross exaggeration, but she hoped it would work. Sharleen and her ex-husband had met him several times socially, but she doubted that he would remember her.

The secretary tried to weigh choices. It was her job to protect her boss; yet, she had forgotten to call for the gate pass. Now, here was the director's friend with an El Lago police officer who was not wearing a visitor's badge and two prisoners. She discreetly turned her videophone in the direction of the four people. Once she got them all to fit into the screen, she figured the director could take a look and decide for himself. She overrode the do-not-disturb feature on the phone and interrupted her boss's lunch. "There's a Sharleen Rothwell here."

The director strode out of his office and said, "Sharleen, how good to see you!" She followed him into his office and behind closed doors quickly and concisely told him about the trajectory data and about her full involvement with LandSkyTech. She rapidly described the break-in to her house and how the El Lago police had caught the two men. She discreetly left out any information about how she, Officer Ontiveres, and the two prisoners had gotten onto the JSC grounds. She ended by saying, "Now, one of the prisoners claims to be working for a CIA agent."

The director said, "One of our astronauts was contacted about a month ago by someone who identified himself as a CIA agent. He immediately reported the contact to me. The CIA is investigating the case." What he didn't tell Sharleen was that the CIA and FBI had already set up a command station right down the hall to handle whatever contingencies the day would bring. He figured Sharleen and her prisoners were just such a contingency.

The director thanked Sharleen for her help and suggested she wait outside in the reception room while he got his people to contact all the right authorities.

As the four waited in the reception room, a man who looked like he had more important things to do brought them all soft drinks. Officer Ontiveres immediately recognized the insulated glasses as standard gear to lift fingerprints. As soon as someone held the glass, the prints on the sensitive cylinder, actually a small computer, were transmitted instantly to an international fingerprint bank for computer identification. Often, enough saliva was left on the container to do a DNA check, too. And if they happened to speak, a voice check could be run, too.

"Are you comfortable?" the officer asked his prisoners, trying to get them to talk.

"Of course not," one replied.

"I guess I can take the Siamese restraint off your arms, for now." The officer removed the restraint, which had held the two securely together, left arm to right arm, one at the biceps and the other one right below the biceps.

"Is that better?" Officer Ontiveres asked the one who had not yet spoken.

"Yeah!" the other said. Then he looked at his empty glass and said, "I'd like some more to drink."

The secretary was not getting any calls, which Sharleen thought was strange until she figured someone else must be handling all the calls. Then, she did get one call and waited several seconds before turning on a TV set and swinging it in their direction. Jana Novacek was on the air, reading, looking directly at the audience. Then, Jana's voice faded, and at the bottom half of the screen Commander Jack Medwin made his plea for help. One of the prisoners appeared agitated and looked away from the screen. Sharleen then noticed the way the phone was pointed toward the two prisoners, set up for observing them.

Less than ten minutes after Sharleen, the officer, and the two prisoners had walked into the reception room, although it seemed like a much longer time to Sharleen, a small woman entered the room and said to the two prisoners, "Mr. Ingram and Mr. Young, if you will please follow me, we'd like to ask you a few questions. Officer Ontiveres, you are welcome to accompany us."

The officer stood up, but neither prisoner moved. One of the men appeared visibly shaken when he was mentioned by name, but the other man blandly said, "Are you talking to us?" He then looked suspiciously at his drink container and sat it on a small end table. Suddenly, he leaned forward, swung one foot back, lifted his other knee, and looked like he was ready to bolt from a sitting position, to try for an escape past the small woman at the door. Abruptly, his foot froze in midair and his knee remained lifted as if in a freeze frame.

Officer Ontiveres said to him, "Naughty, naughty."

Sharleen did not know what was going on. The officer said to her, "They've got on wrist, elbow, knee, and ankle restraints, which are totally comfortable, like elastic bandages. However, if I push my remote control or if I say a certain word or if certain other conditions go into effect, then the restraints become rigid and inflexible. Imagine someone trying to run away with his knees locked in one position."

The prisoner said, "You're just crazy with power. Why should I try to run away? I'm being illegally detained."

Sharleen did not see the officer holding a remote control, but she thought it best not to ask questions of that nature in front of the prisoners. Instead, she said to Officer Ontiveres, "I felt safe, at least about the prisoners, that you were well in charge, but I didn't know you had such control over them."

The prisoner said, "Oh, yuck, first you're making out in the elevator, and now this 'sweetie pie' stuff. You're the ones who should be investigated. When you're sued for false arrest . . . ."

Officer Ontiveres smiled slightly to himself before releasing the prisoner's joint restraints.

The woman at the door said, "Mr. Ingram and Mr. Young, neither of you have a criminal record, but we need to talk to you."

Jana's Journal

Inside the *Copernicus*, Jack, Fawz, Lauren, and I were flying in a curved trajectory toward an empty point in space where we would rendezvous with the Jovian system, Jupiter and its more than 100 moons. Once inside that system, we would continue on our trajectory to our destination: Ganymede, the ice planet. Although a moon, it was far larger than our moon and three/fourths the size of Mars.

As we traveled along, our velocity now more than eighty thousand miles an hour and still accelerating, life inside our ship had settled into a pleasant, although busy routine. Every wake cycle we performed scheduled experiments in addition to supplemental tasks that were continuously being sent to us. We kept our ship in perfect shape and took care of ourselves. It was essential for us to exercise every wake cycle so we would not lose bone mass and our muscles would not deteriorate.

Despite the amount of work, I secretly treated this mission like an extended vacation. Of course, I did not mention the vacation concept to my crew or they might not have considered me serious enough. In truth, I always worked as hard as I could.

We did not have the luxury of a standard flight day, because we had to adjust our sleep to accommodate what we needed to observe from specific vantage points. Therefore, the length of our wake cycles and sleep cycles varied. To make the scheduling even more complicated, one person was awake and on duty at all times because we were too far from Houston to count on their getting our data and alerting us in a timely fashion if we had an emergency situation. Because of the time lag, we could be on our own for more than half an hour before Mission Control could help us. The first time I stood watch on my own was truly terrifying. There were two meteoroid programs to protect us from the outside, so I mostly needed to check the gauges to make sure everything inside was functioning properly. Each succeeding watch became a little less terrifying.

On occasion, we recreated. On my personal computer, I showed Fawz the draft paper that Venzi Suzaky had written on space-time discontinuities. I also showed him the timing progressions and background material that Venzi had sent me. Fawz was as fascinated as I was. Sometimes, we read and discussed the material together. We even made up hypothetical situations and tested the effects of applying various timing progressions.

Exercising was vital to our well-being, but it also was relaxing, and I often thought about the aliens that we could encounter. I resisted speaking to my crew about them because JSC had suggested that we not speak much about their possible existence. The NASA psychologists did not want us overly scared about meeting them or too set up for disappointment if we did not. I could not picture Jack, Fawz, or Lauren scared about anything.

At the beginning of the fourth month into our mission, JSC announced we would begin preparations in the event that we encountered living, intelligent beings. Finally, we could talk about the true purpose of this entire mission. We gathered in front of a video terminal and together watched the animated training material that JSC sent us. What would the aliens look like if we were lucky enough to find them? They might appear insect like, perhaps with hard exoskeletons like ants. If insect-like, they would be relatively small, probably smaller than humans. That was simple biology.

They might be so big that we should be careful not to get stepped on. We were not to cower in fear in front of them, but to be brave and self-assured.

"Sure," Lauren said, "as the alien lifts up our lander in its claws and brings us up to its giant eye for examination, we act brave and self-assured."

We were all in a silly, giggly mood, partly from anticipation, partly as relief from the experiments in which we needed to concentrate so intently, and partly glad somebody back there cared enough to provide truly entertaining training.

I blurted out. "I think about this stuff a lot. What will they be like? I know we are supposed to avoid chauvinistic thinking, but I want them to look like us or at least like recognizable creatures. If they're energy fields or balls of protoplasm like giant jelly fish, then that would be difficult for me to relate to."

"Balls of protoplasm couldn't function on Ganymede at minus a hundred degrees. I hope they're like those who visited Fawz's people," Lauren said.

"Suppose they don't exist where we look for them?" Jack asked.

I replied, "That would be a huge disappointment."

"Their non-existence is the likelihood. We must live with that possibility," Jack said. "After all, we'll be the first people on a new planet. It's potentially habitable for humans and close to Jupiter, a great source of energy. That should be more than enough to keep us happy."

Lauren said, "If we had no hope of finding living beings, an unmanned mission would have been much cheaper, and it still would have provided a huge amounts of data. Our governments would not have spent this much money unless someone believed we would find intelligent beings."

"Correct!" Fawz stated. "I am that someone. Your President wants only a safe mission. Yet, even she would be happy if we found abandoned artifacts. Then, we would be needed, particularly you, Lauren, and not machines to read small clues."

We stopped chatting as the etiquette section of the video began. Assuming we made contact, we were to refrain from sudden movements. We were to allow them to get accustomed to us and not force ourselves upon them. Yet, we were to attempt communication. The video again emphasized that we were not to exhibit fear. There was much more.

227

I understood why discussions about our potential encounter had been discouraged. After only one conversation, I was bursting with anticipation. I wanted to be on Ganymede at that moment.

Fortunately, our heavy workload plus the views from the windows helped time pass more quickly. Day after day, I snatched moments to watch Earth although for quite a while, it merely had been a bright star. I watched Jupiter grow larger and larger until one shocking day this giant planet became the largest body in the heavens, even surpassing the sun in brightness.

A private beach, Hawaii, Hawaii

5:00 a.m. Hawaiian-Aleutian Time

Charlie Darwin owned one of the largest lift-off companies, and when he got away, he could afford to really get away. And he liked it that way, no cell phones, no TV, no air conditioning, just his private home on the big island of Hawaii. None of his employees in Houston knew where he was.

Today, he sensed a strange quiet; he peered with his binoculars up and down the beach. Where were the early bird tourists, those waiting for the sunrise, and the energetic tour guides? No one was out, nobody surfing, nobody walking. A few boats were out, but they were not moving. Each appeared to be anchored in place. The presence of boats ruled out a tsunami. Anyway, he had left instructions to be informed if his life were in danger, such as if a hurricane or tidal wave were approaching. He would definitely want to know about an act of nature.

He figured that the caretakers who maintained his house, a husband and wife team who lived in a guesthouse, had cell phones, battery radios and TVs, and maybe even electricity. But they were discreet and did not pierce his illusion of isolation. If they had electricity, the wires were underground.

He stretched out on his recliner on the big loggia that ran completely around the house. He could have found a more remote place, perhaps a small private island, but he was quite fond of this big island. All those miles and miles of black lava appealed to him and made him feel like he was on a distant planet.

What a great day, he thought, for parasailing, trailing ten stories in the air above a speedboat. He visualized himself strapped in a little harness with a full parachute billowing behind him. Yes, he would like that. If he weighed just a little less, well maybe quite a bit less, he would take it up in a minute.

Then he thought of his last project, launched just four days ago, a quirky little assignment, a satellite to study the moons of Saturn, financed with private funds, an odd thing, heavy on guidance, but light on experiments. After they make it to Saturn, then what?

Darwin had said to B. G. Landres, the owner of LandSkyTech, "You've got a sure thing. Saturn's not going away. It won't do anything strange. Saturn's very, very large, and it won't try to evade you. Neither will its moons."

The man had replied, "What about comets and remote things?"

After that, Landres had rescheduled the launch date and, furthermore, insisted on a peculiar trajectory. Darwin's people had questioned him on the trajectory, and Landres had explained that he needed to fly by certain asteroids. The way the customer wanted it would not be cost efficient, but he readily agreed to pay for the next size larger lift-off rocket.

Landres seemed pleasant enough in a superficial way, but he knew so little. Darwin wondered why the parent company, SpaceTech, did not give its subsidiary more help and direction.

On the other hand, maybe Landres was running some type of tax shelter. Perhaps, LandSkyTech was a limited partnership. The general partner would make a huge profit and the limited partners would invest a lot to write off on their taxes. Yes, indeed, the general partner would make a killing. However, Darwin did not think that type of partnership was legal anymore.

Landres wanted the Saturn probe launched, and Darwin Industries earned a great deal of money launching that practically useless thing. Darwin's company routinely provided the total guidance. For shots within the orbit of the moon, his company insisted on providing the guidance, simply for safety's sake. So many things orbited the Earth. It was crowded up there. His company was liable for anything they might run into. Their impact record was zero, and he wanted to keep it that way. However, once three days out and outside the range of the moon, a customer could elect to have some other company take over the guidance. LandSkyTech had elected to take over its own guidance.

The LandSkyTech people had been so concerned about the launch and guidance as if Darwin's people could not handle it. Landres had brought in his own people to oversee Darwin Industries' very competent guidance team. Darwin had soothed his launch team's egos by telling them that the LandSkyTech controllers just wanted to see how professionals handled it.

One of their people, a young fellow named Russell, had marched into his office late one afternoon and had said that it was urgent. Darwin rather firmly suggested that the young fellow go through his own chain of command. "But, sir, it's critical."

"Then, sit down and talk to your own manager about it. Management has to weigh a lot of factors in making decisions and tradeoffs. Do you know what the goals are for this mission?" Darwin had asked.

"Sir, I'm sure I don't understand what any of their goals are, but something isn't right, and I think you should know about it."

"I'm very busy, now." Darwin started rustling papers.

Russell had slumped forward and turned away. Darwin wondered what that young fellow was doing now. He had wanted to advise him to leave that goofy company right away. Darwin had no idea what LandSkyTech's goals were either. He looked for the young man for the next few days in Mission Control but did not see him. Darwin promised himself that he would not accept goofy launches anymore. His was a private company, and he answered to no stockholders.

He remembered the enthusiasm he had starting the company, the shoestring budget, all the government approvals. Now, it was different. He knew what he was doing, how to routinely get government approval for each launch, and how to get business because he had an impeccable track record.

Now, he was losing interest. Maybe he should sell, go start a new business, but what? He was getting bored, almost suffering a malaise. He needed something to get his blood flowing, to get that vigor he once felt. Not a new wife, he had tried that twice, and his third wife was practically perfect. Sometimes, when he was very quiet and very alone, he missed his first wife terribly. His second wife had left him because she considered him a workaholic, and he did not think about her too much, but if the truth were known, he missed her sometimes, too. Once, he compared pictures of the three wives, and they almost looked like the same person, practically interchangeable. Yes, he thought, his taste in women was consistent, but superb.

Even running away from his staff did not give him that little spark anymore. They could find him if they half tried. He had brought his entire staff here once for a brainstorming retreat and then had justifiably written it all off as a business expense. This, he thought, would or should be the first place they would look for him.

He scanned the beach with his binoculars. It was very still, very strange. He went over to his telescope and focused on the horizon. A tour boat that went between the islands seemed to be moving right along. Then, he saw big ships, moving in an orderly way. Darwin swung his telescope inland. He saw not a tour helicopter in the sky. Then, he saw some motion from the guesthouse. The caretaker was sprinting toward him holding something in his hand that looked like a cell phone.

"You have a call, sir," the man said in a rather sheepish voice.

"Thank you," he replied casually, taking a phone for the first time in this house.

It was his general manager Bob Sandstrom calling from Houston. He did not explain how he had tracked him down or apologize for disturbing his vacation. "I believe we have a problem, Darwin. I'm pretty certain we have a huge problem. It's about the satellite we launched four days ago. I'm going to need some decisions on how to proceed, some rather instant decisions. We can CYA, but I think we should play this one straight. We did everything by the book on that last satellite, didn't we, Darwin."

"Yes, as far as I know. There were some clashes between our guidance people and theirs, but there was nothing irregular." Strangely, Darwin began to feel a vigor that he had not felt in years.

"We don't have much time, but I think if you could find a TV, you would quickly understand what is going on."

"Stay on the line with me, Bob."

The caretaker readily admitted that he had a rather large TV set. Darwin followed the man to the guesthouse through a tropical living room into a well-equipped TV/media room. After watching Jana on one half of the screen and Commander Jack Medwin on the other half, Darwin's thoughts raced, quickly analyzing the situation.

"Okay, Bob, I've seen enough."

"Darwin, NASA's been in contact with us, and they think if there is an explosive, then the probe we launched on Tuesday is the most likely delivery vehicle. Darwin, NASA isn't fully convinced that there is a bomb."

"Those astronauts sure seem convinced enough. And why did they take a kid on a mission? And why in heaven's name would she want to encounter an alien intelligence? Well, these questions aren't relevant. What's relevant is can we recover guidance control of the probe?"

"The answer usually is yes. They've put some kind of code in it, and we're having trouble getting control. That would be the best thing, taking control and making damn sure it doesn't come anywhere near the solarship. I've called in everybody who remotely knows how to break code."

"Call LandSkyTech and tell them we need to take over control. Remind them that we have that option in our contract. Tell them to send their guidance people over right away to get this code thing straightened out."

233

"I've been leaving urgent messages all morning on a recorder, but no response. I sent Isabel Halley over to LandSkyTech this morning, and it's all closed up. That's not particularly unusual since today is Saturday. However, we made it clear to them that we might need to reach them anytime."

"When their guidance people were working with our mission controllers, they all had visitor passes. Have you checked that list and tried to call any of them?"

"Yes, I've thought of that already. Isabel called our receptionist who said that the sign-in log disappeared on their last day, so she started a new one. I personally have been through our logbooks, twice. It's not there. Our controllers are trying to remember, too, but all they can remember are first names."

"Bob, listen to me carefully, B. G. Landres seemed very goofy, but he may have had a goal that we didn't realize, to intersect with the solarship and destroy it."

"That thought has occurred to me, too. This morning, Isabel also went to his home address listed in our files, a very nice neighborhood. You're not going to like this. The house was vacant. Isabel did a little snooping with the neighbors and found the house hasn't been occupied for three weeks. Should we ask the JSC people to help us with the code? I'm afraid by the time we orient them to the way we have things set up, we'd be out of time."

"Hold off an hour calling JSC in. They'd probably just be in the way, but at least it would be a gesture of good will. And if we can't figure anything, maybe some JSC person might have a spark of intuition."

"Darwin, is there anything else I should do?"

"Stay on the line a minute or two. I need to think this through." There was something Darwin needed to remember, something he was thinking about before Bob called, a little thing, probably nothing, but it might be important. For the moment, it was irretrievable. "Bob?"

"Yes!"

"You're doing a really fine job. Carry on." Darwin thought how very competent Bob Sandstrom was, competent and loyal. His calls, even including this emergency, were purely for courtesy. Bob did not need him. Sometimes, Darwin suspected that if Bob had not been quite so competent, then he, Darwin, might not have lost interest in the company. However, at this moment in time, he was totally grateful for thorough, competent, calm Bob who probably did not need to feel adrenal steroids coursing through his veins.

Darwin Industries, Houston, Texas
10:02 a.m. CDT

Isabel Halley wanted to help Bob Sandstrom, but she did not know exactly what to do. Bob had told her only that there might be a problem with Tuesday's launch. She knew better than to pester him with questions about what was going on or how she could help. She would be there if he needed her. In the meantime, she was both scared and bored.

She, therefore, decided to play receptionist until Bob thought of another errand or a new task for her. After taking calls from Director Clayton as well as from several other high-ranking people at JSC, she had the eerie feeling that the Saturn probe launched on Tuesday was heading toward rendezvous with the four astronauts on the *Copernicus*. Between calls, through the supernet on her computer, she watched Jana Novacek read her journal and Jackson Medwin issue pleas for help. She was not helping them by watching; maybe she could do something right now.

She ran a computer report on the phone calls that were not being put through to Bob, mostly spouses of the controllers who had been asked to work today. Then, she computer sorted by phone number. Nothing unusual. Next, she sorted by name. A name jumped out at her, Russell Ramsey, with eight calls from six different numbers. The first seven calls were for Darwin, and the final call was for whomever was in charge of "the emergency situation." The last call had grabbed her attention although she remained calm and said she did not know what the caller was talking about. In retrospect, she should have put him through to Bob.

She called Russell's last number. No answer. Yes, she definitely should have put him through. She wondered if the fate of Commander Medwin and that young astronaut Jana hung in the balance. She closed her eyes and silently prayed, "Please, God, let me find Russell and soon. I promise I'll be a good parent to my children. I'll spend lots of time with them. Please let Russell call back."

Various Cities Surrounding Johnson Space Center
10:12 a.m. CDT

Russell Ramsey felt like a six-foot clown dressed like a female, but better to be a live clown, he thought. His girlfriend had helped him get dressed up in this garb, and she had laughed so hard at him that he had almost forgotten his desperate plight.

Since leaving his townhouse that morning, he had changed locations five times and cars four times. If LandSkyTech people were looking for him, at least he had a head start. He had seen the astronauts on the supernet a good ten minutes before they got on TV, because his artist friend, Marge MacInturff, in Seattle had called him about it. As soon as he figured out what was going on, he gathered up the detailed drawings and quickly left his house. He had parked his car a few blocks from his girlfriend's house because he remembered that LandSkyTech knew his license number, too.

His girl appeared totally unconvinced even after he sat her in front of the TV set. "Get some 20-20 vision, Russell. It's probably a foreign power, not the aerospace company you worked for." However, she was good-natured, took down her red living room draperies, and within ten minutes whipped him up a jumper type dress on her high tech sewing machine. She loaned him a big red canvas purse that almost matched his new dress and borrowed a large pair of high heel shoes from a neighbor in her complex. The shoes pinched his toes.

He left his fourth message with Darwin Industries as soon as he got to her apartment and the fifth while she was making up his face. She then trimmed a wig for him. The wig was a ratty blond thing that

238

she had worn to a costume party. "You don't look like Scarlet O'Hara, but it's not bad."

For the first hour of trying to call Darwin Industries, a recorder answered. After that, a rather pleasant woman answered the phone. It was not until the last call that he found out that Mr. Darwin was out of town. He decided to try his luck in person. As he drove over to Darwin Industries in a borrowed car, all types of scenarios went through his mind. He needed to think positively. What did he want the outcome to be? He needed to get past that pleasant phone voice. He thought of various introductions he could make to her. And then would his information be that helpful after all?

Darwin Industries, Houston, Texas
10:17 a.m. CDT

As Russell walked into Darwin Industries, or rather teetered in on high heels, he was surprised that it was unlocked on a Saturday and that he could just go right in. He said to the woman at the reception desk, "My name is Russell Ramsey."

Before he could get one of the various explanations out of his mouth, she merely said, "Mr. Sandstrom is in charge while Mr. Darwin is out of town. I'm sure he'll want to talk to you. Would you please follow me?" She escorted him to a large, though rather austere office. He could not believe it was so easy. He waited several minutes and was forming the idea that maybe she had just deposited him in this office to get him out of her way when a man he guessed was 40 or so breezed in. "How can I help you, Ms. Ramsey?"

"I was here on Tuesday with the Mission Control team from LandSkyTech, and I believe I have some information regarding their probe that may interest you."

Bob Sandstrom raised his brows. He had not paid much attention to those people. The mission manager was handling them, but by golly, he would have noticed a six-foot plus woman with unkempt long blond hair and a husky voice. Bob did not say anything.

"I came across something pretty irregular that concerned me. I tried to talk to Mr. Darwin."

Darwin basically had an open door policy, but Bob did not know if it applied to interlopers from LandSkyTech. "I'm extremely busy today. Maybe you could get right to the point."

Then the phone rang. "Sandstrom here."

It was Darwin from Hawaii. "I've thought of something else. It may not be important, but one of the LandSkyTech people tried to talk to me on Tuesday. Was a nice, clean-cut young fellow named Russell. I told him to talk to his own managers. I looked for him on Wednesday, but he didn't come back. Got to go. There's just one line in the guest house, and I'm expecting a fax from our attorneys. I'm working on a statement, you know, in the event that . . . ."

The line went dead. Bob took a long look at Russell. At this moment, he needed to follow any lead. "Do you usually dress like that?"

"No, hell no, I'm a guy."

Sandstrom was staring at him.

"My girlfriend took down her drapes and made me this, uh, dress. I didn't want anybody from LandSkyTech finding me." Russell could not tell if Sandstrom believed him or not. "I'm sorry, sir. I sound like a nut. Let's start over. Here's my identification, and here is my badge. I came to work here on Tuesday with the LandSkyTech controllers.

"I saw some things that deeply disturbed me. I tried to talk to Mr. Darwin, but he brushed me off. Do you mind if I take off this wig. It's hot and itchy."

Sandstrom nodded. Russell placed the big, blond messy wig on Sandstrom's neat, polished desk.

"I'm mostly a designer of satellites although I've done a little work on probes, so I get this contract job with LandSkyTech. I'll start graduate school in the fall. Right off, I see that they don't know much about what they were doing, but the pay is good so I think I will just help as I can and keep my mouth shut.

"One day, they give me some drawings to check. I see that there are two separate areas of explosives. When I ask about it, I am told that it is for destroying the probe if it goes off course and is likely to cause any damage to other satellites.

"I explain to them that they can't do it that way, that it is too dangerous. I explain how many satellites are circling the Earth, so I computer generate another drawing for them with all the explosive stuff

241

removed. I explain to them the implosion technique, and volunteer to do the drawings and specs for that.

"Mr. Landres himself thanks me profusely. After that, I'm given mostly drawings of the experiments to check until a few weeks ago. Then I am one of the people asked to review the full package of drawings and specs that are to be sent to you. I see that all of the explosive stuff is removed. The implosive material is pretty sloppy, as if it were lifted right from a software package without any customization. So I write them some notes on how to customize it."

"Then on Tuesday they asked me to come here with LandSkyTech's controllers. I'm not a controller. I wasn't sure why I was assigned to go with the controllers, except my name was one of the names on the signed off drawings. It was pretty embarrassing, being with LandSkyTech's bozos monitoring an organization like Darwin Industries.

"Mr. Landres had brought a little stack of notebook computers, and one was handed out to everyone. Of course, Darwin wouldn't let our people hook into your computers. So we just hung over the shoulders of your people and requested what I thought were frivolous changes. I wanted to be out of there. But a job's a job, so I started playing around with the notebook computer assigned to me, but it malfunctioned, so I picked up another one and started playing with it. I got into an area of the computer where I probably wasn't authorized to be. And then I saw drawings marked "FINAL." All the explosives were back in. I figured I was looking at some old version. You know how drawings are marked FINAL until the next iteration comes along. Since I didn't have anything to do, I started enlarging various areas. It seemed like the most current material with the exception of the explosives, but I couldn't be sure without comparing it to material I had back at the office. I wasn't sure why I zoomed in on the signature box, but when I did, there was only one name, mine, and the drawing was dated just three days earlier, the very last day to submit minor changes to Darwin Industries. But I wasn't aware that LandSkyTech had submitted any minor changes."

Listening to Russell, Sandstrom's head began throbbing. Time was running out. He had to stick to the point. Was Russell who he said he was, and did he know the code to enable Darwin Industries to assume guidance control? Sandstrom asked in his blandest tone, "Would you be willing to undergo a security check?"

"I'm already cleared for Global Top Secret," Russell volunteered.

"Would you undergo another one for me?"

"Yes, sir, but isn't time of the essence?"

"This won't take long. It's my new toy. Please walk around my desk to my computer." Sandstrom brought up a screen called Instant Security Check. A full sized shape of a hand appeared on the screen. "Place your hand over that hand print, say your name into the computer, and then read the words on this card."

Russell placed his hand on the screen and then spoke clearly to the computer. "Russell Ramsey. I am voluntarily undergoing this security check with Darwin Industries for the purpose of potential employment." Within a minute, his photo along with a complete biography came on the screen.

"Neat." Russell said.

Bob decided that Russell was who he said he was and indeed very young, younger than his chronological years indicated. To be doubly sure, Sandstrom found the retinal scan device in his desk drawer and plugged it into his computer. Russell readily agreed to take the retinal scan. That confirmed his identity. "And now you have Global Top Secret, again. Would you like me to read you the responsibilities?"

"No, not now. Is there any way that I can help you?"

"For security reasons, we want to assume control of the probe's guidance. However, the LandSkyTech people have put a security code into the guidance which we so far have been unable to break."

"They won't tell you the code?"

"You're the first person from LandSkyTech that we have reached so far."

"I'm sorry, I don't know anything about the code. I do know that there was a code and that some mission controllers were upset that they didn't have it. I'm sorry, sir. I was hoping I could be of some help to you."

"Do you know the names of the mission controllers?"

"Oh, yes, I'll give you all of their names."

Russell keyed the names and any other information he could think of into the computer, and Sandstrom immediately added, "Isabel, these are the LandSkyTech controllers. Find these people and get them to come in A.S.A.P." He sent her the e-mail marked "urgent."

"It's possible that I might have a lead on the code," Russell said. He reached into his big red canvas purse and pulled out large 22 by 28-inch drawings that were hastily folded and then folded again. "These were the drawings that I found on that notebook computer on Tuesday. I copied them onto a storage stick that I had with me. I went to an all-night copy store and printed them out that night. See, on each of these in the corner is a small black mark. I pulled it up on the computer and enlarged it. It became a solid black lizard." He ruffled through the sheets and showed Sandstrom an enlargement of the black mark. "See, it's a lizard. The code could have something to do with that."

"Do you think the lizard simply could be a company logo? Have you seen it anywhere else?"

"That symbol wasn't on any prior drawings. The first drawings it showed up on were from that notebook computer on Tuesday. Anyway, a lizard would be an odd logo for an aerospace company."

Sandstrom spoke the name "Eric" into his phone. When a voice responded, he said, "Eric, the code might have something to do with a lizard. Come up here a minute, will you, and tell me what you think." Then to Russell, he said, "Just to rule out the obvious, we've already computer checked the words from a standard dictionary and as well as a standard collection of proper names and places. First, of course, we tried any combinations that were personal to LandSkyTech, the street it was located on, the day the company was formed, any information on the owner."

Russell said, "Now, I remember seeing that lizard once before. I walked past Mr. Landres's office late one afternoon. The sun from the window behind him reflected his computer screen on an adjacent wall where there was a glass-covered picture. The reflection from the computer monitor was a large red lizard. I thought it so strange that as rushed as this job was that the owner was playing with clip art.

Eric bounced into Sandstrom's office and said, "I've already got somebody working on the word 'lizard,' like 'onelizard,' 'twolizards,' 'redlizard,' 'bluelizard.'"

Sandstrom said, "It would be nice if it were as easy as "redlizard." He then introduced Eric to Russell, who had forgotten he was wearing a red dress and makeup.

In a totally nonplused manner, Eric said, "I remember you from Tuesday. You were the only LandSkyTech person who wasn't harassing our controllers."

Russell showed Eric the small black mark on the corner of the drawings and then the blow up of the lizard. He also told Eric about the large red lizard he had seen reflected from the computer screen.

Eric leapt into the air. "The passcode could be the computer instructions needed to generate the lizard."

"Then we'd have a real mess on our hands," Russell said.

"Unless, unless we knew the software package used to generate this lizard. If we knew the package, then we'd need to experiment with the size and color. They probably would have shrunk down the lizard to simplify the passcode. Otherwise, the passcode would be far, far too long and cumbersome.

Russell was nodding in agreement. "They had the usual software around."

"We'll go through our libraries of clip art and see if we could find the lizard that matches."

"Or we could work backwards," Russell suggested, "creating a passcode to match the lizard."

"Then we'd have to experiment with the various formats for creating a graphic. We might be able to discard the older methods like bit maps and cgm files."

Sandstrom liked their enthusiasm but he wasn't convinced the lizard had anything to do with the code. He felt it was a slim lead. "How long would this take to check out?"

Eric said, "If we're very lucky and if we find the right software package and the right clip art, then we could take guidance control before the expected impact."

"Go ahead and get started on this lizard thing. Call in anybody you think can help you."

"I'll need Russell's help on picking out the shade of red," Eric said.

"Sorry, that was almost a month ago. It seemed like a deep red. It wasn't this red of my, uh, dress. I can't say that I remember the shade."

Sandstrom said, "I need to talk to Russell now. Eric, go ahead and get started."

Eric bounced out of the room singing, "Lizard, lizard, burning bright, how were you created in the night?" Sandstrom and Eric heard his footsteps echoing in the corridor as he ran down the hall.

Sandstrom leaned across the desk to Russell. "Is there anything else you remember that could be important?"

"There is one thing. I don't think it would make any difference in the end, but I may be able to deactivate the explosives."

"That's vitally important assuming they did put explosives back in." Sandstrom was beginning to feel a little agitated. He did not like that feeling; he liked being in control of himself. He breathed deeply to calm himself down. "How could you deactivate the explosives?"

"When I first saw the explosives in the diagram, before I spoke to Mr. Landres, I went to my line manager, and he said that was the way it should be. I thought there needed to be some sort of safeguard. I talked to the programmer who had written the program for the explosives and suggested some precautionary measures. She seemed a pretty agreeable type, and I sat right down at her computer and programmed in some safeguards. I put in a password for myself, too, so I could get in there, if necessary. If nothing has changed in that subroutine, then I should be able to deactivate the explosives, assuming we can send a message to the probe."

"We can't control the probe, but we're certainly tracking it and we certainly can send a message."

"I don't understand, sir, what good would deactivating the explosives do? If the probe impacts the solarship, the ship will explode anyway."

"Probably. These solarships are made to withstand impacts of micrometeorites," Sandstrom said, thinking aloud. Russell was probably right. The probe was more than 18 inches in diameter. How could a solarship endure something like that? To Russell, he said, "Don't underestimate the astronauts. They're not just sitting around, waiting for impact. They're planning for their survival."

Sandstrom mentally reviewed the situation. In the first place, the probe might not be heading for impact with the solarship at all. In the second place, taking over control made good business sense. In the third place, deactivating explosives if they indeed existed made good business sense, too. Could he trust Russell?

It would be easy enough to find out if the probe they launched matched the drawings provided by LandSkyTech. As a matter of course, Darwin industries x-rayed and took holographic photographs of everything it launched. The company did this for its own protection. The pictures were then filed away in the computer system. If anything went wrong, the computer generated photographic images could be compared with the final drawings provided by the customer. Sandstrom turned away from Russell to his computer and opened the files of the final drawings submitted by LandSkyTech; he then pulled the holographic pictures and x-rays that Darwin Industries had taken of the probe.

Sandstrom would have no trouble comparing Darwin Industries' photographic images with the drawings submitted by LandSkyTech. Working with two totally different programs absorbed him to the point that for a few seconds he blocked out Russell and the urgency of the whole situation. He adeptly took many steps, but he basically gave several ADJUST commands to make the two programs compatible with each other. This was followed with several COMPARE commands.

Within a few moments the computer had sorted out the differences. The only difference was exactly what Russell had suggested, circuits leading to explosives. They seemed to match the drawings that were spread out on his desk. To check whether the drawings with the lizard in the margin were precisely the same, Sandstrom put Russell's storage stick into his disk drive and compared the drawings with the probe. An exact match!

He swung the monitor around so that Russell could see the match. Russell slumped forward and said, "That's what I was afraid of."

Sandstrom had another idea. "Could you make the Saturn probe explode on demand?"

"No, that's protected with a security code. I think it's the same code that protects the trajectory."

"What can you tell me about LandSkyTech's Mission Control?"

"Can't help you there. I haven't seen it, but I've heard that it's very compact."

Sandstrom's instincts said to fully trust Russell, but he knew he must proceed with care. He must move very fast and very carefully. He took Russell down the hall to his own Mission Control and teamed him up with a fast thinking controller, who would observe every step and be able to cancel any questionable instruction that Russell sent to the probe.

After he got Russell started on the deactivation of the explosives problem, Sandstrom checked up on a totally different problem that he had assigned to two controllers. He had asked them to plot the location of LandSkyTech's Mission Control based on the location of the guidance signals coming from Earth. If the signals were not shielded in any way, Darwin's controllers should be able to get an exact location. A Mission Control usually had minimum shielding for its signals, which meant Darwin's people could zero in on a two or three block radius. He then visualized helicopters from above searching for the location. Once the location was found, he planned to merely drive over to LandSkyTech's Mission Control and ask for the passcode.

But his controllers reported to him that the location was changing. That meant it was a mobile Mission Control unit, which was not too unusual, but why would it be moving around during a mission unless it was trying to evade being found. By moving around, LandSkyTech ran a risk of being less accurate. Under the current situation, a lack of accuracy sounded like something to hope for. However, it did not make sense for them to be driving around unless they had locked onto a target. And they would be too far from any target unless it was indeed the solarship.

It was time to report to Darwin. Sandstrom spoke the caretaker's number into the phone, and the phone blinked PROCESSING. Sandstrom thought more highly of Darwin than anybody he knew. Darwin had the uncanny knack of picking people who worked well together and were not backstabbers. Sandstrom marveled as to how Darwin did it. Just what were Darwin's hiring techniques? After all these years, Sandstrom still did not know.

Sandstrom was grateful to Darwin for giving him a job. He had been miserable with his first job out of college. So many of his coworkers had seemed like a band of cutthroats. Then Darwin had hired him, and the company Darwin Industries was so infinitely different. There was a real feeling of camaraderie. Darwin personally acted as his mentor, grooming him, teaching him, but Sandstrom still did not fathom all that Darwin knew. Darwin had an uncanny ability for understanding people.

Sandstrom's thoughts came back to the problem at hand. He did not see how anything could turn out well unless they were extremely lucky. If there were enough time, they could break the code.

He knew in his heart he would take the heat for Darwin. He would resign, if necessary, and shoulder the blame himself. He wondered if he would go to prison, if somehow there had been a criminal offense or negligence on the part of Darwin Industries. He hoped it would not come to that. He liked his job a lot. He liked coordinating the pieces, like a giant jigsaw puzzle. Today would be almost enjoyable if he had not seen Jana Novacek on TV.

Sandstrom liked proceeding in an orderly fashion; it saved time in the long run. He was certainly capable of doing a slipshod job, but it always came back to be redone. No way could today be handled right. It would be only as well as he was capable of doing. He never thought of himself as particularly bright, just extremely well organized, and someone who could see the forest as well as the trees, someone who could see the big picture and act decisively.

The phone was still processing. He pushed the HELP button and a recorded voice said, "Phones all over the world are experiencing an unusually high number of calls. We are processing the calls in the order received."

Sandstrom wondered if Darwin knew the miracle he had created with Darwin Industries, a place people really liked to work. When an employee got bored, which professionals often did, Darwin knew what to do. He watched the arc: the person learned his job, gained proficiency, and eventually became bored. He utilized that employee's expertise in a different position. The employee again was happy, and Darwin benefited from a knowledgeable person. If a suitable position were not available, Darwin used his connections to find that person a job with another company. As these people rose in power in their new companies, they did not forget what Darwin had done for them. He exercised his skill so naturally that Sandstrom wondered if he knew what tremendous ability he had.

Although the two worked closely together, they led their own lives outside of work. Sandstrom noticed a twinge of sadness and restlessness in Darwin, but he did not broach the subject to his friend. They did not discuss personal problems with each other. He felt it would be crossing a line that should not be crossed.

Sandstrom knew he did not have the time to dwell on these personal reflections, but up until this day, there was no indication that his very pleasant life would change, that something might go very wrong with Darwin Industries. He shook his head back and forth and relegated all these thoughts to a little cubbyhole in his brain. These thoughts would not and could not get in the way of his job.

He pushed the HELP button again. A different recorded message responded, "If this is not an emergency, please terminate your call."

Then, his mission controllers who were seeking the location of LandSkyTech's Mission Control called him again. "The mobile unit has stopped, or it has slowed down considerably. We estimate now that it's in the location of Westheimer and Post Oak, give a mile or so in any direction. It's been pretty stable for the last few minutes."

"Can you get the range any closer?" Darwin asked.

"We should be able to; however, LandSkyTech has the strongest shields possible on the signals they're sending; we're having to bounce off the probe itself to locate the source. That's causing some distortion. We'll keep working on it."

Sandstrom wanted to talk to Darwin first before calling JSC, but now there were too many developments. He needed JSC's help. He left the call to Darwin processing in queue and called JSC on another line. Surprisingly, he got right through.

After identifying himself to Director Clayton, to whom he had talked much earlier in the day, he said, "You asked us to check out our recent launches, and I . . . I believe we launched what you're looking for. The Saturn probe we launched for LandSkyTech on Tuesday is heading for rendezvous with the *Copernicus*. We're trying to break the code to take guidance control. We could use your help."

Director Clayton said, "We'll send over our best code breakers immediately. They also have some pretty good techniques for overriding code, too. Hold on while I take care of it."

When the director got back on phone, Sandstrom said to him, "I would recommend changing the trajectory of the *Copernicus*; however, I strongly suspect the LandSkyTech mission controllers would compensate and simply change the trajectory of the Saturn probe. Another thing, the Mission Control is in a mobile unit. We've triangulated the current location to somewhere in the Galleria area. As you know, that's a very crowded part of town on Saturday. We could use some law enforcement help in trying to find it. It's probably in a truck, but it could be in a custom built van."

Director Clayton said, "I just finished talking to a LandSkyTech subcontractor, a woman named Sharleen Rothwell, who somehow had access to our trajectory data. She brought in two other LandSkyTech people who are being questioned right now. They might know what the mobile Mission Control looks like. I'll make sure they're questioned about it. In any case we'll contact the authorities to help us find it."

"Another thing," Sandstrom said, "a LandSkyTech engineer is here trying to deactivate the explosives."

"Could he just blow up the probe now before it gets too close to the *Copernicus*?"

"No, that part is protected through code, the same code, he thinks, that is keeping us from taking over the guidance system. That's why we need your help. It's just a fluke that he may be able to deactivate the explosive system."

When he got off the phone with the JSC director, Sandstrom wished this were a normal Saturday.

Transmission between Houston and Solarship Copernicus

12:00 noon CDT

The four astronauts waited at the main console. Across the cabin, Jack's videos of his pleading for help played over the net. Jana certainly needed a break from reading, but more importantly Jack wanted each astronaut to hear first-hand whatever Houston chose to reveal. He wanted them to judge for themselves.

As Willie's face came into focus, Jack felt relieved that the young CAPCOM had not been replaced by someone more experienced. Jack could trust this young man. How much Willie knew was another issue.

Willie's voice quavered slightly as he announced, "This is the situation, sir. Darwin Industries launched a Saturn probe on Tuesday. The trajectory data you sent us checks out exactly. This probe is on a collision course with your ship. Expected impact is 16:00 today Houston time. Explosives are in the payload. We can deactivate them. So far, this is all we can do. We are working with Darwin programmers to override or break a security code. If we do this soon, we will take control of the probe and destroy it. However, if the probe gets much closer to you, its destruction no longer would be feasible. A debris cloud created from pieces of the exploded probe could pose a great hazard to you. If we take control prior to 1600, we will simply change the probe's trajectory."

As Willie continued speaking, the tone of his voice became bland and neutral as if he did not wish to be judgmental. "You already know the probe's guidance is locked-in on the *Copernicus*. Our data indicates that you have made a course correction and the probe made a corresponding correction."

The fact that Jack had changed the trajectory of the *Copernicus* without either consulting or informing Houston was highly irregular. He decided it would be better to avoid discussion of that topic particularly since he planned to do more without consulting the very people whom until yesterday he trusted. He changed the subject and said, "Darwin is known for its impeccable safety record. I thought those people kept guidance control over whatever they launched."

"They insist on guidance control anywhere inside of the moon's orbit. Then whoever launches with them can continue using Darwin's guidance or not."

"Who is sending us this so-called Saturn Probe?"

"That's the weird thing, sir. It's a subsidiary of SpaceTech called LandSkyTech. But we haven't reached the head person at LandSkyTech, a Mr. Jim Landres."

"Whom have you reached?" Jack asked.

"One person from LandSkyTech contacted us, and another contacted Darwin Industries." Willie glanced down at his notes. "A fellow named Russell Ramsey became suspicious four days ago during the launch of the Saturn probe. When he learned your mission was in trouble, he thought there might be connection. He's a programmer, developer type and has been enormously helpful to the Darwin people.

"A woman who worked for LandSkyTech had plotted some JSC trajectories. The owner had told her it was to talk to 'the astronauts.' I hear she's a friend of Director Clayton and went to him after she saw Jana on TV." Willie referred to his notes. "Her name is Sharleen Rothwell."

"Yes, Sharleen, I remember her," Jack said. "An ambitious woman and very attractive. Not a person one would forget. I think she's been to a reception at my house."

"Then, there's also two ... two ruffians who work for LandSkyTech. They seem to be Mr. Landres' strong-arm men. Rumor around here is that Sharleen captured them single-handedly." Willie stopped talking, and his eyes seemed to glaze over.

"What is it, Willie?" Jack asked.

"Oh, nothing, another rumor, just something weird those ruffians are supposed to have said." Willie squirmed and turned his head away from the camera.

Under normal conditions, Jack would not have pushed, but he needed every clue for evaluation. "I have a need to know," Jack stated.

"Supposedly, they said that their boss—Mr. Landres—worked for the CIA. That's completely untrue and ridiculous. Both the CIA and the FBI are here on-site right down the hall from Director Clayton, trying to help us." Willie assumed his CAPCOM identity, which he had momentarily lost. "We are working the problem, sir. Do you need to know anything else?"

"How did Landres get NASA flight trajectories that he gave to Sharleen?"

Willie ruffled through his notes. "We think it happened like this. An employee right here at JSC named Jerome Westlake was the system administrator for the third-level backup of your projected flight trajectory to return home. He stole the data by copying onto his personal mass storage drives. He stated that he stole trajectory data on many occasions. When he saw Jana on TV this morning, he called his supervisor and confessed.

"He claims that he declassified some of the material by rotating the data points ten degrees. Then, he used the new data to test out a trajectory program he had written. We do know his apartment was burglarized. A professional job, too. A police report corroborates that. He claims these storage drives were stolen from him during the burglary. However, there is a possibility he gave them to a contact."

"That doesn't make any sense, Willie. For starters, JSC protects trajectory data, particularly on-going missions and most particularly our mission."

"I know that. Yet, projected trajectory data for your return mission most likely were stolen." Willie looked down at his notes. "Westlake is being cooperative. He's concerned about Jana's safety. Apparently, he saw her several times in the cafeteria here on-site, I guess, while she was in training." Willie cracked a slight smile. "Westlake timed his lunch breaks, hoping to see Jana. He wanted to ask her out, but couldn't even figure out how to start a conversation."

"Bet you never had a problem like that, Willie." Jack said.

"No sir, can't say that I ever had," Willie said, drawing himself up. "I'm sorry sir, I didn't mean to ramble. It's just that I wanted you to know your broadcast is helping."

"Has anyone else come forward?" Jack asked.

"Not that I know of." Willie checked his computer. "Darwin Industries has been trying to reach several LandSkyTech controllers."

"It would be a good idea to make a TV announcement asking any LandSkyTech people who worked on the Saturn probe to call you."

"Yes, we can take care of that."

"You'll need a dedicated phone number, three or four lines, and some people to screen the calls who know the situation and know what the code breakers are looking for."

"That is a good idea." Willie wrote a note and handed it to someone outside of Jack's field of vision. He then wrote more into his computer. "As soon as we get that number set up, we'll send it to you for your net broadcast. Is there anything else?"

"Call in SpaceTech high level executives familiar with their LandSkyTech subsidiary. Find out what they know that could be immediately helpful."

"I think that's already being done, but I'll check into it." Willie keyed more into his computer and then looked into his camera and said, "So many employees came to work today and offered their help.

Practically everyone from Mission Control is here. I don't know totally everything that is happening. A lot is going on concurrently."

"Is Max Marsh around?"

"I saw him a little while ago."

"I'd feel better if he were deeply involved in everything."

"Sir, we realize how highly you trust Max's abilities. We'll see that he's totally involved."

"Thank you."

"Sir, I'm sorry about all of this. We're doing the best we can."

"I know you are, Willie. Tell me, what are the contingency plans?"

"You mean if we are unable to take control . . . if, if you sustain a hit?" Willie squirmed and then said, "The plans are fluid right now, sir. We have another JSC team at Darwin Industries checking out the probe's capabilities."

"Willie, some of our people must be working on a plan now, regardless of the probe's design."

Willie stared into the camera as if waiting for Jack's words. Jack had the timing of the transmission down perfectly and knew Willie already had heard. He even had ample time to respond. Willie fidgeted, but he neither checked his notes nor looked into his computer.

Jack looked to his crew for their reaction. They had been silently sitting on each side of him intently listening as they observed Willie's image on the screen. Lauren silently mouthed the words, "He doesn't want to tell us."

Jack said, "Willie, we have a need to know the current contingency plans."

Jack carefully watched Willie who still did not check his hand-written notes nor look into his computer. He did not even turn his head to call someone over who would know the plans. Willie already knew! He said, "One idea is to launch the lander with two of you aboard. Two would stay aboard the *Copernicus*. If one vehicle took a direct hit and sustained damage, our hope would be that two in the intact vehicle would survive the dust cloud and rescue the other two. This plan has

257

many variations. Unless we take over the probe's guidance control pretty soon, we'll select the best plan and make launch decisions for the lander. If we take control of the probe before impact, then the lander can rendezvous with the *Copernicus* or land independently at a moon base."

"I see," Jack responded. "You do know that the lander had been reinforced. Make sure the technical people have all the specs that we downloaded?"

"I'll find out." Willie wrote a note and handed it to someone "Sir, when our plans are more firm, we will welcome your input and your suggestions. We are here for you, sir, you know that."

"I hope so, Willie, I truly hope so."

"Anything else we can do for you?"

"Just one more thing. Save our lives."

"We want to. Believe me, we want to."

"I know you do, Willie."

Solarship *Copernicus*

12:20 p.m. CDT

When the transmission with Mission Control ended, three pairs of eyes were glued on Jack. He knew they were all in their own thoughts, just like when they first learned about the possibility of the bomb during their previous wake cycle.

Jack said, "When this is all over, we'll have a big shindig at my house. We'll invite Willie, too. Remember the party when Fawz and Princess Regney were the guests of honor?"

No one responded to such a pleasant recollection. Jack did not have the leisure to allow them to follow through with their own thoughts. It was important, however, for each to briefly express concerns.

Lauren totally ignored Jack's image of a big shindig and said, "The CIA! The two LandSkyTech people said a Mr. Landres, their head man, works for the CIA." Lauren stared at Jack. "I know what you're thinking, Jack. If we survive this day, we'll eventually find out who is doing this to us and why. Now, we must concentrate on the job at hand."

"My exact thoughts, Lauren," Jack said.

"SpaceTech?" Jana asked. "Alan worked for SpaceTech last summer, and we said good-bye at a Gilruth Center expo under a SpaceTech moon." Jana glanced quickly at each crewmember. "We need to get busy, don't we?"

Jack nodded. "If everything goes right, the next moon you share with Alan will be the real one viewed from good old terra firma."

"Fawz asked, "We are not going to wait for Mission Control, are we? We are going to launch the lander on our own, aren't we?" And we are not going to inform Mission Control. Correct?"

Jack nodded, "Under the circumstances, I believe that would be the best to launch really soon, that is, if we are all in agreement."

"I am in total agreement," Fawz said.

"Count me in," Lauren quickly said. "There's too much going on to be passive, even at JSC, like our meteorite detection program being deactivated by someone, possibly that programmer, Denise Morneau, who works for Filbert."

Jana said, "I'm remembering something that happened right before we left on our mission." Jana recalled the waiting room at Cape Kennedy. A person on the other side of a glass wall waved to her. Had Alan come from Houston to Florida to see her off on her secret mission? If so, how had he learned about her mission? He had worked for SpaceTech last summer, and LandSkyTech, a subsidiary of SpaceTech, had launched the Saturn probe. Had the plans for their destruction been underway even before their mission began? In the event their mission was a success?

She looked up and realized that the three of them were staring at her, waiting. No way would she burden her crew with these concerns, not now. Now was not an appropriate time to burden herself, either. Tomorrow, what a lovely word, tomorrow, she would tell her crew. She simply said, "For many reasons, I'm with you."

Fawz rubbed his brambly eyebrows. "The plan Willie told you about is not bad, not bad at all. It would be better if someone piloted the lander. With the lander shielding us, our computer will not have visual contact with the bomb. The computer on the lander will. The person on the lander could make corrections as needed."

"I'll do it. I'll go in the lander." Lauren announced. "You know I'm an experienced pilot, not with Jack or Fawz's heavy piloting experience, but I can certainly follow any instructions given to me from the *Copernicus*."

"That would be a suicide mission," Jack said firmly.

"You all have families." Lauren replied calmly and without emotion. "Jack and Fawz have wives and children, and Jana has Alan."

"You have a man who loves you," Jana blurted out and then hung her head as if she had crossed a boundary and mentioned an issue that all had carefully avoided. Still, something propelled Jana onward into yet more forbidden territory as she softly said, "And you love him, too."

"I have a memory, a magnificent memory," Lauren replied with gentleness in her voice.

"More is still possible. Think about it," Fawz said softly.

"Nobody will fly in the lander," Jack announced firmly. "This topic is not open for discussion." Jack was the commander, and that was that. Jack recognized the strong impact he had whenever he pulled rank, which was only in rare instances since he mostly preferred to achieve a consensus. But, he did not want his crew going down the path of self-sacrifice. Jack was surprised that Fawz had mentioned such an idea. Fawz knew that the computers would do most everything anyway. The bomb and the lander would be moving far too fast for much luck with any manual control. Everything would need to be programmed ahead of time. And the calculations needed to be perfect.

The three were staring at Jack in a state of shock that he had so blatantly claimed his power even though they knew he did that from time to time. He said, "We all have families, that is true, but we four are a family ourselves. We will not sacrifice one of our family members."

"We really are a family," Jana whispered and burst into tears. She blotted her tears really fast but a few still floated into the cabin. "Sorry, Jack. A real astronaut would not have done that."

"Not to appear callous, but a few tears while you read your journal would be a perfect touch," Jack said and patted her shoulder.

Lauren winced at Jack's chauvinistic suggestion, so uncharacteristic of him, but she did not say anything.

Jack spoke to Jana. "When you go back to reading over the net, it will be as important as the lander launch or anything else we are doing. If the terrorists' reason for wanting to destroy us is to keep people from learning about what we found, at this moment they still have that reason. Rumors are floating around, but very few people know our findings. Once you reveal everything, then the knowledge is out there. There may no longer be a reason to kill us."

"You don't need to persuade me, Jack. I'm going to read my journal just like I have been all morning," she replied with a little catch in her voice. Her eyes were still red.

"There's something else, Jana, and it's very important. When we launch the *Falcon*, you must keep reading, no matter what happens. I'll deactivate a few monitors and Mission Control won't know exactly what we're doing, at least not at first. Don't let on that anything is happening."

"You can count on me, Jack. When I read about our mission, I remember how glorious it all has been. I practically forget what a desperate situation we're in."

"When we're in contact with Houston for the next updates, I won't pull you off your reading. We want everyone to know about our mission, particularly if we . . . if we don't make it."

Seattle, Washington

10:35 a.m. PDT
(12:35 CDT)

George MacInturff watched the Commander make one announcement right after another, all slight variations on the same theme. By now George realized they were recorded. He turned off his CD burner. He already had copied each one the first time he heard it interspersed at intervals between Jana reading her journal.

Jana finally returned to the screen. George was pleased to see her. He turned his CD burner back on. Her eyes were red, and there was a catch in her voice, but as she described getting closer and closer to Jupiter day after day, her voice smoothed out, and she eventually regained a bubbly, almost happy tone. After a while, George figured it was past time for another announcement. Had she forgotten to run the Commander's recorded announcement? She seemed completely involved in describing amazing things about Jupiter's magnetosphere. He knew so little about Jupiter.

He swung his chair around, turned to his other computer, and typed in "Jupiter plus photographs." His computer search yielded many choices. He previewed several pictures until he found a magnificent one, all oranges and reds, with big arcs of lightning.

He decided he would like to see Jupiter up close, but that was impossible. Maybe, helping the astronauts survive was impossible, too. He hoped not. The music to the *Impossible Dream* began playing in his head, and he pictured Don Quixote fighting windmills. He tried to block the melody. He needed to stay alert and help them more if he could. He swung his chair back to face Jana on his monitor.

George heard a slight noise, barely audible, above the solarship's background sounds that he had become accustomed to. Jana turned her head ever so slightly and then quickly straightened it so that she was squarely facing into the camera, but her eyes darted twice toward her left. It happened fast, but for a split second, Jana was distracted. As computer security chief for a big Seattle company, George had trained himself to notice the slightest details, things seemingly insignificant.

A number of minutes later, the camera shifted in a jarring manner. Jana's image moved to the right on George's computer screen. The camera shifted again and Jana was partially cut off the screen. The most inattentive person watching would have noticed that. Had the *Copernicus* jolted?

She leaned closer toward the screen and. said, "The camera slipped. I'll adjust it." Her face appeared totally emotionless. He decided she was trying to hide her feelings from the camera. Only because he had been watching her all morning did he believe that something really important was happening inside the *Copernicus*. Had he still been looking at pictures of Jupiter while he listened to Jana, he would have missed the whole thing.

He heard another slight noise, the same sound he heard minutes before the camera moved. Shortly after that, the Commander came on the screen, appearing preoccupied or rushed but just for a second. He regained his composure and asked everyone who worked for a company in Houston called LandSkyTech to call a specific number at Johnson Space Center. George thought of companies in Houston, but he did not remember anyone at his meetings of computer security chiefs from a company named LandSkyTech. On his other computer, he pulled up names of the security chiefs and their companies that he had sent e-mail messages to early in the morning. LandSkyTech was not on the list, a new company, perhaps. Yet, that name seemed familiar.

He darted into the adjacent living room where Marge watched the broadcast on a large screen TV. It was not Jack making the announcement but Michael Trubly, the Public Information Officer for Johnson Space Center.

"Marge, does our friend Russell work for a company with a name like that, like LandSkyTech? I wonder if he saw this announcement."

Marge spoke the name "Russell Ramsey" into the phone. "All of the circuits are busy," she said and waited. "Now, there's no answer. Peculiar, you'd think he'd be watching. Russell seemed so interested this morning when I called him. He thanked me profusely. I'm pretty sure LandSkyTech is his company."

"I like to think he is helping Jana," George said, suddenly feeling uplifted and hearing music in his head again.

Marge picked up her sketchpad and a conte pencil and did several sketches of Jana and the way she held her head. Then, Marge concentrated on individual features, various sketches of the eyes, as Jana glanced down at her notebook computer, and then straight-ahead facing the camera. "Can you imagine this astronaut Jana against the background of Jupiter, so you don't see any of the curve of the planet, just the color, backlit behind her? Are there many pictures of Jupiter?"

"Oh, yes, I think there must be thousands of them right on my computer. I found them just a couple of minutes ago. The colors are magnificent."

"The way Jana describes those colors of Jupiter makes me really sad to be colorblind."

"You're not totally colorblind," George said, trying to console here.

"And you will mix the colors for me, the colors of Jupiter?"

"You stayed home for me today. I told you I would mix colors." George couldn't believe his good luck. Marge's interests were expanding.

"When you asked me to miss our ferry ride to Victoria today, I had no idea of the implication of all . . . all of this. It amazes me. It's all because of you, George, that they're on TV everywhere."

"Maybe," he replied. He liked the way she studied him, with sheer, unabashed admiration, but she deserved credit. "You called the TV stations. You convinced them to put the astronauts on television. I couldn't have done that. And you called Russell."

Yet, George thought, in the final analysis, none of the publicity mattered if the astronauts could not save themselves or if NASA would not or could not save them. Did NASA want to save them, he wondered?

It was sad enough thinking of Jana not seeing the love of her life Alan ever again. But how would Marge respond? Marge had just stumbled onto a whole new subject for her art. He did not want her hurt.

He sat down next to Marge and listened as Jana explained scientific experiments regarding Jovian weather. Across the bottom of the TV screen marched a banner with the general JSC number for anybody who had any information and the special JSC number for LandSkyTech people.

He left Marge happily sketching in the living room, seemingly unaware that what the two of them had done together might not be enough, not enough at all to save the astronauts. He returned to his computer room.

As he listened to Jana, her voice sometimes bubbly and other times sad as if she suddenly remembered where she was, he was beginning to understand why someone would want her information suppressed. What she described now was astounding. Yet, by a sheer act of will, he forced himself to stop listening because there was something more he could do for her, something important he should tell her, but what? It was not a seemingly trivial thing that only George or someone with his training could recognize as significant. No. This was something obvious to anyone. Then he realized. Right in front of him on his computer monitor, there was no banner with numbers to call as there was on TV. A LandSkyTech person easily could have missed the Commander's message.

George would make a banner and send it to them. No, they would be crazy to take software from anyone. Especially in their circumstances!

He typed a message to the *Copernicus*. "Jana, you need a banner with both JSC phone numbers. Good luck from your friend in Seattle, George."

Jana's Journal

At nine million miles out from Jupiter, we flew into the bow shock, an ever-shifting boundary where the solar winds crashed into Jupiter's magnetosphere, a magnetic cocoon that enveloped Jupiter and protected this giant planet and most of its moons from the sun's solar radiation. As the solar winds attacked the magnetosphere, it responded and shoved back, continuing an unending, powerful dance for domination. The confluence of these two invisible electrical forces tossed the *Copernicus* like an insignificant twig. Fortunately, we felt nothing too unusual.

A sound similar to static quickly increased inside our cabin. Because of our equipment, the cabin was a noisy place anyway, but the static soon drowned out the other sounds. Were one or more of our instruments dying? As soon as we flew into the bow shock, every instrument on our ship was in danger of burning up due to the abundance of fast moving electrical particles.

"This is it," Jack said.

He seemed ever so calm. Was this the end for all of us and was there nothing Jack could do about it? We were so close to achieving our goal of putting down on Ganymede, Jupiter's biggest moon. We were less than a week away. Jack and Fawz were at the controls, but our ship continued to fly on an autopilot that was supposed to respond instantaneously to the ever-changing electrical turbulence. They were both studying the controls, and I knew they could take over manually at any time. I held my breath waiting for one of them to take action. Were they frozen into inaction?

Finally I asked, "What should we do?"

"There's not much we can do," Jack replied.

I decided I should say goodbye to my crew. I was trying to frame my thoughts when Jack added, "I'm also surprised that this sound is so loud. It's not a radio that we can turn off. It's the sound of a magnetosphere, and this one happens to be very large. Ear plugs might help a little."

I regained my composure as quickly as I could. Now, I remembered that a magnetosphere had a signature sound similar to static. I found some earplugs and handed them out to the crew. The plugs slightly softened the noise.

I was so relieved that we were okay. Completing this journey through the bow shock would take two or as many as three Earth days. It would be like flying inside a galactic tidal wave that could suddenly reverse its direction.

We took medication and wore monitors so Houston could evaluate how well our medication worked and how we physiologically handled this invisible turbulence. I received a message on a medical channel from Dr. Keenan, our physician, telling me to breathe normally, not to hold my breath any more, and to please take more medicine if I had not already done so within the last hour. All attached to monitors as I was, how easy it was for Dr. Keenan to recognize me as an imposter, who by luck and guile had gotten on this mission.

Last summer, Dr. Keenan had allowed me to take an extra treadmill test because I had told him about my endurance. If not for that test, I could not have been selected to train as an astronaut. Even as we now faced this danger, I still was grateful to him. After I took the additional medicine, I became far less concerned about our plight.

Jack, Lauren, and Fawz thrived on this danger. It was food for their souls and sheer pleasure they would cherish always. They were astronauts to the core, and to them this was a bonus added to the enjoyment of traveling in space for the preceding five months. As much as they loved this extreme danger, they were equally careful and paid strict attention to the monitors. Much less danger would have suited me fine. I had exceeded any need for it by a factor that I could not calculate.

I ranked my crew on a danger scale. Jack went over the top, Lauren required it to a lesser degree, and Fawz liked danger more than I but not as much as Lauren. I wanted to be as brave as they were.

I did excel in a different area. Although Fawz, Jack, and Lauren were in excellent physical shape, I had more stamina. I did not tire out as quickly as they did probably because of my youth. After that realization, I promised myself that I would protect them whenever and however I could. They needed to stay healthy and strong, particularly now that within an Earth week we would put down on the surface of Ganymede. At least, that was our plan if everything went well.

My thoughts drifted. I fondly reminisced on the daily routine in space for the preceding five months. It all was so pleasant, doing scientific experiments, even doing the housekeeping chores, exercising, meditating, and studying the Jovian system, which meant Jupiter, its weather, all the numerous moons that rotated around it, everything in the magnetosphere, and most particularly Ganymede.

I thought of the computer people who made our mission possible: engineers, developers, and programmers who had designed, written, tested, retested, revised, and revised again our navigational and communications programs. I doubted if even Max knew every person involved. More importantly, I wondered if Max was fully familiar with every program that the *Copernicus* needed.

Jack, Fawz, and Lauren were all so incredibly trusting. I guess I was, too. We trusted our lives to the computer people and to all the other NASA workers and contractors who envisioned, designed, fabricated, or simply purchased and tested the millions of the other parts that came together in systems that allowed us to survive.

The astronauts of this century and the previous one had prepared the way for us with their bravery, and some had paid the ultimate price in the Apollo I, Challenger, and Columbia disasters. Although no astronauts had flown through the bow shock before us, it comforted me to know many unmanned space vehicles successfully had crossed into Jupiter's magnetosphere including Pioneer 10 and 11 and Viking 1 and 2 in the last century and the Galileo Jupiter Probe early in this century.

We, however, were the first living beings to cross the bow shock. No, what was I thinking? If Fawz's cylinder had been correctly dated and correctly interpreted, then alien beings whose descendants might still live on Ganymede had gone before us. Aliens with unusual sounding names like Chri Anri had visited Rhatania 500 years ago. They told Fawz's ancestor they were from Ganymede. On the cylinder they described the orbit of Ganymede around Jupiter, and that was before the time of Galileo, who discovered Jupiter's four largest moons in 1610.

As I was coming out of my reverie, Jack invited me to co-pilot with Fawz. I was so thrilled with the offer that I tried my best not to grovel. After that, Lauren and I took turns copiloting with either Fawz or Jack as the pilot so all of us could have our sleep cycles and meals. Even though we rode on autopilot, we constantly were ready to take over if necessary. Jack joked with Lauren and me and said it would certainly look good on our resumes that we had co-piloted through Jupiter's bow shock. The idea of a resume make me think that we would survive and be alive.

At seven million miles out, our monitors indicated that the electrical turbulence had died down. We had crossed the bow shock. It seemed like a time for celebration until I heard Jack say to Fawz that we would wait and see.

We did not wait long until the bow shock smashed into us from behind and continuously rolled over us. The solar winds had gained in the violent dance with the magnetosphere, and again we found ourselves enmeshed in their conflict. The magnetosphere fought back and advanced on the solar winds. We were dragged away from Jupiter as our ship rode a tsunami of charged particles. I consoled myself in knowing there was no craggy coastline to smash into, only more wind.

I held my breath and willed the *Copernicus* and all of its equipment to hold together.

Jack and Fawz were at the controls at that moment. I was glad. I overheard snippets of their conversation. Their words had urgency about them, but their voices and demeanor were as calm as if they were practicing on a simulator.

This was a galactic dance without end. Fortunately, it eventually ended for us after plowing through electrical turbulence for three million miles and for nearly three Earth days. Immediately thereafter, we ran diagnostics on every piece of equipment on our ship. Only after all of our equipment checked out A-Okay did Jack call Houston. He simply stated, "We have crossed the bow shock. We are inside Jupiter's magnetosphere."

Lauren exclaimed, "I've never been so scared. I loved it."

To all of us, Jack said, "Now, we have just gone through one of the most challenging phenomena that the solar system can throw at an astronaut. Nothing on the entire Mars I mission compared to this."

I felt as if Jack were talking directly to me. He knew exactly the right comments to uplift me and not make me feel like such a rookie. Yet, what he said was true.

Jack seemed disappointed to be finished with the dance of the electrical particles, but we were not out of harm's way by any means. While the Earth's magnetosphere shielded its creatures, Jupiter's environment boasted of large magnetic fields and charged particles zipping about wildly. This dangerous environment inside Jupiter's magnetosphere resulted in part from the ongoing game Jupiter played with Io, the closest of the four large moons. The game eventually would end with Jupiter destroying Io. In the millions of years before that doomed moon's demise, large, sulfurous volcanoes on Io would violently interact with Jupiter.

Now that the sound of static was much softer, the relative quiet inside our ship relaxed me. The bow shock danger was the prerequisite for the natural panorama of Jovian weather intensifying before us. We were six million miles from Jupiter, and with the naked eye this giant planet displayed itself like a brilliant gemstone appearing about twice the size of a full moon as viewed from Earth. I clearly saw the great red spot and three white spots accented against muted horizontal stripes and bands of color. The doomed moon Io cast a small dark shadow on Jupiter's surface. However, we no longer saw the other three great Galilean moons that orbited in lockstep with each other, Ganymede, Europa, and Callisto. They already had disappeared behind Jupiter, but in two-and-a-half days when they returned, we would rendezvous with Ganymede.

Houston barely gave us time to rest up from crossing the bow shock before we became inundated with messages regarding our scientific experiments. Many more people at JSC in Houston now were working with us. On several channels, photographs and various measurements were continuously being sent to them. Houston was seeing what we saw with only a 30-minute lag because of our great distance from Earth. How long, I wondered, could the existence of our mission continue being a secret?

Mostly, the people receiving the pictures and measurements were weather scientists with Top Secret clearances. They were told that our purpose was to set up equipment on Ganymede to monitor Jupiter. That was the truth as far as it went. They knew nothing about our major goal of finding living beings or artifacts to prove that living beings once had visited or lived on Ganymede.

Ganymede was a sensible choice as a place to set up equipment. Io was too close with sulfurous volcanoes and chemical interactions with Jupiter. On Io, the monitoring equipment eventually would get fried not to mention what might happen to humans who tried to set up the equipment. Europa could be evolving its own life, and many scientists thought we should not interfere. As for Callisto, it was considerably further from Jupiter. That left Ganymede. If our mission became more widely known, no one would suspect the main reason why Ganymede was picked.

As we drew closer, Jupiter became ever more spectacular. Great flashing zigzags of lightning dominated swirling storms and accentuated brilliant chemical reactions that for centuries held themselves separate from each other like colorful vegetables boiling in a great planetary stew. Because Jupiter rotated on its axis more than twice as fast as the Earth did and because the great storms came and then disappeared, the view before us constantly changed. There were times when we detected no electrical storms anywhere in our view.

Had Jupiter been much larger, it would have been another star orbiting the sun, and the solar system would have been a double star system like so many other stars in the galaxy. As it was, Jupiter boasted its own large family of more than 100 moons that orbited around it. Some were even outside of the magnetosphere.

Our meteoroid detection program indicated a moon was in our vicinity, but we were in no danger of a collision. Fawz thought we should be able to see it with the naked eye "if we keep looking in that direction." He pointed out the window.

"There is it!" exclaimed Jack.

I saw a little speck in the distance. Our meteoroid program estimated that it was the size of a mountain. We magnified the image with one of our telescopic cameras until it looked like a huge rock. Unexpectedly, it briefly turned orange.

"Look at that baby. It's reflecting light from Jupiter. That'll give our weather people in Houston a nice bonus," Jack said.

After we could no longer see it, Fawz researched when it was discovered.

During my next wake cycle, we crossed into an area called the Lion's Roar where we heard distinctive sounds of celestial music similar to a mildly discordant classical symphony. As with the static, these sounds also came right through our ship. The music was cerebral rather than emotional, and it did sound like a lion roaring. Even though I liked the pleasant sound, it gave me a slight headache.

After we crossed out of the Lion's Roar, I caught my first glimpse of Ganymede. It was so very bright because of the reflective ice covering its surface. The ice was estimated to be 500 miles thick. After all this traveling, now, there it was, waiting for us.

I contemplated its grandeur as we descended through Ganymede's magnetosphere. We again heard the static-like sound, only much softer than before. Because Ganymede's protective magnetosphere was far less powerful than Jupiter's, we had few worries about damage to our electrical systems.

Magnetospheres are a rare commodity in the solar system, and Ganymede benefits from two. The big outer one around Jupiter and most of its moons provides protection from the sun, and the smaller, far less-powerful one around Ganymede provides protection from Jupiter. No wonder the beings that visited Fawz's ancestors 500 years ago could live on Ganymede. They essentially were wrapped in two cocoons of protection from radiation. Too bad, I thought, that the cocoons did not offer much temperature protection, but our heated space suits would handle the cold.

Since Ganymede had a thin, wispy atmosphere, we experienced no problems with entry. We had minimal worries about bouncing off the atmosphere or burning up from heat and friction.

Soon, I became aware of Ganymede's incredible size. It was the largest moon in the solar system, twice as big as our moon, and equivalent in size to planets: larger than Pluto, and three-fourths the size of Mars.

As we flew closer, Ganymede's incredible splendor surpassed that of Jupiter. It was not multicolored like Jupiter but elegant in a stark way, a study in grays, lights, and darks with some brighter patches and rays of light. There were similarities to Earth in that it had lots of ridges.

Ganymede was made of two distinct areas, an older one that was full of craters indicating meteorite impacts and another one that geologists called deformed, which simply meant the skin of the moon had undergone some stretching, leaving rectangles pulled apart from each other, which from the air looked something like city blocks. On the side full of craters, the ice was darker. On the side with great stretch marks and deformations, the ice was much lighter.

At thirty miles above the planet, the *Copernicus* went in orbit. We observed no signs of habitation, but since we were so far above, a sign would need to be outstanding, such as skyscrapers or the Great Wall of China. A big obvious sign of civilization would have been nice. I felt a slight pang of disappointment.

Despite no signs, Fawz was undaunted. He said now was the time to attempt contact via radio waves. He broadcast over many radio frequencies and simultaneously recorded his broadcast.

"Greetings, citizens of Ganymede. We have come from afar. We four beings have come from the planet Earth. You invited us to visit you. We now answer your 500-year-old invitation. You asked for a person with a particularly rare blood type to be a crewmember. She is on this mission. You asked for a Rhatanian to be a crewmember. I am that Rhatanian. Please give us a sign that we are welcome."

Fawz spoke slowly and clearly. He chose uncharacteristically short sentences and carefully enunciated each word. His voice was kindly and melodic under normal conditions, but on this broadcast, he sounded soothing, gentle, and even angelic.

"When you visited us, you left us a gift, a musical instrument. On that gift is your invitation to us spoken in the Rhatanian language of the sixteenth century. We will now play that recording for you."

I listened to the Rhatanian words and thought of the English translation. "Fare thee well, dear people, we will meet again in the heavens beyond the broken and jagged rocks torn asunder."

We waited for a response as we scanned radio frequencies. Abruptly, the pang of disappointment left me. Somehow, a strong feeling swept over me that beings were down on Ganymede. They would respond, maybe not this moment, but eventually. However different their communications technology was from ours, they would figure out how

276

to make themselves known to us. Even though I decided against sharing my thoughts with my crew, I somehow knew that Fawz, Lauren, and even Jack felt the same way I did.

After waiting a few more minutes for a response, Fawz continued his broadcast. He compared the Earth to Ganymede. "We inhabit the third planet from the sun. Your home is the third large moon from the planet we call Jupiter.

"We are protected from the sun's solar winds by the Earth's magnetosphere. You are protected from the sun's solar winds by Jupiter's magnetosphere. You are protected from Jupiter's radiation by your own magnetosphere.

"Your planet has an iron or iron sulfide core, which creates your magnetosphere. Our planet has an iron core, which creates our magnetosphere. Our neighbors Venus and Mars do not have magnetospheres to protect them. Neither do most other bodies in the solar system.

"You have an atmosphere of oxygen. We have an atmosphere of oxygen.

"You have northern lights and southern lights. We also enjoy such light displays on our planet. We call them the aurora borealis and the aurora australis.

"One side of your planet always faces Jupiter. One side of our own satellite, the moon, always faces the Earth.

"Your moon is four times further away from Earth than we are from the sun. In inverse proportion, your moon takes one-fourth as long to orbit around Jupiter as our own moon takes to orbit around the Earth. Your moon takes 7 Earth days, and our moon takes 28. Seven days on Earth is called a week, a significant unit of time in Earth cultures."

"At one point during Jupiter's orbit of the sun, you are 365 million miles away from the Earth. That is one million of our miles for each one of our Earth days."

I shivered at all of the coincidences and felt myself being pulled into Fawz's beliefs about fate. What a delightful way to believe. Yet, because my background was so different, I felt myself resisting his magical spell. I realized that Fawz was playing with astronomical numbers and turning them into fate. After all, Ganymede was the seventh moon from Jupiter, not the third, if one counted the four little moons inside the orbit of Io. Besides, practically all moons in the solar system kept one side facing the planet they orbited. Furthermore, Saturn also had a protective magnetosphere. I glanced over to Jack and caught him rolling his eyes.

However, Fawz's conclusion was clear. The Earth and Ganymede were indeed similar. In many respects, Earth was more similar to Ganymede than to any other body in the solar system. Fawz concluded his broadcast by saying, "We request permission to land on your planet and to meet you. While awaiting permission, we will take a closer look at your most magnificent planet."

Fawz then repeated his message in Rhatanian. Afterwards, he said he did his best with the 500 year-old expressions and ways of speaking. That would be like my speaking in Shakespearean English. At intervals, Fawz replayed his message so that it eventually could be heard in every area of Ganymede if only someone were listening. He continued rebroadcasting on all radio frequencies.

We waited for a response on the radio frequencies and checked a variety of light waves for a signal. Lauren and I kept our eyes glued to Ganymede for a visual signal. If the Ganymedians were sending us a message, we did not recognize it. As far as we knew, we received no response.

We spiraled down into a tighter orbit until we were only eight miles above Ganymede. As we flew over the side facing Jupiter, I was thrilled to observe that this huge moon was bathed in an array of soft, subtly changing colors.

Lauren said, "That's incredible. None of our unmanned probes had been close enough to notice these delicate colors."

It took us a few moments to figure out that Jupiter's violent and dazzling weather was reflecting off Ganymede's icy surface in mellow shades of pastel. A large area on Ganymede mirrored Jupiter's red spot but in muted apricot. Even Jupiter's lightning bolts reflected off Ganymede in dozens of barely perceptible flashes. All at once, the flashes on the surface of Ganymede ceased because the lightning storms on Jupiter had stopped abruptly. Jack thought that several separate storms must have been interconnected.

I felt a tinge of homesickness as I thought of Earth and moonlight reflecting off water and shiny objects. As we flew over the side of Ganymede facing away from Jupiter, it still looked like the luminescent grays and whites that we had observed from the higher orbit. We began checking everywhere with sensors that measured heat, oxygen, carbon dioxide, and a variety of indicators of life or simply an anomaly on the surface. We continued checking visually and saw many more details, but since we were orbiting about as high as commercial airlines fly, it would be easy to miss anything that blended into the environment or a habitat that was totally not a familiar style. We used telescopic lenses to zero in on areas of interest.

Our computer-controlled cameras took movies of the surface, and the computers analyzed for shapes considered not made by nature. Fawz adjusted the cameras to account for the lightning, red spot, and other reflections from Jupiter. We orbited around the planet three times but still found nothing that indicated any sign of life. Nothing. Everything looked natural, majestic, but natural. As with the entire mission, Houston also automatically was getting our data on many different channels.

I wanted so much to find life on Ganymede. I knew all of us did. Yet, if life existed underground, we might not see anything from this height.

Finally, Jack found something significant in the computer data, a heat spike and a slightly elevated carbon dioxide level at a particular location. By then, we were considerably past that location. Jack pulled

279

up the area on the computer, and it showed a single circular impact crater located far away from other craters. On the next orbit, we would zoom in and take close-up videos.

As we flew over the horizon approaching that area, I saw something. It was very quick. I was not sure, but I became filled with hope. Had a flash of light like a flare shot up from the crater?

They were signaling us! They were responding to Fawz's broadcast. Then, I noticed that one of our computers analyzed the light flash and listed possible interpretations, including such things as a flare, a beacon, and a reflection from a lightning bolt on Jupiter.

I moved to an opposite window and carefully studied Jupiter. There were no storms in progress. In fact, I did not see one bolt of lightning anywhere on that great planet. I quickly moved back to viewing Ganymede. Now, there definitely were no reflections from lightning.

Jack glanced at the computer reading and said, "What's this mean?"

"I saw something," I said. "It wasn't a reflection from Jupiter. It was a flare or a beacon."

I looked toward Lauren, and she said, "Yes, I saw that, too."

As we passed above the location, we all realized at the same time that the area was not indented like a crater but raised like a dome. Our computers indicated it was about the size of the dome of a sports arena. We took videos until we were far past the spot.

Jack said, "That's a good candidate for a landing site. I wonder if there's life underneath the dome." Beneath his tone of nonchalance, I heard excitement in his voice.

Lauren, also trying to be unemotional and factual, said, "It faces Jupiter. Even if we find no artifacts, it's still a fine location to set up the monitoring equipment."

I resisted the urge to blurt out, "I know they're down there."

Before we had left on the mission, Houston had given us a list of potential places to land. Now, it was our job to suggest several alternate landing spots. Concurrently, from the data automatically being sent from the *Copernicus* to Mission Control, Houston independently analyzed and suggested that we put down relatively soon and not continue searching for other potential landing spots. We were given the go ahead for landing near the dome if that was Jack and Fawz's choice.

I was delighted. However, Jack seemed surprised. He frowned slightly and said, "Houston's seldom that quick in making decisions."

Fawz replied, "On this side of Ganymede, if we land soon, we will have nearly an Earth day for direct communication with Houston. If we are fortunate enough to make contact with residents of this glorious moon, Houston could know within thirty minutes. They are anticipating this as much as we are."

"That's probably it, and we've found a promising landing spot," Jack said. "Yet, I hope Houston doesn't get careless because of communication concerns."

We went up into a higher orbit in preparation for launching the *Falcon*, the landing vehicle. As we orbited Ganymede from fifty miles up, Fawz played his recording one more time and concluded his broadcast by saying, "We request permission to land on your planet. We would like to meet you. If we do not receive word to the contrary, we will land on the side of your moon that faces Jupiter. We will land near the source of heat and carbon dioxide next to an area that looks like a domed city. We accept your flash of light as your welcoming beacon."

We watched and waited for a sign from Ganymede but received no additional response that we recognized. We finally suited up, put on our helmets, and crawled into the lander. What a tight fit! There was no room to spare.

Before we launched the *Copernicus* from the space factory five months ago, the *Falcon* had been packed with a portable communicator in addition to the built-in one, a land rover, the scientific monitoring equipment that we would assemble on the surface of Ganymede, a box of gifts to the Ganymedians, and our supplies.

We did a final mechanical check and paid particular attention to the computers on each footpad. Then, we prepared to launch the *Falcon*.

This was our moment. We undocked from the *Copernicus*, got a safe distance away, and began our descent. Jack put the *Falcon* on autopilot as we curved down in an arc. Jack and Fawz, the copilot, had practiced on the *Falcon* simulator back in Houston, but that was many months ago. During our mission, they often had practiced with the onboard video simulation, but that barely compared to the *Falcon* simulator. Fawz and Jack were both very quiet. I wondered if they were a bit afraid. No, that was not possible. They were just being serious and thoughtful as the situation required.

At eight miles above Ganymede, Jack took the *Falcon* off autopilot and began the manual descent. I dared not say a word for fear of distracting him. I was happy being a passenger and enjoying the view as details on Ganymede grew larger before us. As we descended, Lauren and I scanned for more signs of life. The dome came into sight and took on an artificially made appearance not only because it seemed so much like a perfect hemisphere but also because it glowed a uniform cream color. Our designated landing spot near the dome looked smooth and flat, like an ideal landing pad for the *Falcon*.

Still in an arc, we were approaching from the side when at the same time Lauren and I both saw them, large rectangular blocks, the same color as the ice and resembling giant doors, sparsely spaced around the perimeter of where we intended to land. These blocks were not natural formations. They were made by living, thinking beings. I restrained the desire to yell out. Jack and Fawz needed to concentrate on the landing.

Jack said, "I see them. They're not in our way."

I counted eleven of them. Ten were in groups of two, every 60 degrees, and all faced inward. The eleventh, between two groups and 60 degrees from each, stood alone.

Lauren looked at me and nodded. She did not say anything. We had found artifacts before we even landed. What were they? Were they markers for a landing pad in which we correctly were landing near the middle? Were they monuments? Maybe, the ice doors formed a sacred religious site, and we were committing a social blunder or something far more grievous. Maybe, their signal to us had not been a welcoming sign at all but a warning to stay away. I pushed that last thought right out of my mind.

Jana's Journal

We either would touch down on this ice covered moon or simply turn our downward arc into an upward one and follow the curve. In a moment Fawz would decide.

The computers analyzed the surface density that each footpad was approaching primarily to determine if the ice could support the weight of our well-packed lander? The ice was about 500 miles thick, but how solid was it?

Finally Fawz said, "It's looking A-Okay to land."

I felt a soft thud, and Jack whispered, "We're here."

"The landing was perfect," Lauren murmured.

I did not say a word. I did not even breathe. Would we sink through the ice down into more ice below?

The lander held firm. The computers still were confirming that the ice was dense enough. Jack and Fawz shut down the engine. To Houston, Jack said, "The *Falcon* is on Ganymede."

Relief swept over me followed by the thrill of anticipation. I peered out a window hoping for and almost expecting Ganymedians to approach the ship. Muted lightning flashes and soft hues of apricot, peach, and tan changed quickly as Jupiter reflected off Ganymede's surface. After I mentally factored out the reflections, I saw no motion anywhere outside of the *Falcon*. Were they waiting for us to exit the lander before making their appearance? I wanted to throw open the hatch and go outside immediately.

I unbuckled my restraints and realized that gravity was acting upon me. It was only a fraction of the Earth's gravity, but after living with varying levels of microgravity for so long, this felt strange, but good.

We moved around as much as we could inside the *Falcon*'s cramped space. I leaned close to a window and looked up. Jupiter was majestic, brilliant, and huge. It covered about ten percent of the sky.

I was ready to be outside and felt as impatient as a young child as we ran the preplanned tests. Sensors attached to the outside of the *Falcon* measured the atmosphere to verify that the seals on our space suits would not disintegrate and that the metal parts on our oxygen tanks would not corrode. We determined the atmosphere was what we had anticipated, very light oxygen, about the amount that surrounded the space stations. Strangely, the carbon dioxide level had dropped.

Jack continuously uploaded all of our raw data plus our analyses directly to Houston for its own independent evaluation. Mission Control would make the decision on whether or not we would pop the hatch and go outside. However, the final authority switched to Jack and Fawz if alien beings appeared outside the *Falcon*.

We performed new tests that our situation required, a significant one being remotely analyzing the door-shaped ice blocks. They were not organic or living. Instead, they registered as being the same material as the surrounding ice. One pair of ice blocks was significantly larger than the others, which were all the same size. Those two larger blocks had enough space between them to flank what was beyond: the domed area.

"It looks like the Pillars of Ganymede are framing Dome City," Lauren said, making no effort to conceal the awestruck tone in her voice.

"They're good names," Jack said.

Lauren turned to Fawz, "I borrowed one from you. You called it 'Domed City' during the broadcast."

I said, "The smaller ice blocks we could just call pillars, and all the ice blocks taken together could be the Ring of Pillars."

"So be it," Fawz stated, sounding ever so princely.

"So be it?" Lauren questioned, lightly mocking him.

Finally, we heard from Houston. "Everything looks A-Okay. I would say open the hatch, but we are on a twenty-minute hold here. We have a pleasant surprise for you. Madame President and the King have just landed at Ellington Field. They will be greeting you personally. We've put together an updated agenda for the landing ceremony." Mission Control proceeded to outline our program.

After the transmission with Houston, Fawz fought back tears and succeeded in containing himself before he said, "I have not seen my father since my last visit to Rhatania."

Jack frowned. He seemed concerned and a bit unhappy. Now, he knew why Mission Control had wanted us to stop searching for additional landing locations. It was all for a ceremony.

A bigger safety issue concerned him, too. Under our original agenda, we would have exited the lander, made a few short comments, and then completely unpacked the lander to lessen any chance of a footpad slipping or sinking into the ice. Only after we were fully unpacked would we have continued with the ceremony. Now, complete unpacking would wait until afterwards.

Jack pulled up the data on the footpad computers and studied the numbers. Half to himself, he said, "It should be okay to wait with the unpacking."

Finally, we heard the magic words from Houston that we awaited. "They're at the JSC gate, now. You can pop the hatch any time."

By the time we received Houston's message, thirty minutes had passed, and Madame President and the King probably were already inside Mission Control greeting people and shaking hands.

Fawz clipped on a microphone. He and I went into the airlock. He undid the outer locks, and threw open the hatch. He was the first person off the lander. I followed behind taking movies as he walked down the ladder. Because this live video was being directly uploaded to Houston, I needed excellent footage of Fawz.

He paused a minute on the last rung before stepping onto the ice. I followed him down the ladder and got a great close up of his boot print on the icy surface. The impression was slight because the ice was solid. Then, Fawz pointed between the Pillars of Ganymede to Dome City in the distance. I panned the camera to the dome and then back to Fawz. I handed him the camera and a telescoping tripod that had been attached to my belt.

I stood on the last rung of the ladder and, unencumbered by the photography job, felt free to gaze everywhere. I was awestruck by the sweeping spaciousness as I tracked the horizon. This planet was cheerfully bright, about the same glow as just after sunset on Earth, and also huge, particularly after having been cooped up in the *Copernicus* for five months.

I was so tempted to step onto the surface. I could take that historic step. No one would stop me, but I stayed behind on the last rung. I would abide by our complex protocol.

According to the protocol, if Ganymedians approached the ship or appeared anywhere on the icy surface of this moon and if we felt safe, then I would be the second person to step on the surface. If such a marvelous event as the appearance of natives happened, then we would improvise our entire arrival ceremony. I checked everywhere with a spyglass specially designed to work with my helmet. There were so many pastel reflections that a native could be on the surface, but I did not see one.

Jupiter looked close enough that with one powerful jump, I could touch it, but we were 600,000 miles away, more than twice as far as the Earth was from its moon. At a magical moment, I caught sight of Jupiter's thin gossamer rings.

Reluctantly, I went up the steps. Before going back inside the *Falcon*, I gazed in every direction. Still, I saw no star beings.

I went back into the airlock area. Jack and Lauren were waiting to go out. I refrained from gushing about the beauty and the spaciousness. Soon enough, they would experience it for themselves.

I watched from the airlock window as Jack walked down the steps onto the surface of Ganymede. Fawz pointed the camera at Jack's first boot print.

Then Lauren followed, carrying another video camera. She stepped onto Ganymede. I knew how much it meant to her. My thoughts flashed to last summer at Jack's party. Together with Alan, we longingly had looked at large photographs of first footsteps on the moon and on Mars. Now, not so long after the Mars missions, it was Ganymede, and we were here. That night last summer I did not know enough to even hope for such an opportunity.

Finally, it was my turn. I came back out of the lander, walked down the steps, found a clear place, and stepped onto the planet. My, what a large print, but it was my foot and my weight inside that boot.

Fawz placed his camera on the tripod, and when we all were in a row in front of that camera, he began speaking to Mission Control. He said, "We, the crew of the Solarship *Copernicus*, now stand on the surface of Ganymede, the largest moon of the largest planet in the solar system. On this day, my greatest aspiration stands firmly on the brink of realization because each of you at Johnson Space Center worked hard for us on behalf of all people everywhere."

He then thanked his Father and Madame President for making the mission possible. He ended by saying, "The people of Rhatania thank the people of the United States for helping our countrymen in fulfilling this vision."

Jack spoke next. "We send our greetings to Madame President, who allowed our mission to proceed, to the King, who had faith that such a mission could succeed, to Director Clayton, who saw that our whole mission ran flawlessly, to Max Marsh, who coordinated our many computer operations, to Venzi Suzaky, who stood by if we encountered a problem close to impossible, to Dr. Keenan, who reminded us to breathe, to all the solarship communicators and flight controllers at Mission Control, to all the distinguished guests in Houston now watching our broadcast, to our families, and to all the people of planet Earth."

Jack then mentioned a large number of people at Mission Control by name, probably everyone who had served as CAPCOM, including Filbert, who had frequently served, and Willie, who rarely was CAPCOM. Willie was easy to remember because he so respected Jack and treated him like his hero. "If I have inadvertently forgotten to thank you, tell Director Clayton, and I will announce your name later for all of Ganymede to hear."

Lauren said, "We are standing on what appears to be a landing pad. Eleven symmetrical and rectangular blocks of ice, mostly in groups of two, surround it. Beyond the two larger blocks is a dome the size of a sports arena. All of this looks like it was built by intelligent beings. This could prove to be an amazing archaeological find. Or even better, current inhabitants could occupy the dome. It's possible . . . . It's even likely we have hit the jackpot!" She took a hand-held camera and scanned the dome and the ice blocks for Houston to see.

I gasped at Lauren's words. Had I had seen Jack flinch, too? Even I knew better than to make such statements like that, particularly to the President of the United States, Director Clayton, and the King of Rhatania. We had not yet closely examined the ice blocks. We had not journeyed to the dome.

Now, expectations in Houston would be huge. Lauren's comments had been so uncharacteristic of her. Once, she had told me about the advantages of under promising and over delivering. However, under these circumstances, how could she, a sociologist, be anything but enthusiastic? Yet, Lauren, the astronaut, needed to be more cautious.

I had written and memorized a speech, but this moment called for something more. I said, "I wish all of you were here. Ganymede is magnificent. Right at this moment, we can see Jupiter's thin rings. Walking is easy even after being in the *Copernicus* for so long because we are experiencing only about 15 percent of the Earth's gravity. The temperature outside is very cold, but we are comfortable in our space suits. There is light oxygen and no wind." I followed those comments with my prepared speech.

Then, we waved at the camera. That concluded the first part of the ceremony. Houston had previously told us that eventually they intended to edit our live transmission and make two versions for when and if our mission became more widely known. Jack would be the first to place his foot Ganymede in the American version, and Fawz would be the first to touch Ganymede in the Rhatanian version.

We had an hour before we would receive the response from Houston. During that time, we unloaded and set up outside on the icy surface a large video screen, more video equipment, and a sound system. We checked out all the equipment, and while we waited, Jack checked the footpads.

When the video from Houston began, it about took my breath away. In Mission Control, Madame President, the King, Director Clayton, Max Marsh, Venzi Suzaky, and dignitaries I did not recognize were sitting in the first row of chairs in front of the Mission Control desks. On a second row behind them on a riser were seated many people who worked Mission Control, including Filbert. Director Clayton moved to a podium in front of the tracking maps and introduced the King, who told us how brave we were and how we had fulfilled the yearnings of his countrymen and of the world. Director Clayton introduced Madame President. She spoke of how honored our country was to lend support to the Rhatanian ideas which developed into the joint mission. She wished us luck in whatever artifacts we might find and said we had already achieved a huge goal by extending human space travel into the dangers of the Jovian environment to a place of safety on Ganymede. As far as she was concerned, the mission would be a complete and total success if we lifted off right now and safely returned home. Only for the King and our crew did she wish for more. I thought how graciously she had left Lauren off the hook. Then, Director Clayton spoke glowingly about our achievements. After a while, he gave Jack the names of two people who wanted to be mentioned on Ganymede.

Then he said that now they were going to invite the project leaders and managers who had worked on the scientific experiments into Mission Control and for us not to mention anything about the main purpose of the mission being to find life. We were definitely not to mention the artifacts or to have anything suggestive of an artifact in the background. Those additional people would greet us first and then we would reciprocate.

We watched on the screen as the doors to Mission Control opened and a group of about twenty people came in. I gasped in surprise, pleasure, and shock to see those who were leading the group, our families. It was so good to see my mom and dad but I was overcome with feelings. I did not know what I would say to them. I wished I had known ahead of time. JSC must have wanted a really good surprise for us, and I appreciated their efforts. Still, I would have enjoyed the anticipation. Secrets had their downside in a lot of ways.

First, Regney told Fawz how much she and the babies missed him. Then, Shirl expressed similar sentiments to Jack before she read messages from Brad, Stacy, and Mark. None of the children were present, I guess, because of security concerns.

Director Clayton spoke to Lauren. He said that notifying her family and getting security clearance for them had somehow been overlooked. Once the problem was discovered, he had expedited the clearance, but because of the delay, they were still flying to Houston as he spoke. He played their phone message from the airplane to her, and he assured her that once they arrived, they would be welcomed to Mission Control to watch the video from Ganymede, and then they would be given a VIP tour of JSC.

My parents told me how much they missed me and how proud they were of me. The managers of the various scientific projects clapped when our families finished. Then, each manager thanked us on how successful the projects had been to date and how much knowledge in their fields had been advanced. They each talked no more than two minutes as if they had been thoroughly coached about the timing of the broadcast. It was good to put faces to the names that we had communicated with on the scientific channels.

Their part of the broadcast ended, and now it was our turn. Fawz adjusted the camera so that only the *Falcon* was in the background.

We each talked to our families with that large audience in the background. I wanted to tell my parents how much I loved and missed them. I wanted to ask them if they had talked to Alan. I ended up saying, "Thanks for signing the papers allowing me to go on this mission. I want to make you proud of me. Mom, you would have loved flying through the bow shock. When I get home, I'll describe it to you. Dad, thanks for teaching me how to make good use of my discretionary time. I've been learning about the Jovian system." I so wanted to tell them about the artifacts and the flare. I could extend the secret to just a few more people. My parents both had top secret security clearances. Probably, everybody in that room did. I was tempted, but, instead, I said, "You would like it here. How's the lawn? Is it brilliant green? I'll look for it from the air when the hopper flies over Houston on the way home. I love you both." I waved into the camera. I wanted to say, "Tell Alan not to give up on me. Tell Alan that I love him." Instead, I said, "Tell Alan that I'll be home one of these days."

There was no family member for Lauren to greet. That made me sad, but she seemed okay about it. She spoke directly to her family as if they were already there.

I thought, suppose a Ganymedian walks or flies or ambulates up to us right now in front of the camera? How would we explain that to the people now in Mission Control who do not have a need to know?

That was Director Clayton's problem. He would figure out how to explain that away. That was his job. He could blame it on a glitch in the new light splitting technology that somehow computer animation had gotten into our broadcast. I figured I owed him a lot. I was on this mission in part because he paid attention and checked things out. During my studies at JSC, when I was having problems with his friend Filbert, my celestial mechanics instructor, Director Clayton sent Venzi

Suzaky, the famed physicist, to check on me rather than take Filbert's word for it.

Jack and Fawz wound everything up with a few parting comments to conclude the ceremony. We followed the end of the ceremony with video of Jupiter and nothing of the artifacts. In thirty minutes, Mission Control would receive our message. Because of the time lag, the ceremony had basically been this: we speak, they speak, we speak, end of ceremony.

Jack immediately went into the *Falcon* to check the pressure monitors on the footpads. Everything was holding fine. Our first task was to lighten the load. We carried out the rover parts that we would assemble into a vehicle, the modules that we would assemble into the monitoring equipment, and then a box of gifts for the inhabitants. After that *Falcon* weighed much less. Even through his space suit, I saw Jack visibly sigh. We had not jeopardized our safety after all for the sake of a celebration to fit Madame President's schedule. Next, we installed motion monitors and video cameras to the outside of the lander.

Then we began the part of the ceremony that was directed to the Ganymedians. This video also was being uploaded directly to Houston but fell under the category for only those who had a need to know. It was not part of our official ceremony. I did not know if either Madame President or the King were still in Mission Control.

Jack and Lauren walked up a few steps of the lander so that only Fawz and I stood on the surface of this moon. Fawz spoke using our loudspeaker system, "Beings of Ganymede, you visited our planet more than five centuries ago. You visited our homeland, the country of Rhatania, and were most kind and gracious visitors. All my life, I have yearned to make the return visit to those who told our people that they came from the stars. We finally have the technology, the resources, and the will. Beings of Ganymede, we look forward to visiting with you in the spirit of peace and friendship. We await your visit to us here at our lander.

"The two people you requested on your cylinder more than five centuries ago have now made the return visit. At this moment, we both stand together on the surface of your planet. We hope and anticipate that you will come forward to welcome us to your planet as we welcomed you to our country more than five centuries ago."

Allow me to introduce myself to you. I am Fawzshen, astronaut from the Planet Earth, Co-Commander of the Solarship *Copernicus*, Crown Prince of the country of Rhatania, and direct descendant of Fawzshen, the young boy who escorted you from Rhatania back to your spaceship. At that time, you presented him with a gift, a musical instrument in the shape of a cylinder. On that cylinder you invited us for a return visit when we had the technology. We now have the technology. You requested that at least one person on the crew be a Rhatanian. I am that person.

"You, the beings of Ganymede, also requested on the cylinder that one crewmember have a specific rare blood component and that she could be from a part of the world other than Rhatania. That person now stands next to me on the surface of your lovely planet. She was offered the opportunity to become an astronaut specifically to fulfill your invitation. Allow me to introduce Jana Novacek, astronaut from Planet Earth, mission specialist of the Solarship *Copernicus*, citizen of The United States of America, and daughter of a decorated test pilot and a dedicated Johnson Space Center manager."

I said, "This is an incredible place, ice as far as the eye can see. I saw your Dome City bathed in the Jovian light on one of our orbits. I saw the flash of light, your welcome to us. I hope that you will come out of your underground city to meet us. We are very happy to be here, more happy when we meet you, being to being." Then I ended it with an odd, spontaneous comment. "I feel like I belong here."

At that moment, I did not feel in danger. If the Ganymedians had sent the signal as a warning for us to stay away, then they would know right now that we did not interpret it as a warning.

Then, Jack stepped for the second time onto Ganymede. Fawz introduced Jack. "Allow me to introduce Jackson Medwin, astronaut from Planet Earth, co-Commander of the Solarship *Copernicus*, citizen of the United States of American, Commander of the flawlessly successful Mars I Mission, husband, and father of three children."

Jack said, "We come to Ganymede because we were invited many centuries ago. We come to spread good will from the people of the United States of America, the people of Rhatania, and the people from the entire Planet Earth. We come to meet the descendants of those who visited the Rhatanian people on Earth over five centuries ago. We come to return a social visit."

Lauren again stepped onto the ice, and Fawz introduced her. "Allow me to introduce to you Lauren Adams, astronaut from Planet Earth, mission specialist of the Solarship *Copernicus*, citizen of the United States of America, sociologist, and a dedicated instructor for astronaut Jana Novacek."

Lauren made her speech. She mentioned how she particularly liked to meet people from different cultures and she looked forward to getting to know the beings that lived on Ganymede. "We do not know your customs. If we have done anything to offend you, we did it from lack of information. We would like very much if you would join us in our landing celebration. If you came forward now, our leaders on Earth could meet you by way of our wave transmissions. Now would be a good time." She scanned the nearby areas, particularly looking beyond the Pillars of Ganymede to Dome City in the distance.

"We did not give you much advance notice of our arrival. In retrospect, seeing your habitat and that indeed you do or did live here, advance notice would have been a good thing. Our landing here could be a very large surprise for you, like getting unexpected guests. You may have been tracking our ship and not known that it carried passengers. We have been traveling for more than five Earth months to meet you, the time for nearly half of the revolution of the Earth around the sun.

Possibly, you thought our ship was unmanned as all the preceding ones had been.

"We look forward to meeting whenever you wish during your own timetable. However, if we do not hear from you soon, we will assemble our vehicle and give it a test drive during this wake cycle, and during our next wake cycle, we will assemble our monitoring equipment for observing Jupiter." Lauren thought the Ganymedians should have some idea of what we would be doing so they would not fear us. "We await your visit."

After Lauren finished, Fawz translated the essence of what we all had said into sixteenth century Rhatanian. He then ended our ceremony by reading the cylinder message just as he had done while we were circling above. We all scanned the horizon looking for any sign of movement. In all directions, the environment around us looked serene as soft pastel shadows reflecting off the surface.

Fawz said, "They need to follow a certain protocol to meet us."

I was glad that Fawz believed the Ganymedians were here, too, waiting for something, but what was it?

I said, "Maybe, they are getting ready for us right now." Yet, they could be confused by our behavior. First, we talked to them from the air, and then when we landed on their planet, we called home first before talking to them. What could they be thinking? Rather unpleasant thoughts flooded my mind. They could be preparing to dispose of us. If they had not made contact for 500 years, it could be possible, even likely that they did not wish to be contacted now. Our best chance could be to get into the *Falcon* and liftoff, rendezvous with the *Copernicus*, and go home. Mission fulfilled just like Madame President said!

On the other hand, these unpleasant thoughts bore much less weight in my mind than my more positive thoughts. I actually felt quite safe and even at home on this icy surface.

I was brought out of my reverie by Jack, who asked me to hand him a smaller wrench. Our land rover was almost all assembled, and when it was all finished, Fawz and I went for the first drive while Jack and Lauren waited at the *Falcon*, our preplanned procedure for two to get the *Falcon* ready for lift-off if the other two experienced any danger. The other two would drive back, and, if necessary, abandon the rover and rush back inside.

Fawz and I took a camera, a large portable communicator, and some measuring equipment for our first test drive around in the rover on the slippery ice. The traction was excellent, and the rover worked well. First, we drove in a little circle before driving up close to a pair of pillars. We got out of the lander, walked around the pair, and took measurements and pictures. Some pieces had broken off and were lying on the ice nearby. These pillars were not being maintained. My hopes sank. Had the beings moved on to another location? The arc of light could have been the automatic signal of a wayfaring station for space travelers.

As far as we could tell, the pillars were simply large rectangles of ice. There were no inscriptions or any sign of writing. Were they works of art or markers outlining a perfectly excellent landing pad?

We took turns driving around until all pillars had been checked out, measured, and photographed. Fawz and I discovered that the large Pillars of Ganymede were in pristine shape as if they were being maintained. I was hopeful yet again.

On the far opposite side, the single pillar that stood alone also showed no sign of deterioration. It was set off to one side as if an invisible one stood next to it, but there was no sign that a twelfth pillar ever existed. Thus, of the eleven, three were in excellent shape, and the other eight were slightly deteriorated.

After more analysis, we reaffirmed that the pillars were not natural phenomena. They had been sculpted about 500 years ago, the same time frame as when the star beings had visited the Rhatanians.

We extended our exploration a short distance outside the Ring of Pillars. Once the rover left the landing pad's smooth surface, the terrain became slightly bumpy. In the distance, we saw hillocks. The surface of Ganymede still was cheerfully bright, but the apricot and peach reflections were gone because Jupiter's red spot had totally disappeared from our view. Staying relatively close to the *Falcon* and carefully keeping our distance from Dome City, we spent the rest of our wake cycle checking out possible locations to assemble the monitoring equipment.

When it was time to sleep, I was exhausted. Mission Control concurred with our plan to take turns standing watch even though the scanning cameras and motion sensors attached to an alarm system were functioning quite well. I was the third person to stand watch. Barely ten minutes into my watch cycle, I saw something between the Pillars of Ganymede.

Jana's Journal

Jack, Fawz, and Lauren slept ever so soundly, and for two hours I would be in charge of our safety. Of course, our scanning equipment and motion sensors functioned perfectly, but I kept checking the outside, which glowed pleasantly, reminiscent of early twilight.

Between the Pillars of Ganymede, I observed an oval shape about three feet high and somewhat more than a foot wide. It seemed slightly darker than the surrounding ice. It was not a reflection or shadow from Jupiter. I shivered.

I dared not to move. If a creature were observing us from a distance, I pretended not to see it. Then, slowly, I moved my hands toward a video camera, retrieved it, and smoothly brought it toward me. At the same time, I kept the creature in my view, but I must have glanced at the camera for a second because the being was there, and then it was gone. I did not see it move. The entire sighting happened in a matter of seconds.

I typed the time on our watch log. Using graphics software, I carefully drew a picture of what I had seen. I shivered again. Was I the first Earth person to see an alien life form? I got that one backwards. We were the alien life forms on Ganymede.

I diligently observed Jack, Lauren, and Fawz for the least sign of restlessness. I wondered what to do. After all, at this moment, I was in charge. I could go out by myself and investigate. The airlock door would open without too much noise and probably would not awaken them. I could walk to the Pillars of Ganymede and check. That possibility tempted me, but I reluctantly dismissed it for two reasons. Clearly, the native did not wish to be seen at present and perhaps only needed more time to become accustomed to our presence. As for the second reason, as much as I liked to think otherwise, I did not have authority to leave the *Falcon* and chase a creature on this alien planet.

Instead, I worked at the computer and learned to replay the last several minutes from the scanning cameras attached to the outside. I played the video from the camera that scanned The Pillars of Ganymede and then checked it again on half speed. I found nothing unusual except a blur to the outer left of the left pillar. I enlarged the area. Fast motion could have made a blur like that. From my angle of vision, I had not seen any motion, but the scanning camera did. Now, my only evidence was a blur. Nonetheless, I sent a message to Houston.

"Subject: Possible sighting of native life form.

Attachments: Watch log includes my drawing of life form

Video from scanning camera

To CAPCOM: Scanning video probably did not record life form, but check blurry area that I enlarged. My crew is asleep. Please advise how to proceed. Jana."

Their reply would take an hour to reach me. Again, I debated about waking my crew. If I saw the native again, I definitely would awaken them. In the meantime, I alternated between watching the outside and checking the video from all the other scanning cameras.

An hour later, I started getting messages back from Houston. I certainly had gotten their attention.

A graphics group was analyzing the video to determine if what I saw had been a shadow or a non-shadow. They wanted to figure if the pillars were blocking a shadow and the oval simply was a part of the ice surface not in a shadow. As for the blurry area, they would do color resolutions with that.

Another person suggested that some ice might have broken off the pillar and then rolled out of sight. I thought that could be a possibility.

Dr. Keenan lectured me to use great discretion before deciding to awaken the crew. It was our job to stay well, and enough sleep was a major component.

I also got an anonymous message. "Madame President is most happy with your flawless mission and would prefer if you all just came home after setting up the monitoring equipment. Try to stay out of trouble."

When Fawz took my place to stand watch, I showed him the messages and told him what I had seen. He was so enthusiastic and said he would pay complete attention. I continued standing watch a little longer while he adjusted the timing of the camera that scanned the Pillars of Ganymede. He adjusted the range of another camera to overlap.

Afterwards, I eventually managed to fall asleep but had fitful dreams. In one dream I trudged toward the oval native who waited for me between the Pillars of Ganymede, but the faster I moved, the more the native receded in the distance.

After we all woke up, Jack recommended we eat breakfast first before driving in the rover to look for the native. Jack was right. We needed to be at optimal levels of performance for our momentous meeting.

We reviewed protocol with Lauren. We would make no movements that could seem threatening, and all motions would be very slow. I knew our chance of seeing the native behind a pillar was not high because the blur on the scanning video happened after my sighting, indicating the native had left, but still I had hopes. After all, the native could have returned.

We packed the rover with cameras, tripod, and the communicator. It was a very short drive, only 150 feet, and we took the rover mainly to carry equipment and to make a speedy escape if necessary. We parked just inside the Ring of Pillars.

Jack said, "Jana, you're the one who saw it. You want to be the first to look behind the pillars?"

"Oh, yes, wow, thanks!" I gushed. I gingerly stepped behind a pillar, and nothing was there. I checked the other pillar. Still nothing. "No creature here. It must have gone back to its home," I said, trying to sound upbeat.

My level of disappointment surprised me. Logically, I did not expect to see a Ganymedian. More than four hours had passed since my sighting. If I were given another opportunity, I would not let so much time slip away.

We all carefully checked the pillars and the surrounding ice. There were no creature's prints on the ice and only partial footprints from our boots and tire marks from the rover. In most places the ice was too hard for any print at all.

Nothing had broken off either pillar. Both still were in pristine condition. If some ice had rolled there from somewhere else, then where did it go?

"It could have been a reflection from Jupiter," I said sheepishly but then regained my confidence and said, "but I don't think so. I saw a Ganymedian."

We drove back to the *Falcon*, loaded up the Jupiter monitoring equipment, and delivered it to a prime location 500 feet outside the Ring of Pillars and definitely away from a hypothetical road connecting the Pillars of Ganymede and Dome City. From this vantage point, we had a decent view of our lander and their structures. The portable communicator in the rover continuously checked the motion sensors on the *Falcon* so if an alarm went off, we would know which alarm right away. I felt a little more secure because the rover was right next to us, and we could drive back to our lander quickly.

We began the job of assembly. Despite our precautions, I could barely concentrate on our task and felt rather jumpy because of pleasantly anticipating but also fearing the oval native. Everyone must have felt that way too, because Jack suggested that one of us stand watch so the others could get some work done.

After that, work progressed a little better although quite frequently I glanced up and gazed in all directions, half expecting the native to be peering over my shoulder. Because the monitoring equipment was in modules, assembly was supposed to be simple, but we still had questions. Help from Houston in the one-hour turn around range would have made our job easier, but now the time lag sometimes exceeded two hours.

Of the seven Earth days it would take this moon to complete an orbit around Jupiter, we could directly communicate with Houston from the *Falcon* on days one and four. Our current wake cycle was basically equivalent to day two. Because we were on the wrong side of Ganymede for communicating directly with the Earth on days two and three, we would send our message to the *Copernicus* when it passed within our line of vision, and it would relay the message to Earth as soon as it could. When Ganymede was behind Jupiter on days five through seven, we would be completely out of contact with Earth. Houston had planned for our arrival here so that we would have maximum time for communication before the blackout period.

We finally finished with the assembly. The monitoring station would communicate with Earth whenever it had a direct line of vision. Otherwise, it would store the data and wait. I visualized synchronous communication satellites orbiting Ganymede and even Jupiter itself. When that day came, we would have far fewer gaps in communication.

Working in space suits on an alien planet, we all were exhausted again and welcomed our second sleep cycle on Ganymede. Dr. Keenan would not be pleased with us. When it was my time to stand watch, first I was groggy but quickly became wide awake. The outside looked totally different than it did during my previous watch. Since Jupiter took only ten hours to spin on its axis, we basically were treated to ever shifting reflections. To make things even more interesting, the great red spot within Jupiter spun on its own axis every four days.

I wore a camera around my neck and alternated between checking the Pillars of Ganymede and checking our new monitoring station, which being further away was more difficult to clearly observe but still a prime place for a curious native to inspect. Then, every few minutes, I examined the entire Ring of Pillars.

About an hour into my watch cycle it occurred to me that if the native knew how to avoid a scanning camera, it also would know that I was awake and constantly moving my head, looking everywhere. I positioned myself to face the Pillars of Ganymede, put my finger on the camera's on-off switch, and closed my eyes. Staying very still, I slowly opened my eyes halfway and waited.

Barely five minutes had passed before I saw the oval native. Immediately, I started taking pictures. The native was gone as fast as the first time, but this time it moved rapidly from behind one pillar to behind the other. It definitely was not a reflection from Jupiter. I played the camera back. Nothing. I still had not been fast enough. I checked the scanning cameras, and there was nothing, either, despite Fawz's adjustments. I double checked again looking for blurry areas, and there were none. How could the native know enough about our equipment and me to avoid being filmed?

My crew slept so peacefully after our second full wake cycle. I thought of Dr. Keenan's admonishment. I thought for about five minutes. Nobody liked disturbed sleep. If a Ganymedian were sneaking a peek yet for the second time, it still did not want to be discovered, not yet, maybe not ever. I debated with myself and then woke everybody up. No one grumbled. They all seemed like good sports as we suited up.

We decided to walk to not scare off any creatures by driving the rover. I so wanted to see a native waiting for us behind one of the large pillars. What would we say? What would the being do?

I should have known. Nothing was there. When we checked the pillars and surrounding area carefully, we found something beneath us that looked like a scrape on the icy surface, about three inches long and one-fourth of an inch wide. It was a straight line that had not been there when we previously checked the pillars. No one recalled how we ourselves could have made such a scrape.

Our first communication! We carefully measured it and took several pictures. Fawz compared the length to the width looking for a significant ratio. We considered putting another straight line right next to it but decided against doing that since we did not know its significance.

It simply could be an accidental scrape. The oval alien could have had a vehicle hidden behind a pillar.

"How do you explain the secretive behavior?" Jack asked Lauren.

"They're curious but afraid. Or they're getting ready for us. Or they've decided against making contact, and one is breaking the rules. Or they're giving us a chance to settle in first. Or we're supposed to make the first move, and we don't know the protocol. When I wake up a little more, I'll make a list of possible scenarios."

I was beginning to think all I had seen was a moving reflection that had mirrored something moving on Jupiter but decided against saying that since I had awakened everyone.

We trudged back to the lander. By now, it was Jack's turn to keep the final watch because he and Fawz had switched their schedules. I had just fallen off into a comfortable sleep when I heard the alarm on every motion detector go off simultaneously. I jumped up and said, "They're here. They're everywhere."

Jack laughed. "No, it's snowing."

Lauren said, "Isn't it lovely, snowing under a Jovian sky. Wait, it's minus 100 degrees outside."

Jack checked the outside sensors. "It isn't snowing snow; it's snowing carbon dioxide."

Fawz who now was fully awake said, "But how is that possible?"

Jack replied, "We'll let the weather people in Houston figure it out."

We suited up and went outside and danced in the snow. It was magnificent, the big orb overhead, snow falling on us, the Pillars of Ganymede in the distance, and Dome City beyond them. Gazing up at Jupiter through the snow somehow reminded me of the artificial moon that Alan and I stood under at the Space Tech trade show when we said our farewells. I longed to see Alan again. At this moment, he would have liked being here.

The snow stopped as abruptly as it had started. We decided to stay up. Including our day of arrival, this was our third wake cycle, the time we had planned to visit the dome. We packed the rover with our portable communicator, cameras, measuring tools, and a sounder. At 130 feet from the dome, Jack got the first reading that hollow space was beneath us.

Jack said, "The size of Dome City has just increased."

We drove the rover back to solid ground and began walking while keeping our distance from each other to spread out the weight, taking only the cameras, measuring tools, and a sounder with us. Jack continually checked with our sounder that the surface would support our weight. Falling through the top of their compound certainly would not be a way to make friends. Besides that, it could be fatal to all concerned.

Lauren reminded us that in a much earlier time, Ganymede had been warm and probably more hospitable to life. If intelligent life had evolved way back then and managed to protect itself as the environment grew more and more harsh, now we could be observing the result, an entirely artificial environment.

Fawz said, "Conversely, the residents of Ganymede originally could be from almost anywhere if they are the same ones who visited Rhatania. If they knew how to build a space vehicle, then they eventually would have the technical skills to build a habitat in an alien environment."

"Now is a good time for them to greet us." I said. "We're calling on them. We told them this wake cycle would be our time to visit their

306

city. Even if they don't understand English or Rhatanian, they see our actions. They must know we're here. Where are they?"

"Societies change. Look at Earth," Lauren said. "A society can be very knowledgeable and sophisticated. Then something happens. The inhabitants of this dome might not know anything about a visit to Earth. Five hundred years is a long time."

Feeling optimistic, I said, "There could be a simple reason they're not here. This could be their time to sleep. They could all be asleep right now except maybe for the one who was spying on us."

When we got to within twenty feet of the dome, we stayed that distance while we completely encircled it. The entrance to the complex probably was not on the dome itself.

Eventually, we walked right up to the dome, and Jack pushed the soft, powdery snow off a small portion. I gazed through something very clear, and down far below I saw what looked amazingly like an auditorium. It mostly was empty space, but off to one side were hundreds of things resembling lounge chairs in a semi-circle facing something that appeared to be a stage. When I blinked, the dome was opaque, and I could not see through it.

What I saw was almost too fast to register. Maybe I was thinking that is how it could look. My two sightings of a native also had been very fast. I did not say anything because I was beginning to doubt myself.

Jack ever so carefully laid the sounding tool on the dome. The reading indicated that the dome was about five inches thick where we were measuring and then hollow beneath for more than 100 feet. Jack decided against scraping it to attempt an analysis.

I was overcome with an odd feeling that someone was saying, "Wait for us." It was if I could hear the words in my head. I looked at my crew. It was hard to read expressions through their helmets, but I thought each one seemed bewildered but also awestruck. We were all quiet. I knew we had experienced something together. Yet, I dared not mention the mental message. Then, I remembered that sound enhancing lasers could direct sound to a pinpoint focus, but their technology would not be the same as ours.

Were we to wait for the natives here at the dome or go back to the *Falcon*? How long were we to wait? We had brought microphones and speakers with us in the rover, but now that we were here, no one mentioned using the audio equipment. Maybe, our amplified voices at our landing ceremony had scared the inhabitants. It was difficult to know how to proceed.

What existed were the artifacts, the scrape in the ice and the smudge on the video. A bit more nebulous were the quick sightings and now the voice. Everything beyond that was supposition piled on top of supposition. I kept these thoughts to myself and did not object when we stepped into the rover for our drive back to the *Falcon*.

Jack and Lauren stayed outside to check on the monitoring equipment, and Fawz and I went inside the *Falcon* to uplink video of Dome City to Houston. As we waited for Houston's reply, I again checked my video that I had taken while trying to photograph the star being. I had previously checked the video frame by frame, but I felt the need to look again. This time I stopped cold. I had managed to photograph it. How had I missed that frame before? The native had moved from beyond one pillar to behind the other one. And there in my photo was a bulge at the base of the second ice pillar. It did not look like a shadow at all.

I pointed out the window to the Pillars of Ganymede and said to Fawz, "When I last saw the creature, it had darted from beyond one pillar to behind the other one."

I handed Dr. Fawz my camera with the viewer showing an enlarged portion of the picture. "It's right here. Look at the other frames at this same spot. The small bulge at the base of the pillar is missing."

Fawz studied that frame and adjacent frames for many minutes before he said, "Something is there." We talked about what it could mean.

Jana's Journal
(Not read over the net)

Fawz glanced outside at Lauren and Jack, who still were testing the monitoring equipment. The rover was parked next to them. Fawz flipped off the two-way communication between the *Falcon* and the portable communicator in the rover, leaving the channel open for incoming conversation only. "This frame is our first video of the life form," he softly said. "You might be the one that it awaits. It has appeared twice while the rest of us slept."

"What should I do about it?" I asked, feeling my eyes opening wide.

"Do what your heart and soul lead you to do, what you are destined to do."

"You think I should go out there when everybody else is asleep and meet with the oval native."

"I could not advise you to do that."

"But you're not advising me not to. They're waiting for the one described on the cylinder. Is that what you think?"

"The thought has occurred to me. It could be dangerous for you."

"I'm on this mission because of you."

Fawz looked startled. "I will not comment on that. If you feel you are here because of me, do not let that belief influence your decision in any way. Remember, Jack most enthusiastically approved of the choice. Do not forget the JSC psychologists thought our four personalities could not only endure but also thrive during all these months of being confined together. They were not wrong."

"You're telling me to do what my heart and soul lead me to do?" I asked, giving Fawz a chance to retract what he clearly had stated.

He simply nodded his head in the affirmative.

I pondered on what Fawz had told me. Then I said, "Whatever happens I won't tell Jack or Lauren or anybody about this conversation."

"I would appreciate that."

"Just between you and me," I said and shivered. "We all have our jobs on this mission, and now I realize my job is to make contact. Maybe Director Clayton didn't understand this when he approved my selection, or maybe he did understand. You came the closest to realizing it when you chose me for the training. The beings on this planet know I'm the one because you and I stood alone on the surface of this planet, and you introduced me as the one they were looking for."

He put his hand to his forehead and rubbed his brambly brows. "It can be very dangerous. None of us know where it will lead. According to our legend, good beings visited Rhatania 500 years ago. However, Lauren is correct when she talks about times changing. We do not know who these beings on this moon are or what they are like or why they have not already come out to meet us."

In a sudden burst of honesty, I said, "Hundreds of astronauts are way more qualified that I am. I have two years of college and four months of abbreviated astronaut training. Ever since I began my training and particularly on this mission, I have felt insecure and inadequate because I'm not good enough. I'm not knowledgeable enough because I don't have enough education. I'm not experienced enough because I don't have enough training. Sometimes I act like a child because it hasn't been that long since I've been one. I'm not brave enough like you, Jack, and Lauren."

"You have been carrying a big burden." Fawz said.

I replied, "I already feel better just telling you my secret."

"I understand," Fawz said. "I would like the power to absolve you of feeling inadequate. You could consider me like the Wizard of Oz, and I could bestow confidence upon you."

"Thanks, Wizard Prince, that's good of you."

"Each member of this crew has more major mission flight hours than all the astronauts except for those who went on the two Mars missions."

"That's right," I said, magically hoping to obtain confidence. "It's just that I'm here because of some blood component that I have no control over."

"That is what one calls entitlement. You and I are a lot alike, Jana. Do you feel unworthy?"

"Oh, yes, I certainly do."

"As a young prince, I felt that I had not done anything to deserve my good fortune. Later on, I realized it was not only my station in life, but my parents were particularly devoted to helping me. I learned that not all people with my parents' status took time with their children. I promised myself that I would work hard and be the best person that I could be. With the exception of Regney, I have never told this to anybody. It sounds so pompous."

"Thanks, Fawz, for trusting me and telling me. I definitely can relate."

"So many of my contemporaries just accepted their good fortune and felt entitled to their benefits."

"If I think about it, I guess I was privileged, too, in a much more toned down way. My parents surely love me and helped me all they could. I probably just accepted all of it until I got this opportunity. That's when I started feeling insecure."

"We knew your background. We picked you because you were the person we wanted. At first, you fit the unique profile, but that was the starting point. You performed. You did not get discouraged, and you did not quit. Director Clayton wanted you on the mission. Max

Marsh wanted you on the mission. Madame President wanted you on the mission."

"All those endorsements make me feel like I definitely need to perform. And I want to. If I see the oval native again, if I'm lucky enough to get a third chance, then I'm going for it. How many people get a third chance?"

"Probably you will. That life form seems curious enough. To clarify what I have been saying, the life form wants to meet you. It might be dangerous for you, and you do not need to do this. If you start out and then feel at risk, by all means come back. Remember, do not feel the need to do anything extra to earn your keep. If you go, promise to take the phone-tracker with you."

"I promise." The phone-tracker was not particularly powerful but was something small that I easily could carry in my pocket. I could be tracked by either the portable communicator or the one built into the *Falcon*.

Fawz added, "Another thing, Madame President would be just as happy if you do not find the life form. She is happy the way things are. She is more than a little concerned about our making contact. What is the American idiom? She does not want to open a can of worms."

Jana's Journal

I barely slept waiting for my turn to stand watch. I finally must have drifted into a deeper sleep because Lauren was awakening me, softly calling my name over and over. She reported that she had not sighted a native. Once I was fully awake, I did exactly what had proven so successful during my previous watch. I sat very still and pretended to be asleep. Last time after my pretense, the native had appeared within five minutes. I did not have such luck this time. After thirty minutes, snow began falling. I was so thrilled but still did not move. I wanted the native to think I was asleep and to give me a third chance.

After about 40 minutes, I decided that I needed a new plan. I was dealing with a smart being who seemingly was capable of learning. I reviewed what had happened during my previous watch. After I had pretended to be asleep, the native made its appearance at the Pillars of Ganymede. Shortly thereafter, I woke everyone up, and we left the *Falcon* to go searching at the pillars for the oval native, who by then may have been watching everything from a safe distance. Not a long time later, we had walked completely around Dome City. The native would have deduced that I had not been sleeping but, instead, observing and waiting.

Therefore, this time, I decided to be obvious about not watching the pillars. The video camera watched for me. I angled the viewfinder so I could glance through that instead. Then, I got out my notebook computer and busily appeared totally disinterested in anything outside of the *Falcon*. In fact, I did need to do something personally important to me.

I wrote Alan an e-mail. If all the secrecy about our mission were ever lifted, then I could send it.

"Dear Alan,

I write to you from where there is not day and night, but always a lovely early twilight, like right after sunset. We have variation, however. Jupiter rotates on its axis about every ten hours, but we observe it from this moon as being somewhat more than ten and a half hours because we are orbiting around Jupiter in the same direction as its spin. The great red spot also spins on its own axis every four days. We have not been here long enough to see the full cycle from this vantage point, but I have seen it from space.

We generally operate on a 24-hour cycle, but if extra work needs to be completed or if we need to observe something special, then we still get enough sleep and simply extend the length of the flight day. There is no reason to keep our flight day (one wake cycle and one sleep cycle) equivalent to an Earth day."

I reread the letter. It certainly did not sound like a love letter to someone I cared for so deeply. Was I being reserved because if it ever got sent, other people would read it before Alan ever saw it? I wanted to tell Alan that I missed him. I hoped to see him again and hoped we could pick up right where we left off as if no time had elapsed. I had not managed to put those words down. I hit the delete key and tried again.

"Dear Alan,

I write to you from an incredible place. Jupiter above dominates the landscape. Visualize a moon that looks twenty times larger than Earth's moon, no, a hundred times larger and even brighter. Then, you'll get some idea of this giant planet's presence in our sky. Besides that, there's constant activity on Jupiter. Great electrical storms flash and shimmer almost all the time. The red spot rotates on its own axis and changes shape. Because of all this activity, Jupiter casts amazing reflections on Ganymede's surface.

Ganymede looks like a winter paradise. It is strange how very much at home I feel. I would enjoy living on this moon especially if you were here with me. I miss you very much and want you to know that. You would like this elegantly glorious place."

That was much better, but still I wished to declare that I loved him and would always love him. I could not put those words down because that would be unfair to him considering I was looking forward to doing something incredibly dangerous. If I went outside and were abducted by the apparently timid native, then my e-mail could become my farewell letter. I thought if anything happened to me, my message would have a better chance of eventually reaching him if I did not mention Dome City, the Pillars of Ganymede, and the oval native.

After I finished the e-mail, I had barely started another task when through the viewfinder of the video camera I saw a flurry of motion between the large pillars. The native appeared to be jumping up and down and making no effort to hide from the scanning cameras. Now the oval seemed taller, maybe four feet in height or more. It was as if the being were saying, "Here I am. Don't you see me? Why aren't you paying attention to me? " The oval native wanted the meeting as much as I did, was impatiently waiting for me to look out the window, and did not want me to give up.

I needed to handle this just right. I did not want to go out there and then have the native run away like in a game of hide and go seek. I continued to pretend that I did not notice.

I glanced over at Fawz, Jack, and Lauren. Fawz seemed a little restless like perhaps he was in a light sleep. The impetus for this entire mission was his. He deserved the honor of going out in the snow to meet the native. I could awaken him. No, I wanted this too much, and, besides, with his belief in fate, he would think this was my destiny.

Without glancing out the window, I leapt into my space suit, activated the automatic heater, dropped the phone-tracker into my pocket, and went through the airlock door onto the first step. I clipped two tether lines together and attached one end to my space suit and the other end onto a tether hook on the outside of the *Falcon*.

I could still go back. I simply could turn around and go back into the *Falcon*. Instead, I went down the steps and trudged through the soft, powdery snow. I kept my head down and did not acknowledge that I saw the native. It would be a short walk, only about 150 feet.

I got to the end of my double tether. I unsnapped the tether from my space suit. The snow was coming down a little harder and beating against the visor of my helmet.

I only had a little way to go and still did not look up or attempt to make eye contact if indeed the being had eyes, but I could see the oval native still was there and not moving, waiting for me, just like my dream. It was making no effort to hide. We had both gotten up our courage for whatever was about to happen.

Now, I was standing right next to it. The native looked almost like a small person stooping in the snow. It did not move. Neither did I. It was being very still. I waited.

I touched it softly. It moved. It grew taller, three feet, four feet, and then a few inches beyond that. My heart pounded as I quickly stepped back. It stood up. It was bipedal like a human and even wearing clothes resembling a snowsuit, space helmet, and mittens. I peered through the clear part of its helmet and was pleased that it looked similar to a human with eyes, nose, and a mouth. Above the eyes, there seemed to be antennae. Despite the antennae, it still was very human-like. Had the natives made an android to look like us? It would make no sense for their beings to look like us, but this one clearly did. Dark brown eyes stared at me through the helmet.

I finally made eye contact. "We come in peace," I said and stood motionless, remembering the rule of no sudden movements.

The native was silent. I figured it still was my turn to speak. "We come from Earth." The dark eyes stared up at me. I was thankful the eyes were not staring down. "We are returning a visit from long ago when your beings visited our planet." I did not know how to proceed. I looked all around me for other beings. This one seemed quite alone.

I pointed to myself and said, "My name is Jana Novacek. I invite you to come with me to the *Falcon*, our lander, our house here on Ganymede, and you can meet the other three members of our crew."

The dark eyes still were staring at me. It did not understand me. I did not know what to do next, so I did nothing. I waited. Finally, the creature made melodious singing sounds in a clear soprano voice with the pitch gradually increasing like the notes of a strange scale.

I was thinking what to say in response when the being made sounds similar to humming. The changes in pitch were rapid and not sequential. It was like a song.

I tried to emulate the song. My throat could nearly do it, and it sounded pretty good, too.

In response, first, the being coughed, and then the sound changed into something cheerfully spontaneous like a chortle. To my dismay, I realized the being was laughing at me.

"Say, I tried, whatever you think of the results, now you try."

The creature replied, "Say, I tried, whatever you think of the results, now you try." It was perfect, my exact pitch, every inflection, and even my slight edge of dismay that the native had been making fun of me.

I certainly did not want this encounter to be anything but friendly. I put my gloved hand on my chest and said, "Jana."

The being touched its own chest and said, "Jana."

I put my hand on my chest again and said, "Jana." Then I pointed to the being and asked, "What is your name?"

The being rolled its eyes up and to the left. It seemed to be thinking. Then it said, "Svee Dee."

I pointed at the being and said, "Svee Dee."

The being moved its head, pointed to itself, and said, "Speedy."

I refrained from adding any extra words and simply pointed to the being and said, "Speedy."

The being smiled slightly just like a person would smile, hummed very softly as if to itself, and then said, "My name is Speedy."

I was shocked. "You understand English. You understand what I am saying."

Speedy looked very pleased, pointed to itself, and again said, "My name is Speedy." Then, it pointed to me and said, "My name is Jana."

"Oh, I understand. You are teaching yourself English. You remembered the words I used the first time I said my name. This is simply wonderful. I have not made any progress in your language. I think your alphabet is based on a musical scale."

One second, Speedy seemed happy and pleased with itself, and the next second its demeanor changed from pleasure to agitation. It moved its shoulders or what I thought could be shoulders. It was looking behind me. I turned around and saw someone on the top step of the *Falcon*. I thought it was Fawz but could not be sure because the snow was coming down harder now. I would lead Speedy back to the lander. "And while you've slept, I have made a friend." I visualized myself bragging to Fawz, Lauren, and Jack

I slowly took Speedy's mittened extremity into my hand. It did not refuse and seemed quite willing to hold my hand. I felt what seemed like fingers and a thumb inside the mitten.

Now, one crewmember already was on the ice and another one, probably Lauren, was half way down steps.

Speedy first moved one shoulder in a rotating motion and then the other shoulder. Then the creature started shaking all over.

"Don't be afraid. They're good people. They won't hurt you," I said.

Speedy tightened its grip on my hand, yanked me behind the pillar, and quickly released my hand. A T-shaped pipe about three-and-a-half feet high and not more than an inch in diameter was sticking up from the snow. The top part of the T somewhat resembled the handle bar of a bicycle. The creature bent down and wiped the snow off a flat metal-like surface that was attached to the bottom of the pipe. When Speedy looked away, I slowly took the phone-tracker from my pocket and said, "We have made contact."

The rest happened too fast. Speedy motioned me to stand on the metal surface. What would happen to me if I stepped on that surface? Was it an elevator? Would it sink down through the snow? Was it a vehicle like a sled in which one rode standing up?

I was deciding what to do? I recalled what I had once said to Max, "If I get a chance, I'm going for it. I'm not going to think twice." Then, I had been thinking about the mission, but this was what the mission was all about, finding life on Ganymede.

Not many hours ago I realized my purpose for being on this mission was to make contact with a native. This opportunity now before me probably would never present itself again.

All these thoughts were very fast. My choice was clear. I either stepped on this piece of metal, or I did not. What would happen if I did?

I was pretty sure I knew what would happen if I did not. My crew would get here, and the native would have fled.

I stepped out from behind the pillar. All three of my crewmembers were now getting into the rover. There was not much time. I had to decide now.

Speedy again pulled me behind the pillar and again wiped snow off the flat slab of metal. I stepped onto it and allowed the creature to spin me around until I faced the bar.

Speedy stood behind me on the metal surface and, reaching around me, put its mittened extremities on the outer sides of the bar. As I fumbled to clip the phone-tracker back onto my belt, the creature hummed, and immediately after that we started moving quite fast. I grabbed the bar in front of me with both hands, and the phone-tracker tumbled into the snow.

Speedy really moved on this thing. We went over every hillock in sight, not missing a one, and the creature nudged me with its arms when I needed to lean into the turn. It seemed like a combination of skiing and sled riding. It could have been quite an exciting activity, but I was too tense to enjoy it. "Slow down, slow down," I thought. My hands and arms ached from holding on so tight, and then abruptly without warning we stopped. I went flying over the bar. All I could think of was to roll into a ball. I hit hard on my shoulder and kept rolling after impact. I was at immediate risk of death if my suit were torn or my oxygen tank ruptured. My left foot hurt slightly. I sat very still. Nothing terrible happened, so I could be okay.

The creature hummed and changed pitch at a very fast rate. I recognized a tone of disgust in its voice. I thought how much I wanted to meet the oval native, and now Speedy, this little speed demon, could have gotten me killed. The creature continued humming rapidly while helping me stand. Then, it carefully brushed the snow off my space suit. These seemed like acts of consideration. My left foot seemed okay. "You need to go more slowly," I yelled.

The tone in the humming changed to apology. The creature took my hand and started to lead me. I yanked my hand away. "Oh, no, I'm not going to fall for that again."

Speedy stood on the sled and waited for me. I crossed my arms and shook my head. "No," I said.

Speedy walked back toward me and held out its mittened hand. I did not budge. The native got back on the sled and zoomed off, a cloud of snow blowing behind, abandoning me to this environment. My oxygen was good for six hours with maybe a half an hour used up. How fast had we been sledding? Forty or fifty miles an hour? In retrospect, that little native most likely had not been traveling a direct route but joy riding and looking for hillocks. I could not estimate how far we had come.

I looked all around me, but the snow had cut visibility way down. What I could see was hillier and rougher than the relatively smooth areas around the Ring of Pillars and Dome City. The homing device on the phone-tracker would have led me right back to the *Falcon*.

I thought about my wrist communicator. If I took off my glove, my hand would freeze immediately. If I separated my glove from my space suit, then my wrist would freeze. That would cut off the blood supply to my hand. The heating system in my space suit could malfunction. Still, I considered sacrificing my hand until I recalled that the wrist com only functioned as a communications device inside the *Copernicus*.

If the snow stopped, I probably could see something as large as Dome City even from a distance and then would know the direction to travel. If I knew the way, could I make it back before I ran out of oxygen?

A strange thought occurred to me. If I died here on this moon, my crew would think that Speedy had killed me. I did not want that to happen. This was a kindly native, a bit careless, but friendly. My crew would not pursue making contact with the natives, but they simply would leave. I wished I had not dropped the phone-tracker.

Then I heard a whizzing sound, and a cloud of snow approached me. The sled stopped as abruptly as when it had hurled me onto the snow-covered ice. Speedy moved back on the metal plate and made room for me.

I said, "I'm extremely glad you've come back. I know you don't understand me. But the point is this: I will fly off your sled again when you stop, and that could be the end of me. You must have very strong arms to resist the shock of stopping. Maybe, you don't care if I'm killed. I'm lucky I wasn't hurt. Maybe, my oxygen is leaking out right now. Whatever the case, you are my only chance, but you need to treat me like a treasured guest who has traveled a great distance to see you."

Speedy paid total attention to my words but did not make a sound in response. I did not want to be left alone again, so I kept talking.

"I want to visit your home more than anything, but first I need to return to the *Falcon*, my home, and check my oxygen tank. I need to tell my crew that I'm okay. Is it possible that we could walk to the *Falcon*? No, walking would be a bad idea. I don't know how long that would take. My oxygen tank could be damaged."

Then I had another idea. I held one hand level to represent the sled and another hand perpendicular as the rider. With my hands, I acted out my falling off the sled.

Speedy watched me intently. I wondered if this was making any sense. Then I demonstrated with my hand going slowly and the passenger not falling off.

The native hummed in a tone of understanding, or was it my imagination, my plight being so difficult. The creature again made room on the sled, and I got on. It seemed like the only logical choice. We started off slowly, but pretty soon we were going as fast as before. I leaned into the turns as the creature nudged me. Here a creature and I were sledding together, and I could have relaxed and enjoyed it if not for the anticipation of the sudden stop. We went faster and faster. I could hardly see ahead of me because snow was flying onto the faceplate of my helmet. Then we slowed down gradually and came to a perfectly smooth stop.

"Good show, little alien," I said, suddenly remembering that I was the alien life form and not the creature. I thought we would be getting off the sled when the creature moved the sled slightly forward, and then we descended straight down and fast, too, as if the ground below us had opened up. I never saw an entry. We stopped with a jolt. My hands tightened on the bar, and I managed not to fall.

We were in a glass-like, egg-shaped room that touched another room of the same size and shape. The floor areas in both rooms were flat, but the ceilings were curved like the dome of an egg. Circling on the outside of both rooms were ramps, and beyond the ramps were curved indigo blue walls. The two rooms and the ramps were all bathed in a violet colored light. I thought we still were standing on the sled, but when I looked around, the sled was gone.

Before I knew it, Speedy was inside the second egg-shaped room. The being peeled out of its outer clothing and left them in a pile on the floor. Underneath the mittens were extremities that looked just like hands. Underneath the snowsuit, it wore something resembling a cream-colored metallic body suit with flecks of gold running through it. The only decoration on the body suit was a flat, bright yellow circle about an inch in diameter worn high up on her left chest. Speedy reminded me of a young girl about the age of ten or eleven.

She clearly resembled a human child until she took an object about the size of a pocket comb and moved it near her head, making her hair stand straight out in all directions. She looked like she had stepped into a magnetic field. Then she passed the object by her antennae, making them stand out forward from her brow and perpendicular to her forehead. She touched a side of the egg, which then became reflective. Speedy preened and admired herself before passing the object over her antennae again. Then, amazingly, she moved those antennae in synchronization.

Speedy turned and glanced toward me almost as an afterthought as if I were a toy and already forgotten. She moved both of her shoulders up and down simultaneously and then separately.

"Speedy, is there someone in charge?" I yelled, trying to be heard through the wall.

She put her hands up to her ears and appeared startled, even frightened. Suddenly, she dashed through the egg enclosure, ran around the ramp, and seemed to go straight through the deep blue wall on the outside of the ramp.

I thought she would return momentarily with more natives, and they would greet me enthusiastically. I would say appropriate things and surely mention that we had come in peace. I waited and waited. I did not know how much time had passed. She did not return.

I thought aloud. "Jack, Fawz, and Lauren must be frantic." No, those three would not get frantic. Yet, they could be exceedingly concerned. No way could they follow me. The snow would have blown

323

over any sled tracks, and the entry to this complex did not look like an entry at all.

I explored my egg prison and touched the curved wall cautiously and then forcefully. I went around the egg touching several surfaces. Nothing happened. Speedy knew how to get through the wall. Why not me? How had she done it?

I finally noticed a group of seven identical transparent circles on the wall. Six were arranged in a circular pattern, and the seventh was centered in the middle of the six. Each circle was about three inches in diameter and formed with small one-fourth inch raised circles. In the center of each three-inch circle was a larger raised dot about one—half inch in diameter. None of the circles touched each other. I thought the larger dot in the center of each circle could be a control key or an enter key.

Yet, the circles could be anything: a piece of art, a thermostat, a security system, something that could make part of the wall reflective, something that had the power to make a sled disappear, or all of those things and more. I decided to completely leave the circles alone since I had no idea what they could do. I would consider the circles off limits just like the Prima Donna computer in Max's office back at JSC. However, I did put my hand above the middle circle to check for heat energy and was startled to hear a sound.

I heard a beep, beep, beep but quickly realized the sound was coming from my oxygen pack, announcing 15 more minutes of oxygen. That meant the oxygen had been leaking and would not last 15 minutes, but a minute or two. If I kept on my helmet with no more oxygen, I would die. If I took the helmet off, could I breathe in this atmosphere and for how long? I removed my helmet. The atmosphere smelled not bad but different like good pure mountain air.

I peeled out of my spacesuit and stretched. The NASA daywear certainly was more comfortable than the bulky spacesuit.

"I'm still alive! I'm still alive!" I yelled. I leapt up in the air and hit my head on top of the egg's dome. The egg gave to my touch so my head did not hurt too much. Less gravity! I needed to remember that for however long I survived. I wondered how long that would be. Then, I tried pushing on the surface again but it still did not give to my touch.

Maybe, there was a colorless, odorless something in this atmosphere, like carbon monoxide. I needed to get Speedy back and find out the composition of this atmosphere. We had managed to communicate before. Since my loud voice apparently scared her, I spoke at a normal volume, mostly asking her to come back and saying that I needed her. When nothing happened, I raised my voice a little louder and used the name she first had told me Svee Dee. I kept chattering away, telling why we had come.

Could Speedy even help me? A thought popped into my mind. I remembered a day at Galveston with Jack's children. We were swimming and watching out for jellyfish. When the tide went out, a jellyfish got caught in the shallow water, separated from the deep water by a sandbar. Brad placed the jellyfish into a pail of water, and we took it back to Houston. He held the pail very carefully on the hydro bus. Brad had great plans for the creature. He learned what to feed it and visualized an aquarium for the sea creature. But as might be predicted, it died the next morning. Brad did not want the jellyfish to die. He just did not know what its needs were.

I shook my head from side to side. I needed to get such stray thoughts out of my mind. I had faith that my training had prepared me for this moment. I needed to be persistent and resourceful. I wondered if the message on the cylinder could help me.

I knew some words in the English translation. Would that have any meaning to the creatures here on Ganymede? I said in a clear and loud voice, "We will meet again beyond the torn and jagged rocks torn asunder." I repeated that several times. Nothing happened.

I tried to remember some words in Rhatanian. I could not, but there was a name of a visitor given on the cylinder. Now, I recalled the name and called out, "Chri Anri, where are you?" I repeated that about three times, and, still, nothing happened.

Then I heard a faint hum and looked toward the sound. A larger creature about the size of Fawz leaned against the outside of my egg prison, intently staring at me. The creature had the build of a man. Like the smaller creature, his antennae stood straight out, forming a right angle with his forehead. He wore a metallic blue body suit with flecks of green running through it. He also wore a yellow circle up high on his left chest.

"Chri Anri, I." The voice was the pitch of a grown man.

I rushed toward him. "You're Chri Anri, the Chri Anri who visited Earth 500 years ago?"

"Chri Anri, I. Earth visit not I. Thou be whom?"

"I am Jana Novacek, Astronaut."

"Welcome, Jana Novacek, Astronaut."

"We come in peace to offer solar friendship."

The creature seemed amused. "How get thou here?"

"One of your beings, smaller than you, smaller than I, Speedy, brought me here and then ran away."

Chri Anri made a chortling sound, but he was not laughing at me. "Brought you here by the child Svee Dee."

"That small being was a child?" I figured that might have been the case. I now understood Speedy or Svee Dee's behavior a bit more.

"Decision made by child." Chri Anri lifted one shoulder and rotated it back.

"Is this atmosphere any good for a human?"

"Best in universe atmosphere."

"What about atmosphere where you are?"

"Same, best."

"Then, let me out of this egg."

"Not possible. Kill the beasties."

"What? You're going to kill me? Do not kill me. We could be friends. We are friends."

Chri Anri quickly removed himself from lounging against the egg and stood up straight. "Barbarians we not. Visitor thou."

"Then let me out."

"In two time units. We kill now the beasties."

First rule. Keep calm. Keep rational. Were the beasties Jack, Fawz, or Lauren? "Who are the beasties?"

"Current languages, expert not I. Language expert on trip to Titan."

I was feeling more and more like the jellyfish in incompetent hands. Then he pulled the yellow circle off his body suit and hummed into it. Momentarily, I heard hums, Latin words, and English words coming out of it.

"Mites and microbes. Live in thou eyelashes, mites. Live in intestines, bacteria. Live in thy mouth, bacteria. Sorry, most beasties must die. Afterward, feel thou much better, feel thou marvelous," he said and then placed the yellow circle back on his body suit.

I felt relieved but also somewhat humiliated, like a primitive person with parasites.

"Go now, council meeting call I and about thee decide."

I blurted out, "You certainly don't seem very organized around here. I expected more from you."

My dismay seemed to amuse him. Either that or he was just pleased to see me. He hummed something and then disappeared through the blue wall behind the ramp. "Chri Anri, come back," I wailed.

Two translucent objects magically appeared inside the egg. The horizontal one looked similar to a single bed. The egg-shaped vertical one was somewhat bigger than a large person. The horizontal object gave to the touch while the vertical object felt solid.

Suddenly, a fine blue mist bathed my little egg home. It was dropping all over me, getting my hair wet, falling on my eyelashes, and trickling under the collar of my day wear. It was not at all unpleasant. I became tired and crawled onto the bed-like thing. It gave to my weight and yielded to fit me. My, how comfortable! I would just stretch out for a minute. I needed to stay vigilant.

I was awakened to a chorus of muffled voices. "Jana, Jana, you're okay." Jack, Fawz, and Lauren were leaping around my "bed," being careful, I noticed, not to leap too high. Soon, we all were hugging. They were still in their space suits and helmets, and small bits of snow were falling off them. I was delighted to see them and glad to be around competent people again. With my crew, I already was feeling a lot more secure.

"You made contact?" Jack asked.

"Yes, with two of them. They look a whole lot like us except their hair sticks out straight from their head, and they have antennae."

Jack said, "I wonder if they're robots or androids."

"I don't think so. They're too . . . too imperfect. "What about the ones you met?"

"None, yet," Fawz said with an air of anticipation in his tone.

Lauren said, "We were looking for you when the rover started going faster and faster as if it had a mind of its own. We held onto the vehicle to keep from falling out. The terrain became rougher and rougher when we suddenly sunk right down into the ice, and the next moment we were here."

Neither Lauren nor Jack asked me why I had gone out in the snow on this moon by myself to greet the creature.

Fawz softly said to me, "Congratulations, you did it."

Then, I felt a slight jolt and a feeling of shifting under my feet as the egg expanded in all directions. Three other clear bed-like things appeared. I looked around for my space suit and helmet that had been on the floor, but it was gone. I needed my suit to leave. I needed a properly functioning oxygen tank. Would we be getting out of this alive?

Jana's Journal

Jack, Fawz, and Lauren were thinking about taking off their space suits. I quickly told them that my oxygen tank had sprung a leak and that I felt okay but still was concerned about the air. Fawz whipped a chromatograph out of his pocket and took a measurement.

"This is the purest air I have ever encountered, even better than Rhatania."

"Chri Anri told me it was the best," I said.

Fawz started to remove his helmet.

I offered a word of warning. "Things pop in and out of existence in this egg. I don't know where my space suit is. It's just gone."

"What would you advise?" Jack asked me.

I realized I was the expert in this particular situation. I had been dismayed to discover my suit gone, but after some thought, I said, "It is okay to take off your space suits. When the beasties are killed, we'll have a better chance of getting out of this egg."

"What are the beasties?" Fawz asked.

"They're microbes, bacteria, and eyelash mites," I replied.

"Sounds like a decontamination process," Jack said.

Lauren quipped, "Hope they know what they're doing."

A short time later, a fine mist rained down on each of them but not on me. They became drowsy.

I reassured them. "They showered me in the blue mist, too, and then I soon fell asleep. As you can see, I'm still alive." I pointed to the four horizontal objects. "These things are like beds and very comfortable."

I did not know how long they slept. I dozed a little but thought a lot. They gradually awoke, one by one.

Chri Anri suddenly was inside our little egg prison. "I am Chri Anri. We welcome you to Zalanda." He stood at rapt attention and to my surprise spoke standard American English.

He was the same creature, but his behavior seemed so different, so formal, not at all like the being that had leaned against the egg shortly after I arrived and had seemed delighted to see me.

"I am Commander Jackson Medwin, and these are my crewmembers, Co-commander Prince Fawzshen, Mission Specialist Lauren Adams, and Mission Specialist Jana Novacek, whom you have already met. We come in peace to return a visit your citizens made to our planet over 500 Earth years ago."

Fawz then said, "Many centuries ago, your citizens visited my country of Rhatania and invited us to return 'when we had mastered the art of space travel.' A crewmember on your solarship was named Chri Anri."

"Chri Anri the Elder my grandfather be."

I figured Chri Anri the Elder was no longer alive so was rather surprised when Jack asked, "Is Chri Anri the Elder in your complex?"

"Far away be he," Chri Anri answered. I figured "far away" might be euphuism for Chri Anri the Elder being deceased.

"Are you the leader?" Jack asked.

"Leader, not understand." Chri Anri consulted his circle. "Facilitator the leader. Citizen am I. Time now festival."

"What happens at a festival?" Jack softly asked.

"Zalandans you meet."

"Is that the kind of being you are, a Zalandan?" Lauren gently asked.

"Yes, yes, Zalandan be I," he answered in a softer voice.

She held out her hand, and Chri Anri touched her fingers. They made eye contact. Then, quickly he pulled his hand back and looked away. Lauren slowly moved her hand away. It was a mystical second, and no one said anything.

"Await Zalandans," Chri Anri said in a firm voice.

"How many?" Jack cautiously asked.

"Nine hundred forty three. Now, with me go."

This place was strange, but somehow Chri Anri seemed less strange to me, even with his antennae standing straight out, his hair looking like he had stepped into an electromagnetic field, and his clothes resembling an elegant exercise outfit. In fact, Chri Anri seemed quite likable, and I was not afraid of him or even the situation. If I had any sense, fear may have been the normal emotion, but instead I felt a strange combination of excitement, anticipation, and curiosity dampened by a slight numbness to tone me down so I could function normally.

We went with Chri Anri, not that we had a choice. The translucent egg wall was there, and then it was not. We walked right through the wall with no difficulty and found ourselves on the outside of the egg. I turned back and tapped the egg. It was solid.

The ramp next to the blue wall led to a moving walkway where we traveled fast through a long corridor. Since there was no rail or anything else to hold onto, I concentrated on my balance.

The walkway ended, and the corridor opened onto a spacious hemispheric auditorium. Even though I had seen the dome both from the air and from outside up close, this place perplexed me because it was too similar to stadiums back home and not something I would expect more than 300,000,000 miles from Earth.

Ahead of us a long ramp hugged the wall as it curved downward toward what seemed like the main level of the auditorium where about a thousand natives were seated in lounge-type chairs in a semicircular area that faced a stage. The natives were looking away from the stage and up toward us. They were far enough away that I could not read their expressions.

I wondered if the natives had made this huge arena solely to accommodate our tastes, but how would they know what our tastes were? Was this place really different than what we were seeing, and were we suffering from a mass delusion? I thought not. Maybe things looked familiar because I had seen those chairs before for the briefest moment when I had peered through the dome.

Differences did exist between our auditoriums and this one. Ours would have been packed with many more seats while their seating and stage occupied a relatively small area off to the side and next to the perimeter of this huge, spacious, circular room. This stark grandeur was enhanced a thousand fold when I gazed up through the dome, and Jupiter in all its magnificence gazed back.

When I glanced back down at the ramp again, three adult-sized beings dressed in glittering, iridescent bodysuits began walking up the ramp single file toward us. My apprehension grew, but not out of fear for our safety or life because I did not think they would harm us or dispose of us during the ceremony. This lack of fear was strengthened by remembering Chri Anri's words spoken with complete indignation, "Barbarians we not." Yet, I was tense because I wanted our crew to make a favorable impression in this strange situation in which we did not know the rules. I wanted our meeting in this place to go well. I hoped their customs were things that we could deal with and that our customs would not offend them. Jack, Fawz, and Lauren were intently studying the situation. After consulting his circle, Chri Anri said, "Your guides approach."

The three beings now stood next to us. I studied their expressions. They appeared very happy that we were here and definitely looked friendly.

The first one said, "Visitor from Rhatania, we welcome you to Zalanda." Then, the being took Fawz's hand and led him down the ramp.

The second looked and sounded like an adult woman except for the antennae. This creature said to Jack, "Commander from planet

Earth, welcome to our home." The being took Jack's arm and led him down the ramp.

The third one said, "Mission Specialist Lauren Adams, we hope you enjoy your visit here and find what you are seeking."

Chri Anri longingly gazed after Lauren as she glided down the ramp with her guide. We had traveled these millions of miles, and even a creature in this alien place with totally different genes and thought patterns still found Lauren quite spectacular.

Then Chri Anri took my hand and said, "Mission Specialist Jana Novacek, it is my great honor to be your guide." We walked down the ramp together.

Jack, Fawz, and Lauren were led by their guides onto the stage and toward six lounge style chairs that were placed near the edge. Chri Anri led me to a seat on the third concentric row facing the stage, but we did not sit. Speedy, sitting in the next seat, touched my arm and hummed enthusiastically.

My crew and their guides as well as Chri Anri and I still were standing when all the Zalandans arose and hummed in unison. Next in perfect English and still in unison, they said, "We welcome you, visitors from Earth, to Zalanda. Many long centuries have we waited for such a momentous occasion."

That statement so cheered me that I stopped being disappointed about being segregated from my crew. Jack looked toward me, and I nodded at him, trying to convey the idea that the seating arrangement did not bother me too much.

Now, the walls along the entire 360-degree perimeter flashed the most amazing lights of such color intensity as compelling music bathed my ears. It seemed like ancient music, and then it became more modern than anything I had ever heard. I thought maybe the theme was based on celestial music of the Lion's Roar.

When I looked up, brilliant light bounced off the dome and merged with a lightning storm on Jupiter. It occurred to me that the colors had been planned to coordinate with Jupiter's current activities.

As I observed the dome, it became opaque. Jupiter no longer was visible, and then the flashing lights inside the dome gradually faded as did the ambient lighting until we were in pitch blackness. The music gradually became softer as holographs of twelve Zalandans materialized on the stage for the briefest moment. The audience hummed softly for a few minutes as the music gradually became louder. Then, the auditorium brightened slightly, lights flashed briefly, and the walls became an ever changing palette of delicate pastel colors resembling a giant abstract painting in the round.

I did not understand the lights and sounds, but the combination along with the holographic images captured me on an emotional level the way a good movie or concert involved me. I did not know how nonhumans were able to do that without really understanding the mental functioning of humans. Then I stopped analyzing and became caught up in the moment. I drifted in a netherworld of pure contentment as a sense of belonging enveloped me.

As the auditorium again went pitch black, I pulled myself back into the realm of reason right before a light began orbiting around the perimeter. The light grew larger, and the focus sharpened into a hologram of the *Copernicus*. Then I heard a voice saying, "Greetings, citizens of Ganymede." It was Fawz as he spoke for the first time to the Zalandans all those days ago. When his voice stopped, and an arc of light shot up from the floor to the top of the dome directly in front of the *Copernicus*'s path. It was their answer to Fawz.

The hologram circled another time before a small light separated from it and grew larger and more defined as it turned into the *Falcon*, angled toward the stage, and touched down. In the blink of an eye, images of Fawz and me stood on the ice, and Jack and Lauren waited on the steps. Fawz's words echoed throughout the arena as he introduced our crew to the citizens of this moon. I heard my voice, Jack's voice, and finally Lauren's. She was trying to lure the natives to come outside. She ended by saying, "We await your visit."

These beings had videoed, edited, and condensed our entire arrival into this stirring presentation, but what they had not done was to come out and greet us. Yet, they apparently looked upon our arrival as momentous.

The auditorium was no longer pitch black but now dimly lit when larger than life holograms showed Jack, Fawz, and Lauren dancing in the snow. When only Fawz remained with snow still falling on him, the audience held their arms straight above their heads and swayed and hummed in unison until his image gradually faded from view.

A hologram of me joyfully dancing in the snow came into sharp focus, and on the stage next to me but with no snow falling on her, I recognized Speedy in a metallic body suit, indicating that her hologram had been made inside this complex. There was nothing of our sled riding adventure together.

As soon as the images materialized of Speedy and me, the previously subdued Zalandans leapt out of their lounge chairs, threw their arms in the air, moved their shoulders, and stamped their feet in unison. Speedy touched me on the arm, and I recognized what had to be an expression of pride. She stood up, turned toward me, and took my hand. I stood, and we both swayed with our arms held above our heads and our fingers pointed toward the dome.

After we sat back down, I felt my lounge shift, and a hand touched me. Chri Anri said, "Tight thou now hold."

I must have looked bewildered, because he quickly talked into his yellow circle and then said, "Please hold on tightly."

He pointed to some straps on either side of my chair, which I grasped just in time. My chair levitated about ten feet up and completely circled around the room before flying high into the dome and then swooping down until it again leveled off at ten feet above the audience. Stray thoughts popped into my mind. Was now the time in the ceremony for the human sacrifice? I mentally repeated Chri Anri's words, "Barbarians we not. Visitor thou."

As I zoomed near Fawz, Jack, and Lauren, I saw how concerned they were.

I tightly held onto one strap and waved with the other hand. I even managed to smile, and the smile was not totally forced.

The Zalandans clapped. When the chair finally landed back in the same location, they said in unison, "Your presence brings us great joy."

I nodded my head and waved some more. "They surely know how to welcome somebody, but what was that all about?" I asked Chri Anri

Chri Anri consulted his yellow circle before he said, "You are the child. You have set us free."

"Whoa, wait a minute, Chri Anri. Aren't you free, already?"

Speedy touched my arm and hummed something into her circle. Then she said in perfect English, "Now, we might visit Earth."

"Would you like to visit Earth?" I asked Speedy.

Speedy still was listening to her circle when Chri Anri quickly said, "Yes, yes! Free now Earth visit yes."

"So, you couldn't visit us until we made a return visit to you?"

Chri Anri checked his circle before saying, "That is approximately accurate. More complex. Need verification."

They had their complex protocol, and we had ours. I simply wanted to let it go at that, but their protocol somehow involved Fawz and me.

Fawz, Jack, and Lauren's guides gave long humming speeches without translations, and that was followed by speeches from other beings. I understood from their emotion a tone of jubilation and awe.

Chri Anri now was sitting on the edge of my lounge. "Ceremony this long time last. Permissible now leave."

I followed Chri Anri out of this lively place into a corridor.

"Why was I separated from my crew?"

"Thee a child told them I."

"You told them I was a child?" I said indignantly.

"Child you are."

"Well, yes, no. I am a younger adult." I still was not scared of Chri Anri even after that weird chair ride, which I suspected was his doing. This lack of fear continued to surprise me, but I still felt peeved toward him for classifying me as a child and thought it best to conceal those feelings.

"Angry be thee not. Much more fun with me than visit official be. Dull for Commander Jack Medwin, Co-commander Fawzshen, and Mission Specialist Lauren Adams. Great adventure for Mission Specialist Jana Novacek."

I did not find the ceremony dull at all. I did not understand much of it, but it definitely was not dull.

Soon we were on another fast moving walkway, and again I braced myself to keep from falling. The walkway stopped, and suddenly we were thrust into something like a huge garden complete with waterfalls, a small lake, and trees with hanging vines by the water's edge.

It could have been a magical, wonderful place back home on Earth. Lush tropical plants seemed similar to those from home.

A nagging thought kept bothering me. This was too similar. I had traveled for five months, and the plants looked like those from Earth.

"Wish you concerns talk about?"

Chri Anri certainly was a perceptive creature. "The Zalandans are so much like humans from Earth. Even your ceremony was something like a laser light show or a concert on Earth. That place looked like an auditorium on Earth. We don't have chairs that comfortable, but my Dad has some porch furniture that is the same concept. I don't know what I expected." Chri Anri was staring at me as if maybe I used some words he did not understand, so I said "Your chairs at the ceremony are very nice."

Chri Anri answered, "Chairs the best."

"We thought you would be very different. Logically, we would be different from each other."

"Why be we different?"

337

"Life in the universe evolved differently. Different atmosphere, different sized stars."

"Look we also for universe life. Find it not. Look continue."

"But we found you, and you found us. Are you from the solar system or from another star system?"

Chri Anri seemed bewildered. "Zalanda be we here."

"Were you always from this moon, or did you come from somewhere else and settle here."

"Know you not?" Chri Anri exhibited a look that indicated complete surprise. His antennae fluttered, and his hair swayed. His mouth fell open revealing very nice teeth. "Know you not? From Earth be we."

"What? What? You're Earthlings?" Were we having a communication gap, or could this be true? Then, again, humans did not have antennae.

I must have been staring at Chri Anri's antennae because he talked into his circle before he said, "We brush our eyebrows forward. It is very useful that way."

Yes, of course, those antennae could be eyebrows, but why would grooming the brows that way be useful? I needed precise clarification. "Are you a human just like Fawz, Jack, Lauren, and I are humans?"

Chri Anri's brows moved in synchronization as he hummed into his circle before he emphatically said, "Of course, I am a human. All Zalandans are humans."

"When did you move here?"

"Many years, many centuries ago." Chri Anri pulled the yellow circle off his body suit and hummed into it. Humming came out of it instantly. "About 2,300 Earth years ago."

"I'm stunned and . . . pleased. But Earth people were pretty primitive back then. There was no technology."

"Rest world technology, too, ships, tools, art, architecture, literature, science, mathematics, philosophy. Some people primitive. We technology more, more, much."

"Chri Anri, I like this truth, but it is so awesome, so mind boggling to grasp."

Chri Anri told me that his ancestors liked the primitive people and often visited and helped them. However, sometimes the help and suggestions were misinterpreted or distorted, and the primitive ones got hurt.

His ancestors had superb aircraft and quite an advanced aerospace technology. They lived in northern Asia, and many chose to spend their summers farther north within the Arctic Circle. Most also enjoyed vacation houses on mountain tops in various parts of the world.

We strolled by another section of the park where items resembling fruit and vegetables were growing hydroponically in containers resembling hanging baskets. "But we have no record of your civilization."

"Complete record left in library, Alexandria, Egypt, left in three ancient languages, Egyptian, Greek, and Rhatanian."

"That library was burned."

"Know I. Library for books of the world. Unfortunate. I historian be but small audience, mostly old ones interest have. Great interest have mother my and grandfather. Where now go you next want?"

Not knowing what was around, the first thing that came into my mind was how their computers worked. "Computers, understand not," Chri Anri said and pulled the yellow circle off his body suit.

I did not remember mentioning computers but merely was thinking the word. I must have said it, but still a shiver went up my spine. Chri Anri hummed into the circle, it hummed back, and Chri Anri decided that computers and Center meant the same thing.

He pointed to the yellow circle and said, "Center."

That made sense. The yellow circle was a computer. He said, "More Center." We left the park and stepped onto another moving walkway, which ended at an immense area with spectacular multi-colored crystals of varying sizes.

While the garden area reminded me of home, this was an eerily beautiful alien place. Chri Anri touched a red crystal, and the lighting throughout grew brighter. We walked amid the crystals, and I gawked. I was glad Chri Anri was not trying to explain, because I was on brain overload. I eventually wanted to learn about their computer system to report back to Max Marsh, but my mind kept saying, "They're Earthlings! They're human Earthlings! How is this possible?"

I heard Jack's voice calling my name. "Jana, are you okay?"

Chri Anri handed me his yellow Center just like someone would hand me a phone. To make sure I did not commit a social blunder, I asked, "Do I speak into this?"

He nodded.

"Hi, Jack. I'm fine. Chri Anri and I are taking a tour of the Zalandan Center. It's the computer operations place."

Jack said, "We're going to call Houston now. We think the communicator should work from right here under the dome. Do you want join us?"

Jack's call was more than a courtesy because I did not need to be present for the transmission to Houston. He also was checking up on me to find out if I was okay. My crew was okay, too, because Jack did not have the communicator in the egg prison. That meant the crew must have taken it with them in the rover, and the Zalandans had given it back to them. Perhaps, my lack of fear in this entire situation was justified.

Chri Anri frowned and seemed distressed as if he did not want me to leave. I told Jack I would come back to the dome if he wanted me to, but I was sightseeing. Jack decided to tell Houston that I already was doing research.

Once Chri Anri realized that I was staying, his demeanor changed to his amused self again. "Place next you see?"

"I'd like a small meal. Do you have a restaurant?"

Chri Anri appeared bewildered and talked into his Center. When the response came back, he still seemed confused.

"Chri Anri, I'm hungry. I would like to eat."

"Most personal private business, eating food. In privacy eat. Restaurants have we not." He looked shocked as if I were a primitive savage.

"We have food on our lander."

"Food our the best, the healthiest."

We got on another moving walkway, which began slowing down as we approached a series of ramps. We jumped off the walkway onto a ramp and walked right through an opaque wall. We were in a gorgeous place like someone's living quarters.

"Ready now home for Jana Novacek Astronaut and thy crew."

"This is for us? Is this where we'll be staying? Oh, this is beautiful."

The curved walls softly changed colors except for one translucent wall that overlooked tropical plants in a cozy garden. A small dome above let in the Jovian light that filtered down to four clear Zalandan-style beds. Beyond the beds were four lounge chairs like the ones in the auditorium and an upright capsule that looked like the same object that had been in my egg prison.

Chri Anri led me toward the capsule. "In go thee and food out appears."

"Show me," I said for the first time mildly fearful of Chri Anri.

Chri Anri rotated his shoulders and then walked through the crystal wall into the capsule. Lights from all sides of the capsule started at the top and moved to the bottom, completely bathing him in every color of the spectrum: red, orange, yellow, green, blue, indigo, and violet. Then I saw a clear shelf about waist high with two wafers, one peach colored and one lime green, and a thin cylinder filled with a clear liquid. Chri Anri pointed and said, "Food and beverage." He shyly turned his back on me so that I could not watch him eat and drink. That seemed like a puny amount of food.

He was out of the capsule without my seeing him go through the wall.

341

"Now, you eat."

Chri Anri showed me dots on the capsule's outer wall that configured to my fingertips with my hands stretched outward. I touched the dots and walked right inside the capsule. The lights passed over me, and the shelf appeared holding four wafers, a deeper green one, a yellow one, an ivory colored one, and an orange-red one. My goblet was larger than Chri Anri's. I turned toward him, but he was staring up at the dome. I lifted the green wafer and took a very small bite. It was crispy, slightly sweet, and refreshing. Each wafer had a different taste. The liquid was water with a light lime flavor.

Once I finished eating, I touched the dots on the inner wall and walked out of the capsule without any problem. "Your food was different than mine," I said, trying to sound casual.

"Different needs have thee."

"Why is eating a private thing? On Earth, people eat together unless they are too busy or in too much of a hurry."

Chri Anri shuddered. I decided that was a topic to be pursued much later. He still looked rather disgusted, and I did not want the Zalandans to think of us as Earthly savages. Changing the subject would be the more tactful thing.

Anyway, I was extremely curious about something. "Chri Anri, when your people visited 500 years ago, they left a cylinder with a message on it inviting Earth people to return. They invited a Rhatanian and someone with a certain blood component. Why did they ask those two people to be members of the crew?"

Chri Anri looked so thrilled like he was about to reveal a major secret. "Know why I Rhatanian invited. Know why I you invited. Center go back. Answers show you."

After the moving walkway ride, we walked past the spectacular crystals again.

Adjacent to the crystals were various eggs similar to my prison but larger. We passed through the walls of one and were barely inside when a holographic performance began. A dozen people emerged from something that looked like a lander. As they drew nearer, I saw that all their eyebrows were brushed forward, and their hair stood out straight in all directions. They could have been the same twelve holographs that had appeared so briefly at our welcoming ceremony. Soon, Chri Anri and I were in the center of this group. They hummed to each other and also to Chri Anri and me. Chri Anri hummed statements back to them. I was almost sure a young woman about my age was humming directly at me.

"Your name she wishes," Chri Anri whispered to me.

"I am Jana Novacek, astronaut from Earth."

The hologram held out her arm in greeting and hummed something that ended with "Jana Novacek, astronaut from Earth."

"How did the hologram do that?" I asked.

"Later explain I," Chri Anri replied. "She told you that her name is Hulda."

The lander was no longer visible when another group of people dressed in flowing robes similar to Fawz's native costume greeted the twelve Zalandans. The two groups faded.

I figured the show was over, but now the Zalandans were on ice, back home here on Ganymede, I thought. However, surrounding the ice was water. I saw ice floes in the distance.

Chri Anri whispered to me, "Arctic Circle inside." As he whispered, holographic warmly dressed people came into focus. It seemed like a joyful encounter between them and the Zalandans.

Next, the Zalandans toured Elizabethan Europe. I recognized Oslo, London, Paris, and Rome from old paintings and drawings. In a city that possibly was Prague, Hulda tearfully bid farewell to the rest of her crew. That faded, and in a desolate countryside, the Zalandans handed a rectangular box the size of the cylinder container to a young man dressed in native Rhatanian clothing. The eleven then boarded the lander and lifted off.

Chri Anri had been enraptured with the holographic show, but now he began pacing around. I figured that was the signal that the show was over. "Now, understand thee?"

It was clear to Chri Anri, and I had a vague notion. "Your people went on a vacation. They visited Rhatania, an icy place inside the Arctic Circle, and several capitals of Europe. They gave the cylinder to a young Rhatanian."

"True, understand thee!"

"They left Hulda behind. But why?"

Chri Anri rotated his shoulders. "Very sad. Chose she on Earth to stay. Vacation much longer planned, China, Japan, fearful lose more crew. Return Zalanda crew immediately."

"What happened to Hulda?" That name somehow seemed familiar to me.

"Know we not."

"I still don't understand why your people wanted a person like me and why they wanted a Rhatanian to be a crewmember. Your people visited many other countries beside Rhatania."

He touched the wall of the egg, and several red circles appeared on the transparent wall. "Our archives," he said. "Much information."

He sequentially touched several circles, and then listened to his yellow Center hum a rather short message. He appeared truly shocked. "Tell you I cannot. Secrets not have Zalandans. Not possible information deny." Chri Anri hummed into his Center. "Restrict information Center never before."

I wanted to know, but I became so concerned about his bewilderment that I found myself saying, "It's really okay. Information is restricted on Earth all the time. We're accustomed to it."

He relaxed a little. It did not occur to me that I would be calming down a distressed Zalandan on his own planet. I had not learned that in my astronaut's training but rather from babysitting Jack's children.

"Glad thee guest my unhappy not."

"No, I'm not unhappy at all."

He calmed down more when humming came from his Center. Its message soothed him. He said to me, "Know you will, but wait, protocol follow. Know you soon."

That cheered me. I said, "It took us more than five months to get here. Now we can wait a little longer for the answers to our questions."

Soon, Chri Anri became his amused self again, and we left the egg. We went back into the crystal part of Center, and he explained how the crystals needed to be reactivated every now and then. When reactivation was necessary, they carried a crystal on a spaceship to inside of Jupiter and left it there in a space station for the required length of time while all the molecules become reactivated. Chri Anri admitted to me that there were newer, simpler ways to reactivate the crystals without the trip to Jupiter, but citizens enjoyed the trip, and it was a tradition to make the crystal journey to Jupiter. After reactivation on a space station inside Jupiter, a giant crystal was fully active for hundreds of years.

Later, Chri Anri took me back to the quarters that I would share with my crew. He showed me around and told me how things worked. He asked me if I thought my crew would want to share meals in a communal group. I responded that we would. Chri Anri tried not to look too disgusted. He tried a bland look on his face just like I had seen my parents do, but he was far less successful.

I blurted out, "I'm not a savage."

Chri Anri looked truly shocked as his eyebrows quivered. "Savage, you? No, impossible, you, the child. Understand thee not?"

I did not understand how it could be impossible. Children certainly were capable of behaving like savages. Because I was classified as a child, I could not be a savage. I totally missed that logic. However, I was glad that Chri Anri did not consider me one.

He put his fingers on the circles of the food capsule door and quickly reprogrammed it so that the food could be removed. "When testing food units, this we do." He asked me if I needed anything like a table for meals, and I told him that one was not necessary.

Once he was sure that I did not mind being alone, he disappeared through the wall of the quarters. It occurred to me that I did not know how to follow him, but the thought did not bother me. I was tired. It had been a long wake cycle.

I stretched out on one of the beds and figured I would fall right asleep, but too many ideas swirled in my head, mainly that they were people from Earth, ancient astronauts, so to speak. So much I did not understand. Then, I began forming an idea of why I had been picked for the mission, but that particular thought was too mind boggling to consider.

Jana's Journal

As to the whereabouts of my crew, I was beyond concern but tried not to dwell on scary thoughts of what might have happened to them or what might happen to me. Chri Anri was a completely affable, friendly fellow, who simply wanted to be a good guide. Surely, the other Zalandans must be similar.

Being unable to leave this room bothered me. I tried to look upon my situation positively. This room was considerably more spacious than our cabin on the *Copernicus* and far more spacious than the cramped *Falcon*. I definitely did not feel as abandoned as when Svee Dee had left me alone in the egg prison.

This solitude might have been a nice thing if only I could have shaken the uneasy feeling. Yet, I no longer was accustomed to being alone. I had been around my crew all the time, and I missed them, particularly in this strange situation. I missed my new friend Chri Anri, too.

Maybe, my problem simply was having nothing to do. I wished I had my notebook computer to record the events of this long, amazing wake cycle. A paper and pencil would have served the purpose.

A little distraction also would have comforted me. Right now, I did not want to think too deeply and scare myself. I started a mental list of minor things I did not understand. If the Zalandans had visited Earth 500 years ago, why could they speak current English with just a little help from Center? Why did Chri Anri speak such strange English without using Center very much at all? Still, he could speak my language, and I had not made an effort to understand his.

To my complete relief, Fawz and his guide walked right through the wall. I was so incredibly happy to see them that my anxiety and scary thoughts began evaporating.

Fawz's guide greeted me in humming sounds as his eyebrows waved in synchronization. He studied me with his piercing brown eyes as if something–my thoughts–perplexed him. I understood a message in his humming: "Child, you have nothing to fear. We will not hurt you. We welcome you."

Then, the moment was gone, but the meaning in his humming seemed as real as any words he could have spoken in my language. Because his name was practically untranslatable in English, he suggested that I call him Chief because his title was Chief Engineer. Like Chri Anri, he was an amiable fellow who seemed totally pleased to be Fawz's guide.

Chief said, "We are delighted that you dropped by for a visit."

I suppressed an urge to laugh because I was not sure if he had purposely made such an understatement. I replied, "We are so happy that we found you at home."

He stayed for a short while and told me that he oversaw the functioning of their "habitat carved from ice" which translated in their language to a short one-syllable hum. Although every Zalandan knew how to run the habitat including fairly young children, the chief engineer was ultimately responsible. There were back-up systems for the air, pressure, temperature, power, and water, but still the Zalandans were careful to not become complacent.

Chief's position lasted for 128 revolutions around Jupiter, about two-and-a-half Earth years, but could be extended automatically if there were any current situations regarding comets or meteoroids that possibly could endanger this moon. In that case, the chief engineer interfaced with the chief of aerospace. Fawz said that the chief engineer's job was the most important on Zalanda even though he was not considered the main leader.

As soon as Chief left, Fawz said, "You did it. You went out in the snow by yourself, and because of that we have been welcomed most warmly by these extraordinary Zalandans."

I replied, "You gave me the idea and the courage. Thanks."

From the cat that swallowed the canary look on his face, I knew that Fawz was just bursting to tell me something. He announced, "They are human beings."

I nodded. "I know. That's incredibly amazing. Do Jack and Lauren know, yet?"

"Yes, they do, but I have not seen them since I found out something equally incredible."

"Are you planning to tell me?" I coaxed. "Anytime soon?" I figured he was waiting to tell Jack, Lauren, and me all at the same time. "After all, I did go out in the snow."

"Since you put it that way, I will tell you now. The Zalandans are descended from ancient Rhatanians. In fact, Zalanda means the new land of Rhatania."

If Lauren had been here, she would have asked Fawz an enormous number of questions, but I did not know what to ask or where to begin. I simply said, "That's why they wanted a Rhatanian as a crewmember."

He replied, "I also came to that conclusion. In addition to my father and the Zalandans, you are the only one who knows. I talked to Houston a short time ago, and told CAPCOM, Filbert, only that we had made contact. I requested to be patched through to my father. He became the first person on Earth to know that our ancient countrymen had been bold, brave astronauts and that we now have met their descendants, my long-lost, affable, intelligent relatives. After speaking to my father, I tried to tell Houston, but the transmission deteriorated almost immediately."

"Is this lack of communication going to cause us any problems with Houston?" I asked.

"I hope not. Our transmission after the welcoming festival did not go through either. Jack went to the *Falcon* to send a message from that communicator, and I do not know if he has had any success. The problem seems to be on Houston's end. The Earth is experiencing a solar storm, rare for this time in the sun's cycle, and to further complicate things, today is the spring equinox. My father received his message only because it was his destiny. Director Clayton can call him and get everything straightened out."

"Did you find out from Chief why they wanted someone like me on this mission?"

"No, I did not. Chief mentioned verification."

I said, "Chri Anri said something about verification, too."

"Chief checked the archives for me and was told by Center not to divulge anything he knew about the Zalandan visit to Earth 500 years ago."

"That sounds ominous," I said.

"Indeed! However, Chief thought it was a Center malfunction caused by his putting specific information off-limits at my request. I personally wanted to tell you, Jack, and Lauren that the Zalandans are descendants of ancient Rhatanians, but Chief had seemed bewildered by my request. He spoke into his yellow Center with someone before agreeing to do it. These Zalandans are guileless people."

"I know they are. I think they eventually will tell us everything. Chri Anri showed me a holographic movie, and I'm getting some rather mind boggling ideas why they requested someone like me. These ideas are way too much to consider. Do you think it's better if I simply wait patiently and not speculate too much?"

"Yes, Jana, I do."

Jack burst through the wall with his guide, a woman named Cecil, the leader of Zalanda. Jack was carrying my notebook computer under his arm. I had so much to write.

Cecil was slightly shorter than Chri Anri and Chief, and I noticed that her brows moved much more subtly when she talked. She greeted Fawz and me and said if we needed anything in our "sleep room" to simply ask for it.

I wanted to know how to get out of this room but wondered if the Zalandans would allow us to do that. If not, I did not want to know that.

We all sat down on the lounge chairs, which were arranged in an L-shape. Fawz asked Cecil about her job. She either had an excellent memory or was more conversant in English, because she talked into Center for only a little while and then answered him, speaking for an extended period.

She explained that although the Zalandan word for her position translated into the main leader, it also translated into prioritizer, her primary job. Her title was chief of priority and protocol. Mostly, individuals worked together to resolve their differences regarding priorities and did not seek her help. According to the Zalandan covenant, running the habitat always took top priority, which included normal environmental dangers as well as major ones. Directly related to running the habitat was protecting the health of the people.

Cecil also handled another type of priority. When a decision needed to be made quickly without time to get a consensus or input, then she made that decision. In the event of when to have our arrival festival and the content of our festival, she properly deferred to Chri Anri, who had orchestrated the whole thing very quickly, including selecting the guide for each visitor. She then talked into Center and seemed to be thinking how to phrase something.

Once Cecil had her thoughts together, she said that Chri Anri had done an outstanding job with the ceremony "considering the circumstances."

That comment stopped all of us cold. I could see Jack and Fawz trying to figure out how to ask a question tactfully. Finally, Jack simply asked, "What are the circumstances?"

"The festival was 'spoken' to be two days hence. We would have met you within the Monument of the Lost One when the great orange cloud was at mid rotation. First Chri Anri the Elder would have come forth amid a light snowstorm. It would have been such a beautiful

351

festival." She briefly closed her eyes and her brows waved softly. I saw her as an artist planning and envisioning a beautiful event that was not to be.

Our eyes met as if she understood my thought and it was almost as if she was saying, "Do not weep for me."

Then, the moment was gone, and she said, "Chri Anri made the decision for today. I could not have presumed to do that. It was a good decision considering you already were in the beastie balneary, which you call decontamination.

"Chri Anri the Elder is far away. First, he needs to return. He needed to be at the festival, but now it is over. I must solve this problem."

This was getting a bit spooky. Chri Anri the Elder had visited Earth over 500 years ago. That meant he was dead. I did not want to follow that line of thought, but my mind roamed there anyway. Was he in a deep freeze or suspended animation? Were they thawing him out?

Then, a simpler thought came to me. The Zalandans could be working on a holographic movie of Chri Anri the Elder to honor his life and the last mission to the Earth. That was what would be ready in two days. From the examples I had seen, they certainly were skilled with presenting events holographically.

Jack seemed to be groping for words. Cecil must have realized that we needed to know much more. She told us that all the Zalandans were anxious to meet us and that the waiting had been excruciating, particularly for the child Svee Dee, who had been given permission to discretely observe us at the Monument for the Lost One only when everyone slept except for "the young woman Mission Specialist Jana." She nodded toward me.

Things apparently got out of hand with the observation. When Svee Dee told her mother that she had brought an Earthling back to the habitat, the mother thought that the imaginative child simply was entertaining her with wishful thinking. The child described her usual snow ride, which even more convinced the mother of wishful thinking.

Svee Dee realized she needed to take action on her own. She located the rescue party through observing the outside video cameras and then set the tracking mechanism to guide the rover into the habitat. Svee Dee checked to make sure everything was working properly and safely inside the beastie balneary. Then Svee Dee went to Chri Anri and asked for his help. He also did not put much credence in her words until he heard a voice calling his name. Since Most Zalandans were having a difficult time with patience while waiting to meet our crew, they were pleased with what Svee Dee inadvertently had done.

Cecil still, however, felt sad and concerned that Chri Anri the Elder had missed the festival. That had not been handled according to protocol, and she had been pondering on how to make it up to him. Normally, the Zalandans had no secrets, but when Fawz asked Chief if something temporarily could be held secret from his crew, Chief had consulted with Cecil via Center before making his decision. That gave Cecil an idea. She decided that the related thing could be held secret from the entire crew so that Chri Anri the Elder could reveal that to the Earthlings when he arrived. At least, that would be something left for him, and that way she would have followed protocol.

Cecil certainly had answered a lot of my questions, some that had not even been formulated yet. I was glad that Svee Dee knew enough to take care of us and that we had not been jellyfish in incompetent hands. At the time I had thought she had just lost interest in me, when instead she had been figuring out how to help me.

I still was digesting what Cecil had said when Lauren and her guide Nairme made their grand appearance through the wall. Nairme greeted us and then asked what we wanted to know about her job. I did not know about the others, but my brain overload had returned. She must have sensed that because she briefly told us that her job roughly translated into chief psychologist, which also included education and social events. Her job was to see that the Zalandans were getting what they intellectually, emotionally, socially, and spiritually required to thrive in the society.

Cecil gently interrupted Nairme and told us that she needed to consult with her for a flicker of time. They hummed, sometimes individually like a normal back and forth conversation and sometimes both at the same time, indicating to me that they talked and listened concurrently.

While they were humming, Lauren softly asked me, "Where's Chri Anri?" Then almost as an afterthought, she added, "And Chief?"

"They were here," I replied.

She asked me many questions about Chri Anri. I explained that he truly understood English, and I did not know why he spoke his own version of our language. He rarely used Center to translate.

Realizing that Lauren could be attracted to him, I used my blandest voice and resisted any urge to tease her because I wanted her to feel comfortable asking me about him. I tried to reveal no expression on my face. Fortunately, Jack and Fawz were comparing notes on their transmission problems with Houston and were not listening to us.

I was telling Lauren how completely delightful Chri Anri was when the humming stopped, and Cecil said, "We have solved the protocol situation. We will have a small festival in the astronomical observatory when Chri Anri the Elder and Sedra return." She looked relieved as if a weight had been lifted from her.

Ah, Sedra, a new name! I was ready to pursue that when Fawz asked about the Zalandan political structure.

Cecil explained that there were six main jobs, and the six leaders worked together to run the civilization. Besides those we had already met, the other three were chief of aerospace and related sciences, chief of medicine and nutrition, and chief of humanities, which included music, art, architecture, holographics, literature, languages, and history. When a leader's term of office was over, then someone new who had been in training but preferably who had not previously held that position would move into the office. All six positions had a large body of former leaders from whom to ask for help. Doing one's job well gave one considerable status, and asking for help and other opinions was considered a prudent thing to do. All that Cecil told us interested me in a general sense, but I realized Fawz's interest was in the area of application. Would any of this be useful for his own country?

When Cecil and Nairme were ready to leave, they showed us how to go through the wall. Only at certain places were the wall fibers constructed so they could come apart. After the fibers became stressed and parted, then they healed themselves. Cecil and Nairme invited us to roam anywhere we wanted in the habitat and told us how to get to the auditorium. Cecil announced that our guides would meet us after we awoke.

I thought Chri Anri had done a good job matching guides for Fawz, Jack, and Lauren. Fawz, who loved to solve problems, was matched with the chief problem solver of them all, Chief. Jack, basically our leader had been matched with their main leader, and Lauren, a sociologist, had been matched with a psychologist. I would not have traded Chri Anri with anyone else as a guide, but now realized he could have been anyone's guide or no one's guide, and he had chosen me. I did not know why but suspected that it had something to do with the holographic movie he had shown me.

After they left, we dragged our lounge chairs from the L arrangement into a circle and ate the food that we had gotten out of the food capsule. Mine was quite delicious. We all had different meals. Fawz had seven wafers, the most, and we teased him. Our wafers were all slightly different colors. We commented that eating seemed a precise and for some reason a private activity to the Zalandans.

I thanked Jack for retrieving my computer from the lander. He said, "Cecil accompanied me and was so taken with the *Falcon*. She called it a fragile and delicate thing."

Lauren said, "It sounds like she was being critical of the *Falcon*. Did she express an opinion about our communicators?"

"No. I've concluded that our communicators are working just fine. I've run diagnostics on them twice. The trouble is on Houston's end, what with the solar flare and the vernal equinox. I've sent a message from the *Falcon* over and over again. Filbert was on duty, and I got a partial transmission from him, enough to know that he sounded concerned about us. I don't know how much of my message he received."

Zalanda now was behind Jupiter, and our communication would be down for slightly more than three full days. There was nothing more to do about Houston but wait and let Fawz's dad tell Director Clayton all the glorious things that had happened.

Lauren said to Fawz, "Cecil mentioned you withheld something from us."

Fawz nodded as the cat that swallowed the canary look again spread across his face. He could not wait to tell them.

"Fawz told me. His secret is safe with me," I said in jest and then covered my mouth with my hand.

"Are you going to tell us relatively soon?" Jack asked, half teasing.

"My question was where had the Zalandans come from? Where had they lived on Earth? My guide seemed confused that I did not know. He said, 'Do you not know that the Zalandans came from ancient Rhatania?'"

"Oh, my, that explains a lot," Lauren said. "That's why the Zalandans wanted at least one Rhatanian on the return visit. You and they are the same people. You don't look that much alike. Yet, I'm beginning to see similarities."

He said, "I have been thinking about the same thing. Throughout the centuries, occasional visitors came to our remote country. Some stayed, became Rhatanians, and changed our gene pool. After 2,500 years, we are somewhat different genetically than the Zalandans. We both have a preference for cold weather. Even though we are different, we Rhatanians are the closest relatives on Earth that the Zalandans have."

I had longer to consider all this than Jack and Lauren, but still I said, "This is pretty much to grasp in one day. First, we find out they're

Earthlings, and now we find out that these particular Earthlings are descended from ancient Rhatanians."

Lauren asked, "Is this not in your documented history? Rhatania has a pretty complete set of historical archives that goes back 3,000 years."

Fawz replied, "I'm thoroughly familiar with Rhatanian history. Every school child studies our history throughout the ages. There is no record of this astounding event."

"Why do you believe they are telling you the truth?" Lauren persisted.

I could hardly believe that Lauren would ask such a question. We had all met them, and they seemed so totally guileless, almost as if incapable of lying. It had been such a problem for Chief to briefly suppress information that before doing so, he had requested Cecil's opinion.

Fawz patiently said, "I mentioned to Chief that we had no record, and he explained that this was by mutual consent between the ancient Rhatanians who stayed on Earth and those who left. Back those 2500 years ago before the exodus to a new planet, not all the Rhatanians were so enthralled with our awesome technology, and this became a huge source of contention. Some felt so much power would eventually cause great trouble, and our people would be in danger of losing their integrity and honor.

"Chri Anri told me it was 2300 years," I said.

"Correct! We'll get to that, soon."

"Those who wanted to return to a simpler life looked for ways to validate their desires through an examination of our religious writings. Those who wanted to go full steam ahead used the religious writings for a validation of technology.

"In addition to religious writings, both sides also looked to social issues. Our young people interacted with the primitive people. One side felt we were helping the primitive ones, and the other side felt we were corrupting them.

"Fortunately, these disagreements were done in a civilized way through discussions and analysis because our ancients had great respect for individual rights and desires. At that point in time, they had almost a 500-year history of being a peace loving people. Our ancient ones did not have wars of conquest as so many people of those times did. Instead, they had spent their time on discovery including the mastery of space.

"Both groups kept looking for a consensus and tried to keep from getting any more polarized than they were already. However, this eventually developed into a conflict between people who wanted to charge forward with technology and those who wanted to abandon it altogether.

"Finally, a decision was reached. The technology group would leave the Earth and settle on another planet. Analysis seemed to indicate that Mars could be made quite habitable. The anti-technology group would help them prepare for the trip. Those who were adamantly opposed to technology would help in non-technical ways. Those not so adamant would work with the technology for the last time while making preparations for the trip. That is what happened.

"A very large group of people—more than 10,000—left for Mars. Including the Rhatanians, friends from around the world also were invited on the mission, and a significant number happily accepted."

Lauren added, "That's another change in the genes, the friends who accompanied them."

Fawz continued. "This migration took years to complete, as the spaceships made return trips. Once the group was settled on Mars, by agreement the anti-technology group on Earth destroyed their evidence of technology and purged it from almost all of their records.

"However, by mutual consent, it was agreed that they would leave a record of the migration in the library in Alexandria, Egypt. It would be written in three languages—Rhatanian, Greek, and Egyptian Hieroglyphics—but no record would be left that indicated the people who made the trip were Rhatanians. In addition, the scrolls would be sealed in a special receptacle for 1800 years.

"Once on Mars, the technology group had overestimated their considerable abilities. Many Rhatanians died. Some wished to return, and they did. The others who stayed on Mars persevered and eventually made their technology work.

"After more than 200 years, even with many advances in technology, Mars still had drawbacks for human habitation. It was not as suitable as they had wished. The group considered another mass migration, and, eventually, this moon of Jupiter was selected. They have been here on Zalanda a very long time, close to 2,300 years."

Fawz paused and looked at each of us. I was too amazed to say anything. My thoughts settled on the Rhatanians who had made the space journey so long ago and how the group had dwindled from about 10,000 to around 1,000. I wondered how many had returned and how many had perished. Nobody commented on what Fawz said. I guess we were each too much into our own thoughts.

Fawz said, "Although the Rhatanians who stayed on Earth destroyed their technology and references to their technology, they agreed to abide by two escape clauses. The Zalandans could reveal themselves when the Rhatanians again developed a significant level of technology on their own or with the help of other Earth people. The second escape clause could be activated if a long time, the length of time being unspecified, had elapsed and if the Zalandans needed our help."

Jack said, "It seems that during their visit of 500 years ago, the Zalandans revealed they were star people, but as far as we know, they did not say they were related."

Lauren said, "If the Zalandans revealed that much of their identity, that could mean that they needed help.

Fawz replied, "All that is now off limits to us until the ceremony with Chri Anri the Elder.

Our conversation turned to how there could be such an advanced civilization and no records of its existence even if the civilization itself purged all the records. If they interacted with other civilizations, then records should be somewhere. Because Lauren had such a keen interest in anthropology, she pointed out that records of advanced civilizations existed, and one did not have to look particularly hard. She started reeling off lots of references. She mentioned a model airplane with excellent aerodynamic features found in 1898 in a tomb at Saqquara, Egypt. That plane was more than 2,000 years old. Other model planes were found in Central and South America. She described pictures of aircraft, particularly an embossed one found on a panel in a temple in Abydos, Egypt. She described flying machines in written material such as the Dead Sea Scrolls. Those documents had not been tampered with throughout the centuries. In ancient Indian texts were descriptions and operating instructions for flying machines.

Then she mentioned that the time between the Wright brothers' first flight and the first moon landing was only 66 years, from 1903 with the first powered airplane and 1969, the first landing on the moon. If the ancient people had planes, how long before they had space vehicles. They would need a power source and computers.

I knew about some of her references as I figured did Fawz and Jack. It was just that she reeled them off so rapidly with dates, locations, and opinions of experts. Her material was organized in her brain before she even spoke: actual model planes, pictures, and written documents. Besides flying machines, she reeled off references to ancient technological artifacts found by the thousands in Russia, some very old and very small made of tungsten and molybdenum and small spiral items.

When she finished talking, Jack said, "It only takes one of those civilizations! And we have found one."

Lauren said, "I'm on this mission only for this very moment to show you that such a human civilization is possible here and now as well as 2,500 years ago."

We were all silent. I realized that, as confident as Lauren was, she had questioned why she had been lucky enough to be chosen for this mission. In her mind, she also needed to justify her own selection. That was a rare crack in Lauren's confidence. She even had once said to me regarding my training, "You're here. Therefore, you belong." But for this particular moment, she did not totally believe that about herself.

I had said practically the same thing to Fawz in a different context before my decision to go out in the snow if given the opportunity

Everyone was awkwardly silent until Fawz said, "I am here because of Rhatania's financial contribution to the mission. People have excellent premises they wish to test out, but how many are given the opportunity?"

Of all the months we had spent together, now in this strange room on this strange planet, the veneer of these two brilliant people had been stripped off. At some place within each of them, a little part of them was as insecure as I. Their insecurity would go away with adequate sleep while mine would linger. I realized how much I loved each one of them and how unassumingly brilliant Jack, Fawz, and Lauren were.

Jack pulled us out of this state of bare psyche by saying we had been awake for a very long time, and that it was definitely time to sleep. He thought we had done enough soul sharing for now.

Jack announced we would go on the Zalandan timing for our sleep cycle and wake cycle. Since there also was no day or night here, he found what they translated into sleep cycle was the word "recharge." They called their wake cycle "joytime." The full cycle was approximately the Earth's twenty-four hours.

I said, "I'm almost afraid to go to sleep because I might wake up in Houston and find out that it's all over already. Like a holiday you're looking forward to, then it happens too fast."

"I feel exactly the same way, Jana," Jack said.

Even though the bed was incredibly comfortable as it molded to my every movement, sleep was not imminent because thoughts swirled in my head. When I looked back on that brief moment of Lauren being insecure, I thought she was here because it was her destiny to meet Chri Anri, but that made me feel like I shared Fawz's belief system, which I certainly did not.

I replayed in my mind the events of this long, glorious wake cycle: leaving the *Falcon* and going in the snow by myself, finding Svee Dee, feeling trapped in the beastie balneary, meeting Chri Anri, being reunited with my crew, the festival with the Zalandans, and my sightseeing tour with Chri Anri. Most of all was the fact that they were Earthlings and kind, gentle ones at that.

Instead of relaxing and dozing off to sleep, in the stillness a disturbing concern began growing. Now that all the activities of the wake cycle had ceased, my brain began catching up, and I definitely felt warning lights blinking. The transmission problems with Houston had been at the periphery of my thought for the past few hours.

Filbert had been the CAPCOM at Mission Control. I needed to tell Fawz and Jack what a snake Filbert was. They did not know that he had been mean to me. The brilliant Venzi Suzaky, Max's friend, had guessed it. I had not told anyone that I overheard Filbert deprecating the selection of Lauren and Fawz as crewmembers. Now was Filbert's chance to discredit all of us, particularly Fawz and me. He disliked both of us for different reasons, me, because I was young and did not become an astronaut in the traditional way and, Fawz, because he was a foreigner. The bottom line those many months ago was that Filbert had somehow guessed the importance of this mission and felt he deserved to be selected as a crewmember. Now, of course, he knew what he had missed.

I would tell them while I still had the nerve even though I did not have solid facts. As I was ready to speak, Jack again said that we should get some sleep. We needed to be ready for whatever the next joytime would bring.

I was too tired to get the words out. I would tell them first thing during the joytime, even before breakfast. They could judge for themselves.

Jana's Journal

I woke up the next wake cycle determined to speak to Fawz, Jack, and Lauren about Filbert. They needed to know what he was capable of doing, always something one could not quite prove, but strong and powerful just the same. They needed to know how he had tried to sabotage me.

However, the next wake cycle started with such a whir of activity. First, during a quick conference between the four of us, we again discussed the idea of adapting to local custom if it did no harm. If we all were willing, Jack decided that it was okay to wear Zalandan body suits that had magically appeared in our room. My, what comfortable clothes. Jack, Lauren, and Fawz wore jewel colored body suits with flecks of color running through. I was dressed differently in a cream colored body suit, the color of Svee Dee's. Each suit had a yellow Center on the front near the left shoulder. After wearing NASA daywear for almost six months, it was good to try something new. We all were admiring ourselves in our new clothes, and it seemed like an inappropriate time to mention suspicions about Filbert that I could not quite pin down to anything concrete.

Chri Anri burst in on us and caught us in our circle eating breakfast of wafers and beverages, each with our own specific Zalandan food. Jack invited him to join us, and Chri Anri accepted reluctantly and sat on the edge of Lauren's lounge chair. When Jack offered Chri Anri one of his wafers, Chri Anri adamantly refused with Zalandan hums interspersed with various pitches of the word "no." He fidgeted while we ate and looked like an accomplice to a grave sin. I figured he was trying really hard to adapt to our customs, just as we were trying to adapt to his.

As soon as we finished our wafers and beverages, Chri Anri visibly sighed as the slight frown lines left his face. He began speaking and humming almost simultaneously. "Arrive here Mother mine and Grandfather mine Chri Anri the Elder. Soon, very soon. In now beastie balneary." Chri Anri then hummed along, oblivious that we could not understand him. Whatever the language differences, I did understand one thing; Chri Anri was very excited and happy about their arrival.

"Is this the same Chri Anri who visited Earth?" I asked, the excitement being infectious.

"Yes, yes, same Chri Anri this be. Saw already Chri Anri the Elder and Sedra through walls decontamination. Wishes my asked them for you."

I thought that would make Chri Anri over 500 years old, but I did not comment on that fact.

"Were your mother and grandfather on another part of the planet?" Jack asked politely.

"Be there they Titan."

"You have a settlement there?" Fawz asked, trying to contain his enthusiasm and remain calm.

"Settlement! No. Wish, hope, plan! Small outpost have we there. Future time settlement, yes.

"Mother, grandfather best time yet. Very fast here from Titan. A record in speed. Return they for thee. Earth experts current they. History experts, too."

Abruptly, four smaller Zalandans burst in on us right through the walls. Knocking clearly was not a custom here on Zalanda. They looked like young girls slightly older than Svee Dee.

"We prepare you for the reception," one of them said.

Then, each one in turn said, "My name is . . . ." The words were then followed by untranslatable humming sounds. Each sound was slightly different, but I could not repeat the sounds or remember the differences.

Jack said to one of them. "You have a longer name."

The four of them looked at each other and giggled.

"How do you prepare us for the meeting?" Jack gently asked.

"We groom you," one replied and then giggled some more.

Before I had a chance to object, the smallest one approached me with something the size of a pocket comb without teeth and passed it around my hair. It was the same type of thing I had seen Svee Dee use on her own hair. I pulled back and must have looked displeased because the young Zalandan immediately stopped. The four of them hummed together and appeared concerned. One spoke into Center and then said, "We groom you if you wish grooming."

"What is the purpose of grooming us?" Jack asked in a gentle tone of voice.

The girls hummed into their Centers, and the one with the longest name said, "It will help you with information."

That comment lost something in the translation, so we had another quick conference. Jack decided it was okay to go along with them to a point and continue adapting to local custom if it did no harm. When Jack told them they could proceed, they seemed quite pleased as they hummed happily to each other.

Before my groomer touched my hair again, a wall of our quarters became reflective, converting itself into a big mirror. From the little grooming that already had been done, my hair stood straight out in all directions just like the Zalandans. In fact, my hair looked interesting and actually pretty good. My groomer fussed with my hair some more although I could not see that the fussing changed the look from the original pass of the wand. I nodded in approval. I wondered why they were trying to make us look more like them. Maybe they could relate to us if we resembled them.

Lauren's hair would not cooperate at all. Her groomer got it all standing perpendicular to her head, and then it popped back into its

Linda A. W. King

original style. A little gel or mousse would have helped, but it was not my place to give advice to the Zalandans.

After my hair was done to my groomer's satisfaction, she began working with a smaller wand on my eyebrows, coaxing them to stand straight out. I watched the conversion and decided that I looked quite a bit like a Zalandan. It was amazing what clothes, a hairdo, and a brow brushing could do.

Lauren said, "We've traveled these millions of miles to go to a beauty shop."

The girls listened for their Center to translate; then, they giggled some more and one repeated, "Beauty shop."

"NASA has spent billions of dollars for us to get our hair styled? Senator Quagly would certainly have a field day if he knew about this, and for once I'd agree with him."

Chri Anri murmured to her. "Grooming not reason frivolous." Even though he did not consider it frivolous, he still paced around impatiently. When the four young girls left, Chri Anri said, "For beginners hair preparation much necessary not." Then he touched Lauren's brushed forward eyebrows, and the look that passed between them needed no language. He spoke to Center, and after it hummed back, he said to Lauren, "For optimal transmission, helpful hair your cut."

His statement made absolutely no sense, but they still gazed at each other. Jack, Fawz, and I exchanged rather embarrassed glances, and I remembered Lauren talking wistfully about if she ever met the right person. If any of us had any lingering doubts about Zalandans being human, at that moment, the doubt was gone.

Chri Anri then went back to his pacing as he commented on the whereabouts of the guides. Why we each needed our own personal guide when it was permissible for us to roam freely around the complex, I did not know, perhaps their idea of politeness or protocol. It was okay to burst through a wall, but it was not okay to fail to provide a guest with a personal guide. Chri Anri talked into Center and then

366

explained to us that his mother and grandfather had just completed the abbreviated decontamination cycle required of a mission to Titan.

Cecil, Chief, and Nairme arrived within minutes of each other. Immediately upon the arrival of the last one, we were whisked on moving walkways to the astronomical observatory, a large circular room that seemed to be a combined planetarium and Mission Control. In addition to what I thought was a telescope were many pieces of incomprehensible equipment. Off to one side were several rows of stadium-style seating.

For a moment, our four guides and the four of us were the only ones in this spacious observatory. Soon, three more arrived together, and I met the chief of astronomy, the chief of humanities, and the chief of medicine and nutrition. Next, seven others arrived together, and I had the great pleasure of meeting the remaining crewmembers who had gone with Chri Anri on the last Zalandan journey to Earth those 500 years ago. My crew had previously met them after our welcoming festival. Then arrived Svee Dee and her mother, who was introduced to us as Averg.

Cecil told us where to stand. Jack, Lauren, and Fawz stood with the six leaders, and several feet from them I stood with Chri Anri, Svee Dee, and Averg. Chri Anri told me the placement was because I was the child. The Zalandan crewmembers stood in a little group together.

Through the walls emerged a dignified middle-aged man and a kindly appearing woman. By then I was so accustomed to hair standing out in all directions and brows waving like antennae that it barely affected me.

Before speaking, Chri Anri checked with Center, and with the word order exactly right, he delivered long, elaborate, flattering introductions with the most extreme decorum as he introduced each of us to Chri Anri the Elder and his daughter Sedra.

Chri Anri the Elder responded with a strong voice and simply said in impeccable English, "It is such a pleasure to meet you."

He looked like a healthy person, maybe not much older than my father. We shook hands rather formally, and then he saluted us. As an afterthought, he gave us each a rather affectionate hug. Tears streamed down his face. "We have waited more than five Earth centuries for such a visit. Eventually, we gave up waiting, and the hope faded."

Chri Anri added, "My grandfather was the leader of the last Zalandan voyage to Earth."

Chri Anri the Elder said, "From our home here on Zalanda, our space vessel traversed past the great winds, past the broken and jagged rocks, past the orbit of Mars, our first home in the heavens, and onward to the birthplace of our civilization, Earth. We had returned to our origins. It was a moving experience, so many different people living with a nature they had only partially created, blue skies, green trees, heavy gravity, and freedom to walk unprotected on the surface of the planet. On Earth, we visited our closest relatives of two millennium earlier, the Rhatanians.

"It was a glorious visit on Earth, a tour I would have cherished always except great sadness befell me and all of Zalanda. My first born daughter Hulda chose to stay behind on Earth. It was a shattering experience for me that anyone would choose Earth over Zalanda. That it was my own daughter made the experience more shattering. What had I done wrong that she wanted to leave her family? We take child rearing most seriously. Why would she wish to leave? Was something wrong with Zalanda? What need did we not provide her?"

Sedra's voice was lovely and lilting as she spoke. "I was born eighteen Earth years after the journey. As a young child, I soon learned that there was sadness regarding the Earth visit. I was maybe ten Earth years old before I understood the impact about leaving behind the sister I had never seen. I thought about her and imagined what she might be like. Sometimes, I thought I could communicate with her through the great reaches of space. I still think about her even today. I wonder how long she survived on Earth, and I hope that she had a good life. Sometimes, I think I still can communicate with her."

Chri Anri the Elder said, "Our people have not made a return visit to Earth. All these long centuries, whenever anyone thought of taking a journey to Earth, whenever plans were started, eventually Hulda would be mentioned, and people became concerned. Would someone's child or soul mate choose to stay behind on Earth again? We are a small group of people. To lose one person suffuses us with great sadness."

Fawz spoke, "There was a cylinder you left behind in Rhatania. On the cylinder, you requested that we visit you. You described where you lived, here on this moon of Jupiter, and you requested who two of the crewmembers should be: one a Rhatanian and the other person from anywhere in the world who has a certain blood type. Our astronaut Jana Novacek has the blood type that you requested."

Chri Anri the Elder looked somewhat bewildered. He took my hand and looked into my eyes. He seemed to be quietly thinking. "Child," he said softly, "You could be Hulda's descendant, indeed, if you do have the blood component. It was very rare, originally found only in a few of the Rhatanians who left Earth. None who stayed behind had that variation. Since we are an isolated society, many more of our people now have the blood component. With your permission, we will check it."

I said, "Yes, you may check it. I would be honored to be a descendant of a Zalandan. This is an amazing world you have created here."

"How old are you," he asked me.

"Twenty, sir. Twenty Earth years."

He briefly hummed into his Center and then said, "She was a few years younger when she stayed behind on Earth. I had hoped that my Zalandan child survived the Earth environment. We had left her with potent medicine and a Center filled with valuable survival information. Your being here means she survived long enough to have a child. And her descendants also survived long enough until here you are. You have her eyes and her eye whites. You look like her. It has been a long time. I need to look at one of her holograms, but there is a strong resemblance."

369

I asked, "When you wrote on the cylinder describing someone by blood type, you were describing Hulda. Is that accurate, sir?"

"Yes, yes, it was a last hope."

"Instead, I showed up. I hope you're not too disappointed."

"Jana, your arrival here has raised as much joy as if Hulda herself were on your crew." His strong voice quavered slightly as he spoke with great emotion. He looked at each of us and said, "There are not words enough in your language or ours to express how delighted we are that you four daring space people are here. We are most pleased that all of you made the perilous trip. A first journey is always fraught with unknown dangers."

Then to Fawz, he said, "Not a Zalandan is alive who personally witnessed when we departed our Rhatanian brethren 2500 years ago. We experienced the break in our culture and the division of our people. Now, after all these centuries, our people—the Zalandans and the Rhatanians—are knowingly joined back together. We salute you, Co-commander Fawzshen, Prince of Rhatania, representative of all Rhatanians, and we welcome you, our brother from so long ago."

Fawz said, "Thank you. Our anticipation of what we would find here has been far exceeded. We hoped to find life, but to find Earth people and particularly to find Zalandans, people who are descendants of ancient Rhatanians, is more than I possibly could have desired. To have regained some of our history is special but to have regained the Zalandans is the highest level of jubilation. I am sincerely honored to represent Rhatania at the most significant moment in all of our history." Fawz then spoke in Rhatanian.

Chri Anri the Elder consulted his Center before replying in Rhatanian. When he finished speaking to Fawz, he turned toward me and in English said, "The rejoining of our two peoples in itself is amazing, but because of Hulda and her representative in you, Mission Specialist Jana Novacek, we are rejoined with everyone on Earth. Because she stayed on Earth, she created a bridge between Zalandans and people throughout your world. I always had mourned being separated from

Hulda, but at this moment I mourn no more because she has brought us close to everyone who now walks on Earth. Now on Earth are her descendants, descendants of a space person, descendants of a Zalandan, descendants of ancient Zalandans, some who can know that they are her descendants and some who will never know."

I said, "I too am grateful for Hulda. If she had not chosen to stay on Earth, I would not ever have existed. I don't know how many people on Earth, now and in the past, owe their existence to Hulda." It was a strange thought. If a Zalandan had not chosen to leave her crew and stay behind, I would not be here now. I would not be anywhere. Her family suffered disappointment and sadness because of her decision, but that decision brought life to people, how many I did not know.

At that moment, I felt that I was Hulda's descendant, but things were moving too fast. Chri Anri the Elder had concluded that I was her descendant without my getting the blood test. Maybe, he just wanted it to be that way. We had made the long trip, and believing I was Hulda's descendant could give him some solace. Somehow, I wanted to believe it, too.

Chri Anri the Elder now was talking to Jack. "Commander Jackson Medwin, we are most honored that your space faring country, the United States of America, allowed you, their most illustrious astronaut, to go on such a perilous journey to search for our people. From your Mars landing, you already have filled your people with awe, wonder, and a taste for travel throughout the solar system."

Jack simply said, "I am honored to have been chosen for this journey. To speak with you now, to be the first crew to make contact with people living on this heavenly body is beyond joy. To be on Zalanda with each of you—Chri Anri the Elder, Sedra, Chri Anri, Cecil, Chief, Nairme, Svee Dee, Averg and everyone here in this observatory—fills me with such euphoria." Jack nodded to each person as he spoke the name. He mentioned the other three leaders and then saluted the seven remaining crewmembers of the last Zalandan journey to Earth. He spoke their names as if he had known each of them his entire life.

He said, "As a member of an international crew and as a citizen of the United States, I bring greetings to you from our President. She wishes for a long and peaceful relationship between our two worlds, and she invites you to visit our country, either an announced official visit or a quiet unofficial visit, whichever you prefer."

"Thank you for the invitation," Chri Anri the Elder said. "Many of our people, particularly the younger ones born after our visit to Earth those five hundred long years ago, would like nothing better than a visit to Earth, home of their ancestors. We older ones fear losing citizens to your world. Maybe now it is time for being willing to give up another citizen if that is the person's choice.

Chri Anri the Elder then turned to Lauren. "Mission Specialist Lauren Adams, we welcome you to Zalanda and hope very much that you like our country. We Zalandans are a straightforward people. We recognize such a quality in you. On behalf of all of our citizens, but particularly on behalf of my grandson, Chri Anri, we invite you to stay behind when your crew leaves, to extend your visit, and to consider becoming a citizen of Zalanda."

Lauren glanced shyly at Chri Anri and then quickly looked away. The blush started on her cheeks but quickly encompassed her whole face. On our entire journey, I had rarely seen Lauren blush and never to this degree. She usually was so composed. No nonsense Lauren was caught totally off guard. It was not only Lauren. We all were practically speechless.

"Thank you for such a magnanimous invitation. I hardly know what to say," Lauren replied softly.

"Whenever you wished to return to Earth, we would take you on one of our ships."

Jack, apparently trying to fill in an awkward moment, said, "Have you taken in new citizens in the past."

Chri Anri the Elder answered, "Not in the past 500 years. According to our historical records, when our people moved to Mars 2500 years ago, friends from different places around the world accompanied us on the mass migration and became Zalandans. After that, our people visited Earth many times. Often, there was a full crew, but sometimes it was possible to bring one or two new friends back with us."

Lauren said, "Your kindness in extending such a rare invitation moves me deeply. This is a very new idea to me, something in all my life I could never have contemplated or planned for. I need time to consider this extraordinary invitation."

Chri Anri the Elder simply said, "Of course."

I was shocked that Lauren had not declined the offer outright. I glanced at Jack and Fawz, and they appeared as shocked as I was.

Nobody was saying anything. I think that was why Lauren tried to fill the void with something innocuous and said, "You speak such perfect English."

Chri Anri the Elder replied, "When we visited Earth, we also visited London and became quite entranced with the English language. We recorded it and with the help of our Center, we were able to teach ourselves. It is a rich, vibrant language that borrows freely from many other languages."

That did not explain their use of current English. Almost in response to my unasked question, a wall became alive with the audio and video of an English-speaking world news channel. The words of the broadcaster softly filled in the background until the sound and the picture faded away.

After referring to Center, Chri Anri the grandson spoke slowly, "That was recorded a few days ago. We do not receive Earth TV when we are here behind Jupiter. We could easily do it. We would place craft in orbit around Jupiter. It has been figured out."

Sedra said, "For nearly a century now, we have had access to your TV channels. They help us to keep current with many of your languages and with your advancements in space and technology. Now, you have so very many channels, and several are on aerospace.

"It has been thrilling over the years witnessing your developments in space. Many times, we wished to contact the people of Earth, to congratulate you, so to speak, to visit you, and to reveal our identity.

"We still could surreptitiously visit Earth as we had done so many times in the past if we could get over our concern that someone would want to stay behind. Still, even if we visited Earth again, the people would not know who we were or how we were related to them.

"We wanted an open visit." Sedra looked toward Fawz when she said, "We still were bound by our 2500-year-old contract and were not free to announce our existence to the whole world. None of our escape clauses fit the current situation. The Rhatanians did not need our help. We did not need their help. The Rhatanian technology still was not at the level of our technology even though we had seen documentaries on TV and knew how forward thinking you were.

"Then we had an idea. After carefully reviewing the old document, we decided we could announce our existence by sending a sign to you. If people on Earth recognized the sign and sought us, thus revealing an adequately high level of technology, then we would be free to reveal ourselves."

Chri Anri the Elder spoke. "We still had questions on whether to do this. Would people on Earth wish to know this new and shocking fact? Would it deflate their pleasure in being an advanced civilization? They still had accomplished it on their own, but space travel also had happened long ago. We had other concerns. Would it cause the Earthlings to fear us? We certainly did not want that to happen. Yet, being a society that thrived without secrets, we wanted to end this final secret."

Sedra said, "Late in the last century, we received the most wonderful opportunity to salute the Earth people in a special way and to bestow upon you recognition for your energetic efforts in space, a particular milestone being the moon landing of 1969. We knew that certain dates were important to you, one being a twenty-fifth anniversary of a significant event. If we worked everything just right, we could send a spectacular sign to you.

"We thought that we could get the timing perfect. If people on Earth were receptive, then you would understand. If people on Earth were not ready, then you would not.

"In the Earth year 1994 from July 16 to July 22, we sent you the most flamboyant and marvelous signs to honor the twenty-fifth anniversary of your first moon landing. Twenty-one large fragments of a comet impacted Jupiter in honor of the twentieth day of July 1969, your first moon landing. That message certainly would alert you to our existence. However, on Earth people took our message as a natural phenomenon, which it was, but we had made several adjustments with our tweakers, ships that redirect asteroids."

Jack asked, "How precisely did you do that?" We all knew what she was talking about, but Jack needed clarification because this sounded so astonishing.

Sedra said, "We planned ahead. Years earlier, we tweaked the orbit of the comet. Then in 1993, we sent tweakers to break it into a precise number of large fragments. If we were careful enough, we could break it into 20 large fragments that would be visible from Earth.

"But people on Earth did not understand. The date was totally accurate. The number of fragments was accurate. It was indeed a galactic sign. That nobody on Earth responded was a disappointment, but we decided that the Earth people were not ready. After that, we rather gave up on the idea of contacting Earth. It was in the hands of fate. Maybe, some astronomer in the future would study the comet and understand.

"Little did we ever consider that after these hundreds of years what you call 'the cylinder' would lead you to us. You cannot imagine our surprise and pleasure because there was not a word of your mission on television. When we began tracking your vehicle, we thought it was unmanned although we had not heard of an unmanned one either.

It was not until you began broadcasting from your solarship that we realized you were the Earth visitors that we had hoped to meet."

What Sedra said made me feel so incredibly welcome.

Cecil now spoke, "The finale of this reception will be held in the Shoemaker-Levy 9 area of our spaceship storage facility. There, you will see the same vehicles that directed the comet."

Since we were somewhat of a distance from the facility, Chri Anri and I traveled together standing up in a car that somewhat resembled the food capsule but a little wider. It had curved corners and clear sides. I did not see any controls in the car, and Chri Anri gave no indication that he was driving it. Neither did he explain how it worked. We traveled horizontally on the moving walkways at a considerable speed, went up and down ramps at a slightly lower speed, and on one occasion climbed right up a wall.

When the car abruptly stopped, its walls and floor disappeared, and we found ourselves deposited on a walkway off to the side and high above a huge complex filled with large spaceships. As there was no guardrail, I flattened myself against the wall and looked down as Chri Anri explained that some ships were designed specifically for going inside Jupiter, a few were for flying around Zalanda, and others were for deep space travel.

I pointed to a triangle shaped vehicle that was gleaming almost directly below us. Chri Anri explained that was a tweaker similar to the ones flown to produce the 1994 comet extravaganza. Tweakers routinely redirected comets, asteroids, and other large objects in space. Since Jupiter was such a magnet for these heavenly bodies, each one needed to be tracked and its orbits tweaked as necessary. That fact was too mind boggling to ask questions although I did recall thinking why would a civilization wish to live near a giant planet that attracted large hurtling objects. Chri Anri must have guessed my thoughts because he told me that although comets needed to be carefully monitored and at times an orbit tweaked, their value was beyond measurement, and they occasionally contained unpredictable surprises. The idea of controlling comets with tweakers seemed extremely dangerous.

After I got more comfortable on the walkway, we followed it to the ground level and strolled among the huge craft. We seemed so small, and the craft were so imposing and so numerous. Chri Anri explained that like an airport on Earth, a craft would be moved from its parking spot to a launch and service facility. I wished my mom could have seen all these space vehicles.

There were some smaller ones that could have passed for high tech private planes. Chri Anri said they were like our landers. They were carried inside a mission craft and used for darting around a planet or for landing. A few had the capacity of traveling as far as the Earth and beyond. Chri Anri pointed toward a gleaming red one and said that was his favorite.

We eventually met up with everyone who had been at the reception. Chri Anri told me that they had traveled a different way and had not been given the magnificent view from above that I had seen. I figured they had arrived by a far less scary route.

At our first stop, we were shown a group of special tweakers, the historic ones that had broken up the Shoemaker-Levy comet into smaller comets, of which 21 could be seen from Earth. Chri Anri the Elder explained how the tweakers worked, and it seemed extremely complex. At first, the tweakers merely got close enough to study the comet and take many measurements and holographic pictures before decisions were made how to proceed.

Our second stop was a pleasant surprise to me. We rode on a moving walkway along the perimeter of the spaceship storage facility until we found ourselves in front of yet another gleaming spacecraft. This one, however, had much sentimental value. It was the ship that had made the last journey to Earth 500 years ago. The Zalandans commented on how old fashioned it was, but it certainly impressed me. I estimated that it was somewhat larger than the *Copernicus*.

After the reception was over, we all stayed and talked. I quietly suggested to Chri Anri that Lauren and I could simply switch guides and that he could be Lauren's guide. I thought that would make him happy. However, Chri Anri looked incredibly hurt. I was not sure whether I had committed a social blunder or whether I had hurt Chri Anri's feelings. Was he hurt because Lauren did not immediately accept his invitation to stay on Zalanda? Could that now signal an end of everything between them before it started?

I wondered if I should continue to interfere. I had the immediate dilemma of whether or not to play cupid with Lauren and Chri Anri. I knew they both were instantly attracted to each other, but how painful would it be for them when they parted. I did not think Lauren could stay in Zalanda even if that were her wish. Our crew was too small as it was, and we needed her. At that moment, I decided I would not instigate any further match making, but if either Lauren or Chri Anri asked for my advice, then I would help either one of them the best I could.

I could have stayed for a long time visiting and admiring the craft, but Chri Anri had a special itinerary for us. We went back to the high walkway, got into the disappearing/reappearing car, and whizzed off to our next stop on the tour, the food processing plant, the factory that serviced all the food capsules. Chri Anri compared a food capsule to a CAT scan plus lab work on Earth. The calcium level, potassium level, blood sugar level, and many other measurements were taken. It took less than a minute to evaluate an individual's nutritional requirements, measure and mix the food for the wafers, add the appropriate nutrients to the water, and transmit it to the person waiting in the food capsule.

"Is that why your people live so long?" I asked.

"Long be not so, some merely eight hundred years, a few nine hundred. Physicians our think life span increased could be to 1,200 or 1,250 Earth years. Two physicians life think immortal possible."

"Immortal, now you're talking. I like that idea. Is the secret of your long lives in those little wafers?"

"Reason one. Other reasons, too. Air the best. Water the best. Few beasties here live—few carefully controlled. Benefit humans."

"If we got rid of beasties on Earth, then would we live longer?"

"No, not ethical. Not possible."

I felt the conversation was getting over my head, but I knew it was important and I must pursue it.

"Is it not ethical to kill beasties?"

"On Earth live beasties before people. Their home it is also. Not ethical unnecessary kill beasties."

"In decontamination, your beastie balneary, you killed beasties on and in us."

"Sad to kill beasties but necessary. Zalanda home for humans and plants selected imported we from Earth. Zalanda not home for most molds, viruses, bacteria, and sub categories." Chri Anri hummed into his Center. After the response, he said, "In you lived a virus that would weaken your heart. Die you in sixty-two Earth years. Virus be killed in decontamination. Now live thee longer."

"Thank you. I am very grateful to have that virus gone."

Chri Anri decided we would finish our conversation in the medical unit, which was adjacent to the food factory. I wondered how much longer they would live if they did not whiz around in their high-speed corridors and tubes.

"Fast corridors good, healthy, if muscles strong to hold organs in location."

That was the fourth time Chri Anri had responded to an unasked question.

In the medical unit, five Zalandan doctors greeted us most pleasantly as they gathered around us. They all hummed simultaneously. Chri Anri hummed also, and I got the distinct feeling that he wanted me to speak. I told them how glad I was to be there and how impressed I was with their medical technology.

They touched my face and eyebrows lightly, and then one asked if she could cut a strand of my hair. I agreed as I watched our reflections in the mirror-like wall. They carefully examined my hair as if deciding which strand to snip. It was strange as if hair mattered that much at all. They finally decided on a strand, one located on the top of my head. After they passed the strand around between them, they put it on a clear shelf. The wall in front of us no longer was reflective but became very bright as I saw the greatly magnified strand of hair, which looked like a shaft with things like cereal bowls up and down the sides. Upon evaluation, the cereal bowls resembled TV dish antennae. A strange, eerie thought occurred to me. As if Chri Anri could read my mind, he said to me, "Now beginning thee to understand."

It was a wonderful moment that passed between the doctors, Chri Anri, and me. Brain waves could pass between individuals, and the receiving mechanism was human hair. The wave traveled through the air to an appropriate receiving dish and then down the shaft into my head. I could feel my hair standing straight up on my head as if my whole head was a collection of goose bumps. I felt thoughts coming toward me from the doctors. I felt one doctor thinking, "We can communicate telepathically with each other." I felt great joy. Then it was lost as if I had lost my concentration. Yet, it had been a moment of sheer understanding.

After we left the doctors, we roamed into another part of the medical complex. Chri Anri consulted his yellow Center and announced, "Be here body training like biofeedback places Earth be."

We sat in comfortable lounges in front of circles and dots, their equivalent of monitors. I said, "Chri Anri, I'm in a state of brain overload and cultural shock over this telepathy business."

Chri Anri consulted his Center but when he got his answer, instead of talking to me, he consulted Center again. Finally he said, "Biofeedback or body training decreases cultural shock. Level thou of serotonin goes up, need more for adventure have thee. Then more places take you I."

"I don't want to go against your customs or your plans, but I've seen enough for this wake cycle. Your culture has taken 2500 years to build. I can't learn about it in two days. I appreciate your being a good host. The more I learn, the more questions I have. For example, this telepathy thing boggles my mind."

"Talk we about telepathy." There was a reluctant tone in his voice.

"First of all, you seem to have different feelings about telepathy than your doctors."

"Perceptive thee. True, true. To me a minor thing telepathy be. Brain wave or sound wave, sound wave preferable be."

"You'd rather communicate by speech than telepathy?"

"Yes, yes, far preferable be speech. Speech and brain wave acceptable. Like not brain wave alone. One exception."

"What is that exception, Chri Anri?"

"Usually brain wave works when one meter apart people be. In duress extreme in danger brain wave works for great distances between people who good friends or closely related be."

"Like someone calling for help."

"Called Chri Anri brain waves your from beastie balneary. Brain waves my heard and responded. Hear you not. Sound waves and brain waves each other reinforced."

"But we weren't friends yet, and still it worked for distances."

Chri Anri pointed to my eyes and said, "Related we be." Then he seemed to be studying me, reading my thoughts, perhaps.

"I thought you needed to take a blood sample or do some kind of test to determine if we truly are related, if I have that blood component that many Zalandans have."

"Test completed. Related we be."

"But when, when you looked at the strand of my hair?"

Chri Anri rotated his shoulders and frowned. He appeared bewildered. "Permission give you."

"Yes, I gave my permission, but I thought your medical people would draw blood and analyze it."

Chri Anri shuddered. "Such method necessary not."

"I just want to know when." Suddenly, this was not a safe place anymore. People could read my mind. A component in my blood was analyzed, and I did not know it was happening.

"Here, move shoulders thou like this." He lifted his shoulders and rotated them back. "Tension relieves much."

"I just want to know when." I realized I was not behaving much like an ambassador of the Earth. Maybe, I did not deserve to be an astronaut like Jack, Fawz, and Lauren. They knew how to behave, how to control their emotions, and how to be good representatives of NASA. I blurted out, "I don't understand your protocol. I don't understand why you talk the way you do. You people can move comets, and I don't even know when my blood's been tested."

Chri Anri patted me on the shoulder. "Answer question which first?"

"Blood, blood, blood!" I answered.

"Okey-dokey," Chri Anri replied.

"Okey-dokey?" I mimicked and giggled. "Where did you get that?"

"Earth TV. Faux paux?"

"No, it's not a faux paux. It just surprised me. I've had so many surprises, one after the other. You're an Earthling. You're a Zalandan, who is a descendant of ancient Rhatanians."

"Blood answer?"

"I'm okay, now, Chri Anri. Excuse my little outburst. Yes, blood answer."

"Chri Anri the Elder you talk earlier this wake cycle. Asks you he your permission about blood test."

"Yes, I remember that."

"Then, test then. Optical transmission, beam directed you. Knew he then. Then say he you the bridge between Zalandans and Earthlings all."

"Yes, now I understand. First, he was saying that maybe I was a descendant, and almost in the next breath, he acted as if I already were one for sure. That seemed strange, but everything was moving too fast for me to dwell on any one thing. Can people can be tested with optical beams anywhere?"

"No, organized we not that. Medical facility, food capsule, astronomical observatory, tests these places. Now, other questions answer I?"

"Chri Anri the Elder, your grandfather, seemed bewildered to see me. Why was that?"

Chri Anri explained that was because I looked a great deal like Hulda, and that surprised his grandfather. After all this time, many generations on Earth would have passed. Yet, the blood test indicated that we were quite closely related, more closely related than the genetic math of 500 years would indicate. His grandfather did not understand that.

Chri Anri said that he personally did not need the results of a blood test. He could just look at me and tell that I was the child.

"You have called me the child over and over. Is there a more specific translation?"

Chri Anri talked into Center whenever he wanted to get a translation exactly right. Then he said, "The child means the Zalandan Child. It means Child of Zalanda."

"Oh, wow, now I finally understand. That's why I sat with you during the festival because I'm considered a Zalandan even though only a little bit of me is Zalandan. That's why I stood with you during the reception because I'm related to you and Svee Dee. That's why she was allowed out in the snow to observe me while I stood watch. This is all quite wonderful, Chri Anri. Is that also why you're my guide?"

"More complex." He explained that when new people from Earth had joined the Zalandans, there was a festival, and then guides formally showed the newcomers around the habitat. When the Zalandans stopped visiting Earth, there no longer was the need for the occasional Festival of the Earthlings, but the Zalandans liked the festival and wanted it anyway. They turned it into a festival rehearsal for the time that

Hulda would return. Some people were afraid that the new emphasis on Hulda would make Chri Anri the Elder sad, but he liked keeping her memory alive. He planned what he would do when she returned to Zalanda; he would escort her from the festival slightly before it ended and spend more than two days showing her around the habitat.

Since Chri Anri the Elder had not gotten back yet from Titan, then Chri Anri, his representative, became my guide because I was considered Hulda's representative. No wonder Chri Anri became upset when I mentioned trading guides. There was a complex historic precedent of how things would be if Hulda ever returned to Zalanda.

"Wonderful place take thee I now. Live once there early Zalandans. Called Ancient City. Ornate. Elaborate. Similar to Earth art museum. Ancient Egypt, Greece, Rhatania."

"No, I've learned more than enough for one joytime." I suppressed a yawn.

He coaxingly told me that Ancient City was one of his favorite places and continued to glowingly describe it.

I silently thought, "Brain overload, brain overload."

The hair on top of my head felt like it was being pulled taut as I got a mental message from him. "Biofeedback let thee more absorb."

My brain sent a reply that said, "No, no, enough is enough."

Abruptly, our mental sharing was lost. The telepathy took a certain type of concentration that I apparently could maintain for less than a minute.

He finally gave up trying to persuade me and said, "Mentally say thee absorb not more."

"That's about my limit for today. I appreciate your efforts to want me to see everything here in this fabulous habitat." Those were my words, but my thoughts were that Chri Anri was very persuasive since ten minutes earlier he wanted me to see more sights and I had declined. So, he simply waited ten minutes and then tried again.

"Other Zalandans say I persuasive."

Oops, he had read my thoughts. Chri Anri and I both started laughing simultaneously.

When we stopped laughing, I began getting some serious concerns about potential dangers of telepathy. "Chri Anri, would you use telepathic powers to persuade me?"

He thought a minute and then said that if I were consciously aware of his telepathic thoughts directed toward me, then it would be ethical to try mental persuasion. Otherwise, it would be wrong because the purpose of brain waves was to enhance communication and not to subliminally trick me or anyone else because of a secret agenda or even an overt one.

I was afraid that he could begin viewing me as an Earthly savage who indulged in something as nefarious as secret keeping and who might try to corrupt something as pure as telepathy. As he still was reading my thoughts, he reassured me that he certainly did not think of me as a savage and reminded me that he already had given me the same assurance during the previous joytime.

I asked about going to Ancient City another day, and Chri Anri said that he only would be my guide for the equivalent of a few hours during the next joytime. However, I was free to visit Ancient City anytime. None of us would need guides because we would understand enough and be comfortable enough to roam around the habitat on our own. That was totally new information for me. I would miss him.

Realizing that my time with him was limited, I asked Chri Anri if there was anything he wanted to know about us. He asked me about our Center, and I told him about the supernet and how computers, phones, fax machines, and all types of devices, both old and new technology, could be linked to the supernet.

He pointed to my wrist communicator, and I explained that it functioned as a communications device only inside the *Copernicus* because it interfaced with equipment built into our ship. Some features worked independently, such as the alarm clock that also monitored rapid eye movement sleep. I could set the alarm to not awaken me during REM, but I seldom had that luxury because we usually followed a schedule.

He wanted to know about my notebook computer. Cecil had told him that Jack had brought it from the *Falcon* for me. I said that e-mail could be sent on Earth and even from the *Copernicus* if our mission had not been a secret. He expressed an interest in examining my computer during the next joytime.

Chri Anri checked Center before he shyly asked me about Lauren. "What are the courtship customs?"

Since he had asked first, I decided I was free of the restraints I had put on myself. I would help him. I said, "You watch Earth TV, Chri Anri. You know our customs. You would take her out on a date. You would take her out to dinner."

Chri Anri's eyes grew wide. He looked horrified at the thought of a communal meal. He rotated his shoulders to calm himself down.

"No, I didn't mean that," I quickly said. "No, not dinner. It never has to be dinner, Chri Anri. You would take her somewhere." Then I had an idea. "You could take her to Ancient City. You could explain how the Zalandans used to live. Tell her everything you told me about Ancient City. She's a sociologist. That's archaeology, but she likes that kind of stuff."

That sleep cycle back at our quarters, we were all on brain overload. Lauren said she loved being here, but it reminded her of a whirlwind trip to Europe she had taken. "Travel now, enjoy later." She decided we would be digesting what we were discovering for a long time. She asked me several questions about Chri Anri which I again answered in my bland, neutral way rather than teasing her. I wanted her to continue feeling comfortable asking me whatever she wanted about him.

We were falling asleep in our cozy beds making random comments when Jack became more awake and got into his commander mode. He told us that Cecil had taken him to the auditorium so that he could send a report of his day's activities to the *Copernicus*. The report automatically would be sent to Houston as soon as we came out from behind Jupiter.

He then mentioned some plans he had been working on for when we were no longer with our guides. Finally, he noticed how sleepy everybody was and said we would discuss the plans during the beginning of the next joytime when we all were more alert. I had been treating my time in the Zalandan habitat like a great vacation and hoped to continue to do so even with whatever assignments Jack intended to give me.

Now Fawz was slightly awake and said they were the most guileless and straightforward people he had ever met. Of course, it was their telepathy. If they all could read each other's minds, then how could they practice deceit? But I was too sleepy to explain the telepathy. Anyway, it would be more fun for Jack, Fawz, and Lauren to make that discovery for themselves as I had done.

As my eyelids became heavier and heavier, I slipped into a reverie about my piloting takeoffs and touchdowns in a Zalandan lander that easily could pass for a customized, high tech Earth airplane. I fell asleep with these pleasant thoughts as I looked forward to the following joytime.

Jana's Journal

My third joytime on Zalanda I awoke thrilled to be here, but I needed to recall a dream, not about the Zalandan landers but another one, a repeating one, because now, on this planet, while in the dream itself, I understood what it meant for the first time. It mattered, but I could not retrieve it.

Was it about Filbert? No, I did not think so although I had decided against telling my crew about him. It seemed silly to tell them that he disliked me. I had no proof that he would do anything to discredit us.

We had a breakfast meeting before our guides arrived. The four of us suspected that our time here was limited. We would know when Zalanda came out from behind Jupiter and we could communicate with Houston.

During this joytime and the next, we essentially needed such good information that Director Clayton would want us to stay here for as long as possible. With that said, Jack gave us our assignments. Jack and Fawz would visit the aerospace people and learn about their ships and propulsion.

Fawz had been torn between two goals. He was enraptured with technical things, but on the other hand, he desperately wanted to find out more about Zalandan history, particularly the periods that overlapped with Rhatanian history, such as 2500 years ago and prior to that, going all the way back to the beginnings of the Rhatanian civilization. Of course, he had a keen interest in the Zalandan visit 500 years ago. That had been the impetus for our entire mission. He wanted Lauren or me to take that task.

Lauren clearly was the logical choice with her interest and training. I did not understand why Jack or Fawz simply did not assign her the task, but then after a second I understood. History probably would involve working closely with Chri Anri since that was his favorite subject.

Maybe, Lauren had considered the potential heartbreak of becoming involved with Chri Anri. If she hesitated at all about the history job, then I quickly would volunteer and muddle through it the best I could.

However, the second Fawz finished describing the task, Lauren immediately volunteered. She stared at Fawz and said, "You could have just asked me."

"I wanted you to feel comfortable about your choice," Fawz replied.

"I do," she stated. I knew what she meant, and I thought that Fawz and Jack knew, too.

The final task fell to me. Jack had developed a list of questions regarding daily life in Zalanda. Lauren, Fawz, and I added questions to the list. Then we ranked the questions in order of importance. It was my job to talk to lots of different Zalandans and get as many varied answers as possible. Jack then told me to follow where their questions led me because we did not possibly know enough about the Zalandan culture to ask the right questions, but this list would get me started.

Jack emphasized that my primary task was to be a good ambassador from Earth. The Zalandans would want to know about us, too, and that I should not be so focused on completing the list of questions that I neglected answering their questions.

Since I had typed all the questions on my notebook computer, I asked if it was okay for Chri Anri to examine my computer as he had expressed an interest in it. Jack replied that was fine since our lives were in their hands anyway.

We were still planning the joytime when our groomers arrived and began teaching us how to make our hair and brows stand straight out.

The young girls were pleasant and hummed a lot at us but attempted little English. We gathered that they would not be coming back anymore unless we requested their help. It seemed like we would be on our own with our hair, too. They left us the grooming equipment.

Our plan was to work on our assignments and then meet together for dinner. After that, we would go to the dome to send a joint transmission to the *Copernicus* about what we had accomplished. Our report would include the highlights of the wake cycle. As soon as the *Copernicus* came out from behind Jupiter and was in range of Earth, all of our messages immediately would be sent, including the earlier ones that Fawz and Jack had trouble transmitting.

Chri Anri arrived before the other guides. Although he was gracious to all of us, he could not keep his eyes off Lauren. She reciprocated by making no attempt to hide her interest in him. Jack, Fawz, and I drifted away to other areas of our room to give them a few minutes together. I opened my notebook computer and pretended there was something I needed to check. I so wanted to suggest that he did not need to spend these final hours as my guide, but I now understood the complicated protocol involved in the Festival of the Earthlings. Besides, I needed his help with my assignment.

As soon as the other guides arrived, Chri Anri and I went to the Center with my long list of questions. He was extremely interested in my notebook computer and spent considerable time examining it. I explained basically how it worked.

He asked me if he could check my computer's innards. After assuring me that he would not hurt the memory, I agreed. He held my precious computer against the side of a large fuchsia crystal, and I held my breath. Several line drawings appeared on top of the crystal. He studied the drawings for a few minutes and then said, "Nice work. Now understand I."

The second I got my computer back, I checked to make sure my files still existed, particularly my journal.

"Keys why arranged like that? Very slow."

I was amazed that he could just look at the 26 symbols that formed our words plus punctuation, numbers, and other symbols and realize that the typing would be slow.

"It's tradition. It's called QWERTY." I realized just how smart Chri Anri was. A language he did not even speak in the right order, he knew it would take a long time to type the words. "Early in the last century, keyboards were mechanical, and keys were arranged to slow down the typists so the keys would not jam. Now, for a long time, keys have been electronic, and people could type very fast with a different keyboard."

"Change thee the keyboard. Fix I for you."

"Thank you, Chri Anri, but it already has been fixed. There's a keyboard called Dvorak."

"The Czech composer? *New World Symphony*. Very wonderful. Performance saw I. Houston Symphony."

"Goodness, you learn a lot from American TV." It occurred to me that I might have seen the very symphony in downtown Houston that he had watched on TV. "I think it was the composer's brother who arranged the keyboard, but somehow people keep using this slow QWERTY one."

"Relate I it." Chri Anri then explained that their world was filled with tradition, too. Basically the Zalandans were sane, sensible, rational people, but there were things that made no sense in their culture like honoring the contract signed so long ago between two factions of ancient Rhatanians. The current Rhatanians knew nothing about the contract and clearly liked technology and would have been thrilled to know about the Zalandans.

It also made no sense to not have visited Earth for these 500 years just because his mother's sister, his Aunt Hulda, had chosen to stay on Earth. Even if they wanted to honor the ancient contract, they could have made surreptitious visits as they had done so many times in the past. Now they were free of these encumbrances, thanks to us.

I was ready to show Chri Anri my list when he began asking me more about my computer, particularly how e-mail worked on Earth.

I was beginning to think we would not get to my questions before his time as my guide ended. Then, how would I proceed with my assignment? However, I remembered Jack's words about being a good ambassador from Earth.

I showed Chri Anri the file containing my e-mail address book, and he quickly found Lauren's address. I told him that Lauren also had a notebook computer, but she had left hers back on the *Copernicus*. As soon as I mentioned her name, the information he wanted became precise, detailed, and considerably beyond what we had discussed on the same subject during the previous joytime. He also wanted to know more about telephones and other methods of communication. I showed him Lauren and Alan's phone numbers but explained that one needed to be on earth or near earth for standard phones to work.

Finally, I showed Chri Anri my questions, and he quickly volunteered to answer all of them for me. Did I want short or long answers? I thought for starters short ones would be fine. He talked, and I typed the answers. Within an hour, we had finished my task, and I was free to explore the habitat on my own. Then, I remembered a specific aspect of my assignment. I said, "I'm supposed to get answers from lots of people."

Chri Anri thought a minute and then dictated names for me to type next to specific questions. In a few minutes, every question had a name next to it of a person who had knowledge or interest in the particular question.

He talked into Center before he said, "You have been cooped up in a spacecraft for many months. I know what a short time in a craft is like. Go to the park and take a relaxing swim. Enjoy yourself. Then, the people will come to you. Most everybody roams to the park for a swim. These particular people show up there every day."

I would simply wait at the park. He would call all of them and tell them to help me with the answers. I thanked him profusely.

I had a couple more questions for him that were not on the list. First of all, I wanted to know why Chri Anri talked the way he did. However, I would not ask that question. It seemed like bad manners.

"Fear thee not. Answer I. Earth TV character cartoon, syntax similar to language Zalandan. Fun. Played language. Like a game. Mistake. Entertained Svee Dee and children friends character with I pretending. Stories with character create I."

"I'm sure Svee Dee and her friends enjoyed the game. We've been talking together a lot in English. You have a huge vocabulary, and you even think in English. Otherwise, you would not have played with the language. You comprehend everything I say. Sometimes, you're not happy with Center's translation, and you think how to say something differently. You like the language."

Chri Anri thought a minute and without consulting Center said, "I want Lauren to be proud of me. I speak impeccable Zalandan."

"You just spoke quite perfect English, too."

"I dared not hope I would need it. For Lauren I want to speak impeccable English. What is your advice?"

"Before you speak, just remember the sequence of a simple sentence is subject, verb, and object. I don't think you need Center." I decided against saying that Lauren was quite taken by him and most likely found his unusual English charming.

The time had come for Chri Anri to turn me loose. He no longer would be my guide. He mentioned that I looked very tired and for me to be sure to get a short recharge, his words for a nap.

"What will you do during this joytime?" I asked.

"I will show Ancient City to Lauren."

"That's wonderful, Chri Anri."

Later, when I was on the moving walkway going to the park, I realized that Lauren thought of Ancient City as her assignment and Chri Anri considered it a date. They would figure that out.

When I first got to the park, there were only a few Zalandans there. Svee Dee came up to me and asked, "Want to swim?"

I recalled the wild sled ride over the snow and did not want to become involved in particularly dangerous activities at the moment. Yet, I had come to realize that Svee Dee was not as irresponsible as she seemed. I did not see any Zalandans in the water. Svee Dee was already running toward the lake.

"Is that water safe for humans," I yelled.

"This water is the best and the safest," Svee Dee called back

She grabbed a vine, swung out into the lake, and let go. She made a huge splash. That lake looked so inviting.

I was not sure how uncomfortable a wet body suit would be, but I followed Svee Dee to the water's edge, grabbed a sturdy vine, swung way out, and dropped into the water. My, that water felt soothing. The temperature felt perfect, not too warm and not too cold.

I looked up at Jupiter and thought this was a perfect place. I swam back and forth rapidly. I did a crawl and Svee Dee mimicked me. She showed me a stroke like a sea otter, arms at my side, legs straight behind me, and moving in a type of wave motion.

I thought of the day so many months ago at the pool with Alan when he had given me so much encouragement and hope. Alan would have liked this lake under the dome and the nearby hydroponic garden. I was filled with such happiness thinking about Alan being here with me. Someday, that could happen. We came out of the water and were basking in the glow of Jupiter. My bodysuit was totally dry. It somehow had acted like a big bath towel.

There only had been a handful of Zalandans when we went into the water, but now Zalandans joyfully flocked around me and took turns answering my questions. There must have been close to a hundred now in the park, but a much smaller number surrounding me as they took turns getting up close. After a short time, typing as fast as I could, the answers to my questions were completed.

Then, they had questions for me. Many were fascinated with the communal meal and wanted to know about sitting around campfires. I explained that meals were mostly consumed at tables, and people might even eat a meal sitting in front of a TV. A meal in front of a campfire was a special treat reserved for hiking or camping trips.

Besides mealtime, what else thoroughly interested them were secrets. I knew from my question and their answer that lack of secrets equaled trust and lack of trust equaled secrets. I knew they also equated secrets with power, meaning an unfair advantage of one person over another, one person over many, or one group over another. Secrets had a negative connotation here on Zalanda and definitely were a dishonorable thing to hold and to have. Secrets equaled misrepresentation by omission.

Under these givens, they wanted to know why our mission had been a secret. I did not totally know because layers of secrets were involved. One reason was the finances, but that was incomprehensible to them, since economics was not something that concerned them. They referred to ancient history and mentioned hoarding a metal like gold or in another culture hoarding shells and then using that kind of item as a medium for trade. They knew that our exchanges usually were handled electronically, but this was knowledge in a theoretical sense, not in a daily life situation like having to scrape up enough money to take flying lessons.

Where was Lauren when I needed her? I hoped that she was getting to know Chri Anri.

I told them secrets were used so that an individual or group did not lose face. If we looked for them on this moon and they were not here and no archaeological evidence existed that they had been here, then our countries would look foolish to the rest of the world. If only a very few people knew the purpose of the mission, then only those few would know if our quest failed.

After I said that, they hummed to each other before one of them said, "One can seldom be foolish for trying a new theory."

"Bingo," I said. "That is so true." I was beginning to see why this small group of people was so successful. "On Earth people trying new things often are considered foolish and ridiculed, especially when they are going against established beliefs."

A shared mealtime might be an uncouth or uncivilized thing, but I surmised that they put secrets in a more powerful category of things that were morally wrong. It would seem like all these questions on secrets could hurt my feelings, but the Zalandans were so kindly that it was more like their wanting to understand. I found the whole discussion rather invigorating because I knew they liked us and were very happy to have us as guests.

They seemed really interested in discussing secrets with me until Svee Dee hummed something, and all at once, there was not another question on secrets. Soon, they all said their farewells and drifted away. Again, only a handful of people were scattered around in the park.

"What happened?" I asked Svee Dee.

Svee Dee talked into Center and then seemed to be thinking before she spoke. "Chri Anri asked me to protect you while you were here in the park. Most of these people here have never seen a brand new Zalandan from Earth. Uncle Chri Anri was afraid they would not know how to behave. He watches Earth TV and has some ideas. He said that you would not be accustomed to such blunt behavior. It could be offensive to you. They would talk to you the entire joytime and wear you out. He thought you looked tired and that you needed some rest. He assigned me to take care of you here at the park." She sighed when she finished as if her answer were a lot of words to remember.

"Chri Anri said I'm considered a Zalandan. Am I as much a Zalandan as you are?" I asked.

"Yes, of course. A child of Zalanda." Then Svee Dee consulted Center. She waited. "Anyone who has a Zalandan ancestor or anyone who accepts an invitation to live here becomes a Zalandan by touching our planet. Before your arrival, none of that happened for a very long time, not in Uncle Chri Anri's lifetime, not even in Grandmother Sedra's lifetime. She is extremely old. Then the *Falcon* landed, and you stepped onto our planet."

"Thank you for watching over me, Svee Dee. You did an admirable job." Chri Anri held Svee Dee in such high regard that he had given her the assignment to protect me, and the other Zalandans honored her word.

After assuring Svee Dee that I could get back to my quarters by myself, I said goodbye to her. I was extremely tired as every ounce of energy drained out of me. Chri Anri was right. I definitely needed a nap or as he called it, a short recharge.

Yet, as soon as I was alone, I was plagued with the need to remember something. I tried to shake the feeling. I stepped onto the moving walkway and was surprised that the walls of the corridor glowed in such vibrant colors. No, I was in a different corridor because, being distracted, I had picked the wrong moving walkway. When I got to the end, I needed to choose between two walkways. Neither looked like it doubled back to the park. I was lost. Lost, tired, hungry. Yet, my bigger concern was whatever I needed to remember.

"Stop," I told myself. First, I would find our quarters, and then, using logic, I would recall whatever was concerning me. It had something to do with what Chri Anri had told me, but no, it was an old memory. No, it was both. Being here among the Zalandans reminded me of something at home. That was not so unusual. After all, they were Earthlings.

I picked one of the two walkways and hoped for the best. Fortunately, I chanced upon the big central domed auditorium, and then I knew exactly how to get back to our quarters.

The auditorium was vacant, and Jupiter above in all of its glory seemed close enough to reach up and touch. I walked through the rows of lounge chairs until I found where I had sat between Svee Dee and Chri Anri during the welcoming festival. Then, I did not grasp the full significance of being separated from my crew and being classified as a child. Now, I understood. I thought of the blue tinge in my eyes. I was one of them. I belonged. I was a descendant of Hulda. I sat on my lounge and felt it adjusting to my needs, elevating my left foot slightly more than my right and relaxing me completely.

I wanted to stay on Zalanda for a long time. What wonderful people they were. I was thrilled that the aliens were humans and not giant electrical clouds with intellects.

My eyelids grew heavy and began to close. I would not go back to my quarters now. This lounge chair would be a fine place for a short recharge, but first I needed to remember something. I forced my eyes open. Chri Anri had said that I was more closely related to the Zalandans than the genetic math indicated.

Yesterday, that fact mildly interested me, but after my dream during the last recharge, his comment grew in significance. My dream was the recurring one, and now, as some times in the past, I recalled a strange fragment of it. An elderly woman took off her makeup and then appeared far younger. Afterwards, the woman did a handstand. There was more to the dream, but how could I recover it?

My eyelids again were getting heavy. I could be lucky enough to have the same dream again. It must have occurred during the rapid eye movement level of sleep. I glanced down at my wrist communicator. It knew when I was in REM sleep. I set the wrist com to awaken me after 15 minutes in that sleep. Would that time be too long or too short?

I stretched out comfortably on the lounge chair. I must have dozed quickly. The next thing I remembered was a vibration at my wrist and an annoying buzzing sound. I tried to awaken as quickly as I could. Yes, I had captured the dream.

It was about my great-grandmother's last visit to my home in Houston. I was a young child, and she had acted old and frail around my parents. I had followed her to the guest room where she behaved much more sprightly. After she took off her makeup, she looked much younger. I was surprised when she did a handstand because even as a child I knew that was not something that an old person usually did.

I asked her to tell me a story, and she volunteered to tell me about her life. She was from the Czech Republic, a land that had once been called Czechoslovakia, and before that it had been called Bohemia. Way before that, she came from far away, from the stars, and had spent her childhood on an ice planet. She had worn special clothes to go outside because every part of her body needed to be protected. Now, she was very old and had born many children through the centuries before she bore my grandmother.

She took a cylinder and the container for it out of her suitcase and showed it to me. I heard the voices in a foreign language, and clearly one voice was hers. I asked her for it as a gift, and she told me it was her only remembrance of long ago when she had made an important decision.

In my dream, I told Mom, and she explained that my great-grandmother Hulda simply had entertained me with a charming story. Mom said that Hulda had told her the same story, too.

I tried not to dwell on the dream. Instead, I typed as fast as I could and wrote down the whole thing on my computer. This was not simply a charming story. This was the story of her life. It had been my repeating dream. Whenever I started dreaming about it, even in my sleep I knew that I had dreamed it many times before. In my wakeful state, it was not retrievable except for the fragment. I had finally captured the full memory.

I would ask Mom about her grandmother. Was her name Hulda? Had she told Mom the same life story, too? If these answers were "yes," I would have a starting point.

Hulda still could be alive today somewhere, maybe now a new mother with a young baby. When I got back home, I would try to track her down and find out.

Chri Anri the Elder could get his wish to see his daughter Hulda. I did not know how to mention it to him. I would not raise his hopes based on a dream or even on a story a woman told a young child to entertain her.

I was falling back into another dream, but my sleep was light, almost like a meditative state. I was having a discussion with someone, probably Chri Anri but it could have been Fawz or Venzi. The person's face was in the shadows.

This is what we said: all Earthlings are related to the Zalandans. We are the current intelligent life in the galaxy, Earthlings on Earth and

Earthlings on Zalanda. We are the Galactic Federation, and we will be the colonizers of other planets. Earthlings have already colonized the moon, and the Zalandans have begun on Titan. Someday, we will find life in our or another solar system, and we will help it or benignly let it evolve. When it is ready and wants outside help, we will be there to help it along. We were hoping for help from the outside, but we are the outside. We are the Galactic Federation. Then, I fell into a deep sleep and did not remember anything else.

The next thing I heard was Jack's voice saying, "Jana, it is time to wake up now."

I opened my eyes and looked around. I still was in the big domed auditorium. No one was around. It must have been my imagination. I looked up at the dome. The colors of Jupiter were different. The red spot was gone, and the stripes were so clear. I must have been sleeping for quite a while, but I still was groggy. My eyelids were closing.

Then I heard Jack's voice again. "Jana, we need you. You've been sleeping all afternoon."

I sat up with a start. No one was around. "Jana." The voice was coming out of my yellow Center.

"Jack, how can you do that?" I asked, not at all sure he could hear me.

"Good afternoon, sleepy head," Jack said. "We've had a few lessons on Center. It's quite an amazing gadget. I can speak to anyone in the complex who hasn't notified Center with a "do not disturb."

"Neat, and how did you know I was asleep?"

"Center told me. Beyond that, there's a privacy program. Center serves as a monitor for heartbeat, blood pressure, sleep cycles, and more. You're continuously getting a checkup. Yet, it releases no medical information unless the person needs help."

"Amazing," I said.

"Would you care to join us for dinner, Jana?"

"Definitely. Be right there, sir." Before I left the auditorium, I checked what I had written in the computer. Yes, the whole dream was there, but I would not talk about it until I checked with Mom after we arrived in Houston.

I could not talk about the meditative dream either. It sounded way too arrogant. After all, there are billions of stars in the galaxy.

Jack, Fawz, and Lauren were sitting in the meal circle waiting for me. I was famished and rushed into the food capsule. I realized I had been given almost as much food as everyone else put together, two beverages and eight wafers, including a bright purple one I had not seen before. I noticed Jack, Fawz, and Lauren staring at my food. I was becoming uncomfortable.

"The mystery of the food may be solved," Lauren said, smiling the way she did when she was proud of herself.

I was not going to finish my food with them staring at me. I was hungry but could not swallow. "How do you feel right now?" Lauren asked me.

"Uncomfortable," I answered, "and somewhat angry at you for putting me on the spot like this."

Seeming only mildly sympathetic, Lauren continued. "I think it works like this. Say we were in the JSC cafeteria back in Houston having lunch together. We would all eat about the same amount of food. We would even check ahead of time and ask each other what we were having. We would have different foods and slightly different amounts but rarely would one person eat twice as much as the others.

"But here they've mastered optimal nutrition, and their machine selects exactly what and how much food we should have. Now, Jana, you're probably tired from darting around the habitat so much. I suspect you did not finish the food the machine was giving you."

"That's certainly true. My last meal was breakfast. For lunch, I took a sip of the beverage from a food tube near the park, and that was it," I said. I could feel the knot in my throat relaxing.

"Now, if you didn't have an audience, you'd eat what the machine had given you and not think about it except maybe to be glad you had gotten your appetite back. However, now we're observing you, and that could influence whether you finish your meal."

I said, "I'm thinking I'd like to be by myself." As I gathered up my food and went off to a corner of the room, Jack said to Lauren, "What a brilliant theory. You notice the Zalandans don't talk about health. It is not even on their minds. Come to think about it, I've been feeling so wonderful. I haven't thought about health either. But they don't have to think about it except for their doctors. The air is so totally pure. There are few bacteria or viruses or other parasites. The diet is perfectly designed for each individual for every meal. And Center monitors them at all times. If any problem starts to develop, they can fix it right away."

"It seems like a perfect world in regard to physical health." Fawz who had seemed somewhat distracted said.

"It seems like a perfect world, period," Lauren said, with such wistfulness in her voice.

I strolled back into the group with the purple wafer. "This is absolutely the best thing I have ever tasted," I said, breaking the remainder of the wafer into three pieces. There were no refusals.

Jack said, "Better than peanut butter cups."

Fawz said, "As good as . . . . No, better than my native beverage."

Lauren said, "I rest my case. This was needed nutrition for you but you shared it with us and it became excess nutrition for us. Then the nutrition became a psychological sharing rather than fulfilling a physiological need."

We discussed what we would report to Houston. Lauren said, "I have been touring a most fascinating place called Ancient City with Chri Anri. It was where they first lived when they migrated to Zalanda. The styles are very ornate. Some are right out of the fifth century B.C. It is in such contrast to the minimalistic style of architecture they now enjoy." When she mentioned Chri Anri by name, she looked so happy.

Fawz said, "They so cleverly combine gravity assist with direct propulsion. Jupiter is here, so they use it, but they do not need it." Fawz had been thinking about that during the whole mealtime. I knew his mind had been somewhere else.

"How are you doing with the questions?" Jack asked me.

"They're all done," I said and opened up my notebook computer and scrolled through the questions and answers.

Jack looked really impressed and proud of me. I decided not to tell him how easy the assignment had been because Chri Anri and the other Zalandans had been so incredibly helpful.

We rode the moving walkways to the auditorium where our portable communicator was set up on the edge of the stage. We stood next to the stage and took turns recording our daily report. The minute our ship began passing overhead, Jack sent the messages to the *Copernicus*. In two days when Zalanda came out from behind Jupiter, our ship would automatically send all our messages.

We still were in the dome under Jupiter when Lauren took me aside and said, "I've found what I've been looking for."

She meant Chri Anri, but the words should come from her. I also wanted to be sure that I did not misunderstand, so I played naive. "You mean a space colony like you've always wanted?"

"That, too. I have found Mr. Right. I have found Chri Anri. He is everything I have always wanted."

"That's good, Lauren," I said but I had a sinking feeling about the future of their relationship.

"We have such incredible rapport. He invited me to go with him to Ancient City before I even asked to go. We're on the same wavelength."

I resisted the urge to tell her that he had planned to take her there on a date. She was so happy and bubbly.

"This has been absolutely the best joytime, the best wake cycle, the best day of my life. Hardly anyone on Zalanda shares his interest in history. Sometimes, he feels alone because history is so important to him. Now, we have found each other, and I care about the subject as much as he does.

"The other Zalandans like Ancient City and think it's a fun place. They know the historic significance, but it doesn't affect them the way it does Chri Anri. I understand exactly what he means.

"We looked at the ancient buildings, and he told me how they were built to scale. On Earth today, people know nothing about most of those structures because neither the structures nor art work nor writings about them have survived time. Many were exact replicas of ancient Zalandan residences before they gave up their advanced technology.

"Chri Anri asked me if I had a favorite of the residences I had seen so far. One with wonderful baths and lots of columns clearly stood out. I mentioned that one, and he seemed surprised and said that was his favorite, too. He showed me many other homes, but that one was still my favorite. He told me that some Zalandans lived in other private residences in Ancient City but that most were unoccupied. As the joytime moved along, he mentioned our house hunting together, and somehow, we started calling that residence our home. Then he said that we could live together in our home. I readily agreed, and we started planning how we would prepare it before we moved in.

Practical Lauren suddenly had disappeared. Once, she had told me that she believed in love at first sight, and at the time I thought that had been so unlike her. I had wanted to be their matchmaker, but now it seemed that this attraction was moving way too fast for her. "He lives here, and you'll be going back to Earth."

"Chri Anri said any one of their aerospace people would jump at the opportunity to take my place on our ship."

Lauren and Chri Anri already had begun to work out the logistics, and she definitely was not asking my advice or approval. Instead, she wanted to share her happiness with me. Still, I felt compelled to protect her. I said, "It's a different culture here. You told me that you have not begun to figure out the Zalandan ways."

She said, "I don't want you to mention this to Jack or Fawz, not yet."

"No, of course not, Lauren. I won't say a word to them."

Jack and Fawz were way too well-mannered to ask us what we had been discussing. They probably knew the gist but certainly not the extent.

Jack thought that this joytime had yielded us so much information that we would follow the same plan during the next joytime, and we did. I had a new list of questions, some built on the old questions and other completely new ones. After breakfast, I roamed down to the park with my computer. A few people greeted me but did not come forward. Maybe, I could approach them. While I was working up some courage, I sat on the grass and opened the computer. I reread the questions. I did not have names with the questions. Chri Anri had not prepared the way for me, but when I looked up, maybe a dozen Zalandans were around me. I greeted them and announced that I had some more questions.

They seemed interested. One sat down next to me and started dictating names for me to write next to questions. Soon, it was like the previous wake cycle. We were zipping right through questions and answers. The park was now pretty full of Zalandans, but they took turns sitting next to me and answering questions. This time they gave longer and more detailed answers. They also were a little more blunt than the previous time, but I liked it.

I had more rapport with them than some people on Earth. They understood my words and the meaning. That surprised me. I told them I did not understand how I could have so much rapport with them.

One explained that they were trying really hard to understand where I wanted to go with the questions, and they were supplementing my words with my brain waves. They were looking beyond the words to the underlying meanings.

I complimented them on their English and said how impressed I was that they spoke without an accent. They all became very quiet, and I realized I had offended them. Finally, one said, "We tried to speak English with an American accent and with Jana-style rhythms of speech."

I was so surprised. "You were trying to speak like me. You certainly have succeeded. Earth people often do not consider that their own accent is an accent at all. That is a mistake that I just made. Do you know other English accents?"

One said, "Center knows." That person spoke into Center a few minutes and then spoke English with the rhythm of someone from India. Then, another one spoke with the words and accent of a person from Australia.

"How does Center know?"

They hummed among themselves and then one said, "Sedra and Chri Anri the Elder organized the Earth Language Project after we received Earth TV. Different people helped in their absence while they were away on Titan. It is an important project. Always our hope to visit Earth or for Earthlings to visit Zalanda. We have been reviewing our English since Fawz broadcast from space. He speaks American English with slight British accent. When you stood outside your *Falcon* lander, we heard Jack, Lauren, and you speak with the American accent. We would speak like you."

I was so impressed.

"Your TV actors know many dialects," one said as if trying to understand my surprise.

I then realized that their role models for English were highly skilled TV performers who could switch accents at will or who were trained by accent coaches to learn new ones. I asked them about their knowledge of Rhatanian language.

"Some of us understand Fawz's current Rhatanian because of Earth TV. The current language is far different than the ancient Rhatanian that most of us learn. It is most difficult to comprehend when Fawz speaks the 500-year-old Rhatanian. Sedra and Chri Anri the Elder understand him."

I said, "Fawz would be much happier speaking his current Rhatanian or current English."

I asked about their present language. Historically, after the Zalandans left Earth, they decided they needed a new language because there were so few of them that everyone needed to be versed in many things. They had the opportunity to start from scratch. They based their language on singing because they could infuse everything with more emotional knowledge. Concurrently, the hums and singing lent itself to non-linear thinking which often was necessary in fusing seemingly disparate knowledge. They incorporated the languages of math, science, music, the arts, and human interaction into one language with the technique they chose. The language also would be a good way to get new Zalandans up to speed about their culture and achievements.

I became more and more impressed by the minute. I had learned about their language totally by accident. I wondered how much more I did not know.

Jana's Journal
(Not read over the net)

The Zalandans seemed very willing to talk especially since Svee Dee was not on assignment from Chri Anri to protect me from their direct manner. They told me things that I thought best to not report to Mission Control until I got a feeling how responsive Houston was to the idea of an advanced civilization right in our own solar system. Since most of the Zalandans occasionally watched Earth TV, they had some concept of regional differences between people on Earth and the underlying ideas that different groups and people lived by. They perceived what made groups behave the way they did and why some groups did not get along with other groups. They understood why some individuals were unhappy and did not feel like they belonged in their own group.

I said, "Oh, you all must really be smart. You could help us a lot on Earth."

Several laughed at that, and one checked Center before saying, "It is easier for an outsider to see things. We are outsiders to Earth. You see problems with our society, too."

I said, "This is a perfect society to me, except maybe most of you want to visit Earth. Yet, you are reluctant to do so because of fear of losing another member."

Most of them made comments in agreement. One of them said, "That is over now. You have freed us."

"Svee Dee told me the same thing, but I don't understand why."

One said that would be hard to explain in English, but another said it could be done. He talked into Center, thought a minute, and then said, "If someone is afraid to do something or afraid for others to do that thing, then that person finds a reason. The reason was the pact signed 2500 years ago that the Zalandans could not announce themselves until the Rhatanians had achieved a sufficient level of technology. What is sufficient? That presents a judgment call. The Rhatanians may never have reached a sufficient level, especially after the Earthlings responded not to our meteorite extravaganza on Jupiter in 1994. If you responded not, that presents complete proof that the level of technology is missing. Or you desperately refuse to recognize the sign. Fortunately for us, you Earthlings recognized something else. The cylinder finally was deciphered all these centuries later. Now, we are free because of you, the descendant of Hulda; Fawz, the Rhatanian; and the cylinder."

I said, "You were free all along. But if you want to be precise about a very old covenant, the Zalandans had enough technology for way more than a hundred years so that you could have honored the covenant and still announced your presence back then. Chri Anri understands this. All of you understood this, too.

"You never needed a giant sign. Some of you thought you needed one, and after all your work, the first giant sign failed to get our attention. We just happened to bring you the next giant sign. Visiting Earth was something you used to do regularly, but you haven't done it for a long time so you have become scared. Then, you upped the ante. You decided that you not only wanted to visit the Earth but that you wanted to announce who you are. That was when the ancient covenant came into play."

They were humming to each other until one said. "We all knew this, too, but for you to state it, you as an outsider looking in, you see it with a greater clarity. It was something we all knew and felt, but now that you are here, the excuse to be afraid is gone."

"I need to write all this down," I said. I typed as fast as I could and when I finished, I looked up and all of them either were standing around or sitting on the lawn.

"Are you finished with your assignment, now?" one asked.

I nodded and closed my computer.

"On Zalanda, we recreate first before we work," one said.

I replied, "Good idea. I'm liking this place better and better all the time."

"What would you like to do?" one asked.

I thought of my plan of treating this like a vacation and Jack's idea of doing as much research as possible. Then I thought of Jack's earlier assignment to be a good ambassador from Earth, and I said, "I haven't seen Ancient City, yet."

About a hundred of them went with me to Ancient City. We rode a series of moving walkways and finally arrived at what looked like a thousand years of ancient architecture all coexisting at the same time. It was like a giant architectural history museum that was out of order chronologically and geographically but totally in order aesthetically as one interesting structure looked like it belonged with the one next to it. They told me that most all the structures were done to scale, much full scale and some half scale or less. It was whatever caught their fancy during that time frame, including some things that I knew nothing about. I saw so much so fast. There was the Acropolis with a large statue of Athena. There were Roman Baths, which several people said they often visited. Some of the structures were simply models of private residences, and a few of these were homes to some Zalandans.

This entire Ancient City was all beautifully maintained, even the Hanging Gardens at Nineveh complete with living plants growing on lots of terraces. A woman told me that the gardens were part of their hydroponic vegetable system. I asked about the Hanging Gardens of Babylon and was told that in the ancient world, gardens had been there, too, but those structures probably had been too massive to recreate. Other famous landmarks were not there either, such as the Roman Coliseum.

The Zalandans were all so incredibly kind and friendly as they pointed out buildings and temples and explained the historical significance. I was trying to put names with faces, but I was finding it difficult. Then, I realized it was because they politely took turns walking with me so they all would get a chance to talk to a real Earthling.

For the Zalandans, Ancient City seemed to serve as a nice local attraction. Some visited it every time the great red spot made one rotation, which meant every four days. Most said they visited it about once for every time Zalanda rotated around Jupiter, which was once a week, while a few said what was the equivalent to twice a year.

Strangely, though, when I got back to the habitat in all its stark simplicity, I much preferred it. Ancient City was a nice place to visit.

It would be a difficult job summarizing this entire wake cycle for the report to send to the *Copernicus*. I decided to leave out any reference to a large number of Zalandans now having a fervent wish to visit Earth and now feeling totally free to do so.

Jack was very impressed with my full report and such complete answers to all the questions. Again, I failed to tell him that it had been easy, because the Zalandans again had been incredibly helpful. I wondered if I was being a bad Zalandan to be keeping secrets, but then I rationalized and thought that Jack and Fawz also were probably getting their information with ease.

Jack thought we all had done a significant amount of research, and he hoped that Houston would see the value in our work. He was hoping we would get to stay for whatever Houston thought was the maximum amount of time. We sent our reports to the *Copernicus*, and when we awoke from our sleep cycle Houston would have already received the uplink containing all of our reports. I also hoped they would be so happy with us that we could continue staying here.

Jana's Journal

We abruptly were awakened in the middle of our sleep cycle by Chri Anri, Chri Anri the Elder, and his daughter Sedra who must have burst through the wall of our quarters. They all were humming and talking at the same time.

"Hurry, hurry," Chri Anri said between various hums.

With great dignity, Chri Anri the Elder said, "Please come with us."

After a quick ride on the moving walkway, we arrived at the astronomical observatory. On a large wall, we watched the news from a Houston television channel.

The newscaster said, "We have been following developing events over the past few days regarding the alien abduction of a Johnson Space Center astronaut, Mission Specialist Jana Novacek, who had gone on a secret mission to a moon of Jupiter. A tracker dropped in the snow several yards past the end of a tether line was all that was found of her. Apparently, she met with a violent end. We have further reason to believe that the entire crew was captured by the aliens.

"We have learned from an anonymous source that the purpose of their secret mission was to search for alien life. Apparently, they found it. We have called Director Clayton at JSC for verification or denial, and he has not responded to our request."

I looked at the screen and thought how unfortunate that the commentator had not yet gotten the follow up news about our being safe. What was Director Clayton going to do about this? By now he had the facts. We had resent the old transmissions plus the new daily reports summarizing our activity on Zalanda. This broadcaster clearly was in need of our transmissions to correct his report.

I did not want anyone to think ill of our delightful new friends who happened to be my long lost relatives. I saw no way to solve this misinformation problem other than for Director Clayton to get approval to make an announcement explaining our entire mission. Clayton would start with the Director of NASA and move up the chain of command. He would need the approval of Madame President and probably the King. That might take a few days, but it seemed like there was no other way.

On the TV screen as the broadcaster said, "Our team of reporters has now uncovered the names of the other crewmembers led by Jackson Medwin, the illustrious and beloved commander of the Mars I mission, the first manned Mars landing. The second in command is Dr. Fawzshen, from the small country of Rhatania. Lauren Adams, a young astronaut with many degrees, even sociology, is a mission specialist.

"Now, we have a guest, reporter Eggvar Mesathistle, who personally observed these four going up in the space hopper. It's good to see you again, Eggvar."

"Thank you, Shell. It's good to be here."

"You were one of the last people on Earth to see the four astronauts. What can you tell us?"

Eggvar cleared his throat. "I had been invited to ride on a hopper to the space factory with a group of 15 SpaceTech employees to write about the progress of the minishuttle. In the waiting room, I was surprised that four NASA astronauts were to ride on the old-style hopper with us. Astronauts usually fly to the stations in space taxis, and their missions are accompanied with a bit of fanfare. I had met Jackson Medwin before and thought of him as a gregarious chap. This time he didn't acknowledge me. He didn't want to be noticed. Neither did the other astronauts with him. I thought he might have been embarrassed to be riding on the old hopper along with SpaceTech employees. I thought Jack had fallen from grace with the powers to be at NASA."

"Did you speak with the astronauts?"

"Not at first, but then I walked over to them. They slouched in their chairs as if they wanted to be invisible. I talked extensively to the young woman Jana Novacek even though she was not particularly friendly. I commented to her on how young she looked. At that point, she told me she was married and had a child. You should have seen how that revelation totally shocked the other three astronauts. Over the last few days, I found out she was a college student and a summer hire at Johnson Space Center until she was given some special training. Her official record, which I have obtained, indicates that she has neither a husband nor a child. Yet, as I thought more about her and analyzed my second encounter with her, I came up with a most intriguing hypothesis."

"Before you tell us your hypothesis, do you have corroboration from the SpaceTech people who were on that hopper flight?"

"None of them overheard my conversation with Novacek if that is what you mean. I also don't know if any of them noticed that that they were in the presence of the esteemed Jackson Medwin. They were yakking with each other and revved up about going on the hopper. After boarding, they may have noticed because the four astronauts got priority seating right across the front by the windows. To answer your question, I have learned that SpaceTech has forbidden those 15 employees to make statements or answer questions regarding that particular hopper flight."

Red headed Eggvar looked the same on the Zalandan TV as I had remembered him. I recalled with complete clarity that scary and glorious day when we flew on the hopper to the space factory. We had been warned about the reporter. I must have said less than ten words to him in reply to direct questions and certainly did not participate in an extended conversation as he now claimed. When he questioned my age, unfortunately, to appear older I had told him I was married and had a child.

I looked at the very large TV image of Shell and noticed that he had a gleam in his eye like he was ready to pounce. He said, "NASA would certainly know who was riding up on the hopper with their astronauts. If their mission were such a secret, why would they go up on a hopper flight with 15 SpaceTech employees and a reporter, Mr. Mesathistle?"

Eggvar glared at Shell and seemed at a loss for words, but he quickly regained his composure and said, "That sounds like a question for NASA. It seems like they were careless in that regard, doesn't it? "

"Tell us about your second encounter with Novacek."

"I saw her the next day at a reception held by SpaceTech for the four astronauts. By then I had learned they were at the space factory to give the *Copernicus*, a solarship, its first test run. I talked to Jana Novacek privately, and I can't begin to tell you how much older she looked. Her skin tone was gray, like a sick, dehydrated person. No one could age that much in one day, and a sick person would not be on a mission. I didn't understand it at first, but I declare, suddenly in a burst of inspiration it became clear to me. She's not a normal astronaut. She's an alien from a place other than Earth, and she was having difficulty adapting to the environment of the space station. Momentarily, I became afraid when she realized that I knew what she was."

Shell raised his eyebrows in utter disbelief. "Why wouldn't an alien, of all creatures, adapt to the environment of a space station?"

"I had trouble with that, too, but the answer is simple. It's not an alien space station. It's one made for humans. We all know that space does strange things to people. Our faces look fuller at first. I've done some research and nowhere does it mention a person aging so rapidly. However, if she were an alien in the form of a human, then her aging process would be totally different. When she told me she had a spouse and child, she wasn't lying. It was too fast a response to a comment I had made. You should have seen the shock the other astronauts registered when she revealed that morsel. As an alien being, she has a spouse and a child somewhere, but in the form of a human, she poses as a single college student."

It was way past time for Shell to jump on Eggvar for that perfectly ridiculous thesis, but instead he simply said, "You may have stumbled on valuable information, Mr. Mesathistle."

Jack frowned. The three Zalandans' eyes were wide with a combination between fear and amazement. Across the bottom of the TV screen, a banner announced that the program had been recorded earlier. As if reading all of our minds, Chri Anri said, "It is on other channels, also."

Jack nodded and said, "Okay."

The next channel was a panel discussion. A man with a moustache was speaking. "Astronauts are very disciplined. One would not go out in the snow alone on an alien planet. Yet, Jana Novacek supposedly did that.

"Commander Jack Medwin is a highly skilled leader who never before had to deal with insubordination. I spoke with an astronaut who had been on the Mars I flight. No one went against Medwin's wishes.

"Now, here we have a very young astronaut. That in itself is highly irregular. She most certainly would want to follow the rules and do everything just right. Otherwise, she wouldn't have been selected for the job. You tell me she left the lander and went out in the snow herself? She wouldn't have been given authorization to do such a thing, and she wouldn't have done it on her own unless the circumstances were most unusual.

"Let's think of unusual circumstances? If she were an alien herself, then she would go in search of her own kind. By now, we're all familiar with the Eggvar Mesathistle report, released several hours ago. We know he is a highly regarded science writer. "

The next person on the panel seemed quite disgusted with the mustached man, ignored the Mesathistle reference, and said, "What a huge leap from insubordination to being an alien. Consider that she lacked the maturity to behave like a disciplined astronaut and that she did something incredibly stupid."

Another person with a rather thoughtful expression garnered respect from the other panelists. "Were all the astronauts outside when Novacek carelessly got separated from her group? Only the astronauts themselves and maybe the people at Mission Control in Houston know the answer, and they are not giving interviews."

"Would you care to see another channel?" Chri Anri asked and switched before anybody responded.

Chri Anri the Elder hummed at his grandson and gave him the equivalent of the eagle eye that my Dad used with me. Just for a few seconds, my interpretation of their interaction relieved some of my tension. I wondered if the universe over, there were channel switchers, and other creatures repeatedly telling the channel switchers that they were exhibiting bad manners.

Chri Anri's channel changing had been an act of kindness toward me. He was saving me from unpleasant judgments by people who did not have the facts and who had never met me.

On the new channel, a large picture of Jack filled the screen with "Commander Jackson Medwin, Leader of the Mars I Expedition, first Manned Mars Landing" printed across the bottom. Next, there was a very old picture of Fawz. He looked younger than Lauren. Under that picture, it said, "Prince Fawzshen, Crown Prince of Rhatania. In smaller print, it said, "File Photo."

The most current official NASA photograph of Lauren flashed across the screen. That was quickly replaced with an undergraduate yearbook picture with information about her highlighted. "Strong interest in sociology, cultural anthropology, and linguistics. Ambition: To fly in my own plane and to visit different cultures."

Someone with a know-it-all sounding voice said, "Why would they pick an astronaut with these credentials for this particular mission? Only if they were pretty darn sure of finding an alien life form."

Chri Anri looked away from the TV transmission and toward Lauren. He said, "You found the different culture here on Zalanda. I take you now to spaceship storage and help you select a plane you like. I teach you how to fly it." He checked his Center and said, "The people of Zalanda will give you a plane, and I will teach you how to operate it."

Lauren murmured, "Chri Anri, I hardly know what to say. No, I do know. On Earth, we have a custom of naming boats and planes after people. I would like to pick a space plane for you to name after me, but I want the Zalandan people to keep the vehicle."

Chri Anri replied, "That shall be done."

When my picture came on the screen, I immediately recognized it as the graduation picture from my high school yearbook. The same arrogant voice was saying, "Here is an interesting case, an astronaut with absolutely no experience. Why would they pick someone with no experience for any mission much less a major mission? Things are not as they seem here, ladies and gentlemen. NASA would not pick someone with no experience, not in a million years, particularly for a major mission. We know that aliens walk among us, that they can assume human forms, that they can be our neighbors, and that we would never suspect unless something like this came up. Here is an alien passing herself off first as a high school student and then as a college student, biding her time. Now, NASA is going in partnership with aliens, and they're not telling us. They're doing it secretly, and we're paying the bills. What can we do about this, ladies and gentleman? We don't need to foot the bill anymore. Let them stay with the aliens. Let them stay on the moon of Jupiter. Let them stay with Jana Novacek's own kind.

"We have proof that she is an alien. She helped the world renowned physicist Venzi Suzaky solve a very difficult question on space-time discontinuities. Very few people understand his work"

I said to the TV, "Venzi Suzaky helped me with my physics homework. How could I possibly have helped him?"

Everyone looked at me rather sympathetically. I did not want them to worry about me. I said, "I don't care what those people on TV think. They don't know me. I want all of you in this room to think well of me. I want my family to think well of me. I want Alan to think well of me."

Jack said, "I'm glad you're taking this so well, Jana. Still, a positive public image is a helpful thing. That's a sleazy channel. Still, we need to get this sorted out soon."

I looked at my crew now in our Zalandan clothing with our hair standing straight out and our brows waving like antennae. We fit right in with the three Zalandans who all seemed rather bewildered like they were trying to figure out how to help us. I said, "If you think about it, mostly all that commentator did was call me an alien. I am proud and honored to be an alien even if it is only a little bit of me."

We were all quiet for a minute until Lauren said, "Jack, Fawz, and I are the aliens. A little bit of you is a native. If that commentator were here right now, he would be an alien, too."

"I knew that," I said. "I had that figured out when I met Svee Dee. She is the native."

Jack looked toward Chri Anri and said. "We have seen enough TV."

Chri Anri said that they would record all the broadcasts about us they could find, and we could watch them in the future if we wished. Jack politely thanked him.

Fawz thoughtfully said, "At least JSC knows that we are all fine. They have gotten all of our messages by now.

Jack replied, "We need to clear up this mess. It would be best if the four of us go to the *Falcon* and do a video broadcast even if it means going through decontamination again."

Chri Anri volunteered to accompany us. He also told us not to worry about decontamination. It would be extremely brief because the medical facility had finished examining all the beasties we had

419

brought along as passengers and decided there were none they could not handle.

Our space suits and filled oxygen tanks magically appeared. My oxygen tank had been repaired. We trekked toward the lander with Chri Anri. It was glorious outside walking on the ice with Jupiter above that I pushed the stuff on TV out of my mind. Once inside the *Falcon*, we got out of our space suits and into our NASA daywear. Then we found NASA daywear for Chri Anri, which he seemed quite amused to wear. The four of us flattened our hair and brows. Chri Anri decided he would do that, too. Lauren helped him, lovingly, I might add. They were practically cooing at each other while she combed his hair.

"You look just like an Earthling," Lauren cooed.

"I am an Earthling," Chri Anri replied.

We all lined up near the camera. Jack was directly in front of the camera and spoke into the microphone. "Greetings from Zalanda. By now, you have received the uplinks that we have been sending to the *Copernicus* daily since we went behind Jupiter. We have been having a most pleasant visit with long lost Earthlings. They weren't lost. They knew about us. We didn't know about them.

"This moment we are up linking from the *Falcon* directly to Mission Control. We lived in the *Falcon* for the equivalent of three days and with the Zalandans now for four days. The last time we were in direct communication with you was four days ago, and then the transmission was poor.

"We have been watching some rather interesting things on TV. As you know from our reports, the Zalandans have been monitoring our TV stations for nearly a century. They speak several of our languages, too. We are all fine, more than fine, and ecstatic to be here.

"It appears there has been a large security breach. We are curious how the breach occurred. Was it intentional? How are you going to proceed? Are you going to make an announcement about our mission?

"What can we do to help you? How do you want us to proceed? Do you want us to make the announcement for you to release to the public? About our finding the Zalandans?

"We would like to stay here as long as feasible. The Zalandans are willingly sharing extremely valuable technological information. Can you take care of the situation at home without our making an appearance on Earth? Please advise us."

Then, Fawz, Lauren, and I took turns getting in front of the camera and saying a few words to assure Houston that we were alive and well.

Jack said, "At this point, I would like to introduce you at Mission Control to a native of Zalanda. I would like you to meet Chri Anri. He is the grandson of Chri Anri the Elder who visited Earth about 500 years ago. He has been most helpful in making all of us feel welcome and particularly being a guide to his cousin, our own astronaut Jana."

Chri Anri spoke slowly in perfect English as he thought of the correct phraseology. He did not consult Center. He explained how the Zalandans frequently visited Earth until about 500 years ago and how he hoped the custom would be reinstated. He emphasized that his whole society was thrilled that we had made the journey and he was glad that his civilization was no longer a secret from the people on Earth. He told how much he liked Earth TV, and then he named several programs that he particularly enjoyed.

During the hour that we waited for our reply, Jack, Fawz, and I packed up things we wanted to take with us to the habitat. Chri Anri was entranced by our lander so while he explored, he asked question after question which Lauren patiently answered. Eventually, Lauren got around to packing up, and Chri Anri helped her.

Finally, Mission Control returned our message. We heard CAPCOM announce to Mission Control that he was in visual contact with us and he would project our images on the big screens. Still talking to them, he said, "You will notice that we have gained a new astronaut. We heard cheering in the background. Several people at Mission Control spontaneously came forward to greet us and gave personalized messages to Chri Anri. Several mentioned that they would like to visit Zalanda, and most invited Chri Anri to visit the Earth.

As long and diligently as Houston had worked on our behalf, I was glad that the flight controllers were the first people on Earth to see an alien even though Chri Anri looked just like a regular person now that his hair and brows were flattened down. I still was getting accustomed to the idea that indeed he was a regular person.

After lots of enthusiastic comments, Mission Control got down to business. It had been a tense four days for Houston, one day with either poor or non-existent transmission and the next three days while we were behind Jupiter. They had been extremely concerned about our safety until a short time ago when they received the messages we had re-sent plus three new days of complete audio updates and learned that we were more than fine. At that point Director Clayton had notified our families that we were safe. He suggested they not pay attention to anything on television.

Before that, even though Director Clayton had talked to the King and had been assured that the crew was okay, the director thought that Fawz possibly was saying good-bye to his father in his own way and that the crew indeed was in danger.

In the hours before we disappeared behind Jupiter, Houston had been experiencing major transmission disruptions because of the solar flares. The only thing that came through clearly was that I had been abducted. Later, the transmission between Fawz and Filbert, who had been the CAPCOM that night, had been extremely poor. Before the situation could be cleared up, we were already behind Jupiter and out of range.

As for the security breach, JSC still was evaluating how and when it occurred. Although no one wished to believe such a thing, it seemed most likely that the breach came from someone working Mission Control. Two different shifts at Mission Control had been involved, and both were being questioned personally by Director Clayton to find the source of the leak.

Within hours of my so-called abduction, word had spread to the media, which quickly had acquired a wealth of information. Some of it was correct.

JSC had no plans to make any public announcement at all. They would neither confirm nor deny our mission. They intended to ride out the misinformation. Even if the situation changed and the rumors intensified, JSC preferred to wait until after we returned home before making any announcement. If and when they make a statement, it most likely would be that we had taken the *Copernicus* on a test run, and the solarship had tested out amazingly well.

Regarding our other questions, Director Clayton wanted us to return home immediately or as soon as preparations for departure were complete. JSC wanted to have closure on a successful mission. All of the objectives plus their most fervent hopes for the mission had been reached except for one: our safe return.

The glance that passed between Lauren and Chri Anri was one of such sadness that I could hardly bear it. Under these circumstances, Lauren probably did not feel that she could stay here.

I was not sure if Jack or Fawz noticed, but to distract them, I said, "I wasn't abducted." Jack said, "We'll clarify that during our next transmission. I know we didn't use the word 'abduction' on our end." He moved his bottom lip over his top one, a sign of deep thought and then said, "It's time for this secret to be over. It's time for them to announce our mission. Even Madame President said the truth would come out sooner than we thought."

"Secrets purpose what be?" Chri Anri asked. He thought a minute and then in perfect English asked, "What is the purpose of secrets?" What is the purpose of this particular secret?"

"I don't know." Lauren replied. "It's the way we live. In this particular instance, it's probably about money and approval. The government often does not want to fund NASA missions. Some people in Congress are very much against manned missions and think they're a waste of money. Senator Quagly is one of them. This mission was the search for life that we thought was alien. Some people would be frightened of such a search. On the other hand, those funding the mission would be disappointed and might lose face if we didn't find anything."

"Yes," Chri Anri said, speaking slowly and thinking. "The same with our ancients. Some thought space travel was throwing resources into the wind." Then, Chri Anri looked longingly into Lauren's eyes. "It was enlightening, studying our ancient history with you."

Jana's Journal
(Not read over the net)

Jack said, "Those controllers are disciplined people. They all have top-secret clearances. Why would one have leaked information about us? I certainly would like more details of what went on at Mission Control."

"There is a way," I said. "When I was training with Max Marsh, he showed me how to contact him. He said it was like an unlisted phone number in the event we every needed him."

"Good ol' Max covers every eventuality," Jack said.

"Now is the time," Lauren urged.

It was Alan's name, last name first and the letters reversed. I wrote down the combinations until I got it right. We punched in the code.

"Max will give us the real scoop," I said.

Jack said, "Don't identify us or Max, and keep it short. Keep it vague. Let's turn off the video on our end."

I said into the microphone, "We're in the bird. I'm calling you on the special phone number. We'd like to know what's happening. We'd like some details." Then, I turned the video back on.

They were pretty general comments, but Max would figure out we were in the *Falcon*.

We waited. Meanwhile, we ran some preflight tests, clearly a sign that we were leaving as soon as we could complete preparations. We also unpacked and put away the things we had intended to take to the Habitat. Chri Anri carefully studied the *Falcon*. "This is a very fragile lander," he said to Lauren. "We could reinforce it for you." He then began explaining some things he could do.

425

Finally, Max was on the video. It was reassuring to see him wearing his Stetson and his favorite plaid shirt. "I heard that 'you are more than fine' and that you're having quite an adventure. That's splendid news. Now we have the rumor mills to deal with. So you want to know how it all happened.

"There were five transmissions from you before you went behind Jupiter. The first one came through clearly. You stated that Jana had made contact with an alien. The second message stated that she had dropped her tracking device in the snow and you were going in search of her. You had the portable communicator and said that you would report regularly. However, many hours passed. By then, our communications were pretty bad because the solar flares were aimed directly at the Earth. Then, we got another message from you. We picked up a syllable here and there. We managed to discern that there were three voices, Jack, Fawz, and Lauren's. We did not hear Jana's voice. We knew that the message was being sent over and over, which seemed like an ominous sign, like you were in trouble. I have heard that you sent that message 20 times. But maybe you simply knew that we were having trouble on our end. Then, the fourth message was from Fawz who asked to be patched through to his Father.

"The only words that came through from Fawz's last transmission were these: 'We have made contact.' Lots of static. 'Patch me through . . . my father.' Filbert did a successful patch. After Fawz got back with Mission Control, there was more static, and then Filbert heard only these words: 'Inside their habitat.' We knew Fawz was broadcasting from the portable communicator so that meant he probably was not inside the *Falcon*. Was everyone inside the alien complex? 'Habitat' seemed like a peculiar word for Fawz to select, and people interpreted it as a sign of danger.

"Right after that we got a brief video of Jack from inside the *Falcon*. Had Jack escaped from the alien habitat? Strangely, none of the audio came through except the word "Cecil." What did that mean? We knew

Jack had reset that broadcast to repeat over and over again until you went behind Jupiter.

"At that point, Filbert had a choice. He could have played down the transmissions and hung tough. Everyone in Mission Control would have stayed calm. Instead, he magnified the situation and managed to get all the controllers pretty upset. At some point, someone made the statement that Jana had been abducted although those words had not been in your transmission. Filbert should have squashed that idea right on the spot.

"Then, he could have requested that the director call the King and find out what Fawz told him. That would have been the rational choice. However, Filbert took matters into his own hands and phoned the King on his own initiative. He was more than insistent to be put through, which did not help matters. That wasn't following procedures much less royal protocol, whatever those rules are. It would be like one of us calling Madame President and demanding to be put through immediately.

"Eventually, Filbert got through to the King's personal secretary who reported that Fawz was safe and refused to give any specifics. He also refused to put Filbert through to the King. The secretary also said to direct all other questions to Fawz himself. Of course, that was impossible. By then you were behind Jupiter and out of communication.

"Next, Filbert got angry. He does not take being rebuffed very well. And then he panicked, although he claims he did no such thing.

"After recovering a bit from the anger, Filbert called in a split light technician to restore the broadcasts. The technician quickly realized that the message was coming from millions of miles away. Filbert told her that it was recordings coming from an unmanned satellite being used to test the split light technology. Furthermore, the technician only had a Secret Clearance and not a Top Secret one. Did the security breach come from her? At some point, either the technician or one of the controllers told somebody.

427

"One can look upon Filbert's actions as taking initiative and doing what needed to be done or simply becoming panicky. The outcome was that he made a mess of things.

"Eventually, a phone call through the proper channels between Director Clayton and the King several hours later clarified some issues. We still had many concerns until we got your downlink today, which cleared up everything.

"As far as I can tell, Director Clayton will not announce your mission and will basically ignore the stuff on TV.

"Because of the leak, now we are under increased security. I can keep this channel undetectable if you don't use it too much. Only call me this way if you urgently need to talk to me privately. I suspected that you might have wanted to talk today, and I have been waiting for this call. If I need to talk to you privately, I'll give you a code over our normal channel during the computer check, and then you'll know to call me back on this channel. I'll mention procedure XY12A. That's X-ray, Yankee, One, Two, Alpha."

"Your world is full of intrigue," Chri Anri said, after consulting Center.

I thought to myself, "Maybe more intrigue than you know." I vividly recalled how Filbert had mistreated me, but I refrained from saying anything.

Chri Anri looked right at me and said, "Say it! Say it aloud."

He had been reading my thoughts, and now I read his: "It is important that you tell them."

And I was thinking, "Just because you sent these brain waves to me, I don't need to obey them."

More of Chri Anri's thoughts came to me. "They have a right to know. Jana, you used certain words to describe the control of information? Now I remember. They have 'a need to know.'"

I blurted out, "There are things I should have told you months ago. Filbert made orbital physics very difficult for me, and Director

Clayton sent Venzi Suzaky to check on my progress because Filbert had complained about me. Fortunately, that turned out well because Venzi became my friend.

"There's something else. At the party for Fawz and Regney at Jack's house, Filbert called me the babysitter. He called Alan and me children. After that, I felt like I didn't belong, and I wanted to leave the party. Instead, Alan asked me to dance, and I got over feeling too young and too unimportant to be there. Alan is an excellent dancer."

Chri Anri asked Lauren if she enjoyed dancing, and she replied that she did. His brows, even though they still were flattened down, waved softly when he thoughtfully said, "I did not know that."

"What are you trying to say, Jana?" Jack asked.

I then realized that taken out of context, Filbert's actions seemed like minor things as if I were overly sensitive and bearing a grudge. "I am saying that I don't trust Filbert at all. He could have suppressed or deleted some of Fawz's message."

Jack said, "Filbert has so much going for him, but he does have a distinct mean streak. That streak has held him back a lot."

Fawz added, "A very wide mean streak right down the center of his back. Classifying him as a skunk would dishonor the little carnivore." Fawz took a deep breath. "Filbert is petty and cantankerous, but to deliberately suppress a message is unconscionable."

I had no idea Fawz had such strong negative feelings about Filbert, particularly someone he had not seen for months and someone I did not think he knew very well. Furthermore, I had not heard Fawz say anything bad about anyone before that moment although I surmised that he did not hold Max in as high as esteem as the rest of us did.

Jack said, "Deliberately suppressing a message is not an easy thing to do. When a message from a solarship arrives at JSC, it automatically is stored in three places. Someone would have had to remove it from all three areas."

Lauren said, "I'm sure you all know my feelings about Filbert, but he wouldn't suppress a message. What benefit could he possibly get from removing a message? He eventually would be found out. I know he's an opportunist, but he also is an astronaut and a mission controller. He simply would not have done such a thing."

Jana's Journal

We had hardly gotten back to the Habitat before we were flocked with Zalandans in the moving hallway. They were all humming and talking at once. I heard one say, "We wish you to stay." Chri Anri suggested that we all go to the astronomical observatory so we could discuss the implications. On the way to the observatory, Chri Anri was busily humming into his Center. I surmised that he was making lots of phone calls

Once we arrived at the observatory, Chri Anri began humming with Chri Anri the Elder, Sedra, and the six Chiefs, who were waiting for us. All began humming at the same time to each other. Finally, they calmed down and took turns, although often two hummed at the same time.

Svee Dee arrived with her mother who joined the nine others who were humming together. Svee Dee walked over to me and took my hand. Other Zalandans kept filing into the observatory. Some sat in the chairs and others packed themselves into the room. The wall remained open and more Zalandans stood in the hallway although a few entered, but at this point, it was like being packed into an elevator. The opening in the wall was an arched area about eight feet wide. There was so much humming it was like a huge choir. Chri Anri the Elder raised his arm and a hush fell over the room.

Cecil, the leader and prioritizer, said, "Every one of you now knows that our guests have been requested to return to their home on Earth, effective as soon as they can ready their ship." Cecil looked toward Chri Anri the Elder.

He said, "We now invite each one of you to stay here and to become Zalandans, Commander Jackson Medwin, Co-Commander Fawzshen, Mission Specialist Lauren Adams, and Mission Specialist Jana Novacek. We previously extended this invitation to Lauren and now we restate our wish for her to stay.

"Jana is a Zalandan by birth and does not need an additional invitation to stay here with her people. In fact, genetically, she is more closely related to all of us here than the long centuries would indicate. We hope she will decide to stay here."

Chri Anri the Elder looked directly at me. I knew what it meant to be a child of Zalanda and to be one of them. I could just stay here with my people, the Zalandans.

Chri Anri the Elder now looked toward Fawz and said, "We now extend the invitation to Fawz who successfully found us, his "star people." Our histories diverged 2500 years ago, secretly merged again throughout the centuries until 500 years ago. For the first time, our histories are finally brought back together without secrets and with a full knowledge of the past.

"We extend the invitation to Jack for the person he is and for his dedication to what is so near our hearts, space exploration. We have followed your illustrious career on Earth TV and would be most pleased for you to join us.

"We know that each of you have families and loved ones on Earth, and we would bring them here for you, and under your authority and under their willingness, they would become citizens.

"We have more than adequate facilities for you and your families to stay in Ancient City until we build newer accommodations for you. Or you may prefer to continue living in Ancient City. A few of our citizens prefer its historic ambience and currently live there.

"Think about our offer. If some of you wish to stay on Zalanda, our astronauts can take your place on the return trip. Our people learn very rapidly and are superb astronauts."

The Zalandans who were seated stood up with the ones packed around the room, and all cheered, raised their arms above their heads, and swayed.

As Jack began speaking, again a hush fell over the astronomical observatory. "It so warms my heart to be invited to become a Zalandan. You have created a marvelous civilization here. With sadness, I must decline your offer. I am an employee of NASA, the National Aeronautics and Space Administration. My job is to go on this mission and then to return home safely. I will fulfill my assignment. I do not presume to speak for the rest of my crew."

Jack, our Commander, had turned us free of our commitment to NASA to make our own decisions about this momentous offer. I could hardly believe my ears. I could stay here and live always. I felt very comfortable here like I belonged. It did not seem like a strange place at all. Maybe, it was the stories that my great-grandmother told me. She was Hulda. I was becoming sure of that. What she told me was not something that had been passed down through the generations from 500 years ago. No, it was her own story of her very long life. She had told my mother those same stories when she was a child. I bet Mom had not forgotten, either.

Fawz said, "Meeting you had brought me great joy and leaving you will bring me great sadness, but I will return to my family and the country of my birth, Rhatania. I invite all of you to visit Rhatania and to meet the descendants of your relatives from long ago.

I looked toward Lauren. She was third in rank. It was her turn to speak, but she did not say anything. I knew I should speak. I thought I would like to live here always. I thought about Alan and about my parents. I thought about the garden where Alan worked. I thought about Jack's children whom I considered as my own siblings. I thought about my home in Texas, the brilliant green lawn and the plants on our back porch. I said, "My fondest wish is to stay here longer. I am so honored to be a Zalandan, and I will always cherish being one of you. I have loved being here and am disappointed about leaving abruptly, but

433

I will leave with my crew when our ship is ready for departure. I hope each of you will visit Earth."

I fought back tears and looked toward Lauren. Still, she did not say anything.

Chri Anri the Elder said, "We do have other proposals to present to you. If you ever wish to visit us again, we most assuredly would welcome you. If you desire, we can arrange most speedy transportation for you.

"Now we can return you to Earth in one of our best ships. We could leave shortly, and you would be home within five days. On the other hand, you could stay a while, see some special sights while you are in the neighborhood, and still return quicker than your ship would carry you if you left now."

Jack replied, "Thank you for such a generous offer. The proposal to travel on your ship is tempting. I will check with JSC and ask for their approval. I believe that they will not approve, but I certainly will ask. If they approve, our ship and our lander could return on its own by remote control."

Cecil then announced that our crew would go to the domed auditorium where Jack would call Houston on the communicator. Again, practically all the Zalandans went with us on the moving walkway.

Once we got to the domed auditorium, we went over to the edge of the stage where the communicator was set up. We stood on the level with the lounge chairs and the stage edge served the purpose of a table. They all stayed a polite distance away while we called Houston with what would probably sound like an outrageous request to the recipients. As soon as we were finished, they surged forward to talk to us.

Chri Anri raised his arm in the air, and the others moved back except for Chief and Orval. The three of them explained to us that if we would be traveling home in our own craft, they would like to make the *Falcon* safer before we left. They could reinforce it, particularly the top because they were afraid it was too fragile and could prove a danger to us. This improvement could be done quite quickly, and if several of them worked together on the project, it would not take them more than a few hours. In addition to the *Falcon's* particular function, the Zalandans also looked upon it as a craft that could save us in an emergency.

Orval explained that their next concern was their desire to keep in touch while we were traveling home so they could help us if we encountered any problems. Again, Jack said he would talk to JSC about it if they denied our first request.

We discussed the implications of both plans and thought they were good ideas to present to JSC after we got word back on whether we could zoom back home on the Zalandan craft.

The other leaders were standing nearby humming among themselves. Jack and Fawz still were talking to Chri Anri, Chief, and the Orval while waiting for the transmission from Houston. The Zalandans were milling around. Some were sitting in the lounge chairs by the stage and others were a little distance away in the large open area humming together in groups. This communication would take a while because we did not send our entire message at once.

I wanted to talk to Lauren privately and when I saw my chance, I sidled up next to her. She said, "Director Clayton will never give his permission to ride in their craft."

"I'm pretty sure you're right, Lauren." I wanted to ask her if she was staying behind but I hesitated. I knew how painful it must be for her.

She volunteered. "I'm not staying. Chri Anri knows, too. I was not going to announce it in front of all Chri Anri's people. To say that in front of everybody would make it seem like I don't care about him. I love Chri Anri, and I will love him always. Yet, Jack's right. We have our jobs to do, especially under these circumstances with all the rumors on TV. We have a responsibility to . . . ." She choked up.

I came very close to telling her that she should take happiness where she could find it, which was right here with Chri Anri. I refrained from saying any of that because there was another way. After we were back home, after all the rumors were squashed, after she fulfilled her obligation with NASA, then Chri Anri could come to see her on Earth, and she would come back here with him.

I remembered when we were in training for this mission, Lauren talked about love at first sight, and I thought it was foolish. But now, after seeing how happy Lauren and Chri Anri were together, that idea had been right for her after all.

I noticed Cecil and Nairme busily hummed together. I guessed that they were making plans for something. Then, they laughed and nodded their heads. Cecil talked into her Center.

Barely, a few minutes later, the walls reflected with vivid jewel-tone colors. I heard music, but it was Earth music, Earth dance music. It was a tango. Chri Anri left the group and walked over to Lauren.

"May I have this dance?"

"Certainly," Lauren replied.

Chri Anri led Lauren to the area beyond the lounge chairs. Everyone fell back as they began dancing. First, they were a bit awkward dancing together, but then they got the rhythm, and it was wonderful watching them, pure grace.

Soon, couples who danced the tango most elegantly joined them. Then, children began dancing their own inventive steps, and individuals danced by themselves. It was something like a big family dance. A Zalandan man who had been so helpful answering my questions in the park asked me to dance just as the music switched to a waltz. The man reminded me that there was not much gravity here. I realized why when I looked around and saw that the Zalandans were adding acrobatic flourishes like the star dancers on TV. As we danced, I asked, "Zalandans like Earth dance music?"

"Yes, we are most fond of it."

"I don't believe that was anywhere on my list of questions." They more than liked it. They were totally excellent at it, and then it occurred to me that usually the most excellent, inventive dancers performed on TV. Those performers were their role models for dancing.

Then, country western music started, and the Zalandans lined up in rows. We all were laughing and having such a lark. With western clothes, they would fit right into Texas, and no one would ever suspect they were from another planet. Next, we did a round dance in huge circles within circles. This was different from home in that the dance floor was so incredibly large, with only a small area lost for the stage and seating. An extremely large number of people were dancing at the same time in these huge circles, and the biggest difference was Jupiter above shining through the dome down upon us.

I noticed that Jack and Fawz still were waiting by the communicator at the edge of the stage. When I got over to them, the transmission from Houston was beginning. Jack clicked something that looked similar to a TV remote, and the dance music stopped only in our area. The Zalandans were such good technicians with the music that they could have a totally quiet area.

The reply from Houston was very clear. Of course, as we suspected, we most assuredly did not have permission to come home on a Zalandan craft although Mission Control was amused that we even asked. How could we even have proposed such a thing? CAPCOM, however, admitted he would have liked that, too, and stated how jealous of us everyone at Mission Control was. CAPCOM did go ahead and ask Director Clayton on the outside chance. The director also was amused.

Jack was disappointed even though he knew there had not been much hope of gaining permission. He had tried. Otherwise, he would have asked all the questions at once instead of keeping Houston focused on one exciting concept while he hoped for the answer we all wanted.

Jack and Fawz immediately responded. Fawz set our message to go out on the fastest split light speed that hardly ever worked, and then on the much slower split light speed that usually worked. First, Jack thanked them for evaluating the issues of coming home in the Zalandan craft. He then briefly reviewed the issues. We all figured that no one in Houston had evaluated any issues at all and that we had been victims of a gut reaction.

Houston would see that Jack's thank you was simply last-ditch wheedling, but Jack was such a smooth talker that they would not be offended. There even was the remote chance that Houston would change its collective mind.

Fawz then asked Houston about beefing up the *Falcon*. He mentioned that it would be a prototype if we wanted to adopt any of the changes for other landers. Then, Orval and Chief, who had rather recently served as Chief of Aerospace himself, took turns talking to Houston and explaining the current safety issues with the "fragile and delicate" *Falcon*. The problems easily could be remedied. They explained what they wished to do, particularly to strengthen the top.

Next, Orval requested that the Zalandans stay in touch with us on our way home. They could easily provide their own communications gear to do that. They could be particularly helpful while we were in Jupiter's magnetosphere.

While we waited for a reply, Chief explained what they wished to do with the *Falcon*, and I gathered that they were quite skilled with rapid custom fabricating.

Then we heard from Houston. As for the practical question of our staying in touch with the Zalandans on our way home, surprisingly, the answer was a clear no despite the fact they could have helped us if we needed them. When we left, we would totally break off communications. That was a surprise and a disappointment. The Zalandans were also disappointed but said once we got home they would figure out how to contact us.

There was a time gap, and then we got word back regarding the *Falcon* question.

Amazingly, JSC agreed, but with lots of stipulations. Each change would require detailed specifications of exactly what would be done. Houston did not possibly understand how the changes could be done so fast.

As I was talking to Jack, Fawz, Orval, and Chief, Svee Dee came up to me, took my hand, and wanted me to go with her. I asked Jack if he needed my help right that minute, and he thought not. So I followed Svee Dee over to her lounge chair on the third row from the stage. We sat together in her chair, and then the chair levitated.

"Svee Dee, I'm going to decline this. I've been on a chair ride before. Once is more than enough."

She looked sad. "This you will like, the finale."

Then I noticed other Zalandans were sitting in lounge chairs that levitated also. In some instances two people cozily shared a chair. We were all about twelve feet in the air, just floating when the music started. It was Earth music. It was very familiar. "Wow, that's the New World Symphony," I said.

"Yes," Svee Dee replied. "By Anton Dvorak. He's dead. Very sad. Maybe he's starting a new universe somewhere."

"Probably," I replied with my eyes half closed. Our chair tilted slightly back and I had a perfect view of Jupiter without having to tilt my head. "When he wrote his symphony, he wasn't thinking about this new world."

Svee Dee giggled, and then we both became very quiet and listened as our chairs drifted around like we were floating on a cloud. All the chairs were moving like fractals, none touching the other. What a way to listen to a symphony.

As it ended, the chairs lazily drifted back to their locations. "Do you have musical instruments like we do on Earth, violins, cellos, French horns, flutes?"

"No, different instruments. Flutes, yes, but different. Different music."

The thought flashed into my head to invite her to watch sixty or seventy musicians together playing the New World Symphony at Jones Hall in Houston. But she was a child who would not forget the invitation, and I probably could never honor it.

She said, "Earth musicians playing lots of violins. Good."

"You read my mind. Svee Dee, sometimes I get ideas that won't happen. This was a great event. What do you call it?"

"A festival." Then she talked into her Center and said, "Farewell Festival Impromptu with Music of Earth." "Specific purpose: 'We Hope to Meet Again Festival.'"

"I certainly hope so."

Then, my Center called, and it was Jack. He wanted me to meet him in the astronomical observatory. When I arrived, Jack, Fawz, Lauren, Chri Anri, Chief, Orval, and Chri Anri the Elder were already there along with several of the aerospace people. On the wall were charts, and Orval was explaining the optimal slingshot maneuver for gravity assist. As soon as Jack saw me, he asked me to stand next to him and stated how much he valued my opinion. The Zalandans all took note of that comment. No way could Jack value my opinion on anything technical. Maybe he was just so happy with me that I had decided to return to Earth. I could not imagine how he would have explained my absence to my parents nor could I imagine their giving their permission to anyone other than Jack for such a mission as this. They had trusted him completely.

I dared not let my thoughts roam in the direction of Jack's implications. I just tried to keep positive thoughts and an open mind, which allowed me to understand the discussion.

Later, I thought that was a nice thing Jack did, making me feel like a valued crewmember in front of the Zalandans as if I could contribute to the discussion. I did not want the Zalandans to read my mind, and my thoughts could easily roam into the area of inadequacy.

The slingshot around powerful Jupiter seemed to be something straightforward, but the Zalandans had previously mapped many gravitational anomalies around Jupiter. They showed the best possible approach and slingshot path to provide maximum assist in the precise trajectory that we needed to travel. Of course, they figured our departure time factoring in that we all get a good recharge to be well rested to start the mission. They were every bit as practical as we were. We had a precise departure time. Chri Anri the Elder decided we had thought of everything and that as soon as our crew was away from Zalanda, we would have direct communication with Houston before the slingshot around Jupiter.

As our meeting was breaking up, the two Chri Anris were talking together. Lauren glanced over at Chri Anri and then handed me her notebook computer and asked me to read a letter she was writing.

"Chri Anri, you have this wonderful place here. I am from a different place that I might begin to miss. We had this very special time together, but I have always been a sensible, practical person. This is not sensible or practical for either of us. Whether you or your people choose to visit Earth should be based on considerations other than our wanting to see each other. To say good bye now could make it easier for both of us rather than spending more time together, getting even more attached, and then realizing that other things are important. At present, I like everything about your culture. I like how you value each individual and how your society works together peacefully. This has been the most wonderful time in my entire life, but now I am trying to be logical for both of us. We live by very different rules and systems of logic, although not as different as I might have expected. If we got to know each other more, these differences would become that much more apparent. Zalanda is where you belong, and Earth is where I belong. I am going to try to stop loving you, and I want you to try to stop loving me. You are very happy here on Zalanda. You belong here just as I belong on Earth. I had been very happy on Earth. You know

441

that I will never forget you. Now I have a memory of a perfect time together when we both are so incredibly happy."

The practical Lauren had returned, and I was so sorry. I softly but emphatically said, "Don't do this, Lauren. He loves you. You love him."

"We have so many differences. The man eats his meals in a food tube."

"That doesn't matter. Think! You'll never have to worry about over eating. You won't have to worry about cooking meals or cleaning up the kitchen."

"He believes when people die, they or the energy that comes from them starts a universe."

"That's not such a terrible belief. It just makes them want to be better people. It's like this: are they going to create a heaven or a hell?"

"Stop this, Jana. I need your support."

"You've got my support. I know it's your decision. But tell him in person. This letter is cowardly."

She thought a moment and then slowly said, "You're right on that one. I will tell him."

I so hoped that she would change her mind. I did not get another chance to talk privately to Lauren because we were working diligently getting ready.

The aerospace people liked the rover and used it to drive the fabricated reinforcements to the *Falcon*. A few times I noticed they were driving around simply for the sheer fun of it.

We also used the rover to carry gifts from the *Falcon* back to the habitat. We gave them NASA daywear which seemed to amuse them as a novelty and some packages of our food which we were not sure how they would respond. Then we took the box of prepacked items as a gift. Jack decided that we should not open it because then we would see how inappropriate some of the items were. Some of the gifts explained who we were, but they already knew so much about us.

They gave us several sets of the great Zalandan clothing, lots of their wafers in various colors and flavors, and some dried essence of the beverages to be reconstituted with the purest water. Some wafers came with instructions, such as "no more than once a day." They gave us a food tube, disassembled, with a power source that should last for many years.

It was more than what would fit in the *Falcon*. Then, Jack had an idea. He called Houston and asked if we could leave the rover with the Zalandans to make room to carry the gifts they were sending us. Houston agreed with only a little coercion on Jack's part.

The aerospace people were tickled with the gift of the rover and soon word about it spread throughout the habitat and others came outside to take a rover ride. It was a new toy for people who seemed to enjoy living with a minimal number of possessions, or at least possessions that popped in and out of existence as needed, with the exception of their aerospace vehicles, which seemed to be their only collectibles. The Zalandans said they would take very good care of the rover and park it in a place of honor with their space vehicles.

Jack and Fawz took Chri Anri and two aerospace people to the Jupiter monitoring station and taught them what to do in case it needed servicing that could not be managed remotely from Earth. The three Zalandans promised they would fix it for us if any problems developed. Meanwhile, the other aerospace people continued fabricating custom fitted pieces to make the top of the lander tougher to withstand various problems, including solar flares.

Finally, everything was packed, and we were ready. The only thing left was a restful sleep cycle. Chri Anri said that the wafers for our dinner would enable us to get lots of REM sleep and wake up totally refreshed. I woke up refreshed just like Chri Anri had promised.

The time came, and we walked to the lander for the final time. It was a parade. On the first row Lauren and Chri Anri walked together. That gave me hope that perhaps she had reconsidered and had not told

443

him what was in the letter. On the second row I walked with Chri Anri the Elder, Sedra, Averg, and her daughter, Svee Dee. On the next row Fawz and Jack walked with the six leaders. After them, row after row of Zalandans in white snowsuits followed.

When we arrived at the *Falcon*, all took turns passing in front of the TV cameras for the broadcast that would be up linked to Earth. Then, the Zalandans took holographic pictures of us, and we took pictures of them with our cameras. Then, they wanted the four of us standing together in front of the *Falcon*. Different Zalandans then took turns standing with us. It was just like going on a vacation to visit family on Earth. Everybody wanted pictures to remember. The picture taking which seemed very unstructured and spontaneous stopped in an instant, and Chri Anri the Elder took my gloved hand and lead me toward the pillars directly opposite the two larger pillars. At that point I realized that there were now twelve ice pillars, one being brand new.

Chri Anri the Elder said to me, "We now rename our monument. From the Monument of the Lost One, now we rename it the Circle of Life for you have returned to us. Twelve Zalandans went on the mission to Earth, and eleven returned. Now, the twelfth Zalandan has finally completed the circle." He handed me a stylus, and I printed my first name on the ice. I was tempted to write great granddaughter of Hulda, but I did not know if that was fact or not.

At that point Chri Anri the Elder must have read my thoughts. Even through our helmets, a look passed between us. I said to him. "I don't know. I'll try to find out."

He replied, "Thank you, Jana. After so long, it should no longer matter to me."

"Maybe, some things always matter," I said.

As I turned, I realized many Zalandans had followed us to the new pillar even though they were standing a respectable distance away. I knew these people would always matter to me. I hoped to see them again but did know if that was possible. There was more picture taking at the pillar, and then we trekked all together back to the *Falcon*. Chri

Anri and Chief helped us pack up the video equipment and load it into the cargo area.

Jack, Fawz, and I climbed up the steps of the *Falcon* and waved one more time. Lauren remained at the bottom of the steps with Chri Anri, and I thought, "She's staying here. Good for her."

Then, Lauren and Chri Anri walked up the steps together, but he did not go inside. The four of us now were inside the *Falcon*, and we watched from the window as Chri Anri walked back down the steps. Lauren blinked as we retracted the *Falcon*'s steps. I dared not ask her anything about him, but she simply whispered, "I didn't even tell him that I loved him."

I wanted to yell, "No!" Instead, I simply nodded to let her know that I had heard what she said.

Now, all the Zalandans backed up until they were outside of the Circle of Life. They held their arms up in the air and swayed. Fawz flipped on the outside audio monitor, and we listened to the barely audible singing in the distance.

I thought of Fawz's ancestor of 500 years ago who had walked with the Zalandans for two days back to their hidden lander. Now, the Zalandans had walked us to our lander as a farewell tradition that spanned both cultures.

We had previously done the final reviews with Houston so we could liftoff as soon as the *Copernicus* orbited into position. We had a lot to concentrate on so that would take our minds off this farewell, but still we all had tears in our eyes, particularly Lauren.

Jack said to Houston, "The *Falcon* has lifted-off."

I watched the Zalandans on the ice below until I could no longer see them.

Solarship *Copernicus*

1:59 p.m. CDT

Jana glanced up from reading her journal over the supernet. That farewell with her Zalandan family had been 20 days ago, and she missed them more as each day passed. She wanted to see them again. Would that be possible? Now, the *Copernicus* was decelerating as it streaked toward a rendezvous in four days with the spaceport that orbited above Earth.

Goodness, how could she momentarily have forgotten what was happening? Her crew was in imminent danger. Recalling the glorious time on Zalanda, had Jana temporarily suppressed the fact that that a bomb from Earth was heading toward their ship with estimated impact today at 1600 hours Houston time?

Jana well realized it was not productive to think about who was trying to destroy the crew but to instead concentrate on trying to save themselves. Her job had been to read her personal journal, thereby revealing their secret mission to everyone on Earth who had been watching her broadcast. If the crew were in danger because some powerful group wanted the existence of Zalanda forever secret, then that group had failed miserably. Everybody listening on the supernet now knew. At least, that was something. For that, she felt happy.

Jack, Fawz, and Lauren gathered together by the main console about to begin a transmission with Houston. Already, Jana had missed the last few transmissions, but that seemed okay because Jack had handled them himself while Lauren and Fawz continued working. Now, Jana felt vaguely left out, that she did not matter. She had an urge to put Jack's recorded messages on and join her crew. No, if Jack had wanted that, he would have signaled her. She then recalled Jack saying how important it was for her to keep reading.

She momentarily had stopped. She looked back into the camera and felt an affinity toward so many people she had never met. She thought of those who already had come forward to help. She wondered if she ever would meet George MacInturff.

A few hours earlier, George had sent her an e-mail telling her to run a banner with the two NASA phone numbers, one general number and one dedicated to LandSkyTech employees who might have useful information. Immediately upon receiving his message, she had made the banner. She wanted to thank him over the net but knew that was not wise. Instead, she looked away from her camera as if she were talking to one of her crew and said, "A banner is an excellent idea." Then, directly to the camera, she had said, "Thank you, friend."

Now, she thought about the LandSkyTech employees who already were helping. She hoped that Russell Ramsey along with the JSC and Darwin people working with him would soon break the passcode protecting the Saturn probe. She wondered about Sharleen Rothwell who supposedly had captured two ruffians single-handedly.

Jana looked down at her journal. There still was so much she wanted people everywhere to know about their mission. She recalled her crew had stayed at full alert as the *Copernicus* passed through the asteroid belt. Jack or Fawz had been in constant contact with Houston for the entire duration. It was dangerous but at least none of the asteroids were on a mission to destroy their ship. All of those rocks simply were orbiting the sun, and they were not as densely packed as she had thought.

What had most deeply moved her was the magical wake cycle when the Sun grew bigger than Jupiter. They called that Sun Day. Then, Jana had known with certainty they were on their way home. At this moment, she knew nothing with certainty.

Transmission between Houston and Solarship *Copernicus*

When the transmission started, Jack was disappointed that Willie was not the CAPCOM. The rookie on duty was a thoughtful and completely competent person. However, Jack did not think he could pull information out of him.

"Where's Willie," Jack asked.

"His shift is over."

"Is there anything that we should do immediately?"

"No, not a thing. I'll update you on what's happening around here."

Jack knew that was not a normal time for a shift break even on a Saturday. "Nothing against you, but I prefer dealing with Willie."

"I understand, Jack." The CAPCOM turned his head away from his camera and said, "Go get Willie." Then he whispered, "We need to make them happy. They may not survive this day." He turned back toward the camera and said, "We're looking for Willie."

"I heard what you said."

"Oh, God, I'm sorry, Commander. You know me. I'm . . . I'm a pessimist." The CAPCOM stuttered as he spoke. "I was . . . the only one who never thought you'd make it back from the Mars I Mission. You have no idea how many people are helping and how much they care . . . how much they care about you." The CAPCOM quickly regained his composure, "Willie will give you the update. He'll tell you everything."

"I know! That's why I need him."

The CAPCOM tried to conceal a smile "It's rumored that Madame President said, 'Please don't let anything happen to my precious Jack.' Have you ever met the President?"

"Yes, once for 15 minutes."

"Must have been quite a sizzling 15 minutes."

"Guess so," Jack said in a noncommittal tone for it occurred to him that everything he said to Mission Control on the whole trip but particularly this day would go into the public domain. If they survived, the crew might well need all the public support they could muster. One little careless word or flip comment regarding the President who was immensely popular could easily be used against the crew. Furthermore, he did not feel flip toward her. He felt kindly toward her and quite grateful.

"Willie is running toward us right now," the CAPCOM said.

In a few seconds Willie's face was on Jack's monitor. Willie seemed exhilarated and talked fast. "First, it was good news, then bad, and now it's possibly beginning to look good again. First, the good! Our people are working at Darwin Industries with their programmers and with Russell Ramsey, the developer from LandSkyTech. They have broken the code for the probe's trajectory."

"Hurrah," Jack said. "Our whole problem is solved."

Jack nodded at Fawz and Lauren who were on either side of him. Lauren let out an uncharacteristic squeal of delight, and Fawz said something in Rhatanian.

"Wait, stop," Willie yelled. "Don't celebrate, not yet."

"Change the trajectory," Jack yelled back. "That's nice and clean."

"In addition to programmers and code breakers, we have a Mission Control team over at Darwin Industries. Their own mission controllers are there, too. They had all settled on the trajectory change for the probe when they received an urgent message from JSC not to change the trajectory."

"Why? Why shouldn't they change it?"

"A second code protects the probe's ability to lock onto a target. That code overrides the trajectory code."

"It's fortunate you discovered the existence of the second code," Jack said, feeling both let down and pleased at the same time.

"A LandSkyTech employee alerted us. She was watching your broadcast on her computer. As soon as a banner started running with a dedicated phone number for LandSkyTech employees, she called us.

"When she mentioned two codes protecting the trajectory, her call got the highest priority. Fortunately, we have highly knowledgeable people manning the phone bank. The caller said that although the trajectory could be changed, it would only be for a second or less because a locking-in program overrode it. The probe would search for a target, lock in again, and select its own trajectory.

"And it could lock-in on the *Copernicus* instead of the *Falcon*," Jack stated.

"Yes, that's our concern."

"How credible does the woman seem?"

"What she says checks out. She's coming on-site. May be here already."

"And the good news is that you can override the locking-in code?"

"I wish that were so. Our people are working on it."

"Well, then, have you figured out how to blow up the probe?"

"No. That function also could be protected by the second code."

Jack tried to shake the feeling of discouragement settling over him. He rarely felt discouraged. He did not know how to deal with it other than to banish it. A voice in his head said, "You wanted a challenge. You asked for it. Now, all is hopeless, and you, my man, are going to die." Without saying a word aloud, Jack replied to his voice. "Shut up! If one thing doesn't work, you simply try something else." The voice answered, "Old man, you are running out of time." Jack answered, "Then you try several different approaches all at once. We certainly have enough people." Jack banished his subconscious and turned his attention to Willie.

Jack said, "The second code could be similar to the first one."

Willie replied, "We're working with that idea. The first code was a red clip art lizard of a precise size."

"Thank everyone involved for their diligence."

"Wilco," Willie said. "There's a LandSkyTech mobile Mission Control. We've got it zeroed in to about a one-block area around the Galleria. That whole area is cordoned off, and they're doing a vehicle-to-vehicle search, starting with the larger vehicles, but it could be in a parking garage, too. Which would make for pretty horrible reception."

"That's the good news?" Jack asked.

"That's neutral news. It could be good news. We're not sure how that will play out." Some of our Mission Control team are with the law enforcement ready to take over when they find it.

"That sounds messy. Is Filbert Grystal on that team?"

"I believe he is. How did you know that?"

"Pull him off and have him questioned by . . . by someone . . . as a . . . as a suspect."

"Really!" Willie exclaimed.

"Just do it!"

Willie wrote several notes and handed them to different people. Then he took many seconds keying something into his computer. "Filbert was very concerned about Lauren's well-being. And yours, too."

"We're running out of time, and the LandSkyTech mobile Mission Control is the good news." Jack shook his head. "Willie, I know you and your team are trying hard. I seldom lose patience. My frustration is not directed toward you."

"I understand, sir. Remember, we're Mission Control. We always have contingency plans." Willie was practically grinning. "We can't make the probe blow up on demand, at least not yet, but it would blow up upon impact with something like the lander. The explosion could cause the lander to explode, too, and if that happened, the *Copernicus* could be caught in the debris and dust storm. However, you are aware that we can deactivate the explosives in the probe? Then upon impact, the probe would break apart, or depending upon circumstances, it could catch on fire. The tough top would deflect the debris and dust away from the *Copernicus*. Or the probe could do something worse. It could pass right through the lander's tough top relatively unharmed and lock-in on the *Copernicus*."

"Yes, I know about all that," Jack replied in an even voice, trying not to sound impatient.

"The good news is this. We're getting some numbers that seem to be checking out."

"Yes."

"We're working on a 'soft' explosion in the event that the probe impacts the *Falcon*. Instead of deactivating all the explosives, we would deactivate most of them."

"What?"

"I know it sounds incredulous at first. The soft explosion would be only forceful enough to destroy the probe's homing-in device. That way, if the probe passed through the tough top of the lander, it would not zero in on the *Copernicus*."

"Did Filbert think up this plan?" Jack asked.

"No, no, of course not. Not Filbert. This is a brilliant plan."

"Who, then?"

"I am not supposed to tell you," Willie said, forcing firmness into his voice.

"I have a . . . ."

"I know, sir, 'a need to know.' Do you have any idea how much trouble I'm in for telling you our plans for launching the *Falcon*? I'm being blamed that you launched prematurely and that two of you are not in that lander right now."

"Launching the lander is not an obscure idea. We were certainly capable of thinking that up ourselves. In fact, we did. You know we could not have launched so quickly and accurately without doing our homework ahead of time," Jack said.

"Thanks, Jack, for trying to get me off the hook. But I'm well in the frying pan."

"If you feel that way, you might as well tell me what I have a need to know."

"The programmer Russell Ramsey is working on deactivating most of the explosives so the explosion will be less forceful. If we take over the LandSkyTech mobile Mission Control, no one there can override what he has done."

"Okay, Russell Ramsey thought up the plan," Jack said.

Willie did not say anything but his eyes turned away from Jack to the left and up, and he closed his mouth tight as if to hold the truth inside.

"Tell me, Willie. We who are about to die need to know."

"I salute you, sir. Russell Ramsey did not think up the soft explosion. However, he jumped at the idea and, I heard, berated himself for not thinking of it. At present, we really don't know who came up with the idea. The original plan came in the form of an e-mail to several different JSC addresses all at once. Since so many people were hanging around, wanting to help, several teamed up and started working on those numbers at first simply to give themselves something to do."

"What was the exact message? Where did it come from? Who were the recipients at JSC?" Jack asked.

"I don't know, but I'll find out. However, I've heard that the source is foreign, that the English is rather strange, but the numbers, the math is magnificent. Is there anything else?

"That's it, Willie."

"I'm going to get fired for telling you everything."

"You're not getting fired, Willie. In fact you are going to be a hero for saving our lives. Think about that. You were honest with us. You did exactly what CAPCOM historically does and is supposed to do on every mission. You told us the truth. No secrets. Just the truth. What a concept."

Solarship *Copernicus*
2:20 p.m. CDT

As Lauren prepared to read her reports over the net, she would not mention the best part of a magnificent mission, falling in love with Chri Anri and those glorious times that followed.

If the crew survived, she knew that each of them willingly would be a spokesperson for the Zalandans. If they did not survive, how much jeopardy would Chri Anri and his countrymen face? Her crew had made the long, perilous journey; others could follow. She wondered if in the process of attempting to save themselves, they had thrown the Zalandans to all the fearful and dangerous people on Earth. She hurt inside. Lauren built an isolating wall around the pain. She could help her new friends when she read her reports if she chose carefully.

She needed to protect them from two categories of people, the first category being evildoers who might attack Zalanda for reasons of fanaticism, status, or pure profit, and the second category being fearful individuals who could be intimidated or tricked into helping the evildoers.

To deter the first category, she would emphasize that Zalanda did not have natural resources: oil, precious or rare metals, or anything of material value that could be turned into an earthly profit. She would tell about the incredible danger and expense space travelers faced in reaching that far distant moon.

She would describe all the negatives about living on Zalanda. To go outside, one must wear a heated space suit and carry oxygen as protection from cold far more extreme than Antarctica and from air as thin as that surrounding the space stations. Once inside the Zalandan compound, people adjusted to the low gravity and the effects of Jupiter upon them. However, because humans had not evolved to live on Zalanda, they compensated for the unearthly stresses on the human body by controlling with extreme precision the environmental factors they could control. She would describe the food tube as something eerily strange rather that the novelty that her crew considered it. She hoped her words and reports would discourage the dangerous ones.

The fearful people on Earth who had been thoroughly intimidated by the scandal sheets would be a far larger number than the dangerous ones. For those people, she would explain that the Zalandans had nearly 2,500 years of opportunity to wreak havoc on Earth if they had so wanted. The Zalandan society and their thoughts and beliefs would not impact Earthlings until they chose to let that happen. That was what Jack had said over the net at the beginning of this wake cycle.

She wanted to show what exceptionally admirable people the Zalandans were, but Jana had already done that through reading her journal. Instead, she would show why they were so good and why they got along so well with each other. A major reason was their honesty and lack of secrets. In such an environment, a society could function quite well. A personal relationship could function well and blossom. Their minds were not bogged down with a hierarchy of secrets they held from each other.

She wondered if fewer secrets would work well on Earth, too. She still did not know exactly why their mission had been a secret. It had not been a NASA policy. How could she, an astronaut on a secret mission returning from a secret society, have the audacity to suggest to her net audience that much more openness was desirable? Having no secrets would be a difficult concept to comprehend for a person on Earth who routinely used secrets for a multitude of reasons: to maintain or acquire power and wealth, to protect others, to protect oneself, for the sake of surprise, and for reasons that she had not yet considered.

Even in such a nurturing environment as Zalanda, she had kept a huge secret from the man she adored. She did not tell him how much she ached to stay with him on Zalanda and how completely she loved him. She hoped he had read her mind. On occasion she believed brain waving was possible. Yet, he had verbalized his total love and commitment toward her in perfect standard English. He had waited for her to reciprocate. In retrospect, she realized it was a love or commitment protocol, and she had not known the rules. Instead, she had said that her crew needed her. That also was true.

She wanted to spare him and make their parting easier when she left Zalanda. Afterwards, when it was far too late to make amends, she realized she had hurt him deeply. Now, the least she could do was protect Chri Anri and the rest of the Zalandans from yet unknown dangers.

Exonerating the Zalandans from negative speculations would be a worthy goal. Lauren sequenced her reports to show them as favorably as possible and their environment as miserably as possible. Both things were easy to do. Personally, she thought the environment was just fine. She typed a few notes into her computer on what she would mention extemporaneously. She also planned to describe Ancient City even though that did not bolster either point she wished to make. Her presentation now prepared, she was ready to relieve Jana. Afterwards, her other jobs were to help Jack maneuver the *Copernicus* if and when the lander sustained a hit, and finally to do whatever was needed at the end.

Fawz and Jack had stopped working and waved her toward them. It was time for their food break. Under the circumstances, a communal meal seemed surreal. Yet, they needed to be clear thinking and alert. Of course, they should take a break. Soon, it would happen. The probe would impact the lander. Despite that, she thought Jack and Fawz both seemed amazingly chipper.

She picked a freeze-dried sandwich from the food storage and then floated over to Jack and Fawz. The food choices were slim, as they had already eaten most of their favorites. She wondered if this was their last meal.

"Should we call Jana over?" Lauren asked.

"No, not yet," Jack said. "We will broadcast until the end, but be ready to take over. She's getting tired."

"I know. I've been keeping an eye on her." She wished Jana could have joined them, especially for this meal, but she simply said, "I'm ready to take over whenever necessary."

"When you take her place, emphasize to her that it's time for her food break and a rest. After that, I'll bring her up to date. Fawz and I are almost finished with our work. I still need the information I requested from Houston."

Fawz added, "After we recheck everything yet again, all we will have to do is wait. JSC is rechecking, too."

Jack yawned. "Now is a good moment to kick back, relax, gab a bit, and recharge our batteries. Unless JSC and Darwin break that second code, it will soon get pretty dicey in here. We'll need to be at peak performance. After this meal, I might even catch a few winks."

Lauren almost asked, "Are you going to order us to sleep?" Yet, that seemed flippant. After all these months on the mission, she still treated Jack with the greatest respect, probably even with more respect. She knew Jack could sleep whenever he wished, even on this wake cycle. She admired his complete self-discipline.

The idea of sleep put her in a dreamy mood. Her thoughts drifted. She said, "Maybe there was a peaceful, pastoral existence once. People had enough to eat, enough to keep their minds nimble, something to look forward to, and other people who cared for them deeply."

"Sounds like you're describing life inside this spaceship," Jack said gently. "Speaking about enough to eat, how about a Neapolitan ice cream sandwich? We saved the last one for you."

"Sounds delicious," Lauren answered and retrieved the bar. "That chalky, cardboard taste really grows on you." She was still questioning as she bit into her ice cream and deftly caught the crumbs before they drifted away. "Do you think maybe we should not have done this?"

"Which 'this' did you have in mind? Broadcasting over the net? Launching the *Falcon*? Without a crewmember in it?" Jack asked.

"No, the whole journey, maybe more than that, the whole everything, space travel, airplanes, science, all of it."

"This is our young, ambitious Lauren speaking? You sound like an old man," Fawz said jokingly.

"Maybe, it's the two and three hundred year old people I've been hanging around with lately." She did not want them to tease her out of her mood.

"Or it could be a youngster among them, that 37-year-old juvenile," Jack quipped.

Lauren replied, "I wanted to go. I was so honored to be selected I wanted an adventure. My reservations about this mission never made it to clear cut articulated thought until right now. Maybe, we should not have gone. It wasn't such a good idea to answer a 500-year-old request. No one had answered it before us."

"Late in the last century, the Zalandans sent another message like a beacon to the people of Earth," Fawz said. "They were inviting us again if anyone had been paying attention."

"Nobody then knew it was an invitation," Lauren said. "Why did we do it? Indeed, the mountain was there. Go climb it. The planet was there. Go explore it. Go find out if life exists there. But afterwards, then what? I'm finally getting an inkling why the ancient Rhatanians turned their backs on science. Actions have consequences."

"Are you intending to mention any of this on the net? Jack asked.

"No, of course not. Even if this is the end, even if JSC is doing this to us, I still want funding for the Space Program. After all, I am an astronaut."

"It sounds like you're questioning the path of our entire civilization." Jack said.

"Yes, I guess I am. I am also a sociologist, and I think about these things. With our journey a secret, the implications were far less." Lauren felt herself wavering on the whole concept of secrets. She wondered if freedom from secrecy was possible only in specific, unusual situations.

Fawz said thoughtfully, "Since I've learned my countrymen willingly threw away so much knowledge 2,500 years ago, I believe it was an incorrect decision, an extremely bad decision. We went through famines and suffering and being subjugated, all this unnecessarily. Look how long it took Rhatania to build back what we had lost. All because of a secret, no, a large body of secrets foolishly withheld from future generations."

Jack said, "People by nature are creative. We want to make new things, do new things, and be creators. Sometimes, the society discourages it. Sometimes, the society forbids it. Sometimes, people are their own secret keepers because of their individual personalities. Consider the namesake of our ship, Copernicus. He was too much the perfectionist to get his work published until near the end of his life. Before that, he privately circulated his material among friends. He was not afraid of the Church because he was well connected politically. He was afraid that his astronomy might be considered foolish or that his work was not complete enough. He feared looking like a fool. Those who came after him had other problems. They ran smack into the Inquisition which tried to suppress them."

Then, a look crossed Jack's face that Lauren had seen a few times before, sadness mingled with pride. He said, "Sometimes, a person lives with an enormous secret because he is responsible to others to never reveal it."

Instantly, she knew Jack was talking about himself, but just as instantly she also knew that he would not reveal his secret even if the *Copernicus* were engulfed in flames. It was not something gnawing at him or hurting him but rather something that filled him with pride. She certainly would respect his privacy.

Thinking about Jack living with a secret and thinking about Copernicus not wanting to look foolish helped Lauren understand she lived with a secret every day of her life. Her secret was similar to Copernicus's, one of self-image. Her secret was a filter that all her outward behavior passed through. She perceived herself as a no-nonsense person who did not burden anyone with her personal life. She considered herself a true professional, and like Jack with his secret, she took pride in her behavior. She kept her personal life to herself so much so that Jack and Fawz, her co-commanders, did not know she wanted to stay with Chri Anri. Jana knew, but she could completely trust Jana not to intervene with Jack or Fawz on her behalf. How would Lauren possibly have guessed that Jana would be reading her journal for the entire world to hear? Fortunately, with the little that Lauren had been able to hear, Jana had been circumspect about Lauren and Chri Anri's privacy.

With effort Lauren pushed Chri Anri out of her mind. "I've been asking the wrong question," she said. "The issue is not whether or not we have technology, but the quality of people's souls. Everyone has technology of a certain kind. People living in a rain forest have knowledge of pharmacology. At issue is how people treat each other. Can a good soul work at any level of technology?" Chri Anri was right back in her thoughts again. "Now, with worldwide knowledge, will the Zalandans be safe? Think of Columbus, the explorers who came after him, and the impact on the native peoples such as the Mayans. Their historical records were destroyed. Their leader and many of their people were killed. Now, by revealing the existence of the Zalandans, we have put them at risk."

Jack said, "Good heavens, Lauren, the Zalandans tweak meteors. They are well able to defend themselves."

Fawz spoke slowly and deliberately. "They wanted to reveal their existence to people on Earth before we did it for them. They were tired of their isolation. They did not want to be a secret society, but long ago they had made an agreement to hide their existence. They had faithfully honored the agreement, but now their contract with my people, the Rhatanians of long ago, has been fulfilled because of our visit. I am a descendant of the ancient Rhatanians, and Jana is a descendant of the Zalandan named Hulda, which makes her a descendant of the ancient Rhatanians. You, Lauren, and you, Jack, are people from other places on the Earth. According to the instructions on the cylinder, we are the people whom the Zalandans chose to seek out. We did what they wanted us to do. We have fulfilled the terms of their contract for them. We have set them free."

Fawz's words exalted and soothed Lauren. The ache inside her melted away. She knew his words were true. Still, her thoughts returned to dangers that the Zalandans could face as a choice trophy civilization for an evil country to subjugate. She hoped her reports would be a first step toward deterrence. She said, "They have no idea what they're getting themselves into."

Fawz replied, "They watch Earth TV. They know what our planet is like. Yet, they still chose to send us the message we did not understand: twenty-one major meteors impacting Jupiter on the twenty-fifth anniversary of our first moon landing."

She said, "I hope these peaceful people never need to defend themselves from their brethren, other Earthlings. I don't know if they would do it. They don't like to kill the beasties."

"But they do kill beasties when necessary," Jack said, emphasizing the word "do."

"They have a history. They're explorers, scientists, creators, artists; they're not warriors. We must survive to be their defenders."

"That's a good reason to wish for our survival." Jack said. "I also don't want them to suffer because of our mission.

"Do you visualize yourself as the mother-protector of the Zalandans?" Fawz asked Lauren. It was not said harshly or sarcastically, but as a straightforward question.

"I wouldn't phrase it in those mythic terms. I could picture myself as their public relations person." Lauren thought a minute. "No, it's a stronger relationship than that."

"Remember, they are my countrymen. They are descendants of ancient Rhatanians. We also have their best interest at heart," Fawz said.

Lauren was making strong realizations regarding her relationship with those she had left behind. In a normal situation, she would have kept these thoughts to herself. This was anything but a normal wake cycle. "I see myself as a Zalandan. They invited me to stay with them. I wanted to stay, too. I wanted to stay with Chri Anri. I'd like to be one of them. I am one of them. Not one by blood, but by affinity." She had said it. She had pierced her entire self-image as a professional person. It actually felt pretty good.

Jack and Fawz did not say anything. They just exchanged glances. Finally, Jack said lightly, "We are a family here. Family members tell each other how they feel. At least that is a good arrangement for families."

Fawz said, "Remember, many of the original Zalandans were not Rhatanians by blood but by affinity – people from all over the world, friends of the ancient Rhatanians, people who shared their love of adventure, exploration, and science. Until 500 years ago, a small number of people from around the world continued to join their ranks. You have as much right to their citizenship as their original founders."

"Thanks, Fawz. I am surprising myself that I'm saying any of this to you. I usually keep this kind of stuff to myself. Let's face it. These are unusual times. You are my best friends in this world or any other. Jack, Fawz, and Jana over there by the camera and Chri Anri way, way over there under a dome." Lauren looked down. She raised her hand to her face and touched her cheeks. Her face felt warm. She thought she might be blushing.

"This is an excellent thing you did, Lauren, telling us your feelings. Now that you are a Zalandan, you took a significant first step. They have no secrets." Fawz thought a minute and said, "We can formalize

462

your wishes. There are benefits to being a prince. I can anoint you as a citizen of Rhatania. Since the Zalandans consider themselves Rhatanians, you in essence will become a Zalandan. I do not have my regalia aboard. I do not have my ceremonial sword. Do not have my ceremonial robes and the incense, but we can improvise."

Lauren and Fawz nodded at each other in silent acquiescence.

"Do you Lauren Adams wish to become a citizen of Rhatania with all of the rights, privileges, duties, and obligations?

"Yes, I, Lauren Adams, desire to become a citizen of Rhatania with all of the rights, privileges, duties, and obligations.

"Do you renounce allegiance to any foreign powers with the exception of your native land, the United States of America, and with the exception of the civilization of Zalanda, which is the new land of Rhatania?"

"Yes, I do."

Do you affirm to protect the air, land, and water of Rhatania from industrial and all types of pollution? Do you promise to promote environmental controls throughout the world?

"Willingly, I do that."

"Do you affirm to abide by the Constitution of the Kingdom of Rhatania?"

"I have no idea what your Constitution says, but based on your integrity as a person, I affirm."

"By the power vested in me by the Kingdom of Rhatania, I anoint you a citizen of Rhatania with all the rights and privileges.

Lauren exhaled deeply. "Thanks, Fawz."

Even Jack looked like tears might come to his eyes. He blinked them back and said, "You never know when a prince might come in handy."

They burst into laughter. "It's good to be alive and happy," Lauren said.

Solarship *Copernicus*
2:30 p.m. CDT

Jana read and read. She explained that each day as they drew closer to Earth, the transmission turnaround time with Houston grew shorter, and communication with Mission Control became much more pleasant. She described the back-to-back experiments the crew performed each wake cycle because their return trip was so much faster than the original NASA schedule, thanks to the Zalandan aerospace people.

She sipped water through a straw and glanced away from her notebook computer toward Lauren, Jack, and Fawz who had somberly gathered together for a meal. Her mind flashed to Chri Anri and his shuddering at the very thought of a shared mealtime.

Jana went back to reading and when she looked toward her crew again, they seemed to be having a ceremony. Afterwards, they laughed in unison, and their momentary cheerfulness lifted her spirits.

When she reached the last word on the last page of her journal, she looked into the camera and said, "I have no more to read. I thank all of you, everyone who helped, the people at JSC in Houston, people from Darwin Industries, those from LandSkyTech, and . . . and my new friend." She decided not to mention George by name.

"I think Earth is a good place and that people mostly get along. I'm glad to be coming home. I always have liked living near Houston even though now I know there is Zalanda.

"I was happy there. The Zalandans understand each other so well because there are few of them and they live such a long time. They believe they can read each other's minds. I don't know if they can, but it's an ingrained belief with them. On Zalanda, I thought I could read

Chri Anri's thought waves, but it wasn't easy. I only held the necessary type and level of concentration for about a minute.

"The Zalandans are tolerant of each other. They find each other's quirks endearing. It's a nurturing place, like one giant family.

"That's how I grew up with my family, with nurturing parents who thought well of me. Thank you Mom and Dad for everything. My crew has treated me with kindness and respect. Jack, Commander Jackson Medwin, says that one of NASA's greatest fears is that the crewmembers won't get along for an extended period of time. If that happens, there is no escape for them. Lauren, Jack, and Fawz are people I willingly, even eagerly, would go with on another mission. I've had a good but short life so far.

"If this is the end, then I say farewell. I wish you well. I am reminded of the words on a very special metal cylinder. 'Farewell, dear friends. I hope we meet again beyond the broken and jagged rocks torn asunder.' Those dear friends never did meet again. In their stead, we journeyed beyond the rocks to Zalanda and met with them, and we have returned across the rocks again, past the orbit of Mars, and soon, I hope, home to Earth."

Jana wanted to say more. She wanted to say good-bye to Alan, but words that had been flowing so easily came to grinding halt. Had she embarrassed Alan thoroughly and publicly by telling everyone her feelings toward him and particularly by describing their farewell under a SpaceTech moon? Of course, she had.

Yet, through reading her journal, she recalled so many happy times and often forgot about the crew's desperate situation. More importantly, people had come forward to help. She felt close to viewers all over the world whom she had never met.

Jana looked into the camera. She had no words, just conflicting thoughts. She tried to smile.

Then, magically, a hand touched her shoulder and Lauren holding a notebook computer floated next to her, ready to relieve her. Words came back, and she whispered, "Great timing, Lauren. I was losing it."

Lauren softly replied, "I was keeping an eye on you. Keep an eye on me, too. Things are going to get rough."

To the camera, Jana announced, "Lauren Adams, mission specialist, will read you her NASA reports."

Lauren whispered again. "This is your food and rest break."

They exchanged places, and Jana propelled herself out of the camera's view. She glanced around the cabin. Jack was communicating with Mission Control. She could not hear Jack's words but from the way he was hunched over the console, she judged the conversation to be deep and serious. Fawz was working on his numbers. Suddenly, Jana desperately wanted to know what had happened during those hours that she had been on the net. She knew they were not out of trouble. Jack and Fawz were too somber and too busy. Anyway, they would have told her. She felt left out, but that was silly, she told herself. Time was running short, and her crew needed to do their jobs.

This was her rest and meal break, but she could neither rest nor eat. Her throat was dry, and she sipped more water through a straw. She moved back toward Lauren so she could hear better.

Lauren described the Zalandan complex, enthusiastically dwelling on Ancient City, making it sound better than the current quarters of the Zalandans. Jana herself thought Ancient City was too antiquated for her tastes, more akin to an art museum of ancient Greek and oriental artifacts. However, she knew why Lauren liked it so much. Chri Anri had taken Lauren to Ancient City on their first date.

Next, Lauren read about the religious life of the Zalandans. She made extemporaneous comments directly to her audience, people all over the world. To Jana, what shone through more than anything was Lauren's love, respect, and admiration for the Zalandans. Lauren was doing a terrific job. If their plight was not so desperate, Jana simply could relax and enjoy listening. Lauren spoke in loving terms about the Zalandans but not anything about the love of her life. Lauren was too private a person to mention anything about Chri Anri. In comparison, Jana thought, through her journal she had spilled her guts about Alan.

Jana's reverie was interrupted by Jack. He turned away from the console and said loudly, "You will need strength for what is ahead, Jana." That was the closest to an admonishment that he had ever given her. To appease Jack, she sipped on a space food version of a milk shake. Jana expected Jack to bring her up to speed now that his transmission ended, but he kept working.

Finally, Jack propelled himself toward her, and they both moved away from Lauren. "You've been a trooper reading your journal throughout the launch and through all of our updates from Houston. Your reading has reaped great dividends.

"The launch was good, but not perfect. There was some drift, and we made a course correction. Now, the *Falcon* is not as far away as we would have liked. That could become a problem.

"Regarding the probe, it still is on rendezvous course with the lander. Two codes protect the probe's trajectory and the function to destroy itself. So far, Darwin, LandSkyTech, and JSC people working together have broken one code. If they break the second, they simply change the probe's trajectory, and we're free of that pesky little thing. After that, if we are able, we'll retrieve the lander, and head for the spaceport. That's our first scenario."

"I choose that scenario," Jana said, her voice more hopeful than she felt. She liked the way Jack called the bomb a probe. It made the problem seem manageable. Yet, it was a probe because the explosives could be deactivated. The second security code was new information for Jana. The probe was locked in on the lander, or so they hoped. She wondered if instead it still was locked in on the *Copernicus*, but she did not mention that thought to Jack.

"Our second scenario is far less safe. It's primarily what we talked about last night. The *Falcon*'s top is very strong and well reinforced. Before the probe impacts the lander, its meteoroid shield will be activated. The shield is not strong enough to repel something that large traveling at such a velocity, but it should soften the impact. The lander's soft underbelly with the crumple zone will face the probe. When the probe impacts, it might break apart as it passes through the crumple zone. Or the probe might pass right through it. When it impacts the lander's strong top, we hope the probe breaks apart and the top holds together at a precise angle that deflects the probe's dust particles away from the trajectory of our ship.

"Soon, we will have a decision to make together. I just talked to JSC, and they finally agreed with me that the decision is ours: whether to deactivate the explosives and hope the lander holds the probe particles inside, or whether to allow a soft explosion right at impact. That way, we are sure of destroying or mortally wounding the probe. If the probe breaks apart, the force on the lander's top will be more evenly distributed. Of course, there is so much acceleration already. That LandSkyTech fellow Russell Ramsey can do whatever we want him to do with the explosives. JSC wants him to deactivate most of the explosives and go for the soft explosion upon impact.

Jana visualized the probe passing right through the lander, it's homing-in device still intact, and locking in on the *Copernicus.* The other choice was pieces of a broken-up probe being contained by the lander's tough top. Yet, if the pieces were not contained, surely, the homing-in device would be destroyed or disabled. But there would be lots of fragments. Jana figured Jack had no idea how shaky she was on physics.

"What are the negatives to the soft explosion?" she asked.

"We don't know the source of the information. It could be from the terrorists. From the wording on the message, the source is not a native English speaker. An e-mail message was sent to about ten people at once. At present, JSC can't trace the source of the message. That in itself is highly unusual. The source is still being checked out. JSC will send me a copy of the message and the names of the original recipients. However, the four of us are the ones to decide."

"I'll abstain from voting unless a brilliant insight pops into my mind."

"Another brilliant insight could happen," Jack said.

"You mean going out in the snow alone?" Jana asked. Jack could make people feel really good, but he was not one for massive exaggerations. The whole snow incident could be viewed as an incredibly impulsive thing. She knew it had not been impulsive.

Jack did not answer the snow question. Instead he said, "You were a breakthrough link in getting the whole mission in the first place. Remember the cylinder?"

"Of course," Jana replied, realizing that Jack had not heard her recent comments over the net.

"Do you remember seeing it prior to that luncheon at Fawz's apartment?"

"That's the weird thing. It seemed so familiar, like something I had seen long ago, maybe even heard, but different words. It haunted me sometimes in my quiet moments. Then I remembered the great art catalogues at your house on the coffee tables and end tables. There was an especially fine one from Rhatania on thick glossy paper, the art objects ever so vividly photographed, and I figured I had probably seen it there." Jana refrained from mentioning that her great-grandmother Hulda probably had shown her an identical cylinder.

Jack said, "You picked the cylinder from more than four hundred objects in the catalogue and said it reminded you of a player piano roll. Do you recall that comment?"

"No!" Jana now realized why she would have selected the cylinder and why she would have mentioned its possible musical qualities. She had seen and heard an identical one years before. "Are you saying that nobody in Rhatania made that connection before I did?"

"Not a soul. Who knows, maybe they were looking for a flute-like instrument. Once they had the idea, when someone came across the case, that person already was alerted. Lots of old things came with cases. They could have found the case and still not have made the connection with the musical instrument they were seeking."

Jana knew that Jack was far too busy to give her such non-essential information. She wondered why right now he was telling her this specific bit of mission history if not to build her up so that she would behave like the astronaut she knew she could be.

"You can count on me, Jack."

"I know I can, Jana."

"Thank you, Jack, for believing in me and allowing me to make this journey. Whatever happens, I want you to know it was worth it. It was more than I ever dreamed of, more than I ever knew to dream." She wanted to tell him how she admired him and his abilities, but she started to choke up.

"The *Copernicus* most likely will encounter dust particles. It is naive to think there will be no dust from the probe impacting the lander even if we go with the soft explosion. If our meteoroid shield repels the particles before they touch our ship, we'll hear warning beeps, more like pinging sounds, that things are being repelled.

"If there's a penetration, the compromised panel lights up with perimeter marks. Remember the putty tape for a temporary fix! The tape goes on gently but firmly and immediately. If there's a penetration, we will depressurize. Probably. We'll be in our space suits. We have practiced this same scenario on the trainers back in Houston, and we've done regular drills on the *Copernicus*. Remember that we already are prepared, and right now you have more experience on a major mission than all but members of the two Mars missions. If we are lucky, it's survivable.

"The scenarios get more challenging after that, such as if the lander's top does not withstand the probe's impact and comes apart, or if the angle of the top is wrong. In either case, we get bombarded with debris. Then, there is the possibility that our ship takes a direct hit from the probe. The new training film goes through everything.

"Keep in mind that there's still time to break the second code, and then we won't have any problems at all."

Jana's concerns about being left out of the loop vanished. Instead, she learned all at once about the last several communications with Mission Control. The density of the information reminded her of the time on Ganymede when Chri Anri explained so much about Zalanda all at once. While Chri Anri's information fascinated her, Jana's survival depended on understanding what Jack had just told her.

Jack must have sensed it for he said, "Your jobs are these. Watch the training film. To refresh our memories, Life Sciences sent us a new interactive training film early this afternoon. Lauren, Fawz, and I have seen it already. It's been put together hastily, but it gets the points across. It explains step-by-step everything we may go through. Practice whatever you need. Particularly, practice with the repair tape. Take as much time as you need.

"Then check any new messages from JSC. Upload anything JSC wants, and send it to them. We've sent them all our data already. Everything! We did a huge data dump. A few things may have become garbled in the transmission. They may want particular files. It should be non-urgent stuff. If it is urgent, there'll be the normal warning signal or probably a video transmission. Lauren has sent all of her reports. I'd like you to upload your journal to them, too, off your personal computer."

"What about that stuff with Max, the private code to talk to him and all of that. It's already marked. I can delete it without any trouble."

"Yes, delete it."

"Okay, and I'll send the rest."

Jana sent her journal to JSC before she played the training tape. Jack was right. It was rough, clips from lots of films pasted together. There was Jack in his Mars I daywear discussing how to deal with an emergency. "We need calmness and heightened alertness combined together. We need confidence. Too much confidence and we can become careless. Too little confidence and we are paralyzed into inaction. With the optimal confidence level, we can get the job done. Not that we will save ourselves from every scenario, but we will pull through a lot of risky situations with the appropriate emotional state, a bit of thinking outside the box, and lots of training."

The next part of the film examined the putty tape. It looked like children's clay or repair putty in a roll with peel off backing. A penetration of the *Copernicus* would be covered with the tape. Because the interior of the ship was pressurized and the space outside was close to a vacuum, some of the putty would be pulled through the hole to outside the ship. Once it hit the cold of outer space, the material immediately hardened, and there was a seal. But it was tricky stuff. It was easy enough to work with, but with a bigger hole, all of it could be pulled to the outside before it ever sealed. The stuff had been used in practice situations at the space factory, and it worked about 60 percent of the time. It was good for pinholes. Jana hoped she would not need to use it.

If JSC found the second code, the tape instructions became unnecessary. But she practiced, patting some tape onto the skin of the *Copernicus* and then removing it again.

When Jana decided she knew what she could be facing and knew what to do, she went to the main console and checked for correspondence from JSC. One was marked "Information you requested." It was not marked emergency or priority. She looked around for Jack but he was busy working with Fawz. A picture of the lander was on Fawz's monitor. It seemed prudent to open the file and to not disturb Jack and Fawz.

"Regarding the impetus for the soft explosion, you requested the original message:

> *This is the best. Mathematics the best is. Physics the best is. Tough Top on lander the best design. The best metal. Not indestructible. Need force more evenly distributed on hemisphere of top. Need probe explode on contact. Soft explosion. Force not much.*"

The rest of the message was mathematics and drawings with explanations written in perfect English. At the end of the message, there were several small dots and circles, some imbedded into others.

After the message, the note from JSC continued. "These are the people who originally received the message:

Max Marsh

The four of you (Obviously offsite. Forwarded to your on-site contacts)

Greg Lauderdale

Dr. Tom Keenan

Frank Douglas

Michael Trubly"

Jana read through the message once and immediately knew the author. She read it again so that she would not be overly confident regarding the source. It was so clear to her. She looked at the list of names. She knew exactly where the list came from, all but one name. Greg Lauderdale was her supervisor when she was a summer hire at JSC; Dr. Keenan was the astronauts' doctor; Frank Douglas was her neutral buoyancy instructor when she trained in the big submersion tank; and one name, Michael Trubly, she did not recognize.

Jana printed a copy and took the sheet of paper to Jack and Fawz. "Here's what you're looking for." She smiled broadly.

Jack and Fawz shared the piece of paper as they read. Jack studied Jana before he asked, "You know who originated this message?"

"Yes, and so do you." But then she realized that maybe Jack did not know. Chri Anri usually did not speak his weird way around Jack. He generally spoke standard English. To save Jack any embarrassment, she quickly said, "It's Chri Anri. That's the way he talked when he was around me."

Jack just stared at Jana.

She said, "After reading my journal over the net, someone could have made his language sound like Chri Anri's. But look at the bottom of the message here. This is his signature. He showed it to me. See these circles and dots. This exact configuration is Chri Anri's. But I didn't mention it in my journal. No one could have known his signature."

"How do you think Chri Anri could have e-mailed the messages?"

"I think I've got that figured out. The Zalandans watch Earth TV. They would know we're in trouble."

"Jana, the e-mail messages!"

"One wake cycle, Chri Anri and I were talking about the Zalandan Center, and he wanted to know about our center on Earth. I told him about the supernet and how computers, phones, and TVs hooked into the net. He seemed really interested, so the next wake cycle I showed him my notebook computer. I told him how I could send and receive messages via the computer. I explained how my e-mail program worked and showed him my e-mail address book. He saw Lauren's address and got even more interested. He found out I was keeping a journal and that some of the stuff was about Lauren. We talked about a lot of things. I told him about phone numbers and how people called each other on their phones."

"I remember you asked me if you could show Chri Anri your notebook computer."

"He really studied it. Asked me if he could analyze it and I agreed. He took my computer into the crystal room, and I remember thinking that everything would be demagnetized or erased. Chri Anri assured me that my computer was safe. It's possible that he could have done a thorough analysis then. After all, the Zalandans are pretty clever."

"That's an understatement. So, do you have a magic e-mail address for Chri Anri where we can verify all of this?"

"You mean like the magic address for Max. That would have been nice. I have no way to reach Chri Anri. Sorry. People on Earth were so freaked. Remember, there was that decision to break off communication for our return trip home."

Jana thought Jack would be happy to learn that it was not a terrorist sending the idea. But Jack frowned and his lower lip covered his upper lip. Fawz seemed happier that it was Chri Anri.

Jana pointed to the list of names and said, "I can account for all but one. These names are from my e-mail address book. I showed all that to Chri Anri, too. I don't know about this one name, Michael Trubly. It doesn't fit."

Jack looked at the name and said, "He's a public information officer at JSC."

Fawz added, "His e-mail address could have been on TV."

Jack was saying, "If we could just talk to Chri Anri and find out if the aerospace team worked with him or if he did it himself."

Jana remembered a conversation she had overhead between Jack and Fawz.

Jack had said, "Lauren is such a sensible woman. Now she falls for a flake like Chri Anri."

Fawz had replied, "He makes her happy. He's got a good heart. He's a good man."

Jack had responded, "I guess you're right, but he's still a damn dilettante."

Jana had been surprised because she hardly had heard Jack disparage anyone, but Jack probably had felt responsible for Lauren's well-being. Jana also had been surprised because she thought of Chri Anri more as a Renaissance man who was well versed in so much and not as a dabbler. Jack also was a Renaissance man who had a fondness for music, art, and ancient artifacts. She had thought the two would have some common ground.

Jack asked Jana, "Why would he send e-mail messages to us at JSC. He knows we're not there."

"Maybe, I told him messages could be forwarded. I don't remember everything we discussed.

"Jana, have you checked your e-mail messages."

"No, of course not. My computer can't pick up e-mail from Houston or from . . . . Oh, I see what you mean." She pushed off and retrieved her notebook computer. "Yes, here it is, an e-mail from Chri Anri." She handed Jack her computer.

"Jana, tell Jack and Fawz these numbers are the best. This plan will work. Our entire aerospace team has been working on this. The tough top may hold without the soft explosion, but it is pushing the envelope."

This was followed by various technical notes to Jack and Fawz from the aerospace people. These notes were written in impeccable if not stiff English. Then the e-mail ended with a note from Chri Anri.

"Tell Lauren to read her e-mail. She can answer me using the reply function. You know I can speak standard English. Jack thinks I am an irresponsible human, but this work was done by many of us, mostly by the aerospace people whom Jack has an affinity for. I miss all of you, even Jack."

The three of them were just looking at each other. Jack said, "Damn! I hurt his feelings. I didn't mean to."

Fawz gently said, "They read brain waves. It is a different culture, Jack. On Earth, I ran into cultural situations frequently. You do your best and then forget about it. Chri Anri thinks we all are great, even you." Fawz laughed heartily.

Fawz began thinking aloud. "The Zalandan aerospace people must have lifted the probe's diagrams from the net. Once they learned from TV that we were in trouble, they most likely monitored our communications with Houston and probably monitored JSC's communications with others regarding the probe. Darwin Industries would have the probe diagrams stored in their computer systems. Accessing a secure system would be no trouble for them. Long years of Zalandan history are accessed with a little humming to Center."

Jack agreed, "At their level of technology, they would have found a way to retrieve the diagrams."

"Still, the Zalandans have not seen the probe. Houston has not seen the lander's reinforcements. Our scientists are not familiar with that metallic composition. It is very complex," Fawz said cheerfully.

"Let us return to work. We need to recheck the conversion factors. We worked with the Zalandans on conversions for days. We know how to do it."

Fawz had assumed control of the situation without missing a beat, and Jana knew he would relinquish it back to Jack just as easily. She had two very savvy commanders who also were the best of friends. Her spirits soared.

"I'd like to tell Lauren right away," she said.

Jack nodded in agreement. "Yes, of all people, she should know."

She pushed away toward Lauren. As she hovered next to Lauren, she was not sure how she would tell her. Lauren glanced toward her and whispered, "I am fine and can continue with these reports."

Jana whispered back, "I need to talk to you. I mean, the rest of us are okay, too, but there's something you will want to know, something you need to know, something good."

Lauren announced to her net audience that she would play a recorded announcement from her Commander. She then turned toward Jana who quickly explained the situation about Chri Anri and how the Zalandans were not only watching their plight on TV but were actively helping.

Jana had never seen such a stunned expression on Lauren's face. Lauren was generally so composed, even on Zalanda when the crew was in the egg-shaped decontamination room together. Only twice before had Jana seen Lauren not totally pulled together. During their previous wake cycle, Lauren seemed oddly upset about the classic movie silently playing on the background screen of her computer. Now, Lauren was pale, immobile, and drained of any emotion. She looked like she would faint.

Jana needed to help her friend immediately, but how? She did not know how to help other than to get Lauren involved in an activity. "There's an e-mail message from Chri Anri on your computer," Jana said. "Here, let's look for it." Jana took Lauren's computer out of her hands and checked for e-mail. "Here it is, Lauren."

A personal message Lauren should read herself, but under the circumstances, Jana read it aloud. "The moment I saw you I felt an incredible bond between us, a bond for all eternity. Had I been more persuasive or understood your customs more completely, you would have stayed with me here on Zalanda. Do you have any comprehension how much I grieve over your absence? The light from Jupiter no longer seems as bright. Our marvelous domed city has lost its sparkle. It seems a drab, dreary place now that you are not here to give it brilliance and beauty.

"I cherish our times together in Ancient City and would reminisce on those moments of joy, but you value privacy, and today I have learned your net system, like ours, has practically no privacy.

"The fastest Zalandan ship cannot rendezvous with the *Copernicus* in time to help you. I am appalled that there are such limits to our technology. Still, we help you from afar. All of our aerospace people are involved. The soft explosion will work."

Lauren looked at her computer screen and then at Jana, "Chri Anri is watching us on TV now?"

"There's the time delay. Whatever you were reading a while ago, he is hearing and seeing right now," Jana said in a factual tone in hopes of calming Lauren down.

Jana studied Lauren. The color was coming back in her face. It looked like she no longer would faint. That was good. Yet, Jana thought, the crew needed a stable Lauren, someone who could perform her tasks. In retrospect, telling her about the e-mail was a bad idea. Jana had no idea Lauren would react the way she did. Jana had permission to tell her that the Zalandans were the source for the soft explosion idea, but Jana had taken it upon herself to tell Lauren about the e-mail message.

"Lauren, Jack's recording is over. Shall we play another one? Here, I'll do it for you. Come to think of it, I can take over reading your reports now. It's almost time for me to read while you help Jack."

"No, I'm fine," Lauren said, but she was breathing rapidly. However, as soon as she flipped the camera over to the live broadcast mode, she gave the appearance of total composure as she looked into the camera and said, "Jana will be reading my reports." She paused a moment. "Before Jana begins, I wish to talk to someone on Zalanda who is very special to me."

Jana held Lauren's arm and whispered, "You don't need to do this. Think about it first. A large number of people are watching your broadcast. You can send a private e-mail."

Lauren looked straight into the camera and in a strong voice declared, "Chri Anri, I love you. I will love you always for however long always is and beyond that into a new universe with you, into a universe we will create together."

Solarship *Copernicus*

3:20 p.m. CDT

Jack felt amazingly refreshed, energized, happy, and ready for whatever the next several minutes offered. Logically and rationally, he wanted the Darwin and JSC people to break the second code and simply change the trajectory of the probe. He wanted it to go away. They could even send it to Saturn to do the job it supposedly was made to do.

Yet, all his life he was preparing for a moment he never wanted to see, but did not dread because somewhere within him he thrived on challenge. He wanted not too much action, manageable action, but some excitement. For the sake of his crew and his family and even himself, he pushed those thoughts out of his mind and prayed for the last minute reprieve.

Barring that reprieve, the crew had agreed to go with the soft explosion. Jack was glad they shared in that choice together, particularly since there was no right or perfect choices other than JSC taking over guidance control of the probe. That still could happen. There were so many uncertainties. Yet, the technical stuff was pretty well taken care of, or at least as well as it possibly could be.

Before their joint decision, Fawz had checked and rechecked all the Zalandan conversion factors for the soft explosion. Lauren reviewed Fawz's work and said it looked good. After much analysis, Jack gave his blessing. Many people at JSC had checked it, too, and they mostly were in agreement. A few thought it was a terrible and dangerous idea.

Jack omitted telling Mission Control that the crew knew the origin of the soft explosion plans because there simply was too much fear regarding the Zalandans. Jack doubted that the fear extended to people at JSC, but it was possible. It also was possible that Mission Control knew already. If one of them had listened carefully to Jana read her journal, that person could have figured it out.

The crew all had called their families. Jack's wife Shirl sounded strong and encouraging. What a great wife! He needed to be with her again.

She reminded him about how in a past danger, he had entered the zone, a mental state in which time moved in slow motion and he accomplished everything he needed to do. Once, that probably had saved his life. He had taken a bit of zone training from an assistant coach of the professional basketball team, but years ago NASA had cut that training from the budget. He had rather forgotten about the zone and wondered if he could simply call it up at will. He certainly might need it.

Shirl was so clear thinking. Even under these circumstances, she had given him a great idea. His children sounded like brave little soldiers.

"We're glad you found the aliens," Brad said.

"Please bring one back from your next mission," Mark added.

"I'd like to do that," Jack replied.

Stacy piped up, "Invite one over for dinner."

"They have different customs regarding dinner," Jack said and chuckled, fondly recalling the time Chri Anri reluctantly had sat with them during a meal but vehemently had refused food. "We could hold a reception." Jack visualized food hidden in the pantry for the non-alien guests.

He thought Shirl had coached the children a little. Their voices sounded older and more mature. His family was a good final memory to hold.

He knew Jana was disappointed she had not reached Alan. That was an unfortunate glitch in timing. Lauren had sent her e-mail reply to Chri Anri, and Fawz had talked to Regney and cooed to his babies. Then, Fawz had spoken consolingly with his father.

Now, Jack and Lauren sat at the main controls ready to direct the *Copernicus* to react to whatever the probe and lander did. Fawz sat next to them to oversee the lander and control it if necessary. The three of them already had been working together simulating their best guesses for what soon would happen.

Across the cabin, Jana read Lauren's report on Zalandan meteoroid tweaking, the final report Lauren had selected. While the earlier reports emphasized Zalandan honesty and kindness, this one demonstrated their awesome power. When Jana finished the report, she set Jack's tapes and the banner to run continuously even though it probably was too late for JSC to evaluate a new caller's information.

She glanced across the cabin to her crew. She wanted to say something to them but she did not know what, a good bye or to tell them how good it had been to be with them.

All four astronauts were buckled in place. In fact, the whole ship had been secured, and they were ready and waiting. Alert and ready. At that moment, nothing was happening. Jana recalled another time of waiting back at JSC, waiting for her training on the simulator where she learned responses to emergencies, euphemistically called contingencies. She thought "contingency" was a nice, soothing word.

Jack had decided against a silent time or a farewell between the four of them. Somehow, that would have pulled the emphasis away from survival onto making a peace with the universe. Now, however, he waited for someone to suggest it. Neither Fawz nor Lauren nor Jana mentioned doing it either. Had anyone requested it, he would have agreed.

Instead, Jack told them what he had known since the first weeks into the mission, probably even the first day. "I've never said this to a crew before. You're my best crew ever: the most dedicated, the most selfless, the most team oriented. I've known it from the beginning. Besides that, you're fun to be around. You're my greatest friends, too." Jack moved his bottom lip up, half covering the top one as if he were embarrassed over momentarily abandoning his position as commander.

Lauren said, "We may become swell-headed and insufferable after that compliment."

He did not respond to Lauren because he did not need to. He was reading her every thought. After happily accepting his praise, she reverted to her sociologist-philosopher mode, which she did from time to time. He liked listening to all her theories on life and wondered if that mode was her safe, secure nook in her brain, a place to seek solace.

Lauren's thoughts were these: changes in the world, no, in the solar system, hung by such slender threads. Jana alone had left the safety of the lander and found the Zalandan child. If the child had not ventured outside on that snowy Zalandan day, the entire social dynamics could have worked out differently. In the domed city under the glow of Jupiter, Lauren had found Chri Anri, the person in the universe perfect for her. If there had been a larger crew, as there surely would have been if the mission had not been a secret, Lauren could have stayed behind with Chri Anri. She suspected that the overall effect of most secrets was negative.

Becoming aware of Lauren's thoughts must have been rapid because Jana still was saying the word "thanks" to Jack for his admission that they were his best crew. Jana smiled slightly, and while she waited for Jack's recording to finish playing, he followed her thoughts.

Jack seemed bonded to the chemical traveling down neurons and leaping between synapses as Jana's brain pulsed in a smooth rhythm. An amazing peace and calm swept over her. It was the joy of letting go. She knew in her heart she had done everything she could by sharing her most personal journal with everybody on Earth. She could do no more. The time was getting close. She was ready. Jana had not given up but instead accepted the flowing, inevitable river into the future. Jack felt relieved that Jana, the youngest, with so much potential life ahead of her, was taking this so well.

Jana had been too busy reading over the net to write in her journal. She hoped she would get the chance, that she would be alive and that tonight or tomorrow, she would be able to describe this day. Jana shivered. It was strange that one reason she wanted to stay alive was to write in her journal another day.

She wanted the mission to be a success, but then she realized that whatever the future held, the mission already was a success. Most abundantly and most happily, they had accomplished their major goal, finding life. She wanted more. She wanted the mission to have a successful conclusion and for all of them to return safely to Houston. She wanted to see her parents again.

She wanted to see Alan. She hoped he would forgive her for revealing her feelings toward him over the net. If he would not or could not find forgiveness, she would cherish her remembrances of him: his smirky smile, those dark eyes, that sun streaked hair, Alan leaping high on a trampoline, showing off just for her. Seeing Alan again, even from a distance, would be something, a scrap. She would accept a scrap for starters and try to rebuild a relationship, that is, if she were given another day.

"I hope Alan's love is strong enough," Jack thought. Primarily, he wanted Jana's reading to help them all. Secondly, he wanted to exonerate her from all of the tabloid garbage written about her. He knew that she had been concerned about sharing her journal, but not until this moment did he understand his assignment had caused her such anguish.

He felt something like air swirling around him, even through his spacesuit and helmet, as if Jana were reading his thoughts, too. "I'm sorry I caused you grief, Jana. Even knowing that, I still would have given you the assignment. Whoa! Jana, these pure thoughts are brutally honest."

"I know, Jack, and it's okay. You're the commander, and you made the right choice." Her thoughts were mingled with deep, untranslatable emotion but then he sensed her words. "I admire you more than anybody in the world. I think my parents are great. I shall love Alan forever, but with you it is sheer admiration. I want to be like you, I want to be you, a female version of you." Then, there were swirls of shocked realization. "Jack, not ever would I verbalize these thoughts to you. Not even at the end of time. This brain wave stuff is uncontrollable."

"I care for you like my own child." Jack consciously put on a brake to control his thoughts, and as he did, the swirling increased as if more brains had joined in. Jana recognized that Jack needed a reprieve from such a level of sharing, and without any willed effort, her thoughts focused on Fawz. "You are my spiritual Father. You have imbued me with magical powers. You believe I am the one. Because of you, I went out into the snow."

And Fawz was thinking, "Fate ordained you, Jana, to meet the first Zalandan."

Jack let off his emotional brakes and was back in the mix. "I knew about your discussion with Fawz. He told Lauren and me that you had found proof in the video of Svee Dee spying on us. He told us everything. I explicitly could have instructed you not to leave the lander. Not to go out into the snow alone. As we drove the rover through the snow trying to find you, I realized it had been my job as commander to protect you. And I did not protect you."

For a second, Jana's brain slowed down and processed the new information that Jack knew of her secret conversation with Fawz. "It was your job as commander to allow me to help with the mission. Fawz gave me freedom and wings. You did not countermand that because you trusted me. You believed in me. That was why you let me go. You needed me to do what I did, and you knew that I could handle it. That means . . . that means I am one of you. I am a real astronaut."

There was more beyond words, as Jana's insecurity lessened by significant chunks. Jack looked across the cabin at her, and through their helmets their eyes met as they both confirmed what had just happened. Someone so able had been so insecure, and now during one brain waving session, Jana was developing confidence. It was miraculous.

This brain waving was very intense, Jack thought. It was a pleasant feeling, painful, too, but also exhilarating, cutting directly to the heart of the matter, cutting through social veneer and except in one instance stripping away fear of being too blunt or too truthful, freeing both Jana and Jack.

Then, he perceived he was slipping out of it. No, he was back into it but barely picking up the brain waving from Lauren directed to Jana. Lauren's thoughts were not in words but instead were his translation. "You're here. You're on a major mission. Therefore, you are a real astronaut. We're both rookies on our first mission and I have no basis of comparison, but I bet you are an exceptionally good astronaut." He clearly picked up Lauren's meaning, reassurance to bolster Jana's newly found confidence.

Jana's thoughts to Lauren rang out like a bell. "You trusted me, too. You could have suggested to Jack or to me that I not leave the *Falcon* and venture into the snow alone. You did not do this. You are the big sister I never had. If I did have one, I'd want her to be exactly like you."

"I am honored to be your sister."

There was more to Lauren's response that Jack did not attempt to translate because all of a sudden he felt he was eavesdropping on a private mental conversation. Upon that thought, the air swirling around him became still, and then he was ejected or ejected himself out of the deep, intense sharing. Jack felt strangely disappointed even though he certainly would not have planned anything like this, especially before a crisis situation. Maybe, a more serene brain ride would be acceptable. He wondered about levels of brain waving and if the intensity could be toned down. Almost as if wishing for less intensity, he found himself in a calm place.

In Fawz's brain, Jack felt he was inside the frontal lobe, and from that vantage point, he observed areas on both sides of Fawz's brain serenely working together. Fawz was glad he was with cheerful Americans who exuded such confidence. Jana finally was developing it, too. If only she had understood destiny, she would have realized that she belonged since the beginning.

Whatever happened was Fawz's destiny. His destiny was to work as hard as he could for the crew's survival, and after that he felt his destiny was for each of them to survive. He had never questioned destiny, but, yet, his three friends did not grasp the concept. No, the Americans grasped it, but they thought so differently. Confidence and destiny! In certain contexts, they could be similar concepts. Another day he would think about that.

For now, Fawz would oversee the *Falcon*. The lander's computer was set to do the work because no one could possibly react that fast. After he had learned about the proposal for the soft landing, he had laid out exactly what he wanted, and the JSC people wrote a program for him and uploaded it to the lander. He was glad programs could be done so rapidly, but there had been no time for review and testing.

Immediately upon the probe's contact with the far outer limit of the lander's repelling shields, the contact point as well as the angle of entry (since probe and lander were in a wobble dance with each other) would be fed into the new program. The lander immediately would reorient itself to most effectively deflect particles away from the trajectory of the *Copernicus*. No individual could react as fast as the computer. Yet, even the computer's reaction might not be fast enough because the lander and its onboard computer quickly could become too damaged in the soft explosion to receive and carry out commands.

If that new program did not work, he and Jack already had estimated the impact point, and the tough top already was oriented accordingly.

All that was fairly well worked out. Yet, what could bite them was something Fawz totally did not consider. He, however, felt ready for any contingency.

Through tuning in to Fawz's logical evaluations of his upcoming tasks, Jana calmed down her emotions. Feeling for the first time in her life like a real astronaut, Jana mentally reviewed her duties. She would select more of Lauren's reports to read until near the end. Then, she would check the *Copernicus* for particle impacts and the possibility of micro meteoroid penetrations. She had practiced over and over with the repair tape.

Lauren was still basking in the glow of her big sister designation as her thoughts sped down a runway, took flight, and moved into what the next few minutes could hold. While staying calm, composed, and very alert, her major task was to help Jack with thruster commands so they could maintain as much distance as possible between themselves and the lander.

What an advantage to read minds, Jack decided. It was not merely something the Zalandans thought they did. All four of them were feeling each other's thoughts and emotions simultaneously. They silently held an informal ceremony together after all. He did not consider it a farewell ceremony but a ceremony of hope particularly since Fawz, Lauren, and Jana were mentally prepared for the work ahead of them. That knowledge bolstered Jack's natural confidence, which he quickly reigned in so that he would not cross the line into carelessness or recklessness.

Then Jack's subconscious talked to him. "Old man, you want adventure. You thrive on it. Now, I'm going to give it to you and your crew and everybody watching." And Jack responded, "Know your place, dark and inner thoughts, you are not in charge." And the subconscious replied, "Oh, no! Wanna bet?"

"Be quiet," Jack ordered, but the subconscious said, "You think you're reading their thoughts. You've known that destiny stuff about Fawz for a long time. A prince with a serene mind! How corny!"

"I am busy and do not have time for you." Jack totally banished his subconscious and looked out the window for the lander. The outside was a bit too bright to find it. All the windows still were heavily filtered, as if wearing dark sunglasses, from earlier when the crew had launched the Falcon and then wanted to observe it. He pressed the control for maximum window filtering. Still, he could not find the lander.

With great ease, he brought up the *Falcon* on the computer. As far away as it seemed, it was much closer than their original calculations. Launching had been as good as they possibly could have expected, but not perfect. There had been some drift, and they had made a course correction. He hoped the *Falcon* was far enough away. By now, he and Fawz were working harmoniously with Houston, who did not think the lander was dangerously near their ship.

Even with the beefing up the Zalandans had done, the lander still was a fragile thing, made for a specific purpose, landing on a planet, and not flying for hours through space while wobbling slightly to make the probe do a corresponding wobble, in hopes of slowing down and confusing the probe.

Willie from Mission Control said, "The soft explosion is set. The code still might be broken. Unless it's soon, there won't be enough time."

"Thanks for all of your help, Willie. Thank everyone from JSC, and be sure to tell Max thanks for everything," Jack said and noticed that at his mention of Max's name, Willie glanced away from his camera and appeared a little agitated. Whatever the situation was with Max, Jack did not have time to pursue it.

Willie regained his professional composure and said, "After the impact, your trajectory will bring you closer to the lander as the two trajectories cross. It will happen very quickly."

"I'm well aware of that," Jack commented as his thoughts strangely strayed to Max.

"If you need to change the trajectory," Willie said, "go ahead. Hold off as long as you can. We're all rooting for you and hoping the tough top holds. We'll leave open the option of our taking over control of the lander or your ship or both if you wish. We can take over whenever you wish."

"Yes, that's good," Jack replied. "We are ready. Fawz and I both will be communicating with you."

"We were going to suggest that."

Fawz was monitoring the lander's on-board computer as well as externally tracking the lander from the *Copernicus*. "It is looking good," Fawz said to Mission Control, but he spoke clearly so the crew could hear. "The lander has visuals on the probe. Oh, fate! The lander has begun plotting its own evasion trajectory. I am now deactivating that program. Deactivated. What a surprise! That must have been a default setting."

"Good Catch, Dr. Fawz," replied Willie. "Don't know how we missed that setting."

"The lander's shields are set for a maximum repelling field," Fawz said.

"It's time," Jack announced. "It's T minus ten seconds right . . . now."

Spontaneously, the crew began counting backwards. "Ten, nine, eight, seven, six, five, four."

As Jana swung the camera toward her crew, she quickly told her net audience about the impending impact before joining in the count. Still, she was careful not to say what would be impacted. "Three, two, one."

Nothing happened. Jack hoped Mission Control had taken over control of the probe. How sweet that would be. Then a darker thought, one of his worst case scenarios, came to him that the *Copernicus* could take a direct hit. He rechecked. The anti-meteoroid shields were at the maximum force. Yet, they would not hold.

Jana was speaking aloud, saying "T plus one," but very slowly, her words sounding elongated as if they were coming from far away and echoing out of a tunnel.

Fawz said, "It is happening now. The probe is passing through the lander's meteoroid shield. The shield is slowing it somewhat. The

490

probe now has crashed through the lander and exploded upon contact with something inside.

"The lander has accepted the reorientation command. Lander is reorienting itself. It is oriented exactly at 67 degrees from the midline. That is exactly the correct angle.

"The explosion seems contained within the lander. I still am getting readings from the lander's computer. Amazing! The probe must have crashed through a front window leaving the controls undamaged.

"Oh, fate! Just now, I have sent a command to deactivate yet another program. Another default setting! The lander was or still is programming itself to return to the *Copernicus*, a response to its own injury. Hope the lander took my command. I knew nothing about that default setting either. Lander is changing trajectory. Not responding to my deactivation command. Lander is slowly overheating. So far, lander orientation is still correct. Orientation setting is overriding factor as lander changes trajectory to return to *Copernicus*. Orientation is excellent. New trajectory is bad, very bad for us.

"Lander is quickly overheating. Becoming very hot. I am not getting any readings. I am tracking it externally through telemetry. Lander is on fire."

Quickly, Jana swung the camera toward the window and said, "Everybody watching needs to see this." A billion people worldwide witnessed the exploding lander.

Jack saw a fiery corona around the edges of a dark center but only momentarily. He was glad the tough top was oriented correctly, but was it holding together? Then all was fiery. Was the explosion coming from the inside? The explosion grew larger and much closer. It could be too close for their survival.

Fawz said, "That fireball is completely out of control."

After that, everything happened simultaneously. They lost contact with Mission Control. They began getting hundreds of pings like a hailstorm on a metal roof as their meteoroid shield repelled particles. Concurrently, Jack heard a swooshing roar, a sound he had never heard before, something like the lion's roar around Jupiter, but different, like a bell with the most magnificent clarity, like the sound of a universe being born and welcoming itself into existence. Then, Jack saw a shard a foot in length sticking through the skin of the *Copernicus* and into the cabin. It was shiny like a sword but jagged and two-sided, similar to the edge of a metal picture frame. Jack observed Jana holding repair tape in one gloved hand and bracing herself with her other hand as she lurched in a zigzag fashion toward the shard. He quickly checked the air pressure monitor. It was fine.

At the same time, shock waves from the explosion rolled over the *Copernicus*. The ship convulsed and vibrated before going into a rapid roll. Jack immediately began working on controlling the roll. He knew he would not have much luck until the turbulence outside the ship died down, but still he would keep the roll from intensifying.

Shortly after they lost contact with Mission Control, the lighting system went out. The computer monitors provided the cabin with its only light, an eerie illumination over the keyboards but not much else. As they spun round and round, Jack heard the sound of a seat belt unbuckling. Lauren was thrown about as she quickly retrieved two powerful flashlights. With one hand, Lauren illuminated the myriad of controls for the *Copernicus* as Jack worked on the roll. In her other hand, Lauren held a flashlight over Fawz's keyboard as he tracked the burning lander and thanked all that he held sacred that the computers inside the *Copernicus* continued to function.

"I can see well enough," Fawz said. "Shine the light on Jana."

Lauren strapped down the two flashlights so they illuminated the areas in need. Her hands were then free to help.

Jack glanced over at Jana. She had completely wrapped the shard in repair tape. Her work was critically important but he simply must trust that she was doing a masterful job. He again checked the pressure monitor. The *Copernicus* still had not lost pressure. Yet, a whole panel of the ship could blow out.

The *Copernicus* and the fiery lander appeared to be two ships in tandem traveling on a parallel course, but they were not. The paths of the spinning solarship and the disabled lander soon would intersect. It would be very close.

It was way past time to correct the ship's trajectory, but first Jack had to stop the roll completely. Jack had not anticipated such a powerful roll. Lauren and Fawz were actively helping him. No one talked. They all had worked together so much that they knew what the other wanted. With the presence of a seasoned commander, Jack finally began controlling the roll. What a relief not to be spinning quite so fast! Finally, the roll was controlled, and the ship was stabilized.

Jack needed to correct the trajectory. Yet, there was no time for more work. Then, time almost ceased to exist. Jack seemed far away, like a disembodied spirit. He realized he had all the time in the universe to get everything just right. With Fawz and Lauren helping him, Jack gave the thrusters commands to go into a higher orbit. At the last moment, Jack increased the distance between themselves and the closest rendezvous point with the lander.

Barely a moment later, they closed on the fiery lander, the trajectories of two spacecraft intersecting, the *Copernicus* in control and the lander completely out of control and still on fire.

"Good work, Jack, and very fast work, too," Lauren said. "I don't know how you did it."

"We did it together," Jack said. "I was in the zone. We all must have been in the zone, but it still will be very close."

Fawz was tracking the lander on his computer screen although all three of them were watching it from their front window. The lander looked huge and so close. As it drew even closer, they saw that it had held together and that the fire was coming from the inside. On the side of the cabin, Jana had a better view from her window as she continued tracking it with her camera. She was pretty sure she had totally lost contact with her net audience, but she had set the camera to both record and do a live transmission in the rare instance their connection to the net continued to function.

"And the lander is going to get closer than this?" Lauren half asked and half stated. She knew that it would.

"If the lander had not changed its own trajectory to return to the *Copernicus* before the explosion, this would have been much easier," Fawz mused more to himself rather than as an explanation to the crew who already knew. "We are at our closest point right now."

"I'm feeling warm. Is this my imagination?" Lauren asked.

"Not at all," Jack replied. "It is getting hot in here. The computer is correcting the temperature of our cabin. I am overriding and pushing the temperature much lower. Don't know if that will help."

The ship was in imminent danger. Each astronaut knew but not one mentioned that fact. With so much space between molecules of matter, the heat from the lander came right through the metal and into the *Copernicus* and through all the protective clothing of their spacesuits. Would the intensity of the fireball envelope their frail spaceship. Or would the heat cause a delayed explosion?

Finally, the lander drifted past them. The flashlights and computer monitors softly illuminated the four space travelers, Jack, Lauren, and Fawz at the controls and Jana across the cabin guarding the shard, as they held their breath and waited. Gradually, each astronaut felt the heat subside. The *Copernicus* still was intact.

Jack, Lauren, and Fawz visually tracked the lander as the fire lessened until it practically went out. The lander grew smaller in the distance. When it became too small to see, through the telemetry on Fawz's tracking screen, they observed the charred hull and noted that the tough top still held together despite the fire and the explosion. The angle of orientation had changed slightly but still was satisfactory. Particles continued falling away from the lander, and occasionally the *Copernicus*'s meteoroid detection program made a pinging sound as an auditory notification that a particle was hitting the shields and bouncing off. The velocity of the particles was not terrible. The tough top of the lander mostly was doing the job they had planned for it to do as it deflected the dust away from the *Copernicus*.

"I could have been inside that lander," Lauren softly said. "I even volunteered."

"No, Lauren, no way! That was not an option," Jack emphatically replied.

Suddenly and unexpectedly, the auxiliary lights came on. Everything in the ship looked so bright that they had to blink their eyes. The brightness gave them a sense of safety. One by one, they realized that they were past the urgent and immediate dangers: the vibration and rolling of the ship, the main power going out, the close contact with the lander, and the intense heat.

Jack, Fawz, and Lauren went to work on correcting the trajectory and stabilizing the orbital path. They tried again to rouse Houston for some help.

They clearly were on their own. As they continued correcting the trajectory, they talked concisely to each other about orbits, propellant expended, and propellant needed to reach the spaceport. Unlike a few minutes earlier when they needed to get away from the burning lander, they now had the luxury to carefully plan each thruster command.

Jack said, "We've done it. I'll download this trajectory data to JSC. If they're not happy, they can take over control of our ship."

Jack again tried to get some video or voice contact. There was no response. "If they get this download, they'll know we're okay."

Fawz and Lauren appeared jubilant so Jack decided against saying, "So far we're okay." They needed to concentrate on their next two tasks, re-checking the skin for any more shards and doing diagnostics. He said, "The diagnostics should uncover the communications problem with Houston."

Jack also was feeling jubilant about their last minute maneuvers that had barely gotten them out of fiery harm's way. He so enjoyed that feeling of danger and high adventure as the adrenal hormones pumped through his body. He particularly was relieved that his pesky subconscious had totally nothing to say. Ha, ha, maybe that subconscious was scared speechless.

He was extremely proud of his crew, too, but he already had blown his wad telling them they were his best crew ever. He had no more superlatives to heap upon them.

He marveled how Fawz had dealt with the default settings on two different programs with such speed and ease. When the lander no longer responded to Fawz's command and he could do nothing to override the default setting on the second program, he had maintained his calm and equanimity.

Lauren had been right there helping without Jack needing to ask her for anything. Although Lauren was classified as a mission specialist and was not expected to be extremely facile with maneuvers, she proved to be better than many full-fledged operations members. And Jana had been left to her own devices to literally hold the *Copernicus* together. He wanted to say, "I can't begin to tell you how magnificent each of you are." Instead, Jack simply said, "Good job, everybody. We've earned our paychecks today."

Lauren unsecured the two flashlights and playfully tossed one to Fawz. As she tumbled, she tossed the other flashlight to Jana. "Come join us, Jana," Lauren called.

Jana deftly caught the flashlight but did not look happy or playful. "Ahm, uh, as Jack says, we have an opportunity." Jana moved aside to reveal the penetration of the ship's hull, now wrapped in duct tape.

"Oh my!" Lauren exclaimed. "Sorry, I should not have thrown that flashlight."

"Jana, you've created a duct tape sculpture," Jack joked as he, Fawz, and Lauren all moved closer, their eyes wide in amazement as they allowed themselves to realize the gravity of the situation. A whole section of the ship could blow, causing immediate depressurization. They could be blown out of the ship into the enormity of space. Their only protection would be their spacesuits. "We should attach to our tethers now," Jack said.

Fawz snapped on his tether and then drifted back toward the controls. "Our air pressure is nominal. There are not any leaks."

As Lauren snapped on her tether, she said, "We promise you, Jack, not to use this part of the cabin to push off as we're moving about." Lauren looked around the cabin. Repair tape was around the doors and edges of every storage compartment. "That's an interesting decorating job you did, Jana. Are there more penetrations?"

"Not that I saw. I was following procedure: seal all the storage bins in case there is a penetration we can't see.

"Jack closely examined the skin of the *Copernicus* around the protrusion. He did not see any signs of stress.

"Were there any rips or tears or pinholes at the point of entry? Did any repair tape get pulled into space?" Jack asked.

"No, I carefully applied the tape around the base of this art work where it intersects the skin of our ship, but I don't think it needed any tape. It looked like a perfect seal. I never saw a bubble or the least sign of depressurization, but nothing about the penetration happened the way it was supposed to. The panel around the shard did not light up. I just happened to see it."

"Did you hear that sound," Jack asked.

"Oh, yes," Jana replied. "The sound was beyond anything I could explain. It was a sound of deep space."

"What do you think happened?" Jack asked.

"I think the metal from the shard was so hot as it cut through the metal skin of our ship that it made a seal, like a solder."

"That is what could have happened," Fawz said, trying to see the joint but there was just too much repair tape. "Was the shard red hot at first?"

"I don't think so. It seemed shiny and metallic, but I'm not sure how long it was there before I noticed it."

"What does it look like under all this tape?"

"It's sharp and jagged. I think it's a part of a metal probe that was attached to a footpad. It has two perpendicular sides like an "L." One side is about two inches wide and the other side is an inch or less, and the whole thing is about twelve or thirteen inches long. But somehow it reminds me of a knife or a dagger, no, a sword."

"Ah, yes, the ceremonial sword I needed for Lauren's citizenship ceremony."

"So that is what you all were doing, having a citizenship ceremony. If you still require that sword, its jagged edges need filing and buffing," Jana said without missing a beat.

Jack was happy to see them bantering about although he knew at some level Fawz was serious. It was his destiny to have the ceremonial sword.

Jana said, "The ship was rolling, and it seemed possible someone could fall against the . . . uh, sword. It could have sliced through a space suit and impaled one of us. With that thought in mind, I covered the sharp edges with repair tape and kept adding more to act as padding. Then I remembered duct tape."

As the crew leaned closer to the well-wrapped sword, Jana said protectively, "I don't think anyone should touch it."

Fawz said to Jack, "I can help Jana check the rest of the ship for shards."

"Yes, do that. Lauren and I will run the diagnostics."

Then Jack noticed something for which he had no experience and, worse yet, no confidence. None of the others had yet noticed. He hoped he would figure out how to proceed. He always did, but this was way beyond anything he had ever studied or practiced on the simulator. It was beyond anything he had ever considered.

Solarship *Copernicus*

Time: unknowable

Lauren and Jack returned to the main controls by the front windows. He hoped that Lauren was so intent on starting the diagnostic programs that she would not notice the obvious problem right in front of her. However, she noticed immediately. She frowned as if she were trying to figure out what she was seeing. She did not say anything.

Jack said, "These diagnostics should uncover the problem."

"That problem, too? " Lauren asked, nodding toward the window.

Before Jack could reply, several gauges and controls started going berserk. Jack knew what he should not do.

He was glad Fawz was busy inspecting the ship because technically Fawz had an equal rank with him. Fawz deferred to Jack but he did not need to. Lauren as a mission specialist would go along with Jack's decision. She asked, "Should we reboot or shut down part of the system?"

"Not without discussing it with Houston first. And we still can't rouse them."

"I realize these computers control everything on our ship and they're all networked together. But now, they've run amuck. It seems like we should take action."

"We should not touch anything," Jack said. "The controls are doing what they need to be doing."

"That sounds mystical, Jack. Couldn't we say the computers are malfunctioning, and we need to fix them?"

"No! What they are doing is way beyond our abilities," Jack said.

"You're the Commander but you are acting, how should I say it, non-commander like, and I rarely have seen you afraid of anything, but you are afraid to take action."

"We could say that, but you and I have noticed something very peculiar."

"You mean outside the windows?" Lauren asked. "Is that what you're talking about?"

"Yes," Jack replied.

"There is no sun. The moon or the Earth could be eclipsing the sun, but there is no moon. There is no Earth. No stars either."

"Just blackness," Jack replied.

"The windows could be dirty, or all that heat could have done something to make the windows opaque. Or the window filtering could have malfunctioned."

"Look outside. Can you see any of our ship?"

Lauren leaned forward and tilted her head. "I see the outside of the ship very clearly. I guess the windows are not dirty after all. What do we do?"

"We wait."

"Shouldn't we make plans now?"

"Plans lead to action. Inaction is our best course right now. Remember, our computers are connected to a Prima Donna computer that does nothing unless there is an extreme emergency. Then, it totally takes over. That computer rewires itself as it goes along. Its actions most likely are not transparent. I mean there is probably no interface with our computer screen."

"I know what a Prima Donna is supposed to do," Lauren said, keeping her voice non-confrontational. She tried another tact. "We've just finished dealing with one emergency after another. We're capable of resetting the computers. For that matter, the Prima Donna itself could be causing a malfunction. What about our two separate computer stations? They're not networked to the main controls. We could program one of them to take over guidance control."

Jack suspected the problem was vastly more ominous than a computer malfunction. He thought the computers were functioning perfectly but that their task could be nearly impossible. He wondered if the *Copernicus* had somehow entered a space or time discontinuity. He decided against verbalizing those thoughts.

"How long are we going to wait?" Lauren asked.

"If the gauges and monitors haven't stopped spinning by the time Fawz and Jana are through checking the skin, then we'll consult them."

"What do we do now while we wait? Chit-chat?"

"That would be good. It would take our minds away from the need for immediate action."

"What do we chit-chat about?" Lauren asked. "That awesome brain sharing? It was so amazing-knowing what everyone was thinking."

"We were all there together. The four of us had a . . . a ceremony of hope before everything got so rough."

"You didn't cause any of this, Jack. It wasn't your fault."

"I thought our brain sharing was over by then. You were still there? You read those thoughts, too."

"They're just thoughts, Jack, even those you call your subconscious. Young children think they're all powerful and that they're responsible for all sorts of things. Under the stress of everything, the young child in you popped out."

Jack did not admit to Lauren that relief swept over him. He quipped, "They teach you this in sociology school?"

"C'mon, Jack, you knew all this already. It's psychology 101. The great and powerful Jack needed reassurance. Oh, my! I'm sorry, Jack. This new me is a problem. I apparently say whatever pops into my head."

"I liked the old you. I like the new you, too," Jack said, trying to be truthful but not patronizing.

"Fawz is too polite to mention your subconscious thoughts to you. He's wrapped in layers of protocol on how a co-commander behaves, even under these extenuating circumstances if indeed he has noticed just how extenuating they have become," Lauren said as she pointed toward the window. "Jana still is in awe of you even after all these months, but the new me mentions everything."

"You would make a good psychologist, Lauren. You gave me comfort, and I was not going to admit that to you.

"You've not told anyone about your talking subconscious, have you?" Lauren gently asked.

"No, I haven't. It feels really good that you know. A weight has been lifted from me."

"You haven't mentioned your subconscious to the JSC psychologists either, have you?" Lauren asked.

"Are you kidding? They'd not put me on any mission at all much less this extended one. Anyway, it doesn't seem like a serious problem to me. After all, I don't obey the voices."

Lauren realized Jack's answers were none of her business even though he seemed happy to discuss them with her, but, still, she persisted. "That's not your really big secret, is it, Jack?"

"No, it's not."

"Can your big secret be how very much you love danger? We already know that about you. It's no secret at all. None of us would be here if we didn't need to be right on the edge."

"Lauren, I wouldn't tell you or Fawz or Jana even if this ship were breaking apart. I would take it with me to the end. There are people to protect."

"I'm sorry, Jack. I had no right asking you these questions. I need to learn how to deal with this new person, this new me."

"Now for more psych 101, the old you and the new you are the same person. You've expanded your repertoire of behavior. Under the special circumstances of the last twenty-four hours, you've developed some skills in being more open about personal stuff."

"Apparently, even your personal stuff! And you find my gooey behavior acceptable?"

"I find it charming. If it becomes unbearable, I'll let you know," Jack said.

"You could ask me what I didn't tell the psychologists or the medical doctors. Then, I'd feel a little less like I was prying."

"Okay, I'm asking."

"I've never mentioned going to a chiropractor. Many times. That didn't seem like a problem to me, either." Lauren chuckled.

"Several astronauts I know go to chiropractors."

"I didn't know that," Lauren replied. "Somehow, that makes me feel better, too."

As they talked, they watched the controls flying like dozens of simultaneous computer checks on fast forward.

"How much time do you think we'll have in this netherworld?"

"I don't know."

"Will we get back?"

"I hope so. The shard tore into the skin of the ship, and we didn't lose any pressure."

"That's very peculiar. Some cultures don't think someone has died until after they've been dead for a while. Do you think we're maybe, uh . . . gone?" Lauren softly asked.

"I don't think so. Everything's too much the same."

"Except no sun and no Mission Control. We made it through the pings, the shard, and the heat. Maybe afterwards, the heat caused an explosion. And it was instant, no pain, and no awareness. Where are we?"

"We're somewhere safe for the moment."

"I bet you told your children the ghosts in the closet and the dragons under the bed were friendly and would not hurt them."

"Something like that! They were friendly." Jack smiled. That was exactly what he had told Mark, Brad, and Stacy.

Lauren looked toward Fawz and Jana who still were carefully inspecting the inside of the ship. "I don't think they've looked out the windows. They're deep in concentration. They don't know, do they?"

"There is no need to mention it to them, not just yet." Jack said.

"Maybe we are somewhere. All that exists is us in this ship. We are the all of existence. Do you think the universe said, 'Since they like being together so much, let's just see how they'll manage all eternity? Just how perfectly suited is this crew after all?'"

"That would certainly change the parameters," Jack said. "I think the Neapolitan ice cream is gone."

"Now, that would be a problem," Lauren replied and giggled. "I'm feeling joyous right now like we have no control over our destiny and we have total control all at once. Like we're all powerful and powerless all at once. Everybody knows everything, and everybody knows nothing."

"That's pretty heavy duty, Lauren."

"How about you, Jack."

"I'm sensing the love of everyone on this ship, the love of my family in Houston, the love of Mission Control and everybody helping at JSC, the love of the Zalandans, and the love of everyone on the net pulling us back from the abyss. We've fallen a bit. We've gotten scraped. We haven't fallen all the way. Time is moving backwards to rescue us. No, we're moving forward at an incredible speed to catch the next moment on the forward spiral of time."

"That's beautiful, Jack."

Fawz and Jana finished the inspection and seemed quite jovial as they drifted over to Lauren and Jack at the main controls.

"Except for that major penetration, the skin looks fine," Fawz said. "We left all of the cabinets taped closed. We should do an EVA and check from the outside. As for the net broadcast, we have lost connectivity. We could try to reestablish it. How are the diagnostics?"

Fawz drew closer and studied the wildly moving gauges and controls. "It appears that the Prima Donna is in control," Fawz nonchalantly said. "It is calculating far too rapidly for any meaningful interface with our computer monitors. Correct?"

"That's my guess," Jack replied.

504

At some point, Fawz glanced out the window and said, "It is possible we are in a space time discontinuity. Interesting physics problem," Fawz cheerfully remarked.

Lauren resisted the urge to burst out laughing. "We probably are in a different space and in a timeframe that has no correlation to the twenty-first century, and you think it's an interesting problem. And you, Jack, love dangerous situations a bit more than your average adventure-seeking astronaut. Somehow, I think you guys just might be able to save us. Either that or I am experiencing oxygen deprivation."

"Did you touch any controls?" Fawz asked.

"No, nothing," Lauren replied and sheepishly looked toward Jack who simply winked at her.

"That's very good," replied Fawz. "The Prima Donna should override commands sent to it. Yet, it is a finicky thing. I would not want it compromised by our interference. If we are in a discontinuity," Fawz said thoughtfully, "I like to think the Prima Donna is fixing it. Let me think. If we have lost or gained only a little time relative to the Earth, then we could contact Houston or they could contact us. Except we do not want to interfere with what that computer is doing."

Fawz looked at Jana and then over across the cabin to her supernet setup. "We could try sending Houston an e-mail and tell them to contact us through the net system. That system is independent of the main computers. It would not compromise the Prima Donna. Yet, if we were able to send an e-mail message, Houston would not expect one from us and may not think to check for it. We could ask our friend George MacInturff to have JSC contact us directly through e-mail. Tell George that it is vitally important that he reach JSC and for him to do whatever it takes."

"There is a timing difference," Jana added. "I mean, JSC can't just send us an e-mail without making some timing adjustments."

Jack said, "George knew how to contact us. So did Chri Anri. Yet, that was before the sun disappeared."

Fawz rubbed his forehead. "We shall send them the instructions. Yet, we do not wish to insult them. Correct?"

"We could send it as documentation for their files," Lauren said.

"Yes, Lauren, that is good. Jana, write up the timing instructions and clearly mark it as documentation. We will send that as an attachment." Fawz suddenly remembering protocol asked. "Do I have your approval for all of this, Jack?"

"Absolutely," Jack replied, happy to be sharing responsibility. He was pleased to see Fawz as cheerful as a new pilot practicing touch and go landings. He was glad that Fawz seemed so totally at ease with the discontinuity concept.

Fawz and Jana drifted over to the supernet equipment. They wrote the message with the instructions disguised as documentation and sent the e-mail to JSC. Then, they sent a second message to George. They waited and waited. There was no response.

"We still could be in a different time or place," Fawz calmly said.

"I could keep resending the e-mail," Jana suggested. When the Prima Donna fixes the time-space problem, JSC should receive the message."

"Yes, do that," Fawz replied. He drifted back toward Lauren and Jack who were rambling about whether the controls were spinning faster.

"I could experiment a bit with the timing, too," Jana called across the cabin to Fawz.

"Fine," Fawz answered.

"I'll write a little program that will do it automatically."

"That is an excellent idea, Jana. I will be back in a minute to help," Fawz replied. To Lauren and Jack, he said, "So good that you realized the Prima Donna was in control. How did you resist doing anything?"

"We told secrets," Lauren replied.

"Speaking of secrets, when I spoke to my father today, he told me something rather disturbing. Remember when the security breach occurred, all four of us so hoped that both governments would jointly announce the existence of our mission. The US government wanted to do exactly that. My father talked them out of it. He is rather persuasive."

"Why would he do that?" Jack asked.

"It is not my place to question him," Fawz replied, "but he did tell me. During the initial negotiations with the US government, one of my father's main reasons for secrecy was our country's impending trimillenium celebration. Originally, he wanted to reveal the mission at our 3000th anniversary celebration to pleasantly surprise our people. After we found the Zalandans, our kinfolk, then he looked forward to totally astounding our countrymen. He loves doing wonderful things for our people, but I did not know how strongly he felt about the surprise until today.

"We have so many state secrets that I had not thought about their implications. Perhaps, Lauren is correct. Have as few secrets as possible, even good secrets. I like to believe there were other, more sensible reasons for our mission's secrecy other than a surprise for an upcoming party. In retrospect, my people would have experienced much more pleasure learning about our mission on a day-to-day basis. Now, my father thinks the secrecy is what jeopardized our safety. We must survive. I do not want him to feel responsible."

"We certainly don't want your father feeling responsible," Jack said with sarcasm in his heart, but his words popped out as those of kindly concern.

Fawz stared at Jack for a few seconds before he replied, "I also was rather angry with him." Upon that admission, Fawz floated over to help Jana.

About a half hour later by whatever time the *Copernicus* was experiencing, Jana yelped, "We've got a reply. It's some weird formulas. Pages of them."

Solarship *Copernicus*

They all gathered around the e-mail message on Jana's monitor. It was pages long. Jack glanced at it, and to him it did not look like weird formulas at all but like pages of physics equations. At the end, there was a note.

"This should take care of everything. Your clocks were out of sync. We're fixing everything from here. Be patient. Thanks for all the calculations. The timing progressions helped a lot. Keep the automatic e-mails coming." It was signed "Venzi S."

"I know he's Jana's friend, but what's his job. Who is he?" Lauren asked.

Jack replied, "A brilliant astro-quantum physicist who works on site. I've heard hardly anybody understands what he's talking about, but he's very friendly. Supposedly, nobody has a clue what he's doing, except Max. He and Max are great friends."

"I've met him before," Fawz said. "He has a stellar reputation in the physics community and spends part of each year at an international physics research center. His recent paper is the one Jana and I sometimes study and discuss. "

"I met him at Max's computer lab," Jana said. "Venzi helped me with physics and told me about his theoretical work on space and time discontinuities. He explains things very clearly, so he doesn't deserve the reputation of people not understanding him. He even taught me timing progressions."

"And Jana taught me. We'd make up potential scenarios, apply various timing progressions, and test the effects." Fawz added, "It was fate that we learned it."

"You were playing games. All along I thought you were doing something useful," Lauren quipped. "Wait, here's more message coming through."

"Tell the astronaut Jana that some theoretical physics will cease to be theoretical in a few minutes. She'll know what I mean."

Suddenly, across the cabin the monitors and controls stopped spinning. The crew rushed toward the main controls just as most began functioning properly. The air pressure still looked fine. The time clocks were maxed out. Then, suddenly the clocks were reset. It was almost 1700 hours, and Houston was contacting them. Jack took his place in front of his monitor.

"Jack, it's so good to see your face. Are you all okay?" Willie asked.

Jack heard cheering in the background. "Yes, we're fine. Now, we are more than fine."

"You gave us quite a scare. We lost you on our tracking screens for practically an hour. We'll be sending you help. Don't know the plans yet. At the minimum, it will take about 36 hours to reach the *Copernicus*. Can you hold out that long? What shape is your ship in?"

"My guess is pretty good shape. It's almost ship shape," Jack said, feeling silly and a bit giddy. Then, he regained his dignity and said, "There's a three-inch gash in the skin, but it is perfectly sealed. A piece of debris from the lander is sticking out into our cabin. We'll send you pictures."

Jana retrieved the camera and began taking pictures as Jack continued. "We need to check the modules in the cargo bay. We need to do an EVA. Don't want to go into our cabinets, which are sealed until after the EVA. What do you want us to do? Should we run diagnostics?"

"We're taking care of your diagnostics from here as we speak," Willie replied. "Then we'll develop an action list for you. Probably, the first thing will be the EVA."

"What was our problem?"

"We needed to reset your clocks."

"Is that all there was to it?"

"No, it was far, considerably more than that."

"Is there any way we could have fixed it from here?

"You did. You sent us all your timing progressions. Dr. Venzi Suzaky took those series and ran them through thousands of calculations and uploaded the results to your Prima Donna computer."

Jack wanted clarification. "You mean our e-mails?"

"Jack, you're being modest. Even Venzi said your work was very clever. I suspect he looks upon most of us as cute, affectionate pets who really try. He said those evenly spaced e-mails along with the timing definitions, precise timing variations, and documentation were exactly what he needed."

"The credit on those e-mails goes to Fawz and Jana." Jack knew it was mostly Jana's work and that Fawz merely oversaw it. He was so proud of Jana, but still Fawz had supervised it. "It was totally their idea."

"I'll tell Venzi that." Willie keyed something into his computer.

"Would our Prima Donna have fixed the problem on its own?" Jack asked.

"According to Venzi, it needed points of reference. However, it would have kept trying to find them on its own.

"Would we have hurt anything had we touched any controls?"

"That was one of Venzi's concerns. Even he wasn't sure. He said it was critical not to do anything on the computer during our upload to you with the reference points."

"When did we disappear off your tracking screens?"

"We knew you had sustained a hit, and it was right after that. We thought that . . . . Then, we got a call from the director saying you were okay because he had personally checked e-mails from you and why hadn't we thought to do that. Apparently, a call from a woman named Marge MacInturff in Seattle was put right through to the director alerting him to the e-mails. No one around here has heard of her.

Don't know what she said to the operator to get immediately through to him. She must have been very persuasive. Do you know her?"

"I know a George MacInturff from Seattle. My guess is that he is a computer systems expert. I know he's a resourceful and dedicated citizen. Someday, I hope to meet him." Jack realized he had said more than enough about George for he certainly did not want to jeopardize George's safety. "Speaking of computer experts, how is Max doing?"

"You're not going to like this. Director Clayton found out that Max had not reported his transmissions with you yesterday. The director concluded that Max had spooked all of you so thoroughly that you didn't come to us for help. I've heard that Clayton is personally hurt that you didn't trust him enough to turn to him and to all of us for help."

"That's unfortunate," Jack said in his most bland voice.

"The director's more than miffed at Max. The front gate logbook indicates that Max had a visitor yesterday morning, a Sol Fetterstein, who turns out to be the Kazimier, the renowned religious leader. Had the Kazimier learned something about the terrorist attempt? And if so, why did he go to Max and not to the director? No one knows what Max and the Kazimier discussed. I'm sure all of that will come out."

"What is happening to Max?" Jack asked.

"I've heard that the director is way too busy with this mission and also far too angry with Max to speak to him today, and an appointment between the two of them is set up for tomorrow morning. In the meantime, Max was escorted off the premises about the time you launched the lander. He objected vigorously saying he had important work to do for your mission. Right before you were lost off our tracking screen, Max finally got a call through to one of our mission controllers asking us to check all of the default settings on the lander. We told him that Fawz had corrected two settings barely in time. Then the controller let it slip that you had disappeared off the tracking screen, and Max was devastated.

"Call Max and tell him we're okay."

"Venzi already did that. He just told us that earlier Max had called him and requested that he come help us." Willie looked down and turned his head slightly away from the camera. "When Dr. Venzi showed up this afternoon, nobody here would allow him to help because we usually don't understand what he's talking about. Apparently, Venzi called Director Clayton and complained. Then, the director ordered us to get him involved. In retrospect, we're glad about that."

Lauren nudged Jack and whispered, "Ask Willie who did this to us."

Jack was simply relieved that they were safe. However, their continued safety rested on someone not trying anything else to harm them. "Have you found out who is responsible for this?"

"We're working on it. So are the FBI and CIA. This is what we know. The firm LandSkyTech is completely involved. The FBI believes that the owner of the firm, a B.G. Landres, has total and full knowledge of this terrorist attempt. He may be the leader of the plot. The FBI has an APB out for him. We still have not located the LandSkyTech Mobile Mission Control. The search continues.

"The FBI cannot find anything yet to connect a JSC programmer named Denise Morneau with B.G. Landres. She deactivated one of your meteoroid detection programs that was uploaded to you in the form of an update. Apparently, that's what got Max so rattled. The FBI believes she is hiding in Tennessee."

Jack did not volunteer that Max had already told him about Denise Morneau. Instead, Jack said, "Ah, yes, the update that Filbert uploaded to us! Looks like a smoking gun to me: a meteoroid detection update programmed to deactivate itself at the very time we need it the most; the wrong person, Filbert, uploading it to us; and the wrong time, toward the end of a mission when the old program is totally fine. What's Filbert's status?"

"I did as you asked. At my request, he was pulled off the team looking for LandSkyTech's Mobile Mission Control, and he was questioned by the Houston police."

Jack waited but Willie did not continue. "And?" Jack asked.

"Filbert was immediately released because the director intervened on his behalf. Third and fourth hand rumors are floating around and merging into a heavy fog. Supposedly, Denise told Filbert that Max wanted him to send you the update. She had paperwork with Max's signature. Another version is that Filbert can't exactly remember his conversation with Denise that led him to send the update. Also, he is quoted as saying that except for Lauren none of you like him, but he wants to assure you that he is totally not involved."

"Do you have anything that's more than rumor?" Jack asked.

"Several weeks ago, a man who claimed to be with the CIA phoned Filbert and wanted to set up a meeting. Filbert did not meet with the person and immediately reported the contact to Director Clayton. The director turned over the information to the CIA who said no such person worked for the agency.

"As far as anybody can determine at this point, Filbert is not involved. He's in a minor bit of trouble over not following procedure in sending you that update. Think he'll get a letter of reprimand for his files. You must know that the director thinks highly of Filbert.

"As for me, the director was distressed, actually very angry, that I authorized having Filbert questioned, but Clayton's a bit off my case now because he's so pleased that you are all alive. However, everything I do other than my routine duties for the duration of your mission needs his personal approval unless it's an extreme emergency."

Jack put his negative feeling about Filbert aside and asked, "Are the diagnostics completed yet?"

Willie checked his monitor. "Almost. So far, the problems have been pretty minor things that we are fixing from here. Know you'll feel more at ease once you do the EVA. Wait, I'm getting an e-mail marked urgent."

"What is it?" Jack asked.

"Russell Ramsey, the LandSkyTech fellow with our people over at Darwin Industries, wants me to convey his apology to you. He is extremely sorry that he made a terrible mistake. And he is so relieved you are okay. Here's another message from one of our controllers at Darwin saying Russell is a young fellow who has never worked a mission before. Now, he is overcome with guilt and shame and all that baggage."

"What mistake?" Jack asked.

"Russell suggested slightly increasing the explosives for the soft explosion, and there was agreement to do that."

"Was the soft explosion not executed according to the original plans?" Jack asked.

"No," Willie replied, "It was changed. In retrospect, now we realize that's why the debris impacted your ship. The original plans would have been much better, probably perfect."

"Can you patch me through to Russell?"

"I think so. I'll check on that right now." Willie must not have turned off the sound completely because Jack barely heard Willie saying, "Yes, Director Clayton, that's what the Commander wants. Yes, sir, I also believe Russell Ramsey has no reason to feel responsible. Yes, I know he has been a pillar of strength all day, and I don't know why he's crumbling now, either. I would guess he's a conscientious person who doesn't make too many mistakes. Yes, I definitely will tell Russell Ramsey to keep the conversation short." Then Jack could not hear any more until Willie at normal volume said, "Russell is on the line now, sir."

"Russell, this is Jack Medwin."

"Commander, I am so sorry I made a mess of things. I truly wanted to help you and your crew."

"Russell, listen to me. You did help us. You are not responsible for the shard impacting the *Copernicus*. If anything, I am responsible. Or secrets are responsible. I didn't tell Houston that I knew the source of the original plans: Chri Anri and the entire aerospace team on Zalanda. They're the same people who reinforced the *Falcon*'s top and who have more than 2,500 years of space travel experience."

"What they must comprehend!" Russell exclaimed. "If only I had known . . . ."

"If JSC had that information, no one would have considered changing the plans. Why didn't I tell Houston? Why did I keep such a secret from them? It wasn't much of a reason. I knew there was fear regarding the Zalandans. I didn't think the fear extended to JSC, but it could have even though JSC had allowed the Zalandans to modify the *Falcon*. Then, our engineers evaluated and approved each change in advance. Russell, are you okay?"

"Yes, I am. Commander, it was good of you to call and to tell me about the Zalandans. I'm so glad your crew is okay despite my actions. I am feeling much better, now."

"That's good, Russell, and I tell you with all sincerity that your help to us today was of the utmost importance for our survival. I want you to remember that, Russell."

Jack rather wished that he had a video hook-up with Russell so he could have better gauged his reaction. He thought of Russell as someone who had absolutely no mission training volunteering for this emergency situation. Russell probably had not piloted a plane before, probably had not even stepped into a simulator, and maybe did not even yearn for danger.

As soon as Jack was back with Mission Control, Lauren nudged him again and whispered, "How could SpaceTech let its subsidiary LandSkyTech run amuck. Wasn't somebody overseeing what was going on? If people at SpaceTech know, then the conspiracy could be vast."

"What's going on with SpaceTech," Jack asked Willie.

"LandSkyTech is not affiliated with SpaceTech. B.G. Landres told the Darwin people his company was a subsidiary of SpaceTech, and Darwin never checked that out. We believe Landres told them that so his company would have an instant creditability.

Willie continued. "The SpaceTech executives and public relations people are mortified to be associated with the plot. They have taken action big time. At first, they went to the airwaves with large ads denying any affiliation with LandSkyTech. Their plans grow more elaborate by the minute. They were going to send a group of their minishuttles out to meet the *Copernicus* and escort you back. They were trying to get governmental approval. They wanted Jana's friend Alan piloting one of those shuttles to show that they are so easy to use even a non-pilot could control one."

Jack knew that would not happen. He glanced toward Jana who looked ever so happy. He did not want her getting hopeful. "Alan will not pilot a shuttle. Someone will nix that idea, probably Director Clayton."

She whispered, "I am aware of that, Jack. I'm just happy that we're here, now."

Willie said, "Once you disappeared off our tracking screens, everything with SpaceTech moved even more quickly. They approached the government with the idea of a search and rescue mission. Now Madame President has become personally involved. She is in consultation with NASA and Homeland Security directors.

"I'm getting a beep with urgent information to relay to you."

Jack waited while Willie read from his computer.

"Hey, listen to this! Madame President will speak to you tonight at 20 hundred hours, 8 p.m. Houston time, over live TV and tell the nation the plans for your rescue. I am authorized to tell you now. She has approved the SpaceTech rescue mission with conditions. Only minishuttle certified pilots who have met the most vigorous security checks are being selected for the mission. They will be used in an escort capacity only unless you get into trouble. You will be escorted to the space factory, not the spaceport. Your destination will not be made public. The highest level of security will be observed at all times."

Willie went back to reading.

"What is it, Willie."

"Don't understand this one. It's supposed to be a personal message from Madame President to you. I'm to tell you that Madame President said she appreciates such brilliant and creative preemptive damage control."

Jack smiled to himself. He hoped Madame President was not being sarcastic. It would help to be in her good graces.

"This next message is one I understand. After you hear this, delete it from your records. Director Clayton said Madame President can good and well speak to you at your convenience, not hers. The space walk around the *Copernicus* is of the utmost importance now. He does not want you talking to her until after you have thoroughly checked your ship. He doesn't want you jeopardizing your safety."

"I am sure Madame President would not want us jeopardizing our mission either," Jack said. He wished the director had been slightly more tactful because deleting every copy of any transmission, particularly today's, would not be easy.

"There's more. Our director says that when those 'little toy shuttles' arrive, he doesn't want anyone frivolously transferring into one of them."

Jack said, "Tell the director we await his instructions regarding the minishuttles."

Willie was reading his computer screen again. "What else is it?" Jack asked.

Willie said, "We've finally finished running the diagnostics. All of our readings are nominal. From here, most everything looks A-Okay. A few minor things need to be done from your end. You can fix them after the space walk and after you've checked the cargo bay. You're now cleared for the EVA."

"We'll prepare," Jack said, looking forward to the new danger.

"We'll stay with you throughout," Willie said and then read something from his computer. "This is from NASA headquarters in Washington. Whatever problems you encounter, at all times you are to refer to the minishuttles as an escort mission and not ever as a rescue mission."

"Got it," Jack replied, and then to his crew he said, "We're definitely back in our own universe, now."

"I'm glad," Lauren said. "Personally, I welcome the minishuttles under any classification. Maybe, SpaceTech is doing it as a big publicity bonanza, and they probably feel like they have inherited a gold mine. Yet, they want good publicity, so they will be careful."

"I also welcome the minishuttles," Fawz said, "My father and Madame President will prevent SpaceTech from doing anything too flamboyant."

Lauren said, "All of a sudden, now that our survival seems more likely, I am realizing how much I miss life on Earth. I think Chri Anri will like Earth . . . a lot."

"Whoa! I think I missed something!" Jack exclaimed. "Did all that happen in your e-mail to him?"

"I did invite him for a visit."

Jana said, "Hope he doesn't take 500 years to reply."

"Don't worry about that," Lauren confidently said.

Johnson Space Center, Houston, Texas
Sunday Morning

Max Marsh waited outside the Director's office. He figured he would be fired for breaking the chain of command. He did not want to be fired. However, all that really mattered, he thought, was that Jana, Jack, Fawz, and Lauren had survived the attack of the so called "Saturn probe." They were safe, at least for the moment anyway, safe and three days from rendezvous with the spaceport. If all went well, they would be docking there on Wednesday.

Max could not remember if he had ever seen NASA so abuzz with activity on a Sunday. Some people were at work because they had been called in, and others were there because they were bursting to know all the details of yesterday's barely averted destruction of the *Copernicus*. Many who had disregarded the tabloid reports had just found out yesterday that indeed the astronauts were returning from a secret mission to Ganymede.

Max fingered the recording he had made on his phone. He had played it over and over. Smart move of the Kazimier, asking him to record their conversation. It was difficult for him to fathom that just two days ago, Friday morning, a call came from the guard at the North gate that Sol Fetterstein wanted to see him. Sol did not go by that name anymore but by the name Kazimier.

On Friday morning, his old friend the Kazimier had walked into his office in a business suit, rather than the flowing robes that he had seen him wearing when doing TV interviews or lecturing at a university.

519

Max and the Kazimier had been childhood friends. Max remembered a sincere little kid who followed his own convictions, even then. Like Max, the Kazimier rarely needed to be one of the in-crowd. He could be totally alone and confident. The most striking difference between then and now, Max thought, was that melodious baritone voice, a rich timbre, easily the voice of God's messenger. For someone with the Kazimier's calling, Max thought, that voice indeed was a gift from heaven.

Over the years they had followed their own paths, but whenever they saw each other, it was if there had not been the intervening years apart. Their meeting on Friday had been no exception. They both were delighted to see each other. Quickly, however, the Kazimier got down to business. At that point, he suggested that they record the conversation. "It's about our church finances, an embezzlement, but there may be further implications, and I need information from you regarding the secret mission."

"You know I would do anything for you, but there are things I can't reveal. Someone higher up could authorize me, of course." They both chuckled. Max had not meant to make a joke. "Someone higher up here at JSC, I mean."

"Our donations have been dropping for the last eight weeks. Donations fluctuate, so at first it was nothing to be alarmed about. I usually let my business people handle the money matters, but a few days ago I decided to look things over myself. I ran a computer check, and it seemed to be a pattern. Some big contributors had stopped giving altogether, not all the big contributors, but basically the ones who . . . . How shall I say it tactfully?"

"We go back a long way. Just say it."

"As you know, some people our religion attracts are not too stable. They have serious psychological problems. These people are members of God's flock. They need a church, too, and maybe we can help them.

"The big contributors who stopped giving were basically those in the group we had referred for psychological counseling. These people needed more than the pastoral counseling that we offer to any member. Had I offended a whole group of people? I read my most recent sermons, nothing offensive. There were a few in this group who had continued their regular contributions. I decided to pay a visit. I picked two people who I was sure did not know each other. They both told me the same story.

"Each one told me that my chief financial officer, a new fellow who had replaced my CFO of many years, had approached him about giving money to a foundation in lieu of the normal donations to the church. They further told me that the CFO stated that he was acting on my behalf. The purpose of the Flame Foundation was to see that the astronauts not return from space, that they stay on the planet they are visiting.

"Then, he fed them double talk about evil influences in the universe that needed to stay away from earth."

Max asked, "Why do you think he did this?"

"I don't think he believes what he told them. But why wouldn't he want the astronauts to return?"

"I don't know," said Max. "If there were a mission, and I'm not saying there is, then NASA would protect the astronauts. Outsiders would not be able to harm them."

"My concern is straightforward. Is my CFO stealing money, or does he have a more sinister plan? My question is simple. Is there a mission?"

"I can't tell you either way."

"Yesterday, we convened an emergency meeting of the board, met with our attorneys, explained the CFO's legal rights to him. Our major goal was to recover as much money as possible. The CFO stated that I had requested that he collect money for the foundation. We sent e-mails to our local members: he no longer is our representative; he no longer has authority to collect funds on behalf of the church; and we have no affiliation whatsoever with his foundation."

"You had a busy day."

"Early this morning, I got a call from one of our members, a former big contributor, demanding his money back from the foundation. Apparently, the CFO had promised him destruction of the spaceship by tomorrow afternoon. The member told me of an angry argument between the two of them. 'We'd better deliver,' he had said to the CFO. The CFO had yelled numbers to him and had said they were the time and celestial coordinates for the destruction of the spaceship. That is when and where the ship's explosion is supposed to occur."

"Do you have those numbers?" Max asked.

The Kazimier pulled a computer printout out of his suit pocket and handed it to Max. "I often take notes on my computer when having phone conversations with church members."

"These could be celestial coordinates," Max remarked. "I'll run them through the computer." He fully and completely trusted the Kazimier. The Kazimier had enough to worry about dealing with the embezzlement. He wanted to put the Kazimier's mind at ease in this one category, but he would need to divulge highly classified information. "First, I have a question for you. How can I become a member of your flock?"

"We have classes."

I would need to become a member pretty instantly. As my religious leader, you would be obligated to hold what I tell you in secrecy. I could tell you confidential information."

"I see. Would you please rise?" They both stood up, and the Kazimier held his hand over Max's head. "My son, do you affirm to hold life sacred, to put the needs of living beings above material gains, yet recognize the world has reached maximum population capacity, recognize and rejoice in genetic diversity among the human population, care for the earth, the sky, people other than yourself as well as your immediate family, love and respect your immediate family, even though this command may be more difficult than to love and respect a stranger, love yourself, strive to fulfill your potential to yourself, spread good in this world whenever you can, always remember that you are a unique individual, yet, you are part of a whole. Do this in remembrance of all the good and loving people who came before you and in anticipation of the unbroken chain of all the good souls who will come after you." The Kazimier looked into Max's eyes. "Now, you say, 'I do.'"

"I do," Max said in a strong voice. Then he added, surprising himself, "With all my heart." Max felt a feeling of peace sweep over him.

"Then I pronounce you one of the children of the earth to go forward to spread joy, understanding, and affability among all your brothers and sisters."

The two friends who grew up in the same neighborhood, the Kazimier and the computer flight analyst, sat down, and Max told him that indeed the mission was returning from Ganymede, known to the inhabitants there as Zalanda, and that some of the information in the electronic tabloids was basically true. Max ran the numbers though his super computer. Two numbers were very close, but the third was way off.

Max did not like it. How could someone be that close on two of the coordinates? Even for an amateur astronomer, finding and tracking something that small and that far away in the skies seemed highly unlikely. "What do you know about your CFO?"

"I try to stay at arm's length from the money people. The board hired him. Brandon Lane—that's his name—came with the highest recommendations and the best credentials." The Kazimier frowned. "Recently, I've become aware of his arrogance. He's bright, no doubt. Have you noticed when someone perceives himself as being smart, sometimes that person grossly underrates the abilities of those around him?"

Max nodded in agreement. "Yes, I've noticed." An image of Filbert flashed before him.

"I eventually realized that he didn't think much of the board or even of me. Still, it's a stretch from arrogance to embezzlement and possibly much worse. In contrast, he got along well with his staff. I recently found out they willingly did all of his work for him.

"When Brandon was hired, his previous employer had faxed us a glowing reference. It couldn't have been more positive, sorry to be losing him but glad he was getting an opportunity to work for such an outstanding organization and so forth. Yesterday, I called that employer in hopes that I could figure out what went so very wrong. That employer had never heard of him. Neither had any of his other references."

"Wow," Max said, "You've got a mess."

I guess my concern goes back to this. Are we dealing with an embezzlement, or is it more far reaching? Is the spaceship in danger?"

"I'll check everything out this morning and call you back."

The Kazimier slowly said, "There's another thing. "Our previous CFO died under rather unusual circumstances. He had been with us many years, and we were devastated. There was a boating accident in Galveston Bay. Yet, he had been so careful and so competent with his boat."

"I remember the accident, about six or seven months ago," Max said. He had read the article in the paper and had written the Kazimier a rather long condolence letter.

"On that particular day, our CFO had taken a potential new VP of Finance out on a fishing trip. The CFO's body was recovered but that of the potential employee was never found. All we had was his resume. When we tried to notify the man's family, nothing checked out. None of us had seen the man; we didn't even know what he had looked like. It was as if he never existed. The police didn't think that much of it, just that sometimes people try to start new lives with new identities. In fact, the police thought it rather surprising that the CFO's body was recovered."

"So you think that . . . ."

"I don't know. It's possible we may be dealing with a very dangerous man, one who is capable of anything."

"He would need access to a lot more than embezzled funds."

After the Kazimier left, Max looked at the coordinates again. Strange that the two should be so very close. It might not be a coincidence. He went down the hall to report the conversation to Jean, his boss. He needed some ideas on how to proceed. Should the astronauts be alerted, or would they be needlessly worried?

Her office was empty, and her computer screen was blinking, "Back in 10 minutes or so." Max sat down to wait. His feeling of inner peace was still there, but it was being edged out by a concern. The CFO in anger had yelled out coordinates. The church member had memorized the coordinates and then repeated them to the Kazimier who had keyed them into his computer. Somebody easily could have transposed a number.

Max rushed back to his office and took another look at the three coordinates. He ran a printout with NASA's projected coordinates. Then he started moving backward and forward in time. Bingo, for fifteen minutes earlier, the first two coordinates were almost exact. The third coordinate was different. Max began transposing numbers. It took him only a couple of minutes before he saw a close match.

Someone outside of JSC had the three projected coordinates for a moment in time tomorrow, Saturday afternoon. How would that be possible without help from someone inside JSC?

He called Jean. She still wasn't back. On her phone, he left a message, "It's urgent that I see you."

Sitting at his desk, he began making a list of concerns to discuss with her. A voice interrupted his concentration.

"You seem deep in thought," Filbert said. He leaned against the door jam.

Max looked up. "How're you doing," he said, hoping Filbert would not stay.

He slithered into Max's office and sunk into a chair. "I'm standing in for Jean today. She's tied up with meetings this morning, and then she leaving for Washington at noon."

"Washington?"

"It came up all of a sudden. Now, how can I help?"

"I need to talk to her."

"It'll have to be Monday then." Filbert thought a minute and then said, "Maybe I can get you five minutes right before she leaves. What it's about?"

Max did not like dealing with Filbert at all, but he particularly hated that phony helpful voice that Filbert had slipped into. He forced himself to be civil. "I'm concerned about the safety of the astronauts. I want to know what security measures have been taken."

"It might be better if they didn't return," Filbert said.

Max's mouth flew open.

Filbert laughed. "I've never seen you shocked before. Hey, buddy, it was just a joke. Don't look so upset. I'm sorry. It was in poor taste. It's just that their return will open a can of worms. To make it up to you, I'll get you in to see Jean this morning for sure.

Sometimes, one random or thoughtless comment has irreversible consequences. The thought jumped into Max's mind that someone at JSC indeed could be involved in a deliberate act of sabotage. Max tried to push the thought away, but the idea wedged itself securely in his brain and took root.

When Jean popped into Max's office between her meetings, she seemed distracted and annoyed. "Filbert said you needed to see me."

"Is there any way someone outside of JSC could get the flight path?"

"I guess an amateur astronomer could find the ship and start tracking it."

Her answer was too fast and too glib. "Wouldn't that be terribly remote? The ship is small, and it's still four days from the spaceport. And what about the anti-detection shield?"

She stared at Max. "Is that all?"

This was the moment to tell her what he knew. She was behaving so differently toward him, but he had not interrupted her schedule before. Usually, if someone were trying to tell her something, she would dig in and find out why that person was concerned about a particular issue. A question swirled in his mind. Could Jean be involved in any of this?

After she was gone, he considered the possibility that he may have overanalyzed her behavior. People went to Jean; she did not usually drop in on them, and, after all, she had been in a hurry.

The doorknob to the Director's office rattled. Max stood up and took the phone out of his pocket. His conversation with the Kazimier two days ago on Friday would be the easy part to explain. He would have a harder time explaining why he did not report the Kazimier's conversation to Jean. He had discussed coordinates with her, barely, in a vague way. Even after she had gone to Washington, Max still could have gone to the Director on Friday afternoon or at least made an attempt to reach him.

The Director strode out of his office and said, "It seems you created quite a commotion, Max."

"Yes, sir," Max said.

"Did it occur to you that there may have been a more straightforward way to handle all of this?"

"I believe there's some JSC involvement in this, sir." Max hoped he could trust the director. He needed his help to proceed any further.

Galveston, Texas
Sunday Afternoon

Jim Landres wanted to be away from this whole thing. Nothing had gone as he had planned. They would be looking for him at airports or along the border with Mexico, not here at the beach 18 miles from Houston. He did not think they could trace the money to his Swiss and offshore bank accounts, but he wanted to move on to something new.

He fit in like a tourist in a visor hat, sun glasses, unbuttoned shirt, bathing suit, and sandals. He bought six prestamped post cards in a souvenir shop built on stilts that hung out over the gulf. He would send one to that woman who had made the trajectory calculations to locate the *Copernicus* for him. Sharleen even had outsmarted his muscle men.

First, he addressed a tanned muscle man card to her and wrote, "For a job well done." Below the message, he jotted down three Swiss bank account numbers and pin codes. Below that, he listed three offshore account numbers and ID codes. Her only weakness, he could tell, was her greed. Ha, that would make her squirm. Would Sharleen turn down so much money? A woman like that certainly appealed to him.

He addressed the second card to his mother and wrote, "Remember our family vacation in Galveston."

He wrote and addressed the other cards and put all of them in his shirt pocket. He got into his rental car and drove west along the main road of the island until he reached San Luis Pass at the west end. He did not cross over the bridge that connected Galveston Island to Surfside but instead turned off. He remembered a little fishing village from a long time ago when he was a young child. His family had been sunning on the beach, and he explored on his own, crossed the highway, and stumbled onto the village. It had been a special place where he lingered too long. His family was in an uproar when he returned, but they easily believed him when he said he had gotten lost and scared. Had he dreamed the whole thing, or had it happened? Maybe the incident had happened to his father. His father had told him so many stories about his childhood, pointless stories it seemed.

Jim thought his own childhood had been so bland, his parents so passive. His life had seemed like one huge pastoral scene out of a French painting until he discovered that he was capable of stirring things up, little stirs at first like putting his family in an uproar, but later, making things happen, pulling the strings that controlled peoples' lives. Even that seemed pretty meaningless after a while. He tried to think up bigger stirs; the execution of his plans, even perfect executions, fell short of what he was going after. And what was that? He did not know.

Then he came up with a better idea, a legitimate business, a small space exploration firm. Space exploration interested him, and he originally thought of the firm as a place to launder his money. He bought an off-the-shelf probe at a vastly reduced price (because it had not met the specifications for the original buyers). His employees customized it to explore Saturn and Titan. He started an educational foundation to help fund his space firm. It all might have worked out, too, if his new idea had not been so tempting.

In retrospect, he realized his plan had been too ambitious and had kept him too busy. Once he added his new idea, he was far too exposed. The scheme was costing him far more than he had expected, and he started taking chances with the educational foundation. LandSkyTech was a huge sponge sucking every donation out of the Flame Foundation. Sometimes, he used his own money garnered from previous schemes to make payroll.

The area around the San Luis pass was filled with high-rises that appeared to have been there for a long time. He drove around the inlet looking for the fishing village. If it had ever existed, it was gone now. He crossed back over the main road, drove to the end of an access road that lead to the beach, and parked the rental car. He got out and walked toward the water. As he passed the sand dunes, he took the post cards out of his pocket and threw them to the wind. That life was behind him now; it was time to move on, assume another identity, and stir another pot.

He took off his shirt, folded it neatly, placed his sandals on top for a weight, and started walking along the beach. He felt his feet make impressions in the damp sand. Where would he go next? He would wait until things calmed down and then go somewhere that offered new possibilities. England? Australia? New Zealand?

He thought of Jana Novacek reading. On the day of her probable death, she was reading her journal. That took courage. He wanted to get the image of the girl out of his mind. She was not begging or pleading, merely telling her story. None of them begged or pleaded. He could have imagined them suffering and whimpering, but they were brave, in charge, taking action. He was not getting the reactions he wanted from people. If the astronauts had not been on TV, things would have gone better for him.

He felt the sun bearing down on him, searing his skin. Out of nowhere, a lifeguard ran toward him. "The tides are dangerous here. The red flag is up. And your arms are turning pink."

The lifeguard handed him a sample of sunscreen. Did the person recognize him? He did not think so.

Jim was a powerful swimmer. He could outswim the rip tide. He walked out into the water. It felt cool on his skin. He kept walking further out. As he got into deeper water, the salt lightly stung his newly pink shoulders. A powerful wave claimed his visor hat, sunglasses, and the sunscreen sample that he had been clutching in his right hand. Soon, the tide carried him out. He knew how to handle the tide. He was way offshore, now, and still afloat, still doing fine. He could handle it. He could handle anything. He felt something on his toe, a nibble. Then he felt an excruciating pain in his thigh. Shark bites are rare worldwide, he told himself. He could handle a shark; sharks are stupid. He was smarter than anybody and anything. It was probably just a cramp. He could swim with a cramp.

On the beach under a blue umbrella, a four-year-old boy patiently waited until the slightly sunburned man was deep in the water and then so deep that the boy could no longer see him. The boy glanced at his mother and determined she still was absorbed in reading her paperback. He slipped away toward the sand dunes and retrieved the post cards. By the time his mother looked up, the boy sat passively at her side, his post cards safely stashed in his sand pail under a collection of broken shells. His mother suggested they get some pistachio ice cream, and the boy nodded in agreement.

Swimming with his arms and one leg, Jim involuntarily thought of Denise Morneau, the JSC programmer. She was a strange one. She did not believe fully that he was with the CIA, and she did not succumb to his romantic overtures. Yet, she had helped him, anyway. First, she had gone through mental gymnastics, he thought, that he was not privy to. She refused money but readily accepted an all-expense paid hiking trip to the Smoky Mountains. He felt absolutely nothing toward her.

He wondered where that young probe designer, Russell Ramsey, had gone on Saturday morning and if he had been apprehended yet. The minute the broadcast for help from the *Copernicus* had come on TV, Jim dispatched his muscle men to Russell's apartment to delay him. Then, he made an anonymous call to the police, saying that Russell had masterminded the sabotage plans for the *Copernicus* and that his name was on the final drawings. He also gave the police the number of Russell's auto license plate. Jim did not mention anything to the police about LandSkyTech or Darwin Industries.

He would merely disappear, and Russell would take the blame. But nothing had gone as he had planned. Russell had not been at his apartment, and Jim's muscle men could not find him anywhere. Russell was a loose end.

Jerome Westlake, that JSC young man, merely a boy, who stole the flight data, was another loose end. Surely, by now, NASA would have figured out that Jerome or someone who worked at JSC deliberately and with forethought had stolen sensitive flight data. Yet, Jim's curiosity was waning. He wanted to be through with this entire *Copernicus* episode; drop the whole thing, evade capture, and get on with his life. Except for Sharleen Rothwell.

He tried to conjure up an image of Sharleen swimming next to him, no makeup, nude, and encouraging him. But he only could see her perfectly groomed, too well made up, wearing an impeccable, yet feminine business suit, and presenting him with the trajectory of the *Copernicus*. He wished he had not thrown away her post card.

When the image he wanted did not present itself to him, Jim's thoughts roamed, and he vaguely wondered why his probe had not succeeded in destroying the solarship. If he were caught and if asked why he did it, he would say to protect the people on earth from aliens. What could their intentions be toward humans? To be served tasty humans for breakfast. The renowned physicist Stephen Hawking said that searching for intelligent aliens was a bad idea. Why would we think that their intentions toward humans could be good?

That was what he told church members when he collected money for the Flame Foundation. Not at first. He was more careful and simply stated that the purpose of the foundation was to support private space exploration.

How could he possibly have known that the aliens were ancient earthlings who wanted to announce their presence and reestablish ties with people on earth? Yet, the astronauts still could be full of dangerous germs that take a longer time to incubate than three-and-a-half week return flight. He had still done a humanitarian thing. He had been in a position to keep the astronauts from returning. It required sacrificing his Saturn probe, and at first he did not want to do that. However, the idea quickly grew on him.

This was the major reason he did it, to protect people on earth, particularly those who donated to the Flame Foundation. However, he knew the Center for Disease Control was taking appropriate action, and contagious astronauts would not be exposed to the general population.

There were other reasons. The idea of an explosion in space seemed particularly appealing. Another reason, he was tired of running LandSkyTech, and this was a way out. These were both pitiful reasons.

If he examined his motives more closely, he could reach back into his past to an old lady, her beloved cat, and three nine-year-old boys. One of the three boys had stolen her cat and taken it to the pound. He was that boy. Minutes before the cat was to be euthanized, the other two boys finally located the animal and paid the fees to get it released.

When he was considering a move to Houston, he decided to find out what had happened to them, Sol Fetterstein and Max Marsh. He was surprised to learn that Sol had become the Kazimier. Since their lives had intersected briefly, he figured that neither would remember him. That proved to be the case.

Sometimes, he felt he was in a game that they did not know they were playing. They had won round one and saved the cat. They would not win round two and save the solarship. They each had much to lose: the Kazimier, his reputation for financing the destruction of the ship, and Max, his career, for his inability to protect the ship. However, the ship had been saved. They had won round two. Jim looked forward to round three.

This was crazy. And he was not crazy. He hardly ever thought that way. There was no way anyone could learn that he did. For some, he might be considered a sociopath, but that was just a word.

The sun was setting and he was shivering. The Gulf waters had not yet warmed sufficiently. He was getting tired. He needed to return to shore quickly and not become exhausted in the process. He was too far out. He would swim at a steady pace until he reached the cross current, and then he would swim diagonally and more energetically. He needed to stop thinking and concentrate on reaching the shore, but thoughts would not stop.

He should have returned the money to the Flame Foundation contributor instead of feigning anger. That had been a tactical error. He had yelled the time and place for the destruction of the ship. That was hubris gone wild. Had that been Tuesday or Wednesday? He could not remember now.

On Thursday, the Kazimier had fired him. Two in-house lawyers were polite and professional. All they wanted was the money, but there was no money. It was sunk in the probe. He did not intend to replace that money with his funds from previous schemes.

He simply said that he misunderstood what the Kazimier wanted and that they could find all the records filed under the Flame Foundation. That was true enough. They would find the original articles of incorporation. He had made a quarterly tax filing and listed the name and amount from every donor. He even had the letter authorizing him to start the Flame Foundation with a window pane signature by the Kazimier. Everything was there but the money.

At that moment, he hoped that he had taken enough care to keep his identities separate. He had many aliases. As the Chief Financial Officer for the Kazimier's church, he was Brandon Lane, a brown eyed accountant. When he stepped into his role as owner of LandSkyTech, he combed his hair differently and became Jim Landres, an engineer/businessman and wearer of blue contact lenses. When he involved JSC employees in acts against the *Copernicus*, he was Lincoln Listle, a no-nonsense CIA man. Even his given name, Lester Longworth, came in handy on occasion.

No wonder he had no time for his swimming. He was out of shape. A wave washed over him, and he briefly went under water. He remained calm and focused. With the sun down, he was chilly but too tired to swim vigorously to warm up. He had stopped shivering.

Reflections from the moon flickered on the water. It was not a night to become fish food. He swam steadily toward the lights of Galveston until he got to the cross currents, but the lights were going out. People were going to bed and turning out their lights, or was he drifting in and out of consciousness?

Then, he finally saw Sharleen Rothwell, dressed in white like an angel, holding out her hand from the end of a long, bright tunnel. As he swam toward her, she turned into his mother, who plaintively called his name.

He focused on swimming and eventually got past the rip tide. He was thirsty, and his head hurt. He would drink a bit of salt water. No, that was a bad idea. He caught a sparkling wave and then another, and they carried him to shore.

He dragged himself onto the beach several miles away from where he had started, exhausted, his face, shoulders, arms, and hands sunburned, his lips parched, his thigh badly cramped, and his right toe throbbing. It appeared a crab or small sea creature had taken a bite. A person jogging along the beach at midnight found him and took him to John Sealy Hospital where he checked in under another alias.

While a worldwide search was going on for him, he watched it on TV from his hospital bed in Galveston. It may not have gone as he had planned. Yet, he had made a sufficient mess of enough lives. When he was feeling better, he would go to Cannes and then in June or July, perhaps the tennis games at Wimbledon. Yes indeed, he liked games, all kinds of them. He decided he was not quite through with his current scheme. He would buy a phone without GPS tracking and find out how many followers he had left and what they were willing to do.

Great Smoky Mountains, Tennessee
Monday

Denise Morneau, the NASA programmer who attempted to deactivate the micrometeoroid detection program, had been hiking for three days in the Great Smoky Mountains, cut off from what was happening in the world, and she liked it that way. She ran into only a few people.

When she passed a young couple on a remote trail, the woman asked, "Wanta hear the news?"

"No, thank you," she had replied. The woman looked oddly disappointed, and Denise later wondered if anything significant had happened.

After those days of being one with nature, she still could not get the dealings with the CIA man out of her thoughts. He had all the right credentials, but still she felt queasy that what he asked her to do was something really wrong.

Now, driving back to the motel in the rental car, a slight drizzle fell on her windshield. She passed the trail to Laurel Falls and remembered the good payoff, a view of a lovely falls for a rather short hike. As she turned the car around and parked, she figured the light rain would keep most tourists away. She sprinted up the trail, inhaling deeply and listening to the splashing and crashing of the falls, yet unseen, echoing through the trees. At the top, she was disappointed to find nearly a dozen people.

Denise balanced on a rock directly above the shaded falls and peered down at the water rushing into the gurgling creek below. Carefully shifting her weight, she turned around. A short distance from where she stood, water tumbled from above over a smaller falls into a natural wading pool. Two boys, barely teens, seemed engrossed in a small TV. Why would anyone take a TV on a hike, she wondered, and with such a view? As she glanced their way, one of the boys called out to her, "Wanta see the man who about blew up the solarship."

"What?" she asked as she swayed precariously above the falls.

"You'd better be careful. Them rocks is slippery," the boy admonished as he carefully made his way to her side, took her hand, and led her over to his friend who sat on a huge rock with his feet dangling in the water.

"Oh, shoot, he's off the air," the other boy said, "I'll do an instant replay."

She was feeling very confused, and, suddenly, her feet ached. She sat down next to the boy, took off her hiking boots and socks, and eased her feet into the cool mountain water.

"Here 'tis," the boy said and showed her his TV.

It looked like Lincoln Listle, the CIA man, but the screen was very small. "It looks like somebody I might know," she said softly. She quickly pulled her feet out of the water and stood up on the slippery rock. As she felt the rock disappearing from under her feet, she was aware that one of the boys grabbed her and tried to break her fall right before her head contacted hard rock.

"It's okay, ma'am, I gotch ye."

That was all she remembered until she heard voices. "What's the matter with her?" a woman's voice asked.

"She slipped and hit her head," one of the boys said. "Her heart's beating. She's breathin'."

"I caught her afore she fell very far. I hope she didn't hit her head too hard," the other boy added.

"Maybe it's the thin mountain air," a man said.

Such a ridiculous comment made her stir and moan. These mountains are under 3,000 feet, she thought. There's plenty of air.

"She's a commin' out of it. Ma'am, ma'am, wake up," the boy said.

She opened her eyes and looked around. Several people were peering down at her.

The boys took charge. "Please back up and give'er some air," one of them said.

"Maybe we should find a forest ranger," a woman suggested.

"No, I'm okay," she said, but she was not okay at all. She needed to get another look at the man on the TV.

The boys helped her to sit up. After she was feeling somewhat steady, she leaned toward the water and splashed some cool water in her face.

The group around her eventually dispersed, leaving her in the boys' care. She said, "I'd like to see the TV again, the man who almost blew up the solarship."

From a slot on the side of his small TV, the boy unfolded a thin two-foot screen that became rigid around the perimeter. He did a freeze frame of the man.

Yes, she was sure. It was Lincoln Listle. The man had convinced her he was a CIA agent, and she reluctantly had agreed to help him. She refused to take money. However, she so enjoyed hiking and had accepted this all expense vacation. To get out of the heat of Houston into the mountains seemed so perfect. "Are the astronauts okay?"

"They're fine. There was a big explosion near them. I guess it was the probe blowing up. NASA's not a sayin', but it was all on TV, a huge explosion, almost got all the astronauts, too.

"What day was that?"

"'Twas Saturday, two days ago."

Denise tried to remember. Was Saturday the day? She had programmed in the deactivation of the automatic sensors for micrometeoroids. The deactivation was for twelve hours and time-dated into a subroutine. The so-called CIA man had told her the sensors interfered with reception from inside the spacecraft, and the CIA needed to eavesdrop on the astronauts to determine if they had been unduly influenced by the aliens. The CIA man had told her there was no way NASA would ever know that she had helped him. The subroutine to her program would be time-dated, and she could code it to leave no evidence, to disappear out of her program without a trace.

Until that conversation, she had not believed there was a secret mission. She had thought it was only unfounded rumors that somehow had been elevated to fact.

She did not want to help Lincoln Listle. However, as she talked to him, she decided that what he was asking her to do was of no consequence and that he did not understand enough about a mission to realize this. Unknown to Listle, she had worked on a second, completely independent program for detecting micrometeoroids anywhere within a two hour range of a ship; she figured that backup system would give the astronauts plenty of warning if they needed to change their course. Furthermore, Mission Control would be unlikely to send a new program to astronauts on a mission when they already had a fully functional and well tested system. Her modifications to the program would be used on a future mission, she figured, and the first time it was tested, the time-dated subroutine would merely disappear out of the program. After rationalizing those things in her mind, she had agreed to help him. Now, after the near destruction of the solarship, she thought that what she did may have had major consequences.

One boy started talking confidently. "He named his corporation LandSkyTech. That din't take no time, jest going to the courthouse in Houston and doin' the paperwork. He also paid somethin' called the Texas Franchise Tax."

"How do you know all of this?" she asked.

"I seen it on the TV."

"Rich wants to run a big business someday. He pays 'tention to things like that. Rich would like to see his name on top of a tall building in downtown Maryville."

539

"Good luck, Rich," Denise said. Then, a thought occurred to her. "You don't look up to this man, as a . . . a role model?"

"Oh, no Ma'am! Don't ye wanta know more?"

"Yes!"

"He bought hisself an off-the-shelf probe and hired some people to add explosives. He paid them lots of money." As Rich talked, he carefully folded up the large TV screen until it fit in the slot on the side of the small TV. "Then the man he contacted Darwin Industries to launch the probe. Darwin Industries checked his references with the bank, and he had a very good financial statement."

The other boy, not to be outdone, chimed in, "Betch'ye don't know what a financial statement is." When Rich ignored his friend's comment, the other boy said, "At the same time, he was the Chief Financial Officer for the Kazimier."

"The Kazimier's involved?"

"No, he didn't know what the guy was doing 'til it was 'most too late. That guy had phony credentials."

"You can say that again." She thought of his CIA credentials. "What is his name?"

"His name as owner of LandSkyTech is Jim Landres. But when he worked for the Kazimier, his name 'twas Brandon Lane. They think he might have lots of aliases."

"And there's some folks at NASA involved."

"Who?" she asked, feeling her head pain intensify.

NASA won't say, but they're workin' on it. Say, you're beginnin' to look sick. Want some 'mella wafers?

"Yes, that would be fine."

As she bit into a vanilla wafer, she wished it were a communion wafer, absolving her of any wrong doing.

Later, after she told Rich and his friend that she was okay, the boys waded in the water and splashed each other as she guarded their TV for them. They had no way of knowing that she had made a very poor guardian of something far more important, the solarship and its crew.

She wondered if she should call Johnson Space Center and explain. As she absently ate another wafer, she rationalized that the astronauts were safe and the authorities were seeking the man responsible. Indeed, she had nothing further to tell NASA. By getting involved, she could only heap much trouble upon herself. NASA would not have sent her program to the astronauts in the middle of a major mission, she decided.

Abandoning the small TV set, she lowered herself off the rock into the shallow water. Yes, she would do nothing, at least, not yet. As she took a deep breath absolving herself of any responsibility, moldy, woodsy air filled her lungs.

Later, the boys walked down the trail with her. As she got into the rental car, she thanked them for their help and assured them she felt fine. Driving on the mountain road through the light mist to her motel in Townsend, she wondered if she should find out what was happening with the astronauts and with the so-called CIA man. No, she did not want to think about it. Anyway, her head was aching. She would not watch the TV news; she would not call her supervisor at NASA. Instead, she would take a long shower before enjoying some Southern cooking in the motel dining room. Then, she would fill her back pack with clean clothes and fresh supplies, get a good night's sleep, and leave early the next morning from Cade's Cove, hiking along the AT trail to Spence Field. Denise had planned that particular hike even before leaving Houston.

She parked her car, hefted her back pack lopsidedly onto one shoulder, and ambled toward her motel room. She did not pay particular attention to the two police cars in the parking lot. As she put the key card in the door slot, a deep voice asked, "Are you Denise Morneau?"

"Yes," she said weakly.

"We have a warrant for your arrest. Please raise your hands and turn around slowly."

As she turned around, she saw two guns pointed toward her. A policeman began reading her rights to her. The backpack on her shoulder suddenly felt too heavy, but she dared not move or shift her weight. It all seemed so surreal. A random thought that popped into her head: "I guess this is the end of my vacation."

Jana's Journal
Private Entry
Monday

Two days after our near incineration in space, six SpaceTech minishuttles arrived as our escort right before we crossed inside the moon's orbit. Each vehicle circled the *Copernicus* before settling down to fly in formation. We observed them through our short-range telescopes. They had to keep their distance.

They continually checked the condition of our ship's skin through their short-range telescopes and sent us lots of clever correspondence reporting everything was A-Okay. This was quite pleasant except that it reminded me that something could happen where the shard abutted the skin. The *Copernicus* could come apart. I dared not mention it to Jack or Lauren or Fawz.

Jana's Journal
Private Entry
Wednesday

The *Copernicus* swung into earth orbit as we prepared to dock with the space factory. The SpaceTech minishuttles were still with us. Ten minutes before we were to dock, a minishuttle pilot noticed a small crack on the skin where the shard had penetrated our ship's hull. She sent pictures to us and to Houston.

The minishuttle pilots were given the option of leaving us because their crafts could be destroyed by the ensuing dust cloud if the *Copernicus* blew apart. They all elected to stay.

None of our monitors registered any danger. After consultation with Houston and after alerting the space factory, Mission Control determined that we should dock as planned. We already had been in our space suits. Lauren and I duct taped that entire wall in hopes it would hold before buckling ourselves into our seats.

Jack and Fawz were at the controls. Jack went for as light a touch as possible, but expectedly the space factory moved slightly. The docking maneuver was practically perfect. The *Copernicus* held together. We disembarked quickly.

Once we were safely in the space factory, we tumbled for joy and hugged, which was fairly awkward in space suits.

I did not know if the space factory had been in danger because of us. The crack in the ship's skin was on the far side away from the factory, so maybe they had not been in danger. The implications were too much to consider. They might have refused to let us dock. In any case, we were here.

Only seven months ago we had drifted away from here, our mission veiled in secrecy. Now, upon our return everyone knew about us. They supposedly did not know specifically where we were.

I had heard that docking areas often were festively decorated, especially for major missions. However, the spaceport was the usual location for a returning solarship, not here. I did not know what to expect.

We passed through the air locks and entered a stark docking area. Not a decoration in sight. What I did not expect was one sole individual dressed in white medical garb. He wore eye goggles, and a surgical mask covered his mouth. He did not introduce himself, but the name on his uniform read, "James Angle, Medical Technician."

"Welcome to the space factory," he said in a monotonous voice as if we had just dropped by from the Space Tech section of the space factory. "Here are some injections you must take." No expression was apparent through his eye goggles. Such a strange technician. What a weird homecoming!

I did not like our reception. A thought popped into my head that I most certainly did not want. James Angle was our executioner. The end came right here, right now. I hoped I was wrong. There were four of us. We could overpower him.

Jack must have been picking up my brain waves for he said, "It's okay, Jana."

We took off our space suits which we had worn for the docking and transfer maneuver and rolled up the sleeves of our daywear. We were jabbed in both arms with various needles. "What's this?" I asked.

James Angle read the names on the vials: "Vebramycin, amantadine, and clatromazole."

Lauren said, "They're antibacterial, antiviral, and a type of fungicide. We don't need any of this. We're the most germ-free people anybody would want to see, but it won't hurt us."

It would not hurt us if it were what the labels read, but it could be anything. We were given huge pills to swallow, the size of which should have required gravitational assistance. I struggled to get my pills down.

James Angle abruptly left the room. If we started keeling over one at a time, then I would know. But what could I do? Prick my finger and write in blood, my blood but the similar blood all humans share: "The Zalandans are people like us, kind and loving. Do not harm them."

Fawz floated over to the door and grasped the handle. We all made eye contact, but no one spoke. After coming so far, was this the moment of truth? He turned the handle, and the door opened easily. That was reassuring. We were not prisoners in this docking area, and we were not going to be done in, at least not here.

None of us felt much like talking. I thought the room might be bugged, and that somebody could be judging us and deciding whether we should live or die.

The medical technician returned, carrying four Velcro-handled sacks of food. He stuck the sacks on a wall track and disappeared. After retrieving my sack, I was pleased that it contained my favorite space foods. We had depleted our stock of these choice tidbits months before reaching Zalanda. Someone cared about us. With that reassurance, I calmed down and almost enjoyed my meal. Luckily, I was finished eating when I thought about a prisoner's last meal before the execution.

James Angle returned and led us through several corridors to another air lock and into a space taxi, a medium sized older one, not the oldest, yet one that had no distinction to call attention to itself. We buckled ourselves in. A pilot and navigator boarded the shuttle and greeted us warmly. They both knew Jack and one knew Fawz. Things seemed more normal now.

"You always did get the plum assignments," one pilot said to Jack.

The other said, "We'll be taking you to Edwards."

"Why not Kennedy?" Jack asked. At that moment, I saw the look of genuine concern on his face. It made me shiver since Jack is mostly fearless.

"I don't know. There are security issues. Very few people know you're on this taxi, and most would expect you at Kennedy. The weather today is ideal at both locations. Whoever planned this operation seems to be hoping surprise will minimize your risks."

I interpreted his answer as sincere.

"You'll be the only passengers," the navigator said.

"I resisted the urge to ask, "Is this taxi going to blow up?" Somehow, labeling my fears so concisely made me giggle.

"How long do we stay in California?" Jack asked.

"We don't know anything about your schedule after Edwards. This whole operation is a few ratchets above Top Secret. If the term 'need to know' ever applied, it applies now."

Lauren said, "The technician James Angle was very strange."

The pilot chuckled. "We ran into him in the corridor. He was practically shaking, babbling about meeting real heroes. He's not much with social skills. Sometimes, he clams up. Did he withdraw into his shell?"

"I guess so," Lauren replied. She looked so pensive before she said, "I hope that won't happen to me."

I thought, "Oh Lauren, you could have stayed on Zalanda with Chri Anri."

Fawz took her hand and tenderly said, "Let him be a joyful memory and go forward."

Lauren and I worried about survival in different ways. She was concerned about the quality of her life without Chri Anri, and I was concerned with actual, physical survival.

As soon as the pilot got the go ahead to undock, we drifted away. When the shuttle rotated, from my window, I saw Earth in all its fragile beauty. It supported life naturally on its own.

I did not tell myself to calm down. It just happened. My fears dissipated. The oceans and land masses were clearly defined. Water, the thin layer of soil, a larger layer of air and creatures who thrived on that mix. As we drew closer, it all looked blue, green, and brown with only an occasional cloud cover. Houston was down there. I was going home to blue skies, clear water, green grass, my home planet.

Another softer voice in my head said, I have a second home now, too, an ice planet circling around Jupiter. That is beautiful, too, but so different.

I had been looking out the window the whole time. Green was moving by fast. We were getting lower and lower. Then the wheels were let down and we touched down, rather gently for something as big as the taxi.

I was aware of something pulling me, holding me to my seat, even after I had undone the seat belts. It pulled on me so hard, and my muscles had to resist. It was gravity, and I did not like it. I suddenly was thankful we faithfully had done all of our fitness exercises every day with the exception of this past Saturday.

We shook hands with the pilot and navigator, patted each other on the shoulders, and hugged. It was a festive moment.

The pilot unlatched the door, and down below all was quiet. Not a soul was there to greet us. The navigator let down the stairs and popped up the hand rail. As I stepped out of the taxi, the sun felt so oppressively hot. Gravity and the sun both assaulted me. I did not want to tumble down the steps. I concentrated on each step as I held tightly onto the rail with one hand and shielded my forehead from the sun with my other hand. The sun was almost blinding.

In the distance a jeep was speeding in our direction. It stopped, and a passenger in full military regalia leapt out and strode toward us. Jack introduced us to the base commander. He greeted us warmly with what I thought was a lovely prepared speech.

Two vans pulled up near the shuttle, and about ten people rushed forward across the airstrip. Then I saw my parents. I hugged my Mom and Dad. It was nice to feel wanted.

My mom said, "I thought we would never see you again." My mom had not cried in front of me before.

"You look wonderful," Dad said. They looked haggard.

She said, "It's so good to see you face to face. Did the Zalandans take good care of you?"

"Oh yes, the best possible care."

My Dad announced, "We will be going to Rhatania."

Rhatania, Fawz's country. Why not stay in the United States? What was wrong with going home? My head was whirring around. It was like being in a fast forward movie. Maybe, it was the heat coming up off the runway. Maybe, it was the gravity. I was vaguely aware that Jack was surrounded by his wife and kids. Lauren was hugging her family. Fawz talked very fast to an older man in a flowing robe and headgear, the same kind of native garb Fawz wore at his luncheon in Houston. That seemed like a long time ago. We were introduced to the older man, Fawz's father, the King of Rhatania. He shook each of our hands and said wonderful things about how brave we were and how we were the people who made legends. The King had the same trait as Jack, a gift to make someone feel wonderful and important with just a few words.

I had become so accustomed to Fawz that I did not think of him as a prince. I was not sure how to handle being around a king. I would try to think of him as Fawz's dad rather than a king. That same technique had worked last year when I had first met Fawz. I remembered telling myself to think of him as Jack's friend.

There was a brief photo session. Then, our families were whisked away in the vans to a waiting plane on another runway for the trip to Rhatania. After we boarded the plane, Fawz's dad said to him, "A fine banquet tonight, a good night's rest, and then tomorrow you will meet with the press. That meeting is crucial. We do not want to put it off any longer than necessary."

"We're pretty tired, sir. We've been on the *Copernicus*, the space factory, a space taxi, and now your jet all in one day."

"Madame President and I thought the safest thing was to keep you moving and have you in a safe place before anyone could figure out the schedule."

"We appreciate all of your precautions. Everything worked perfectly so far. However, it has been a long wake cycle already. It would help the weary travelers to keep the banquet tonight short." Fawz spoke firmly but still in a deferential manner.

"I have already thought about that, minimum speeches, no entertainment. Darwin Industries requested a video hookup tonight to wish us well. I believe they are trying to take credit for the rescue. If they had been more careful in the first place . . . . We have agreed to a brief video visit. Besides our normal banquet guests, our inner circle, I have invited some people who were instrumental in saving your lives. The Kazimier sent his regrets. He has his hands full with the embezzlement problem caused by the terrorist. We will do a video hookup with the Kazimier, too."

Fawz and his Dad switched into a foreign language, Rhatanian, I presumed. It seemed neither was aware they had changed languages right in the middle of a conversation. They switched just as easily as I've seen the Zalandans go from halting English into their native humming.

Once buckled in leather seats arranged like a long, narrow living room, the plane took off and reached cruising altitude most rapidly. Fawz's dad turned his attention toward his guests, and we quickly were enveloped in a warm, pleasant conversation. I felt truly safe for the first time in five days. After a short time, Fawz's dad announced he would fly the plane himself for the rest of the journey. He went into the cockpit.

I rambled on to my parents, giving them a day by day description of our visit with the Zalandans. I finally took a breath and asked them if they had seen Alan.

They looked at each other a second too long before Mom said, "No, we haven't seen him."

I tried to read their minds. They were worried, but not for me, for Alan. "Okay, tell me."

"Jana, it could be nothing. We don't want to worry you."

I waited. Finally Dad continued. "There was a seat for Alan on this plane. As far as we know, he intended to board."

"I've thoroughly embarrassed him, and he doesn't want to see me."

"He'll get over it," Mom said. I had not seen my mom in many months, but those words were not like her. Where had my sympathetic Mom gone? There was more to this than Alan missing the plane.

Dad said, "In Houston, the pilot held up the plane for a short time waiting for him. We called his home. His mother said that he had gotten a phone call earlier in the day and left immediately. He has not been heard from since the call. Because of his close ties with you, the CIA is now involved in trying to find him."

Alan not wanting to see me sounded like a better alternative than being missing. I found myself so hoping that he was okay. I would mentally hunker down and live with the possibility that Alan could be in danger. It had not occurred to me that my reading about Alan on the net could place him in the cross hairs of those plotting against us. I hoped the CIA would find him and protect him the way the four of us now were being protected.

Jana's Journal
Private Entry
Thursday

We flew over the Pacific Ocean for long time. At some point we crossed the International Date Line, and Wednesday magically became Thursday. I learned that a rescue plane had been flying about five minutes behind us for the entire flight. It was protocol for whenever the King flew. I munched on warm mixed nuts and dozed on occasion. When I awoke from one nap, we were served a delicious meal of real food that did not float off the plate. We flew over rolling hills and eventually above high, craggy, mysterious mountains. After clearing a particularly steep mountain, below us on a plateau and surrounded by more mountains were three magical castles with tall spires. I thought, "These castles are reaching for the heavens, and Fawz, the native son has found his bit of heaven beyond the asteroids."

The plane swooped almost straight down, reminding me of the weightless maneuver in the KC135X. For sheer thrill appeal, the descent ranked with the hopper liftoff from Kennedy seven months ago and the space taxi reentry into the atmosphere today. The solarship maneuvers all the way to Zalanda and back, even our evasive action above the fiery lander four days ago, had been milder in comparison to this descent. I looked over at my mom and she, the good pilot, said, "Wow."

I knew she liked that descent. I on the other hand tried to concentrate on the view.

We landed very quickly on the shortest runway I can remember. Fawz's dad emerged from the cockpit appearing exhilarated. As we filed off the plane, Fawz bolted away from the group toward a young woman in native dress who held a squirmy toddler in one arm. A three or four year old held her other hand, and in the child's free hand was a bouquet of flowers. She and the children were a safe distance from the runway, but still I recognized Regney from that party at Jack's house.

Fawz's Dad announced, "This is our summer retreat. We vacation here, but it's also a place for governmental meetings. The third castle is often available as a conference center."

People were commenting about how beautiful it was. Fawz's dad said this place primarily could be reached by air unless one wished to travel on winding unpaved roads. Hikers also found it a good destination.

Fawz's dad chuckled gleefully. "We picked this place for our press conference because of its seclusion. None of the reporters know this location. They will be flown here from our capitol tomorrow. Right now in our capitol a final security-stability check is being run on every reporter."

Fawz's father seemed pleased with his thoroughness but a shiver ran up my spine. All this security meant we were not out of danger yet. We walked toward the largest of the three castles through a formal, symmetrical garden between box hedges which framed bright exotic flowers. The air was thinner here than either in the spaceship or back on Zalanda. Walking was an effort again after living in microgravity. I concentrated on walking and breathing. It seemed strange to be concentrating on two natural things. The odor of the flowers was so pungent. Instead of enjoying the flowery perfumes, I reacted almost as if the air were contaminated. The air on Zalanda was so pure and clean, something I did not even appreciate then.

The sun seemed to be in almost the same place in the sky as when we left Edwards Air Force Base in California. The plane and the sun had both traveled west in tandem, and now day was extended for almost the length of the plane trip.

A strange feeling was sweeping over me. In the midst of all this beauty, I was missing Zalanda and their perfectly controlled environment. I was lonely for Chri Anri, Svee Dee, Sedra, Chri Anri the Elder and several of the other Zalandans. I glanced over at Lauren and could almost read identical feeling. No, hers were more intense. She had lost Chri Anri, her true love. I tried to pick up more of her thought waves, but there were too many people not tuned in for me to concentrate any more.

That evening passed rather rapidly. First, we went to our rooms to rest and to prepare for the banquet. I took a long, warm relaxing shower and chose from an assortment of spiffy bath gels and shampoos. What a luxury, and what a huge difference from bathing on the *Copernicus*.

After admiring the view, the room, and the palatial furnishings, my loneliness intensified. It was a vague, jumbled loneliness: for my crew Fawz, Lauren, and Jack whom I had shared close quarters with for so long on a journey that could not ever be replicated, for the Zalandans whom I probably would never see again, but most of all for Alan.

I had lived constantly with being lonely for Alan, a background feeling that I was almost accustomed to, a screensaver of the soul, but this was different. Alan knew the plane he chose not to board would have brought him to me. What kept him from boarding? What possibly could have been so important? Except for the obvious that he did not want to see me. And that crossed the boundary from intensification of the loneliness to outright loss.

He received a phone call, and that was more important than boarding the plane. Or there was the other thing that I dared not even think, that he was in danger?

After a few minutes, I searched out my parents' room. With them, the loneliness, loss, and gloom faded as happiness bubbled forth for seeing my family and for knowing my crew had survived safely so far.

"Despite everything that happened, I'm glad you gave your permission for this mission. Are you sorry you gave your blessing?"

"If you had not gone, the mission may have turned out quite differently. You were the one who saw the first Zalandan. If you had not gone out in the snow, they may have decided not to be discovered."

"I appreciate that evaluation. However, they were planning to come out and meet us. My actions merely advanced their schedule by a few days."

"They may have reconsidered and decided not to do it. Their revealing themselves to you was fraught with yet unknown repercussions."

One of the many good things about my parents was they usually saw me and my actions in the best possible light. While they were acting so positive, I decided to mention something that disturbed me.

"I read my journal for the world to hear about how I tried to manipulate you into letting me go."

"That helped convince people you were who you said you were."

"A weasel?"

My dad laughed, "No, merely a person who desperately wanted to do something more than anything in the world and a person willing to live with or die with whatever results those actions lead to."

"In the past, sometimes, I hated you for saying no."

"Of course!"

"But you came through when it really counted." I hugged Mom and Dad and asked, "May I go live on another planet."

Neither one was sure if I was joking or not. Come to think about it, the words just popped out, and I, myself, didn't know if I was joking.

"You proved you're capable of making your own decisions and living by them," Dad said in his most serious voice.

At the banquet that night, Jack, Fawz, Lauren, and I wore our NASA daywear. In addition, Fawz wore his native headgear with brightly covered scarves trailing, and somehow it looked like it was meant to be that way. As the four of us entered a large banquet room, everybody in the room stood up and cheered. We sat at a low table of honor on bright, puffy pillows. There must have been eighty or ninety people, many in the native costume of Fawz's country. I remembered the Chancellor from the party at Jack's house. Some were from a neighboring country. At our table was Fawz's father, Fawz's wife Regney, the chief aeronautical minister, the head of state from the neighboring country, the four of us, and four empty places. Fawz's father indicated the empty places and said that another plane was due in momentarily. Food had not yet been served, not even appetizers or rolls. I certainly could have used a Zalandan wafer right about then. However, the special beverage was at every place although I noticed no one had touched the drink, yet. I sipped on water, figuring there was protocol involving the beverage.

To the right of the head table and slightly forward was the podium. One person after another stood up and gave speeches which were translated into English. Most of the speeches stressed our bravery and the advantages of the two planets working in cooperation. A few speakers hinted that we still were in danger and that they hoped the reporters at the press conference tomorrow would diffuse the dangerous situation and not intensify it. Fear welled up inside me. And I thought to myself, there I go, getting afraid again. What kind of astronaut am I anyway, surely a fraud.

Then the other thought came back to me that was so powerful that I almost leapt off the pillow. It's okay to be afraid. It's normal and even sensible to be afraid. I thought of all the times my heart did somersaults with fear. Somehow, I thought I would be a real astronaut if I could get over being afraid, as if being fearless would instantly qualify me as a real astronaut in my heart to myself.

I had been a real astronaut all along, even with my fear. That was the key, being fearful but doing what needed to be done anyway. As long as my fear did not paralyze me into inactivity, then it was okay to be afraid. I had been through this thought process before and now realized that I might go through it every now and then, and that was okay, too.

I felt eyes boring down upon me. I looked up and met my mother's eyes. She was nodding and smiling slightly. I thought to her, "You're reading my thoughts, aren't you, and you're happy that I know what you've tried to tell me. You probably don't understand you're reading my thoughts but just that we're sharing this moment, as pilot and astronaut, as mother and daughter."

Then, the people were on their feet, cheering again. I scrambled over to Mom and gave her a hug. I hugged my Dad, too. In the earthbound world, there must have been plenty of times he was afraid, like waiting for his wife to come home from testing an experimental jet and then later waiting for his only kid to come home from a strange planet.

The cheers were growing louder. I scooted back to my pillow at the head table. The people were chanting. It sounded like "Maaax, Maaax." Someone had entered. It was Max Marsh, waving his cowboy hat in the air. He wore a spiffy black western-cut suit and looked quite handsome. This was the first time I had seen him dressed in anything other than blue jeans and a faded plaid shirt. Max was special to me, but now he was special to all of us.

The man who served as both master of ceremonies and translator left the podium and went over to Max. As he was leading Max over to the head table, the King stood up and strode over to meet Max. The master of ceremonies backed away as Max and the King spoke privately for a few minutes. A hush fell over the room. Then the King pointed Max in the direction of the podium. There was more cheering for both of them.

Max sauntered over to the microphone, hat in hand, cowboy boots shined for the first time that I had seen him in shiny boots. "Your accolades are appreciated. However, I must say I merely was doing my job. When the Kazimier came to me on Friday, I checked some celestial coordinates that he gave me. I was surprised. How could someone outside of NASA know of the flight path of a secret mission?"

Max explained how difficult it was to find an object in space as small as the *Copernicus*, especially when it was using techniques to avoid detection. As much as I wanted to hear everything Max had to say, I was extremely hungry and hoped for dinner to begin.

. Three people I did not recognize were ushered toward the podium. They were introduced as George and Marge MacInturff of Seattle, Washington, and Russell Ramsey of Webster, Texas. Russell was quite good looking, but from his manner I surmised he was not aware of his looks.

The King said, "These people have traveled far to be with us tonight and are probably tired and hungry. Before the food is served, our guests are most anxious to hear about their experiences."

George MacInturff looked a little stunned by the surroundings but acclimated quickly. He spoke in a clear, confident voice. "Net surfing is a great joy. I'm pleased that because of this passion, I found the broadcast from the *Copernicus*. It was the merest stroke of luck that I found the flicker on the screen. The good that happened because of this, I defer to my wife Marge, the most persuasive person I know. She convinced the TV stations to play the message from space, and you know what happened from there."

Marge MacInturff waved at the audience. She started to back away from the microphone without saying anything, but then she spoke. "At first, I did not believe George was picking up a broadcast from a solarship. I called the TV stations because George asked me to do it and because he convinced me that what he saw was authentic. I did not call just because George promised to take me some place quite spectacular."

"After I called the TV stations, I called my friend Russell before contacting other friends." She nodded toward the young man next to her. "I didn't know that he could deactivate the explosives."

She quickly backed away from the microphone, and all eyes turned toward Russell. Before he could speak the King stood and said, "Russell Ramsey, you are directly involved with saving our astronauts. You deactivated the explosives in the LandSkyTech probe, thus keeping the ensuing explosion smaller and preventing it from engulfing the *Copernicus*. Would you care to say a few words?"

Russell moved forward toward the microphone. He seemed to be a confident person but one unaccustomed to attention. "I'm glad I was in the position to help." He started to move away but then added, "Because Marge MacInturff called me, I got out of my apartment fast and evaded the LandSkyTech people before the astronaut's message played on TV." He started to move away again but then said, "I was toward the end of a chain of people who helped. The Kazimier risked loss of his prestige by alerting Dr. Max Marsh of the potential danger; Dr. Marsh did not brush off the Kazimier's concerns but instead checked out the situation and then risked his career by alerting the astronauts; the astronauts put forth great effort to save themselves. Bob Sandstrom of Darwin Industries believed what I told him and gave me a chance to help, and Eric, a great Darwin programmer, worked so hard with me to deactivate the explosives. I thought deactivation would be easy, but that didn't prove to be the case." Russell looked around at the audience. "Now I will tell you what few people outside of NASA know. I did not fully deactivate the explosives. I went for a soft explosion, and how did I know to do this? I had help from a descendant of ancient Rhatanians, a Zalandan named Chri Anri who sent an electronic message to JSC telling them what to do. I didn't know the message was from a Zalandan so I modified his calculations slightly, almost causing a disaster. However, a physicist named Venzi Suzaky came through in the end and corrected a timing problem by using the advanced computer aboard the *Copernicus*. And that, honored guests, is some of what happened this past Friday and Saturday."

People were clapping and cheering. I was shocked. In a matter of minutes, Russell had managed to reveal much classified information. I hoped the Rhatanians did not understand what he meant about Max risking his career.

Still, we were alive tonight in large part because of Russell and the MacInturffs. Those three people did not know us and did not even work at NASA. They were doing the job of being good citizens. I felt a bond with them. It seemed like a Zalandan thing to do, no, a human thing to do. If we had not broadcast over the Supernet, they would not have known we needed help. Yet, if we had not launched the lander, their help would have been in vain.

The moderator directed them toward the head table. Russell sat next to me. I thanked him profusely for all of his work on our behalf. I dared not mention top secret things that he had revealed, such as Chri Anri helping JSC and the hint of Max not following protocol. For that matter all of his help on Saturday surely was classified, too.

The King nodded to his spiritual leader who stood up and said a long blessing in Rhatanian. Then, waiters began to file into the banquet room, balancing trays of food on their shoulders. The food, reminiscent of the luncheon at Fawz's apartment in Houston many months ago, included delicate leaves wrapped around vegetables and an exotic variety of rice molded into the shape of the *Copernicus*.

It smelled and looked so good. Jack whispered to me about trying everything so as to not offend our host. I felt an envelope of security, like an island of safety between the trip back to earth and the press interview tomorrow that I had begun to dread.

Russell was talkative. He and Max had flown from Houston to Seattle where they picked up the MacInturffs before proceeding over the Pacific on the journey to Rhatania.

He told me the FBI and CIA were concerned that four people who had partial knowledge of the attempted sabotage had left the country. However, Max, the MacInturffs, and Russell already had made extensive statements to both the FBI and CIA. None were told not to leave the country. The MacInturffs had made the mistake of returning a phone call to the FBI before disembarking from the plane this evening; the FBI wanted them to stay on the plane and immediately return to the US. After phone conversations between the CIA and various officials in the Rhatanian government, an agreement was reached that Max, the MacInturffs, and Russell would all return to the US early tomorrow to render whatever assistance they could. However, that was quickly superseded. Homeland Security was coming here instead to interview them and to advise the astronauts.

I was not being much of a dinner companion. It was like the wake cycle had extended right into the middle of the sleep cycle. Russell did not seem to mind that I was rather quiet. He cheerfully chattered. His voice helped me relax. He also seemed totally recovered from his dismay about incorrectly changing Chri Anri's calculations on Saturday. I wondered if that was why he made a public declaration about changing the numbers. Was it a public confession? Whoa, tonight, I could turn off being analytical and just relax and let him talk.

He told me that his girlfriend had made him a dress out of her window draperies and disguised him as a woman. He said, "Women's shoes are very painful." He added, "I wish she could be here tonight, but this trip was top secret. I couldn't tell her I was going."

I had just taken a gulp of water and almost choked when he said that. He asked me if I was okay and I nodded. I still would not comment about what he said at the podium. He studied me a moment before he asked, "Do you know what the inner circle means?"

"I guess it means close friends," I replied, recalling that the King said the inner circle would attend the banquet tonight.

"It means that and more." Russell put his hand over my water glass. "I don't want you to choke again. The Rhatanians here know that whatever is said tonight will not leave this room. Inner circle is their equivalent to our top secret. None of these people will reveal that you and the other astronauts are here. Have you noticed that no one is taking pictures? No one is sending pictures to friends."

"I noticed."

You will recall that the King spoke immediately before I did."

"Yes."

"Something he said or did was a double code. I had previously asked permission to tell that Chri Anri helped me. I thought the Rhatanians would be happy to know. Permission was granted, and all my words were elevated to the highest level of secrecy."

"I totally missed that exchange. I wish we didn't need this secrecy, but they're trying to protect us. They're trying to protect you."

"I know." Russell dropped his voice to a whisper. "You, all four of you, discovered and released huge secrets about both worlds."

"We really did, didn't we? The Zalandans wanted it done. The US government wanted to do it, and now the Rhatanian government is happy, too, because Prince Fawzshen returned home safely."

"The Zalandans tried telling the whole world in 1994 about their existence. I've been reading a summary of your journal."

"Ah, you mean the Comet Shoemaker-Levy 9 fragments. The Zalandans thought that would be a clear sign for Earthlings. They said, 'Here we are.' No one on Earth was ready to interpret the message."

"What about the security leak a month ago? I didn't pay attention to it. Someone wanted to tell everybody."

"That was horrible. Somebody wanted to impress one person. It turned out to be the wrong person."

"I'm all ears."

"Sorry. Even with your high level of security, I can't tell you." Our crew had found out recently. When I took the sled ride with Svee Dee, a flight controller at JSC quietly called his new fiancée. He swore her to secrecy. She called her cousin who also was sworn to secrecy. The cousin just happened to live next door to a news reporter whom she could not resist telling. It grew and mutated exponentially from there.

Russell did not seem to mind that I would not tell him. He asked, "When the secret broke, is that when Jim Landres found out about the mission?"

"The investigators think so. He might have known earlier. Some JSC people are involved."

"Before I accept another job, I'm going to check it out so carefully and not end up almost being responsible for . . . ." Russell's voice quavered. "I'm going to look into every owner's background and the goal of the project I'm working on. For that matter, the goals of all the projects in the company. A week ago, I thought a job's a job. Not anymore. It's important to know whom I'm working for and what's the purpose of the work they do. When I see the four of you and realize what I almost did, it makes me see jobs in a different light. "

I hardly knew how to respond. I could have said that the stated goal was to explore Saturn, but that response seemed puny. I thought of several things to say but finally settled on the truth. "I totally agree with you, Russell." I slightly changed the subject. "Do you think your disguise helped you evade the LandSkyTech people?"

"I think it did. When I went inside Darwin Industries on Saturday morning, two men were sitting in a car near the entrance. I recognized them, but I didn't want them to recognize me. I glanced away, the way a woman would do, and concentrated on walking like a woman. "

"Wish I had seen that," I said.

From his pocket, Russell removed a picture torn from a magazine cover. It was of four people. "These two men are thugs who work for Jim Landres. This is an El Lago police officer, and the woman is Sharleen Rothwell, an employee of LandSkyTech. Rumor has it that she captured these two thugs single-handedly.

"My apartment manager gave me the magazine. The thugs were waiting for me early Saturday morning. Afterwards, they must have gone after Sharleen. I couldn't have captured them even though I'm young and strong."

I examined the photo carefully. Sharleen Rothwell was beautifully dressed in a peach suit and perfectly groomed. "Maybe, that policeman plus a couple other officers had something to do with the thugs' capture," I suggested.

Russell laughed, "I thought the same thing."

"What about the ones waiting in the car at Darwin Industries?"

"They were different, but I've seen them at LST, too. I'm glad I showed up in a borrowed car wearing a red dress and blond wig."

"Were you scared helping us on Saturday?" I asked. It was a rude question but I thought he would answer me truthfully.

"I didn't have time to be scared. There was too much to do. Until it was all over." He thought a moment and asked, "How was it for you on Saturday?"

"It was the same. There was too much to do. Other times, I was scared."

He studied me a minute. "You went outside the lander, the *Falcon*, on Ganymede alone to meet an alien. I think you don't have a scared gene in your body."

After dinner, from large video screens behind the head table, the Kazimier in Houston offered a benediction. When it was over, the King cordially expressed his appreciation to the Kazimier.

Also from Houston, Charlie Darwin, the owner, and Bob Sandstrom, the general manager, of Darwin Industries wished us well. I knew that the King held Darwin partially responsible because they had not checked out LandSkyTech and its owner, Jim Landres, more carefully. From what I had overheard on the plane, what dismayed the King the most was that Darwin Industries had not compared the final submitted drawings with the pre-launch X-rays of the Saturn probe. Despite the King's feelings, he politely thanked them both for their assistance on Saturday.

After the banquet, people stayed and talked. I expressed my gratitude to the MacInturffs. George said his biggest inspiration to help was my love for Alan. He wanted me to return safely to my love. I could not possibly tell him that Alan chose not to board the plane that would bring him to me.

The more I tried not to think of Alan the more I saw him before me. We said farewell under a SpaceTech moon. I closed my eyes, magically hoping he would stroll into this banquet room. I opened my eyes, and he was not here.

I examined the facts. Alan was scheduled to fly on the plane with the families. He did not cancel. He simply did not show up. That was not like Alan.

Before the flight, he had received a phone call and immediately went somewhere. The call may have been related to his not boarding the plane. At present, other ideas were supposition.

I looked for Fawz. He was surrounded by a group of Rhatanians who were hanging onto every word he said. He left the group and came over to me. After I told him how lovely the banquet was, I said, "Alan would have cancelled. I'm concerned. He could be in danger."

He said, "We've thought of that, Jana. Homeland Security is looking for him."

"It also could be that he doesn't want to see me."

He patted me on the shoulder and said, "People sometimes make foolish decisions."

"What should I do?"

He thought a moment before he answered. "For the time being, let him make the first move. Let him contact you."

"How long should I wait?"

"Give him three or four days."

I thanked Fawz. I had a plan. After those few days of waiting, I would track Alan to the ends of the world. He was not an astronaut. He could not leave Earth. I would find him, and I would grovel, if necessary. I was thinking in hyperboles, but it made me feel good. I felt exhilarated. I would get Alan back.

Jana's Journal
Private Entry
Friday Morning

I briefly considered pleading sick and missing the press conference. I did not want to meet with the reporters. Suppose I said something stupid and jeopardized the Zalandans or ourselves.

The King had hired a media advisor named Helmut from Germany to help prepare us for the press conference. Helmut decided I was the token kid. "Guileless" was his word. He showed me facial exercises to practice to achieve an expression of wide-eyed wonder. I hated it.

The clothes he selected for me were worse than his advice. I wore a blue and white dress with stiff petticoats. Even more insulting was the big bow in my hair. After the comfort of the NASA clothes and the even greater comfort of the Zalandan body suits, this outfit was scratchy, only suitable for a kid too young to revolt. I felt like a giant toddler.

I arrived at the small auditorium where the press conference would be held later in the morning. We were getting together here before proceeding to our breakfast meeting. The stadium seating held about 45 people although there would be 20 reporters. Like the rest of this castle, the auditorium exuded the feeling of another century, making it quite suitable for a conference pertaining to another world. I was the first one there. On the stage was a table for five speakers.

I sat down in the audience area in a seat marked with a reporter's name from Houston. The seat reclined and conformed to me. From the wings, Lauren walked onto the stage wearing a low cut, tight emerald green dress. Not that I had anything against emerald green, but she would not have picked out a dress like that. She looked like a gaudy doll. She looked terrible. I never had seen Lauren appear anything other than stunning, even on our mission when we often were really busy. I got up and climbed the few marble steps past an orchestra pit onto the stage and sat at the table next to her in the place marked with Jack's name.

Jack and Fawz roamed in from the back of the auditorium, looking over a sheet of paper and pointing to the seating for the reporters. I was ready to join them but Lauren made no effort to budge. Two ushers followed behind them, and Fawz called one of them over to make seating changes.

Fawz was wearing his traditional Rhatanian garb, and then I noticed Jack was wearing cowboy boots and a western cut suit. Had I ever seen Jack in cowboy boots? I could not remember. Then I thought about Helmut. I was the young one, Lauren the glamorous one, and Fawz was the prince. Jack was the Texan.

We were a team. We were astronauts. We were explorers. We needed to be in our NASA day wear, not dressed as Helmut chose.

Lauren covered her microphone and said, "I can't do this."

"Sure you can." I had not bothered to cover my microphone. My words echoed through the auditorium.

Fawz glanced at me and chuckled. "I'm not laughing at what you said. We will have our moderator to protect us from any abuse." Even without a microphone, his voice rang out with perfect clarity. He thought I was giving myself a pep talk.

"Stand up," I whispered to Lauren as I stood up. She complied. I wanted Fawz and Jack to see how ridiculous she and I looked in these costumes. "Now, say something," I whispered.

"The sound in here is amazing," Lauren said as her own voice filled the room.

Fawz glanced over at us and again laughed. "When I was a young child and learning English, I had a storybook. You look exactly like the Little Bo Peep character." Fawz usually was so tactful.

"Your media person Helmut picked out this silly costume," I said indignantly.

"So, that's it. Helmut is not one of our permanent staff, but supposedly an expert in media situations." He glanced at Lauren and frowned ever so slightly. "Let's go to the press conference in our NASA daywear."

"Good idea, Fawz," Jack said and looked toward Lauren.

She nodded in agreement. "That's what I've always worn for press conferences. And if you care to know, Helmut picked out this thing for me. I can barely wait to wash my face."

Then Fawz said to all of us but I felt to me in particular, "If Helmut has given you any ideas that you feel are helpful, use them if you wish. Otherwise, feel free to disregard anything he suggested to you."

"Thank you," I said.

JSC had more substantial ideas on preparing us for the press conference as opposed to our dressing in inappropriate clothes. First of all, JSC and the King had worked together to select top quality reporters from prestigious newspapers. Several were science and aerospace reporters. They were all required to read background material about our mission. They were also required to sign statements saying they would not reveal where they had been taken for the press conference.

We left the auditorium and went to a nearby room where trays of breakfast had been set out for us. The coffee and tea smelled good. Lauren and I still were wearing our foolish clothes.

Each reporter had submitted five questions ahead of time that had been combined and whittled down to a total of 64. JSC had worked around the clock preparing answers for us.

Last night, tucked in a large, comfortable bed, propped by fluffy pillows that did not float away, I had read the questions and answers until I fell asleep. Now, as we sat in that room eating real food, we reviewed the answers. We made a few changes, put those changes onto a computer, and sent the document back to JSC for approval.

The reporters would receive the questions and answers in their packets. During the press conference, we were free to answer these same questions any way we wanted. The reporters were free to ask us anything else.

While going through the questions and answers, even though I was reading and thinking as fast as I could, one answer stood out as clearly as anything. "No evidence whatsoever links Astronaut Filbert Grystal to the act of terrorism against the government of the United States and the government of Rhatania. He is not a target of any investigation." I was stunned, but there was not time to dwell on him now.

We had our own rules that the reporters would not know. Our tasks were to make NASA look like an exemplary agency as well as to make us look like responsible astronauts. However, we felt our most important tasks were protecting the Zalandans and making them look like the kind, loving, non-aggressive human beings that they were. Of the 64 questions, there was not one about whether the Zalandans could be a danger to people on earth. We needed to dispel the idea about their being a danger, but we could not bring it up. We needed to wait patiently for a reporter to ask the question. We called that the 64,000-dollar question.

JSC had retroactively approved everything that we did on the mission, including reading my journal and including the delay in their being notified that we were in jeopardy. The reporters did not and would not know we had delayed notifying JSC.

Lauren asked, "If we do good work with the press conference, do you think we'll keep our jobs?"

Jack said, "I imagine that decision has already been made." Quietly, almost to himself, he said, "I love my job."

I so wanted Jack and Lauren to keep their jobs. We had gone public instead of asking JSC for help first. Because of what we did, our mission was saved. We were saved. The existence of the Zalandans was made public. They wanted their existence known, or they would not have tweaked the comet in such a dramatic manner. Would JSC see things the same way?

As for me, I had signed a contract for one mission and one mission only. I wanted to continue being an astronaut, but I had gone out in the snow on Zalanda and gone off with a Zalandan. That was when the secret first had leaked at JSC.

We went back to our rooms to change for the press conference. Even though I had been concentrating deeply while reading the material, I could not forget the itchy, scratchy dress I wore.

Dressed in our NASA daywear, we waited in the wings outside the stage area of the auditorium with my parents, Jack's family, Lauren's parents, Princess Regney, and that Helmut person. A live orchestra played the Rhatanian National Anthem as the King entered the stage. He made a short welcoming speech to the press, telling them how each reporter had been individually selected, based on his or her esteemed reputation. Then we marched onto the stage right before the orchestra began *The Star Spangled Banner*. We stood at attention. When the anthem ended, the reporters clapped politely, not anything like the enthusiastic cheers that greeted us last night.

The master of ceremonies from last night's banquet was the moderator. His presence quickly alleviated some of my apprehension. After he introduced us to the press, we each read statements about how beneficial our mission would be to all the citizens of the world. I breathed deeply.

The moderator ran a highly edited version of a video we had made about life in the Zalandan complex. When the film was over, Fawz promised a souvenir copy to each reporter.

The moderator reminded the reporters about questions they had submitted beforehand but also said they were free to ask anything.

"Why are all of you here in Rhatania in this resort city hidden away, rather than in Houston where most of you live?"

"Due to circumstances we could no longer control, our people learned far ahead of time about the surprise planned for our three-thousandth anniversary. We decided our people would enjoy a surprise right now by meeting the other three astronauts fresh off the mission: our Commander as well as the Commander of the Mars I Mission, Jackson Medwin; astronaut Jana Novacek who traces her lineage through the Zalandans right back to the ancient Rhatanians; and astronaut Lauren Adams who gave us so much hope through her wide range of historic expertise that ancient people were smart, creative, and inventive and that they could accomplish space flight. I'll not forget her examples of modern times, from the first flight of an airplane at Kitty Hawk, North Carolina USA in 1903 until the landing of a man on the moon in 1969, the timespan was only 66 years. Modern man has existed at least 100,000 years.

"People will be hiking in to meet the astronauts. This is a choice destination for hikers."

In Fawz's capable hands, a lie sounded truthful. We were here in this lovely, isolated city solely for protection from Jim Landres and whatever other terrorists were involved with him. Homeland Security wanted to get more of a handle on the investigation. Madame President wanted them to get busy so we could come home, but there were no clues. Landres had simply disappeared.

Jack answered the next question about the status of the investigation. "We have not found Jim Landres yet. We think he is still in the US, maybe still in Texas, but he could be anywhere. Every border crossing has a picture of him. Every airport has a picture of him. That's why we think he is still in the US. We could be wrong. Please distribute your pictures of him everywhere you can. He wears contact lenses. His eyes could be a different color. His hair could be a different color."

The next question was directed at me. "Why hasn't Filbert Grystal been arrested yet?"

We all were well prepared for that question. I had written so much against him in my journal that I had read over the net. We also knew we would be asked this question. "Filbert Grystal was the supervisor of the programmer who was arrested, Denise Morneau. She had given him an altered program to send to the *Copernicus*. A correct version of the program had been checked off as complete and ready to go." I had memorized my answer. I slowed down to pace myself. "She claims she had been influenced by Lincoln Listle. He had approached her under the identity of a CIA agent. Was she working with him as a terrorist or had she been tricked by him? It is a complex issue. The altered program uplinked to the *Copernicus* was very important as it supposedly alerted us to micrometeoroids and also in our situation, a bomb. Instead, it deactivated our micrometeoroid protection exactly when we needed it the most."

I did not tell the reporter that Denise claimed Lincoln Listle looked like Jim Landres. From pictures she thought they both were the same person.

The reporter had a follow-up question. "It seems like you don't like Filbert Grystal very much."

"My personal journal was meant for my own reflection."

The reporter requested one more follow-up question. "Are you aware that Filbert Grystal was interviewed on a Houston TV station recently? He admitted that on the day before the *Copernicus* came under attack he had said and I quote, "It might be better if they didn't return." During the interview, he explained that he had been joking and that he meant that all of you liked Zalanda so much, it was a shame the mission was cut short. Were you aware of his comment?"

I pasted on my blandest expression and said, "I was not aware that he made that comment." Something was occurring to me. Filbert probably had said those words to Max on Friday, the day before the bomb destroyed the lander. It was just enough to keep Max from going through the proper channels with the Kazimier's information. Was Filbert now closing ranks and trying to protect Max from being fired? As arrogant and selfish as Filbert was, he was doing the right thing for Max if my thought was correct. Until this moment, I still had thought Filbert could be involved. I realized I had been silent and all of the reporters had their eyes intently focused on me. I said, "People say the darnest things, don't they? I should know. I certainly did in my journal."

The reporters laughed. That was good.

Jack said, "Her journal was enormously helpful. People realized that they could help us and quickly came forward. These people performed heroically. Because the investigation is ongoing, for their protection, we are not releasing their names at this time."

The moderator said, "Next question." We moved on, and that was that.

"Why didn't NASA simply make an announcement and request help."

Jack answered again. "NASA was working at the top level, asking corporations that inadvertently could be involved. We were working at the individual level. JSC couldn't possibly ask every single individual who worked for all of the companies, especially on a Saturday. Some individuals who worked for LandSkyTech realized they had been involved."

Reporters asked more questions about LandSkyTech and Darwin Industries, a launch company. Jack explained the relationship between the two companies. Darwin launched probes and satellites that other companies manufactured. Darwin Industries did not know a bomb was on LandSkyTech's Saturn probe because drawings had been switched. Darwin was supposed to know precisely what it had launched.

Because it was classified as top secret, Jack did not mention Russell Ramsey, the LandSkyTech programmer who had gone to Darwin Industries on Saturday morning disguised as a woman. Jack simply said that Darwin Industries had cooperated fully with JSC in saving our mission. Neither did Jack mention Sharleen Rothwell, the other LandSkyTech employee who had come forward.

A reporter raised his hand and produced a picture. The picture was passed toward the front and one of the ushers handed it to Jack.

"This picture has been in papers all over the world. Can you identify these people?"

Jack said, "I believe most news sources have identified them. As part of the ongoing investigation, I cannot confirm or deny their identity."

I had first learned about the picture from Russell Ramsey at the banquet last night. It was of an El Lago policeman, two thugs who worked for Jim Landres, and Sharleen Rothwell, a contract employee of LandSkyTech. Sharleen had convinced the police officer to break onto JSC grounds to take the thugs to the Director's office. As soon as the picture appeared, Sharleen Rothwell and her child Emily were put under protective custody.

The questions turned to why we made the mission, and Fawz told the reporters about visitors to Rhatania 500 years ago who may have come from the sky. He then produced a replica of the cylinder and the container it rested in. Seeing it practically took my breath away. Fawz handed the cylinder to an usher for the reporters to hold and pass around to each other. Words in ancient Rhatanian filled the room. Fawz translated. "We will meet again beyond the broken and jagged rocks torn asunder."

When the question turned to why I was selected for the mission, Fawz again answered and explained about Hulda, one of the visitors to earth, a teenager who requested to stay behind. A woman walked out onto the stage. Fawz introduced her as an esteemed geneticist from the Rhatanian Technical Institute.

She sat down next to me and turned up her name plate. She told a few jokes and then said that she mainly was going to talk about simple arithmetic. That put everyone at ease. She explained that I was a descendant of Hulda, the teenager who had been left behind over five hundred years ago. The only way at present to know was the BLU2 factor that had shown up in my blood. Both of my parents carried the recessive gene, but that did not show up in their blood.

The chromosome for the recessive gene was known but not the gene's location on the chromosome.

The reporters asked her many questions. She explained that most people who had blue sclera did not have the BLU2 factor and were not descendants of Zalandans. It was simply used as a broad screening tool. In fact, people who had it should be checked by an eye doctor because it could indicate a serious medical condition.

One reporter said, "The Zalandans live a long time, eight or nine hundred years. Hulda could still be alive."

That made the hairs on my arms stands up. What a thought. On Zalanda, I had thought that it all could be possible and that my great grandmother could be Hulda, but now back on Earth, I thought that she was probably a descendant. I had even promised Chri Anri the Elder that I would check it out.

Lauren answered. "They live under pristine conditions, pure air, pure water, and specifically monitored food. They need to live that way because they are away from the nature in which they evolved. They had to be very careful simply to survive. It turned out that they were able to thrive."

The reporter persisted about Hulda's longevity and the geneticist said, "Of the Rhatanians who left earth 2500 years ago, many died. It is likely that those left in the breeding pool were heartier. However, you will recall from your reading material that bacteria, viruses, and fungi are highly controlled on Zalanda. When Hulda came to earth, she encountered many organisms for the first time. That factor also must be considered.

"All we can say for sure is that Jana and her parents are descendants of Hulda. We don't know how many other descendants of Hulda are alive today. It is highly improbable that Hulda is alive, but what an interesting idea. I like it." The geneticist nodded at the reporter who asked the question.

I noticed that several reporters were getting squirmy. It was past time to end the press conference, but we still hoped to say that the

Zalandans meant us no harm. Yet, they were not defenseless if some group or government decided they were a threat. On our private agenda, this was listed as protecting the Zalandans. However, a reporter had to ask us.

Fawz stood up and said, "I believe we could all benefit from a short break. You will find refreshments set up in the lobby outside this auditorium. Please be back in a few minutes. The press conference is almost over."

Most of the reporters left the auditorium. A few sat in their seats. A petite woman surreptitiously took pictures of us.

The break was preplanned if the press conference went long. We stood up and moved around but did not go into the wings to talk to our families. I felt more refreshed. I waved at my parents who now were sitting on folding chairs. More people were now in the wings. Jack whispered that they were from Homeland Security. The orchestra played another movement from Dvorak's New World Symphony.

The reporters all came back at the same time. "Why are the Zalandans not far more advanced scientifically. They had a twenty-five-hundred-year head start."

We took turns explaining the reasons as we perceived them. They had moved from Earth to Mars and then from Mars to Zalanda, both highly complex ventures. They spent their time and energy working on their survival, in itself a huge scientific feat. Now, well settled, there were too few of them to pursue each complicated technological issue that interested them.

Another reporter thought they were considerably advanced and pointed out how they could tweak meteoroids, something we sorely needed to achieve. I said, "Tweaking is easier on Zalanda than it would be on earth because Jupiter acts as the vacuum cleaner."

Jack explained further about Jupiter's gravity pulling in the comets. "The Zalandans keep comets from slamming into their own planet but allow them to slam into Jupiter."

Then came the question we were bracing ourselves for, the 64,000-dollar question. We knew it could be phrased many ways. "These Zalandans are advanced enough that they could take over the earth."

Lauren said, "If that had been their purpose, they would not have waited until people on earth had nuclear weapons. They worked very hard to create a civilization on another planet. That is their home."

The reporter's follow-up question was, "What guarantee do we have that they will stay on Zalanda?"

Fawz spoke. "I will make this very clear. Zalanda is the new land of Rhatania. We Rhatanians consider these people citizens of Rhatania with all of the rights and privileges of citizenship. They can visit Rhatania any time they wish. They can stay as long as they like, or they can all move here if they wish. We as a sovereign nation welcome them.

"They are no threat to the Earth. They will be an immeasurable benefit to our planet."

No one said a word. Finally, the moderator said, "This is a good point to end the press conference unless there is one last question." Every hand shot up. "Who has asked only one question or less?" Only one hand remained.

"There are new solarships at the spaceport that have never been flown, and the US is implementing austerity measures at present. On Zalanda, Old Town is unoccupied. Tourists could visit. Our engineers and scientists could live there and help them with their scientific endeavors. My question is this: Do these things sound feasible?"

Fawz said, "This is an excellent question to end the press conference. A question for the Zalandans. A question for the Rhatanians. A question for the American taxpayers. Or a question for the readers of your paper."

I figured that Fawz could have talked thirty minutes on that question without taking a breath. I was rather surprised at his brief answer until I realized we were on a schedule, and this had indeed been a long press conference. There was a quick picture taking session with the various reporters.

After the press conference, we rushed down corridors to a conference room and were introduced to the team from Homeland Security who had flown in from the Houston office. We all sat around a large oval table. I was surprised at how happy they seemed, and then I found out why. They finally had gotten a break in the case from a four-year-old child who placed Jim Landres solidly in Galveston on Sunday, the day after the lander explosion. Following through, they placed him checking out of the John Sealy Hospital two days later using yet another identity. They had missed him by ten hours.

We were introduced to a young FBI agent named Camille. They were so impressed that she did not let the lead slip through her fingers. They reminded us of the sensitivity of the material before telling us. The receptionist in their Houston office had gotten a call from the four-year-old child in Galveston who had said, "Mommy wants to mail my postcards." The receptionist played along and suggested that the boy listen to his Mommy. The boy then said, "Postcards are mine. Terrorist threw them away." The minute anyone mentioned the word "terrorist," it was the receptionist's job to transfer the call to an agent and not do further screening, even if the caller were a young child. Camille got the call and decided to follow through. "Listen to me very carefully," she instructed the child. "Hide the postcards in a safe place where your mommy can't find them. My name is Camille. Don't show them to anyone else but me. I will be at your house as soon as I can. I need to talk to your Mommy now." The mommy did not come to the phone. Camille ordered the FBI helicopter and flew with her more senior partner to Galveston.

The postcards led them to the terrorist's true identity: Lester Longworth. With painstaking round-the-clock work, they were able to place him as a child in the same neighborhood as Max Marsh and the Kazimier for a short period of time, approximately four months. The agency had developed one theory that something happened during that period between Lester Longworth, Max, and the Kazimier. The agency had acquired photos of when LL was young and had an appointment with the Kazimier as soon as it became morning in the US. At this moment, an FBI agent was interviewing Max here in this castle.

I realized their giggly behavior had disappeared. "None of this leaves the room," the senior agent said. We are dealing with a sociopath who lives with some strange code of behavior. Part of it is to take no prisoners. His code may simply be to cause as much trouble as he can. However, he did zero in on the Kazimier and Johnson Space Center, probably Max Marsh. He is reasonably intelligent, a good swimmer, and highly unpredictable. He understands business and develops his plans as he goes along. He also has posed as a CIA agent."

"Word has filtered down to us that Madame President wants you back in the US. It makes us look bad with you here, like we can't protect you."

Jack said, "We've had the Rhatanian banquet to attend. This was a joint mission. We're ready to return home now."

The agent's face turned slightly red, "Respectfully, Commander, you don't need to play act with us. You're in Rhatania for your own safety. Those reporters didn't buy that window dressing either, or if they did, they're in the wrong business.

"I need all of you to be honest with us. We're here to protect you. We think LL acted alone, but he may have acquired followers along the way.

"We're prepared to offer each of you Secret Service protection around-the-clock. That is a not requirement for returning home, but we strongly recommend it. Please do not try to solve things on your own. Please do not keep things from us."

"What kind of things?" Lauren asked.

"Well, let's see. Say you smuggled a Zalandan aboard the *Copernicus*. That friend of yours, Chi Chi."

An agent sitting next to him with his computer open said, "His name is Chri Anri, sir."

"As long as Chri Anri's here, he's the responsibility of the Rhatanian government. That's fine and dandy. However, if he comes to the US, he will be in need of Secret Service protection. Do you understand me? Whatever it is, come to us."

Lauren suppressed a smile. It was good to see her even want to smile.

"Now, some of you may have secrets. We probably know your secrets already." He looked at Jack who did not change his expression. However, for barely a second Jack glanced toward me. "Do not succumb to blackmail."

"LL must be stopped. He has probably done horrendous things before. He will do them again. Our advantage: he is no longer under the radar. We have his prints, we have his picture, and we have his true identity. His picture is everywhere. Later, we will show you how he can look with theatrical putty, a little bit to change his nose, a little to change his chin, but he cannot change the distance between his eyes.

"I may sound harsh, I have been told, but I assure you those Secret Service agents are a different breed. They will deal with you on a day-to-day basis. They will treat you much more delicately, so do not think they are like me. My people will serve more in the background."

"However, it also is our job to protect you. We have been and will be monitoring your phone calls and other forms of electronic messages. You can opt out of having your electronic communications monitored. Try thinking of it this way: your lives are more important than your privacy. When LL is caught and we determine that his followers, if any, are caught, then you will have your privacy back. If you are dealing with classified NASA material, use their phones and computers. Do not use your own.

"Go ahead and live your lives. LL may have no interest in any of you at this point, but his unpredictability is a problem. You are all friends with Max Marsh. Maybe there is a pattern we don't see. That's why you need to contact us with anything."

There was a knock at the conference room door. Fawz said, "The food has arrived. Do you mind being interrupted while they bring in your lunch?"

One of the agents pushed his chair back and jumped up. "That's a Homeland Security reg. Don't refuse food."

Another said, "Especially in a castle."

The food was all the fancy Rhatanian stuff that the servers had arranged on a wall credenza to form a buffet table. It smelled like real food, not rehydrated packets. I promised myself not to overeat.

The agent in charge was not through yet. "We need to know what you are going to do before you do it. That's our job to figure you out." He pushed his chair back from the conference table, stood up, walked over to the buffet, looked over the morsels of food, and took a plate. He stopped cold and said to Fawz, "Your Highness, what is the protocol. Do you go through the buffet first?"

Fawz said, "This is an informal meal. I believe Miss Camille should go first. She surely earned it." Then he lifted his water glass and said, "Here's to audacious agents who commandeer helicopters."

We all lifted our glasses. I took a big gulp, but it was not water. It was not alcoholic. It was light and beyond delicious.

She took her plate and led the line. The agents made a point of sitting with us. I figured every word we said to them would go into their reports. Camille sat next to me and asked me, "How did Prince Fawzshen know I could have gotten in a bushel of trouble taking our helicopter to Galveston?"

"We all knew that," I replied.

"I could have been wrong. Hunches often don't work out."

"Like our hunch about Filbert. It was stronger than a hunch. We believed it."

"With the limited facts you had, it was logical to believe. Besides, you don't like him. You had a hypothesis. In our line of work, we must be careful not to let our emotions influence our hypotheses."

"Just like science."

"I'm curious," she said. "Did you learn how the ancient Rhatanians developed such a level of technology?"

"From what I gathered, they didn't risk a reprimand for taking the helicopter to Galveston."

"That would be a pleasant environment."

We talked a little before she said. "We made a little bet about you. Strictly lunch hour stuff. Guess we can't get our minds off work. Will you pick the physicist or the botanist? It's seven to two that you'll go for the botanist. Personally, I would pick the physicist."

I had a sick feeling in my stomach and wondered if I would ever get my privacy back. I said, "You do read our e-mails. I haven't heard from Alan. He's a student, not a botanist yet. JSC is not allowing me to contact anyone electronically because our whereabouts could be traced." She caught me off guard. I did not expect such a question. "As for Venzi Suzaky, he contacted me and invited me to dinner. My account is blocked, but that was no problem for Venzi. If he went through official channels, JSC would have lifted the block for him. Everybody treats him like a god. He will be remembered for saving our mission even though he was the last of many people. Without him, our ship would have been lost. But you know all of this already."

"Venzi Suzaky invited you to the most expensive restaurant in Houston."

"He was invited to last night's banquet, too, and sent his regrets. He was presenting a paper somewhere, I've heard."

He has sent you seven e-mails. So who are you going to pick: the botanist or the physicist?"

I laughed, "You're Homeland Security. You figure it. I'm not going to interfere with your bet or give you an unfair advantage."

"You already have."

I wondered if Camille knew that Alan was supposed to be on the plane with our families. I already had picked Alan. Venzi was simply a surprise. I would not lead him on. I would not use Venzi to get Alan back if indeed I had lost him. That would not be fair even though the though seemed tempting. Venzi was a super guy, maybe someone to help Lauren get over Chri Anri. Would a match be there? Lauren and Venzi?

I glanced toward Lauren. An agent was sitting on either side of her, each trying to impress her. Maybe a Homeland Security agent could make her happy. But she already found the man she wanted. He just happened to be out of range. Smuggling him aboard the *Copernicus* would have been the ideal choice, but at that point, it would not have occurred to us to break any NASA rules.

I looked back toward Camille and asked if she had any estimate about when we would go home. She said, "You'd like to find Alan." Then she winced.

Her choice of words was scary. She could have said that I would like to see Alan rather than I would like to find him. That implied that he still was missing. I waited, but she did not explain her meaning. Squeezing every drop of emotion out of my voice and putting on my blandest expression, I asked, "How long has he been missing?"

She turned pale. "Not long. It's not like that. We simply lost track of him."

I tried not to think about what that could mean.

Jana's Journal
Private Entry
Friday Afternoon

In a magical Rhatanian garden outside the palace Jack's three children and I sat at a glass table shielded from the mid-afternoon sun by a multi-colored silk umbrella. We were reading newspapers from all over the world. The papers we had not yet read were weighted down by a big bowl of fruit. We sipped the Rhatanian juice for special occasions, the same drink we had toasted with in Fawz's apartment in Houston seven months ago.

I wore an elegant sundress with a coordinating lightweight cardigan that Mom had loaned me. She had hesitated a second before agreeing since she had brought me a small suitcase full of my own clothes. Somehow, her clothes seemed more appealing. The sun barely was warm enough for such a dress. In addition, the air here in the mountains had a chill to it.

"Do you know how we got these newspapers," Jack's son Brad asked.

"They come electronically," I said absently while reading a report from Australia.

Brad persisted. "We've been upstairs in the communications tower. Signals travel through the air and go into a receiving disk.

Mark added, "That's right, receiving disk, converter, computer, and then the best thing, the high speed printers. In a second, no less than that, there's a whole page of newspaper."

"Why don't we read the news on our computer or phones like we do at home? Why is it on this strange paper? Stacy asked.

"That's special paper for news," I said. "It's called newsprint."

"Killing all those trees. Why would anyone do that?"

"These are special, commemorative, souvenir papers. After your dad, Lauren, Dr. Fawz, or I read something in one of the papers, then it's been read by an astronaut who made the Zalandan mission, and the King or any of us can give it to our friends as a gift."

"Weird!"

"Why were Dad and Helmut arguing?" Mark asked.

Brad said, "Helmut wanted us to dress in funny clothes and stand around the reporters and look winsome and say a lot of things he was going to coach us to say. Dad said absolutely not. It was after that that Dad talked to us. Remember, he told us to stay away from the reporters and to stay away from Helmut, too."

Mark said to Stacy, "And you talked to them anyway."

"I didn't tell them anything important."

I loved those kids. I knew them all of their lives and watched them grow. I asked, "Have all the reporters left yet."

"There's one more planeload. They were boarding when we brought you this last batch of papers. I said to Stacy, 'Keep moving, don't even look at them.' She wanted to tell how we got you to be an astronaut, because we told Uncle Fawz about the blue in your eye whites."

"Thank you, I'm very glad you told your Uncle Fawz about my eyes."

"Even with everything that happened?"

"Almost everything."

Thoughts of Alan were all around me. In a garden I could not help but think of him. This garden was formal with hedges and large groupings of flowers. Alan's garden was tropical and asymmetrical, more of a well-loved jungle.

The roar of a jet broke into my thought. We watched the jet rising in the sky. Brad breathed a sigh of relief.

Stacy said, "Now you can take me for a walk in the mountains."

"What?" I asked.

"Dad said when the reporters leave, I could hike in the mountains if I found someone responsible to take me."

"Brad or Mark can take you hiking," I said.

Both boys were shaking their heads. "No, we've got other plans. We can't be slowed down."

"The last time I took a walk on strange terrain, look what happened."

"You were kidnapped." Stacy proclaimed.

"No, I went willingly."

Stacy coaxed me. "Something exciting like that could happen to us in these woods."

"Don't be goofy," Brad said and pulled a paper out of her hands. "Let me see this paper."

"No," she said, grabbing it back. "I want something exciting to happen to us."

"You don't know what you're talking about."

"I'll tell you what. Let's be real quiet, and I'll read the paper for a little bit. Then we'll see."

"All the reporters were at the same press conference. Don't all the papers say the same thing?"

"As a matter of fact, they say good things. Most all of them quote your Uncle Fawz. Listen to this headline. 'Zalandans Declared Citizens of Rhatania.'"

"Is it true?"

"I don't know," I said. "I certainly hope so. I think the Rhatanian parliament would formalize it. Maybe that's happened already. The Zalandans were Rhatanians a very long time ago."

"So let's go for a walk in the woods."

"First we'll explore these gardens."

"I told you something would happen," Stacy piped up. They were all staring over my left shoulder, Mark's mouth dropped open in amazement.

I looked over my shoulder, then quickly jumped up and turned around. It was Alan standing right in front of me with a man in a dark suit.

I blinked my eyes a couple of times.

"Hi, Jana," he said casually.

"Oh Alan, it's really you. You're here." We hugged each other. "I've missed you so much. Nobody knew where you were."

"I've missed you, Jana, every day."

Alan looked wonderful, better even than I remembered him. We were holding hands, staring into each other's eyes.

Jack's kids flocked around the man in the dark suit, touching his hands, acting rather rudely, I thought. They were generally well mannered, especially to strangers. "Are you really the alien?" Stacy asked.

"Alien, no! Zalandan I be. Chri Anri be I."

"You look almost just like us."

"Yes, be I like you. Human beings all we be."

"Except your eye whites are blue like Jana's."

"Yes, whites blue all Zalandans. New Zalandan's whites white."

I said, "Chri Anri, I'm so happy you're here. I hope you'll stay a long time."

"Zalandans all miss you, cry when you go. Miss you I. Also miss others I."

Particularly Lauren, I thought but he was too shy to say.

"You look like our dad's CPA."

"CPA be what?"

"A CPA handles financial things, money matters," I said.

"He does our Dad's taxes."

"Taxes, money matters, telephone money, understand I not."

"It doesn't matter, Chri Anri. They mean you're dressed like everybody else. You could walk down the street in downtown Houston. You could visit the Space Center, and nobody would notice you."

Chri Anri rotated his shoulders, seeming quite pleased. The fabric of his dark suit sparkled in the sunlight.

"Where did you get your suit?"

"Clothing creators our made it. American TV studied they. Look it earthly?"

"Oh, yes, it looks earthly, classy, but definitely earthly."

Mark piped up. "We'll take you to see Lauren."

He smiled, hummed, rotated his shoulders, and quickly regained his composure. "Lauren, yes, Center, call Lauren." He shielded his eyes and quickly checked the three kids and me for Center.

"There's no Center here, Chri Anri."

I noticed a look of panic quickly followed by an expression of relief. Mark and Stacy each took one of his hands. "We know exactly where Lauren is." They took his hands and started pulling him.

"Wait, more slow. Here for me gravity heavy. To walk difficult." He lifted his knees as if he were marching.

"No, no, you don't need to walk like that. Swing your legs like this," Brad instructed.

They trudged off, Brad leading the group. I heard him saying to them. "So bright the sun in my eyes, on my face. So heavy the gravity. So many smells in the air. No Center. No Center. I cannot imagine. A wild and wonderful place this Earth be."

"He likes it here," I said.

"He is ecstatic," Alan said as we ambled through the garden.

"How did you get here?"

Alan laughed. "It's just amazing. We flew in Chri Anri's ship."

"The red ship, the one that looks like a private plane?"

"Yes. Have you flown in it?"

"No, but I saw it parked with lots of ships, and I commented that it looked like a private plane."

I realized that Alan was leading me somewhere. "Where are we going?"

"I saw this spot from the air. I think you'll like it."

We arrived at a series of reflection ponds surrounded by lush foliage and statues. It was magnificent. Lilies floated in one of the ponds. I said, "It's not the SpaceTech gazebo in Houston, but it'll do."

We sat on a wooden bench facing the lilies, and Alan described meeting Chri Anri. "I got a call from a man at an airstrip in Friendswood.

The man identified himself and said, 'Your friend asked me to call. I think you should get right down here. He's strung out on something, maybe alcohol, I don't know. Alcohol and flying don't mix. Don't know how he managed to land his plane, didn't see the landing. He's got a really nice plane, too, something new. I've never seen anything like it. But your friend claims he doesn't know how to use a pay phone, doesn't have any money, doesn't know his charge code. Phone won't accept his voice print. No wonder with the shape he's in; he can't put his words in the right order. And he's dressed in an expensive suit, probably high-end designer duds, not normal clothes for flying, but who am I to tell somebody with a plane like that what to wear. Don't know what kind of drug he took. He wanted me to call that astronaut Lauren Adams. I told him I thought she was on the moon or at the spaceport. Then, he asked me to call you. Had your phone number on some weird gadget. You'd better get right down here. I'll stay with him a little while, but I've got to leave.'

"Then I heard the man say, 'Hey buddy, talk to your friend. Here, take the receiver, no, the other way, put it closer to your mouth.'

"Another voice said, 'Alan, help need I Chri Anri.'

"I said, 'Chri Anri, just stay there at the airstrip. I'll be right there. And try not to talk too much to anybody.'

"I rushed over to Friendswood. By the time I got to the airstrip, a small group had gathered around Chri Anri's vehicle. There were asking him questions all at once. As I charged up to the group, I heard someone say, 'Who's the manufacturer?' And he answered 'Zalandan craft it be.'"

"'That's a new SpaceTech design,'" I said in as authoritative a voice as I could muster. Then Chri Anri said, 'Yes, yes, space technology.' Then somebody said that he talked like the Zalandan that you read about on the net, and I announced, 'He's my cousin.' I whispered to him to be quiet, but he said, 'Yes, yes, related we be. All Earthlings related.'

"At that point, I decided not to let him out of my sight. He needed my help.

He repeated a couple of times, 'Earthlings nice, helpful, friendly, like they my craft.' I hope this great person doesn't need to learn our guile and deception."

"You rode in his craft?"

"Yes. That's how we got here. You weren't easy to find. Rhatania's bigger than I thought."

We talked for a little while. I told him how scared I sometimes was during the mission. He said fear seemed like a totally sane reaction, and since I had carried out tasks despite being scared, that meant I was braver than someone who was fearless.

"What a lovely analysis," I said. We both chuckled. "You make my fear sound like extreme bravery. Jack and Lauren like danger a lot. Prince Fawzshen likes danger, too, but not as much."

"I like a sprinkle of danger," Alan said.

"A sprinkle? You rode in an alien spacecraft with an alien."

"I rode in a private plane with a friend."

"That's an interpretation."

"We were chased by an F-18. Maybe it was an old style F-16."

"Oh, were you scared?"

"I should have been, but I was focused on convincing Chri Anri to speed up. The fighter pilot wasn't playing games with him. He eventually accelerated, and we easily got away."

"Wow! I'm glad you're okay."

"Maybe it's all serotonin."

"What do you mean?"

"I've heard people with high levels of serotonin seek out danger."

"Jack and Lauren don't seek out danger. They're happy when it finds them."

"They're astronauts. They chose that field. You all chose it."

Our eyes met. "Interesting," I said.

"I bet you all were tested for serotonin levels. There's probably a range, not too much and not too little. NASA isn't going to choose someone who's going to be reckless with the solarships or space taxis. On the other hand, they're not going to choose someone who won't do what's required."

The sun dropped behind the mountains. The temperature plummeted. I shivered. I did not need to track him to the ends of the earth. I merely needed to wait for him to find me.

He looked at me longingly and took me into his arms. He drew me close and waited. I nodded slightly in acquiescence right before he kissed me. I was no longer cold. I felt fire and passion. I put my arms around him and kissed him back. I did not want to stop.

A rustling from a nearby hedge about 20-feet away got our attention. The cold wind gusted. We pulled back from each other.

"It's only the wind," I said, but it could have been an animal, probably only a small animal.

"You're shivering. We can go back."

"No, I'm fine. Let's stay a little longer. It's so good to be here with you."

"You're wearing next to nothing."

"I'm wearing a sundress and even a sweater."

Alan looked in the direction of where the sun had been. Then he touched my sweater and said, "This is a faux sweater."

It was dusk. Little lights around the reflection ponds blinked on. An early star twinkled. It was a magical moment in the entire universe.

Alan said, "This place is not the ends of the earth. It's the beginning. And you knew I would track you."

My heart stopped beating. "Why did you mention the ends of the earth?"

"I don't know. Because you were thinking it, I guess."

"You read my thoughts?"

"Sometimes."

"I didn't know."

"Even before you went away. Even when you were there."

"I'm surprised." I was more than surprised. I was stunned.

He whispered, "It's because we're in love."

The universe propelled forward in all of its swirling glory for this very moment. Alan never before had declared his love. He had shown his love. I had felt his love. I hoped that he had felt my love. But now he had put words to it. We began to kiss again.

One minute, our lives were perfect, and the next minute a petite woman jumped out from behind the same hedge and started taking pictures of us as she rapidly approached. We stood up, and Alan spun me around so our backs were to her. "She's one of the reporters from the press conference."

"I'll take her camera if you wish," Alan offered.

"She's pretty small. I don't want her hurt."

"I won't hurt her."

We heard a commotion and turned around. Camille, the Homeland Security agent, had the woman's camera in one hand, and with the other hand, she held the woman's arms behind her back. The reporter did not resist. I explained to Alan about Camille and suggested she may have been following the reporter.

The reporter admitted that she had rushed off her plane before take-off when she caught sight of the red vehicle landing on another runway. Through clever questioning, it was determined that she had not seen Chri Anri.

Fawz said she would be driven to the capital to join up with the other reporters. He apologized that most of her pictures had been deleted. I understood his actions were diplomatically soothing.

She apologized for scaring the couple in the garden. The only people who suffered were Alan and I because our relationship abruptly chilled. I felt a wall between us. Our love needed to be stronger than one reporter. I wanted to tell Alan there would be no reporters jumping out from behind hedges in Houston, but he surely knew that already. For now the less we talked about the incident the better. I hoped time would take care of us.

Jana's Journal
Private Entry
One Week Later

A woman observed me from across the room. She looked familiar, maybe Mom's friend from my childhood. I sat at a square table for four in the student center at the University of Houston at Clear Lake looking over my schedule and waiting for Alan and Chri Anri.

My Secret Service agent stood at a nearby wall, constantly observing everybody in the room. I knew she had already taken several pictures of the woman and had probably sent them for identification.

NASA had decided to keep me as an astronaut. I was overjoyed with their decision, especially after being written up for not properly editing what I had read over the NASA channel on the day of the explosion. I was formally told that anybody with any sense of propriety would have known better. Conversely, Jack told me not to worry about it. My journal not only got the job done but went beyond expectations, and Director Clayton had to tell me what he did.

JSC would be sending me to the U of H at Clear Lake to get a degree. I thought my first courses would be in aerospace, but JSC wanted me to take writing courses, including one in interviewing techniques. Director Clayton had assigned me to interview George MacInturff, the computer security expert from Seattle, his wife Marge, the artist who called the TV stations on our behalf, Russell Ramsey, the LandSkyTech programmer who deactivated the explosives, and Sharleen Rothwell, the LandSkyTech contractor who along with an El Lago policeman delivered the two LandSkyTech thugs to Director Clayton's office. Since Sharleen was under protective custody, that interview would be on hold. JSC had a huge oral history library, and these interviews would be added to the history of the *Copernicus* Mission. If the director liked the interviews, maybe he would assign me to interview more people involved with the mission.

The woman was now right beside me. "I'm Mrs. Lin. I remember when you were a little girl." Her lovely voice harked right back to my childhood.

"Please sit down," I said.

She had not seen my mother in years and asked how she was doing. After I told her that Mom was just fine, she asked me about the mission. It was my job as an astronaut to be a good ambassador for the space program. I said, "Many things are classified. Ask me anything you want, and I'll answer whatever I can."

"Did you find the Zalandans to be responsible?"

"Yes."

"How did it feel seeing Jupiter in the sky above you?"

"I miss looking at that huge planet with so much activity going on all the time. That big orange-red spot changed before my eyes."

"I liked that smaller yellow spot and all the bands of striations, too." She closed her eyes momentarily before she said, "I've seen pictures on the net."

I shivered. Was it possible that she was Hulda, or was I simply indulging in wishful thinking because her voice seemed familiar? I wanted so much to find Hulda, and I would do a proper search, too.

It occurred to me that she might be a reporter or a blogger. "This is beginning to sound like an interview," I said in my blandest voice. I was supposed to get clearance before talking to any reporter.

"Oh, I'm sorry. Zalanda is a special place, and I wanted to talk about it. You said to ask you anything."

I told her it was okay to ask me more questions but instead she told me what a cute little kid I had been. I was beginning to think the questions were over when she disguised a question as a statement. "It must have been a real treat flying with Jack."

"He's the best!"

I looked up and my Secret Service agent was signaling me. Mrs. Lin had not passed a basic security check. It simply meant the agency could not easily check every moment of her life back to her birth. For me, it meant to be prudent.

"There is something I haven't told you. I am under Secret Service protection. My agent is in this room as we speak. Every word you say is being recorded. Your picture may be taken. If you are a reporter or a blogger, your phone will be confiscated. Other electronic equipment will be confiscated. You may wish to leave at this time."

"I'll take my chances, Jana. I am more modern than you know, but at present I am not involved with reporting, blogging, or social networking. Perhaps, you could teach me social networking."

"Maybe someday," I said vaguely. Social networking was strictly off limits for me.

Mrs. Lin touched her ring, a work of art with an interesting rectangular stone. I looked up toward my agent as she touched her ear. She had lost the sound.

"Tell me what it was like flying with Jack, flying with your own father."

"Jack is not my father. Where did you get such an idea?"

"Your Secret Service agent can't hear us now. It's okay, Jana, I'm one of the five people who know."

"You're very mistaken."

"They planned to tell you. I thought they would have done so by now."

"Plans change."

Mrs. Lin was telling me other things, but I was trying not to listen. I looked a little like Jack. I had chalked that up to coincidence. Maybe, I looked more than a little like Jack. We almost have the same name. Jack is a form of John, and Jan is a form of John. Jana is the feminine of

Jan. But Jack's name is Jackson, son of Jack. When I started listening again, she was telling me that Jack was my parents' best friend, and they had asked him to be their sperm donor.

I was tempted to stand up and walk away, but my heart was pounding too hard to move. When I calmed down a little, I asked, "How can my parents continue to be close friends with my biological father?"

"Your parents have a strong marriage. They asked for my advice, and I thought that it could work. I have been married many times." The woman appeared to have a serene temperament. Why had she been married many times? Being a busybody and interfering in other people's lives could be a reason.

"I don't want to hear this. My father is the man who raised me. He will always be my father."

"I'm glad you feel that way."

"Does he know that I'm Jack's child?"

"Of course. They all know. They always knew."

I felt my eyes narrowing. "Who are they?"

"Your mother Myra and your father. Jack told Shirl before they married."

"Who else knows?"

"I know. That's all."

"This was none of your business. You interfered." Still, I did not walk away. I felt like screaming that I hated her but that seemed like a childlike response.

"Secrets are hard to live with. I've had some experience with secrets throughout the years."

You seem to have had a lot of experience throughout the years."

"I'm pretty old."

"You don't look so old."

"I'm sorry, Jana. I wish our first time together in years could have gone better. I assumed that you knew about Jack. It caught me off guard. Your DNA is in the astronaut's database. Jack's DNA is in there. I've been reading how they look through that database for genetic markers sometimes, for example, BLU2. I had wanted to talk to you about something else."

I would not blindly believe this woman with the lovely voice that reminded me of my childhood. I could get up my nerve and ask Mom.

How does someone with no degree, no pilot's license, no Olympic-level physical endurance, and no area of expertise fly on a major mission? It helps if her father had commanded the Mars I Mission.

Almost in response to my thoughts, Mrs. Lin said, "Everyone stands on the shoulders of many others, Jana. Sometimes the connection is clear. A person may be born at the right place and time in history for her abilities. Sometimes, she's lucky enough to inherit beneficial genes."

She talked on in that vein. I was beginning to like her now. I was tempted to tell her so.

"JSC tested more than 50 people for the BLU2 factor, and you were the only one with it."

I did not realize more people had been tested after my eye test. "How do you know that?"

"I read it on the net."

I noticed that her eyes had a bluish tinge. "Did you get tested?"

"I didn't know JSC was conducting tests."

I saw Alan and Chri Anri across the room and waved at them. Their Secret Service agents marched in a respectable distance behind them. "I see my friends now. I thought that Mrs. Lin would leave. "I'll tell my Mom that I ran into you," I said, waving my hand as if to dismiss what she had told me.

"Yes, please do," she said. All I needed to do was get up and walk toward Alan and Chri Anri. They were rapidly approaching. Neither Mrs. Lin nor I left the table.

Now Alan and Chri Anri were standing at the table.

"This is mom's friend, Mrs. Lin," I said. "These are my friends, Alan and Henry." That was the name we had agreed to call Chri Anri.

"Pleased to meet both of you, Alan and Henry." She pronounced Henry strangely like a French name. In fact, it sounded a lot like Anri.

Chri Anri took one look at her and sat down adjacent to me, moving his chair closer to me. Alan looked happy to see me and disappointed about sitting across from me rather than next to me.

Chri Anri was examining Mrs. Lin. Then he would look back at me as if I had something to do with her being here. "I ran into Mrs. Lin and she remembered me from my childhood," I said, feeling some explanation was necessary.

I did not want Chri Anri to feel uncomfortable. I could simply say we needed to leave. He had been fitting in so well, speaking standard American English, not reverting much to his own version that he had patterned after a character on an American TV show. I had not seen him stare at anyone on Zalanda, in Rhatania, or here in Houston, with the exception of Lauren. Many men stared at her.

"We need to go now. We need to get over to JSC," I said. That was not quite true. We had some time yet.

Chri Anri was so concentrating on Mrs. Lin that he did not hear me. Chri Anri said, "I seen pictures of you when you were much younger." Then he corrected himself. "I have seen pictures of you."

She replied, "I have not been young for a long time."

Chri Anri politely asked, "May I sing a song to you? It is a very unusual song."

"I must leave now," she said. She took a deep breath and then a second one. "I don't want you young people to be late."

Now, we would get rid of her. In a way I was afraid I would not see her again, and deep inside me, I knew I needed to see her again.

Chri Anri persisted. "It is my song for you."

Mrs. Lin could not politely refuse him. She nodded and sat back in her chair.

Chri Anri began humming in his native language. It was melodic and beautiful.

I pasted on my bland expression so she would merely think that it was a song and not realize that he was a Zalandan.

When he finished, she did not move a muscle. She seemed deep in thought. Her brow furrowed. She took a sip of water, waited a moment, and hummed right back at him. It sounded Zalandan. When she stopped, she asked, "Did you understand me?"

Chri Anri replied, "Few words understood I. I understood a few words.

"It's difficult keeping up a language with no one to talk to. From time to time, I taught my children, but it often was not safe to do so."

Chri Anri said, "Did you understand my words?"

She replied, "Some words. Enough to know you are Zalandan. How did you recognize me?"

"First, by the smell of another Zalandan, then I noticed your eye whites, and then I remembered the pictures my grandfather had of you. Tried I visualize look your age. I tried to visualize how you would look in middle years."

"Who are you?"

"I am your nephew, Chri Anri the Second. Chri Anri is my grandfather. My mother is your sister, Sedra. You have never met her."

How did you get here? Were you on the *Copernicus*?

"I came alone in my own ship."

"That's quite a feat."

Chri Anri began telling her about his ship until she pointed out that it had been a long time since she had been immersed in aerospace and interplanetary flight and that she had been only an apprentice. He glowingly told her about Lauren, and Mrs. Lin said that earthlings usually made excellent spouses except they eventually died despite the wafers.

Soon, Mrs. Lin started asking Chri Anri questions about her father. Once she was satisfied that Chri Anri the Elder was quite well, she said, "I heard on TV what Jana wrote about my father and me." Her cheeks became crimson. She turned her head toward me. "What he told you is a lie." She spoke as if five hundred years had not intervened to soften her feelings. "True enough, I wanted to stay on earth, and my father agreed. I was too young to make such a decision. After the ship left me, I realized I had made a mistake. I knew the crew had flown to Rhatania to say good bye, so I called on my transmitter for the ship to come back for me. It did not come back. Father never returned to find out if I was okay or if I had changed my mind.

"Jana read about a cylinder describing the mission and me through my blood component. My Father didn't need to write that cylinder. He needed to come back and get me."

No one said a word.

Finally Chri Anri said, "I am distressed to hear that."

She had regained her composure. "Later, I thought the ship had crashed and that my father and our team hadn't made it back to Zalanda.

"Have you talked to anybody about this before?" Chri Anri gently asked.

"Not really. I've disguised some of this into stories I've told my children. In some periods of time, I couldn't even do that. Telling someone who understands feels like a burden evaporating into the air."

"I'm glad I could help." Chri Anri patted her hand, touching her ring.

"That was a very long time ago. I've had a good life on earth. Mostly. Still, on rare occasions even through the nineteen eighties, I would enter a dark place in my mind and wonder if Zalanda had ceased to exist. If that were the case, I would be the only one on earth who knew of the magnificence that had been Zalanda. When a man landed on the moon in 1969, surely if Zalanda still existed, people on earth had reached a sufficient degree of technology so that the Zalandans could reveal themselves. I could tell everybody, but who would believe me. Then, I thought, this was a time for earthlings to bask in accomplishment and not be upstaged.

"Twenty-five years later, Zalanda sent the signal. It was glorious. Zalanda lives. Zalanda thrives. The timing was perfect, honoring the twenty-fifth anniversary of NASA's first manned moon landing. Twenty-one large fragments of Comet Shoemaker-Levy 9 slammed into Jupiter. Zalandan tweakers at work. Never before had there been such a 21-gun salute.

"Nobody on earth understood. They were looking for a signal to come a specific way, by radio frequency from far away."

We were quiet for a few moments until she said, "I may not have much longer to live."

Chri Anri pursed his lips and frowned. "You look so healthy."

"I've run out of the Zalandan wafers. I've been out for over a year. I used so many during the influenza epidemic of 1918. It protected my husband and children. I gave it to others, too. Many of them survived."

"There's nothing wrong with you?"

"Not that I am aware of."

"Worry you not. Don't worry. I have a ship full of wafers."

He reached into his jean jacket and pulled out a fabric envelope and handed it to her. I looked up and turned my head quickly. Three Secret Service agents were converging on us.

"Open it," I ordered. Chri Anri and Mrs. Lin glanced up. They had forgotten that Alan and I were at the table with them.

Chri Anri unsealed it and it opened flat into a small napkin, exposing eight purple wafers. "You have enough of these on you?" I asked.

He said, "Yes."

"Now, offer them to us." From the corner of my eyes, I saw the three agents had stopped. They retreated.

Mrs. Lin gratefully took a small bite out of her purple wafer. What she said about knowing a lot about marriage made sense. What she said about knowing about secrets made sense, now. I knew who she was in my life. My initial realization had been correct. I had denied it to myself because it seemed too marvelous to be possible. She had searched for me.

"Take a wafer, Jana. It'll be good for you," she suggested. "This is a particularly delicious wafer. I've been using the miniature travel-sized ones for the last couple hundred years until I ran out of them."

"I don't want to waste the wafers. I'm only a little bit Zalandan," I said, but I already knew better.

"You are one-eighth Zalandan plus whatever your father is. I'll figure that out."

"You told me stories about space when I was a little child. My mother said they were only stories, but they were your life of long ago. You did a handstand in my bedroom. You are my great-grandmother Hulda. You wore make-up that made you look older. You disappeared from our lives, and Mom couldn't track you down. That made her very sad. Now, I understand why. You were not an old person then. You're not an old person now. You didn't want to keep disguising yourself as an old person."

"I've left people I've loved many times. Leaving you was one of the hardest things I did because you believed my stories. I'm glad they came true for you." She blinked back tears and said, "I could do a handstand right now on this table."

Chri Anri said, "Take wafers for a few months before trying that."

With authority in his voice, Alan said, "Gymnastics are strictly against the rules in this building. Students need to join the health club."

She seemed relieved. "Take a wafer, Alan," she said. "Prevaricators particularly benefit from Zalandan wafers."

603

"Yes, Ma'am," he said sheepishly and lifted one from the unfolded envelope.

"I like you, Alan. I could have broken my arm or worse, showing off. You stepped up. That's a good trait. You . . ."

I knew what else she was going to say, but it was better left unsaid. Instead, she turned to Chri Anri. "You haven't shared a wafer with us."

Chri Anri shuddered. "It's so disgusting, so primitive, sharing a meal. I can do it." He picked up a wafer.

She said, "I had almost forgotten about that custom, eating alone in a food booth."

When it was time for us to leave, she promised to keep in touch and even said that she would contact my mom someday. I was concerned that I would not see Hulda again until I realized that the Secret Service most likely knew or most certainly would find out where she lived. Chri Anri told her that his ship was at Ellington Field and he would make arrangements to give her a large supply of wafers. They exchanged phone numbers.

Alan and I took Chri Anri over to JSC for him to meet with Venzi Suzaky. Venzi greeted me affectionately and was enthusiastic to meet Chri Anri. He looked Alan over from head to toe before he said, "Somehow, I expected you to be more dashing."

Allan smirked and said, "Is a 'dashing' faster than a neutrino? Oh, now I remember, that's the vehicle that carries a neutrino into the fifth dimension."

Venzi did a double-take because people usually treated him like a god.

Everyone laughed politely.

I was peeved at Venzi for behaving shabbily toward Alan even though this world honored physicist had protected me from Filbert Grystal during training and more importantly had saved our crew after the lander explosion by correcting a "timing" problem aboard the

Copernicus. My crew had used other words to describe the problem, namely, rescuing us from another dimension.

Alan and I walked outside onto the JSC grounds.

"That Suzuki guy likes you," he said.

I was ready to deny it, but instead I replied, "I know."

"He treated me like an insect."

"That's because you have the girl. If you want her. And he doesn't."

"Of course, I want her. Of course, I want you."

That was all I needed to hear, but Alan did not stop talking. "You read about our afternoon together at Gilruth under that SpaceTech moon. You read it because you were required to do so, not that you felt it any longer in your heart. It did the job, too. George MacInturff, that security expert from Seattle, said your love for me inspired him to contact everyone he knew."

"I was afraid I had thoroughly embarrassed you." There, I had said it.

"Maybe, a little." He thought a moment and asked, "Are you planning to read more of your journal on a social network?"

"No. Even if I wanted to, which I don't, JSC has put that strictly off limits for me."

"Good. That's very good. I'm better looking than he is."

"That's a matter of taste." I felt the wall between us collapsing. "You were at Kennedy Space Center when the hopper took me to the space factory."

"Of course, I wouldn't have missed that for all the moons of Jupiter."

"How could you have known?"

"Easy. Lauren and Jack arranged for us to meet at Gilruth to say good bye. Before that, the three of you along with Prince Fawzshen were seen training together in a solarship mock up. After that, no one saw any of you. Four SpaceTech employees were informed that they would be bumped from the hopper flight to the space factory in two weeks. SpaceTech was unhappy about that. Two weeks is the isolation time. I didn't need help from an un-dashing particle physicist to figure that one."

"It's a wonder the secret held as long as it did."

"I was motivated to find you."

"Look, Alan, the moon's out already."

"Where?"

"Over there, right above the Gilruth Rec Center." I raised my arm and pointed toward it.

"It looks like a real moon to me," Alan said. He reached up to take my hand and a spark of electricity joined us.

Linda A.W. King
Houston, Texas
Photo by R. David King
Background painting by Rose Davis